MW01622847

ASHES OF BLACK OAK

A BLACK OAK NOVEL: BOOK FIVE

MONIQUE EDENWOOD

ASHES OF BLACK OAK

Ashes of Black Oak is the fifth book in the Black Oak series. It is not the final book in the series.

The novel is a dark romantic suspense and features scenes involving characters in states of physical and psychological distress.

Reader discretion is advised.

Copyright © 2022 by Monique EdenWood

All rights reserved.

This book is a work of fiction. Names, characters, businesses, places, events, and incidents are either the products of the author's imagination or used in a fictitious manner. Any resemblance to actual persons, living or dead, or actual events is purely coincidental.

No part of this book may be reproduced, distributed, or transmitted in any form or by any means, including photocopying, recording, or other electronic or mechanical methods, without the prior written permission of the author, except in the case of brief quotations in a book review.

Cover design by Monique EdenWood

Photo Credit - Front cover:

Mask: depositphotos.com/outsiderzone

Roses: stock.adobe.com/Kevin Carden

ISBN (electronic format): 978-1-7772249-8-1

ISBN (paperback): 978-1-7772249-9-8

Proofreading by Potter's Editing.

For more information, please visit MoniqueEdenwood.com or Facebook.com/MoniqueEdenwood

ACKNOWLEDGMENTS

I would like to thank every reader who has taken this journey into the Black Oak.

This is such a personal series to me and it means more than I can really put into words to have people connect with these themes and these characters.

I am incredibly blessed to have the loveliest and sassiest group of readers in my Facebook group, Monique's Clique. You very often make me cry with laughter and your enthusiasm and passion gives me so much strength. Getting to know you through these books has been an incredible honor.

I would particularly like to thank Penny Betcher, Cheryl Woodward, R.J. House, Jennifer Chris, Shreya Basu, Gisell Butler, Violet Gillis, Jaclyn Combe, Rabea McGhie, Rachaell Askey, Gina Whited, Jean Sweeney, T.D. Ratcliff, Kathy Gentry, Terri West, Glenda Johnson, Devon Beirne, Patricia Dawes, Melissa Leslie Bramall, Patti White, Yumnah Isaacs Hajwanie, Angela Ortiz, Giselle Mendieta, Jill Williams, Jess Clanton, Marie-Hélène Hébert, Beryl Robinson, Karen Warner, Nikki Pruett, Shafeequah Slarmie, Kelly Marie Gregory, Sue Graham Edmondson, Ella Ravicovich, Shianna Keegan, Trisha Benton, Anne Lucy-Shanley, Kimberly Piasecki, Savannah McCann, Cassandra Yorke,

S. Keller, Patricia Johnston, Jacqueline Hylands Gough, Melody Steele, Brenda Durell, Tamyrh James, MaRci Ya, Linda Edwards, Poppy Hopper, Zoe King, Marie Boag, Michelle Crosnoe, Jane Loveday, Angie Hathaway, Maria-Luminita Lungo, Gayle Murphy, Jane Hope, Azucena Uctum, Leia Moten, Arleene Rickard, Dorothy Sankey, Leigh Todd, Lixx Luna, Lynfa Dahlstrom, Michala Jury, Siobhan Royle, Sandra L., Jennifer P and Nichole as well as all other members of the group.

Some of you have joined recently and I hope to thank you in the next book!

Thank you to everyone who took the time to write reviews for books 1 to 4. Reviews and ratings make such a huge difference in the lives of small independent authors and I am so grateful to every single person who took the time to leave one.

Thank you to Poppy Hopper, Bea and Vivi for being so vocal in your enthusiasm on Instagram and beyond. Your support means so much and gives me so much energy!

Thank you to my group of lovely author friends, Sophy Bannister, N. Dune, Anna White, Margot Swan, Katie Rose, Anouk Roche, E.A. Pierce and E. Broom for your daily support and encouragement not to mention all the much-needed silliness we get up to. You mean so much to me.

Thank you to all the new authors I've met in our support groups.

Thank you to the heavenly R&C Christiansen, an incredible friend and one of my favorite authors who has shared my series about so much and who fills me with laughter, love and support every day.

I'd like to thank my lovely and talented author friend, Lynn Rhys, for patiently tolerating all my questions about American English and giving me so much support and encouragement with the series.

Thank you to another incredible author friend, Shantel Brunton, for all your encouragement and for answering all my special questions in such detail!

Thank you to my amazing proofreader, Potter's Editing for all of your love, support and hand-holding in the final week. You've made it so much easier.

Thank you so much to my wonderful author friend, Linda Pankow, for your incredible support and encouragement on Instagram and for sharing the book so much! Thank you for ARC reading and for helping us find those scraggly typos. Your help has been invaluable.

Thank you to my amazing PA, Zoe Knight. I'm beyond thrilled to work with you. Thank you for everything you do. You've made the last few weeks so much easier.

Thank you to all the incredible authors and bookstagrammers of the Rice Tribe. Your friendship and support has meant so much.

A huge thank you once again to the incredible Sophy Bannister who always gives me so much love in the last week and helps me to have the courage to publish.

There are other people whom I would like to thank, but am not able to this time. I would like you to know that if you have reached out to me, commented on one of my posts, left me feedback or a rating or review, I have seen it, and I am eternally grateful to you and just beyond thrilled that you have enjoyed the series so far.

Ashes of Black Oak is very dark romance. Lines will be blurred and crossed. Things will get messy at times, but I hope any challenging emotions that come up make the adventure more moving, memorable and thrilling.

Monique xxx

If you want your light to reach me, you have to meet me where I dwell.
In darkness.

PROLOGUE

Manhattan
Twenty years earlier

"I'm gonna tell my dad."

"No! You can't! If my dad finds out, he'll take it out on me."

"He can talk to him. Get him to stop."

"He won't stop! They'll just take me and my brothers away. We'll never see him again."

"Your back's covered in them now, Jack!"

"He only does it when he's drunk."

"We need to tell someone. Let's just show my parents the bruises. They'll help him."

"They won't! They'll just fire him! He told me. Then they'll send me to some foster house. I'll never see you again."

"I can't just not do anything! Why don't we tell a teacher or something? It's been ages now. It's not stopping. We can tell Mr. Davis or something."

"We can't. He'll lose his job."

"What am I supposed to do?"

"We just need to wait. He said he was gonna stop drinking. Let's see if it gets better."

"It's not going to get better, Jack. Let me just tell my dad."

"What do you think he'd do?"

"He'd try and get your dad help or something."

"No, he wouldn't. He'd call the police and fire him and then they'd send me to live in some home."

"It'd be better than living with that monster."

"He's not a monster! It's only 'cause he's drinking. He just needs to stop. When he's sober, he goes all quiet. He says he's gonna stop."

"You can come and live with us. I'll ask my parents. I know they'd say yes."

"Your parents wouldn't want me, Cam."

"They would! I'd beg them. Please. Just let me say something. I can't stand this anymore."

"No. They'll take me away from here. I know they will. We'll never see each other again."

"Jack..."

1

"Hello, Jessynia."

I know my fingers are clutched around my blanket, but I can't feel them.

I feel the wooden panel at my back but can't move from it.

I know my heart is beating out of my chest, but for a moment, it feels like it's stopped.

I peer into his face, unable to comprehend how he can be here.

His bronze eyes bore into me as I glance at Sebastian next to him who eyes me curiously, watching as a fat tear spills over my waterline.

How could you?

"What is he doing here?" My voice is so thin it's a miracle the words came out at all.

The man pulls his hood down to reveal striking eyes which bore into me—eyes I sometimes see in the dark, glowing like embers.

He's taller than I remember, his body stockier. His brown hair is thinning at the front and he looks so much older than I recall, but I will never forget that face. It etches itself into the bark of trees I pass, meeting me in my nightmares.

I believe that the trauma of that day was so great because the incident was so unexpected. He was one of the young leaders of the camp.

We trusted him. He seemed so plausible. There were no alarm bells at all. The shock, the split-second journey through the murky veil separating my innocent reality, and the cold bleakness of the outside world was part of the trauma.

The other part came from the true abject powerlessness I experienced for the first time. He was so tall, so strong. I'd never had my limbs restrained like that before. Once his arm was around me and his hand around my mouth, I couldn't move, no matter how much I tried. I didn't have control of my body, and it was the first time that that had happened to me.

And then came the powerlessness I felt afterwards when adults dissected my story and deemed it unworthy of contacting the authorities. The fallout would be too great. For the camp leaders, it was damage control. My parents thought they were protecting me, preventing me from going through months of questioning and reliving, only to have the authorities deem that there is not enough evidence anyway...

And then the rumors, and the whispers and the loss of self-esteem, the decay of self-image. And the panic attacks constricting my throat when I would walk through the school gates afterwards.

How can one event, one short incident, affect a person for so many years?

His beady eyes gleam as his mouth twists into a smile dripping in the kind of malevolence that you couldn't believe unless you saw it with your own eyes.

"Can I have her now?"

Oh my God...

His voice. I'd forgotten it...

"Jess, can you help me carry this to the other camp?"

"Um, sure."

"Do you think you could carry this one?"

"Okay."

"No, not that way. It's heavy. We'll take a shortcut through here. It's much quicker."

"Okay."

"You looked like you were enjoying yourself this morning."

"Um, yeah. It's fun here."

"You like fun, don't you?"

Jessynia...

I retreat into the wooden panel at my back, my eyes pleading with Sebastian's.

It's impossible.

He wouldn't allow this...

The man takes a step towards me only for Sebastian's hand to snake over his thick, cloaked shoulder, stopping his advance. As he does so, I glance to my right at the glass bottle of water, deciding it will be my weapon of choice if he comes near me, hoping the red coat I'm still wearing doesn't restrict my movements.

"Not yet, my friend," Sebastian replies as the man glares at me in the same way Stephen Frost does—lascivious delight unabashedly carved into his face in a way that makes your skin crawl.

"What are you doing?"

"She looks afraid," he moans to the trembling of my body. The guy is huge, way over two hundred pounds. "This is gonna be good. You have no idea how much trouble the bitch caused me." As he pulls apart the front of his cloak, footsteps approach.

"You know what I'm doing..."
"Stop!"
"That's it, pretend you don't like it, you little slut."

"Stop! Stop!"
"Have you ever been—"

Vallen Markov enters, his muddy eyes glittering as he observes my silent terror.

"Stop!"

He holds out a box for the man. "They're all mild," he says. "But it'll make it... more intense... for both of you."

The man doesn't hesitate, dipping his fat fingers into the metal box, only to be stopped by Sebastian Gravier who winds his fingers around the man's wrist.

"Are you sure you want it?" he asks. "You may not be able to fight as well."

"Fight? Fight *her*?!" he sneers, derision dripping from him. "Oh, I won't have any problems in that department."

Sebastian nods, letting the man bring it to his lips. He takes the bottle that Vallen holds out to him and drinks down the pill, letting out an audible groan as its effects begin to kick in.

Sebastian eyeballs Vallen who holds out the box to him, allowing Sebastian to follow suit, drinking down a pill himself.

"We want it to be a fair fight, don't we, Mr. Markov?" he says to Vallen's dark grin.

What is he doing?

The gleaming silver discs of his eyes meet mine, remaining affixed to my face at all times as my gaze wanders haltingly from the man I prayed I'd never see again to the man who has brought him into my room.

The scent of roses jolts me for a moment, snapping my spine up straight.

Don't show fear...

"What's he doing here?" I stammer, wishing I could summon up my mother's bold voice on command.

"Oh... this is so fucking perfect," the man grins, breathing heavily as the high of chemical-induced euphoria makes the skin on his chest flush. His voice is raspy, but with a high-pitched tinge that clings to the end of words. His skin is misting already, the heat from the drugs no doubt surging through his stocky frame. "*What am I doing here?*" he repeats, mocking the fear in my voice. "Bet you didn't see this one coming, did you?"

His words make me shudder. "Why is he here?" I repeat to Sebastian.

"Retribution, Jessynia," he replies solemnly. "It comes to us all."

"I did nothing wrong!" I respond.

"Nothing wrong?" the man sneers. "You caused me no end of shit, you worthless little bitch."

I can't speak words to him. I can't address him directly. Not like this. He barely looks like the man I knew. He's taller than I remember, easily over six foot two, but the biggest difference is his body. Where once he was lean, he's now bulky and muscular with a thick layer of fat sheathing his muscles and turning him into some ogre of a man. His dark hair is thinning noticeably and his face, once oval, is now square—chubby almost.

The man has taken enough from me.

I won't address him.

I cast a glance to my right again at the bottle of water and out of my left peripheral vision, I spot him taking a step closer.

"You're gonna pay," he pants, and I turn in time to see Sebastian coil his thick, strong hand around his shoulder.

"You're going to step outside for a moment, friend."

The man spins quickly to face Sebastian. "Why?"

"Because I need to speak to her first. Prepare her for what's about to come."

The man pants audibly under the curse of the chemicals. "After that, I want to be left alone with her. No interruptions. As promised."

Sebastian smiles, but I spot it—the narrowing of his lucent eyes.

"Mr. Markov, please escort our friend outside while I speak to our guest in private."

"How long?" the man asks.

"Just a few minutes. Then you'll get what you came for...."

The man's glare returns to me, morphing into a smirk of heinous anticipation. "Don't warm her up too much," he hisses as he turns to leave the room.

As Vallen closes the door behind them, Sebastian begins to walk towards me as I edge further into the wood against my back.

"Stay away from me!" I exclaim, to his stone-faced regard.

As he makes it to within a foot of the bed, he holds out his hand for me to take and I shake my head at him, unable to steady my breathing. "You can go fuck yourself!"

In response, he reaches down and yanks the blanket off me, grabbing me by the waist and lifting me to my feet. I push against his chest, but he wraps the hard muscle of his arms around me, caging me in against the wall until I realize the futility of struggling against his physical superiority.

A tear spills from me at the sensation—the prison, being unable to move but for a man's say-so.

"Let go of me! I don't like feeling trapped, *asshole*."

"You feel him on you, don't you?" he responds grimly. "When you're held..."

"Why is he here?!"

His eyes roam over mine, taking in my distress, tracking the slow trail of the tear down my cheek before finding me again. His eyes glitter despite the solemn note to his countenance.

The dark notes of his voice shudder through me. "I made you a promise, Jessynia. Remember?"

My heart sinks into the wooden boards beneath my feet. There's only one promise he's ever made to me about that man. "What promise?" I ask.

His eyes narrow. "You know what it is."

My respiration shallows at the gruesome oath he once spoke to me, despite the protective heft of the human scaffolding holding me up.

"You're not serious."

He eyes me sternly, his gaze falling to my lips.

"Sebastian..."

His fingers slip up my back.

"No." I shake my head. "I don't want that! I don't want that on my conscience! Just send him back!"

He drinks me in for a moment as I peer up into the storm brewing in this rugged features. "That isn't an option. Every aspect of him being brought here has been meticulously planned out for months so that his connection to us is untraceable."

"No!"

"We must all pay our debt at some point, Jessynia. *All* of us. He will not be returning home."

I push against him, but his grip tightens. "You realize what you're saying?!"

His head dips into mine so that his lips are hovering just over my mouth. "He has brutalized over a dozen young women that we are aware of, several underage. He has forfeited his rights."

"You didn't care when Alexandra was seducing underage boys!"

He grimaces, his face hardening. "I wasn't aware of her *proclivities* for men so young until several years ago. She has been banned from seducing those under seventeen for some time now."

"She must love you for that," I sneer.

"She didn't force herself upon those young men. That's the difference."

"*Yes she did!* Not *physically*, but she coerced them. She took advantage of their weakness and their youth."

"She may yet pay a price for that."

"Listen to me, Sebastian. Please. I don't want this. You know this would cause me even more trauma, right?"

He soaks in my wide eyes. "In the short term, yes. In the long term, it will free you in ways you could not fathom now."

"Like killing your mother freed *you*? You have to hurt people to cope with that!"

He shakes his head slowly. "My trauma is not from her death, Jessynia. Her death was the only source of light I'd ever felt. The damage done to me happened in the years prior to it. The poison had already entered," he responds. "Healing is too late for me. You are still pure,

Jessynia. The memory of *him* is what taints your purity, contaminates your mind, forces you to live in fear. I intend to take the touch of him from your body."

"Why?!"

His right hand slides up my neck where his thumb pulls back the creamy skin of my face, as if wishing to expose the bone beneath it.

"They didn't believe me either," he responds, robbing me of my breath. "I know what that does to a child. I intend to correct the self-doubt he left you with."

"Look, I'll go to the police," I barter.

"Your word is not enough evidence. You know that, Jessynia. Don't play games with me. You know very well they won't even press charges."

"I don't want this, Sebastian. *Please*. Please listen to me. Just send him back."

His eyes half-close as he watches a tear spill onto my cheek, plunging us into deathly silence but for faint wisps of voices seeping into the room from outside. "Did you doubt me, Jessynia? When you saw him?"

"I... I don't know... Please just send him back."

He shakes his head slowly. "No."

2

He grabs hold of my hand and pulls me out of the room as I try to resist in vain against his physical strength. A wooden gangway falls into a peat-covered path lined with conifers on either side. Voices floating in the gusty wind emerge from inside the forest.

"Where are we going?" I ask to his silence.

His fingers, interlaced with mine, grip me more strongly as the woods wrap around us, imparting the scent of pine and sap on us.

And a moment later, a clearing emerges.

The man—Adam, though I can barely bring myself to think his name—sits on one of a dozen stumps of trees brutally sawed down in their prime which join together to form a circle.

Seven unmasked people stand around, long cloaks concealing their frames—Isaiah, Grace, Vallen, Ilya, Alexandra, Dominic Becker, and one of the men I saw standing in front of the car when I left that building Nathan took me too. And then finally, there is another man—tall and wearing a cloak, his identity concealed, eyeing me from behind his full-face mask as we arrive. I would care more about who it was if I wasn't so terrified about what Sebastian is planning to do...

"Are we doing it out here?" he asks. "Are you freaks gonna watch or something? Hey, I mean, the more the merrier."

But Sebastian doesn't answer. No one does.

He pulls me to the side of the circle, positioning me between Grace and Alexandra Frost—just as I was placed that day they took me to that house and made me watch that heinous initiation ceremony.

He turns to face the man, legs apart, staring at him without moving.

"Hey, what is this?" the man says, the two eye-balling each other for a while before he begins to walk towards Sebastian who, in turn, stalks him slowly, each step measured, his hands curling into fists beneath the sleeve of his cloak.

"Oh my God, I'm going to fuck you so hard..."

"Stop! Please! Stop!"

"What is this?" Adam repeats, darting a glare back at me. "You said you were gonna give me the bitch."

"I will, friend. You just have to do one thing first."

"What?"

"It's very simple. You can have her, but you have to take me out first."

"What the fuck are you talking about?" the man snarls.

He doesn't interact with Sebastian in the reverent way most Society members do. The version of events that got him here must be different from reality.

"No prize as sublime as this comes for free, Adam. That's not how life works, now, is it?"

The man's shadowy eyes flick from one person to another, as if stunned into silence. I watch his throat contract and his eyes dart nervously before he finally lets out a hiss of frustration. "You know what? *Fuck* this shit. The bitch isn't worth it."

As he sidesteps Sebastian and begins to walk to the edge of the circle, he's stopped in his tracks by Isaiah who moves his mammoth frame to stand before him. The man readjusts his trajectory but is stopped by Vallen Markov and then again by Ilya Markov who looks bulkier each time I see him—forced, no doubt, to work out tirelessly to prove he's worthy of being the Council member he has just become.

The man turns back to look at Sebastian. "What the *fuck* is this?"

Sebastian doesn't answer but slowly peels his black cloak from his dense frame and throws it onto a wooden stump nearby, eyes fixed on the man who takes a slow, unsteady step backwards. He's almost as tall as Sebastian, and as bulky but not as in shape. Sebastian's body is a sculpture of hard peaks and troughs. I can't see this man's, but he is clearly carrying a little extra weight.

In a staticky blur of movement that makes me gasp, the man turns to run through two stumps at the back and into the forest. With no sound uttered other than a growl from Isaiah, he, Vallen and Ilya take off after the man, their rabid bursts of movement that of ravenous wolves chasing prey.

"Sebastian"—I notice Grace turn swiftly to look at me as I take a step towards him—"Please. Just let him go! He isn't worth it!"

"He will be let go," he snarls, "once he makes it past me. It's only fair he occasionally has to fight a man, Jessynia."

The sharp stab of panicked shouts from the forest informs me that they've caught up with him. The man's deep voice thunders through the woods as Sebastian's flaring eyes, peppered with shards of metal, scald me.

"Stop! Stop!" His pitiful pleas pull me back to my own in that forest as I begged and pleaded to be let go.

Sebastian throws a glance at Grace next to me. "Hold her. Don't let her loose."

"No!" I take a few steps back only to have this giant of a woman lunge towards me, grabbing me and pulling me back into the circle, holding her arms tightly around me as I squirm to get loose.

"Grace, you have to stop this!" I plead as my eyes are pulled to the sight of Isaiah and Vallen dragging the man back towards us as he tries to tug against them. My eyes are caught by the sight of the muted crimson line carved into Sebastian's chest—the one he made before me with the knife, barely grimacing as it sliced into his sacred flesh.

"I don't want this!" I exclaim. "Please."

"You will once it's done," he replies. "You won't be free until it is."

"Let go of me, you motherfuckers!" the man shouts as he's pulled into the circle, the faint wisps of desperation clinging to his voice.

Sebastian's eyes peer into mine, his face hardened by anger as he slowly turns around to watch the man be thrown, breathless, into the center of the ring.

He staggers to his feet as Isaiah, Vallen and Ilya spread out to bar him from attempting to run again. In any case, he looks too out of breath to attempt it.

"What do you want?" he pants. "I told you you can have the fucking bitch. She's not worth the trouble."

"And I told you that you can have her *yourself*. You just have to get through me first, Adam..."

"Who the fuck are you?!"

I hear the snap of twigs nearby. "I'm the man who's been watching you," responds Sebastian grimly. "The man you've been waiting for..."

"What the fuck is that supposed to mean?"

The cavernous notes of Sebastian's voice echo through the forest, punctuated only by the man's desperate attempts at bravado and the occasional sharp caw of crows in the woods. "I want to hear what happened that day."

"What?!" the man shouts.

"You heard me."

"Don't fight. You know you want this, you little slut."

Without warning the man lunges at Sebastian and throws a punch, and in an instant, an image flashes before me, hauling me back to the horror of seeing Cameron ambushed in the woods and beaten by Isaiah and Leon, a beating overseen by Sebastian himself, this man who would purport to protect me. For a brief moment, the cognitive dissonance makes me feel like I'm falling through space.

Sebastian blocks the man's punch with his forearm and delivers one of his own, knocking him to the floor, the thud of his fist so loud that it reverberates through the clearing and into my flesh. The man, dazed, lifts up a hand, realizing in record time that he's outmatched by the leaner, stronger, fitter Sebastian.

"What do you want?" he pants, and I close my eyes at the ache of desperation clinging pitifully to his voice.

"I want to hear what happened that day," Sebastian sneers. "From your mouth. You're not leaving here until I hear it. Until you say it. What did you do to her?"

"I did nothing!"

I open my eyes and the smell of the woods invades me, but this time, it's the scent of the woods in Albany—the fragrant pines, their sweet sap and heady fragrance aroused by the muggy August heat. I remember how bright the day was, how hot. The sky looked like it was burning and the flaming sun peeked through swathes of leaves and branches, illuminating the ground, turning it vibrant shades of amber and gold... until we ventured further and shadow encased us...

And suddenly, the taut prison of Grace's grip on my body transforms into the skin-crawling touch of his huge hands as he spun me around and into the tree, scraping my skin, cursing foul words into my ear as he did so, the change in mood so chilling that the world turned to black in an instant. One hand wrapped around my mouth as another lowered to the button of my shorts which he undid before grappling with the zip as I twisted my body to stop him.

"After this, I'm gonna fuck you in the ass, you little whore."

I'm going to lose my virginity like this...

I still hear the scream muffled by his strong hand. He felt so strong back then, as if powered by supernatural forces, born of something not human.

I'd never really felt evil before. I'd heard of the concept, but I'd never experienced it firsthand. Those meager few minutes took me into the cold black the likes of which I never knew existed. It opened some portal into a world that had been there all the time, but which I'd lived blissfully unaware of.

Vague voices from somewhere on the outskirts of the forest made him pause for a moment and the shift had him loosen his grip on my mouth.

As he did, a voice, so different from my own, whispered to me...

Bite.

I bit so hard I could barely believe it. I remember clenching my jaw so feverishly, desperate to snap the skin, which I did. I sunk my teeth into the flesh between his thumb and index finger, grinding so hard that I felt bone and tasted blood.

A dragon must have helped me bite that hard...

He snarled his anger into the skin on my neck. "Fuck! Fucking bitch!"

But somehow, doubt pervaded him, just enough for his fingers to untense and for his guard to drop and for him to let go for long enough for me to swing back and hit him. He pulled me back, but I kicked, and at some point, he stumbled, just a little, and I ran, running as if demons were chasing me to drag me into hell.

I was free.

Or I thought I was...

It wasn't the triumphant end of the journey out of trauma. It was only really the beginning. What happened next changed my ability to trust myself for a short while. It took something from me that I've never fully gotten back.

"What happened?" Sebastian repeats, taking a step towards him.

"Nothing happened! The little slut was parading around, flaunting her ass all weekend."

I shake my head.

That didn't happen.

"How?" asks Sebastian.

"They were swimming in this lake. Bunch of little sluts. They all knew what they were doing, believe me."

I swam twice, the day before. I wasn't even wearing a bikini. I'd forgotten mine. I was wearing a sports bra and shorts. I wasn't flaunting anything. I was being a dumb, barely seventeen-year-old with my friends. It was stupid, and innocent... and beautiful.

Sebastian turns to look at me and I grit my teeth and shake my head.

"You took her into the forest, didn't you?" he asks the man. "Why?"

"The bitch wanted it!"

No.

I DID *NOT*.

"Then why did she bite? You still have a scar from that day. Just where she said it was. Women who *want* it don't bite and grind their teeth till they hit *bone*."

"Look, I don't know why. They're all the same these pr... these teases. They smile at you and then play innocent when it comes down to it."

"What did you say to her?"

"I said *nothing*."

"What did you say?"

"I told her... I..." He drops his head. "Look, she *wanted* it. They all pretend they don't, but once you get going, they turn into whores. *All* of them."

"You admit that she fought you?"

The man drops his head... "Look, maybe I misread her, alright?"

"You either did or you didn't."

"Fine. I *did*. I fucked up. I thought she was up for it. I'm... I'm sorry."

"You are?"

"Yeah, I am, okay?"

"Say it to her."

"What?"

"Apologize to her for what you tried to do to her. What you *did* to her. You tried to take her soul from her. You almost succeeded."

"Fine." He finally makes eye contact with me. "I'm sorry." He hisses the word before collecting himself, as if realizing he's supposed to be conveying contrition.

I don't respond. I *don't* believe him. And I don't care what he says.

"Can I go now?" he asks, turning to look at Sebastian whose hands ball into fists by his sides.

"You're sorry?"

"Yes!"

"If you're sorry, Adam," Sebastian asks. His tone is smooth, but his breathing is rabid and his body tense, as if containing anger. "Then, why are you here?"

"I'm... You told me I... You... you *entrapped* me."

"No," Sebastian responds, his tone as if carved from ice. "I *tested* you. And you *failed*."

"I... I wasn't going to do anything..."

"We know of some of your other victims. One is now dead. Two were fifteen. We imagine there are many, many more. You've been doing this your whole adult life, haven't you?"

"Look, I... I... I've got a fucking problem, okay? It's not my fault. It's a fucking disease! I've tried. I can't stop it!"

"Tried? A young woman went to the police about you *four* months ago, later retracting her statement, no doubt upon intimidation by your family."

"Look, it's my dad's fault, okay? He's got the same disease. He gave me a taste for it."

"And what can be done about men like you who can't stop?"

"I'll... I'll turn myself in... to the police."

"It seems a little late for that, Adam. So much damage has been done." He takes a step towards the man. "Now *get* up."

"No!"

"Get on your fucking feet," Sebastian growls.

"No!" the man whimpers, raising his hand in the air.

Sebastian's eyes flit to meet Isaiah's. "Get him up."

Isaiah and Vallen walk over, sliding their hands under the man's armpits, lifting him onto his feet before tugging his cloak off and throwing it onto the ground nearby to reveal a white T-shirt over black jeans.

"Look, I'm sorry for what I did, okay? It's a fucking illness! Do you think I wanted to be like this?! I can't control it!"

Sebastian's head tips slightly forwards. "It's taken you a while to come to this realization. Blood has been spilled along the way..."

"Look, I'll stop, okay. I've been wanting to stop for some time."

"Why haven't you?"

"I... I've tried, okay. It's like... demons inside me. I can't stop them."

For a moment, I see a vision before me—some dark figure standing, watching over both men, its body tall and black, bent over, hooved, black wings folded behind it.

Jess...

"What do you have to say to her?" Sebastian's thunderous timber shakes my body.

The man looks at me, glaring for a moment as he takes in my face, before softening his countenance, clearly deliberately. "Look, I'm sorry, alright. I... I got it wrong. I thought... I made a mistake." He turns back to Sebastian. "Look, I just wanna get the fuck out of here."

"*Out?* I've told you the conditions for leaving."

"Sebastian, please," I beg, only to be ripped from Grace's grasp by harsh hands in cruel movements which pinch into my skin despite my coat.

"Help me with her," Alexandra snarls as she tries to wrangle me into position. I manage to fend her off until Isaiah's hand snaps around my wrist, yanking it up behind my back. She takes it from him, winding her fingers roughly around my wrist and tugging my hand upwards until I wince in pain.

At the sound, Sebastian turns to look at me before finding Alexandra's eyes behind me, his glower eating into her until she releases me just a tad, enough for the pinch to subside. She wraps her other hand around my body, imparting that same perfume—heavy, spicy, pungent, the kind I'd never wear for the life of me. It takes me back to that initiation I watched, the first time they gave me their potent drugs, the first time I saw Sebastian's naked body, saw the dominant way he owns any space he's in.

When I try to release myself from her grasp, the pinch has me fearing that my shoulder will dislocate and I stop. As her pronounced chin meets the top of my shoulder, the swipe of a blow shudders through me as the man punches Sebastian hard in the jaw while he was looking in our direction.

As if afraid, he doesn't throw a second punch but peers up into

Sebastian's eyes as he slowly turns his head back to face the man who holds his shaky hands up as if ready to punch again.

"You really *are* a coward," Sebastian utters coldly. "Do it again."

"What?"

"You're not making it out alive unless you take me out. They've been instructed"—he gestures towards the men on the periphery—"to not intervene to rescue me under any circumstances. So… take me out..."

The man's fist flies at Sebastian's face again, only this time, I see the faintest stain of blood as his lip is sliced open.

No...

Sebastian lifts his fingers to his lip, bringing them down slowly to observe the blood. "Again," he orders.

"No!" I shout as the man rams his fist into Sebastian's face. I try to advance, but Isaiah winds his hand around my bicep, stopping me as Alexandra pulls me into her body. "Stop!"

The man punches five times, taking a breath between each one as Sebastian takes it, bracing himself so as not to fall until blood finally flies from his mouth, and on the sixth punch, Sebastian blocks it, waiting a moment before landing one of his own.

The man yelps in pain as Sebastian's fist collides, taking steps backwards before turning to run. He's stopped by Ilya and Vallen Markov who throw him back into the circle where Sebastian punches again before turning to look at me, blood trickling from his mouth.

"Close your eyes," he orders.

"No!" I shout, but it's too late.

The next few minutes flash before me as if in bursts of gunpowder, for Sebastian, who had once administered measured punches to exact locations, loses control, his breathing tenebrous rasps as he punches over and over again until the man's knees hit the dirt.

"Stop!" I plead before closing my eyes tightly, only to have Alexandra's lips brush against my cheek.

"You bitch," she snarls. "You're not going to manipulate our president with that nauseating compassion of yours like you do everyone else. Do you realize how lucky you are, you ungrateful little *bitch*? Do you know what I would give to have the men who stole the last years of my childhood in front of me now...?"

No...

My senses are muted, replaced by the horror of hearing Sebastian beat the man. I can't help but open my eyes, just a sliver to see his movements so dynamic that they melt into a murderous blur.

A dragon, thirsty for blood...

His growl is almost a snarl, the heft of his feverish stamp to the man's face so unyieldingly brutal. The man's yelps and pleas reverberate through the woods, followed by thuds and cracks of bone, and then finally, the savage kicks by Isaiah, Ilya and Vallen to the lifeless body as Sebastian stands back and heaves heavy breaths to calm himself down.

I wasn't supposed to see it. He told me to close my eyes.

But I couldn't help but have them jolted open for split seconds by the horror of the sounds, the desperation in the unintelligible groans, the high-pitched whimpers, the crack of bones in his face...

Until...

Finally, there is no more noise.

The woods tumble into eerie silence as I tremble in Alexandra's arms, opening my eyes fully to see the man lying face up on the ground, his mouth open, his face a bloody spectacle of gore. Sebastian stands over him, his knuckles stained with blood, his face injured, as he catches his breath.

"*You'll never unsee it,*" Alexandra hisses into my ear, her final parting words before letting go of my body and standing to the side.

Sebastian turns his head to meet my gaze and I take a step back at the sight of the wounded animal, the murderer as he walks towards me. Stumbling backwards, I turn and run only to hear his growl.

"She's mine."

I don't get far—twenty feet maybe, until I'm caught and spun around to face the man who whose blood seeps onto his pale skin like petals of rose falling into ivory snow.

His teeth are stained with blood, his eye swollen, his lip cut, the sight of him making me tremble as he walks me backwards, pinning me against the thick trunk of a conifer.

"Why?" I ask, peering up at wild eyes flecked with glistening shards of silver.

"When that man touched you like that," he breathes, "he lost the right to live."

I watch in horror as trickles of crimson drip down his face, observing the swollen skin, the pink flesh which will soon turn to black.

"Your face," I utter.

"I don't care," he responds.

"I didn't want that, Sebastian," I whisper.

"Yes you did. You just didn't have the strength to ask me for it." I swallow hard as he peers down at me. "No one will ever hurt you like that again."

3

"Baby?"

Jack's voice echoes around the apartment as the door bangs shut. Upon the clunk of keys in a bowl, my breath hitches as the apartment dissolves into silence.

"Baby?"

"I'm... in the bath, Jack. Just give me a few minutes." I realize my voice barely carried as I wrap my arms around my bent legs tightly, willing myself to leave the grotesque comfort of the bathtub.

I stare at the now-cold water, the suds having dissolved to reveal clear liquid that distorts my legs with shadows which dance and flicker courtesy of two large candles placed around the otherwise unlit bathroom. It's been an hour since I was dropped back off at the apartment and ran a bath in the hopes of cleansing myself of what I saw today.

Murder.

Not just a murder, but the beating to death of a man by another man who believed, somehow, that he was healing me by doing it...

I don't fully understand why Sebastian did it. I feel more trauma now than I've felt in years over what happened. Or maybe, as he says, it's acute trauma that I can heal from rather than the chronic unhealed trauma from that event.

Is this why Sebastian did it? To heal me? To free me? Or was it to pull me into his world? To haul me through some invisible veil so that, bit by bit, in the face of shadows bearing down on me, I succumb to the promise of release from pain, and become part of the fabric of the underworld he reigns over with such malicious grace.

Or was he really killing someone else? He killed his mother once, the ruthless child abuser. The man was an abuser of children too. Did Sebastian need to kill him to attempt to snuff out the dregs of the thing that crawled from her into him? Was he trying to stamp her out? I've never heard Gabriel speak of him wanting to heal the part of himself that is so malevolent. Why now?

The horror I feel is mixed with guilt.

He did that for me...

But I never asked for that...

At the low thud of footsteps on the stairs, I peer down at the tepid water. The suds have now all vanished, exposing my bare legs, the ones I've stared at for the last half hour as I've relived the events of today, which are constantly infiltrated by images of what happened to Rose, leaving me unable to reconcile that act with what I've seen of Sebastian.

I shiver at the sound of the bedroom door opening, and then the bathroom, taking a deep breath and smiling as brightly as I can in the circumstances as Jack enters wearing the designer suit he wears on Wall Street with such savage equanimity.

Hold it together, Jess.

He looks at me quizzically as he pushes the door closed before removing his tie and draping it over the back of a chair in the corner.

"How was work?" I ask, my attempt at sounding breezy coming off ridiculously stilted.

"The usual pigfest," he replies, sliding the wooden chair across the room so that he can sit right next to me. He never talks much about work. It's as if he's trying to shield me from the demons he encounters there... I guess we try to do that for each other...

His eyes narrow as his gaze sweeps up my body before soaking in my face. "What's wrong, baby?"

"Nothing," I respond swiftly.

"You're shaking. Why?"

Jack...

How do I begin to tell you...?

Why can I tell Sebastian dark secrets about myself and not tell my own husband who has so many of his own? What it is about Sebastian that makes me want to tell him everything? That makes me want to *know* everything. Even his secrets whisper to him, a fact that makes me feel so lost.

I find Jack's lingering gaze for a moment but can't speak for my senses are muted and replaced by the momentary horror of seeing Sebastian beat the man to death, his movements so dynamic, his growl almost a snarl, the heft of his stamps to the man's face so unyieldingly brutal.

I hear the man's yelps and pleas, and the thuds and cracks of bone, and then finally, the barbarous kicks by Isaiah and Vallen as Sebastian stood back and heaved heavy breaths to calm himself down.

I wasn't supposed to see it. He told me to close my eyes.

But I couldn't help but have them jolted open by the barbarity of the sounds.

"What is it?" he repeats.

Lying to Jack's face is almost impossible. Despite everything that's happened between us, this raw, gritty, honest bond we share never seems to dull. He seems to be able to read me, see into me, feel things about myself that I haven't uttered yet.

"I've just been in the water too long," I respond.

He dips his hand in, his expression perplexed. He reaches for the faucet against the wall and turns on the hot water whose current warms my legs.

"It's cold," he says, curiosity clinging to the word.

"I've gotten used to it," I smile, trying to drown out the visions playing over and over in my mind of blood and torture.

Without another word, he gets to his feet, unbuttoning his thick white shirt and peeling it off the slabs of muscle that make up his torso. He watches me with the eyes of a predator as he slides his belt out and then unzips his pants, pulling them and his briefs down off his feet, revealing his semi-hard erection. He removes his socks, throwing all the clothes into the wicker laundry basket in the corner of the room.

Without asking for permission, he climbs into the large tub, his massive bulk filling up so much of it that it shifts the water up a full six inches or so. He places his feet between my legs, spreading my thighs apart as he studies my face.

"I haven't seen you take a bath in a long time," he says. He glances at the bottle of Bordeaux standing on the wide rim of the large tub next to a half-full wine glass. "Nor drink strong red wine alone."

"Well," I respond, my voice small even to my own ears. "I was just in the mood for it tonight."

He picks up the bottle and swirls it a little. He must feel that it's at least a third empty. I don't like to drink alone, and especially not red wine on an empty stomach, but I'm no longer processing everything that's happened lately fast enough for my nervous system to catch up. I grabbed the bottle after trying and failing to text Gabriel in the hopes that I could talk through the man's murder with him... but I'm so afraid of what he'll tell Cameron about what happened or that Sebastian will learn that I told Gabriel that I chickened out at the last minute.

He puts the bottle back down, eyeing me sternly as he turns off the hot water now that the temperature in the tub has gone up a few degrees. His eyes tighten into slits, his features blackening as he takes me in.

"How was your day?" he asks, though it sounds more like a test than a question.

"Okay," I say, my heart beginning to race.

"Hmm. Come here," he orders, glancing down at my nipples just hovering above the surface of the water.

Something about his tone takes me aback. "No," I respond, glaring back at him in defiance.

Stealing a gasp from my throat, he reaches forwards and grabs me, pulling me into him, bending my legs and lifting my feet so that I'm sitting between his inner thighs with my legs wrapped around his waist. He hauls me into his body so that my taut wet nipples slip against the wall of his chest as he threads his fingers into my hair and tugs my neck back.

"Your defiance will get you into trouble one day."

"What the fuck's got into you?!"

"Me?" he retorts, his glower like glowing charcoal. "I don't like the word *Okay*, Jessynia, as you fucking well know. I don't like the civility of it. The banality. It's nauseating. Vapid. You don't use words like that. *Ever*." He pulls at my hair until I wrap my hands around his thick wrists. "I feel like you're hiding from me. *Again*. I don't know how much longer I can take it."

I whimper as he extends my neck backwards so that I'm forced to peer up at him. "You're hurting me."

"How do I get inside your head, Jessynia?" he asks, his frustration morphing into what looks like anguish, not an emotion a man like Jack is used to being vulnerable enough to show. "There are secrets in there. I feel them. Ones that weren't there before. How do I know them? Do I have to have you followed again?"

"What?! No!"

"Then tell me. How? I never used to feel that you were hiding from me."

"I'm not... I'm... I don't want to subject you to every stupid thing I'm feeling."

"I want to be fucking well subjected to them. I want to know what's in your head. I've told you that before. How do I get in there, Jessynia?"

I swallow hard at his solemn concern. I want to tell Jack so much. About that man. About Cameron. About Sebastian. About what I saw him do today. I'm just... afraid. What if I set off some war? Or trauma? What if I implicate Jack in what happened? I've dealt with that day back in Albany by not telling the men around me, by not letting myself be seen as weak. I don't know how to share everything I've experienced in the last year.

I want to... but I don't know where the chips will fall if I do.

His brutal lips slip against mine. "How do I get inside you, angel? How do I get you to open up and trust me? What do I have to do?"

"I *do* trust you."

"Not enough," he snarls. "Not enough to tell me what's on your fucking mind. Why? Trying to protect me from something? Is that it? Well, in the process, you're hurting me."

"Jack, stop," I plead at the flicker of distress in his face. "I'm not trying to hurt you. Ever."

"Well, you *are*. I'm trying to control the animal inside me, Jessynia. The savage who wants to chain you up and lock you in this apartment so that I never have to fear losing you again. I'm trying to be civilized, but I can't feel like you're hiding from me. I can't allow it. I know you too well. I feel when you're not there. Do you understand that?"

I nod slowly, sinking into the deep cerulean pools of his eyes. I slide a hand onto his bicep, the hard girth of it soothing me despite its innate savagery. My lips part at the flex of his muscle.

At the taciturn gesture of awe at his brutish masculinity, he loosens his grip on my hair and slides his thumb over my jaw and onto my lips. He pushes into them, moving his thumb gently from side to side, exploring the slippery amaranth flesh of my wet lips.

Without even meaning to, upon years of training, I part them, an invitation for him to push the digit inside, just a little... and then more, slipping his thumb against my saliva, gliding it left to right before pressing further, the tip touching my tongue, invading more, until finally, he penetrates my mouth fully, watching me, testing me as I begin to suck, my eyes wide on his. He's always evaluated my willingness to submit like this, my willingness to let him invade my body when he needs to.

His eyes half-close and he lets out a rough exhalation as my lips clamp around his thumb and my tongue slips against the underside as I suck.

His hand winds around my back and suddenly, he releases his thumb from my mouth and I am hauled into his hard chest so tightly that I can't move. His hard sex, a smooth column of wood, slips against my pussy as his hands weave into my hair, tilting my head back.

"You can't hide from me by giving me your sex," he utters sternly.

"I'm not trying to hide, Jack. I... I want to tell you everything I feel. I just... I need to feel that it's... safe."

"You still don't fully trust me?"

It's not just you I don't trust, Jack...

It's myself.

It's everyone around me...

"Do you trust me when I fuck you, Jessynia? Do you trust me not to hurt you?"

"Yes," I respond, realizing that I do.

"Hmm." The low groan drops from his throat. "I can fuck you whenever you want. My body belongs to you, angel. But at some point, I need you to feel that you've given me your soul as well as your body, Jessynia, just as I have given you mine. Do you understand that?"

"Give it *back* to you," I correct softly, for he once owned *all* of me.

His large cock, fully hard, slips against the entrance to my body in the water. He could take me now, but I know what he's thinking. It's not enough.

"I'm going to make this work, Jessynia," he says, the bite to the affirmation making me swallow hard. "No matter how much you fight me. Or how much you hide from me. Or how much you hate me, or want to run from me. I will be getting you back. *All* of you. I hope you know that. I won't give up. Not on us." I peer into his earnest eyes as his strong wet hand slides up my slim back. "And before you ask, *no*, you don't have a fucking choice in the matter."

I can't help but smile. Maybe it's a nervous smile but the boldness of his dominance and the certainty with which he talks about our marriage helps to relieve the wiry ball of tension knotted in my gut.

"Is that clear, Mrs. Wilder?"

I nod, praying for the day I can really believe in us like I did before.

God, please let it come...

He looks to the side and grabs a bottle of shampoo, pulling my hand up and dropping a dollop into my palm.

"Wash your hair," he orders.

"What?!"

The ghost of a smile on his face shows me that he's at least attempting to lighten the tension billowing between us like the most unforgiving of gales.

"You heard me."

"I've already washed it," I sigh out with a rueful shake of the head.

"Do it again," he instructs sternly, though a glint of mirth makes his voice less gravelly than usual.

"May I ask why?" I respond, adding on a coat of attitude in an effort to allay the strain between us at unspoken words, at the veiled secrets blocking the path to one another.

"Because I like watching you."

I shake my head at the sinful tone and lift my hand. The fresh scent of mint floats between us as I apply the pastel-green shampoo to my hair, massaging it into my scalp as he slides his hands down the side of the tub and leans back, fucking me with his eyes.

"Is this some weird kink of yours, Wilder?" I ask with a nervous smile.

"I'm not sure," he replies. "We'll have to see."

His gaze wanders onto my tits which bounce as I massage the shampoo into my hair.

"I know you're getting off on this," I chide.

"You turn me on, Jessynia. Everything you do makes me hard. Especially when you follow my instructions like a good little girl." He slides his finger underneath my body and locates my sex, sliding his index finger up and down my clit.

"Jack..."

"Don't fucking stop," he orders as the sensation makes me stop rubbing.

I continue to work the shampoo into my hair as he twists his wrist and curves his finger and pushes it into my sex.

"Don't stop." The severe bite to his words steals my breath.

He inserts a second finger and I bite my lip at the delicious stretch, at the threat in the invasion. He pushes halfway to my cervix and withdraws before taking a plastic container sitting on the side of the large white tub, dunking it into the water and rinsing my hair, watching as water spills over my face.

"Fuck." His thumb traces the wet skin on my cheeks. "Your beauty is insane," he whispers. "Do you know, I sometimes wonder whether you're real, Jessynia."

"Nice line, Wilder," I scoff with a smile.

He takes the bottle of shampoo and squeezes some into my hand. "Wash my hair," he instructs.

The order makes me grin nervously and his eyes gleam at my hesitant amusement, albeit one tempered by the frankly diabolical way his eyes are devouring me.

"This is definitely some weird kink, Wilder," I smile.

"Could be," he replies, his lips curving ruefully. "I'm trying to figure that out."

I press my palms together to distribute the shampoo and then lift my hands to his thick dirty-blond hair. I rub my palms over it and my fingers through it as his fingers locate my nipples and tug... hard.

"Ow," I moan only for his lips to curl into a smile that should be illegal. His greedy hands knead my slippery breasts as I massage the shampoo into his hair, taking care to work his scalp.

"Do you like it?" I ask and he tips his head slowly to indicate yes, only for goosebumps to draw my skin tight as I recall what happened today in an unexpected detonation of gunpowder that makes the scene around me turn to white.

I feel my hands in his hair, but for a moment, realize they're not moving.

"Jessynia..."

I blink only for him to fall into focus, concern painted onto his face.

"Baby," he says.

You'll never unsee it...

Taking a deep breath to steady myself, I grab the gray handle of the plastic container that Jack placed back into the corner of the tub, fill it with water and use it to rinse his hair, watching the rivulets trickle down the breathtaking planes of his face. His angular cheekbones are stunning, carving through his broad face. Droplets of water cling to his dark lashes, framing aquamarine eyes which pierce you mercilessly.

Without a word, he cups and lifts my ass cheeks and tugs me into him until the head of his cock rests against the entrance to my sex.

"Grab my cock and sit down on it," he orders and I bite my lip as I reach down to grab the hard column with one hand while curling my palm over his other shoulder.

He watches me, eyes wild, as I slide down onto him, gasping as he fills me up. He contracts the muscles in his thighs, core and arms to pulse deep into me. My wet tits slip against the huge, heavy armor of his chest and my eyes are drawn to his full pale pink lips, glistening in the dimmed light of the bathroom.

He leans back against the tub, his gaze wandering greedily down my body. "Ride my cock, angel," he orders.

I hold onto the sides of the tub and contract my thigh muscles and my glutes to lift and lower myself onto him, closing my eyes at times as I feel him strain against my cervix.

"Don't take your eyes off my face," he instructs and I comply, feeling myself blush profusely as he takes in the spectacle, groaning audibly at the sensation until...

I blink several times, peering into him, as the clear water on his face turns to wet branches of blood before my eyes.

I stop all movement, waiting for the vision to disappear. My name is spoken by him but turns into a drowned blur and a moment later, he sits bolt upright, coiling his hands around me, pulling my hair back so that I'm forced to peer up at him, relieved to find the blood gone, replaced by clear, glistening water.

At my sudden inertia, he pulses inside my open sex, studying my face, pinning me against him so that I couldn't get away if I wanted to.

"Where the fuck are you, Jessynia?" he snarls as he thrusts deep into me, not moving for a few seconds before pulling out and driving back in again.

"I... I'm here."

His face hardens. "You think that being inside you is enough?" he asks, the words pouring out as if molten metal.

"Jack, stop..."

"It isn't," he growls. "I need *all* of you, Jessynia. I need your mind. Your soul. Your heart. I need you to only see me, the way I only see you."

"Jack..."

"Who is it inside your head? I no longer know."

I swallow hard as he evokes not one man, but two...

"Jack..."

"How do I get inside you the way I need?"

In a burst of anger, he lowers me down onto him hard, his cock pushing against my cervix with a pinch which makes me gasp.

I so desperately want to tell him that I belong only to him. I want to rewind time to a year ago when the thought of other men never crossed my mind, when I hung on his every word and melted under his every touch. I want so badly to get back to that.

His brow furrows. "You still don't trust me, do you?"

I close my eyes as the vision of Sebastian striking the man's bloody face jolts through me like a jolt of lightning.

I open them after a moment, stunned to see Jack peering at me, feeling like I've lost time...

"I do, Jack. I'm trying to."

It's not just Jack I don't trust anymore. It's me. It's Cameron. It's Sebastian. It's my friends, at times. Maybe I've lost my ability to trust anyone...

He contemplates the reality that we're not fully healed, that the hurt over him fucking Alexandra and so many other women and my affair with Cameron have chipped away at a bond that once tied us together unyieldingly, allowing water to trickle into the cracks, and rot to sink in that I'm trying to scrape away.

I love Jack and I forgive him for what happened, especially in light of my own sins, but I can't escape the fact that finding that phone or seeing him on that balcony or watching him fuck that woman with my own eyes has left me unable to believe in him with my whole heart the way I used to... and I so want to.

A minute passes during which he fucks me in silence but for light splashes of water that glisten around us. He holds me so tightly that I can't move, giving him the access that he needs to my sex into which he pulses, getting so hard and thick that the stretch begins to sting a little.

"You're going to trust me, Jessynia."

I frown as he begins to lean into me.

"Jack!" I exclaim as he begins to push me backwards, holding me as I brace myself against the sides of the tub. "What are you doing?"

He withdraws from my sex and pushes my torso down in the huge white tub and climbs on top of me. He's so heavy that I'm pushed to the bottom of the tub and I have to brace against the sides with my hands to keep my head and neck above the water.

"Hey!"

"Open your legs. Give your husband his pussy."

"No!"

"Now!"

Upon my refusal, he slides his legs between mine, forcing my knees to bend and my legs to part further as he rams his hard length into me, glaring down at my face as he does.

"Let go," he orders.

"No!"

"Let go, Jessynia. Don't make me make you."

"What is wrong with you?! You're scaring me!"

I grip the sides of the tub tightly but he pries my hands off before grasping the back of my head by my hair and pushing me down with his body until just my chin and face are above the water.

"Stop!"

But my exclamation is swallowed by the tepid water as my head goes underneath, yanked down by his merciless grip. He fucks me slowly as my legs flail and my hands try to push him off me. He's too big, too strong, his muscles too dense, his torso too large. I can't move him.

A moment later, he slides me forwards, lifting my head above the surface of the water as I take in a lungful of air.

"What is wrong with you?! Stop!"

Before I go under again, he utters words that Sebastian Gravier said to me a few hours ago—words I wonder if he once said to Rose...

"I won't hurt you."

"No!"

As my head is fully submerged once again, I flail beneath him, my eyes wide on his, seeing him through the distortion of the tumultuous water as he grips my hair with his hands, stopping me from coming up. His hard dick burrows deep inside me as he keeps me under water for ten seconds, maybe more, until he suddenly yanks me up and I take in air.

He watches me until my breathing calms and then slowly pushes me back under... although this time, I panic a little less, watching his face through the veil of the water as he evaluates mine for a few seconds before pulling me back up.

Amidst what seems to be one of the two candles in the room burning out, the shadows begin to play tricks on me and moving pieces of another man's face float into view as he begins to fuck me faster, harder, longer.

Thick shoulder-length hair flops over his face as he drives into me, taking pleasure from my vulnerability, my submission, my compliance... and the fact that my survival depends on his graciousness—on his decision to bring me back up for air.

Sebastian...

My hands reach for the slippery sides of the ceramic tub as he takes my body, groaning loudly, the silver threads of his eyes alight with white flame as he revels in the desperate state I find myself in, in the threat of the crawl towards death...

As my fingers grab the side of the tub, they collide with something hard, knocking over my half-full glass of wine and causing the deep maroon liquid to fall into the water, turning it the faintest pink.

At the sight of it and the thought of Rose, panic grips me, making me fight underneath him. As my body begins to flail more desperately, he withdraws from my sex and pulls me out of the water, lifting me and sitting me on top of him as he bends his knees underneath me and his arms wrap tightly around my dripping body.

"Jack," I pant, my lips finding his shoulder as he holds me against him for a long minute until I catch my breath.

"You're looking for monsters, Jessynia," he finally breathes into me. "And you'll find them while you try to make them human. While you try to solve puzzles which will end up killing you. This is the reality of them. This isn't a fucking game. I need you to understand that."

I close my eyes, holding onto his shoulders as his hands knead my back.

"I'm here, angel. I've always been here. No matter what I've done, I've always been here. Can't you see me anymore?" The low plea into my ear denotes throughout my body, but the possessive strength of his tight grip calms my heart rate.

After what feels like an eternity, he tilts my head back with his hands, his dark gaze roaming over my face, as mine does his. "Do you see me?"

I nod slowly.

"You have to trust me," he utters. "You *have* to. Nothing can work without that."

I nod, swallowing down a tear that trickles into the seam between my lips.

He exhales a weighty breath before dipping his head towards mine. "Who do you see, Jessynia? When I fuck you like that?"

The realization that he knows that Sebastian owns part of my consciousness skewers me like a knife.

Pain registers in the crease between his brows as I remain silent. "Did you see him?" he asks. "Alone?"

I gulp down nerves as I nod my head.

"Why?"

I don't answer and a low rasp of anger leaves his throat. "You're trying to save people somehow," he snarls. "I know it. I can feel it. You have no idea what you're doing. You have no idea how dangerous he is."

"I do," I retort.

"No you *don't*," he growls. "If I find out that you've seen him again, he and I will go to war, Jessynia. I promise you that. Do you want that?"

I shake my head. "No, Jack."

He slides his hands up the sides of my body as he tries to temper his breathing. "Do you understand how much I love you? Do you know that you are the only thing that exists in this world to me? That every breath I take is made possible because of the thought of you, that every day I work, I do it so I can always keep you safe, that every woman I talk to, I see your face?"

"Jack, stop."

His stormy eyes clash with mine. "You are the only source of light in the darkness. Do you know that?"

I nod.

"Then show it to me, baby. Show me you feel it."

"I'm trying."

Without a word, Jack pushes me off him, causing water to splash all around as he lifts his mammoth body out of the bathtub, and reaches for me, dipping his hands back into the water and yanking me up. He picks me up and carries me to the bedroom and places my naked body down onto our bed.

He doesn't bother with a towel, and I'm not capable of the speech needed to protest about making the sheets wet, nor do I care right now. Everything fades into insignificance amidst recurring flashes of that man's blood spattering onto Sebastian's skin.

The mattress shifts as Jack climbs onto the bed and on top of me, pulling the covers over us. He tugs my face to look at him, his gaze soaking in my features.

At the sight of his eyes, I tremble internally, feeling my muscles quiver as I recall the vicious blows dealt by Sebastian. I felt them in my body. I heard them. I heard the man fall.

"What is it?" Jack repeats, his glacial eyes flaring like errant embers in the dim light. "What do you see?"

I don't know where to start...

I saw a man be murdered in front of me.

A man that once tried to hurt me.

"Jack... Hold me," I say.

He slides his hand under my back, cradling my neck, holding me, watching me. His other hand reaches down and feeds his cock into my pussy as he begins to fuck me gently. I peer up at him as he glides into and out of me so softly, the movements precise, meticulous. He angles his hips in a way which stimulates me differently with each slow drive into my body, his fingers slipping between our torsos, down to my clit which he begins to press into... over... and over as I close my eyes, desperate for the relief I know he can give me.

"Do you feel me, angel?" he asks into my ear.

"Yes," I reply.

"Do you like being fucked by my hard cock?"

"Yes."

"Good." As he increases the cadence of his drives into me and presses into my clit, sliding his fingers up and down with my own wetness, I grab the sheets with both hands and pant loudly as the orgasm rocks through my quivering core, relieving me of what feels like a century's worth of suffocating black tension.

Despite my closed eyes, light erupts before me and I relax my body, hearing Jack groan like a beast through explosive thrusts which shake me until he finally collapses onto me, expelling rabid breaths as I melt into the sheer beautiful weight of the man.

I finally open my eyes to find him peering down at me.

"I'm here, Jessynia. I'll *always* be here. And I'm taking you back. Every single piece that I've lost."

4

I have to see you.

My hands quiver as I press Send on the message to Sebastian Gravier.

I've spent the last two hours pacing the apartment, trying to think of anything but what happened. It's been two days during which I've barely slept. I know I'm experiencing an acute trauma response. I know it will calm in the days and weeks to come, but right now I feel as if I've just journeyed into hell and the things that live there won't let me out.

I keep hearing the noises, seeing the vicious blows meted out by

Sebastian over and over. I see the blood pooling onto the floor, taste it in my mouth.

What's more, I can't tell anyone. Not Jack. Not my friends. Not my parents.

Not Cameron...

I feel like he'd understand it, maybe—the darkness of it, the need for retribution. With Jack, I'm so afraid of triggering his childhood trauma, of awakening the beast inside him that whispers uncivilized words to him, that taunts him about being too weak, that I fear telling him anything like this.

I can't even confide in a therapist without being afraid they'd contact the authorities.

The only person I know to turn to is the man who designed it. The man who designs everything.

My breathing grows shallow as a reply pops up on my screen.

Someone will pick you up. He is safe. Ten minutes. 87th and Columbus.

Pick me up?

What if Leon's around? What if he sees me leave?

He hasn't been around much in the last few days, thanks to Jack's orders, but I never know with him. He's so unpredictable.

As the vision of them driving me back to QN rolls across my mind, I hear Sebastian's voice, his previous utterance echoing through the room.

One day, you will beg to see me...

Is this how he intended to make that happen?

Was he trying to heal me by killing that man? Or entrap me? Make me need him... Make me depend on him to stay sane...

I change from my nightgown into black leggings, a navy camisole, and one of several crocheted beige sweaters that Babs made for me years ago when she knew they comforted me. I don't care how I look when I see him...

I don my faux-suede ankle boots, loose denim jacket and the now-tatty turquoise scarf that I've had since I first met Jack, grab my phone and purse, and leave, taking quivering breaths as I lock the door behind me and head into the mirrored elevator.

I don't leave through the foyer for fear of our concierge Tom seeing me, but instead, go down into the garage and leave our building through the side door.

As I walk down 87th Street in the direction of Columbus Avenue, I see the car as if trained to constantly be on the lookout for them.

A large black SUV.

Tinted windows.

A tall stocky man stands out front on the sidewalk—the same man that was standing next to Isaiah when I left the house Nathan took me to. The same man that watched the man be beaten to death. Sebastian must trust him...

He watches me, his glare unflinching, as I approach. His skin is olive and his eyes like discs of varnished mahogany. He opens the back passenger door and I swallow hard as I peer through the windshield into the back of the car. It's empty.

He watches me as I hesitate. "Get in, Jessynia," he says as I find his eyes. He has the same impossibly unflinching glare that all of those who frequent that place seem to have...

"What's your name?" I ask.

His eyes narrow. "That's a pointless question. I could say any name I like."

"What is it?"

"Dimitri."

He watches me as I appraise the angles of his stern face. I look behind me for a moment, contemplating whether I should go back—back to pacing my apartment, back to seeing the blood drip before my eyes and hear the gurgling sounds of desperation and death...

I turn back around to face him and take a step forwards. He moves to the side so that I can get in. Before the events of last year, I wasn't in the habit of getting into cars with men I didn't know. Now it's becoming the norm, though it never fails to make my stomach lurch the second I get inside.

As I buckle my seatbelt, I flinch as the man slams the door shut, before getting in himself, observing me through the rear-view mirror before pulling away. On Columbus, he turns left in the direction of Tribeca... as expected, only to take another left onto West 86th, continuing onto the 86th Traverse, one of only four roads that cut through Central Park.

"Where are we going?" I ask, urgency plundering force from my voice, only to repeat the question when he doesn't answer.

"I'm taking you to see our president," the man replies as my heart begins to race in frantic beats.

"Where... where is he?" I ask.

"He's at home."

As his words pour out, I realize that I'm going to Sebastian Gravier's home. I don't know exactly where it is, but I know it's on the Upper East Side, Fifth Avenue, I think.

"Who else will be there?" I ask as we make it through the park and I peer up at the pale stone billion-dollar apartment buildings that line the most expensive residential street in Manhattan, one overlooking Central Park, just as our apartment does on the more humble other side.

He doesn't answer and a few blocks later, as we pull up at a traffic light, I barely dare to look, for the building is that of my friend.

Cameron...

For a second, I fight the impulse to get out of the car and run in to see him.

But I can't...

No matter how much I may want to some days.

A dozen or so blocks later, we pull up to a building and drive into the garage hidden beneath it. The underground cavern is dark and empty and I shudder as the man turns the engine off and watches me through the mirror, plunging us into silence.

"Ready?" he asks.

Jessynia...

Of course I'm not ready, asshole.

I drop my gaze, staring at my hands as the memory of the gruesome slaying of the man hits me once again with unwanted clarity—the crimson specks cascading through the air, the crunch of bone as Sebastian's fist broke his face, just as he had done to his mother two decades earlier, though this time he used his bare hands, his movements rabid, as if possessed by some unearthly thing that needed blood to survive through the night...

"Ready," I respond as boldly as I can. He gets out and opens the door, holding it open for me. He leads me into the elevator—all glossy gold and black—and I close my eyes for a second as he turns a key and presses PH.

Penthouse.

The same letters Cameron presses when he enters his elevator not fifteen blocks down...

As it chimes our arrival at the top floor, I wait for him to get out, but the man bows his head for me to. I do and turn to see the doors closing on him.

"Hey!" I pant, more out of surprise than anything else.

"Goodbye, Jessynia," he responds, and a moment later, I find myself alone.

I turn all around, taking in the striking black wallpaper weaved with threads of gold. As I pivot, my eyes are drawn to the peephole in the black door—the only door on this floor. Silence deafens me as I peer into the hole. I don't see cameras anywhere, but if he really does live here, they must be concealed around the place.

I feel like I'm being watched...

I glance back at the elevator, contemplating whether I should leave or not. On instinct, I press the elevator button, only to find that it doesn't light up. I wait for what feels like a full minute, but it doesn't come. You must have to tap the card on the card reader next to it to go down or something. There's a staircase at the end of the landing, but if you wanted to get away fast, you'd have to run and hope you could do it faster than the person behind you...

Up above, there's a cavernous white ceiling and a tiny window at the top of the wall through which streams muted sunlight, but other than that, the floor is elegant but featureless.

I take a step towards the door, armored from the looks of it, only to see that there is no bell.

For fuck's sake...

I glance behind me at the staircase.

Should I go back?

Do I really need to see this dangerous man?

Can he relieve me of some of the trauma I feel possessing me?

Hasn't he hurt me enough?

I glance at the peephole again, the hammering of my heart echoing through my ears. I know he's watching me. I can feel him.

Courage, Jess...

I bring my hand up to the door and knock, quietly the first time and more loudly the second and third.

And a moment later, a click...

The door opens as if in slow motion and I'm stunned into inertia at the sight of the man standing before me. I glance down at his loose black shirt, its sleeves rolled up to the elbow, and his loose black pants. Nothing adorns his feet and his hair is loose and slightly damp, brushing his shoulders.

There are bruises around one of his eyes and cuts around another and on his lip. His jaw looks slightly swollen, all fading evidence of that man's desperate punches to his face. I wonder for a moment if that's why he brought me here... so that he's not seen at the Society with his beaten face.

His eyes form into serpent-like slits as he watches me while holding the door open for me without a word.

I swear he whispered to me without speaking.

Come in...

I take slow steps towards him, our eyes connecting until I make it through the threshold of the doorway and my gaze is drawn away by the sheer expanse of the room.

The charcoal-gray walls sweep up to a lofty white ceiling with dark beams stretched across it. Huge oil paintings of trees and forests line one wall and on another, a mammoth painting of an ebony mask in shadow.

Intricate rugs of gold, burgundy and beige thread are scattered over the dark hardwood floor. To the left are loveseats and sectionals of black leather surrounding low tables in dark wood. There are brushed metallic accents dotted around and large white candles in glass bowls.

It's decadent but elegant.

As the door behind me clicks shut, I drop my purse and crouch down to remove my ankle boots, placing them next to the wall to reveal goofy socks that Kevin once gave me, my style so at odds with the sheer elegance of this man.

As I stand back up, my hands reach for my scarf only to stop as I find him observing me in tense silence. As I lock eyes with him, I feel the ghost of the thing that has been haunting me for days—the image of him bludgeoning that man to death in front of me. It's a specter that has been hiding in shadows, watching over me since that day and I need it *gone*...

My body freezes as his metal-hewn eyes scrutinize me, and as if realizing my inertia, he takes a step towards me. I step back in defiance, removing the scarf myself, pulling it from my neck. He glares down at me, his face softening a little as his eyes drift over every inch of mine.

I know he can read me. It's disconcerting how much...

I lift my numb hands to my top button and unbutton it. This time, he doesn't encroach into my space and I remove my denim jacket, hanging it onto a hook next to the door.

I feel his eyes bury into me as I turn and begin to take halting steps deeper into what passes as his living room, trying to get accustomed to the dark, dungeonesque colors.

I feel him walking behind me.

I don't know what I'm doing.

I don't even know who I am anymore.

I make it past a coffee table of glistening epoxy resin encapsulating the twisting roots of a tree, with several files atop it. I wander to the far wall that is annihilated by a painting of a hideous black mask. Or maybe to Sebastian, it's beautiful...

In a burst of frustration tainted by a wash of blood before my eyes, I pivot to come face to face with him, our gazes colliding as I make a concerted effort to stand my ground in light of the otherworldly potency and beauty of his rugged face and whatever is etched into it—concern, maybe. Frustration? Or something more sinister...

With Sebastian, there's never just one emotion—concern may appear chiseled into the stunning angles of his face, though you can sense the malevolence at war with it. Sadness may deign to erupt from time to time like magma from a deep crack in the Earth, but it can cool into the rigid tar of intransigent wrath in the blink of an eye. You never know where you are.

"Are we alone?" I ask.

Fuck, my voice sounds small.

He nods slowly.

"There's no one hiding in some room somewhere?"

"I'm not sure I appreciate the question," he retorts.

"I don't give a fuck if you appreciate it!"

Great. Look unhinged right from the start.

"We're alone."

"How do I know you're telling the truth?" I ask.

His features storm, obfuscated by the shadows he toys with so deftly. "I always tell you the truth, Jessynia, no matter how hideous. Just as I expect you to do to me. We are *alone*."

He takes a step closer towards me and I inch back until my back hits the wall, raising my chin. I'm not showing this asshole that I'm afraid. If only my fucking body would cooperate...

"Why did you want to see me, Jessynia?"

"You don't want me here?"

His lips curve slightly at the corner. "That sounds particularly insecure of you. It would disappoint me if that were your nature."

I shake my head at the man's never-ending riddles. "I didn't mean it *that* way."

"You know full well that I have desired you to come to me willingly since I met you," he adds.

"I'm not here to *be* with you," I counter, hoping my tone doesn't ring hollow.

"Not yet," he responds, his voice as cavernous as the room we're in. "That day is coming..."

"I feel trauma, Sebastian. Trauma at what happened. I can't get it out of my fucking mind!"

"That's a normal response, Jessynia. An acute trauma response, like I told you. It will pass with time."

"Well, it's been four days and it doesn't feel like it's passing!" I retort. "And what's it going to leave me with? Post-traumatic stress?!"

"Only if you don't get it out."

"That's the point! I can't get it out! I can't tell anyone!"

"You can tell *me*."

"Is that why you did it?!" I shout, panic surging through my body in relentless swells of roaring water at the thought of going home and facing those visions again. "To leave me traumatized and dependent on you to heal from it?!"

His face tenses, the angles harshening, as if incised by a blade. "*No*." He breathes out the rough word as if consumed by bitter outrage at the accusation.

His rancor silences me but I hold my glare. I can't soften around this man, nor convey contrition the way I do with Jack and Cameron. I'm already on the precipice and aware of the perfidious pull of him—a being who would promise to erase my pain. I need to keep my wits about me.

"Tell me about the trauma, Jessynia."

"Why?! So you can feast off my pain as you love to do?!"

"So that I know how to help you."

"Help me?"

"Yes."

Be careful, Jessynia...

"I... I can't sleep. I can't think. I keep seeing it and hearing it over and over again! I'm afraid of being stuck like this forever. I know that to shift trauma you have to get it out, to tell people, and I can't!"

"You could go to the police," he suggests flippantly. "You could tell them what you saw."

I pause for a moment. "You know I won't do that."

"Why not?" he asks.

The truth is that the thought of him going to prison for taking out that monster makes me sick to my stomach.

"You know why not..."

He inhales deeply, his lips parting as he contemplates my words. "I want you to get it out with me," he says, edging towards me.

"I shouldn't have to get it out with you!" I shout. "I wasn't even given a choice! You just decided that today is the day that I murder a man with my bare hands, oh and just to make it extra spicy, I'll make Jessynia watch his face be caved in!"

I jump as his palm nails the wall behind me and the fingers of his other hand curve around my throat, holding me in place. "I don't allow men to hurt you and get away with it. From the day you met me, what happened was beyond your control to prevent."

"So why did I have to see it?"

"Most people would want to see those who have harmed them suffer, no?"

I shake my head in outrage. "I think you're confusing me with your friend Alexandra Frost! I didn't want to see that!"

He leans into me, forcing me to peer up at a man whose size and presence make him feel like a giant. "Yes, you did," he utters softly. "You wanted to see it, but as usual, Jessynia, you can't face the reality of who you are. You can't face what hides in the darkness. You can't embrace it. You're afraid of what you'll see there... so instead, you hide, you hide from me, from the world, from yourself. You extinguish your own flame out of fear. I won't allow it anymore. You had to see it. And one day, you will revel in the memory of his light extinguishing before you."

"Well, right now, all I feel is terror and trauma. I can hear his voice, Sebastian! I can see his blood pouring from him. Everything feels black! And I don't know how to make it stop!"

His fingers slip across my jaw as he leans into me. "You will share it with me, over and over again, until it has no power anymore and you feel relief flood your body. You will speak the things to me that you won't with anyone else. I want to hear them. *All* of them. No matter how heinous."

"Why?"

"Because I want you freed. I want you strong. And because knowing you, all of you, the darkest parts... it soothes me, Jessynia."

"How?"

"It dulls the rage."

"You don't have to live with this rage..."

"You can't give me advice when you can't even heal yourself," he snarls, dragging the room into cold dark. His shifts in mood are not as extreme as those of Alexandra Frost, but they are as unsettling, for you know that there are forces at work inside him that even he is not in full control of. "Now tell me what you feel. All of it."

"What, are you my therapist now?"

His glower stiffens like metal cooling. "I'm the man trying to help you. And I would advise you not to water it down. I will *know*. And you won't get away with it. Now speak to me. Tell me what you see."

I close my eyes for a second, steeling myself to recall that day. "I... I keep hearing him... screaming and then... the thuds, and the cries. I can't hear anything else. I can see the blood... and his face, and his misshapen bones. It keeps playing over and over in my mind. It won't stop!"

"It will with time."

"How do you know?!"

"It always does."

"And what will it leave behind?"

"Liberation."

"And I suppose the cost of this so-called liberation is checking my soul at the gate and living in darkness like... Alex... and Vallen... and—"

"They were born into darkness, Jessynia. It would take more than this for you to become like them."

"Do *they* feel trauma at what they saw?" I ask, recalling the enthrallment with which they seemed to observe what was happening and the enthusiasm with which Vallen joined in at the end.

"I would highly doubt it," he replies.

"Why not?"

"Because they feast off torment, Jessynia. It energizes them."

A frigid fog rolls through my body. "Then, maybe you need better company, Sebastian," I suggest and his eyes gleam just a little—he doesn't smile the way Jack and Cameron do, but occasionally the sides of his perfectly sculpted mauve lips curve ever so slightly, and his eyes glisten, as if sheathed in morning dew.

"You may be right," he concedes ruefully in that deep, elegant voice of his.

"Do you ever get tired of being around people like that?" I ask.

"No. The way they are helps me feel sane."

Silence encases us, punctuated only by the dull ticking of some clock somewhere. My gaze drops to the thick muscle of his neck, to the curve of his broad shoulders, before daring to lift to meet his eyes again, the skin around them swollen and stained as if with charred wood.

"Does it hurt?" I ask softly, the injuries paining me despite him being a willing participant in them.

"I've had much worse," he responds slowly and the thought weakens me. "How did it feel, Jessynia? To watch him die?"

I shake my head. "It felt... like a fucking nightmare! I didn't want to see that!"

"You must have dreamed of it before..."

"So?! We all dream of things like that! It doesn't mean we really want it! It doesn't mean we want to see it! Most people aren't forced to experience *murder*! I mean, the man had a family."

"A family who knew what he was and who actively fought to discredit every victim who dared to come forwards. A father just like him and a mother who looks away despite knowing what he and his son are and who would hurt anyone who dares to damage their perfect life by speaking out."

"Would she do that?" I ask.

"There are women like that out there. I can promise you that. I feel no pity for them. Nor should you. You're not some common or garden empath, Jessynia. If you were, I would have no interest in you. You are an educated one. You know how dangerous it is to show compassion to the wrong people..."

"Like you?" I counter gruffly.

"Like me," he nods.

A tear born of overwhelm and fear escapes me—fear that I'll never be free of seeing him die, that I'll forever be bonded to Sebastian due to the horror and isolation of seeing that act. "I'm scared now."

His brow furrows as he drinks in my distress, his steady gaze dropping to the tear dripping down my cheek. He strokes my flushing cheek with his fingertips before gliding his thumb over my skin, wiping the tear away and leaving a white-hot cinder in its wake.

And I let him. Goddamn it, I feel safer when he touches me...

He speaks in a timber so low, so deep, that it soothes the ungrounded energy twisting my insides into some raging tornado that propels me off balance. "Tell me what you're afraid of."

"You *know* what," I answer as another tear trickles over my waterline and a low groan escapes him at the sight. "I'm afraid of seeing him be beaten to death for the rest of my life. I'm afraid of never being able to go back to being a normal person anymore. I'm afraid of you getting caught. And I'm afraid of only having *you* to talk to about it all."

My sorrow morphs quickly to anger as I watch him observe the droplet of saltwater, the manifestation of my distress, with utter focus, mesmerized.

"I suppose you want to taste it?" I sneer, shaking my head at his malevolent desire.

"Do you want me to sanitize myself for your benefit?" he spits back. "Erect the façade that men do around women they want to fuck... only for it to come crashing down when their woman can no longer leave? Would that make you feel better about being in my presence?"

"How do you expect me to feel safe around you when you're turned on by my fucking tears?"

"Most men are aroused by women's tears, Jessynia. We are aroused when women are weak, vulnerable. It's in our DNA. Designed by a universe that wants men strong and women enfeebled, that wants humans to procreate. Most men just don't have the guts to admit it to their women."

"You're wrong," I retort.

He shakes his head slowly. "Allowing you to maintain the woeful delusions about humanity—about men—that you have has its benefits to me... but I don't want you naïve. I want you raw. I want you facing reality, and that means hearing the truth about men. What's more, I believe you know it. I know your men well, Jessynia. I know how deviant they are. I know what they enjoy."

The sharp breath that flutters from my chest leaves me panting as he conjures up both Jack and Cameron.

Oh my God, he's right: they both turn into animals in the face of my tears. When I first learned of his affairs, I would cry as Jack convinced me to let him fuck me—and from what I know of his body and the gluttonous way he would enter and ravage me, my tears only seemed to make him more ravenous.

And then, when I was taken from Jack by him and the resistance, Cameron didn't make it one full hour before ripping my robe off and fucking me. The fact that I was mute but for tears that were so copious that I would swallow them didn't stop him. In fact, it turned him into a beast that couldn't restrain himself. He fucked me three times that night despite the flood of my tears seeming interminable.

How could Sebastian know that?

I feel my body wilting in the face of his utterance.

"So, I'm right," he says softly as he observes my surely ashen face. I remain unspeaking as he drags his thumb over my cheek, studying the glistening droplet lingering on the pad of his digit. His skin feels cool, the touch of it allowing energy to trickle into me that feels... unfamiliar.

Our eyes lock as he lifts his thumb to his mouth where his tongue licks the tear slowly away. I can't help but watch the movement—the thick pink muscle undulating, feasting on salted water that encapsulates the pain in my wounded heart so perfectly. His eyes close for a moment as he savors the taste. It's as chilling as it is impossible to look away from...

Before I can stop him, in a sudden loss of control, he dips into me fiercely, grabbing my arms with his hands and licking the remnants of tears from my face with the full flat surface of his tongue. He grunts his pleasure so unashamedly.

I push into his chest. "Stop!"

"Why?" he asks, lifting his head as he pants through his arousal.

"Because I said so!"

"The fact that I'm aroused by your tears doesn't mean you aren't safe with me, Jessynia."

"Of course it does! My tears come from distress. If you're turned on by them, you'll want me in that state!"

"Your tears also... pain me."

"Oh really?" I scoff. "I haven't seen any evidence of that."

"Maybe I conceal it... Maybe I conceal it the same way you conceal your arousal at mine over your tears, the way you try to conceal that you are dripping wet and desperate for me to fuck you against this wall." My lips part, causing him to drink them in. "We *all* hide, Jessynia. Even you."

5

The deadlock has lasted over a minute—him glaring down at me, his face unflinching, eyes wide as he studies my descent into anger, and fear.

"How did it feel?" he asks. "Hearing him die?"

"Like a nightmare," I whisper.

"The man hurt you. He degraded you. He wanted to take something from you that would have colored your entire life and left part of you fractured until the end of your days, and seeing him die was a *nightmare*?" he asks, incredulity dripping from the word. "I thought you smarter than that."

"Well, sorry to disappoint. I guess I'm supposed to be just giddy about it, am I?"

"You will be one day."

"What if you get caught?"

"It won't happen."

"Surely his family will be looking for him?"

"It's not the first time he's disappeared. His relationship with his family has been rocky for a long time. This trip, he won't be returning from. Every aspect of this operation was carefully planned. We have police on standby in case he's declared a missing person."

"Police who are members of the Society?"

"Yes."

"How many do you have?"

"Many."

His mercurial glare strays to my lips. "You didn't tell your husband, did you?"

I shake my head.

"Why not?"

"I don't want him to get in trouble for knowing."

He shakes his head slowly. "That's not why, Jessynia. I don't enjoy you withholding the truth from me."

"What do you mean?"

"You've been with him for almost four years and have *never* told him about that man. And yet, you are very bonded to him. Why not?"

"I… I was afraid he'd… try to find him. Hurt him. Or that he'd treat me differently."

"Or maybe you're just afraid of your husband's more savage side? The side of him that is like his father…"

"Jack is nothing like that animal!"

"Cain was once a civilized man, before the death of his wife. That triggered the descent into brutality. You're afraid that that could happen to your husband, aren't you?"

My stomach sinks at the very thought of it. "Jack may lose it," I respond. "But he will *never* be like Cain. Ever."

"I hope you're right," he nods. "But you didn't inform Mr. O'Neill either. You clearly don't trust *either* of your men to be *civilized*."

"That's… That's not it. I… I just wanted to move on."

"Pretending something didn't happen to you isn't moving on."

"Sebastian, you're the one that has made me relive that fucking event! Not to mention that you haven't even gotten treatment for what your mother did to you… or for how… you… made it stop."

"I have seen more so-called professionals than I can count. The damage is done to me, Jessynia. I'm no longer fixable. Nor am I redeemable."

The cruelest of biting chills freezes my skin. "That's not true."

His lucent eyes glisten. "The fantasy you have in your head where you turn me into something palatable would be laughable if it weren't so fucking predictable."

My cheeks burn hot at the insult. "Well, sorry that every single utterance of mine doesn't blow your fucking mind with its originality. Oh, and by the way, you *can* heal. I can help you... unless... you're a *coward* who isn't willing to try..."

As the word leaves me, I regret it instantly. Shaming abuse victims into action is never much of a plan. I know he hates the word. I know it will make him disconnect from me.

Smart, Jess, I groan as he takes me in, his anger seeping into the shadows of his angular face.

"I'm sorry. I... retract that word."

"It's not the first time you've said it to me," he replies.

"I don't mean it."

My eyes soften in contrition as he removes himself from me, standing straight up to peer down at me, holding me hostage with his irascible glare.

"Why did you do it?" I finally ask. "I want the truth."

"Retribution comes to us all."

"No matter the consequences?!"

"The way he hurt you... I can't allow it."

"I'm hurt *now*. I can't sleep. I can't eat properly. I can't stop thinking about what happened. I need to understand how you thought it was okay to do that. Was it just about me... or did you need to kill someone again?"

His eyes narrow. "If I needed to kill, there are easier targets. As for *him*, when he did that to you, he signed his own death warrant."

I drop my head only to have my jaw lifted by him. "You feel guilt?" At my silence, he continues, "The guilt you carry around for things that you are not culpable for, it's pitiful to see it in action."

"I suppose you'd think more highly of me if I felt no guilt or remorse like the rest of the psychopaths you frequent?"

"You remember what he did to you?" he asks.

"Of course I fucking well remember."

"Well, you are one of many victims."

Hearing him repeat that hollows me out from the inside. "How can you be sure?"

He grabs hold of my hand, pulling me towards the coffee table. When I resist, he lifts me across his arms, carrying me over to the coffee table despite my protests. He places me onto the floor, straddling my body from behind. He bends his legs, spreading them wide on either side of me and hauls me back so that I'm sitting against his chest. I curse, trying to fight, but he wraps his thick, hard arms around me, hemming me in, caging me against the bars of his body.

"Let go of me!"

The side of his face brushes against my cheek as his hands wrap around my wrists, holding me firmly in place. "Don't fight me, Jessy-nia," he snarls. "You can't win." The greater I struggle, the greater he affirms his hold. "Stop." His brutal lips set my skin on fire. "I won't hurt you. You know that."

Sebastian's words are so treacherously beautiful. So seductive. He appeals to my need for safety, my need to not have my sex be the only thing the man I'm with wants. When I'm with Jack or Cameron, I know they love me. I know they'd kill to protect me. And nonetheless, their need for my sex colors our every interaction, and they're not subtle about it. They both know I crave their dominance, for reasons I don't fully understand, and they both know that if they pick me up and rip my panties open, that I won't resist them. They know how to get me to drop to my knees and gag on their cock until my eyes water. They know how to get me to take them until my legs are too shaky to take my weight.

As much as I know from their demeanor that they are enjoying a meal with me, or a movie, or a hike, I also know that once it's done, they hunger to impale my body, to fuck me, to shoot their load into me, growling their menacing desire to impregnate me into my ear.

I know that's normal. That's what men want when they desire a woman. I'm not complaining.

I know it's what Sebastian wants too. The charge clings to us, crackling like the errant sparks of an electrical storm. Every glare of his leaves me panting. The touch of his skin sets off fireworks that feel like they could light up city hall.

And yet, he doesn't even try...

If it had been Jack or Cameron holding me, they would have sat me on top of them and rubbed against me while they were soothing me until they were hard. Once they'd calmed me down, my top would have been pulled open and a hole torn in the crotch of my leggings. Both men would have sunk their cocks inside me before I could think and at some point, pushed me face down onto the floor and ridden me while grunting sinful promises into my ear.

I know Sebastian wants that. I feel it in the tension of his muscles. They almost quiver. It's as if he's fighting himself, stopping himself from doing what comes naturally to him—what he does to every other woman.

I want that too...

Or at least, part of me does.

The shameful part of me that I can barely face. The part that wants to forget. To not care anymore. The part that wants to be held by the devil. Kissed by him. Fucked by him. To have every minute of suffering I've felt blasted away by the terrible heat of his potent body.

The way he restrains himself around me makes me trust him, connect to him... when it may just be a trap all along. I can't tell. Does he care about me? Or is he just attempting to care in the hopes that the by-product of his experiment is my succumbing to him?

I stare at the swollen red skin on his knuckles before my gaze finally drifts to the red and blue files on the table as he releases his grip on my wrists, leaning around to watch me from the side as my respiration tempers.

Satisfied with the stillness in my body, he reaches forwards and picks up a file, opening it to reveal a wall of text but for one picture at the top—a young woman. Dark-blond hair. Gray eyes.

"We did our research," he says. "He targeted young women. Many have made complaints. Only one was taken seriously as it was filed in a different state than the others. His family harassed her into backing down. This girl." I stare at her picture, her eyes so vivid it's as though she's looking at me. "Sixteen years old," he continues. "She is now dead by her own hand."

Aubrey Downey.

I stare at her name and then at the notes from a police report, my fingers tracing the words.

Raped

Accused

Swab

Bruises

Suspect

And as I skim through the pages, I see a certificate.

Cause of death: Suicide

Her obituary. Pictures with her mother.

"Why did she do it?" I ask, my voice empty of force.

"They had threatened her mother with a lawsuit for slander by her daughter."

"Is that even possible?"

"No. She had a small family. She, her mother, and a younger sibling. Her young brain couldn't take the pressure they applied."

I grab the file from him and slam it shut, placing it back down onto the table as my breathing accelerates.

He pauses for a moment before picking up another file and opening it, only to reveal a picture of another girl—curly black hair, dark skin.

"This one was fifteen. She explains what happened in great detail in the police report. Sometime later, she withdrew the complaint."

Oh my God...

"His family got to hers, we believe."

"I should have gone to the police..."

"That decision was taken out of your hands," he replies stiffly.

"I should have fought harder. I should have insisted. I knew it was wrong! I knew he was dangerous! I just... wanted it all to go away."

"You were a child, Jessynia. They took the decision from you in the hopes of saving you from trauma. But they made you powerless, removing choice from you over whether to inform the police."

Putting the file back, Sebastian opens a third one to reveal the face of a young woman, tanned skin, brown eyes, short brown hair.

"Can you close it please?" I ask as my blood spills from an invisible wound.

"The man got what was coming to him," he says. "He would never have stopped. There would have been more victims, maybe dozens over his lifetime. His time had *come*." He closes the folder, placing it back down on the table.

As the images of the girls' faces sear into me, I realize that the memory of the blows rained down on him by Sebastian's wrath doesn't slice through me like a machete in the way it did a few hours earlier. Maybe it will when I get home tonight, but for now... it feels... bearable.

I don't move as he slips his fingers across my neck, pulling my long brown hair backwards and behind me to reveal my bare skin. The warm breeze of his breath caresses my nape and without meaning to, I close my eyes at the sensation, the proximity, the intimate gestures of a man so dangerous. A murderer. My lips part as he breathes in the scent of me, exhaling audibly.

My eyes open.

"Why did you... have to kill him... like *that*?" I ask, staring at the untameable sinewy roots encapsulated into the clear resin of the table. "Beating him to death. It was... barbaric."

"You feel sorry for him?"

"I mean, I think I feel sorry for both of you!"

"*Don't*. I enjoyed every drop of blood."

"You looked like you were out of control. Were you?"

"Does it matter?" he asks roughly, his breath hitting my neck.

"Yes. If you beat someone that savagely. Why did you?"

"You know *why*, Jessynia. Don't play coy with me." I swallow hard as he leans forwards and his lips scrape against the shell of my ear. "Tell me why I lost control."

"You... don't like child molesters."

"No. I don't. But I don't have a habit of beating them all to death."

"Why did you? Like that?"

"Tell me," he whispers, and my eyes fall closed for a moment.

"I don't know," I say.

"Yes you do. Tell me." At my silence, he begins to spill treacherously seductive words into me. "Let me tell you what you already know... I feel out of control when it comes to you, Jessynia. Your suffering pains me."

"As much as it pleases you?" I ask.

"Almost as much," he answers and my body seizes at the words.

"I can't tolerate what he attempted to do to you," he continues. "The people that hurt you will suffer for it."

"*You've* hurt me, Sebastian."

The shudder in my body is matched by the shaking in his breath. I quiver as his hands slip down my forearms, winding around my wrists, using them to pull me into him further, closing off the space around us, leaving us in this bubble where his body feels like armor.

"Yes. And I have a price to pay for that," he responds.

"What price?"

"The *torment* you make me endure. What you do to me is most unwanted."

"Why is it?" I ask.

"Because you make me *feel*. That's most unwelcome... and very dangerous of you. And you make me *care*." He spits out the word as if it were poison on his tongue. "Caring about another's well-being is abhorrent to me," he scowls. "It weakens me, especially when I don't believe I own all of the person. What would it take for me to *own* you, Jessynia?"

I pause for a while before speaking, knowing my answer will grate on him. "They'd have to be free, forever."

"Your men..."

His hand slides up my arm, finding my shoulder, and then my neck, and then my jaw. "What else?" he asks.

"I'm scared that I..."

"What?"

"I wouldn't come out alive..."

He doesn't speak, doesn't protest, doesn't offer any reassurance. It's as if he knows those fears are justified.

"Do you ever fear that?" I ask. "That I wouldn't make it out?"

"Yes," he replies upon a pause. "That is part of my torment."

"What's the rest of it?" I ask.

"That I don't want you in exchange for anything. I want you to hunger for me the way I hunger for you. Nothing less than that will satiate me."

"Then let them go, Sebastian. For good."

His breathing is heavy on my neck. Hot. The scent arouses me against my will. The muscular sheathe of his body softens mine, making me feel tiny. I wait for him to speak, to tell me the words I've wanted for so long—that he'll release Jack and Cameron for good—but he doesn't. I know full well that the dregs of the human I'm trying to revive are still too enslaved by things inside him that I don't understand.

"Do you feel trauma?" I ask after a moment. "Over his death? Over how brutal it was? The blood?"

"No," he responds. "The blood was meager compared to what I've seen myself."

"You mean, your own blood?"

I close my eyes at the vision of blood trickling down his chest.

"I want you to come to me when it gets overwhelming," he says, ignoring my question. "Is that understood?"

"Is that why you did it?" I ask, staring at the closed files on the table before me. "To leave me bonded to you? Dependent?"

"As you are experiencing trauma, I will forgive you for the question," he spits out.

"So, what, is it just a perk? Me needing you like this."

His brutal lips caress my ear. "We both know that you were already beginning to need me..."

"Yeah, keep telling yourself that, Sebastian."

"And keep denying it to yourself, Jessynia. Keep denying that you meet me in your dreams. Keep denying what happens to you when I touch you." His palm slips up my neck, his fingers finding my jaw. He moves them across it slowly, as if discovering the skin of a species not his own. "Why do you let me touch you?" he asks.

In a flash, I see two eyes—one deep amber, and the other the brightest of pale blues—sear into the somber wall on the opposite end of the room.

Thoughts of Jack and Cameron plague me constantly—their well-being, their protection, their extrication from this maze. But it's not the full truth of why I yield to Sebastian's touch...

"I don't know," I respond, the beat of his heart hitting my back.

Static crackles through my body at his touch... and he can feel it. I know it.

"Did you like it?" he asks. "Did something inside you like watching me beat him to death?"

I close my eyes, barely able to believe what I saw, or to face the burgeoning swell of relief flowing beneath the trauma and the horror of it.

He's gone...

At my silence, he asks, "Are you afraid, Jessynia?"

I nod.

"Of me or of yourself?"

"Both," I reply.

"Why do you fear me?"

"You know why, Sebastian. You know the things you've done. You know you take pleasure in hurting people, in controlling them."

"Yet unlike your men, I won't pressure you. They have coerced you into sex since you first met, haven't they? Because you like that, Jessynia. You need your men dominant. You require them to take charge. That's how you feel safe. That's how you feel pleasure. I could use that to make you succumb to me. It wouldn't be hard. But that would not be satisfactory to me. That means that you only have to be afraid of yourself. Are you?"

"Yes."

"Good." As Sebastian drops his mouth to the side of my jaw, something on the opposite wall catches my attention—causing my breath to hitch. A large painting—a flower, black. A rose, misted in droplets of dew or rain. The sudden scent of roses floats through the air as if a vase of them were in front of me.

Jessynia...

I glance around, looking for her in the corners of the room...

Nothing.

Rose...

"Did she die here?"

He pauses at my indecent non-sequitur, lifting his lips from my skin. The way he breathes the word into me leaves me shivering. "Yes."

"I want to see where..."

"Why?"

"I just need to see it."

The low ticks of a clock somewhere punctuate the dread I feel and the tense silence engulfing us.

"Very well."

I get to my feet after him and he holds out a hand for me. I take it and he pulls me to stand up before turning to walk me through the expansive lower level and to the foot of some hardwood stairs. For a moment I'm transported back to Cameron taking me up those secret stairs at Blackwood and showing me that room made of glass through which we peered out onto the star-kissed firs standing sentry around the house.

He gestures for me to go first and I do, climbing up with leaden feet. As we make it to the top, he overtakes me on the landing, leading me into a bedroom.

His bedroom.

Not dissimilar to the one he has at QN Tribeca, although no cage this time, or at least, not one on display...

Dark gray sheathes the walls, punctuated by various oil paintings of contorted bodies half-hidden in shadow.

My pace falters as I take in the imposing bed filling the far side of the room. The bedframe is made of dark wood but there are metal bars with circles as the foot and headboards—designed to bind you easily.

On the wall to the left hang shackles attached to chains of various lengths. Some shackles hang near the ceiling, others lie on the floor. Next to them are disciplining devices the likes of which I've seen at the Society.

I didn't know rooms like this existed. Not even Cameron, for all of his unabashed dominance, has outwards signs of his tastes in his bedroom—all toys and props are hidden away in drawers or cupboards and the room, though displaying hints of devilishness, are still sophisticated enough for a random stranger to walk through without alarm bells going off.

Sebastian doesn't care. It's as though he's unable to be affected by what others think...

He turns his head to look at me, his regard solemn.

"Did... Did Rose sleep here?" I ask.

"Yes."

"She didn't mind the... décor?"

His eyes narrow. "She was my *wife*, Jessynia, which means she was my submissive. She submitted to my needs, as I explained to her in detail that she would need to do in order to be my wife. She agreed... most willingly, I might add. Once we were married, what she *minded* became entirely irrelevant."

"Did she like being that way with you? Submissive?"

"Yes... for the most part."

"Until things went too far," I suggest and he bows his head in agreement.

"Did you have a safe word?" I ask.

"Yes."

"Did she use it?"

"No. She wasn't like you, Jessynia. She didn't have your limits."

"Would you have stopped if she had used it?"

"Of course. But I informed her in great detail before she agreed to marry me what my tastes were. She knew that her use of it would be... *disappointing* to me."

"Disappointing, but you would allow it?"

He bows his head to confirm.

"Is it when *I* use it? Disappointing?"

He contemplates the question for a moment. "I do believe I still take pleasure in your use of it."

"Why?" I ask.

"Your resistance won't last forever, Jessynia. I will be patient until the fight itself ravages you so much that you can no longer resist the inevitable..."

I swallow hard and glance at a white door to the right of the bed.

"She died there," I utter, losing my breath.

He nods solemnly, almost as if it wasn't really him that killed her. As if he had no choice. As if he were condemned to let the demon inside him take someone else so that he could live...

Or maybe I'm just desperate to find some excuse for the evil that this man was capable of...

I take a step towards the door and push it open to see a standing tub—white ceramic with curved legs, and much larger than most.

In a momentary pull into some parallel world lost to time, I see drugged limbs twitching under the water and hear faint splashes as Rose attempted to fight for her life with the meager strength that the drugs left her with.

As I stare down at the tub, blurry flashes of movement whirl before my eyes and I see Sebastian carrying her inert body into the water. I know it was cold. I can feel it on my skin.

I can see her face—her azure eyes widening as she realized how he was going to do it, as he parted her legs and entered her body, pushing her head under the water, and pulling it back up to prolong his pleasure.

A droplet of crimson drips from her nose.

I see her face under the water as life ebbed from her as he fucked her into the next life.

Rose...

"She knew she was going to die," I utter.

The voice of the devil emerges from behind me. "Yes."

Panic rises up in my chest as I see her face and watch the last dregs of life extinguish like the final valiant efforts of a dying flame.

As my chest tightens, I take a step backwards, my panting visibly louder. I shake my head and utter her name, only for Sebastian to wrap his arms around me.

This time, I don't bother to fight when I know how unyielding his strength is. He's too strong. Nothing a woman can do could prevent him from doing what he wants to you.

"Did she know that she was going to die?" I ask.

"I told her she would die before she married me," he breathes into my ear. "I told her I'd seen it. I told her I wouldn't be able to stop it. And she begged to be my wife anyway, Jessynia."

Tears spill onto my cheeks as I see her taking her last breath. "Is that true?" I ask.

He wipes it from my skin and as he does, I realize he is trembling. "I don't lie, Jessynia. Ever."

"You told her that?"

"Yes. Just as I told her I would cut her, and bind her, and choke her... and confine her."

I close my eyes as I try to understand why any woman would allow that to happen...

"Was it you?" I ask. "Who killed her? Or was it *her*? The thing that was inside your mother..." I conjure up the demonic thing he called a mother, the dark thing that slithered into him upon her murder after years of abuse and invalidation.

His deep voice cracks as he speaks—the first time I've heard it falter. "I don't know."

"Do you regret killing her?"

He tightens his hold on me, his mouth finding my ear, breathing into it in labored breaths. "I regret everything that has taken me away from you."

6

Did you go to see him?

I stare at Gabriel's message on my secret phone the next day, unsure how to answer. I finally pluck up the courage to type.

`No.`

His response is swift.

Why not?

`I couldn't.`

Can I call you?

`Yes.`

As Gabriel's name flashes on the screen before me, I take a deep breath.

"Why not?"

"Hello to you too Gabriel," I shoot back with an internal eyeroll.

He lets out a sigh of contrition. "I'm sorry, Jess. I'm just... *stressed*. I haven't heard from him for days."

"Nothing?"

"Nothing," he replies.

"Have you spoken to Charles or Aaron?" I ask, anxiety thinning out my voice.

"Briefly. They both said the same thing—he's closing himself off from the people around him."

"God. That's not good."

"No. Why couldn't you call him?"

Why?

Where do I start, Gabriel? The kidnapping didn't help. Neither did the drugging nor witnessing murder before my eyes. Kind of threw off my plans a little.

I wonder for a second if I could tell Gabriel. Would he be bound by client-therapist confidentiality to keep it a secret? I'm guessing he's so used to the insanity that goes on in that place that maybe it wouldn't phase him.

I shudder in a breath, preparing myself to tell him that Sebastian had me taken back there... but I lose my nerve.

"I'm going to call him," I say instead.

"Are you afraid of Sebastian finding out?" he asks.

I contemplate the question, feeling in my gut that Sebastian already knows I've seen Cameron. He's either accepting of the idea, enjoying the show, or waiting to mete out punishment for my insolent disregard for his clear orders.

So, yeah, I am afraid of him finding out, but the fear doesn't really compare to the fear of something happening to Cameron, something irreversible; to the fear of him listening to the voices that I know whisper to him in the dark. Of him falling. I'd never forgive myself if that happened.

Plus, I have this feeling in my gut, naïve as it may be, that Sebastian wouldn't hurt me. Not anymore. I know part of him wants to, but something has shifted between us, and I have to believe that that part is no longer as strong as the part trying to protect me...

"I'll call him now," I decide, glancing out of the window. It's only just after 8 a.m. and despite daylight arching over the Upper West Side, the sky is swathed in ashy clouds which stop the light from blazing into our apartment.

"You still have his number?" Gabriel asks.

"Not in my phone, but I know it by heart," I respond. "It's still the same one, right?"

"Yeah."

"Should I use my regular phone?" I ask.

"Yeah," he replies. "Just block the number first, otherwise expect endless calls from him. Things will get messy."

"I'm just thinking, maybe he won't pick up if it's a blocked number."

"Hmm. I'm not so sure, Jess. When it comes to you, he seems to sense you in his blood."

"Let me call him," I sigh out.

"Let me know what he says."

"I will."

I clasp my hands together for a moment before grabbing my phone and fiddling with the settings until my number is blocked.

He won't pick up...

He won't pick up...

It rings for what feels like forever, and just as I'm about to stop the call, the dial tone stops and I peer at the screen to see... one second, two seconds.

I wait for a voicemail message but there is none.

Someone's on the line.

Waiting in silence.

Gathering the courage to speak, I utter one word.

"Cam..."

Silence.

"Are you there?"

Silence.

"It's me."

As if he hadn't figured that out by now...

Goosebumps trickle down my spine, drawing my skin taut.

Is it really him?

What if it isn't?

What if it's Charles? Or Aaron? Or... someone else who is able to access his phone?

I'm afraid to say too much until I know it's him.

And yet, deep down, I know that it is.

"Cam, speak to me. Please."

Leaden silence stretches between us as I listen in the desperate hope that he'll speak. Cameron isn't the type to play games or do things for effect. He mustn't be well.

"Cam, I'm worried about you. I worry about you all the time. You need to talk to me. Please."

I almost gasp at the sound of his voice. "I can't."

My eyes close for a second, my brain short-circuiting at the sound of anguish deepening his voice. It's almost hoarse, as if he hasn't spoken for a while.

"Cam," I exclaim breathlessly. "Please just... just talk to me."

"Why?" he utters, his timber hollow. "So that you can tell me you're there for me? That you're my friend? So that I can listen to you speaking from your husband's house? Is that the torment you want me to experience?"

"I... I'm not trying to hurt you. I'm trying to not get us into more of a mess. I'm worried about you, Cam. Please just talk to me so that I can help you."

"*Help* me? How? What I want from you, you refuse to give me."

"I *can't* give it to you. You know that."

"So you throw me crumbs, Jessynia, and expect me to survive off them..."

The bitter rancor of his words stuns me for a second. He's never spoken to me this coldly before. "Cam, if you were healthy and happy, then I wouldn't call like this. I'm afraid. I worry all the time."

"Were you worried when you left me, bloody and beaten, to go back to him?"

The floor falls out from under me at his brutal words. "It wasn't like that. They had my godmother's kitchen burnt down. They had my brother drugged and followed! They gave me three days. I waited as long as I could. I was... so scared of what they would do. Look what happened to Luca, to—" I stop. "Please try to understand."

"I understand, Jessynia. But you can't tell me how to feel about losing you like this. About watching you return to a man out of terror, living with him because you don't feel you have the right to leave. Telling me how to live with that is not within your power."

"I'm not telling you how to feel. I'm telling you that... I'm here. I'm always here."

"As I friend?" he scoffs.

"I can't do it any other way. It's too dangerous. I don't know how."

"And I don't know how to navigate the world without you. I told you that without you I'm lost. I don't lie. And you made the decision that you did, Jessynia. You can't take it back. You can't heal me from the violence of what happened. And I can't reason with you when you don't realize you need to be saved. I can only take matters into my hands to free you from these people."

"What?! No! Cam, I told you to just keep away."

"I don't care what you told me," he rasps, the sound emerging as if his teeth were clenched. "I can handle losing you if it's your own choice, but I will not accept the only woman I've ever loved being a prisoner. Not anymore. I'll be handling things myself from now on. Goodbye, Jessynia."

"No! Cam!" I drop my phone to look at the screen and realize that he has ended the call. "Cameron," I whisper. "Fuck!"

I try to call back, once, twice, a third time, but he doesn't answer.

Fuck.

In a burst of anxiety, I get to my feet, pacing the apartment for a few moments before making a decision I'll no doubt regret. I take both phones and shove them into my purse. I don my puffy black coat with a huge hood that I hope I can hide under if need be, and leave, marching through the foyer without a glance at the concierge, and crossing the street into Central Park in the direction of Cam's apartment.

Time passes in frenetic beats as I march determinedly, quickening my gait, desperate to see him so that I can stop this descent into insanity, this landslide that I feel shifting the earth beneath me. I can live with being part of the Society, but not if he's like this. Something bad is going to happen; I can feel it.

My feet rush over gravel and grass, slipping on a wet leaf in one place, stumbling over a branch in another as I walk too quickly.

"Shit," I mutter, my fucking ankle beginning to smart as always happens when I give into my heedless impatience.

I reduce the weight on that ankle, walking stiltedly for the last fifteen minutes as I get closer to his apartment, my feet slipping against the damp soil as I enter a flower bed behind the outer gate of the park, half hiding myself behind a large shrub, a butterfly weed, out of bloom.

My fingers coil around the black bars of the fence as I run my gaze up and down the street, checking if anyone is around. I peer over at his apartment—half a block away. Two doormen stand in front of the iconic Art Deco building in the most opulent district in Manhattan, one home to billionaires, moguls, politicians and other people who bury secrets that they have the means to keep concealed.

A little further down sits a parked SUV with two men standing next to it, tall and strong-looking. I squint through the bars, waiting for cars to pass by to get a better look. One of the men is huge with buzzed black hair and, by the look of his neck, olive skin. It can't be...

"Fuck," I mutter as he turns his head, just a little.

Aaron.

Fuck.

I take a few steps to the side, hiding behind a black post in the gate, watching him as he turns back to talk to the other man.

I peer up breathlessly at the window on the top floor—Cameron's apartment—realizing in a moment that hollows me out that what I'm doing isn't going to help. If anything, it will make everything ten times worse.

"Shit," I mutter again as Aaron turns his head in my direction. I duck out of sight just in time, pulling my hood up and keeping my head down as I turn to walk away, quickening my pace. The force of my boot hitting the earth sends the stab of a dagger into my ankle.

I'm never gonna be free of this fucking injury...

Blasts of gunpowder detonate in my body as I walk away, scared to look around just in case he saw me. He didn't. I'm not that unlucky.

My insides twist as I get further from Cameron's place. I don't even know if he's there. For all I know, he's with some woman who's merrily giving him what I can't.

And I couldn't blame him...

As my ankle begins to throb and each step becomes more painful, I slow my pace, the unsolvable puzzle leeching light from my cells: I can't be with one man without hurting the other; I can't be with Jack without being connected to Sebastian, and I can't be with Cameron without putting my family in danger.

I know full well that the best thing for me is to be with neither of them. And I would do it. In fact, the idea plays over and over in my mind day and night. Leaving Manhattan. Alone. For good. I would just need to get Sebastian to agree to leave them both alone for good if I do. That's all that matters now.

I have to talk to him about it.

Good luck with that...

As my cadence slows further, I glance around me, trying to shake off the paranoia—this unsettling feeling that I'm being watched... or followed. I feel it in the lump of coal forming in my stomach, in the sudden beat of my heart in my ears as I tune out the sounds of passersby around me, in the unease I feel creeping into my body like a spider slipping through an open window.

As I make a turn along a gravelly pathway through the park past a pond to the left and stunning elms and tupelos to the right, I glance behind me quickly to allay my fear... only to spy a figure beyond the hood hiding me, dressed in black.

"For fuck's sake," I mutter, knowing full well that my mind is playing tricks on me. I see ghosts around every goddamn corner these days.

I accelerate a little, glancing behind me again, only to spot his silhouette out of the corner of my eye, but this time, he's closer.

Groaning internally at my ridiculously jumpy state, I turn around to have a sharp breath flee from me at the sight of the man bearing down on me.

"No," I utter, shaking my head, walking backwards as he marches in determined strides towards me.

Without a word, he grabs me by the waist and lifts me, one arm slipping under my knees, ignoring my protests as usual as he carries me off the path, over a small metal fence, into an area shrouded by a mammoth black tupelo topped with a vast canopy of branches that almost falls to the ground, forming a rare private space in this ever-mystical park.

"Let me go!"

Setting me down on the roots of the giant tree with its enormous cloud of budding branches which block out part of the sky and the tops of passersby around us, he pulls my hood down and searches my face, his eyes darting to and fro, dropping to my lips, examining me as if I'm some thing he can't understand.

"You shouldn't have followed me!" I exclaim, hating myself for doing so.

"You're limping," he responds, ignoring my protest. "Why are you limping this badly?"

"It doesn't— You shouldn't have followed me! I mean it!"

His amber eyes darken, his face twisting in sorrow. "Why are you limping so badly, Avery?"

I scope the surrounding area for signs we may be being watched before turning back to face him as he repeats the question. "Because I've just walked forty minutes!"

"So?"

"So, my leg's been playing up recently. It's not a big deal."

"Does *he* know? That so-called *husband*. Does he know that his wife is still maimed like this?"

"It's only today that it's gotten bad like this. It comes and goes in waves. Anyway, that's not the fucking point! We can't be seen out here like this."

His scalding eyes zoom in on mine as I try to catch my breath, withering under the heat radiating from him. "I knew you'd come, Avery. I could feel it. I can feel it when you're near me."

"I... I made a mistake," I stammer. "I shouldn't have come. They could see us!"

"My men are on it. Three of them. I'll know if we're being watched."

I peek through the low branches suspended around us, not seeing any of them. "It doesn't ma—"

"I'm sorry," he interrupts, his voice grim. "I'm sorry for the way I was on the phone. I shouldn't have spoken to you like that. I didn't mean to. I'm just... not always civilized when it comes to accepting life without you."

"Well, seeing each other isn't going to help."

"Jessynia..." He shakes his head slowly, stunning me with the flames crackling in his eyes. "It helps *me*. Seeing your face helps me. It helps me to stay sane."

His words make the ground beneath my feet crumble to nothing. "Cam, please don't say that."

"I don't need to say it. I know you feel it. Don't you?"

Upon the guffaw of some passersby on the path, he lifts his eyes from me, glancing around for a moment as I take in his profile—his straight nose, his high cheekbones that swoop back to a thick, prominent hairline, his strong chin, his beautiful golden skin. He catches me watching him as he turns back to face me, studying me as if I'm a solitary candle left aflame in a dark room. Sometimes I think I imagine the yearning in his face, but today it's unmistakable. It never seems to abate with him.

His eyes dart over my face. "You've lost some weight," he utters, concern engraved into the words. "Why?"

Since I saw that man being beaten to death, I've barely eaten. I don't have much weight to lose so when I lose a few pounds, you can see it easily.

"I've had a... weird few days," I reply.

His brow draws tight as he leans into me. "Why, Jessynia?"

"I... I can't explain it."

"Try," he orders. "Please."

Try?

How?

How do I tell him that I witnessed the bloody slaying of the man who tried to rape me when I was a teenager, at the hands of a man who seems to also want this one dead?

"I can't."

"You don't trust me again?" The question is steeped in anguish.

"*Again?* I've *never* not trusted you, Cameron. Never."

He lets out a halting breath as my eyes wander over a face so masculine, so breathtaking that I can barely comprehend its wild beauty. "You didn't trust me to keep your family safe from him."

"I *did* trust you. I've always trusted you, Cam. It was just... too great a risk. My brother... I... panicked. I'm sorry. I'm so sorry. I never, ever wanted to do something like that to you. Leaving you like that felt a nightmare."

His gaze strays over the panes of my face, taking in my lips before finding my eyes. "I know that." His whiskey-hued eyes blast heat. "I know you, angel."

I nod. I hope so...

"How are you?" he finally asks.

"I'm... okay," I respond, once again unsure what the word even means anymore. After the trauma and insanity I've experienced in the last nine months, words like "Okay" seem utterly vapid.

As I try to stay afloat in the deep wells of Cameron's soulful eyes, I realize that I'm afraid to ask him the same question, afraid of hearing an answer which will cause me pain, or stress, or make me worry even more. But I do it anyway. "You?"

He lowers his gaze for a moment before lifting it to find mine. "I'm not sure you want to know, Jessynia."

"Of course I want to know! Do you think I don't care? Do you think I don't worry about you?"

"You think it's your concern that I want?" he retorts stiffly. "I *don't*. It doesn't help me. You know what I want from you. Something you refuse to give me."

"*Refuse?* It's not that simple, Cam. Nothing is when it comes to that place."

"And if that place weren't in the equation, and it was just a choice between me and *him*..."

I close my eyes for a moment at the brutality of the question. The truth is that I don't know. I don't know how it's possible to worship two men so completely. I never could have thought it possible. The thought of hurting either rips apart my insides. "I can't answer, Cam. It won't help."

"Do you think of me... when you're with him? Do you feel me, Jess? Do you feel me holding you?" He stretches the words out as I peer at the dusty pink of his perfectly sculpted lips before panning up to meet eyes that stun me with their ferocious focus.

"You know I can't answer these questions. Please don't ask them. I'm trying not to make it all worse."

He closes his eyes for a moment before opening them, his gaze roaming over every inch of my face.

"Cam, I really should go—"

"I don't like you not eating, Avery. I know how you like to eat. Something bad must have happened for you to lose the little weight you have on you like this."

"I didn't realize it was that much. I just haven't eaten much for a few days."

"Did he notice? Your *husband*? Does he give a fuck?"

In truth, Jack has said something, handing me fruit twice yesterday and standing over me until I eat it.

"I think so," I respond.

"Being away from you like this is enough torment for me to endure. If I know you're not looking after yourself on top of everything—"

"I'll make myself a huge bowl of pasta every night for a week," I interrupt, forcing a smile, "and pack on the few pounds I've lost. It'll only take me a few days."

"Are you sleeping well?"

I nod, but perhaps the pause I took beforehand was too long, for he asks, "You're still having nightmares, aren't you?"

Cameron's always been able to read me, ever since we first met when we were in college when he seemed to understand things about me before I'd even spoken them.

"Yes," I reply. "Are you?"

He nods slowly.

"Just as bad?"

His silence gives me my answer and I drop my head, shuddering through the thought of them. His fingers find the side of my jaw, setting my skin ablaze as he lifts my face to peer up at him. "Are you still seeing the therapist?" I ask.

"Three times a week," he responds. "I no longer want to. I no longer want to do much of anything, but... I'm seeing him because I need to know that when you finally come back to me, I will be healed. You will sleep in my bed, next to me, as my wife, not afraid. And I will never hurt you like I did again. Nothing else keeps me sane but the vision that I can see... of *us*... one day." I feel the gentle pressure of his fingers behind my neck. "I see it, Jess. I see us. Far away from here. In a cabin in the woods. It's safe. We never worry. We just... lose ourselves in each other day and night. Do you see it? Can you see us the way I can?"

I close my eyes, opening them to find my breathing quickening. "Cam, I can't hear this."

"I don't care," he replies. "You're going to. I'm not hiding the truth. Not from you."

"Are you still seeing Olivia?" I ask.

"I still use her to cope with the fact that you're trapped with those people. I feel nothing for her. As she knows."

"Jesus, why does she even go along with it?"

"I've given her an out more times than I can count. She won't take it. I compensate her. She has safe words which she can use whenever she needs them."

"Does she ever make you feel like... you want to move on?" I ask, swallowing hard at his coarse glare.

"No." Dregs of low flame smolder in his charred timber. "Nor do any of the other many women that I *fuck*."

Before I can stop it, jealous rage has me shoving him hard in the chest, trying to push past him in a moment of unjustifiable indignation that I can't tame. Blocking me, he pins me back against the tree, wrapping his arms around me, his mouth dropping to my cheek as he lets me breathe through the ire that I know full well I have no right to.

My body trembles as I try to calm down. I have no right to be jealous. I know it. Jack fucks me every day—more than once, some days. We don't only fuck, but we make love so passionately that I can barely move afterwards from the sheer visceral overwhelm of the experience. Cameron has every right to do what he wants. I just wish my heart would catch up with my brain.

"I hope you're happy," I scowl, shuddering out frenzied breaths that he inhales, watching the side of my face with his usual tempestuous grace.

God, I groan internally. *Why can't I control how I feel about what he does?*

"I like your storm, Jessynia," he whispers as he holds me. "I'm not afraid of it. You on the stormiest of nights is where I feel *home.*"

As his grip on me loosens, I look up to find his eyes gleaming, just a little.

"That's a nice line, O'Neill… And by the way, you're still an *asshole.*"

"I know that," he responds, his lips curving at the corners.

My breath leaves in a burst of frustration as I try to temper the hurricane. "And even though you're a *prick,*" I continue to the glitter of mirth in his eyes, "I'm sorry. I know I have no right—"

"Don't be," he shoots back. "I like to see what it does to you. It would *kill* me if you didn't care. I'm tormented at the thought of it. And you have every fucking right to be jealous, Avery. Just as I have every fucking right to be enraged at that man you call a husband touching you when you are still not free to leave him if you desire…"

My eyes soften in contrition at the solemn plea in his voice. He tightens his grip around him, breathing into me as I peer up at his soulful eyes.

"You remember how they took you, Avery?" he continues, his demeanor suddenly altogether more grave. "Do you remember it or do you pretend it didn't happen?"

The moment Leon dropped me back off at Jack's place after Cameron's beating flashes through my eyes. "I remember, Cam."

"Do you remember us before they took you?" His lips hover over mine. "Do you remember the way you touched me? The way I held you? The way we loved each other? The way we *fucked*."

I nod, my body softening until it barely feels there.

"Do you know that if that hadn't happened," he continues, "if they hadn't beaten me, and threatened you, and taken you, that you would belong to me now? Do you know that you would be spending every night in my arms, Jessynia? You would be trembling as I tied you up and fucked you? Do you?" At my silence, he continues, "You know it, and I know it. And no matter how much you deny reality, nothing will stop the rage we feel at other people touching us. Do you understand that?"

He asks the question with such earnest sorrow that I feel my body wilting from the force of it.

"I spoke to Gabriel," I finally say in lieu of a response. "He says you haven't been answering his calls, or seeing the resistance. Why?"

I lose myself for a moment in his face, in the taciturn anguish staining it, some incongruous mix of storm and grace. His energy feels volatile and yet his body still, as if through years of conditioning, the product of being the famous son of one of Manhattan's most prominent families.

In moments which invariably leave me ungrounded, I see him in the Society section of certain upscale magazines, usually with Olivia on his arm—the ultimate expression of male beauty, power, composure and strength. Despite having known him for so long, I'm sometimes taken aback to see him in the flesh, glaring down at me as if wanting to devour me.

"Why?" I repeat.

"I haven't been myself. Nor in the mood to see people."

"That's no good. You can't shut yourself off!"

"I feel safer that way, Jessynia. And maybe the world is safer without my rage."

"For fuck's sake, Cam, you can't do that! You'll end up in..."

A dark place...

I stop myself from saying the words, for I know from the brush of mauve under his eyes and the length of his stubble that he is already there.

"I don't want you to be this way, Cam. It torments me to even think about it."

I try to stay strong under the weight of a glower so ferocious that it makes me feel like I'm sinking into quicksand.

I whisper the word "No" as he watches me, leaning into me, gently brushing his lips against the flushing skin of my cheek. He doesn't kiss but the touch of him sets my flesh alight, causing staccato flashes of white to blur my vision and my limbs to tingle. His lips find my ear, his voice the most seductive of low breaths. "No words will ever be enough to express what you are to me. There is no life for me without you." *No...* "Be with me, Jess. Let me worship you. Let me protect your family. I could put millions into it. You'd never have to worry about them again."

The sight of determined flames licking the baseboards of Babs' house flickers before me. Unease drips into my body as I realize that Sebastian allowed that to happen.

He has to pay for that...

"I can't, Cam."

Cameron

The huge eyes that I see in my dreams peer up at me, searching mine. "I have to go back," she whispers, contrition hiding in her tone. "We can't do this again."

"I miss you, Jessynia," I utter and her lips part on a loud inhale which makes my body stiffen. "I know you'll hate me for it, but I'm going to tell you what I feel anyway."

"Cam—"

"I ache for you, day and night. I ache for your touch, for your voice."

"Stop."

"I ache to hear what you have to say about the world. I hunger for the taste of you. My body is restless, as if constantly searching for something out of reach."

Her eyes mist over. "Cam, please."

"We could meet," I add swiftly, aware of the wretched desperation in my words, desperation that I abhor but can't control when it comes to this woman, a woman who blazes as if the only source of light in the world I inhabit. I don't want to pressure her, but I have to make it clear to her that she has a choice, that she's not stuck, that she doesn't have to pretend she isn't trapped. I know that's what she does. She applies her love and compassion for the people she loves and uses it to excuse behavior that is beyond words. "I could arrange it. It would be safe. I have the means to protect you and your family forever."

"It wouldn't be—"

"Fair?" I seethe, unable to control my jealous rage over a man who should have had the guts to let her go and allow her to come back of her own accord if she so wanted. "On that fucking man you call a *husband*."

"*Safe*," she corrects.

She swallows hard and it takes all my strength not to carry her away from the insanity she spends her days rationalizing away.

"Jess, meet me again. Please. Just to talk."

She closes her eyes and I see her tremble for a moment which forces me to restrain myself from touching her to soothe the squall. Finally opening misty eyes, she whispers. "I have to go, Cam," her plump lips barely moving. My gaze drifts up her sharp cheekbone and onto turquoise eyes that have held me captive since the day I met her. Her beauty is beyond what can be put into words.

I take a breath before telling her something she must already know I have the means to find out. "I know your number, Avery."

"What?! How?"

"I haven't called yet," I respond, ignoring the question, "because I don't want to put you in danger, but I've stared at that number so often that I know it by heart."

"You can't call!" she insists, shaking her head. "For all I know, those freaks could have hacked it!"

"Which is why I haven't, despite the pain of being unable to hear your voice. If you could just speak to me, Jessynia, it would help m—"

"I have another phone," she interrupts, her face dropping as if immediately regretting having said it.

"The one you speak to Gabriel on?" I ask, knowing full well that he's been speaking to her for a long time.

"He told you about that?!"

"No," I say, "but I knew he had a way of contacting you. I want that fucking number, Avery."

"What are you going to do with it?"

"Speak to you. Check that you're eating. That you're sleeping."

"I don't need you checking up on me like a child!" she exclaims, shaking her head in outrage.

I can't help but smile internally at her vibrant indignation. She always could tell me when I'm being an asshole.

"And to check that you're not in danger," I continue. That you're okay."

"I'm *always* okay, Cam."

"No," I sneer and she gulps down my irritation. "I don't mean this bullshit appeasement you do to me to stop me from doing what I should. I mean, *well*. That's how you're supposed to be, Jessynia. You're not supposed to be *okay*. You're not supposed to be afraid. You're not supposed to be appeasing anyone, and that includes me and the so-called man you're forced to stay married to. A woman like you is supposed to be *free*. And thriving. And happy. Deliriously fucking happy like I want to make you... if you'd let me." My fingertips find her slim hand. She pulls away but I slide them between her fingers, gripping her palm tightly, glaring at her until she stops the resistance. It doesn't take long. "At the risk of making you want to throw up, Avery," I continue, "that's how an insanely beautiful, ridiculously smart, vibrant woman like you is supposed to be. You're not supposed to be cautious or afraid or walking on fucking eggshells. You're supposed to be... *you*."

Every messy, messed up piece of you...

"Cam, stop," she whispers as I dip my head towards hers, forcing her to peer way up. "Please. I don't want to be cruel, but I can't hear this."

"I don't care what you want to hear," I shoot back. "You coping with what's happened to you by pretending to be in control is not something I'm going to be enabling, Jessynia. You went back to a man after your family was threatened. Their lives, their homes were threatened. The fact that you can't face that, and that you still *care* about him"—I spit out the word—"is irrelevant. I can't stand by and watch the only girl I've ever loved be swallowed up by sick people. I've watched it happen to someone before. I'm not making that same mistake again."

"I *won't* be swallowed up," she responds, eyes glistening despite the thick clouds above. "I'm never tempted to become like those people, Cam. Ever. Most of them sicken me."

"But you're tempted by *him*, aren't you? That monster that runs the place. That hurts people." Her eyes close softly as her lips part. I hate speaking to her like this. I hate making her upset, but there are some things I need to know. She has no idea what she's playing at by trying to negotiate with Sebastian Gravier. "Your judgment is adulterated by your need to save him. To make him human. To negotiate, isn't it?" I lift her jaw up, forcing her to peer into me. "Look at me. I know you, Jessynia. I know how you love. I know that you are willing to sacrifice yourself to save the people around you. No one wants that. Not me. And if he's as honorable as you think he is, nor does Jack."

"I have to do *something*," she responds. "You've both been entangled in that place your whole adult lives. I can't do *nothing* while he takes another decade from you."

"If you end up *dead*, or *broken*, then it won't be another decade I'll lose. It'll be the rest of my life."

"Don't say that."

"I mean it. I intend to handle this."

"How?"

"It doesn't matter how."

"It matters to me! It gave me anxiety, what you said on the phone. I don't want you getting involved, Cam. I'm serious. You'll end up getting hurt."

"I'm already hurt," I snarl, though the word doesn't come close to how I feel. "The pain of being without you would be bearable if I didn't know you were in this fucking mess partly because of me."

"It's not like that."

"Yes it fucking well is."

Before I can stop myself, my lips drop to her pale cheek and her breathing becomes audible. "Do you dream of me, Avery?"

She pushes against my chest... but not hard enough. "Cam, we can't do this. I'm not kidding."

"Do you?"

"Cam—"

But she stops speaking as I gently brush my lips against her skin, right to left, taking in her scent. She shuts her eyes as my lips fall to the corner of hers, and I kiss her, as gently as I can. I know I shouldn't. I know how she'll feel afterwards, how she'll torment herself over allowing it—the result of a misplaced sense of guilt because she's entirely ignorant of the extent of Jack's infidelities during their marriage, and I don't have the heart to tell her how many women, how many times, how many months. I imagine that the little I've been told doesn't come close to reality.

Her chest rises and falls and her eyes remain tightly closed as I kiss from the corner to the center of her lips, the contact with her setting my body on fire.

It takes all my strength not to lick the full length of them, not to find where they part with my tongue, and push inside, a little, then more... and more.

I know she'd let me.

But I don't want to push her again... It's not enough.

"Look at me," I say and after a moment, her eyelids lift, her gaze at first hovering over my neck, then slowly creeping upwards onto my lips and then finally meeting my eyes.

"I have to go, Cam," she breathes out.

"I want to see you, Jessynia. I don't have to touch you. I just need to see your face. I know how you feel about us seeing each other, but it keeps me sane. It tells me the truth about what's going on with you. It's the only thing that does."

"Cam, it'll just make everything a big mess." My body stiffens as she pushes me away gently. "I have to go."

"Go *where*, Jess?" I ask.

She shakes her head slowly. "You know where."

"I can take you back with me," I respond. "You get to have a choice, you know? Every fucking woman should have a choice of who she lives with. Do you know that?"

"I'm working on it, Cam."

"So am I..."

At the thought of her walking the five or so minutes back on the ankle that is clearly not healed properly, I tuck my arm under her knees and lift her up, carrying her over my arms.

"Hey! Put me down!" she orders, trying to wriggle out of my grasp, but she knows she couldn't get free from me unless I let her.

My legs feel like dead weight as I carry her in the direction of Jack's apartment when every fiber of my being wants to take her back home with me.

And I will... soon.

I just have to take care of Sebastian Gravier... once and for all.

"Cameron, stop!" she repeats but I ignore her, carrying her past passersby on the path. I know that if Jack's men were around, mine would have told me by now.

"I don't let my woman walk when she's limping like that," I respond roughly upon another plea for her to release me.

"Someone could see us," she says, peering all around us.

"I don't give a fuck. Let them see us."

"God, men are such Neanderthals," she mutters under her breath, her reproachful tone making me smile for just a moment.

As we finally arrive at the metal gate near Jack's apartment, she wriggles, ordering me to set her down, for I'm sure she could sense from my momentum, that for a moment, I had no intention of stopping.

I put her down as gently as I can, watching as she finds her feet on the grass. We both turn our heads to look through the bars around the park, concealed partly by large evergreen shrubs. "I have to go," she says breathlessly as I pivot her to look at me.

"I need you to do something for me," I say as she stares up at me, her face so earnest, her expression so open, so vulnerable, so pure, her mouth so plump, so fuckable.

"What?" she asks.

"He's at work all day. We pick a time. Midday. You take off your clothes, and you make yourself come."

"What?!"

"I'll do the same," I continue. "I'll work my cock while thinking of your wet pussy. We do it every day at the same time. I imagine you... tight and wet and open for me. You imagine my cock driving inside you. You don't stop until you come. I won't either."

"Look, I can't."

"Please. I need your help, Jessynia."

"I have to go," she responds with a shake of the head.

"You're not going anywhere until you promise me you'll do it," I growl.

"Jesus, Cam—"

"I'm going to make myself come while picturing your body. Midday. Every day. I want you to do the same. Tomorrow I'll be in my office. I'll make it clear I'm not to be interrupted. I want you to lick your fingers and rub them up and down your clit. I want you to play with it until you're nice and juicy, and then close your eyes and penetrate yourself, push two fingers inside, imagining my cock is sliding into you... and out, over and over."

She swallows hard and her lips part.

"I want you to feel me fucking you. I'll work my shaft until I shoot my load."

"I can't—"

"It's not a request, Jessynia. You're going to do as you're fucking well told. Midday. Every day. I want your pussy nice and wet and ready for me. Is that understood?"

"Cam—"

"Is that understood?"

"Fine!" She glances all around. "Look, I have to go."

My hand coils around her tiny wrist. "I won't have you feeling guilty about seeing me as usual, Avery. I know what that man was doing during the second half of your marriage."

"Stop!"

"He doesn't deserve one ounce of your fucking guilt. And this was *my* doing, not yours. Understood?"

She pulls my hand off her wrist. "I have to go. Cam, just, please... be strong. For me. Okay?"

"As long as I know you're there, Jessynia, I can make it through this."

Jessynia

As I turn to leave, trying to ignore the desperation in his face, I limp as I make my way tentatively through the gates of the park, looking all around to see if Leon is there or another of Jack's men.

As I make it back inside, up the elevator and into our apartment, I close the door, sliding down it breathlessly onto the floor. I pull out my secret phone, bringing it to my ear as I wait for him to pick up.

"Jess."

"I need to see you, Gabriel. It's urgent."

"You know that's risky."

"I know. I don't care. I'm not coping as well as I have to. I need help. I need to talk. I have no one else I can get this out with..."

No one except Sebastian...

7

I reach for another handful of cashews as I stare at the screen in front of me. I've been loading up on nuts and seeds in the last few days, trying to put on some of the weight I've lost since watching that man be... murdered by Sebastian.

Some days I barely believe I saw it, wondering if I conjured it up in some nightmare. Everything feels different now, as if I'm seeing the things before me through some ashy filter with mysterious dust billowing above me like a cloud of burnt, pulverized wood.

I just pray that with time, the visions will disappear, not to mention, the worry, the guilt, the fear over what would happen if someone found out...

As I crunch my way through a few nuts, drinking them down with some cold-pressed apple, carrot and ginger juice which I hope will help soothe my fluttering stomach and give me some extra calories, my eyes float over the words I typed earlier.

Today's subject of research:

Dominic Becker.

Surgeon, multi-millionaire, friend and confidant of Sebastian Gravier.

He's been married three times and has two grown-up children.

I've noted down his marital history, what I can find out where he's lived, what boards he's on, the names of the people I see him with at functions of Manhattan's high society, as well as any business partners, and other things of note, before turning my attention to another man.

Silas.

He seems to have joined the Society over forty years ago, when, from what I've gathered, it was basically just an upscale swinger's club, before Sebastian got hold of it and turned it into something entirely too dangerous.

I peer over the medical examiner's report that I managed to get a copy of.

Accidental overdose of insulin.

Presence of opioids.

Is that true?

Was it really that simple?

He seems to have been ousted from the Society not long after Sebastian became president, which only happened after Cam and Jack had *already* been taken there—over a year after their initiation. It was eleven years ago, when they were around eighteen years old, and Sebastian was just twenty-four.

How the hell did he become president that fucking young?

There must have been someone behind it, someone who believed in him, who vouched for him, who wanted the Society to become a more dangerous place.

Dominic, maybe? Alex and Stephen, surely? Who else would have the kind of power needed to make him president of one of the most elite societies in New York by the age of twenty-five?

I know that Alex met him not long after he left Chicago, upon his release from the young offender's institute, and finally got his hands on his father's fortune. He moved to New York, no doubt into an area of affluence and influence.

Did he meet her then? Did he meet her at special gatherings while searching for submissives who would enjoy his sadism and acquiesce to his tastes, share his vision?

He's a powerful man, his presence bold, his poise unflinching, his wit and charisma almost incomparable, but I always assumed these were gifts he'd developed with age.

He was released from the young offender's institute at the age of twenty-one. His birth name was Stefan Koval, and despite hours of searching, there's literally nothing on his former life online, not even the usual prisoner info from the corrections institute, or at least, I can't find it. I imagine he paid to have every trace of himself removed.

I learned from Gabriel that he was on probation for five years after release. How could he have become president within three years of being released, and while he was still on probation? It makes *no* sense. I mean, was he really just that ruthless and ambitious?

There must have been people behind him, people who knew of his trauma, of his malevolence, of his craving for blood, for extreme sex. They must have championed him. He couldn't have made it alone, surely.

I peer at a photograph taken fifteen years ago at a charity function that I scoured from the deep dregs of the internet after hours of searching: Silas standing next to a man on one side and a thirty-something Dominic Becker on the other. As I stare at the picture of the man, my heart rate quickens and I zoom in.

I feel like I've seen him before somewhere...

I glare at the notes beneath the picture.

Darragh Finnegan.

I think back to... that day.

The church...

No.

It can't be him. My mind is playing tricks on me.

I turn to my Word document, ready to type some notes from today, but once again find my hands weak, my enthusiasm for the project waning, siphoning strength from my body as I attempt to write.

I was once so sure of what I needed to do: expose them, all of them, even Sebastian; make sure that place never sees the light of day and again.

As I've connected to Sebastian, I've found myself struggling just a little, and wondering how the hell I can feel the need to protect this vicious man who has hurt so many people, including myself…

Why am I suddenly struggling like this?

As my fingers hover aimlessly over the keys of my keyboard, another man's name seers itself into my field of vision.

Adam Kroenig.

I dare not type his name. In fact, I haven't in years, never wanting to remember any more about him than I had to. Only this time, it's for fear that one day, the police could come knocking on my door, taking my computer as evidence, asking why I suddenly typed his name. And goddammit, the thought of Sebastian—the man who I was once desperate to expose—being caught by them makes me sick to my stomach.

Fuck.

I save the document and shut off my computer, feeling like my body could explode from nervous energy, and from the constant threat of the images of that man being beaten to death which lurk in the shadows of my mind, just ready to imprint themselves on me once more when I dare to close my eyes.

I spoke to Gabriel briefly but he can't see me in person for another three days. I just have to last that long because every second of the day, I'm tempted to call Sebastian to talk through what happened that day… but I know that's what he wants. He wants me caught in the web.

I glance at the clock on the wall.

11.53 a.m.

It's been two days since I saw Cameron in the park. Yesterday he texted me just before 12 p.m. telling me to think of him. I know what he meant. I didn't answer. I can't answer anymore. I can't keep this triangle going. I need him to free himself from it once and for all.

That didn't stop me from closing my eyes and breathing through the thought of him pleasuring himself, thinking of his strong hands coiled around his thick shaft, sliding up and down, bringing himself to orgasm and letting out a loud groan of pleasure, just as he knows I like.

I tried to watch a documentary, but could barely focus on it, seeing his hard cock over and over in my mind as he ejaculated onto his taut stomach.

As the thought of it mixes with the horror of the blood I saw the other day dripping down Sebastian's savage face, I get to my feet, restless, unable to sit still or concentrate, feeling like there is a scream trapped inside of me that I can't get out.

Contemplating whether I should just get in my car and drive somewhere, anywhere, to a place where I can think, I decide I need to calm down before I start driving, and head upstairs, throwing off my clothes and hopping into the shower.

The water mingles with tears of frustration that seep from under my closed eyelids as I picture the man, feel the brutal blows that Sebastian bestowed upon him, picture Jack's face, and then Cameron's... and then his hard body, his thick shaft engorged with blood, smooth and long and perfect.

I see him closing his eyes, leaning back in his chair, his designer suit covering his body. I picture him undoing his belt and unzipping his pants, taking out his cock and gripping it firmly, gliding his hand up and down the rigid column as he thinks of my pussy.

I hate that I still ache to touch him, to kiss him, to wrap my lips around his shaft and bring him the pleasure he needs...

Taking the showerhead out of its dock, I drop it to my clit the way Cameron did in his shower at Blackwood. I part my legs a little, keeping my eyes closed as I let the tepid water pulse over the tight knot of nerves until my sex begins to throb in pleasure and my body tightens, desperate for any release it can get.

Running on fumes of frustration, I leave the shower, grabbing a towel as I do so, which I lay messily on the bed.

As I sit on top of it, the beep of the phone I plugged in to charge earlier sounds and I grab it from my nightstand, my eyes widening and my respiration accelerating as the words float before me.

How are you, Jessynia?

Sebastian.

I contemplate responding with a few choice words, but don't, putting the phone back and lying down, my body simmering and my legs parting as relentless images dance before me—the man, the blood, and then Cameron working his cock, hoping I'm tending to myself as he asked me to do.

I don't want to.

I don't want to be locked into this energetic bond with him, but my body is a tornado of volatile energy and I feel like I'm on the verge of losing my mind along with my senses.

Needing a release, my fingers slide down to my clit and I tip my head back as I press into it over and over as I picture Cameron's body, causing my sex to open up, unfurling, wet and warm and just ready to be fucked.

Lick your fingers and push them inside your pussy until it's nice and juicy.

Imagine it's my cock fucking you...

I lick my index and middle finger, pushing them inside me, just an inch, and then another, opening myself up as I pant to the image of Cameron sliding his cock into me.

A moan escapes me as my clit engorges, pleasure seeping through my core in sweltering breaths of summer breeze that blow away the cold gray clouds muddying my thoughts.

And in a sudden unwanted burst, I see Sebastian's silver-gray eyes watching me, and begin to picture his cock—longer and thicker than even Jack's and Cameron's.

The thing is deviant, with angry veins that snake up the sides, and as I rub my swollen clit, I imagine dropping to my knees and sucking on it as I peer into his eyes, being watched by him for every lash of my greedy tongue, being studied as I suck on the head, being scrutinized as the thick length slides down my throat and I gag.

At some point, I see him tying my hands together and fucking me, stretching me out in a way I've never felt before. It feels like being fucked by the devil.

Jesus...

As I'm turned over by him, I see Jack's face watching me, stroking his erect cock, stepping forwards slowly and positioning it at my mouth. Watching his eyes, I begin to suck as Sebastian pulls my hair back and pushes all the way into my cervix. I moan as I tend to Jack's cock while being taken from behind only to have my attention called to someone to my right.

Cameron.

He comes to stand next to Jack and I begin to suck his cock, and then Jack's and then his again, moaning as I take slow licks up both erect shafts.

Jack stays standing, ready to fuck my mouth again, as I'm hoisted up by Sebastian, my hands still tied behind my back as Cameron slides beneath me and begins to fuck my pussy, grunting loudly with each impalement. Sebastian takes up position behind me, running his tongue up my back before entering me from the back, something I've never let a man do before.

Only this time, I'm not afraid.

I like it.

Pleasure undulates through me as the men groan like savages, positioning me how they want, yanking my legs apart, using my body unashamedly, ravenously licking my skin, brutally biting my flesh, pulling my hair, snarling deviant words, driving into me hard and fast like unapologetic beasts reveling in their shackled captive held in some dark cave that no one will ever know about...

And as I picture the moment they climax in bestial grunts, I'm tipped over the edge myself and let out a groan of relief as I succumb to much-needed pleasure which allows my body to finally relax a little and for tingling warmth to spread throughout my cells.

My breaths slow as I finally open my eyes to contemplate how long I can keep going like this, tortured, wracked with guilt and entirely ungrounded, the foundation eroding under my feet.

I need help...

8

My hand delves into his thick long hair as he wraps his lips around my clit, contracting them as he begins to suck.

I thought he would be rough. He always told me he would bite and cut and make me scream. Instead, he's given me more pleasure than I've ever felt, teasing me until I feel like I'm losing my mind.

His tongue flicks my clit—up and down, side to side. His lips wrap around the bundle of nerves again, and he begins to suck as I tip my head back on his mammoth bed and gasp, my body undulating in beautifully treacherous waves at the nirvana building.

His strong tongue thrusts inside me, and he groans as he fucks me with it. It feels so deviant. So good.

I close my eyes and pant as he lashes my clit once more, running the velvety muscle up and down, his brushes fast and then slow, hard and then soft as a feather.

My legs try to bend but are stopped by the cuffs tying my ankles to his bed.

"Please," I gasp as he stops short of making me come once again. He's been torturing me for time that I couldn't calculate, building up the orgasm and then denying it, agonizing me with surges of bliss that stop just short of ecstasy.

"Say my name, Jessynia. Say it and I'll allow you to come."

"Sebastian..."

Upon hearing his name, he presses into my clit with his tongue rhythmically several times until I tip over into ecstasy.

"Oh my God," I whimper, keeping my eyes tightly shut, as merciless tides of heat lap at my body. I feel him watching me as I breathe through an orgasm so intense that the high hits my brain, causing lights to flash before my eyes and warmth to pour into my chest.

My hand reaches forward to touch his and as they do so, the cold sensation of a thin strip of metal startles me for a moment, taking me back to Rose...

I slide my fingers up onto his knuckles only to feel them slick with some thin liquid—sweat, no doubt. Trepidation makes me shudder inexplicably as I slowly open my eyes and glance down at his hand to see it shimmering in dark blood, and behind him, spy the movements of a dragon, breathing fire with cruel, ferocious equanimity.

No...

My eyes pan slowly upwards, over the unassailable ridges and buried valleys of his potent body, over his chest, up his thick neck and onto his chin, stained crimson with blood.

At the sight of the demon staring down at me, eyes red, teeth dripping in blood, I stagger and begin to tumble through space...

Until my eyes open and I find myself panting, propped up on my elbows as I look down to see the top of Jack's head between my legs and feel the frantic lash of his tongue against my clit.

I glance at the neon numbers on the alarm clock to my left and see that it's just before 9 a.m., a late weekend wake-up call before my yoga class.

"Jack," I pant, finding my bearings as my sex begins to throb and the orgasm trickles through my cells, untangling some of the hard knots running through my body. "What are you doing?" I exclaim as my body, misted in perspiration, quivers through the pleasure.

He lifts his head and props himself up, spreading my legs and moving his knees between them. He places his hands on either side of my shoulders, scanning my face as I breathe through the unexpected assault to my senses. He drops his torso onto me and bends my left knee up so that it's near my breast as he pins both my hands to the mattress next to my head.

His reprobate smile hauls me out of my nightmare. "I'm waking my wife up. The way a decent husband should." As he pushes his cock into me, driving deep inside me hard and fast, a sharp exhale slips from me at the unexpected invasion of my flesh. I try to sit up on instinct, but he holds my hands down more firmly. "Don't fight me, beautiful. This is what you were made for."

I shake my head in incredulity as his sinful smile sears me, and he begins to fuck my docile body while I try to shake out these recurring nightmares involving Sebastian Gravier which are showing no signs of abating.

"Lie back, angel. Let your husband wake up his wife properly."

"You're a fucking animal, Wilder," I chide as he slides his hand under my pajama top, snaking up my abdomen before finding my naked breast as I cut up some tomato to go with the scrambled eggs I'm making him. His other hand pulls the mint-green cotton all the way up so that my breasts are exposed as I attempt to pull away from him with a moan. I can't help but let out a playful grumble as he peers over my shoulder at my breasts, tugging my nipples as he exhales in pleasure.

"You only have yourself to blame with those tits of yours, Jessynia."

I lower my head to look at my exposed breasts which Jack is kneading with his strong hands.

"They weren't exactly an option," I shoot back. "Fuck's sake," I chide in jest as he slowly pulses his cock against my ass while observing the body he's displaying for his own personal amusement. He's hard again and the way he rocks himself against me from behind feels ruthless and unforgiving.

"I'm never cooking without a bra again," I announce loudly. "I hope you know that. Also, correction, you're a *deviant*. How are you already hard again?" I admonish, just thirty minutes after he fucked me in his bed in the kind of wake-up call that we haven't had since last June.

"I've told you what you cooking for me does to me." His nimble breath blows hot on my ear. "Especially when you cook with your pussy naked."

"I have pajamas on, Wilder," I counter, assuming my most berating tone. "I'm hardly naked."

"You are in my mind, beautiful. As far as I'm concerned, when you cook for me, you become my personal little slave." He grips me tightly from behind, licking the side of my cheek with a moan. "I'm going to reward you for looking after me by fucking you on that table once we've eaten, Jessynia. I hope you know that."

"You realize I'm gonna need medical intervention if you keep this up?"

I feel him smile against my cheeks as he observes the nipples he's tugging into hard points.

"Ow," I breathe, and he presses his cock into me, a guttural breath of pleasure breaking from his throat. "God, don't tell me you enjoy hurting me."

"All men like to know that women will take pain to give them pleasure, angel."

"You're all messed up, you know?"

"Indeed. You'd better get used to it, Jessynia. I intend to make your pleasure my personal project over the next few months."

A shiver rolls through me and I close my eyes to shake it out.

Don't get me wrong, I'm relieved to find myself so turned on by Jack, but I still have fleeting moments when his touch hurts me somehow. It makes me feel like I'm being touched by *her*. Alex. I feel like the years he spent with her, precious young years when that predator had no business going anywhere near him, have penetrated him, allowed her serpentine touch to imprint on his skin. And while I adore Jack, sometimes I feel her scales on me. I hate the feeling. I always wonder if Jack feels it on him too, but I don't dare ask. *God, I hope he can't feel her on him...*

Jack has done everything in his power to recreate a sense of intimacy between us, giving me space to breathe when I've needed it, taking charge when I've been reticent, fucking me in a way we haven't managed since last June. The reality is that nine months on, I'm still not fully there with him... but I'm trying.

I so want to get back there...

To get back to a time when everything between us was effortless, every touch of his set my cells on fire, every word would leave me desperate for more, and I would melt into the safety of his arms, never once thinking about any other man.

I remember tumbling into warm seas of laughter, our energy seeming to quadruple in each other's presence, whisking us gracefully along in the lightest of dances.

Occasionally, my body freezes as I wonder if getting back to the ease and flow that we had before is possible or whether we will always see clouds encroaching after a while, always feel like we're climbing the cold, dark north face of a mountain where storms have their hold, our footsteps heavy and somber as we ascend while their echoes die on the rock.

I feel the cracks around us, fissuring our bodies. Do those cracks fill in with time? And even if they do, do you always feel their presence? Do the cracks leave a couple eternally weakened, or is our relationship like some work of Kintsugi, the broken pieces of pottery put back together with gold, embellishing the flaws and imperfections and damaged pieces to create more robust, more beautiful works of art...

As Jack's hand finds the elastic of my pajama bottoms and slides inside and onto my pubis, we're interrupted by some insufferable pop jingle, courtesy of a ridiculous ringtone that Kevin put on my phone when I wasn't looking. I lean over and glance at it lying on the mottled granite countertop to see my mother's name pop up onto the screen.

"I'll call her later," I decide, chopping up the last tomato.

Jack releases my body and I barely have time to say a word before he's picking up my phone and answering it.

"No!" I mouth as I drop the knife and turn to face him, grabbing a tea towel and wiping my hands as he takes a deep breath and says, "Hello, Diana."

Shit!

"Give me that!" I mouth, reaching for the phone, but he takes a step backwards, putting his hand out to stop me.

I still haven't mustered up the strength to tell my parents that Jack and I are back together. My dad, I can just about cope with, but my mom is another story altogether. I can just hear the irate lectures now and envision Vera the vein popping up on her forehead. What's more, I'll never be able to fully explain it to her, or to pretty much anyone who has no knowledge of QN—a fact that never fails to leave me feeling hollow.

"Yes, it's me, Diana."

I open my mouth in outrage, mouthing for him to give me the phone. I try to reach for it again, but he takes a step back.

"Jack!" I whisper.

"We're back together, Diana," he says slowly, moving the phone from his ear for a second as if to spare his eardrums from a yell I can hear from five feet away.

Fuck.

"Not long," he says after I hear her yell, "For how long?"

I shake my head at him, despite knowing he's probably doing me a favor. I mean, the woman had to find out at some point...

"I'm aware of my failings as a husband, Diana. The word *Sorry* doesn't come close to conveying how I feel about my actions. I am going to therapy every week and intend to put all that behind me. I will never hurt your daughter again."

Oh Lord.

Frankly, the declaration would sound mawkish from any other man, but Jack has this graceful and yet assertive manner about him that never stops you from being affected by him.

From the exclamation that I hear through the phone and the sight of Jack raising his eyebrows at me, I can tell that his words did little to assuage my mother's affront at this unexpected turn of events.

I *was* planning to tell the woman myself. She just truly hates feeling out of control and I really wanted a team of negotiators on standby when I did it.

"I understand your misgivings, Diana," he replies coolly. "But I love your daughter more than I can express with words, and I intend to make our marriage work. I hope to earn back your trust with time."

He drops his phone a little, pressing a button, presumably to mute her.

"Your mother wants to talk to you," he says.

"Thanks, asshole. Tell her I'll call her back," I groan with a sigh, deciding to give her half an hour to cool off before I get on the phone so that she can unleash World War Three on my behind. He presses the screen again.

"She'll call you back after breakfast, Diana." He squints as if taking an atomic bomb of an insult. "It's been a pleasure to speak to you too. I look forward to seeing you later this month."

I lift my palm to my forehead, groaning at the awkwardness. "Oh, fuck, you know she's gonna take it out on my poor dad now?"

"Your father's too passive with her," Jack retorts. "Too submissive. He has to pay the price for that."

He smiles as I whack him with the kitchen towel, handing me back my phone which I place on the countertop with a groan of mortification and dread. "God, why did you tell her?"

He slips his hand around my waist, yanking me into his hard frame. Another hand slides up the side of my face, lifting it to peer at blue eyes which startle me with their solemn entreaty.

"Because you're my fucking wife, Jessynia. And we're going to make this work, out in the open. No more hiding. Your parents have to know about us. It had to happen."

He speaks with such earnest fervor, as if willing me to be there with him.

I am.

I want to be.

I dream of the moment I fall into him like before, my heart consumed only by him, my body enslaved to his, his savage face playing over in my mind day and night.

I'd do anything to get back there. I know if I can get there, everything else will fall into place.

"I need you with me, baby," he says tenderly, dropping his lips to mine, brushing them with his before gifting me the gentlest of kisses, one impossible to imagine that this powerful, ruthless man is capable of. "Are you there?"

I nod as he kisses me again to the sound of a phone ringing, this time, his. I peek at the phone on the kitchen table behind us to see Cain's name emblazoned on it like some dark threat.

"God, I think it's parental torture day," I moan, trepidation churning in my belly as he smiles at the jab.

"Apparently," he says dryly, releasing me to pick up his cellphone, watching it for a few moments before bringing it to his ear.

"Cain," Jack says.

My body freezes at the sound of that sick man's name and at the unbidden sensation of the stone carcass he calls a body straining against mine, at the horror of his erection rubbing up and down my ass. Every time I think of it, my mind short-circuits, forcing the memory out.

I turn to the counter and pick up my phone and type a message:

Dad, I'm sorry about mom. I know she's gonna ruin your morning.
I am back with Jack. I'm sorry I didn't tell you before. We've been trying to work things out the last couple of weeks.
Everything's okay. Don't worry about anything.
I'll call you later. Love you.
Sorry for unleashing the beast.

Oh, Lord...

Putting it back down, I pick up the knife, slicing into a tomato which falls into perfect focus as Jack slowly walks away. I stab into the delicate red film, pushing the knife through the tender flesh as juicy seeds spill out onto the teak cutting board.

Oh, to be able to do this to your testicles, asshole, I mutter internally about my father-in-law as I slide the knife and make another cut through the squishy red fruit which squirts its juice out onto the rich wood beneath it.

I hear Jack speak over the sound of the knife scraping along the cutting board.

"How do you know?"

"That doesn't sound like her."

"Has she ever taken it before?"

Gina?

"Why would she start again?"

"When?"

"I'll speak to my wife about it."

"Fuck," I mutter as, distracted by Jack's last sentence and him placing his phone back down onto the table, I slice into my finger with the sharp Japanese knife, watching as if in slow motion as my skin parts into a deep valley only to fill with red liquid.

Jack is behind me in an instant, his shadow darkening the countertop. He curses as blood drips from my finger onto the chopping board before I can catch it.

"Jessa," he says roughly as he lifts my finger towards him, placing it in his mouth and sucking the blood from it. He turns to grab some paper towel and wraps it around my finger tightly, pulling me over to take a seat at the kitchen table, holding the paper towel in place.

"Stop," I laugh as his grave eyes watch it turn crimson, my blood seeping into the ivory. "It's nothing."

"I'd rather you cut me," he sighs out roughly, grabbing the first-aid kit from the cupboard above the fridge.

He unwraps my finger and wipes it with a disinfectant wipe before applying a ridiculously large Band-Aid to it.

"You'd make a good nurse," I sing.

"You need to be more careful, Jessynia."

"Sorry, the sound of the asshole makes me want to stab flesh."

"Well, you're not alone on that one," he responds through gritted teeth.

I peer into his eyes to find his expression grave. "What's wrong? What did he say?"

"It's Gina," he replies. The solemn note to his gravelly voice makes my stomach tip. "He... says she's taking opioids."

"What?! That's ridiculous. The woman's a health nut!"

"Yeah. It does seem strange."

"Why on Earth does he think that?" I ask.

"Apparently he found her stash. He says she's been acting strange. She passed out last night and he couldn't wake her. He almost called an ambulance."

"She wouldn't take that shit," I announce, alarm bells sounding off in my head. "Unless life with that *asshole* has finally pushed the poor woman to the limit." I lift my chin in defiance at the insult to his father and Jack's eyes gleam before a cold shadow swathes his face.

"We all have our breaking point," he says. "Maybe she's reached hers. I'm gonna go over there today."

"Okay," I nod, sliding my hand onto his. I know I should go with him. I just can't face the thought of seeing that abusive thug of a husband of hers.

I still feel him on me.

I just... I can't.

"Do you—" Jack stops the sentence short. "Nothing," he says with a shake of the head.

"You want me to go with you, don't you?" I ask.

"I... I thought maybe Gina would be more likely to open up to you than to me."

I swallow hard at the thought of seeing his father. At this point, I'm not sure that even the thought of Alexander Frost spurs such murderous urges in me.

"I... I..."

"I know you don't want to see that prick, baby. I don't blame you. I don't want to see him either."

"I'm sorry," I say as Jack's eyes scour my face.

He leans forward, sliding his hand behind my neck and pulling me towards him. "Jessynia, I need you to tell me the truth. Did he... hurt you... in some way? I mean, not just your wrist."

Jack's stunning masculine features fade out of focus as I think back to being pinned against the wall by Cain. It didn't feel dissimilar to being pinned against the tree in that forest all those years ago. My heart rattles in my chest at the thought.

I know Cain is unlikely to have done anything in light of Jack coming home. I suspect it was all done just to intimidate me over my attitude and to piss his "disrespectful" son off, but the thought of it has panic and claustrophobia constricting my throat.

I want to tell Jack the truth, but I can't. He's already suffered so much at his father's hands. It's the same reason I couldn't tell Cameron everything about my life when we were friends. I just can't subject them to more pain than I know they've already endured.

There's only one person I can tell all my secrets to. One person who can absorb the pain of others without it hurting him. One person who may very well feed off it...

"Jessynia..."

"No. He didn't hurt me."

I see relief loosening his body, the muscles softening as tension uncoils from his chest.

Maybe I should go there after all, look the ape square in the eyes, face that so-called man and not let him yield the power over me that he has now, not let him infiltrate my thoughts, let him know how much he affects me, let the touch of him contaminate me.

Take some power back.

Plus, I like Gina. She's always been so kind to me. I can't stand the idea of her not doing well. "I'm gonna come," I decide, slapping my thighs with my palms.

Jack pauses for a moment. "You're sure?"

"Yeah. I want to see Gina. Plus I may get to call your dad a *prick* again. That always makes me feel better."

He bows his head. "I won't object, baby."

9

I glance through the kitchen door at the men sitting at the dining table. Jack gripped my hand tightly as we entered and even more so when his prick father's beady eyes locked onto me and his lips twisted up at the corners in malignant satisfaction at my presence, one I'm sure he'll know will be tricky for me in light of our last encounter.

The tension is palpable even if Leon is on hand to watch over this father-son stand-off and try to prevent me from throwing a drink in Cain's face as I've dreamed of doing for months.

Truth be told, as much as I hate the tension, I'm kind of relieved it's there. When I first got together with Jack, it wasn't, for Jack seemed almost submissive to his father. Afraid.

I'd never, ever seen him like that before. He's one of the most self-confident men I've ever known. So dominant. So powerful. His eye contact is unflinching, his stance bold, and yet around his father, he became smaller somehow, weaker, and I hated witnessing it.

Now, the atmosphere is weighty and awkward, but I know it's because Jack is slowly taking his power back and asserting himself against a man who took so much of his childhood from him in such brutal blows. And I can live with that.

Leon, sitting on the opposite side of the table, strategically positioned between a bristling Jack on the left and his rancorous father on the right, seems to be watching me through the doorway as I help Gina prepare lunch in the kitchen.

"Here, sweetie," she says, placing some carrots on the chopping board in front of me. "Chop these for me."

"Sure," I reply, positioning the carrots in a line and grabbing a knife. I cut the heads off while imagining I'm chopping Cain's thick skull off his neck as Gina pours herself a glass of wine. It does seem early for her to be drinking, but I still can't believe what Cain said about her using drugs...

The man is full of shit.

"So, how've you been, honey?" she asks, holding up my dangly citrine earring with one hand before taking a generous sip of white wine...

"Oh, I've been... okay." As I say it, I realize that a year ago, I used to beam with enthusiasm when she asked me that question and proclaim that life was great.

"How's life back with Jack?"

I take a breath before resuming my chopping action. "You know we separated?"

"Of course, honey. It lasted months, no?"

"Yeah."

"That must have hurt?" she suggests.

"Yeah," I nod. "It was agony."

"You met someone else? This *Cameron* guy."

I throw a glance through the door to make sure no one is within earshot.

"Jack told you?"

"Let's just say that he was the subject of numerous debates around here. Cain wanted to solve the problem... old-school style."

"God, what a fucking neanderthal," I groan, trying to mask the staticky panic that invades me every time I think of it.

"Indeed."

"And what stopped him?" I ask.

"Jack. Just about." My heart aches at the thought of Jack protecting a man who had taken me from him, a man who was once a brother to him.

"I'm amazed Cain respected Jack's wishes," I scoff.

"Well, let's just say it's a good job you went back to Jack when you did."

A tremor of angst rattles me at the thought of Cameron being in Cain's crosshairs. "Anyone would think this is the Wild West," I moan, trying to maintain my composure.

"Oh, to our men, it is," she replies.

"Sure. Until their luck runs out."

"Oh, I've tried telling him," she responds as I down the rest of my glass of water. "May I?" I ask, reaching for the bottle of Moscato.

"Do you want a wine glass, honey?" she asks.

"No, fuck it. This'll do fine."

She smiles as I pour myself a glass and down half of it. *I'm gonna end up an alcoholic myself if this goes on much longer,* I mutter internally.

"How about you, Gina?" I ask. "How's life with the asshole?"

She chuckles good-naturedly, and I sigh out, "Sorry."

"Don't be," she replies. "He doesn't try to hide it."

"No, he does *not*," I retort with an eye roll. "Are you happy?" I finally ask, but in lieu of a response, she turns to take a colander full of parboiled potatoes from the sink to my right and pours them into a metal pan, seasoning them and drizzling them with olive oil.

I lift the lid off the boiling water and throw the carrots in upon her instruction. "Isn't the wedding coming up soon?"

"Just a few more weeks now," she responds, turning the extractor fan on.

"Excited?" I ask, watching Gina as she sprinkles some dried herbs onto the potatoes. She has this way of moving that's so graceful. Her tight black leggings compliment her thin pink sweater, its sleeves rolled up to the elbow to show off strong, lithe arms. Her thick chestnut-brown hair is tied into a high ponytail and she has just a little bit of make-up around her eyes. She's in her early forties and simply gorgeous, and from everything I know of her, even lovelier on the inside.

I asked the question with an internal groan for I don't know how any sane woman can be excited to be legally bound to that gesticulating ape out there. I can only pray he's gentler when it's just the two of them, though I doubt it somehow.

I know from the assertive way that Jack is in public compared to the gentle way he is with me in private, that people are not always the same behind closed doors, although I suspect that Jack and his father are very different in that regard.

"Weddings are always exciting, aren't they?" she replies as she douses the potatoes with some more olive oil and rolls them around the pan.

"You're not... nervous at all?" I ask as she pops the tray into the oven.

"Nervous?" she smiles. "Honey, we're all nervous when we get married. Remember the wreck you were just before yours?"

Despite the wide smile and the light demeanor, there's something behind her eyes—some solemn note that Gina's always been so adept at concealing. Only on this occasion, it seems harder to ignore.

How do you ask someone that you like and respect if they need help? If they're on drugs? If they're trapped?

I can't even fully help myself...

I head over to her as she finishes her glass of wine and places it down onto the counter. Looking at her more closely, I see that her face is more gaunt than before, more lined, not quite as vibrant as when I first met her a couple of years ago.

My eyes roam over her skin—it's olive and beautiful but thinner somehow. I've always wondered if that baboon she's engaged to makes her watch her weight or something. It never seems to fluctuate.

I take a greedy sip of wine.

Come on, Jess. Do it...

"Gina, I—" *Holy fuck, I can't do this*—"I... I know this is so inappropriate and you can throw me out of your house, but... are you *really* okay? You can tell me. We won't tell Cain, ever."

She pauses for what feels like half a minute before smiling. "You're a sweetheart, Jessie. You always have been. But I'm fine. Honestly."

"Does..."

"What?" she smiles, though it doesn't quite reach her eyes.

"Does it ever scare you? Being with such a dangerous man?"

She looks down for a moment. "Yes. But then"—she tucks a strand of loose hair behind my ear—"I think you may understand the appeal of dangerous men better than most."

Her words take me aback. Living with a man as ruthless as Jack has become the norm. I don't really remember anything else, nor do I really think of him as being dangerous, especially when the only other man I've shared my heart with has his own danger label attached.

Sometimes I forget that I too have chosen men that live on the edge. Not all men are this dominant, nor possessive, nor love this passionately. Explosively. Insanely.

"Gina. I know you'll hate me for this. I know I'm in your house and you can throw me out whenever you want, but..."—I shudder in a fluttery breath—"does he ever *really* hurt you?"

Her eyes soften as she watches me. "I can't answer that, Jessie. You know that."

Oh my God...

I look back briefly at the animal sitting at the head of his table. I picture myself grabbing the wine bottle and making my way over there. If I'm fast enough, I can smash the thing over his thick skull before Jack or Leon can get to me. "We can get you out of here," I say softly. "We can help."

"And have Jack face his father's rage? His brothers'? No. I've made my bed. I'll lie in it."

"Do you love him?"

"I live with two men, Jessie. The sober one and the drunk. The sober one is loving. He's almost gentle. The other is..."

"A monster."

She nods slowly. "And you love Jackson, don't you?"

"Yes. But he's not—"

"A monster?" she suggests. "Are you sure?"

I frown and her face softens.

"Yes," I reply.

"He's certainly a league apart from his father, but I've seen him when he loses you, Jess. When he's without you, he is unstable. While women deal with that pain and process it, these types of men don't. That's when the monster can come out. If you have to stay with him to keep him sane, that isn't healthy either."

I watch her beautiful face as the reality of her words sinks in, as does the reality that Jack isn't the only man who loses his mind like that when he's out of control. Cameron is not that much different, although I expect he would not resort to violence to get me back, nor allow me to be threatened the way Jack did.

Though I could be wrong...

"I know," I nod.

Her keen brown eyes glitter. "You really have the most beautiful face I've ever seen, Jessie. I like to think that if I'd had a daughter, she would have looked like you."

"You never wanted children?"

"I did once. But I couldn't bring a child into this. I love the boys, Jack especially. That's good enough for me."

"Gina?"

She nods for me to speak.

"I hate asking this fucking question."

She smiles. "Ask it anyway."

"Have you ever... turned to... *substances* to cope with... life with Cain?"

Her face falls into shadow, suddenly grim as she eyes me curiously. "You know, you're the second person this week to ask me that question. Did Cain say something?"

"No," I respond after a moment, remembering Jack's instructions not to let Gina know that Cain brought up her alleged drug use for fear of her getting into an altercation with him.

"Then, why ask?"

"You just... look a little thin," I explain clumsily.

"Oh, that's because I've been working out, honey. I don't take drugs. Never have, never will."

"Okay," I sigh out, praying it's true.

I rattle out a halting breath, and as I do so, my eyes pan down her neck.

And my heart stalls in my chest.

I frown as I peer at a black bead on a silver chain—a single bead sticking out of her pink sweater. It's nestled next to others hidden underneath the woolen fabric.

No.

My palms turn clammy and the floor falls out from under me, making my stomach drop a thousand feet.

No.

She eyes me as I lift a quivering hand to the necklace and pull it out from her sweater, my body inert, the room spinning as if seized by the first dregs of a tornado.

Two obsidian spheres on either side shield five rose quartz ones in the center.

Cameron...

I hear her voice, but the words are drowned out, as if uttered from deep under dark water. Splashes of light flash across my field of vision.

Leon...

By some miracle, I manage to collect myself and glance up to meet deep, soulful brown eyes.

"It's beautiful, huh?" she says, smiling broadly. Her face morphs as she watches what I imagine is the color draining from mine, leaving me a ghost stuck in some world which no longer makes sense. "Jessie? You okay, honey?"

"Where... where did you get it?" I ask.

"My mom gave it to me. Stunning, huh?"

As I try to formulate the words, a tenebrous shadow catches my eye as it looms towards us from just outside the doorway. My tempestuous glower lifts to see Leon leaning against the white door frame of the kitchen, his eyes fixed on me, narrowing slightly as he takes in my obvious distress.

"You need anything?" Gina asks him.

"More beers please."

"Coming right up."

I try to breathe through brutal blows of panic as Leon's lips curve at the sides while drinking in my face as if it were the smoothest of aged whiskey.

He gave it to her.

There's no other way she could have got it.

But, why?

Oh, my God...

"Two?" Gina asks, popping the cap off a large bottle of brown ale.

"Two," Leon responds as my features steadily furrow in anger, my nervous system unable to keep fending off the shots fired into it.

Gina heads over to him and hands him the two beers, announcing that lunch will be ready in fifteen minutes.

"Sounds good," he smiles, watching me, his eyes gleaming like setting tar in the moonlight until he turns and walks out of the room with a smirk.

He can't be...

Not him and... her.

He'll get her killed...

Leon's eyes barely leave me as we eat lunch. He's sitting opposite me and Gina with Jack at the end of the table to my left and Cain to my right.

I can't taste the food. I can barely feel my hands as I bring the fork to my lips, trying to ignore the oppressive miasma, the invisible poison of foreboding settling over the dining table.

All I can think of is Cameron's necklace and why he would have given it to her.

It doesn't help that Jack has been eyeing me intently for the last ten minutes, no doubt in response to my sudden selective mutism. The thought of Jack having to look at a necklace that Cameron had made for me makes me sick to my stomach.

I was looking forward to glaring at Cain with contempt as he eats and throwing jabs whenever I could get them in, but right now, force is evading me and I feel myself wilting under a sense of foreboding so thick that it feels like acrid smoke is billowing into the room.

I can't breathe...

"How's the *journalism* going, Mrs. Wilder?" Cain asks, drawing my attention as he spits out the word in derision before glancing at Jack opposite him, his lips twisting in contemptuous satisfaction.

The asshole just can't help himself.

"It's going well," I say, lifting my chin despite my moxie wearing thin.

"I hope it keeps you occupied, at least," he shoots back. "And out of *trouble...*"

His harsh eyes scald me and right now, I'm wondering why I agreed to come here. It's way too soon to see him again after his unwelcome visit to our apartment. If it weren't for my concern over Gina, the most decent human in this family, I wouldn't see the prick ever again...

"Out of trouble? Sounds a bit dull," I sigh out.

"Jessie's blog gets thousands of visitors a day, no?" interrupts Gina, squeezing my arm.

"Well, I've always believed there's no shortage of fools that need to be told how to think," snarls Cain.

"That's enough," retorts Jack.

"I don't tell people how to think, Cain," I pipe up. "I'm just... sharing information. Sharing my viewpoint on issues that matter, in my opinion, anyway."

My heart sinks as he drinks down the rest of his beer, banging the bottle back down onto the table with a thud. I hate knowing Gina has to deal with him when she's alone and he's wasted.

"Like what?" he scoffs.

"Never mind," I sigh.

"A journalist who can't even explain what she writes about," he sniggers.

"Oh, I can explain it. I just know what you'll think of these issues and I don't like wasting my breath."

"How are you liking the roast, boys?" Gina asks to slice through the tension as Cain eyeballs me.

"It's delicious, Gina," Jack replies. "Thank you."

As I turn to smile at her, my gaze is once again drawn to the necklace that Cameron designed and had milled for me.

Only this time, it seems someone has spotted my interest...

"Pretty, huh?" asks Cain and my heart rate begins to careen.

I peer at him, locked in some unholy standoff as his eyes draw thin.

"The necklace," he clarifies. "Her mom got it for her, didn't she, Gina?"

I shudder internally as he speaks. It's not like Cain to notice, much less care, about what necklace his wife is wearing, and he certainly wouldn't point it out.

My eyes stray to Leon whose face is suddenly hard, carved in lines of rigid concern.

I don't know what's going on here, but if it's what I think, someone is going to get hurt.

Gina turns to me and smiles broadly, always so willing to lighten the atmosphere, but there's something hidden in her eyes—fear, doubt, this never-ending need to smooth things over so that Cain doesn't unleash whatever monsters he is brewing that day.

As I think of the threatening thundercloud that she lives under, I turn to Cain, meeting his glare head-on. His indecent, unflinching eye contact only pisses me off more despite my stomach churning in trepidation.

I want to finally say everything I feel about this violent child abuser, but I know he'll take it out on Jack and later Gina.

One day, Cain.

Yours is coming...

Once we've finished eating, Gina and I take the plates to the kitchen and begin to load the dishwasher, only this time, we're plunged into weighty silence. Neither of us talks. Occasionally she meets my eyes, but now, fear taints the air. God knows what it must be like when she's alone with the man.

"Are you okay?" I ask her.

"Sure, honey," she says after a pause that felt *way* too long.

"Look, sorry if I was a bit blunt out there. I wasn't trying to provoke him. He just really gets under my skin."

"Honey, that man doesn't need *you* as an excuse to be a prick. He'll always find one." She squeezes my arm as I search her soft face, wishing she could be with anyone but him. "I'm going to the washroom," she says, pulling a bottle of malt whiskey and a tumbler out of a cupboard. "Can you pour Cain a glass?" she asks.

"Are you sure? I feel like he's had enough to drink."

"He has," she replies with a half-smile. "But telling him that doesn't usually end well."

"Okay," I nod, rinsing off a couple of plates before loading them into the dishwasher and grabbing the bottle, pouring in the bronze liquid. I'm not handing him the drink till Jack's left.

I glance through the kitchen only to see Leon walking towards me, leaving Jack and Cain alone and facing one another.

My cheeks burn hot as he approaches, his eye contact lethal, his mammoth body owning the space the way an ancient tree would a barren field.

"Enjoy lunch?" he asks as he takes slow steps inside.

"Why does she have it?" I spit out in as low a tone as I can muster.

"Have *what*, Jessynia?" he smirks.

"Cut the shit! Why?!"

"The necklace, I presume."

"Why?!"

"You won't be wearing it ever again. It seems a pity to let it go to waste."

"You're sleeping with her, aren't you?!"

His lips curve in malignant amusement as the foreboding drumbeat of raised voices drifts across from the open-plan dining area.

Wow, they made it a full five minutes...

"You're going to get her killed!" I whisper.

"Or myself," he retorts, "though I don't suppose that would bother you much."

"No, it wouldn't! What the fuck are you thinking?!"

He takes a step towards me, his huge frame bristling as if a lone tree on a rugged heath wracked by unforgiving winds, twisting his features. "You think you have the right to demand answers from me, little girl?"

"When it involves people I care about being put in danger, yes!"

"You know, I'm still convinced that some discipline is all you need," he responds contemptuously.

"You couldn't handle it, Leon," I sneer to the glitter of mirth in his narrowing eyes. "You realize it's only a matter of time before you get caught, right? Do you realize what that neanderthal would do to her if he found out? Do you even give a fuck?!"

"Careful, Jessynia," he growls and my lips part in incredulity.

"What, don't tell me you have feelings for her..."

As footsteps approach, he leans into me. "I'd strongly advise you to mind your own fucking business... for your own safety, little girl."

I avert my glare to the shape approaching.

Jack.

His arrival is greeted by palpable tension between Leon and I, and I consciously soften my features as Jack's eyes flit between me and Leon who turns to face him.

"We're leaving," Jack says. "Now."

"Why?" I ask.

"Because my father is still a prick, believe it or not, and I don't want to break my knuckles today."

"Fair enough," I sigh out in mock-exasperation, throwing Leon a look as I wonder for a second if Jack knows.

He can't do...

It would be suicidal on the part of Leon to tell *anyone*...

I'm tempted to tell Cain what a talent he has for clearing a room as we leave, but decide to keep that insight to myself just this once. It feels painful to leave Gina, especially seeing her place the tumbler of whiskey onto the table for Cain to glug down. I don't know how in God's name a beautiful, smart, caring woman like her ended up with a man like him...

Maybe I'm not one to talk, although Jack is not like Cain. Not even close...

Upon finally saying our goodbyes, mainly to Gina, with a cursory *thank you* to Cain to hopefully prevent the ego monster from being unleashed on his long-suffering fiancée, Jack and I don our coats and leave their large house.

We make it a few steps out of the gate before my breath is stolen from me as Jack pins me against the brick wall surrounding their property.

"Hey!" I exclaim, pushing against his chest. It's at times like these that I realize just how tall and strong he is. I somehow forget it, for he handles me gently despite his dominance, lifting me carefully, placing me down cautiously. Even when he throws me onto the bed or pins my limbs to the mattress, he does it in a way that won't cause me pain, never bruising me or squeezing too tightly—just enough to restrain me so that my body can serve his needs.

He ignores my attempts at pushing him back.

"What?!" I ask, with as much attitude as I can muster in the face of his storm cloud of a glower.

"What were you discussing with Leon?"

"Discussing?" I stammer. "That ape doesn't have the cognitive ability to *discuss*. He just comes in and verbally urinates all over the place as usual."

"Answer my question."

"Just... just the usual."

"And that is?"

"Him being a *prick*. He can't help himself."

"You looked shaken," Jack counters. "I want the truth. I don't like feeling that my wife is hiding things from me."

"I... I'm not." *I hate lying to him.* "Look, we always have these verbal spars. We've never had a single pleasant conversation. It's not a big deal."

His luminous glacial-blue eyes form into tight crevasses. "My job is to protect you, and when you hide from me, I can't do it as well. If I find out you're lying to me, I will make you pay so that you don't do it again. That's my job as your husband—to keep you safe. And I intend to do it, no matter the cost. Is that understood?"

I nod slowly as his countenance softens, exposing the wild beauty of his wind-lashed face. His eyes don't move from mine, not for a second and as he shields me from the outside world with his body, I succumb to the protective armor he always tries to place around me.

"Is that your only job?" I ask in a clumsy attempt to lighten the mood.

His eyes fall to my lips. "Not even close..."

"What's your other job?"

"I have several. I'll be showing you one of them the second we get back home... up against the door, if we make it through it."

I smile, breathing out a sigh of relief at signs that his tense body is unwinding... just a little.

His hand lifts to my face and his thumb strokes the skin of my cheeks. "When you disconnect from me, I lose control."

I nod and stand on my tiptoes as I bestow a gentle kiss on his brutal lips. "Can we get out of here?" I ask, peering up at him through my lashes as a low groan escapes his throat.

He takes a step back, finding my hand and interlacing his fingers, walking me in weighty silence back to the car as an image of Leon and Gina floats through my mind.

What are they thinking?

10

Leon

My eyes don't leave hers as she approaches the table. I'm normally careful not to look at her too much, but today, I can't seem to stop myself.

Something's wrong.

Cain.

That motherfucker.

There's something in his tone that isn't usually there. If the prick knew what self-restraint was, he'd hide it, but I know his type. I was raised by them. I know he can't help himself.

Fuck.

I don't want to leave her with him. He's had too much to drink as fucking usual. He can't help himself in that department either.

"Do you boys want anything?" she asks as she reaches the table, her hands gripping the top of her wooden chair.

"Sit down," Cain says.

"Oh, I don't want to cramp you boys' style," she sings. She's so good at putting on that wide smile around him, but I know she's nervous. I can see it. Her hands shake, just a little, and her voice gets breathier.

Her shoulders tighten without her realizing it. Hell, I can feel what she feels in my body.

"I was going to leave anyway," I say, not wanting to.

I don't want to leave her with him when he's drunk, but I don't have much choice. I've gotten used to this by now—leaving her in the clutches of a maniac and hoping that when he hurts her, it's not too much, that this time, things don't go to a place there's no coming back from.

I could take her far away from here, but I know he'd find us. He's rabid that way, just like the men I grew up with. Once he latches on, once the venom has entered his veins, the prick doesn't let go, no matter what the cost to him or anyone around him. He'd see himself in a cell before he let her taste freedom.

I don't know how I got into this fucking mess.

I only wanted to fuck the bitch. He deserved it. I never meant to feel this. I never meant to feel anything for her.

I'm half-tempted just to quit, pack up my car and get the fuck out of here, leave her to him. She chose him after all. She knew what she was getting herself into. I keep telling her I'll take her away, but the only way I'll be able to pull that off is if he's in a body bag… and I don't know if I can manage it without getting caught.

I have someone who could do it, but it's risky. I don't have the means to pay for the professionals that Cain hires to solve his problems. It'd have to be someone good, smart, someone I can trust never to breathe a word of it. The risk is just so fucking high…

His gray-brown eyes narrow. "I haven't finished with you yet, Leon."

I'm used to men like him—rough, damaged, bitter, violent. The fuckers don't phase me.

Hell, I'm one of them.

But there's something that unnerves me about Cain's face—his strong jaw, his deep-set eyes, the shape of his mouth. And the way he glares at you. Jack has it too, but it's less primal, less violent of a glare, and Jack is smarter. He can reel in his emotions—or at least he can as long as it doesn't involve his wife.

Cain can't. Once the fuse has been lit, you can't put the thing out.

He's gone, and no amount of reasoning can stop the explosion once the flame has taken.

It's partly the alcohol, but it's also the bitterness and resentment that corrupts him. Life didn't pan out how he wanted and instead of the fucker seeing everything he has—the wealth, the power, the beautiful wife, the healthy children, he sees everything that was taken from him —his first wife, his youth, the respect of his son... and the changing status of men like him.

He thought he'd be head of an empire by now, but he's still a low-level mob boss sending out his men to steal, deal drugs and blackmail. He's lucky he's not in prison serving a life sentence. But then, this man wouldn't be able to identify fortune if it fucked him in the ass.

I don't blink as he dares me with his eyes. If he didn't pay me, I would already have put a knife into him for that glare. I've done that to men for less. No one else dares look at me like that... perhaps with the exception of Jack's untrained wife and even then, she's usually shaking with so much outrage that it's borderline amusing to witness.

His eyes slide slowly towards Gina. "Sit down."

"I'm sure you don't want me listening to—"

"Sit. Down."

I have to hand it to him; the man has a voice that can plunge any room into silence.

Gina glances at me for a reckless split-second that I've warned her about repeatedly before staring down at the table as she takes a seat opposite me.

Cain leans back in his chair, sliding his hands along the arm rests until he reaches the ends that he grasps firmly with thick fingers.

"Did you enjoy your little chat with Jessynia?" Cain asks as Gina swallows down nerves that there's no way that Cain can't see. She needs to pack it the fuck in and fast...

"Yes, she's lovely," Gina replies, gulping down clear anxiety, the type that Cain will feed off of.

Hell, so do I, usually.

Except I don't like seeing it in *her*. This fucking woman does something to me that no other has. I don't know why it had to be *her*. I wish I could get her out of my fucking head. I don't like feeling out of control. That's what she does to me.

At first, it was about the fantasy—taking your prick boss's woman from him. The ultimate victory. A reversal of roles. The ultimate ego boost.

I wish it were just that now. I've never been kept from sleep before, wondering what he's doing to her, picturing her face. I see her eyes looking for me, and later, staring up at me softly as she sucks on my cock. She does it for up to an hour some days, depending on how long the fucker will be gone. She never complains. She wants to give me pleasure but never acts like a whore. It's gentle. It's everything I thought I despised.

I hear her voice, feel the touch of her on my skin. No woman has ever touched me the way she does. Seen me.

How?

I want to go back to when I didn't give a fuck who she was. When I saw her as this fucker's bitch.

I've seen it with Jack. Men lose their power when they fall in love. It makes them weak. Soft. Vulnerable. Everything I fucking well hate.

And now, suddenly, I'm starting to understand him when I don't want to. I don't want to be like him—enslaved to his feelings for a woman to the point of stupidity.

I can't allow that to happen to me...

If only the bitch didn't see me the way she does. Didn't look at me like that. Didn't smile at me the way she does. Didn't care for me, worry about me... and love me despite everything she knows about what an unpalatable prick I am.

The way she loves is not something I remember since... I last saw it... in my mother's eyes.

I was four when my father lost control...

I haven't seen that look since.

Even now when she's looking back at him, careful not to make eye contact with me, she's speaking to me. I can feel it. I can hear the words. I know she's unsure. I know she can tell something's going on with him. I know she needs me here.

She needs things from me that I don't know if I can give... or if I want to.

It will mean life as I know it is over...

Am I even capable of loving another human being?

Do I want a life I've mocked and pitied for as long as I can remember?

Cain's beady eyes narrow. "*Lovely?*" he repeats, his thick jaw tightening. "Is that what you think? You think the bitch who disrespects her father-in-law, your *fiancé*, is *lovely*, darling?"

"I... I'm not saying she's lovely to *you*, honey. I just mean... she's always been kind to me. I can only judge her on that."

"Really? You clearly don't understand loyalty, Gina. Where I come from, when a man has an issue with someone, his *fucking* wife supports him and *only* him or lives to regret it. That's what we would expect from our women." His cold eyes shift to me. "Wouldn't you agree, Leon?"

I want to take this fucker out...

My body tenses as I realize with disgust that I want to defend her, to contradict everything I know about the role women should play, right to his fucking face...

But I can't...

I can't bring myself to say the words. I can't let him think I'm defending his wife. He knows me too well. He knows how I believe women should behave around their husbands.

"Right," I nod, and my insides tear a little as I say it. I'm suddenly aware of how callous my voice sounds.

How the fuck did I get here?

Her eyes lift to meet mine solemnly. She never seems to get angry. She's always understanding. She always has compassion for my fuckery.

I wish she didn't. It makes it so hard not to just walk away...

"What did she ask you?" Cain asks.

"Oh, just small talk, you know," she replies. "About her work. Her writing. Jack. The usual."

"You're lying to me, Gina."

"I… I'm not," she stammers, glancing at me again, as if I might save her. I don't know if I can.

"Yes, you are. Apart from the fact that that girl doesn't do *small talk*, she went into that kitchen being the insolent little bitch I've come to *know and love*, and came out of it as pale as Leon's ass, and barely able to talk. You think I don't notice these things? I see more than you think, sweetheart." His frigid eyes wander to me and without meaning to, I glance at the knife he keeps next to him at all times, its wooden handle taunting me. I'm not that far away. I could grab it first. "I want to know what shut our little friend up like that. I know you're not going to lie to me again."

"I—"

"Or perhaps *you* have an idea?" he asks, directing the question at me as he reaches forwards and lifts a glass of whiskey to his lips. The half-melted ice cubes rattle as he tips it up and drinks down the brown liquid.

The thick glass bottom hits the table with a clunk that makes Gina jump. He fixes his eyes on me as his hand moves to the right, his fingers finding the handle of the knife, wrapping around it. He bends his elbow and the tip of the blade finds the fingertips of his other hand.

He knows.

I can feel it.

I've never felt tension with him before, despite months of fucking his wife.

Something has shifted.

It's too early.

I don't have things sorted out.

Plus, there's another matter in motion that requires my concentration.

"I gave her some grief over Cameron O'Neill," I lie, meeting his glare head-on as his eyes form into slits and the fucker studies me as if I were some diamond he's planning on stealing. Wouldn't be his first…

"Hmm… You must have really pissed the little girl off, Leon, for her to come out of that room unable to talk."

"I guess I pushed her a bit far," I respond as his dark glare meets the submissive gaze of the woman he intends to marry.

"Is she seeing O'Neill? Do I have to take care of that as well?"

"No," I respond, though I'm not entirely sure that's true.

But I know one man who will know...

He breathes out a heavy breath. "Good. That bitch has been asking to be taught a lesson for a long time. It seems she's escaped it for now." An indecipherable smile plays on his mouth as he eyeballs his wife. "Did she like your necklace?"

Gina's usually tanned face looks pale. "Yeah."

"Good."

What is he playing at today?

Or am I just being paranoid?

We've been careful. I don't see how he could know...

There's no real reason to think he does, other than that bit at lunch over the necklace. It just seems out of character for the mindless grunt to give a shit what people think of his wife's jewelry. He normally doesn't like men looking at her, even his own son.

"We have our other little matter to attend to," he says, turning to me.

"Should she leave?" I ask, gesturing to the woman sitting opposite me, the woman who shouldn't have to hear men plotting murder.

Gina moves as if to stand but is interrupted by that rumbling voice of his. "Sit. The. Fuck. Down." She swallows hard and takes a seat. "I don't hide secrets from my women. I go down, *they* go down. We trust each other, don't we, beautiful?"

"Of course," she replies.

"Now. How much does he want?"

"Three fifty," I reply.

"Three hundred and fifty thousand dollars?"

I nod slowly. "He can get it done cleanly within three months. No trace. He won't exist after it's done. He's pulled off *six* so far. No arrests. No one has even looked into him."

"You could kill a fucking president for that amount," Cain snarls.

"That's the price to get rid of a man like Sebastian Gravier."

Though my eyes remain fixed to Cain, out of my peripheral vision, I see Gina taking her glass of wine and downing it, placing it back onto the table as gently as she can, as if afraid of making a sound.

"See if you can get the price down."

"I've tried," I reply. "He doesn't negotiate."

"Hmmm."

"Do you want it done?"

He toys with the knife in his hand, running his finger up the flat side of the blade, staring at the metal. "When does he want an answer?" he asks.

"He'll give us two weeks to think about it. After that, he's out. What's stopping you? I thought you wanted it done."

"I do. It's just... there's another urgent matter I have to attend to."

If I'm not mistaken, there's a slight lift to the edge of his lips.

"What?" I ask.

He eyeballs me for way too fucking long, the silence twisting in my gut, making my hands ache to form a fist, the tension turning to fever pitch despite neither of us moving.

Finally, he drawls, "I won't need your help with this one."

Sometime later, my stomach sinks as he stubs out his cigar and polishes off his second glass of whiskey that Gina served him with a smile. I know full well what she thinks of his drinking. "You can go now, Leon. I have some business to attend to with my fii-ann-céééé."

My breathing quickens as he draws out the word, his eyes glassy.

My body remains inert.

How do I leave her with him?

He watches me as I remain seated.

How the fuck did this happen to me?

How could I have been so goddamn stupid?

I throw a quick glance at her and she gives me that fucking smile, one of reassurance, the same one she gives me every time I leave, to tell me it's okay... when I full well know it's not okay.

What do I do?

Pull out my knife and do battle to the death? Part of me wants to do it. Part of me no longer cares if I end up a bloody pile of dog meat on the floor. I've had it coming for a long time. I just don't want it to be at the hands of this twisted fuck.

Do I drag her out? Do I call the police? The same police I've loathed my entire fucking life?

Do I wait till he leaves and then take her, imploring the God I've ignored since I was a kid to stop Cain from burning her parents' house down in retribution? He's capable of it. He's done worse before.

"It was nice to see you, Leon," says Gina, as if willing me to leave.

I get up, saying stiff goodbyes. I put on my coat and get the fuck out, pressing my back against the door as I close it behind me to have a sharp blast of wind cool my skin.

My car is just down the street.

I could get in it, go home, pack a few things and get the fuck away from here for good. I have enough savings to start a new life. I don't have to put myself through this anymore.

But... *her...*

I walk down the path, open and close the gate behind me before heading to my car and getting in... only I don't leave.

I wait.

11

Gina

He knows.

I stare down at Leon's text message, knowing that each second that Cain is waiting for me will make him more and more suspicious.

He left ten minutes ago. I know he didn't want to. I saw it in his faltering movements. But he had to go.

Of course he did. I get it. Cain can't suspect… or suspect anymore.

With hands quivering a little, I manage to text back:

What do I do?

He replies:

I can come and get you.

Me:

No. It's too dangerous. Maybe we're just being paranoid.

In truth, I've dreamed of him coming to save me and us riding away for months, but I'm so afraid of what that mad man will do to us. I know he is too. He doesn't like to show fear, but occasionally I see fleeting glimpses of it where I never did before, even when he was carrying out Cain's most dangerous orders.

I could never ask it of him. He has to make that decision on his own... and I'm afraid deep down that part of him just wants to run away and not face what I know he feels.

I don't believe that I'm just another fuck to him. He doesn't need me for that. Women throw themselves at him in the circles we move in. He has a side-piece, Misty. She'd do anything for him. I know it's about more than just the satisfaction of nailing the boss's wife. I see it in the way he looks at me, the way he touches me, the way he worries despite trying not to show it.

Should I even let him keep this up? There's nothing he does in any part of his work that's as dangerous as this...

From outside the washroom, the clunk of glass against the wood of the table jolts me. He's losing his patience.

I send another message.

I have to go.

Leon:
Text me later.

OK.

I put my phone on silent and tuck it under some folded towels in the cupboard next to the sink. I flush the toilet and wash my hands, checking my reflection in the mirror. For a second, I realize that the figure staring back at me looks haunted.

Where did she go? That vibrant woman with shining eyes? My eyes look hollow, as if I've seen too much...

I take off my nice thin sweater and hang it on a hook on the door. I know he's in a mood. I know how he gets himself out of those moods, and usually my clothes are the first things that get it.

I plaster on the smile I use as some kind of armor to protect myself and unlock the door of the downstairs washroom, glancing behind me quickly to check that everything is in its rightful place.

Towel.

Faucet.

Toilet paper.

Check.

Deep breaths...

In one of those recurring moments I experience a few times a day, I wonder how I got here. It's one thing being afraid of occasional fights like most couples are. It's another being scared every moment of every day, walking on eggshells, listening out for noises, deciphering imperceptible twitches in the man's face.

I smile as breezily as I can as I make my way over to him, still sitting at that chair, eyes sunken in shadow, owning the room as he always does. It's as if everyone else is there by his grace.

My hands find the top of the chair as he watches me.

"Come here, Gina."

He shifts back in his chair, pushing it backwards, the rubber pads under the feet scraping against the floor as he makes space for me between his legs and the table.

My heavy feet lead me to stand before him as my ass hits the narrow edge of the table.

My heart stalls as he slowly gets to his feet, towering above me, glaring down at his possession. His chest rises and falls slowly under his white shirt—the sleeves rolled up to the elbows, as always, as if he's ready to get stuck into the action at the drop of a hat. I peer up at him, trying to smile as he takes in my face.

Despite the fear he arouses in me, I'm sometimes taken aback by what an arresting man he is. His jaw and nose are strong, his eyes piercing. His graying hair and short beard are thick. His cheekbones could still cut glass. He looks like a more brutal version of his sons, especially

Jack, but with darker eyes and hair. I don't know if it pleases him to look in the mirror and see his youngest and most defiant son.

"Did you enjoy our chat with Leon, Gina?"

I swallow hard without meaning to. "I can't say that I enjoy hearing you talk about taking out contracts to kill people."

He tips his head slightly to the side. "Why not? You don't like bad men, all of a sudden? I think you do..."

"It's dangerous, baby. You never know what could happen."

I shudder inside as his hand reaches for that damn fucking knife. The thing is almost a part of him. Sane people don't keep knives next to them like this. It's almost as if he needs to feel the potential of its violence in order to feel alive. He needs everything to feel extreme. It's as though he needs the shadow of death around him to feel alive.

At the scrape of metal across the table, his other hand reaches up to my throat. His thumb and fingers coil around my neck as I peer up at this man who was once gentle with me.

He tips his head towards me, a splash of whiskey on his breath mixing with the ashy odor of his cigar. He squeezes my neck, watching for my response, and my eyes soften—I can't show too much fear.

It doesn't protect me. He gets off on it too much.

"You like the danger, though. Don't you, baby?"

"Some danger is good," I reply. "But..."

"It's too much for you?"

I shake my head. "I just worry about you."

I shudder as the tip of the knife makes its way across my cheek. It doesn't hurt or cut—the damage is in the threat, not in the pain, and he knows it. He knows the horror resides in the fear above all else. The act that hurts me is never as painful as the terror I feel beforehand.

The knife ventures over my jawline and down my neck. He slides it under my necklace as my breathing quickens. He lifts the chain a little so that it's draped over the blade. "Do you enjoy wearing it?" he asks.

"I don't have to, honey. I know my mother annoys you. You don't need a reminder of her every day."

"You won't take it off unless I say so. Understood?"

He knows...

He has to.

Either that or this is his way of soothing his rage over my mother giving me a necklace that I dared wear in his house. He can get that way at times. He knows she doesn't like him, so will get moody if I see her or talk to her, tolerating it on the surface, but brooding over it for days during which he makes his rancor known in various ways. I've learned to speak to her only when he's out, to visit her only when there's no chance he'll come home early. Maybe he is just still irritated that I had the audacity to face him wearing a gift from her... or so he thinks.

God...

In a movement that grips me with fear, he grabs the top of my T-shirt.

"Baby—"

Ignoring me, he plunges the knife through it and slowly slices all the way down to the bottom. The man's never been good at leaving clothes intact when he wants them off me. I couldn't even count the number of tops and pants I've thrown away after he's ripped them to shreds. I don't bother buying quality leggings anymore. They'll usually have a hole in the crotch within days if he catches me wearing them.

Gripping the knife, he tears open my T-shirt before pulling the strap of the bra between my breasts away from my skin and slicing through it. The cool metal tip of the blade traces a gentle path over my breasts before finding my leggings.

"Baby," I breathe, but his vicious eyes dart up to mine and I stop my protest.

Satisfied with my silence, he pulls at the fabric between my legs, inserts the blade and rips apart the crotch so that my sex is exposed before raising the knife to my throat.

The words Leon has spoken to me so many times play over in my mind.

Don't show fear...

"Do you think I've been bad to you, Gina?"

"I... I don't think that, honey."

"Sure you do," he retorts grimly. "Why wouldn't you? I've hurt you. I've been a bad man. I know that. Has it been too much?"

"No," I reply gently, though we sailed past "too much" a year or so ago when he left a bruise on my face that took a week to heal when I dared to question him about sleeping with his sons' wives—or two of his sons anyway.

Everything since then, every word spoken, every time he's fucked me, every kiss I've given him with a smile, has been a move in a waiting game that seems interminable as I try to find a way to get out.

"I've tried to be a good man to you, Gina. I've tried to protect you. To house you. To feed you. To provide for you. To fuck you well. I've done my job as a man. And I don't always feel that it's appreciated..."

"*Of course* it is, baby."

"Do you think you've done your job as a woman?"

"Yes," I nod as my exposed nipples harden into points. "I've tried to."

"Hmm. I hope so, Gina. For both our sakes..."

"Baby, what's gotten into you?" I ask, terrified of the answer he'll give me.

His muddy eyes siphon the breath from my lungs. "I just... want to understand."

"Understand what?" *Jesus, my voice wavered.*

"Hmm... You'll see soon enough. In the meantime, I still have faith that you can be a good wife. Can you?"

"Of course I can, honey."

"Do you want to be my wife?"

I swallow down the answer I want to give. "Yes."

"What does a good wife do, Gina?"

Does the prick want a list?

"She..."

"She what?" he snarls, his breath a blast of ethanol on my face.

"She takes care of her husband."

"How?"

The questions he asks me always reduce me to the pitiful state of simpleton, to the messed up twenty-year-old I was before I got my act together and became someone, someone that unraveled under his guidance bit by bit. I was once a smart ass with a sharp tongue. I could give as good as I got, banter with the best of them. That's part of why he liked me.

At some point, I became so afraid of pissing him off that I stopped trying to tease, to be playful, to answer back. Now I just respond to his asinine questions like some automaton, some Brooklyn Stepford Wife that I play like some role I was cast for and can't get out of.

"She... she cooks and cleans."

"What else?"

"She looks after him when he's sick."

"What does a man want from a wife, Gina?"

"He wants... to be satisfied."

"That's right. How?"

I don't answer. Occasionally the humiliation is too much, and I can't bring myself to say the degrading thing he wants from me, even when there's a knife to my throat.

"Let me tell you, baby," he growls. "She offers up her body like a good little whore. She gets on her knees whenever her man wants and sucks on his cock until she gags. She'll swallow his cum if he wants it. She'll bend over and take it in any hole he's in the mood for and won't bitch about it if it hurts. Do you think you do that for me?"

"Yes," I reply, strength seeping from me as I degrade myself by admitting the truth in front of him.

"Hmm... How about we check whether you're still marriage material, shall we? Get on your fucking knees." When I hesitate, he growls, "Now..."

I kneel down slowly, my knees instantly sore against the hardwood floor. The prick doesn't allow rugs in most of the house. He likes it to hurt when he's on top of me. He likes the hard wood to press into my bones, especially now that I have no fat on me, courtesy of him and his "standards" for my body—ones he doesn't apply to himself. He's stocky, full of muscle, but he's allowed an inch or two of fat on top. I'm not.

I stare up at him, just as he likes, and flinch as he grabs hold of my ponytail and extends it back over the table, holding it in place with his left hand, laying my hair along the dark wood riddled with stains and scars. I feel him pull the elastic loose, just a little. My chest tightens as he lifts the knife into the air, and without warning, stabs it into the table just behind me.

I can't stop the scream from leaving my throat as, for a second, I think he's about to stab the knife into my skull. I lean forwards, panting audibly as I realize that I can't move and that the knife is embedded through the hair above the hair band and pinned into the table that he's already defiled in more ways than I can count.

He stares down at me coldly as a single tear trickles down my cheek. "You're shaking. Why so afraid, Gina? You don't think I'd hurt you, do you? My soon-to-be-wife..."

I shake my head slowly and his lips twist into a malicious smile before darkness comes over him again, his mood blackening further. He spreads his legs apart before me as he reaches for his belt buckle, glaring down at me as he unfastens it and pulls the belt open.

He unbuttons his dark-blue jeans and unzips them as I prepare to pleasure a man I no longer want to. I've loved his dominance since the day he first made love to me, but now... it's too much. I want to be dominated by someone who loves me, who respects me, who protects me. And the vestiges of those things are drowned out by the fear I feel every day.

As he pulls out his erect cock, my sex—exposed through the hole he so elegantly tore in my pants—pulses despite myself. I glance down at the pronounced veins running along it. The head of it is swollen, the hue mauve, as if manifesting his anger.

"Now, be a good little girl and stick out your tongue."

I do as he wants, picturing the body of my lover as I so often do these days to get through sex with Cain. The thought of Leon removes weight from my body. It transports me to a place where I feel safe and wanted.

Maybe this is my fate. Maybe I no longer deserve to be free. I gave my power up out of fear and because I extended empathy to someone incapable of returning the favor. Maybe I deserve to pay the price for my stupidity.

Cain wraps his stocky fingers around his shaft and taps the head on my tongue over and over.

"Get comfortable, beautiful," he purrs. "You're going to be in this position all night."

A tear falls from me as I realize he's going to take his time. For my exes, fellatio was a ten-minute preamble to get them ready to fuck. Cain can happily draw it out over an hour until my jaw is so sore that I can barely open it. That's the part he likes the most—when I'm flinching in pain and begging him to come.

He taps his cock against my cheek. "Who's the obedient little whore I'm going to marry, Gina?"

Fuck you, Cain...

The first few times he said that word during sex, I stopped the act, protesting profusely. He told me it was just something men say to get them in the mood. Now I daren't question him. He calls me the most degrading names you could imagine, and I just have to take it.

I've never lost power like this before. How do I get it back without running? If I run, can I hide? Will he find me? Will I see my parents again? My friends? Will he take it out on them like he's threatened to do so many times before?

I know he would.

I can feel it...

He can't let anything go.

I often wonder if I can ask Jack for help. He's always offered to help me. Beyond a few punches, his father would never really hurt him, I don't believe. Can he protect me if Leon can't? Can someone else? This Sebastian guy that Cain wants dead? If I gave him information, would he protect me? If I told him of Cain's plans?

Upon another hard tap of his cock against my face, I respond, "I am."

"What is the point of your mouth, Gina?"

"To pleasure you," I say, hating the words.

"That comes before eating, before drinking, before any fucking thing. Are we clear on that?"

"Yes."

With that, he plants his huge palms on the table on either side of my head and slowly slides his cock deep into my mouth. I loosen my throat and he begins to thrust deep inside. The gentle movement only lasts a few seconds until he's ramming his cock inside me in a frenzy, making me gag as saliva drips down my chin and onto my bare breasts.

"You're going to show me how lucky you are to have me as your man, woman."

Half an hour later, with tears running down my face from the constant gagging and the assault to my throat, he finally comes all over my hot face, smearing his cum all over my skin with the head of his cock.

He stands back as he exhales his pleasure, watching me in my wretched and humiliated state—the state he likes me in above all others.

"Hmm. You look good like that. That's the only facial you'll be getting once we're married, darling," he sniggers. "Do you understand that?"

I don't answer, glaring up at him as he grins wildly, enjoying my degradation.

"Do you think you deserve to be let free, you little whore?" he asks.

For a second, his wording confuses me until I realize what he means. Based on past behavior, I know he's capable of leaving me like this all night and coming downstairs to fuck my mouth whenever he's in the mood.

"Yes," I reply softly, gazing up at him, trying to hide the plea in my face. It only makes him more ruthless.

Upon a moment's reflection, he grabs hold of the handle, drawing the knife out from the wood and throwing it onto the table with a clang that makes me wince.

He grabs me by my ponytail—Cain's version of hand-holding—and pulls me to my feet, using my hair to tug me in the direction of the staircase.

"Ow," I cry out as strands beneath my ponytail are pulled from my scalp with a sharp pinch.

He stops in his tracks just as we reach the bottom of the stairs. "Is there a fucking issue here?" he snarls, eyes like frozen winter earth.

"No. It's just... It hurts."

"It's *supposed* to hurt. A good husband knows how to hurt his wife. And a good wife knows how to take it. Are you going to be a good wife, Gina, or am I going to have to teach you another lesson?"

"I—"

"What?!"

"I... I'm gonna be a good wife," I reply breathlessly as he tugs at my hair again, yanking it upwards for no reason other than to prove a point. The indignation of debasing and dehumanizing myself always comes second to the fear that seizes me when he's in moods like this.

"Good. But by all means, cry like a little bitch. I enjoy your pain, sweetheart. Makes my dick nice and hard."

Without another word, he pulls me up the stairs. At the top, I'm dragged into our bedroom where he shoves me onto the bed, some of the cum on my face splattering onto the duvet cover.

I scoot backwards until my back hits the pillows in front of the headboard, but instead of turning his attention to me, he opens a door on his side of the closet, pulling out a little black bag—velvet by the looks of things. He marches to my side of the bed and grabs my wrist, pulling out a thick leather cuff and winding it around it.

"Hey," I whimper.

He's never done this before...

He stops, staring down at my wrist, eyes wide. "Do you have something to say to me, woman?"

"I... I just... We've never done this."

"Well, we're doing it now... or do I have to teach you another lesson?"

"No. It's just—"

"Just *what*?"

"Nothing. I... I'm sorry," I reply, though I'm flooded with unease at the sight of the handcuffs tightening around my wrist and his sturdy fingers closing the fastening. The cuff is heavily padded on the inside—I guess I should be grateful for that, at least. I wouldn't have expected that from him. I'm surprised they're not sharp metal rings that dig into me.

Don't get me wrong—Cain has bound and restrained me more times than I could possibly count, but he's never bought toys like this. If he wants my hands tied, he'll use rope or a necktie or a piece of clothing. If he wants a collar put on me, he'll use his tie or my own belt. If he wants me gagged, he'll shove some material into my mouth—my panties, a small towel, some crumpled up banknotes on occasion—his way of handing me my monthly allowance, something that he never does without sodomizing me just afterwards. It's the obligatory *thank you* I have to give him each time.

The man takes *old school* to ludicrous heights. He doesn't buy "toys," nor will he allow me to have any vibrators in the house. What he's doing now is new, and he's not a man open to change. He's a creature of habit who likes things done in the same way each time. This change has my insides twisting in trepidation.

I expect him to tie the other cuff attached to the chain to my other wrist, but he doesn't. Instead, he pulls my arm back and cuffs it to one of the hardwood posts in our bed frame.

Shit...

As the asshole moves swiftly around the bed with purpose, I pull my other hand away.

He moves to grasp it but misses, his muddy eyes blazing at my insubordination.

"Five seconds, Gina," he growls and after two I slip my hand back towards him, giving him the access he wants. He yanks my arm roughly, fitting the cuff around it, fastening it, and then attaching the other cuff to the opposite bedpost.

He stands back once he's done to admire my work. My breasts—surgically enhanced as per his wishes—are falling out of my top, my nipples contorted into hard points because of the chill in the air. His cum still clings to my face. The most humiliating part of it all is the hole that he ripped in my crotch. I keep my legs clamped tightly together as his thighs hit the short footboard at the bottom of the bed.

"Open them," he orders.

"I—"

"Don't try me, woman. Open your legs like the obedient whore you are, or I'll open them for you. Five seconds."

Fuck...

I'm hit with one of those recurring moments of cognitive dissonance that knock me over several times a day. How did I, a smart, formerly self-sufficient woman, wind up in this unholy mess with a man who feeds the monster inside him, who takes pleasure in tormenting me, debasing me, using me like some woman he picked up off the street? I can't even find the pieces of the puzzle to understand it...

I snap my spine up straighter and slowly slide my legs apart.

"Wider."

God, it's humiliating.

He groans in enjoyment—both at my naked pussy being exposed while I'm bound like this, and, since I know him, most probably at the debasement, the dehumanization I give unquestionably to avoid his brand of *punishment*.

"Wider."

He begins to rub his hand over the black denim over his crotch. He's wearing a shirt with short sleeves that show off the grotesque tattoos snaking up both arms—half mobster, half businessman, the image he likes to portray.

In reality, he's just a thug, even with his endless "meetings".

I glance down to see his erection despite the fabric covering it. It's thick and hard, and it's contours are visible as he slides his hands over it, squeezing his sack for a moment before sliding back up to rub his cock with a loud exhale.

"Handcuffs suit you. You'd better get used to them..."

Save me from this...

"I'm going out," he continues. "I'll be back in an hour. And you'll be sitting here like a good little wife when I get back. Is that understood?"

"You're gonna leave these on?"

"Of course."

"Baby, it's not gonna be comfortable. What if I need to... go to the toilet, or... drink something? Or if there's a fire? It's not safe."

"It's not supposed to be *safe*. Nor *comfortable*. Your purpose is to serve my needs. The discomfort serves me, and you'll deal with it like a fucking woman. If I find out you've taken these off somehow while I'm gone, I'll make you pay for it. I promise you that. Understood?"

"How long will you be gone?"

I can ask that much, I hope.

I've learned better than to dare ask him where he's going, or to question the fact that he's driving after consuming alcohol. I learned *that* lesson in a way that took me days to recover from.

"You know," he breathes in that rumbling thunderstorm of a voice of his, "I'm in two minds whether to gag you."

"No, baby," I reply instantly, trying to maintain my composure. This man feeds off fear like no one else I've ever known. "Please don't. I won't be able to breathe properly."

"You not breathing makes me hard, darling. That's one of the issues I have..."

Cold mist invades me. "Please, baby..."

His eyes trail greedily down my body as he considers my plea. "I'll save that for next time," he says. "One hour. I'll deal with you when I'm back..."

Five minutes later, upon the click of the front door and the turn of the lock, I tip my head back and let out an exhale so loud I'm sure the neighbors could hear it. It's as if the whole house exhales in relief.

I glance around the room, my gaze coming to land on my cuffs lying on the pillows on either side of me. I pull a little but they're fastened tightly. I follow the chains to the cuffs around the bedposts. My only hope is if I could lift them up and over the top of the posts somehow, but the posts are really tall, and my wingspan isn't wide enough to allow it. And anyway, what if I couldn't get them back on before he's back...

I keep thinking of Leon. My phone is downstairs in the washroom.

Normally after he leaves, he makes me text him to tell him everything's okay. I usually manage it. I go to the washroom or sneak upstairs or wait until Cain's taking a call or has passed out drunk. On the days that he decides to fuck me as soon as Leon's left, it sometimes takes me an hour before I can get to it... but I always do. And he waits for the call, I know he does.

Cain fucked my mouth for at least half an hour after Leon left. What if he's gone longer than an hour? I'm always so afraid that Leon is going to lose control and come to the house one day... a day that I know will end in disaster.

I keep having nightmares—Leon lying on a slab, eyes open, a bullet put between them, stained with blood. I never used to have them but in the last two weeks, they've become a constant.

I just can't shake this feeling that Cain knows somehow...

I prop myself up, sliding my feet under me, trying to use the headboard to brace myself with. I push my back into the black wood, attempting to get to my feet. I manage to, just about, in shock that I'm able to stand. I coil the chains around my wrists over and over again until they're taut, and then I pull upwards to try to get the cuffs off the bedpost. As they reach the top, I have to pull, trying to figure out if, once they're off, I can get them back on somehow. One of them I can, but what about the other? I'd have to throw it over.

I can't refasten the ones around my wrists—the chains aren't long enough to allow that. I'd have to somehow throw the cuffs and hope they landed over the posts and slid down.

God, what if they don't...

As panic pulls me under, I lean back, sliding back down, letting the cuffs settle back in position.

Don't cry...

He knows what he's doing. He knows there's a chance I could get free—he tied them in this way to allow that possibility. It's part of the torture; freedom is just there. You can taste it, smell it. Only you can't touch it.

I slump against the pillows, listless and defeated, trying to get as comfortable as possible. The alarm clock tells me ten minutes have passed since he left. It feels like an hour and a second at the same time. Trauma does things to time, I've realized of late—it makes it meaningless, endless and impossible to calculate.

I close my eyes only to have them open a few moments later.

I thought I heard something...

12

A click.

The thud of boots hitting the ground.

A zip.

I'm imagining things...

"Fuck!" I mutter, my breath suffocated from my body, at the sound of the door to the mudroom opening. If you don't turn the handle in a specific way, it will creak.

I glance at the nightstand to check that I didn't nod off without realizing it, listening out for further sounds.

Nothing.

And suddenly, panic surges through me at the sight of a shadow lurking outside the half-closed bedroom door.

Did he come back early?

"Baby?" I whisper.

Upon a moment's pause, the shadow disappears and after a moment, there are noises—clicks and taps.

"Baby, you're scaring me."

My heart flurries in my chest as the shadow approaches, and a man fills the doorway.

"Oh my God," I pant. I bring my legs firmly together, shame leaving me mortified as he walks into the room. "What are you doing here?! You can't stay here! He'll be back soon."

But he doesn't answer. He walks towards me, his expression sober as he takes in my pitiful state, staring at the cuffs, his gaze tracking down the chains, my naked breasts, the hole in my leggings that I'm doing my best to conceal. I glance down—you can see the smooth pubis from between the large hole, despite me clamping my legs together.

"Don't look at me," I plead, dropping my chin, horrified that he could see me in this wretched state. "Don't look at me."

I stare down at my legs as he stands next to the bed, not speaking for what feels like forever. *I can't look at him.*

Suddenly he's gone, and I lift my head, watching as he enters our bathroom. I hear the sound of water running and see the small wet face towel in his hand as he comes out.

He sits down on the side of the bed and lifts it to my face, rubbing the remnants of what he knows must be Cain's cum off my cheek. God, I'm mortified.

"Baby, he'll see it's gone," I mutter in a panic.

"I'll be replacing his with mine," he retorts coldly.

"You have to put the towel in the laundry basket, or he'll see it," I say, still not daring to look him in the eyes as he rubs the other cheek, and then my chin, my lips, my forehead, everywhere Cain decided to leave his mark. "You have to hide it under the other clothes in there."

As he places it down onto the nightstand, I see his hand lift and feel it on my jaw, jolting it up.

"Look at me." Anger roughens the order.

I can't...

"Look. At. Me."

Lifting my eyes to his makes silent tears fall down my face and onto my bare breasts.

I hate crying in front of him...

He grimaces at the sight, as he has always done, ever since that day that he caught me sobbing in a corner, my eye pink and swollen.

He closes his eyes for a moment, taking a silent breath before opening them, lifting my face when I drop my gaze again.

"Has he done this before? The cuffs?"

I shake my head and his eyes pan down to the chain attached to the thick leather straps around my wrist. He lifts it, inspecting the cuff, sliding the tip of a finger under it.

"It's padded," he says, curiosity morphing the words.

"His form of mercy, I guess."

His eyes narrow as if in suspicion. "Maybe..."

I dare to watch his face as he studies the cuffs, turning my wrist over so that he can inspect them. As he sees me watching him, his eyes dart to mine, just before mine fall to my thighs.

I'll never be able to look him in the eyes again.

"What do you mean?" I ask.

"I've seen cuffs like these used before."

My heart sinks to my stomach at the thought of the women that throw themselves at him. I've seen it with my own eyes. I know I have no right to be jealous, but the thought of him with them is hard to bear.

"Where?" I ask, not wanting an answer.

"They are used to restrain people who won't make it out of a room alive."

"What?"

"Unlike rope," he continues grimly, "they leave no ligature marks. Regular cuffs leave marks, even thick leather ones if you tug on them enough. The padded ones don't."

"You've seen people be—?"

"Yes."

God...

He reaches for the buckle.

I try to stop him, but he ignores me, unfastening one cuff, and then walking around to the other side of the bed where he undoes the other.

I rub my wrists on instinct despite the padding protecting them and scoot back into the headboard, keeping my head down. I bend my legs in the hopes of concealing the hole that Cain has left for his pleasure, that he will soon make good use of, no doubt.

God, I feel like a child...

The weight shifts on the mattress as Leon sits down, grasping my neck with his hand.

"Look at me, Gina," he orders roughly.

I lift tear-filled eyes to meet his, only his are filled with concern and anger, his brow furrowing, his lips thinning. A thumb swipes a tear from my face, its gentle brush so soothing.

Every sign I can get that he still feels the same way, that he feels one tenth of what I do for him, fills me with the only light that seeps through the empty darkness of life with Cain.

His words emerge through gritted teeth. "He's gonna pay. On my life, I'll make him pay."

"You have to go," I mutter as tears pool into my mouth. "He could be back any minute."

"I know where he's gone. He won't be back for another hour."

"How can you be sure?"

"Because I helped him set up the appointment. I followed him by car for a few minutes to make sure he was going in that direction. He won't be back for an hour at least. I've erased the last fifteen minutes of footage and turned the cameras off. He still never checks them?"

"Not unless he hears a noise or something. He's usually too hammered when he comes home to bother."

I lift a shaky hand to his neck, sliding my fingers down his long dirty-blond hair. "I've missed you, baby."

"I was here less than an hour ago," he responds.

"I know, but it's not the same." I peer up at him as his gaze sweeps over my face. "Can you hold me?" I ask, aware of how needy I must sound to this man. I long to show him the woman I once was...

"I told you before," he responds, "I'm not the hugging type, Gina. If that's what you're looking for, you're gonna be disappointed."

I nod. "I know. I'm sorry. It's okay."

But without warning, I'm pulled towards him and his arms wrap around me, his lips finding my neck as he inhales me in loud pants. "I get scared when I have to leave you," he whispers, his gravelly voice hoarse. "I can't take this much more."

I wilt into his arms, letting his body shield me, if only for a moment. I hate crying, but I can't help it today. I feel my tears slip against his skin. "I get through it by thinking of you," I respond. "You're all I think about, baby. You're the reason I still hold on."

I know that's a weight too heavy to put on someone's shoulders, especially in the case of someone as emotionally unavailable as him, but I can't help myself from speaking the truth around him. I lost the ability to speak the truth around Cain over a year ago. I used to, in the beginning, until it became too risky, his reactions too volatile. So now I walk on eggshells like a Stepford Wife, unable to say anything that could evoke the slightest discord between us.

With Leon, as afraid as I am of pushing him away with my openness, of freaking him out, of making him want to run, I can't help but want to speak the truth that I keep hidden from everyone else. I hide from my friends, from my family, never telling them what life is really like with Cain Wilder, for fear of a confrontation, of them getting hurt, of him banning me from seeing them. He barely tolerates me seeing them as it is.

Leon's fingers find the hole in my leggings and I flinch at the humiliation. "He does this a lot?" he asks, not lifting his eyes to look at me.

"Yes," I reply as he slides his fingers up my taut abdomen, finding my breasts through the torn fabric of my T-shirt. He kneads them for a moment before tugging at my nipple and then gliding his palm up my chest where he finds the necklace he gave me, one that Cain suddenly doesn't want me taking off.

He fiddles with the spheres. "You wear this for me?"

"Of course, baby."

"He still thinks your mom got it for you?"

"I hope so. That's what I told him."

His eyes lift to mine. "Why did he bring it up at lunch?"

"I don't know. It was... weird. Do you really think he knows?"

"Has he said anything else?" Leon asks.

"Not really. Just... going on about whether I'm a good wife or not. The usual sick games..."

He looks down at the remnants of clothes that Cain has so courteously left for me to wear until his return. "Did he hurt you?" he asks, the words eking out despite the tension tightening in his jaw.

"No, baby," I reply. "He didn't."

"You always say that, Gina. You always try to protect me from the fucking truth."

"I made my bed," I respond softly. "It's my mistake. No one else should have to pay for it but me. That's why I get so worried about you. That he could know."

His intelligent hazel eyes land on mine. "Something feels *off*. I'm going to try to have him watched."

"Is he strange with you?" I ask.

"A little."

"Maybe he just suspects something," I suggest.

"Maybe."

I nod, and after a moment, his head dips to mine, his lips hovering an inch from my skin as he stares down at my mouth. "I want to take you away from here... It's just... getting rid of him isn't going to be as easy as I'd hoped. I don't have the same means that he does. I'd have to take care of it myself or trust some fucker with half a brain to do it."

"No, baby." I rub my hand up his thick bicep. "No. You can't do that. It's too dangerous."

"There may be another way."

"What?" I ask.

"There's a man that he wants gotten rid of."

"This Sebastian guy?"

"Yeah. I know him. A little. I can talk to him. He tolerates me better than most. He could afford it. He may do it if he thought he were in danger."

"Can you trust him?"

"That's the problem. He isn't like normal men. He's a *bad* man."

"What, worse than Cain?"

"Smarter. Much smarter. He doesn't play by the usual rules. He's unpredictable."

"God, doesn't sound like someone we can put our trust in..."

"No. But Cain has been disrespectful to a woman he cares about for years."

"What woman?" I ask, wondering if he's referencing one of Cain's many messy affairs.

"His daughter-in-law."

My heart begins to race. "Bri—" Suddenly, I know who he means. And I hate that I know it. Not her. "Jess?"

He nods. "Cain wants to fuck her. Jack's told him that will never happen."

"Are you serious?! I fucking well knew it!"

"Yeah. But I'm not sure that Cain has given up on that fantasy. If Sebastian knew that he had such intentions, maybe that would make him react."

"Why would he care?" I ask.

"He seems to have grown attached to her."

"Jess?!"

He nods.

"Oh my fucking God. Does Jack know?"

"Not the full extent of it."

"How... how did it happen?"

"It seems that since finding out about Jack's affairs, she's not been as *devoted* to her husband as she once was."

"Well, I guess that's kind of understandable..."

I peer up at him, knowing full well he won't like what I'm saying. He's old school, believes that women should tolerate men cheating if they treat them well in other areas. I watch him exhale a breath of irritation, letting my opinion slide this time.

"But, he's not in love, right?" I ask. "This Sebastian guy?"

"He's not a normal man. He's... *evil.* I'm not sure being *in love* is something he's capable of... but he's close to it from what I've heard. Or to his version of it, anyway."

"God. Does Jack know you're friends with him?"

"We're not friends," he retorts gruffly. "But we talk occasionally. He listens to me, and I could use Jessynia to get what we need."

"God, baby, I hate the idea of Jess being involved in any way. She's always been so good to me. Is there another way? Couldn't we just... run away?" I suggest.

"I've told you before, Gina," he retorts with a shake of the head. "Running won't help you. Maybe me, it would. I don't have family, or at least, none I give a fuck about. *You* do. If Cain couldn't get to you, he'd get to your parents or your sister. I know you. You wouldn't survive it. The guilt would be the end of us. There is no running with a man like him. We keep going like this... or we find a way to take him the fuck out before..." He pauses, staring down as he composes his breathing. "Before something goes wrong..."

"You shouldn't have got messed up with me," I whisper.

"I know," he responds gravely as I peer at the thick stubble over his lip and around his jawline. "It's not your fault. I didn't plan any of this. I didn't expect to feel this."

I close my eyes, melting as he seals his lips over mine and pushes his tongue into my mouth, sliding it in and out before climbing on top of me and pinning my hands over my head with one of his. His other fumbles with his belt and then his zipper and a moment later, he pulls out his thick hard monster cock, all twelve or so inches of it.

As it finds the hole in my leggings, I take a breath, preparing myself for the sheer size of the thing.

"Baby?"

He lifts his eyes to look at me.

"Can you... get the taste of him... out of... my mouth?"

He pauses for a moment, his face registering anger before he slowly makes his way up the bed on his knees.

He glares down at me as I open my mouth for him, and pushes his cock inside. I wrap my lips around him in utter relief at feeling him there, his rock-hard shaft taking the place of Cain's. My eyes flick up to find his hands gripping the headboard as he peers down at me, watching as I lift and lower my head while he pulses inside me, letting out a groan of pleasure as I let my tongue dance against the smooth column. I can never get enough of him. I could suck his cock all day long. If we were together, I'd do anything to keep him happy... just as I once wanted to do for Cain...

A few minutes later, after letting out a grunt of pleasure, he withdraws from my mouth and lays his bulky body on top of me, lifting my knee and finding my pussy with his cock. He pushes in a little, stretching me open, and then more, and more, until finally, he has inserted his whole hard length into me through the hole in my leggings.

I gasp as the head of his cock pushes into my cervix with a pinch. I don't mind the pain. It's nothing compared to the pain of Cain's so-called technique.

Leon's hands slide up my arms and he grabs my wrists, pinning them to the mattress as he begins to thrust inside me, anger roughening the movements.

"Who does your body belong to?" he asks.

"You, baby. You know that."

I peer up at him nervously as he glowers at me, driving his cock inside me in hard thrusts for a few seconds, before slowing, his face growing more tender as he watches me.

"Gina..."

I smile up at him, letting my body go limp and parting my legs further, giving him the access he deserves.

The sound of a noise outside has both of us turning to the window for a moment.

"It's just a car," he says, turning back to face me.

"He could come back," I whimper.

"I don't give a fuck," he snarls. "You're gonna take your man. All of him. Until he's ready to stop. I want you feeling me when he comes back... and only me. Understood?" I run my hands up his arms as he begins to fuck me more slowly. "I can't handle the thought of him fucking you anymore, Gina. I'm gonna have to kill him myself..."

"He's not here now, baby. It's just you and me."

"Who do you think of?"

"You. Only you. Always you. I close my eyes and picture it's you."

"I'm gonna take you away from here."

I nod. "I know."

"In the meantime, I want you seeing me when he..."

"I already do, baby."

"No," he growls, driving into me a little deeper. "I want you feeling me. It's my cock fucking you, not his. It's my cum you'll swallow. Is that understood?"

"Yes."

"Open your legs wide for your man, Gina."

I do as I'm told and he straightens his arms, looking down at me as he slides deep inside, stretching me out so deliciously. As he fucks me, his expression morphs, sometimes angry, sometimes pained, sometimes softening, but his eyes never leave mine for a moment.

I stare up at him adoringly, desperate to soothe him. These nightmares I've had of late have unsettled me—seeing the man I love dead on a slab.

The strong part of me wants to just tell him to run away, to forget me, to forget Cain, to forget that either of us existed. Maybe I'll find the strength to tell him. Maybe once I give up hope and accept my fate, things will get better. Or maybe once Cain stops drinking, he really will behave better.

Leon's eyes pan up to the cuffs lying on the pillows on either side of me and he suddenly stops all movement, pulling out of me, his cock, glistening in my own juices, pointed upwards. The thing is huge—easily three to four inches longer than Cain's, though not as girthy, thank God. Cain's thickness is the source of never-ending pain, especially since foreplay to him means bending me over and occasionally spitting if he's in a good mood.

Leon's not the biggest on foreplay either, but he's gentler, and the way he touches me, looks at me, places me down, it makes me instantly wet. With Cain, I haven't really been fully aroused for months, which only makes his brutal style of "love-making" all the more torturous to endure.

He kneels up, grabbing one of the cuffs.

"What are you doing?" I ask as he wraps it around my wrist and fastens it. He ignores me, doing the same with the other before positioning the swollen head of his cock at the entrance to my sex.

His hair flops over his face as he watches me while I pull against the chains on instinct. "If you're doing this," he growls, "you're doing it with me first. You'll know what to expect. You'll be seeing me. Tasting me. Feeling me when it happens. Understood?"

"Yes."

"Now open your legs like a good girl."

He's never let out groans like this before as he fucks me. His eyes bury into me as he takes me in Cain's bed, his boss's bed, the one his wife is handcuffed to.

When it comes to sex with Leon, I don't make that much sound. I'm always so afraid of Cain coming home early that I spend half the time listening out for unexpected noises and the other half ensuring that this beautiful man gets the pleasure he deserves.

He could get it from other women. I'm sure he probably does. After all, Cain fucks me, usually several times a day, whether I want it or not. I don't expect Leon to endure that and not have some form of relief elsewhere... even if it hurts.

"Do you like my cock, Gina?" he growls after a few minutes of increasingly rough fucking.

"I love it, baby. I dream of it day and night."

"This is the last year you'll be with that man. Soon, it's my cock you'll be sucking day and night. Understood?"

I nod and he withdraws from me with a groan, straddling my arms with his knees and sliding his hand up and down his cock, aiming it at my face as he works his shaft, increasing the pace.

He glares down at me, letting out rough breaths as he prepares to ejaculate.

"Close your eyes," he orders after a moment, and I do, waiting until I feel the cool liquid hit my face, accompanied by his loud grunts of pleasure.

I keep my eyes tightly closed as he slides his cum all over my face with the head of his cock, just as Cain did... only this time, no matter how humiliating it is, I don't mind. It feels like relief compared to having Cain's mark left on me like that.

When he finally stops moving, I open my eyes to find his soft on my face, his expression pained almost.

"I had to do it," he says, as if losing his breath.

"I know, baby. It's okay. I know."

13

Twenty minutes later, I buckle under the weight of a silence so heavy that it stops me from drawing but the shallowest of breaths. It took me over ten minutes to convince Leon to go, to leave the house and not hide in some room. Cain has guns everywhere—in locked cupboards, but also hidden around the place.

I find the things when I'm cleaning. They're always loaded, always weighty. I think there's one in every room in the house, sometimes several. I know there are a few in this very room. He moves their location about almost obsessively.

Short of Leon waiting for him and putting a bullet into his head, and then spending the rest of his life in prison, there's nothing he can do.

I told him I love him.

I know I shouldn't have, but I couldn't help it. I do. I love every fucked-up piece of that man. The way he looks at me when he's inside me is like nothing I've ever experienced. I tremble when I feel his gaze settling on me. It's not the terror that comes with Cain's glare, but the flutter of butterflies that occurs when someone you love can't look at anything but you...

He didn't say it back. That's okay. I'm not sure that's his style, and anyway, I'm a married woman. Why would he want to put himself out there like that?

"Shit."

The word escapes me without my meaning it to at the sound of the metal clicks of a lock being turned and the slam of a door.

I can tell what mood he's going to be in by the way he shuts that fucking door, and half the time, my heartrate doubles just from the aggressive bang. My fiancé doesn't believe in subtlety...

Leon took his time to ensure the room was exactly how Cain had left it, putting the wet towel at the bottom of the laundry basket—I'll deal with it later. He brought me a glass of water, and I drank it down, despite the humiliation of having his drying cum on my face.

But at least it wasn't Cain's...

After I finally begged him to go, and upon setting the timer for the camera system, he watched me from the doorway for a full minute, unspeaking. It was intimate and yet petrifying. I know he thinks his life would be simpler without me in it.

He's right.

I'm really trying to find the strength to tell him to go. If he wanted to leave, I wouldn't stop him. I just pray that he doesn't. I pray that by some miracle this will end up alright...

Just breathe...

I try to calm my breathing as the thuds of Cain's heavy footsteps hit the hardwood stairs.

I know it's him.

I can feel it.

He shifts the energy in any room he's in, transforms it into a place which matches his moods—sometimes light, usually as black as the barrels of his guns.

He pauses at the top of the stairs for a moment like some predator scoping out his surroundings. I see his shadow before I see him, watching it loiter in the wood beneath his feet.

Then a hand, an arm, and finally his face comes into view, his expression rough. Even if he doesn't show it, I know he'll be pleased by the sight of me, pleased that he can use me to knead out the irritations that plague him constantly as he rolls them over and over in his mind until they become the stuff of nightmares.

He walks over to stand at the foot of the bed, his eyes raking over my body in its humiliated state—a hole torn in my crotch, my T-shift ripped open, exposing my breasts.

Please let nothing be out of place...

I know how he operates. I know he'll be hard. Anything that degrades and humiliates me turns him into an animal.

"Did you have a fun time, Gina?" he asks, eyes glacial.

I'm just being paranoid...

A few months ago, I'd have taken the question as one of his woeful attempts at dark sarcasm, but now... I can't help but wonder at the delivery, at the riddle in the question.

"No," I answer, raising my chin. He doesn't tolerate defiance, but I don't fancy spending my days chained up like this every time he goes out. Knowing how his mind works, he'd be capable of it...

"Are you sure about that?"

"It's not comfortable being chained up, baby," I say. "I can't even lie down properly."

"One hour is not much of a sacrifice for your man's pleasure, is it? Or is that too much to expect from you?"

"No. It's not too much. It's just... what's with the handcuffs, baby?"

"You'll be getting used to them. I may well be putting a collar on you soon."

"Why?"

"Because you deserve to be fucked like a bitch in heat. Chained to a post. And because I need you to get used to being tied up, Gina."

The way he says it makes me shudder. His tone is cordial enough, but something is simmering beneath the words.

I need you to get used to being tied up...

The phrasing is off. He doesn't usually say things like that. He just... *does.*

His eyes wander down to my crotch. "Why are your legs closed, Gina?" he growls.

"I—"

"Get them open. Now. I've had enough from you today. You're going to be paying for your sins, woman. I promise you that."

I can't help but squirm internally at the indignation of opening my legs for this ape... but I do it anyway.

"Wider, you slut."

As I part my legs wide, he begins to unbuckle his belt. He always does it the same way in moments like this—his movements measured, methodical as he prepares to obtain the pleasure he craves day and night.

"You're gonna get it, Gina. I hope you know that."

He slides his belt out and drops it to the floor, undoing the top button of his dark-blue jeans. He leans forward, placing one hand onto the bed. I scoot back on instinct but he grabs my leg, yanking me towards him.

He lifts his frozen eyes to me. "Do that again, bitch..."

I remain silent in the face of his need to dominate, watching as his hand creeps up my leg as he studies my pussy.

"You're wet, you little whore. Why are you wet, Gina?"

"I—"

But before I can answer, his finger advances, opening up the folds and sliding into me.

"No, baby," I plead. He's always rough when he does this.

He slides his finger inside me and then out. "You must enjoy being chained to the bed. Is that it?"

I remain silent, wincing as he pushes two fingers inside me, and then three. *Fuck.* I would protest that it hurts but I know he'll only get off on that so I breathe through it, watching as he feels my wetness.

I'm not wet for you, asshole.

"Hmm. Haven't felt you wet like that for quite some time."

"You once told me you don't like me wet," I respond solemnly. "You like me dry. Hurting."

"You're right, sweetheart. The drier the better. But I'll take you like this today. Makes a nice change." He pulls his fingers out of me and stands back up. "Are you ready to do the job you're paid for and suck my cock?"

I don't answer. I've noticed my ability to placate him waning in the last few weeks. Maybe it's because I taste the very edges of freedom for the first time in over a year. I taste the promise of life with a better man. I'm still just as afraid but the love that kept me captive, the need to try to understand him, it's vanishing like sand slipping from an hourglass the more I see him for what he is—a bully and a coward.

At my silence, the skin around his eyes crinkle and his lips twist maliciously.

"You know," he smiles, aware that I'm displaying some small sign of so-called insolence for the first time. "I've learned some things about women over the years, my love. Want to know what they are?" I can't believe it but I dare to glare back at him, with the thought of the man I love coursing through my veins. "They all complain about wanting a good man, but when they get a really good one, a gentle one, a kind one, they treat him like *filth* they scrape off their shoe. Their men treat them nice, and they lose their fucking minds. The bitches turn into monsters who want more... and more... and more... until they suck the life out of their men who are doing everything they can to please them. But if you treat a woman like a dog, good for three things and three things only, she'll step into line like an obedient little whore and do what she's told. And she'll like it. Why is that, darling?"

I shake my head at him, pulling against the chains. I can't even believe I'm doing it.

"It's because... women were made to be *owned* by men, my love. That's how humanity has survived. The universe wants us to take a woman and fuck her whenever we want, to impregnate her over and over again. Her needs are irrelevant. We are designed to *own* you. All of you."

I can feel it bubbling up, the words *Fuck you!* I feel them in my throat, in my chest, on the tip of my tongue. I want to scream at him for the first time. I want to tell this pig to go fuck himself.

I just have to hold on a little bit longer...

I feel the muscles in my face tense as I hold the words in, and suddenly, the prick bursts into low, eerie laughter. His laugh is guttural and always dark, always born of amusement over someone else's distress.

"Go on, say it," he laughs grimly. "You have something to say to me, don't you? Spit it out. I'm allowing you to spit it out for once," he sniggers.

I feel my face twisting in hurt, in anger, in indignation at how I got here. "You're a coward," I finally whisper, regretting it instantly as his eyes flare wildly and the smirk lingering on his lips disappears.

"A coward? Is that what my soon-to-be-wife thinks of me?"

"You hurt me," I backtrack. "That's what I meant."

"So, the man that provides for you, that protects you, he's a coward, hey?" The room has never sounded so silent... "I think I've been lenient enough with you, you ten-dollar hooker. What do *you* think?"

I begin to pant as he walks over to the closet, rifling for something, his huge back contorting as he reaches deep into a shelf and draws something out.

I gasp at the sight of the gun in his right hand. A Glock, I think.

I want to beg, to try to appease him, ask for mercy. But I can't do it. No more.

Instead, I sit, watching him silently, hoping I can subdue the never-ending bitterness which fuels his every move.

Or maybe I no longer care...

Maybe he can put me out of my misery...

Only the thought of one person stops me from wanting that.

A man I pray isn't still here somehow...

Part of me keeps expecting him to burst in at any moment. The other part of me wants him to run away from here as far as he can. To forget I ever existed. To be free. I know he's torn, but I so want him to be free. I'll love him the same no matter what he does. These past few months with him have been the greatest source of light I've ever felt, and I don't regret one minute of them.

"Baby, please." The humiliating plea falls from me unconsciously as he jumps onto the bed and comes to stand before me, straddling my legs with his feet.

A tear falls from me as he points the gun to my head, the metal end of the hard gun pressing into my forehead. "Maybe you're right, Gina. Maybe I am a coward. That's what you think of me, isn't it? The man who goes to work for you every day, who provides for you, who houses you, clothes you, gives you money, fucks you properly, I'm just... a fucking coward, right?"

"Baby, stop."

"Open your fucking mouth."

"No."

"Open it or I'll make a fucking hole in your face and open it for you."

He slides the muzzle of the gun down my face until it reaches my lips where he presses it into them until they part. I squirm as he pushes the barrel into my mouth.

"Suck it."

I battle against my tears as I glare up at him. I try to shake my head but he pulls the barrel of the gun out and then thrusts it back in.

"Suck it like the whore that you are, sweetheart. Suck it so that that cunt mother of yours doesn't have to see you with your face blown off."

I taste the salt of my tears as I suck the thick metal barrel as he groans his appreciation at my utter humiliation.

"Lick it, bitch. Lick it like you're about to lick my cock."

My eyes half close as I begin to lick the underside before he pushes it deep into my throat in a black move that makes me want to die.

"That's it," he groans. "Good girl. You think you're so tough, don't you? You won't be so tough with a bullet in your throat. Now look me in the eyes and suck, baby girl."

I shudder through it for another minute or so, praying his sturdy fingers don't do what I know he wants to do.

"Wasn't so hard now, was it?" he smirks as he slowly slides it into and out of my mouth for a long minute, finally withdrawing and holding it with one hand as he unzips his jeans and pulls out his fat, erect cock.

I turn my head to the side but he grabs my hair and tugs my head back to face him, bringing the gun to my temple as his smirk sets my body alight in rage.

"Open your mouth."

The muzzle presses into my head as I begin to suck his cock, wincing at his orders.

"Moan like a whore, Gina."

Upon my refusal to comply, I hear a click next to my head. I know the sound—the safety being turned off.

I think of my mother for a second before seeing the face of the man I love.

I cringe as I moan, closing my eyes and imagining it's not him.

"Louder, you whore. I know you like it. Moan like a hooker I'm paying double."

Please...

"I should put a bullet in your head and fuck you as you bleed out."

God, help me...

Sometime later, as if in a fog, I find him on top of me fucking me with his usual grace, only this time, his eyes are wide in delight at the sight of the gun to my head.

"Turns out I do like you wet... when there's a gun to your head," he sniggers, grinning at me as I try to maintain my composure despite the rough drives into my body. "Do you know that I'm half-tempted to blow your fucking brains out?"

"Baby..."

"Baby," he sneers, mocking my tone, and I jump, a yelp falling from me, as he pulls the trigger, the click echoing through my body.

Realizing that it didn't go off, that it may be empty of bullets, I begin to cry and he puts the gun down onto the mattress, wrapping his hands around my throat and starts to squeeze, cutting off air and forcing me to gasp.

"Stop!"

"Why do you make me hurt you like this, Gina?" he asks, the sneer suddenly gone as he glares down at me. "I didn't want to hurt you. I *didn't*. Why can't you just *behave*? Why do you break the rules?"

What is he talking about?

It can't be *that*...

"I *do* behave," I reply in a moment when he lets me breathe. As for his so-called rules, they are too numerous to count, and he makes me abide by them when he himself does *not*.

"No. Not well enough. *You've* done this, Gina. You force me to hurt you. You make me a bad man. Why do you do it?"

No.

"I don't make you do anything," I dare to say and he begins to squeeze harder as I kick my legs underneath him.

As pressure builds up in my head, he fucks me harder and harder, increasing the speed of his thrusts until he finally lets out a long grunt, pulsing inside me as he deposits his cum.

It's only when he's ejaculated fully that he releases his grip from my throat and I take in loud air in desperate breathes as he watches me.

"I hope you've been a good woman, Gina. If not, I will be forced to make you pay for it. I'll make everyone pay..."

14

Jessynia

"*Stop!*"

The crunch of Sebastian's fist into the man's cheek has the cry falling from me. I pull against the shackles binding me to the wall as I watch the snarling beast's movements become more frantic, each punch more brutal, the groans of pain from his victim louder, more desperate with each minute that passes.

Dark blood drips from under the hood of the man onto the bare floor of the dank room. The victim tries once again to get to his feet, his legs straining, but he's too weakened by the assault of his assailant, a man who never seems to lose strength, to lose stamina, to lose his breath. His movements are fluid, violent, merciless, his wrath so overwhelming that no amount of pleading from me stops him.

Masked spectators all around us take in the spectacle in eerie silence as the wounded man lifts his face, shrouded by shadow and the hood of his cloak, his eyes watching the man who stands over him, heaving heavy breaths.

"Please don't," I beg, but on the plea, he delivers one final punch, knocking the man to the ground.

As he does so, his head shifts towards me and his hood falls, uncovering the man whose beating I've felt in every cell of my body.

I scream as the fabric falls away from his face and his swollen eyes blink slowly as he watches mine.

"Cameron!"

"It's okay," he manages to utter, his body shaking.

I pull against the shackles as I watch Sebastian glaring down at his victim, pleading for him to stop. He turns to look at me and I gasp at the sight of his eyes—mottled in blood-red hues.

A demon's eyes.

"Please stop!"

His lips curve into a sinister smile. "No..."

As his boot lifts into the air above Cameron's face, my scream fills the air. "No!"

"Jessynia!"

Wild blue eyes blaze into view.

Jack.

"Another fucking nightmare," he snarls.

He wipes the hair off my face, his fingers slipping against the slick sweat dripping from me as he does so.

"Jack," I whisper as I try to catch my breath.

After watching me for a moment, he shifts the covers, lifting his tree trunk of a thigh over my legs and wrapping his naked body around me, gripping tightly with strong arms that make me feel tiny.

"What was it?" he asks into my neck.

"Nothing," I breathe.

"Tell me. I mean it, Jessynia."

"I saw him... beating... someone."

Shit. I shouldn't have said that.

"Beating who?"

I don't answer, shuddering in his arms as I become aware of his erection pressing into my leg. It's not his fault. He's always as hard as wood first thing in the morning, as my regular morning wake-up calls have proven of late.

After over a minute of silence during which he asks me again to tell him what I saw, he climbs onto me, grasping my wrists and lifting them onto the pillow. He stares down at my face, some silent plea hidden in his eyes.

"All I want to do is protect you, and all you want to do is hide from me."

"I'm not trying to hide, Jack. I'm trying to..."

"To what? Save me from the truth? I don't want to be saved. I want to know you. I want to understand, and you're stopping me from doing that."

"I'm trying to—"

"And I don't want your fucking protection either. You're my woman, Jessynia. My heart. My soul. My property. I need you to feel safe, or I can't myself."

"It's not about—"

"About *me*? I can't allow other men inside your head, Jessynia. You know that about me. You're my wife. I have to own you. Just as you own me. I want to hear these secrets. Tell me what you dreamed. I won't fucking well tell you again."

I contemplate telling him of my fear for Cameron, but how can I? How can I even tell him that I still think of him?

"I can't."

"Very well." He places the full bulk of his body on top of my slim frame. His fingers wind into my hair, pinning them to the pillow roughly. "I'll claim you in a way you understand until you stop hiding from me. Open your legs for me." He hitches my nightdress up to my waist.

"Jack—"

"Now," he snarls and I part my legs, allowing him to slip his cock between them, finding the opening which he pushes into, just the tip.

His wild eyes clash with mine as he pushes just the head of his cock inside me, over and over, until my core tightens and my sex pulsates.

I frown up at him as the frustration of being simulated like this begins to build. "Jack?"

His eyes narrow. "What?"

"What are you doing?"

"I'm doing to you what you do to me," he deadpans.

"Stop," I breathe out with a smile, grabbing hold of his ass and pulling it into me.

But he doesn't let me get far, glaring down at me.

He pulls out of my body, letting the head of his cock lie on the outside of my pussy. "What did you dream, Jessynia? I want to know. No more secrets."

"Jack, I can't control these fucking nightmares. Do you think I want to have them?"

"I want to know what you see."

"I… It doesn't matter. They're just dreams."

"Bullshit." He tightens his grip on my hair until I moan at him about the pain. "If they didn't matter, you'd tell me what you fucking well see. Who did you see being beaten?"

"Jack, please don't make this a thing! I'll have to start sleeping in the guestroom if you do."

His face hardens, fury distorting it. "Like *hell* you will. You're my fucking *wife* and you sleep in my fucking bed, Jessynia, and nowhere else."

"Let me go," I order, disorientated from the dream still wreaking havoc on my system, coupled with the ignition of Jack's jealousy. "I'm not apologizing for having nightmares that I can't control!"

His lips scrape mine as he speaks, the words barbed. "I'm not asking you to apologize for them. I'm asking you to tell me what you dreamed of tonight."

The murky glow of twilight sharpens the shadows of his face as he scowls at me, his energy dark and distrustful.

"I dreamed that… Sebastian was… beating someone…"

"Beating who?" he asks solemnly.

I don't answer, shaking my head slowly, giving him his answer. "I… I can't control what I dream, Jack."

"Do you dream of me too?"

"Of course I do! All the time. Jack, I can't control these fucking dreams. I never used to have them, and I hate them, okay? I just want them to go away."

Without warning, he slides his cock into me, his breathing quickening as he does so.

"Jack!"

He thrusts into me deep, staying there, not moving.

He pushes his tongue deep into my mouth and begins to fuck it as the meticulous thrusts of his cock accelerate. My tongue dances against him and we kiss passionately, pawing at one another despite the image of Cameron's face hitting the floor running through my mind. Jack always kisses me as if it may be the last time he ever does, and today is no exception.

Pulling out of my mouth, his face softens as I stare up at him, trying to convey my contrition as he slowly glides into and out of me, but in flashes of vision that I can't temper, Cameron's bruised and bleeding face flickers before me.

I have to do something.

I have to stop him...

15

Jessynia

My hand shakes as my thumb hovers over the Send button.

`I need to see you.`

I stare at the same fucking words I typed to him as last time, building up the courage to send them.

The nightmare that woke me from my sleep is still coursing wildly through my veins, pulsing its poison deep into me despite Jack's attempts to relieve tension from our bodies...

Visions of the murder, as well as those of Cameron's bloody face, are still just as relentless, as graphic, toying with me, catching me in some whirling maelstrom I don't know how to swim out of.

What's worse is, I don't know who to talk to about it, and I know enough about trauma to know that if you don't get it out, it stays stuck in your cells, turning you into its unwitting slave.

I've contemplated telling Gabriel about the murder, but what if Sebastian were to find out? Would that be a betrayal of trust?

Taking a deep breath in, I press the Send button and watch as the blue tick appears.

The words he spoke to me not long ago play over and over in my mind.

One day, you will beg me to see you.

Is this what he meant? Do I want to see him because of this godforsaken trauma, or is there something else? Do I want to see him to free Jack and Cameron from his hold, or because... I crave his presence? His strength. His protection. His body...

The thought of the latter makes me shiver, the shame of it leaving me feeling paper-thin and brittle as winter leaves.

I *can't* want this man—this man who has hurt the two men I love so much. When it comes to Vallen or Alex or Dominic or Stephen or Ilya or any of the other sick people that frequent that place, I want one thing—to never see or hear from them again. But with Sebastian, perhaps the most dangerous of them all, I ache to see him. It's as if my body yearns for his presence. My mind hungers for his words, so bold, so elegant, so brutal. Some nights I'm tormented by the thought of him, the man incapable of artifice, of small talk, the man who cuts to the heart of who you are in a way that is so chilling and yet makes you feel so alive.

Is it part of the trap? The devil making you feel understood? Or is part of him still human? Can I bring out the human side of him? Can I heal him and set him and the people around him free?

I cringe at the naivety of the idea, but I have to believe there's some reason for all of this, for the fact that I'm drawn back to a man so deadly.

The Society has no need to be so dangerous. It could function just as well if it were an upscale swingers club like it was before he took over and implemented less forgiving "rules" and consequences.

Can I make him see that? Am I foolish to even think I could influence a man as sophisticated as this one?

My heart stalls as a message appears.

Ten minutes, Jessynia. Same place as before.

As we continue south past West 58th Street, I realize that we're not going to his place this time, but are driving in the direction of Tribeca. My heart races at the thought, thumping in my chest like the staccato beat of a relentless drum.

Each time I've been there I've experienced things I never wanted to —from the first time Cameron took me there and I panicked at the sight of naked bodies reduced to their basest of purposes, to Alexandra's glass-to-the-face attempts at conversing, to watching Sebastian fuck a woman in front of me, pressing her face into shards of glass upon slicing his own chest open with a knife.

I realize I'm steam-rolling over repeated traumatic incidents, absorbing them as if they're nothing. In reality, I'm not absorbing them. The trauma is getting trapped in my cells, causing nightmares that punctuate the once-perfect stillness of my sleep, making my body seize when I least expect it.

"We're going to Tribeca?" I ask Isaiah who eyes me in weighty silence every time he stops at a red light. "Not much of a conversationalist?" I suggest as his discourteous glower eats into me, but he doesn't answer.

I glance out of the window as we drive through SoHo, not far from Kevin's apartment. At the thought of his no-nonsense bullshit, ripples of unease wash over me, followed by stronger waves which knock me over, causing nausea to flood my system until it suddenly hits me with clarity what I'm doing.

"I've made a mistake," I blurt out, realizing I'd be better off spending the day in SoHo than seeing this dangerous man. Isaiah watches me in silence before taking off as the light turns to green. "Hey, can you stop the car? I'm sorry, I've changed my mind. I need to get out." Two blocks later, as we come to a halt at the next red light, I unfasten my seatbelt before pulling on the handle. It doesn't open, and there's no unlock button. "I want to get out, Isaiah. I made a mistake."

His eyes draw thin through the rear-view mirror. "There is no getting out, Jessynia. Now put your fucking seatbelt back on before I do it myself..."

Standing outside the car and holding the door open, Isaiah glares at me in the closed parking garage underneath Quercus Velutina Tribeca, watching as I unbuckle my seatbelt and get out.

I jump as he slams the door shut behind me and slides a card through the reader next to the door, taking me on that familiar trek along the industrial-looking corridor that leads to the elegant changing rooms of this place. I've been here several times now, but the scents, the sounds, the light, the décor, they never cease to unsettle me, eroding the foundation from under my feet as if loose earth giving way in a landslide.

We make our way to a room, and he taps the card again, holding the door open for me. His eyes don't leave me as I step inside and turn to watch him close the door behind me as he utters, "Fifteen minutes."

I breathe a sigh of relief to find myself alone for a moment, scanning the room—the tigerwood table with a stark bronze sculpture of a prostrate female body; the elegant burgundy chaise longue sitting against a wall sheathed in gold and cream wallpaper; the changing cubicle behind thick velvet curtains and the shower and toilet behind a frosted glass door to the left.

My eyes are drawn to the wall to the right, from which hang a cobalt-blue cloak and matching mask with embroidered trim and a slip of a white dress suspended from a metal hook next to it, twisted into some grotesque vine.

I take a step towards it, conscious that I have less than fifteen minutes left until someone comes to get me. My fingers find the white silk, running along the satiny fabric as I wonder if he picked the dress out himself... and why the fucking thing is always white. I mean, is it some symbolic thing to him, or does white just show off my tits better?

I pull off my scarf and coat and hang them up, before peeling off the rest of my clothes except my panties.

I scrunch the long dress up and lift it over my head, allowing the delicate fabric to settle over my body. The thing seems to have been made for me. It's not too tight or too loose anywhere, allowing me to move freely but not giving me so much room that it swamps me. The straps are spaghetti straps, and as usual, the thin fabric over my bare breasts leaves little to the imagination. I reach for my back with one hand and realize that the dress is completely backless, with three small, round pearls sown vertically below the bottom of the cut-out. I glance down at my body.

What am I doing?

Occasionally the insanity of this place hits.

This is how they do it—a war of attrition, habituating you in small increments. First, you find the mask normal, then the cloak, then the rituals and routines, the dress, the fucking in dark rooms... and finally, one day, you're walking willingly into a lair you have no guarantee of getting out of...

I close my eyes and remember what I need from him—to talk through what happened with that man before it drives me out of my mind, and most importantly—that Cameron and Jack be let free from his grasp for good.

You can do this...

You can do it.

I head over to the washroom cubicle where I find the mirror, staring at the reflection of a woman I don't fully know anymore.

I'm more scared of that fact than anything else—the fact that I'm losing myself, or opening doors to places that a year ago, I would never have walked into. Am I just stepping into who I truly am, or have the trauma and pain of the last year led me to places I have no business being in?

My compass is off. I feel untethered, floating like driftwood in an endless ocean of frigid water and fickle currents. My ability to trust my own instincts is skewed so badly that only the months after that summer in Albany can compare to how lost I feel, how disconnected I am to my inner self. And I hate that feeling more than anything.

Peering at my reflection, I see that my cheeks are flushed pink, and my eyes and lips are large and gleaming, and yet, I look haunted somehow as if I'm seeing things I can't process. I sweep my gaze down my body, absorbing quite how indecent this dress is, but then I imagine his eyes on me and... *God help me*, but I want him to see me.

How is it possible?

I'm not oblivious to the pull I've felt towards Sebastian since witnessing him take out that man. As horrific as it was, I know that *some* part of it was birthed of his need to protect me, or his outrage at the events of that day, at his desire to punish the man that hurt me, that hurts children, just as he was once hurt. As wrong as it was, I can't help but weaken at the thought, sinking into the inexorable riptide of his perilous protection.

Jessynia...

My hair is tied into a neat bun at the back of my head, and for a second, I contemplate pulling out my hairband and letting my hair fall loose to cover my breasts... but I don't.

A while later, as I'm silently following an imposing-looking masked and cloaked man down increasingly dark corridors, I say a silent prayer for strength.

16

The faceless figure opens the door to Sebastian's room, holding it open for me.

I glance up at the man, shivering internally as I take slow steps inside. I remove the slippers that they provide for me and that I sometimes wear, putting them next to the door, my bare feet pressing into the hardwood beneath them as I do.

I flinch as the door behind me closes, walking tentatively inside. The room is dimly lit with wooden blinds drawn and only slithers of warm light making their way through the thin wooden slats that conceal us from the rest of Manhattan. The place feels like another world...

Today the cage is on full display—uncovered. It's empty, but that does little to dampen the unease I feel at the sight of it—the place that he stores women for when he requires them.

Through the metal rings in his headboard lie a pair of handcuffs attached to chains, the thick leather cuffs sitting on the dark-gray pillow cushion lying before the slats.

Turning to my left, I take in the huge ebony mask suspended from the wall, its sinister features causing tiny bumps to crawl down the skin under my cloak.

And as I pivot once more, my stomach plummets to the ground at the sight of a dark shape in my peripheral vision, and I spin around to see him.

Sebastian Gravier.

Standing silently in the shadows in the corner of his room, watching me—a lion tracking its prey.

Except this prey has some game...

He's maskless and wearing a loose cream cotton shirt, its sleeves rolled up to the elbows, the hem tucked into black cotton pants. I stand completely still, shuddering as he takes his first step towards me, his vibrant starlit eyes holding mine hostage.

Every time I see him, I feel awe at the size of him. He must be six foot four, just slightly taller than Cameron and Jack, and his frame is huge and dense with muscle. My body wilts at the sight of it.

I gulp down my nerves as he stalks towards me, even though I know nothing can happen without my consent.

In truth, I'm as afraid of myself as I am of him. I'm afraid of how far I'm willing to go to get him to do the only thing that really matters anymore—to relinquish all debt and all claim to Jack and Cameron.

As he makes it to within a foot of me, his hand lifts to my hood, and he slides the fabric down the back of my head before tugging my cloak open at the top. Next, he ventures to my mask and pulls it off in deliberate movements.

Dammit, I feel my cheeks positively burning as lucent eyes peer down at my naked face, studying it in a blaze of hissing fire. His eyes roam at leisure, feasting gluttonously on my lips before finding mine. As I peer up at him, I realize I'm blinking fast under the heat of his implacable scrutiny and statuesque frame. He barely blinks, and when he does, it's slow and measured, even if I spy his chest rising and falling faster than usual.

Before I can protest, the mask in his hand that he removed from my face tumbles to the floor, and I'm spun around so quickly that the movement steals my breath. A sharp intake of air punctuates the silence of the room as my cloak is ripped off me and thrown onto a black chair against the wall.

"Hey!" I try to protest, but his palm snakes over my mouth, and his other arm pulls my body into his chest as he wraps around me, stopping me from moving.

"Don't fight me," he utters until I stop resisting, waiting for my respiration to temper. "You can't win."

After a minute or so of struggling, finally stopping all movement as I come to accept the superiority of his strength, the feathery brush of his lips adorns the nape of my exposed neck. He doesn't kiss me, but his mouth grazes my skin, and the sharp inhale informs me that he's smelling my scent.

My lips part on an audible breath as he moves one hand onto my bare back and begins to trace, delicately exploring the naked skin exposed by my backless dress with his fingertips as his lips drop to my shoulder and he breathes me in audibly, taking in my scent with unabashed fervor.

My eyes close before I can stop them as the fingers of his strong hands begin to explore me with a softness that rocks me to my core, touching as if to see if I'll crumble to pieces.

I feel the puff of air as he sniffs the skin on my back, and hear the low, guttural groan he emits as my head drops back, just a little. And for a moment, my mind's eye sees the eyes of a dragon flare in blood-red flames from deep within murky caves hiding centuries of deathly secrets.

His fingertips caress my skin with impossible tenderness as he works his way down to the center of my back, his brutal, treacherous lips stroking my flesh, setting it alight as if sparking it with errant surges of electrical current. As his fingers play me like some delicate string instrument, my nipples twist into hard points under the slender fabric of my ivory dress and my own wetness seeps into my beige panties.

His parted lips lift to my shoulder and then stray across the side of my neck as he breathes me in with a rumbling inhale.

So, the man can make me ready just by touching me—that's one of the things that make him so dangerous to be near. No matter your principles, he is designed to steal your sanity from you deftly. Things that seemed logical become inconveniences under his touch, and you want nothing more than to give in to reckless abandon, to your secret desires, the ones that are the most shameful and terrifying to admit to anyone, but that make you feel the most alive...

In a moment of fear, I summon up the things that are stopping me, clinging to the vision of them like lifeboats in a torrid ocean.

Jack and Cameron, both men whom I worship.

Morality.

Fear of what he'd do to me. And of what I'd become.

Rose...

Would she want this? Would she want me to try to heal him somehow? Or would she want retribution for what he did to her?

I feel like I'm losing my mind...

I shiver as his hand delves into the back of my dress and finds the side of my body, sliding down and then back up, missing the side of my breast by inches. He hesitates for a moment before withdrawing it as the side of his cheek finds mine from behind. I feel him watching me but keep my eyes tightly closed, my body pulsing as if on the verge of tipping into ecstasy that will waken it from eternal sleep.

Soft ridges of pleasure undulate through my core as he makes his way around me, taking in my scent in loud inhales... and a few moments later, I feel him standing before me, feel his mouth dropping to my cheek.

His lips slip against my skin as I pant through my arousal at being handled so delicately by a man so savage in his danger, so brutal in his instincts, so strong in his body that he could tear me to pieces if he chose to.

He won't hurt me...

I hear the whisper, the ebb, and flow of his breath, feel the warm air on my cheek, as if he's breathing life into me... or his brand of life—one that burns so brightly only to extinguish when you least expect it... or when he gives in to whatever monsters dwell inside him.

His hand slides up my neck, the touch of it singeing my cells, igniting them in precipitous flames. "Open your eyes," he whispers, his low voice an earthquake fissuring the root-laden ground beneath me.

I draw in a silent breath and comply only for my eyes to collide with a gaze so impossibly incandescent that it feels like the only light in the room. His eyes are unlike any I've seen before, their luster so at odds with the obscurity of his mind. They look like they're lit by dragon flame, illuminating a face whose rugged beauty is impossible to behold.

As his thumb drifts against my cheek, my gaze is drawn to his strong jaw and his mauve lips. It sweeps over his dimpled chin and down his thick neck which fans out to meet broad, muscular shoulders.

And then... I see it—the muted crimson line of a scar between the unbuttoned sides of satiny cotton at the top of his shirt. I'm drawn back to watching him take a knife and slice through his own flesh, barely flinching at the gruesome desecration of his once-sacred body.

I tremble at the heinous memory—the blood that spilled from the wound in slow drips, and of his wild eyes as he watched mine. Did he want me to understand who he really is, to understand his demons? Did he want to traumatize me some more as Cameron said, leaving me dependent on him to try to heal? Or does he reach points where he just can't hold in his pain and fury at the world anymore?

The weight of his glare almost stops my fingers from reaching up to the scar, but somehow, they have the audacity to do it, and somehow... he doesn't stop me.

A crackling bolt of lightning incinerates the pads of my fingertips as they enter into tentative contact with the raised line, evidence of a wound still somewhat raw. He watches me watching him, observing a vein filled with fresh blood flowing beneath his skin.

"Does it hurt?" I dare to ask, but he doesn't answer, regarding me in silent menace as I peel back the top of his shirt to reveal the scar stretching all the way to the bump of his shoulder.

And there... I spot another scar, this time old—maybe a decade old. It's nude in color and thin, almost imperceptible.

Oh my God...

It could only have been carved by a knife.

As the cotton of his shirt stretches no more, I do something that I can barely hold myself together to do. I peer up at him, my fingers quivering as I reach for the top button of his shirt, watching his eyes as I undo it, as if afraid that at any moment, he'll lose control and teach me a lesson in respect. I keep expecting him to pull my hand away at the brazen intrusion into his personal space... but he doesn't.

What are you doing?

As I reach the bottom button, I begin to peel the thick, soft cotton off his torso, reaching up to the tops of his shoulders which seem ten storeys high, pulling it down the thick, sinewy muscle of his arms and off his hands, dropping it to the floor in a move I feel sure he'll punish me for.

But he doesn't.

My core tightens despite myself as I drink in the defined ridges of a body so honed it would put the most famous statues to utter shame. His arms are about five times thicker than mine, but hard with muscle, with barely any fat on them at all. His pecs are strong, the grooves of his abdominals pronounced, stretching down to a defined V etched with several pronounced veins which delve under his black pants under which I see the ridge of his erection.

I can't shame him for that in light of the unwanted arousal besieging me. I'm shamefully aware that every cell in my body feels alive, is vibrating, humming, bubbling with a brand of corrosive heat that feels unfamiliar to me despite the years of dark pleasure I've shared with Jack and later, Cameron...

That's the trap...

The threat of sex so deviant that you are no longer yourself at the end of it.

Your rational mind says no. Your body and soul want to experience being taken to the edge.

No...

I run my gaze along the wound in his chest, lifting my eyes to his for a moment to find him glaring down at me, his body tense. I know he's struggling to accommodate my need to expose the incisions and the reasons for them.

As more scars float into view, my hands weaken. Each new line is shiny and thin but for a couple on his arm and another on his chest which look newer, less pale—months old, perhaps.

The thought of the horror that carved these grotesque branches into his skin depletes me for a moment. I know by how narrow and pallid some are that they may date back to when he was a child...

The pads of my fingers tentatively skim a scar on his arm and he instantly goes rigid, his body hardening as if molten metal suddenly plunged into ice water. My eyes widen as I see it split open before me to reveal the incision of crimson muscle beneath. I blink and the sight disappears, reverting back to the thin pale line which I run my fingers along. I'm so afraid of making him feel like a freak, but I can't stop myself—I need to know who he is, to comprehend the kind of soul-fracturing pain that causes this, or allows it to happen.

In reality, I know... or at least, to some extent. Not long after the incident in Albany, in the midst of the panic disorder that emerged afterwards during my last year of high school, I cut my arms a few times. The cuts were not as deep as his, and I don't have scars to show for them, but for a short while, I did something to stop the alienating shame and isolation I felt, the unexpected void. My young brain led me to a knife which I hid in my room, and then to scars which I hid under clothes, until Babs saw them and insisted I get help.

I had an adult who cared about me, who made me feel like I was worthy of existence, that my flesh was too sacred to desecrate—not just Babs but my parents too.

He never had that. In every single interaction that that so-called mother had with him, she let him know that she despised his very existence, that he, her own son, made her skin crawl, that his wounds were a source of indifference, or worse, of pleasure.

I don't know how a mother, or father, for that matter, can do that, but I do know it happens *all* the time, and that the children of those parents don't even begin to start processing the abuse until years later —or, as in the case of Sebastian, they take matters into her own hands.

I swallow hard under the turbulence of his glare as I deign to brush my finger across what must once have been a deep scar inscribed into his bicep. The static of thunder sets my skin alight as I touch it, as I try to control my breathing as this man—this monster—tolerates my impudent exploration... for now.

Seeing a scar twist around his arm like a cruel axe blow to the bough of a beautiful tree, I take a tentative step to the side of him, following it as it curves around his arm.

My God...

A faint gasp floats from me as the scars on this back spill into intolerable focus. I've seen him naked before. Sebastian seems to feel no shame about his naked form—not exactly surprising for a god-like man with a body like his—but it's only when you look very, very closely, in the right light, that you see shimmery wafer-thin bands, slashes engraved into the sacred wood of his body.

He couldn't have made these himself.

Some of the lines go from right to left across his back.

Someone else did this to him.

My panting is audible even to my own ears as I dare to trace the lines stretching into a pallid web of torture, wondering how old he was, when they were inflicted upon him. Were they put there by his command, or against his will?

And then... I see something else, in the center of his back—a raised scar, the same color as the intact skin around it; a circle with something languishing inside—a tree, maybe, though it's difficult to decipher as the scar looks old.

A brand.

No...

It must have been burnt into his skin.

"What... what is this?" I whisper.

As I touch the edge of it, a scream is ripped from me as he spins around in a burst of violent rage and lifts me, pivoting me as he pushes me against the wall in a loss of control that I felt coming from the second I dared to expose him like that. My dress is hitched up, and my legs wrap around his waist as he pins me to the wall behind my back, glaring down at me, his face twisting in fury as he loses his patience at my boundaryless audacity.

Breathe...

As he sandwiches me between the dark wall and his hard pale body, suspending me at his will, my eyes soften—a tender plea of contrition and capitulation that always works on Jack and Cameron, subduing their rage when I push them past the point of comfort. Except this man, I don't know if he works by those rules. Every single thing about him is utterly unpredictable in a way that even Jack or Cameron aren't.

My hands curl around his shoulders as his glower eats into me, his chest rising and falling heavily, his respiration breaking against my breasts as if the tips of ocean waves rolling onto the shore in a cacophony of ghostly-white foam.

"I'm sorry," I say as his eyes eat into my lips.

"Why are you sorry?" he growls.

"I know I… invaded your space. I don't mean to. I'm just trying to… know who you are."

"So that you can save your men?" he asks bitterly.

I shiver at the sight of the lucent silver irises flattening into serpentine slits before me.

"Not only that."

"Why else?" he asks. One of his hands is cupping my ass, and another snaked around my back, holding me up. For a second, I feel the caress of his fingers against the exposed skin of my back. I wonder whether he meant to do that…

"So that… *everyone* can be saved…"

I close my eyes for a long second, shuddering at the banality that comes out of my mouth in his presence. With anyone else, I wouldn't be this self-conscious but this man sees through you. He holds himself as if he's been alive for hundreds of years and grown exhausted by the tedium of humanity. I hate the thought that my words are hackneyed or predictable or overly simplistic… but then, maybe I need to speak to him earnestly. Around the likes of Alex and Vallen, he'll only hear snarling cynicism. Maybe he needs to hear something else…

"That would suggest, Jessynia, that you see your fate as inseparable from mine…"

"Yes," I reply softly. "Am I wrong?"

He remains silent as he examines the curves of my blood-flushed face with reptilian curiosity. "What do you feel when you see my scars?"

"Pain."

He dips his head into me, his mouth hovering over mine. "Do you think I want to be pitied, Jessynia?"

The harsh bite to the question makes my pulse skip. "No. But... I think... you want me to see you... don't you?" The glossy charcoal mirrors of his pupils dilate, forcing me to gulp down the nerves lodged in my throat. "You have scars on your back," I add gently. "Knife scars. Did you cause them?"

He shakes his head slowly.

"Then who did?"

His lips encroach further into the space between us until they're an inch away.

His silvery-gray eyes, like a shimmering lake in the muted winter sun, flare for a moment as he speaks a word that makes my heart stall and my limbs dissolve into nothing.

"*Demons*, Jessynia."

17

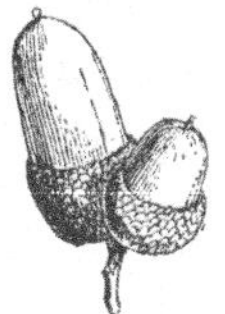

Silas
Quercus Velutina
Eleven years earlier

Sebastian grimaces, a groan tearing from him, as I plunge the sharp blade of the dagger into his flesh, slicing open the pallid skin.

Blood seeps from the wound, trickling in grotesque streams of crimson sap down his back. He doesn't scream nor cry like the other men did.

But then, bringing back the old ritual—Sanguis Quercus, the Blood of Oak—was his idea, championed by him and him alone for months.

It had been banned over a century ago for being unnecessarily cruel and barbaric. Sebastian's takeover of the position of President was assured upon his ousting of David and what will certainly be the majority vote of the Council next week. There was no need to do this, and yet he insisted it be brought back to test the mettle of any future president of Quercus Velutina.

The two other candidates for president who challenged the takeover of the role by Sebastian bowed out of the ceremony as soon as the knives came out. One stomached a single slice of the blade into his flesh, another broke down crying before it had even been drawn from its sheath.

The disgrace of their perfectly justified cowardice in front of the Council members earlier today will ensure that they don't nominate themselves again for a long time, no matter what they think of Sebastian's future presidency, although he knows nothing of their surrender. He wasn't witness to their swift capitulation earlier. All he knows is that to ensure that he is worthy of the position of President, he must out-tolerate what they managed—the thirteen carefully chosen cuts sliced into select parts of his flesh, some deeper than others, depending on how likely we are to nick a vein by mistake...

Sebastian's hands strain against the ropes tying him to the huge rosewood chair—too large and heavy to tip over. His head hangs low, his face covered by his thick hair. Occasional grimaces eek from him but are barely audible over the dark instrumental music and the occasional mutterings of awe from Samara, his long-time confidante. As much as I'm sure it pains her to see this man whom she seems to care so much about cut open in front of her like this, I know she will approve of the sight, of the knowledge of his dangerous devotion, for it is she, Dominic, Alexandra and Steven who have been the driving forces behind Sebastian's rise to power.

I wonder if that bond he has with her will remain as strong once he is made President.

God, I pray somehow that that doesn't come to pass.

Just one more cut...

Perhaps due to years of studying the most gruesome of religious texts, I have been gifted with the ability to cut into a living human's flesh without flinching, but it's not lost on me how dangerous this is, this precedent, this descent into barbarity. Despite veiled warnings about my dissidence, I voted against the reintroduction of such a brutal ritual. It has no place in the modern world. Not only that, but it appears to me that it foreshadows the way Sebastian intends to run our Society, distilling it to the archaic rules of a bygone area, rules relaxed many times due to the inevitable consequences of tyranny.

Unfortunately, what can only be described as veritable human vampires now dominate this Council. They've slowly worked their way in, and support each other, nominating one another until the place has become riddled with them, and I barely recognize what was once a safe haven of pleasure and liberty.

If it weren't for my concern for some of the younger members, I would have left already. I may have even left that a little late. Sebastian seems determined to make leaving a more complicated affair than it has been in the three decades I've frequented this place and made it my home of sorts, a place which once catered to my needs, but which now leaves me afraid.

I watch as his perspiration-soaked skin twitches under the gashes in his flesh.

He wanted this...

He needed this.

No one else did.

No good can come of this.

I glance over at Darragh, wondering how he feels about a ceremony he voted *yes* to. This so-called man of God. Does the sight of this desecration of flesh soothe him somehow?

My gaze slides to the masked observers standing in a circle around the almost bare, dimly lit room. Some have retreated and are sitting on the floor, backs against the wall and heads down, presumably to stop themselves passing out at the sight of blood, as advised. They will not face consequences for being human.

A few are left standing, including Steven, another sadist who is no doubt reveling in the extreme brutality that he was so enthused about. The young Vallen—about the same age as Sebastian—is watching in enthralled silence.

To an outside observer, our group may look harmonious. In reality, the tension is brewing between the old school and those who require more extreme measures to obtain the pleasure they seek, and who would rule through intimidation, threats and violence.

Francis, equally concerned about the direction the Society is taking under Sebastian's influence, has retreated and is standing against the wall, her head bowed in some silent protest that I know Sebastian will feel even if he can't see it. The tension between them is reaching fever pitch amidst whispers of Sebastian's plans for her expulsion in dishonor...

"As per the decrees of the ritual," I declare to the faceless members —a mixture of Council and a handful of special guests who have proven their loyalty over the years—"an observer may volunteer to provide the final brand. Would anyone like to perform this sacred ritual?"

Silence fills the room with its stifling weight... until...

"I would."

No...

My heart sinks to the floor at the sound of the young man's voice. I observe his friend, standing next to him, turn to face him, shaking his head.

They're still in their late teens. They should *never* have been invited in the first place—as I was very vocal about—but Alexandra insisted that they watch today's proceedings. She has plans for both of them, and the realization thereof depends on their gradual dehumanization.

As current vice-president and de facto president until final voting takes place, Sebastian is also taking their education and integration into our Society seriously. They are two huge draws for this place, the likes of which cannot be bought. The number of female patrons with full membership has increased since their arrival here with no signs of abating.

Sebastian has invested considerable time in training both of them, not something he often does. While they both show potential for the dominance needed among the men here, it is Cameron who shows a more natural aptitude for sadism. It is also he who has a more tense relationship with the woman who brought him here, and by extension with Sebastian, Alexandra's lover and confidant, and a man she worships above all other... including her husband.

I can't ask Sebastian if he is willing to have his flesh cauterized by Cameron. It would be a humiliating affront to his dignity to ask such a question in public. He will have to take it.

Who knows? In Sebastian's twisted mind, maybe this is a victory of some sort—witnessing the decay of the O'Neill scion and his descent into degradation and disgrace. Maybe he will secretly revel in seeing Cameron's boundaries and penchant for decency erode as he burns Sebastian's flesh.

Sebastian must know full well that the other two candidates will never have gotten to this point, will never have been able to take the cutting of their flesh. He could stop now in the certainty that he has been victorious. But he won't. I knew from the start that he wouldn't, no matter how much pain he has to endure. One thing I know about him is that he is not afraid of pain the way most of us are. His early life was spent in the kind of hell most can't conceive of, and nothing he suffers as an adult seems to come close to the purgatory of relentless psychological abuse inflicted upon the unformed, unfinished mind of a child by a parent of the most heinous variety. Not only can he tolerate more pain than most, he seeks it out, he studies it, toys with it, tries to understand it, to master it...

Cameron is a tricky young man. He's only eighteen, but has a strong character, as does Jackson. The difference is that Cameron has expressed to me in private some concern at the consequences of seeing so much on his young mind, on his young life. He's barely an adult but unlike Jack, already seems aware of the danger this place may cause him.

Many of us have been vocal about changing the age of entry to twenty-one. Technically, there is nothing illegal about bringing a seventeen-year-old into our family in the state of New York, but psychologically, many do not seem to fare well, which is exactly what some of the people around here want. They want the people at the top to be fractured in youth, with nothing left to bind them to any sense of morality, to tether them to any anchor of weight. They want them left with no real sense of who they are, perfect fodder to be molded into the much-needed soldiers of this place.

It never used to be like this...

Something so dark has gotten in...

Cameron seems as fascinated by Sebastian as he is weary, perhaps recognizing his own darkness, his own penchant for sadism in Sebastian, a penchant that, unlike our president, he seems to be fighting not to succumb to. It is a fight we all must bear, including me, for, on occasion, I feel the treacherous pull into the transcendent agony of hell and all of its pleasures and freedoms...

All watch in silence as the young man, cloaked but unmasked, walks towards us despite his friend's silent protests. His steps are hesitant, his countenance somber as he makes his way over, his thick brown hair shading his young face.

I'm tempted to veto this heinous act, but I know that Sebastian would not approve of breaking protocol in such a manner. Technically, anyone watching can volunteer to complete the trial, to brand the skin with the mark of the Black Oak. Cameron's age isn't an issue, not on paper anyway, nor is the fact that he is not a Council member. Special guests are allowed to witness and participate in the ceremony upon approval by the Council.

I don't know why Jack and Cameron agreed to attend, but I have no doubt that Alexandra, who they are both still besotted by, poured her special brand of insidious poison into them, whispering dark promises laced with hidden threats, playing on their endless desire to please her, to compete with one another, to gain approval that her pathology is not designed to grant.

Who knows? Maybe they enjoy being pulled to the edge, witnessing the abyss, the things that the average person would not get to experience. God help me, but I know full well that sometimes, it just makes you feel alive...

The young man comes to stand next to me, his fiery eyes widening as they drink in the dripping scarlet striations incised into Sebastian's back and shoulders, and the blood welling, coagulating—horror spilled in hues of somber crimson, as if blood drawn in moonlight.

Before he can brand the flesh in his back, he must perform one cut —a vertical line running from the vertebra that protrudes at the bottom of the neck down one inch, just enough for blood to seep into the oak to be branded on the skin below.

I hand him the handle of the blade—wood, stained black and

engraved with twisting branches. The young man scrutinizes the blood pooled at its metal tip.

"You draw the knife down, Mr. O'Neill. One inch. Not deep. We're not cutting muscle this time. We're only cutting skin. Is that understood?"

He nods, his hand quivering for a moment as his fingers clutch the handle. Sebastian flinches, pulling on the ropes as Cameron inserts the cruel tip, closing his eyes for a moment before slicing down, one inch, the cut shallow, just enough to let a droplet pool at the bottom of the laceration.

I walk over to the fire and withdraw the branding iron, handing the twisting metal pole to him as the end—shaped into a flat circle with an oak inside—burns red hot, as if in flames of hellfire.

God help us...

I press my finger into the spot on Sebastian's back where the brand should go. His body is trembling, from shock and loss of blood maybe, and just the trauma of a ceremony so brutal, one so wanted by him. The undulation in his rippling muscles mimics the quivering of Cameron's hands. From across the room, my eyes are drawn to the sight of Jack stepping forward as if to stop him, only to have Alexandra swiftly wrap her hand around his bicep, holding him back.

Cameron lifts the brand, positioning it over Sebastian's pale skin. We wait, collective breaths baited, for him to press the scalding metal into Sebastian's shuddering body.

Instead, a low breathless utterance falls from him. "I can't."

As I peer into his ashen face, watching horror spread over it, the vision of a man approaching distracts me.

Darragh.

He takes the poker from Cameron quickly, easing him to the side and stabbing it into Sebastian's flesh as fast as possible, not to draw out the agony any longer.

At the heinous hiss of singeing flesh, Sebastian's body seizes, his hands pulling against his binds as Cameron steps backwards, watching as the blood from his cut trickles into the burnt flesh.

The blood of Black Oak.

A while later, Darrah and I gently untie the ropes from Sebastian's wrists and ankles in silence, lifting his head as Samara begins to tend to his cuts, and I whisper to myself, "All hail the President of Quercus Velutina."

18

Jessynia
Quercus Velutina, Tribeca
Present

"Cameron?"

Sebastian nods slowly as tentacles of nausea creep into my belly.

It's impossible...

How much horror can these three men have seen?

"He stopped," I utter.

"He was weak."

"He was a *child*."

"Who cut me."

"Are you angry that he cut you?"

"I'm angry that he stopped," he responds, his jaw tight.

"Why?!" He doesn't answer as I search his face. "You're angry because *you* wouldn't have stopped, and you wanted him to be like you, didn't you?"

"You see too much, Jessynia."

"Why did you bring that fucking ceremony back?! You knew what they were going to do to your body! It didn't have to be that dangerous!" His eyes flare at my accusatory tone. "You did it so you would feel something, didn't you? You can't feel anything unless it's really extreme, can you?!"

"I did it because I knew that I would soon hurt people," he spits back. "If I cause pain, I have to be willing to take pain myself."

"Sebastian, they cut your body open! It isn't normal! You shouldn't have had to endure something like that. You must have some trauma from it!"

He dips his head as he takes in my lips. "I live in trauma. I can't remember existence without it. My heart beats to it..."

My fingers grip his shoulders tightly. "*No*. It doesn't have to be like this. There are other ways."

"Amuse me, Jessynia."

"Trauma therapy. And I'll help you. And I'll never invalidate or downplay what happened to you, or say that the evil bitch was doing her best, or didn't know any better, or all the other bullshit rationalizations you've had to suffer through! I can help you. Please. Just let me."

"The hope you feel is so alluring. It's so pure. It's so fucking *naïve*. Do you think I haven't endured the miserable path of so-called *hope* before?"

"This time, I can help you."

He scrutinizes my face, his expression so difficult to read. "When you look at my scars, what do you see?"

"I see blood."

"You taste it?"

"Yes."

"What do you feel when you taste it?"

"I feel... pain. It's horrific, Sebastian. That should never have happened. This place doesn't have to be this dangerous!"

"Pain makes people do strange things, Jessynia."

The ghost of something rolls through me as a realization dawns. "You said thirteen cuts," I whisper, "but you have more than that on your body. Did... the others take place as part of another ceremony?"

He shakes his head slowly.

"How did you get them?" I ask, barely knowing if I want the answer. Some of them look so old. Could that thing he called a mother have made any of the cuts to the body of the boy whose existence felt like contamination to her? Or did he cut himself to relieve the agony of a childhood so desecrated?

He doesn't speak, but reaffirms his hold on my suspended body.

"What does my pain make you feel, Jessynia?"

"Pain," I reply.

His brow furrows in something akin to consternation. "Despite everything you know that I've done..."

"Yes," I reply. "Despite everything."

And in a sudden loss of control, he slips his lips against mine before peering down to watch my panting mouth.

"Sebas—"

His name is swallowed as his tongue emerges from his mouth and gently pushes into the seam between my lips, slowly flicking up and down, sliding left to right before pushing through... a little... and then more, just about touching the tip of my tongue before pulling out to observe me.

Not removing his eyes from my lips, he utters, "How can you feel pain at the suffering of a monster?"

Mine fall to his. "I don't know."

He inhales my breaths for a moment before his tongue once again slips across my lips before pushing into me slowly, my lips parting to accommodate him as I fall into a deep, slow kiss, the type of which it seems impossible for a man this brutal to be capable of.

In a wanton moment that I can't control, my hands find his thick long hair as his arms wrap around me, pulling me into him as the dense bulge of his erection presses into my clit—firmly, deliberately, over and over.

His mouth tastes divine, his scent is masculine and strong, dizzying me, stunning my senses. The way he holds me is possessive, protective almost, even as his tongue delves into and out of me amidst deviant groans which leave his throat and mingle with the high-pitched exhalations I can't stop.

My body is a helpless mess, enslaved to arousal stoked by months of psychological and physical foreplay which have left me desperate to feel the invasion of his body into mine.

But I'm so scared.

And it's so wrong.

And so dangerous.

I could do it if he promised to let Jack and Cameron go forever... but I feel in my gut that once I allowed him inside me, I'd never be able to get out.

There has to be another way...

He has to be able to heal...

As he presses his erection into me once more, I drop my palms to his chest and push gently.

The words stumble from me messily. "White Oak."

He arrests the fucking of my mouth and drops his forehead to mine, staring down at me, his arms tensing in frustration. He holds me there for what feels like a minute as I tremble under the rancor of a glare holding me immobile.

I know what he thinks. He thinks I'm playing games with him. I don't mean to. I just... need to be sure of what I'm doing when it comes to a man this dangerous. And right now, I don't know...

"You're very lucky that I still find your resistance pleasing, Jessynia."

19

Sebastian

Her eyes—as large and deeply blue as the ocean—widen as she peers up at me.

"Why do you?" she asks. "Find my resistance pleasing? Is it just because you like the challenge? Would you get bored if I stopped resisting?"

"I believe that what you're trying to get me to admit, Jessynia, is that I feel protective of you. That part of me is afraid of hurting you, and that is why I like when you stop me..."

She swallows hard. "Do you? Want to protect me?"

My body tenses, for I've battled with this godforsaken and unexpected need to protect her for some time now, a need only mitigated by my desire to inhale her suffering.

"I believe so," I respond slowly, watching the frown that comes over her. "Does that reassure you? Does it allow you to convince yourself that the bad man has a soul?"

"You do have a soul, Sebastian. It's just... fractured."

"Held together by the scraps you would offer me..."

Her breathing quickens, her eyes softening as she searches my face, her misplaced contrition as foolish as it is breathtaking.

"That's not fair. You know full well how dangerous you are. Am I supposed to ignore that? You've hurt people I love. And I'm not a free woman, Sebastian! I was brought back to Jack by *you*, remember? And I love him. I don't want to hurt him."

"You don't want to hurt the man who I've witnessed fucking dozens of women during your marriage, often several at a time."

"Stop!" She pushes against my chest, hurt flooding her delicate body. "I don't want to know these things! We're moving past all that."

"You're not a coward, Jessynia. You would have me face truths that hurt me. I will insist that you do the same. Your desire to be a good wife is admirable, but the fractures left behind by Jack's actions have consequences. Would you have found yourself in my arms a year ago? Would you have let my tongue fuck your mouth back then, before you knew the truth?"

Her eyes mist over as they drop to my lips, still coated in her sweet saliva.

"I didn't think so."

"Why did he... come back?" she asks, a single tear welling in her eye. I throb at the sight of it.

"Have you not asked your husband that question?"

She shakes her head.

"Why not, Jessynia?"

"I don't know. I think... I was afraid to find out."

"Living in fear is a pitiful state for a woman as powerful as you."

Her hands tighten over the bare skin of my shoulders. "Well, sorry to disappoint," she pants, ire making her body tense.

"I have no doubt that with time you will stop being enslaved by fear."

"You supposedly want me free from fear, and yet you still want to hurt me?" she asks.

"Yes. Part of me does."

The tear teetering on her waterline trickles onto her flushing cheek, tracing a perfect shimmering path.

Drink her pain...

I lean forwards, my eyes studying hers to look for signs of reticence, but there are none as I slowly lick the saltwater droplet from her face.

Her bottom lip crumples as I savor the delight of her tears, my body hardening.

"Why do you let me?" I ask.

"I don't know."

"Why?" I repeat, wondering if she has the courage to say it.

"I want to help you— To help *both* of us to heal. That means I have to sacrifice something to get you to listen."

"What a cop-out, Jessynia. The pitiful denial of a woman who can't admit to her desire."

Her breaths shallow, her body succumbing to indignation. "Maybe you're right, Sebastian. But it doesn't change the fact that we have to try to heal... finally."

"*We*? I believe you mean *Me*, Jessynia. Is the pronoun some attempt at inclusivity? If it's designed to stop me from feeling like a problem case, I hate to disappoint you, but I am beyond repair."

Her spine straightens and the plea in her face becomes more desperate. "No. You don't have to live in trauma anymore, Sebastian."

The words would sicken me with their banality if they were uttered by anyone else. There's something about the earnest force with which she speaks them that touches me more than I can usually stomach.

"I don't?"

She shakes her head, her breath escaping her. "No. You don't. There are ways out. I can help you." Her fingers dig into my skin, blanketing my scars.

"You are drenched in trauma yourself, Jessynia."

"We can help each other," she replies, forcing me once again to call upon a degree of self-restraint that is painfully new for me. I harden at the naïve beauty of her words, at the nauseating purity with which she searches my eyes, pleading silently for me to meet her on a path that only she can see. I know she must feel how thick and hard I am against her, how desperately I hunger for her, how I yearn to drink her blood as she gives me her body, and yet she would still try to meet me...

"How?" I ask, endlessly curious as to the inane dregs of hope she will find.

"We can talk to each other, in safety." Her breath caresses my face. "We can get out the things that have damaged us. I won't judge you for them, Sebastian. I've studied narcissistic abuse by parents. I won't rationalize or invalidate what you want through. *Ever*. We can heal."

"You would heal me, Jessynia, even though you know I may hurt you for it?"

Fear makes her shiver in my arms. I imbibe every shudder of it, drinking it in as if blood. I consume the terror. The doubt. The reverence she's always shown me despite her attitude.

My lips fall to her ear, brushing gently against the soft, milky skin. "Don't you want me to hurt you?"

She thinks I don't hear her almost inaudible gasps. What she doesn't know is that I feel them rippling through my body—every quivering note, every breath that is swept from her and into me.

Out of my peripheral vision, I see her plump lips part at the question. Mine skim the pale cream of her outer ear. "Tell me the truth, Jessynia. Do you know I may hurt you?"

"Yes."

"And you would take the risk of conversing with me? Dissecting years of my life which were utter torment?"

"Yes."

"Why?"

"It's the only way, Sebastian. We have to recover. Both of us."

"And while we do so, we may hurt..."

"Yes," she replies. "But it will be worth it..."

I study the most breathtaking of faces, falling for a moment in eyes so blue, so honest, eyes that peer into me so deeply, that shine light, that see me, that it's all I can do to resist the urge to close them forever.

"Do you believe pain can be worth it, Jessynia?"

"Of course."

"Then answer my fucking question." A whimper escapes her and my body hardens at the exquisite sound. "Do you want me to hurt you? Do you want to feel the pain that I like to inflict as I enter you?

Do you want to experience sex as it was meant to be? Savage. Brutal. Primal."

Tilting my head slightly to the side, I observe her eyes drop and her cheeks become washed in mouth-watering hues of pink as she contemplates the reality of her longing for submission... and for the pain that is a non-negotiable part of that. I already know her tastes—no woman who can handle Cameron O'Neill is afraid of some pain. She's just afraid of how much I need to inflict...

It is a concern of my own...

"Do you? Crave the pain I wish to inflict? Do you want my demons to dance with yours?" I whisper into her lips and she lifts her eyes, astonishing me once more with the earnest truth of her gaze.

I'm rarely rattled by humans anymore. Amidst years of agonizingly vapid social interaction, I lost my faith in their ability to behave outside a nauseatingly predictable framework of sanctimony and hypocrisy. There are a few exceptions—she is one of them. Her men are others. I have no doubt they enjoy the way she is—erratic, illogical, unstable at times, humorous, unpredictable, sharp, passionate, emotional, naïve, foolish. Her whims would be intolerable if every interaction of hers wasn't colored by her endless compassion and need to care. To heal. And by the fact that she is the singularly most arousing creature I've ever encountered.

Her body and face are uniquely fuckable for she seems to not fully comprehend the magnitude of her beauty. The shape of her body. The curve and color of her lips. The sickeningly pure flame glowing in her eyes laden with an innocence that all men are programmed to want to defile. To debase. To infiltrate. To fertilize.

As her skin heats against mine, I'm aware of the warmth I feel when I hold her, aware of how deeply it hurts me to feel it, aware of the invisible screams of wretched creatures which writhe in agony at the sensation.

I want to hold her.

I want to understand her mind.

I want to fuck her.

I want to reward her for becoming a vehicle, a conduit.

I want to bite into her flesh as I ravage her, drinking in the warm metal of her blood.

I want to tear her to pieces until she is nothing but a memory, an artifact of a time lost.

Her light burns more brightly than most.

Its flame is unpredictable. Beautiful. Warm.

The light it shines on me is *not*. She forces light into the dark—light that is most unwelcome.

Holding a creature such as this so gently while yearning to rip her throat out, to drink her blood until she's empty of all life—it is a fight I had assumed I would have succumbed to by now. In truth, I have no idea how I've managed to keep her intact for so long... especially when I know of the endless black torment that Mr. O'Neill will endure if she is no more. That is a temptation I have struggled to resist.

The beauty of her way of existing grates on me endlessly. It awakens things inside me that twist in torrent agony at the godforsaken farce that humans would call joy and curiosity. At her innocence. At her fucking purity.

And yet the thought of her evisceration haunts me in a way that no one else's does.

Tear her apart...

"Does pain have to be a part of... sex?" she asks.

"In my world, yes," I respond, observing the pink of her cheeks grow pallid as she contemplates the suffering that I require. "You have loved Cameron O'Neill. I know the tastes of that deviant, Jessynia. Our types recognize one another fast. I've seen what he needs. I watched over it for years. He was merciless in his need to cause pain to procure pleasure. And I have observed the faint glimmer of bruises where his teeth have bitten into you, the desecration of your flesh that you have allowed. You cannot tell me you don't enjoy pain."

"He's... about as much as I can handle."

"How do you know? A year ago, would you have imagined letting a man bite into your skin, bruise you, brand you the way he does? Jack uses discipline and dominance but he doesn't bite. I know that much. That was new for you, wasn't it? And yet you accommodated it? Why?"

"You want me to discuss sex with a man you hate?"

"I want to understand why *him*. I want to understand where the line is. Why is *he* allowed to bite you? You realize that he doesn't only get pleasure from the bite? He also likes to *brand* you. He wants to mark your perfect body to ensure that you are his property. Why do you allow it?"

"He doesn't puncture my skin," she replies solemnly. "And he stops when it's too much."

"I allow safe words, Jessynia. I stop also."

"But they're frowned upon?"

"No. Not in my private life."

"But do they use them? The women you—"

"They are informed of my tastes beforehand... in great detail. They know what they will experience."

"Sex with the devil," she suggests softly, shifting her body in my arms, causing her to rub against the hard ridge of my erection before collecting herself, closing her eyes and shifting her pelvis back.

"Is that something you wish to experience?"

The tiniest of gasps escapes her.

"Tell me the truth. The *heinous* truth. Do you want to be fucked by a man as evil as me, one who desires you to the point of insanity? A man who will open you up to worlds of pleasure you could not conceive of?"

"I can't."

"Why not?"

"I'm afraid I'll be... lost... for good."

"Or you'll find yourself, Jessynia. Become more yourself than you've ever dreamed of. You'll let go of the chains of torment, of conscience that taunt you."

"And become another one of your mindless subs?" she suggests, daring to lift her eyes to meet mine. "They hardly seem human anymore. That one that you... you made me watch, she barely seemed like she was even there. She was cackling like some demonic invertebrate. It was like her soul had left her body or something. You want to turn me into some drone like them, don't you?"

"A mindless drone," I repeat, drawing out the words. "That would suggest I don't give a fuck what you think, what you feel. You would ignore the hours I've spent talking to you, listening to you, questioning you so that I may learn who you are, how your mind works. Do you think I hunger for every word *they* have to utter as I do yours? To understand how they think? How they function? I don't."

I glower at her, the heat of anger rioting through my tense, unsatisfied body as she utters words which undermine my ability to stay in control. "I want you to put me down, Sebastian."

I bow my head slowly. "Very well."

I reaffirm my hold on her tiny body as I carry her towards the door, pressing a button on the wall which plunges the room into darkness but for daylight penetrating through the wooden slats of the blinds covering the window.

"Hey," she exclaims, and I press another button, drinking in the exquisite fear and confusion on her face as the metal shutters separating the room from Manhattan slowly descend, taking all remaining light with them.

"Sebastian!" she shouts as we are plunged into utter darkness but for the faintest sliver of light emanating from underneath the door, a meager glow that I will see better than her, for I have spent months in darkness, my eyes getting accustomed to functioning in quantities of light that would not permit others to see.

She twists in my arms, reaching out, grappling for the button I just pressed. Before she can push it, I haul her away, carrying her across the room to a wall adorned with objects of which I know she will be afraid.

"Sebastian, stop!" She tips her head forwards, her forehead pressing against the top of my shoulder as her hands wrap around my neck, panting into the dark. The fear in her breaths arouses me, forcing me once again to breathe through the unfulfilled torment caused by the proximity of her body. "I don't like the dark."

Tear her apart...

"Why don't you like it?"

"No one likes the dark!"

"That's where you're wrong," I sneer. "Your fear of it is unusual. Why?"

"We all hate the dark," she whispers, her scalding breath heavy on my shoulder.

"Not like this. You feel things in it, don't you? You feel beings watching you. You see their faces, don't you?"

"Yes."

My lips find her temple. "You will get used to it."

"I don't want to fucking well get used to it!"

"If you want your light to reach me, Jessynia, as you say you do, then you have to meet me where I exist. In darkness. This is the place I understand. Only in this place will you see who I am... and who you are. If you refuse to meet me there, you can't understand me. You can't help me."

"Do you want to be helped?" she asks, her voice frail as she grips me tightly as if afraid to be placed onto the ground in the black. "Really?"

I consider the question, contemplate my loathing for her naïve attempts to tend to wounds so deep, so heinous that I feel the incision of each one with every step I take.

And yet... I feel pulled into the current of her blind hope against all reason. And I abhor the promise of something so duplicitous.

I breathe in her panting breaths. "I don't know."

With that, I let her go, placing her down onto the floor against the wall, ensuring that her feet are steady in the pitch black.

I feel blasts of her panting breath on my chest as I run my hands down her slim, smooth forearms, parting her arms, helping her to locate two diagonal bars fixed into the wall on either side of her. My fingers wrap around hers, winding them around the bars.

"Sebastian."

"Don't let go," I order. "The dark is disorienting. Hold onto the bars. If you don't, I will chain you to them."

"Like hell you will!"

I step into her, pulling her jaw up, forcing her face upwards. I just about see the faintest glimmer of her eyes as they blink into the blackness. "Don't tempt me, Jessynia. My self-restraint is hanging by a thread as feeble as yours. Is that understood?"

I drink her racing breaths, parting my feet and finding the tops of her hands with my fingertips. I slide them up her arms. Her skin is as smooth as silk but for goosebumps which prickle on her upper arms. I slide my hands back down, closing my eyes as I take in the touch of her.

"What are you doing?" she asks, her breath warm on my neck.

I dip my head to find hers, the neck I dream endlessly of biting into, of tearing a piece out of, of drinking the red liquid that will gush forth from it, filling my mouth with life force that I know would sustain me for a decade.

"I can't fuck you yet, Jessynia. You're not ready. Neither am I. So, in the meantime, I will teach you to exist in darkness." I feel my hot breath on her face as I speak. "That's the only place you can meet me in. I will teach you how to embrace it, how to no longer be afraid of it, how to hunger for it. You will show me, in the dark, who you are."

I feel the tremble of her body in my fingertips as I brush them down her arms, wrapping them around her fingers. The feeling is unfamiliar to me. Alien. Everything about her makes me behave in ways I abhor... and yet I can't resist the urges plaguing me.

I close my eyes for a moment, opening them to find her looking up, the sheen over the sphere of her eyes barely visible in the void.

"You sanitize people in your head," I whisper, inhaling her exquisite scent, a fragrance that haunts me in rooms where she is absent, a ghost conjured up in my mind. "Convince yourself you are safe with them." I reach for something on the wall, bringing its dull edge into contact with her face. She flinches as she feels the hard wood.

"What is that?!"

"Have you ever seen a wooden blade before?" I ask, knowing full well that that man who contaminates her had one made to ensure her safety around him.

"Stop!"

I draw the smooth wood slowly across her skin. "I want you to see the truth," I whisper. "The truth about me. I want you to know that I dream of cutting your skin and drinking your blood."

I slide the flat side of the blade across her bottom lip, resisting the urge to slowly push it into her mouth.

"That's enough, Sebastian. I didn't come here for this."

"No, you didn't." My lips hover over her temple. "But when you play with the devil, at some point, you get burned."

"Fine, you've made your point, okay?"

"Which is?"

"That every time things get uncomfortable, and you have to face the idea of trying to heal, you deflect, and do something like this! You scare me! You tap into your dom side. It's a cop-out, Sebastian. Anyone could do it."

"Are you calling me a coward?"

"Of course not. I know what it's like to not want to face what we've been through. No one wants that. It's messy and uncomfortable and we're going to do it anyway, no matter what you say, or how many times you try to scare me."

I release the knife from her skin, throwing it across the room with a clang that makes her jump, the kinesis of her panic so exquisite.

The dark and the noise must disorientate her for a moment, for she releases one bar and grabs onto my arm, gripping it so tightly for such a small creature.

"See, that's where you're wrong, Jessynia," I whisper, my body throbbing at the closeness with hers, at her fear, at her rapid breaths. "I'm not trying to scare you. I'm trying to *warn* you. I'm trying to protect you. There are things inside me that want your death. I need you to know that."

I see her blink into the darkness as she tries to find me. "I know. I'm not afraid."

Her impudent words cause wrath to rage through my body. "You should be," I snarl.

"I want you to put the light on," she pants. "This isn't how civilized people converse, you know?!"

"Well, I think we both know I'm not that," I retort.

The hint of saliva glistening on her mouth draws my eye as I breathe through my need to fuck the wet pink hole before me with my tongue. It's another sensation that is new to me. I don't usually fuck with my tongue, and yet with her, I can't seem to be able to resist the wretched urge.

"Look, I didn't come here for this, Sebastian."

"Are you sure about that?"

"Yes," she replies defiantly. "I'm *sure*."

"Why *did* you come? To negotiate an exit strategy for the men you love? Do you think of anything but that when you are with me?"

"I think of freeing you..."

20

Jessynia

As my eyes become more accustomed to the dark, I see his, just the faint sheen of them, as if glowing in the dark.

I hate the way I speak around him. I hate that I may sound trite or insincere; that my wit and sass escape me and that my sentences are suddenly peppered with platitudes. I don't recognize myself around this man.

"Free me?" His words drip with disdain.

"From needing them," I continue. "From needing to control *anyone*. There's no future in that path, Sebastian. You can't control people forever! At some point, they'll rebel. That world will come crashing down. It can only lead to..."

"To what, Jessynia? Say the word."

"To *death*."

"Whose death are you concerned about?"

"All of yours!" I exclaim, realizing that I can't feel my feet. "Sebastian, this thing with Cameron, it has to stop! There's already been enough blood shed."

"I decide when it's enough," he rasps, his breath a blast on my face as I strain my neck to look up at him, trying to find his features in the murk of the room.

"You're not rational when it comes to him," I dare to say.

"Nor is he when it comes to you..."

"It's not the same," I counter.

"*Isn't* it? Do you think his love for you isn't dangerous? For you? For Jack? For himself?"

"I'm having nightmares," I admit as I try to ignore that I'm standing before this infamous sadist, in his sunless bedroom, no less. Little things that once seemed unfathomable have now become commonplace. "They're scaring me."

I see the glistening of his teeth as he speaks. "We all have nightmares. It's not something humans have the privilege of escaping from."

"Not like this," I snap. "I've never experienced *anything* like this."

"Tell me about them."

I pause for a moment, wondering if he's asking out of concern, curiosity, or whether he secretly derives pleasure and satisfaction from knowing my pain.

"I wake up... shaking. Covered in sweat." Despite the dark, I observe those singularly reptilian eyes of his sweep over my face as he takes in my distress. I know he can see me more clearly than I see him...

"Like someone else you know," he suggests coldly, conjuring up the man he despises—a man whose nightmares stem from his dealings with Sebastian and other patrons of the Society.

"Yes. Like *his*. They feel so real. I never had them before all of this."

"You had one before you came here, didn't you? That's why you called me, Jessynia, isn't it?"

"Yes," I concede.

"What about?"

"About... *him*... The man you beat to death."

"For hurting you..."

"Yes. For hurting me."

"You can't say his name, can you?"

I shake my head, trying not to allow the full blaze of that man's heinous face to enter my mind as it so often tries to do.

"Why not?"

"I don't know."

"What did you dream?" he asks.

"I dreamed of you... beating him. I can see the blood, Sebastian. I can hear the noises. I can see his face caved in. I can't get it out of my mind. It's haunting me! And I can't talk about it to anyone!"

"You can talk about it to me. You know that."

"Well, there shouldn't be things that I can only talk to *you* about. You're not my husband, Sebastian! You've hurt me and the people around me. You shouldn't now be my confidant, for fuck's sake! You've pulled me into places I have no business being in!"

"You haven't stepped willingly into any of those places?" he counters bitterly.

"I have," I confess. "But it doesn't change the fact that I've now got a man's brutal murder playing over and over in my head."

"It's a trauma response which will dissipate within weeks. And when it does, you will feel a liberation you never knew was possible... or is that what you're really afraid of? Who you'll become once you free yourself of the shackles that keep you enchained..."

"Free myself so that you can stick your own shackles onto me?" I scoff.

"I have no shortage of *mindless subs*, Jessynia, as you so graciously call them," he retorts solemnly. "I have no desire to turn you into just another one. That would be tedious in the extreme, and I would be highly disappointed if you let me."

"Well, that's not going to happen, *ever!*"

"I should hope not..."

I take a moment to feel the floor under my feet, peering down, unable to see them, before looking back up to find the only source of light in the room—the faintest of glows that bounces off his huge body. "He's not the only thing I have nightmares about."

I just about see him bow his head to urge me to continue.

"I can see you... beating Cameron."

A swift shadow plunges his luminous eyes into utter blackness. I scour his face once more, trying to find them, but I can't. "Do you know what your concern for that man does to me?" he snarls.

"I can't help it. I need this war, or whatever the fuck it is, to be over."

"And you'd put yourself in danger to inform me of your fears for him."

"It's not just *him* I'm worried about. It's *you*. Everyone's luck runs out at some point, Sebastian. Things happen that we hadn't planned."

"And what neat little solution would you suggest to solve the problem?"

"I want you to let them both go. Cancel all debt and ties to the Society on their part. Never speak to them again. Never go near them. Never have them followed, or bothered. Just... let them go..."

His strong fingers find the hand clutching his arm. He envelops it, forcing my hand to slip up his bicep, to feel the density of the muscle, to understand its strength, to learn the bumps of his scars. As shameful as it is, my sex pulsates at the sheer size of the hard, sculpted mass of his body. "That's quite a bold request, Jessynia. What makes you think you get to demand such a thing of me?"

"I'm not *demanding*. I'm... *asking*."

"In exchange for what?"

I stare back at him defiantly despite the dark. "My gratitude."

And suddenly, his eyes flare, inches from mine, so impossibly luminous, the only sign of light in the dark. I see some vague reflection in the obsidian glass of his pupils, barely able to believe where I am... how close I am to a man so infamously ravenous for brutality.

"Why would you think that your gratitude is enough for me?" he asks.

"You told me you don't want exchanges. You don't want me in exchange for their freedom."

"No. That would not be acceptable. I need you to *yearn* for me, the *monster* and not the man you would invent in your mind, until nothing else exists in your world."

"And I told you that that's impossible if you hurt either of them, or threaten them in any way."

In the shadows, the lean angles of his rugged face harshen at the reiteration of my conditions. "I'm not so sure, Jessynia." He dips his mouth to my ear, his hot breath caressing my skin. His scent is unique —fresh yet musky, the notes deep, unfamiliar, stunning, dizzying. "You're close already. I don't know how much longer you will resist," he whispers, pouring his seductive poison into me. "The forces at work here are stronger than you are, or than I am, for that matter..."

I can't stop the whimper from evading me as he takes a step forward, his bulky frame pressing into me, the hard cock under his pants touching my abdomen, moving in gentle pulses that are both deviant and civilized—the devil attempting to be human. The movement is positively restrained in comparison to the rough way that Jack and Cameron grind and groan against me seconds before bending me over some object and ripping my clothes off so that they can fuck me.

That's part of the trap, Jessynia...

The fact that he restrains himself the way he does when I know what he wants to do to me.

Jessynia...

His thick hair caresses my face as he speaks. "You desire me despite all logic, despite all red flags telling you to run, don't you?" At my silence, he repeats the question roughly. "I think highly of you, Jessynia. I expect you to have the guts to admit the things you wouldn't to others."

"You're asking me to admit to things you already know full well, Sebastian," I spit back.

He lets out a low groan of satisfaction at the confession. "And why does that still make you feel ashamed?" he asks, referring to my previous answer to this same question.

"Because I'm *married!* To a man that you've *hurt!* You've hurt several people I care about. Do you think I'm proud that you have this power over me?!"

"Power?" he sneers. "This isn't about my power, Jessynia. This is about *yours.*"

"What are you talking about?"

"This is about you taking what you want for once, and not being baited by the pain of men who have not cared to spare you yours. You refuse to step into your power, your right to experience pleasure the way a woman like you should. It's pitiful to observe."

"You use that word a lot," I scowl.

"I yearn to set you free, Jessynia." He utters the last words violently, the force of his voice so palpable, so vulnerable for a composed man like him—a man who dominates every room he's in, who can infiltrate minds like no one else.

"Is that all you want for me?" I ask.

His hand winds around my neck and mine moves to pull it off... but I can't. "You know full well that I am at *war,*" he growls into my ear. "Two pieces of me wage war on each other day and night. Do you know the fucking torment of that, Jessynia? Do you understand what it means to desire something to the point of insanity while wishing to consummate the act by ripping that person to pieces?" I gasp and try to pull on his wrist, but he holds me firmly in place. "Do you know the hell of wanting to protect the thing you want to destroy? Do you understand the agony I feel every day that you torment my body and mind?"

"Stop!" I respond. "You're scaring me."

"You're not a coward, Jessynia. Nor are you afraid of the truth. You *will* hear me. You will hear what you do to me. You will hear the godforsaken *torment* I feel at being *near* you, at being apart from you, at your touch, at your absence. You will hear me despite your fear that what we share will become as inextricable for you as it is for me."

"I want them freed," I declare as loudly as I can muster. "For good."

"Is that the only reason you would give your body to me?"

"Yes," I say, willing myself to believe it.

The tremor of anger reverberates through his limbs and into my body—anger at my admission, or perhaps anger at my refusal to admit the truth about how dark my desires go.

A low growl emanates from this throat as his other hand slides onto my taut belly.

"Stop! White oak!"

Within seconds, both my arms are lifted into the air. In a frenetic movement that I feel but can't see, something clicks into place around one wrist, and then another. Chains jangle as I pull down furiously only to find my hands bound.

"Let me go!" I pull down but am stopped by the shackles. "I said the safe word!"

His lips slip against mine. "The safe word will stop you from being penetrated by me, Jessynia. Penetrated and *cut*. Nothing more."

"Well, I'm not consenting to either!"

"I don't force women," he counters, his voice a hoarse groan. "Such an act is forbidden by our Society... and by my code."

"I came here to talk to you," I insist. "Seriously."

"And this is how you'll do it."

"What, handcuffed to the fucking wall?"

"There is a price to pay for being with me."

"I can't talk like this!"

"Observing women tied up before me is nothing new to me."

I shake my head as the rage of jealousy surges through me at the words, causing my breathing to quicken and my face to burn hot. I feel him watching, knowing that he has caught me in the act, drinking in the unexpected shock and anger I feel at him conjuring up the women he's bound for his pleasure.

I can't feel that...

"You came here to speak to me. I want to hear it."

"I can't talk like this. It's not even comfortable," I protest, yanking down on the chains, to no effect.

"If you're *comfortable* with *me*"—he spits out the word as if it sickens him—"then you should start being *scared*. Now tell me what you want. What you came here for."

"I want them freed. For good. Both of them."

"Do you even give a fuck what happens to yourself in the process?"

"No. Not anymore. I want them freed from the Society permanently. They've given enough of their lives to this place. No more following them, no threatening them. They'll be banned, and left alone for good, as if they never existed."

He sniffs the skin over my jaw. "Why the fuck would I do that?"

"So that you can be free too," I respond, cringing at the platitudinous plea. "We *all* can."

"We don't see freedom in the same way, evidently."

"That's because you're still functioning from a place of trauma and abuse. I want to... talk about your mother again," I say, shaking my head internally at my woeful attempt to deconstruct this man's pain.

"Another therapy session?" he smiles. "I do so enjoy them."

"I want to heal you, Sebastian."

"And I want to *fuck* you, Jessynia." I gasp internally as my body begins to pulsate despite the ire singeing my cells. "That would help to heal me."

"Well, sorry, but in the meantime, you'll have to just go fuck *yourself*!" I respond, closing my eyes, breathing through my frustration, at the situation, at my own ineptitude, at the dark derision in his voice.

I don't know how to handle this man. I don't even fully trust myself around him. I want him to let them go, but I'm fighting something ancient and bitter and burnt that I have no idea how to negotiate with.

A minute passes as I breathe through my vexation at my own inadequacy, wondering what other options I have.

He once told me that men and women sometimes resist this place, resist allowing their spouses to fuck other people, before slowly coming around to the virtues of it and then reveling in its freedoms. Would it be easier to become like everyone else around here? To succumb to forces greater than me? To keep him placated that way?

Jack hasn't said a word about coming back to this place for weeks. He hasn't even hinted at it. I have to believe that he wants to finally be free as well...

I open my eyes to find two tears born of overwhelm falling from each eye, dripping down onto my jaw where they linger before tumbling onto my breasts, one of them soaking into the ghostly-pale fabric over my nipple.

"Why the tears?" he asks soberly.

"Why do you care?" I ask sharply. "Don't you get off on them?"

"Yes," he breathes out. "I do."

"How do you think that makes me feel?"

"You are designed to want to give pleasure to men like me. Fighting that reality is futile."

"I don't want you to get pleasure from my tears, for fuck's sake!"

"And yet, I do."

"And it pisses me off!" I exclaim. "It scares me."

"You're supposed to be fucking well scared. Now, why did you cry? Why now?"

"I... I don't know if you even want to try to heal or if you're just toying with me, if I'm just wasting my time to end up in the same position as before, or worse. I can't understand how your mind works."

"You wouldn't want to," he utters and my body shivers as if plunged into a desolate lake of icy water.

"Do you want to heal?"

"To be a better man?" he scoffs.

"You may mock me, Sebastian, but something bad is going to happen if we don't try to stop it. No good is gonna come of this war you insist on waging. Not for *anyone*, *including* yourself. At some point, you'll become too dangerous and someone will do something about it."

"Would you care?" he asks.

"Care? I'd be *devastated*. I don't want you *dead*, Sebastian."

"Your endless compassion... If anyone deserves *death*, Jessynia, it is *me*. What's more, as a rare educated empath, you know it."

"I'm trying to find some path that doesn't lead to that for *anyone*. Can you help me? Just... meet me halfway or something?"

"I believe I already indulge you sufficiently."

I want to ask him about his mother, his trauma, to untie him from it, to lighten the darkness, but I can't do it like this, chained to his wall. I have no power like this, no credibility. And he knows it...

"Unchain me, Sebastian. Please," I implore, trembling under the dark menace of forbidden pleasure hanging over us.

"I intend to."

With that, his lips slide to the side of my bare neck and he hesitates for a moment, as if readying himself to do something unnatural for him. After a moment during which my own heartbeat thuds through me like the unforgiving beat of a drum, his lips brush against my skin, and the gentlest of kisses is adorned on my neck... and then another... and another, the contact so tender that it causes my cells to tingle from my head to my core. My back arches a little at the sensation of this beast untying himself before me—dropping the mask he uses to keep his subs and his subjects in place.

Or pretending to...

His brutal body seems to quiver as he slides his mouth down my neck, falling into the crook between my neck and shoulder which he breathes in audibly, his breath hot, his respiration labored, as if he's not in control. He kisses me once... and then again... and finally, I pull against the chains as his tongue leaves his mouth and brushes my neck in one sinfully slow wet lash of velvet muscle.

"Sebastian," I pant.

"Say the safe word again, Jessynia, and I will stop."

Say it...

Say it...

His hand slides up my flank, his thumb skimming the side of my breast, straining against my body as if stopping himself from sliding onto it, from finding my taut nipples with his strong fingers.

God help me...

He breathes me in through his nose, the draw of air audible as he inhales the scent of my skin between my breast and my shoulder, freshly showered but most certainly misted in perspiration from my hour of verbal and quasi-physical foreplay with a man I feel powerless to fully resist.

I squirm as he inhales the smell of me.

"Don't be afraid," he whispers. "I can smell your scent, Jessynia, whether you wear clothes or not." He dips his head and licks the exposed skin to the side of my breast, releasing a loud groan of pleasure at tasting me. "I can taste you..."

My fingers wrap around the metal bars attached to the wall as the palm of his hand finds the top of my abdomen, sheathed as it is in a slip of ivory silk. The movement is slow, soft. His huge palm, with fingers fanned out to make a hand that feels almost as wide as my waist, makes a halting path down my taut belly. His fingertips press into my flesh, as if trying to feel what's underneath me—where my organs are, where my womb is, my ovaries, my cervix—or at least, that's what it feels like.

With eyes now accustomed to the dark, I take in the shadows cutting through his savagely beautiful face as he studies the body he's palpating.

Without warning, his eyes lift to mine as he presses into my lower abdomen with his fingers, trying to feel what's beneath the skin and muscle and silk separating his flesh from the intimate parts of my female body.

I know what he's thinking. I know from the numerous times that Cameron and Jack have demanded they be allowed to impregnate me, and from Sebastian's own admission of his desire to do the same, that he's imagining what it would be like to fertilize my body. To watch over me as I grew his child inside me.

The idea is utter insanity.

I'd never do it...

Jessynia...

Removing his hands from me, he asks, "If you didn't want to save them, would you care about saving me?"

"Yes," I respond.

"But you think of them, don't you? When you're with me."

"Yes." I feel his body go rigid. "Do you expect me not to?"

His glare flares at the question. "I'm not accustomed to women thinking of other men when they're in a room with me. Not even their husbands."

"There's a way to solve that, Sebastian. Let. Them. Go."

His head drops to the bottom of my jaw, his strong jaw brushing mine for a moment as his lips find my cheek, forcing me to grip the bars more tightly.

My nipples tighten into hard points as I pant through the proximity with this dangerous man who owns darkness in such a singular way.

"And what if I don't?" he whispers.

"Then I'll never consent. Nor will I be able to keep seeing you like this."

"Or maybe you will, Jessynia." His wet lips brush against my skin as his hand reaches for my bun and pulls it back, cranking my neck backwards.

"Stop!"

"I know what's happening to you. I know what's happening to your body. I can see it, Jessynia. I can taste you."

I whimper at the unabashed insinuation.

"Maybe you won't have the strength to stop it," he continues as he licks my bottom lip from left to right and back, doing the same to the top.

I close my eyes, trembling as he slowly pushes his large tongue inside my mouth. In the dark with my eyes closed, I see nothing; I feel nothing but the strong push of his wet muscle into my mouth. It enters slowly and fills me fully, moving before withdrawing from me, leaving me a panting mess.

It must take me over a minute to open my eyes, a minute during which there is silence but for my breaths. I feel him watching over me, studying me while knowing full well what is happening to my body. The knowledge of his mercy hangs over us.

My eyes meet his to find them unblinking, studying me curiously. "Shame? *Still?*" he murmurs, eyes drawing thin. "I see it will take a lot to rid you of it."

"Why wouldn't I feel it?" I shoot back, my voice small.

"Because you're not responsible for the way our bodies react to each other, Jessynia. Resisting something as powerful as *this* is beyond mortal control."

I flinch as his hand slides down the bottom of my arm, unwinding my fingers from the bar and drawing my hand towards him.

I know what he's doing...

I can't stop it...

White oak.

Say it...

A loud gasp emerges from my throat as my fingers collide with the hard ridge underneath the thin cotton of his pants. I feel the heat of his scrutiny as he slides my palm up and down his erection. I shiver internally at the feel of it, my eyes locked onto the glassy sheen of his, one of the few things I see in the near-black.

The thing is huge. I've never felt anything like it. It's thicker and longer than both Jack and Cameron who are already much bigger than average. And it's rock hard, as if made of smooth wood.

My mouth waters at the feel of it, and for a second, I feel the urge to drop to my knees.

But I don't...

I *won't.*

I will never do that.

He leads my hand down to cup his large sack, squeezing my fingers around him. God, the thing feels huge, firm, full. I whimper as he slides his hand backwards and forwards, curling my fingers around his sack as my sex begins to throb.

After a moment, he guides my palm back up to his thick, hard cock, the length of which I can't really believe despite having seen it before. It feels even bigger.

God...

"This is the state you leave me in from the second I see you to the second you leave me," he whispers. "What's more, I know your body endures the same torment when you are near me."

I swallow hard for what he's saying is true. My sex is wet from the moment I see him, constantly throbbing, pulsating, opening, aching for him.

I crave his penetration.

It feels like torture to resist.

But I'm going to resist...

"White Oak," I whisper, my eyes closing and then lifting to take his in.

He releases my hand instantly and I pull it away though the feel of him is imprinted on my palm and fingers.

My words are but a whisper. "I have to go home."

21

I take a deep breath as I glance up at the apartment building Gabriel gave me the address to on the far north edge of the Upper East Side. Its walls are of elegant pale stone, its windows bearing the types of frames you'd see in an apartment building in Paris.

After getting the cab driver to drop me off a few blocks away and spending five minutes darting across crosswalks, taking small side streets, and looking around and behind me constantly, I've felt confident that no one is following me.

Or at least, confident enough to muster up the strength to go inside. I can only pray that Sebastian never finds out, but then, somehow, I feel like he knows everything—my meetings with Cameron, my secret conversations with Gabriel. I feel watched and listened to everywhere I go, but I guess I don't feel as afraid I should. As delusional as I may be about him, I don't think he'd hurt me... Not now.

I scope out the quiet street a final time before dialing the buzzer number Gabriel gave me. A harsh buzz jolts me and I push the door open, shuddering in a ragged breath as I make my way to the elevator as instructed.

I peer at my reflection in the mirror inside. My eyes look huge today, popping out from the brush of mauve skin beneath them—the result of another sleepless night punctuated by nightmares that left me panting in the pitch black. My lips are chapped and I pull out the cherry lip balm from my pocket and apply it as I study the flush of pink caressing my cheeks.

I don't entirely know what I'm doing here...

I don't fully trust Gabriel, but I know enough about trauma to know that I can't keep this inside anymore. The nightmares where I see Sebastian caving the man's face in don't seem to be getting any better and sometimes whole days pass without me being able to think of anything else. I have to get it out...

Not to mention that my anxiety about Cameron follows me around like the most unrelenting of shadows. I'm determined to regain my strength and stability, but I clearly need help and going to a regular therapist to tell him stories of bloodlust and murder would probably not go down very well...

As I leave the elevator and look around the elegant landing, I hear the click of a lock.

"Over here." Gabriel's rich, confident voice steers me to the right. As I reach the corridor, I see him down to the left, one hand holding the door open as his eyes land on me, a smile on his face, albeit a muted one.

A small ripple of anxiety rolls through me as I see him—a man part of me fears, mistrusts... There's nothing in his expression or the way he holds himself that would suggest he's hiding anything. His stance is open and relaxed, his face warm, caring almost.

Maybe he's just a master manipulator. He's certainly been studying people long enough...

He puts a hand on my shoulder as I make it to the door. "It's good to see you," he smiles warmly, his curious brown eyes glistening.

I've never been able to get the image that I saw at Blackwood out of my mind—vines enveloping Gabriel's face, transforming into an obsidian mask that cloaked him like the bark of an ancient tree.

I never used to have visions or feel the presence of things that weren't really there before getting tangled up in that place. Sometimes I wonder if that place really has chipped away at my sanity...

"You too," I reply as he closes the front door behind me and opens the door to a closet next to it as I take off my coat and boots. As I place my boots against the wall, I notice an array of shoes inside the closet—both male and female, all expensive-looking.

I can only see the entranceway but the place is clearly worth millions, just based off its location and the sumptuous decor and the length of what I can see of the living room with its tall balcony door on the other side, cloaked in a frail tapestry of lace.

"Nice apartment," I say.

"It's not mine," he replies as I head towards the living room with him walking behind me. "We rented it for today."

My heart skips a beat. "We?" I ask as I turn around to face him.

He gestures towards the living room and I turn, walking with leaden feet a few more steps until the room opens up before me. I stop dead in my tracks at the sight of faces staring at me.

Francis.

Remi.

Charles.

Beth.

Nathan.

I turn back to look at Gabriel and he eyes me resolutely.

"You're an asshole, you know that?" I whisper.

"Oh, I know," he responds with a wry smile. "But we had to do this."

"We didn't mean to ambush you, Jess," says Francis as I turn back round to face her. "We just felt it would be safer for everyone if we do things this way."

Gabriel walks around me and gestures to an empty cream loveseat. My glare makes him smile as I take a moment before sitting down to face the resistance...or what's left of them. It's not that I don't want to see them. I just know that this would not be appreciated by Sebastian. Plus, after being ambushed several times over the last few months, I now have anxiety over entering new places and unexpected *surprises* like this don't exactly help matters.

I cast a glance over at Charles who smiles at me warmly, his eyes gleaming. I exhale in relief at the sight of him. I've wanted to speak to him for so long, to ask him how Cam really is, to have him reassure me that he's okay, but I've been too afraid to contact him.

Gabriel sits down next to me. "Do you want some tea?" he asks as my eyes drop to the clear glass teapot with loose tea leaves steeping at the bottom of the hot amber brew.

"Sure," I say and he reaches forward and pours tea into a small beige ceramic cup with no handle, placing it on a coaster closest to me. "Thank you."

My eyes wander to Beth. The last time I saw her, she seemed petrified, convinced that she couldn't trust Gabriel. Today, fear appears absent in her and her borderline-uncivil eye contact is making me feel uneasy...

What the fuck is she even doing here?

And don't get me started on Nathan who led me to a house where the Society's goons ambushed me not two weeks ago... He's eyeing me discourteously as always. The prick's consistent, I'll give him that. As per usual, his unflinching eye contact is doing little to soothe my malaise around him. What's more, he knows I don't trust him. He's too smart not to pick up on it. I know these people are the resistance. I know I'm supposed to put my faith in them, but at this point, I no longer know who to trust...

"How are you, Jess?" asks Remy, her long navy kaftan showing off her gorgeous curvy frame.

"I'm... a bit shaken, if you'll bear with me..."

She smiles warmly, her cocoa skin glistening as her cheeks plump. "We felt it was necessary."

"How do you know you weren't followed?" I ask.

"I checked," replies Charles. "So did a couple of our men. They're outside."

"Outside? I didn't see them."

"You weren't supposed to," he replies with that smile of his that always soothes me. "If you'd have seen them, we'd be having words with them..."

"How have you been?" repeats Francis.

"I've been—"

I pause. I don't really know an adjective that could fully convey the events of the last few months—the kidnappings, seeing Cameron being beaten, being taken back to my husband by coercion, being drugged, watching a man being beaten to death by another... "I don't mean to be rude, but... I honestly have no idea how to answer that, Francis," I respond. "Thanks for asking, though."

"We can't imagine how hard it must have been to leave Cameron like that," she replies. "You did the right thing."

"I did?" I reply. "I still feel tormented by it."

"You had no choice," replies Nathan and I frown as I lock eyes with him, glancing sub-consciously down at the top of his shirt. The last time I saw him, there was wavy blond hair clinging to it. I'm too far away to see this time.

"We just hope Jack didn't take what happened out on *you* when you returned," Remy says.

The memory of a glaring Jack mercilessly restaking his claim to me when I returned arrows through me...

But he did ask for consent. He always does. And honestly, I don't expect any less than what he is. I don't know if I'd want any less than his possessive dominance, however unhealthy that may seem.

"No more than what I expected," I reply and Charles drops his gaze as he lets out a deep breath.

"How have you guys been?" I ask, my eyes wandering slowly around faces that seem more concerned than the last time I saw them.

"We've..." Francis stops speaking.

"It's been a tricky few weeks," takes up Charlies. "Silas. Cameron. You. What happened with your return. It's shaken us all up."

"Charles, my family were—"

"We understand, Jess," he interrupts. "Not one person is judging you for what you had to do. We'd all have done the same."

Remy and Francis nod as I look down for a moment. "I'm so sorry about Silas. What did the medical examiner conclude?"

"Accidental overdose of insulin," responds Nate, "due to acute intoxication."

"Of what?"

"Heroin."

"What? Did he take heroin?" I ask, bringing the cup of tea to my lips in the hopes of quenching my sudden thirst.

"Not that any of us have ever seen," replies Remy.

"God… It must have been horrible to lose your friend like that," I suggest as I take in the thin lines etched into the pale skin surrounding Francis's intelligent blue eyes.

"It was," replies Charles. "We're still processing it."

"Of course," I reply, suddenly feeling the gaping hole left behind by Silas' bold, warm, soothing presence. "He was a wonderful man."

"He was," replies Francis. "He liked you a lot."

"Well, it was mutual," I smile.

"Jessynia," Francis continues and angst ricochets through me at the ominous way in which she says my name. "We wanted to talk about Cameron."

"Okay."

"Have you seen him?" asks Nathan. As I peer at him, I'm tempted to ask in front of everyone if he knew they were going to take me to that house in the woods after I saw him…

"We agreed we weren't going to ask that," chides Gabriel sternly.

"Well, sorry, but this isn't a joke anymore," counters Nathan. "The loss of Cameron to that place will mean the failure of the resistance. It will mean the fall of one of the most high-profile men in the city. It will change *everything*. Everything we've worked for will have been for nothing."

"I've told you before, Nathan," says Charles softly. "Cameron will *never* go back."

"I wish I had your confidence," replies Nathan, regarding me with circumspection.

"Have you guys not seen him at all?" I ask.

"No," replies Beth swiftly, her serial-killer eye contact still just as combative as ever despite the slight hollow under her eyes. In spite of the liberal application of make-up over her beautiful face, she looks almost as haunted as the last time I saw her when she acted as though she were being watched, hunted… "Except Aaron and

Charles, I believe. And Gabriel"—her cold eyes flit to him—"*of course.*"

God, the woman has about five different personalities, and just from her tone, I sense that today's is not the agreeable one.

"What's he been saying?" I ask, swallowing down my disquiet at the thought of Cameron being disconnected from people who were once so close to him...

"Not a great deal," replies Charles. "That's why we're concerned. He's never been this quiet, this... secretive..."

"I mean, you see him every day, right?" I ask Charles.

"No. I see him once a week if I'm lucky. He assigned me to Valentina and Evie. I'm not privy to everything he does anymore."

"Maybe he just needs some space," I suggest, aware how thin the idea is.

"There are dangerous people who want to hurt him, Jessynia," retorts Charles. "Being without proper protection is not what he needs right now."

"Sebastian won't hurt him for as long as I keep going back to that place, and stay with Jack."

"And Cameron won't tolerate you sacrificing yourself for him," replies Charles. "At some point, things will come to a head."

"Look, I'm trying my best to hold it all together as it is," I say. "I've been told of the consequences of seeing Cameron. I... I want to help him but, I just can't do what he wants me to."

"You could just talk to him," suggests Remy.

"I want to, Remy. I think of him all the time, but Sebastian made it clear that there would be consequences for that. I'll have to pay the price for them. My family. My friends."

"It can be done without him finding out," replies Francis. "Our biggest concern is Cameron going back to that place."

"He wouldn't do that," I retort, though my words ring hollow, for as I utter them, the recurring image that visits me in my dreams of Cameron, cloaked and masked, marching down the corridors of that place drifts into view. I see it clearly—his tall, solid body, the onyx mask covering his breathtaking face, the black cloak floating behind him as he enters a room to be serviced by any number of women who would treat him like the God he is. "He... he hates that place. Those people."

"Our concern is him returning to be close to you," says Gabriel.

"Sebastian would never allow that," I reply as a sharp ray of sunlight slips through a gap at the side of the lace veil over the window, hitting the huge golden-framed mirror behind Francis and Beth opposite me. "He hates Cameron. Why on Earth would he let him back?"

"Precisely because he *does* hate him," replies Nathan. "Sebastian likes nothing more than to watch the people that he destroys close up, to see the effects of his work on their face. We know you've seen him."

I glance around the room to meet looks of concern on the faces of some... and suspicion on the beautiful, angular face of Beth...

"How do you know that?" I ask.

"We can't tell you that. For your own safety," replies Francis.

"I'm sorry, but fuck that! I want to know!"

"It's not just about *your* safety, Jess," she adds softly and I realize that someone else may be at risk if she told me.

"What did he say to you?" asks Beth, her heavily lined jade-green eyes narrowing as she speaks.

Where do I begin?

"I... I'm trying to get him to leave Jack and Cameron alone for good."

Nathan shakes his head as if in contempt at the idea. "You're way out of your depth, Jessynia. You have no idea what you're playing at."

"I'm not *playing* at any—"

"He's not redeemable," warns Remy. "Not even close. We've seen him try to be saved once before. That person lost their life to the effort. You need to stop whatever you're doing. Now."

"And have Jack be his slave forever? And have him fantasize about Cameron's death until he finally snaps? I'm supposed to just sit back and let it happen, right? Well, sorry, but no fucking way."

"If you want to help," replies Nathan, "then you'll speak to Cameron. Give him some hope."

"False hope?" I scoff. "Would that really help?"

"Where there is life, there is hope, Jess," he adds. "We need him convinced to file the complaint against Alex, like he planned. Seven other men will do it if he will."

"What's stopping him?" I ask, afraid of the answer.

"You know what it is, Jess," replies Charles, his doe eyes laden with concern. "He's afraid that Sebastian will make him pay for it by hurting the person he loves the most. You."

"Would he?" I ask, my breathing shallow.

"Once the complaint has been made public, others will follow," says Francis. "The Society will be exposed and the scrutiny will be so strong that Sebastian won't be able to do anything. We'll protect you. Cameron will."

"And Jack?" I ask.

"Sebastian won't hurt Jack," replies Gabriel. "He enjoys his trauma too much for that..."

"There are no absolutes when it comes to Sebastian," I counter. "It's totally impossible to know how he'd react."

"We don't believe he'd hurt Jack."

"Unless he wants to hurt *me*. Punish me."

"Jessynia, you were once for Cameron speaking up," says Remy quizzically. "What's changed?"

Everything...

"It won't work unless he's committed," I answer. "He clearly isn't anymore..."

"Has Sebastian said he wants Cameron back?" asks Nathan.

"No," I respond. "He doesn't want that."

"How do you know?" asks Gabriel.

"It wouldn't make *any* sense. They hate each other."

Gabriel lets out a breath of frustration. "Sebastian doesn't choose his patrons based off how much he likes them. He does it based on how discreet they'll be, how powerful they are, how interesting, how much material he has on them, and how much fun it would be to toy with them. Him hating Cameron is no obstacle to having him be a member again."

"I'm going to ask him," I respond, riddled with fear at the very thought of Cam ending back up in the place he battled for so long to get away from.

"You shouldn't be seeing Sebastian at all," shoots back Francis, roughly scraping a lock of her auburn hair off her pale face with a slim hand adorned with a large ring, the top of it shaped into the head of a snake. "Nathan's right. You don't understand what you're getting yourself into."

"I'm not *getting* myself into it," I reply softly. "I was pulled into that place *months* ago. You don't just get to walk away. I can live like a prisoner, or try to do something to—"

"Fix him?" sneers Beth. "Fix the *devil*... You're so fucking naïve."

Christ, this woman has personality shifts that could give you whiplash. At the church she said she was pleased to see me. Today that's clearly not the case.

My eyes wander to Gabriel who is glaring at his lover. He turns to look at me, his eyes softening in a silent apology for his part-time girlfriend's brick-to-the-face delivery.

"I'm *not* naïve," I retort as boldly as I can. "I *know* very well what he is... but..."

"You think he's still human?" Beth spits out. "After everything he's done to Cameron... To you. To me. He is *irredeemable*."

The way she stretches out the word makes me want to challenge her to an impromptu boxing match, Brianna-style, starting immediately.

"Look, I'm not trying to invalidate or make excuses for the things he's done to the people in this room. There is no excuse for *any* of it. I know that, but... maybe the fact that everyone thinks he is beyond hope is part of the problem. He's been seen as some freak, some monster, since he was fourteen years old when he finally took out his abuser after years of being tortured while being abandoned by adults.

"Maybe having someone who actually *hears* him and believes him instead of writing him off will make things less... risky... for everyone. None of this has to be this dangerous. He's made the Society way more dangerous than it needs to be because, I don't know, maybe he's still driven by rage and a need to take control. If we can heal him somehow, some of that rage will dissipate, and things can get back to the way—"

"You sound like one of those fucking morons who write to men in prison," Beth spits back. "Thinking that the big bad man can be saved."

"*That's. Not. It,*" I exclaim firmly, shaking my head, ire surging through my body. "This isn't just about Sebastian. There are other people's lives at stake here, and I'm not just gonna sit back and do *nothing.*"

"Well, it doesn't look like you've accomplished much so far... apart from destroying Cameron."

"That's enough," warns Charles roughly, staring Beth down as her stilettoed fingertips wrap around the ends of the chair she's sitting on. "Jess saved Cameron's life, as he's told us repeatedly. She's never tried to hurt him. He knows the threats she's living under."

Don't cry...

I feel my eyes burn hot at the assault of her merciless words. My stomach aches as I think of Cam. His pain. The consequences of everything that's happened. I can take my own pain, but the thought of his... or of Jack's, for that matter... is unbearable.

"Why am I here?" I finally ask, squaring my shoulders, refusing to be beaten down by a woman who can't extricate herself from victimhood or seem to tolerate anyone who doesn't want to meet her in that space. I can't allow her poisonous bitterness to affect what I know can be accomplished... or hope, at least.

"We're asking you to open some line of communication with Cameron," says Remy. "To keep him from losing himself. From going back to them."

"He would never go back," I insist.

"They've reached out to him." Gabriel's rich voice next to me rumbles in my chest. "He's considering it."

"What?! Why?!" I ask.

"To be near you. To stop the pain," suggests Gabriel. "To protect you from them."

"Or maybe"—Beth's vibrant eyes glow as she stares me down—"he's as naïve as *you*, and thinks that he can do something to tame the *devil.*

Outwit him. Or maybe," she smirks contemptuously, "he's just finally facing reality and embracing his inner freak. Perhaps he's come to accept that he likes being treated like *God* with a harem of submissive little whores he gets to fuck as roughly as he—"

"That's enough!" interjects Charles, the only time I've ever heard him raise his voice. "We didn't come for this! We're trying to find solutions here. We're not losing Cameron. And he *won't* go back."

The room is encased in silence so heavy that I almost want to get up and leave. These meetings have never been pleasant but the group is clearly now fractured, and without the graceful but soothing power of Cameron and Silas, and with Beth clearly rattled by my presence, it feels like the resistance is hanging on by a thread.

Swallowing down what Beth said about me, about Cameron, I decide to speak to break the intolerable silence. "Does he not talk to you at all anymore?" I ask Charles again.

"Not about anything personal. Sometimes I don't hear from him for days. It hasn't been that way for years. The last time was when..."

"He was back there," I suggest.

"Yes. When he was still a patron."

"What do you want me to do?" I ask.

"Can you talk to him? Just a little? Just enough to keep him sane?" asks Nathan.

"What if Sebastian finds out? What if he takes it out on my family like he threatened?"

"We don't believe that's a credible threat," replies Nathan.

"They set fire to my godmother's house, for fuck's sake! They had my brother followed. They drugged him!"

"Things have changed," replies Francis.

"How, exactly?" Jess asks.

"They did that to get you back," she answers. "You *are* back. Sebastian and you have grown... closer... since then. We don't believe he would sabotage that by hurting your family. Plus, the Council would never agree to it."

"Look what they did to Cameron's father... and—" I take a deep breath as I conjure up Gabriel's father, and the fresh wound of Silas. "I'm sorry."

"It's okay," Gabriel replies, watching me with gentle eyes.

"I'm just... so worried about— I'd never recover if they hurt my family."

"Joseph and Luca were actively trying to take the Council down, Jessynia," says Francis. "It's not the same."

"Look, sorry, but they set fire to a house for fuck's sake."

"It was a warning designed to stoke fear," says Nathan. "It worked. If they'd wanted to harm your family, they could have done so. Easily."

"And the Council will never approve of any actions that could truly harm your family, in our opinion," adds Remy. "We know the vote to intimidate you into returning only just snuck through on the proviso that your family will not come to real harm. He won't try it again."

"They voted on that?!" I exclaim, sitting up in a snap. "Are you serious?! What is wrong with these people?!"

"It's not the full Council," says Remy. "It's the inner sanctum. There's only about thirteen of them. The full Council has thirty members. The inner circle all have unclean hands. They're rabid in their loyalty. They trust each other. They are all deviant people to varying degrees. They take care of matters which it may be unsafe to let everyone know about."

"And they voted to burn down my godmother's fucking house?!"

"From what we've been able to ascertain, they voted to allow Sebastian to order his men to use non-lethal methods to procure your return, including intimidation towards your family. They were not informed of the methods to be used."

As if blood were spilling from me, I weaken once again at the thought of it. He allowed that to happen... He allowed them to set that fucking fire. He allowed them to drug my brother! Sometimes I forget, caught in the web of a presence so unique, of torment so raw, that I don't process the horrors he's capable of.

He has to pay for it...

I turn to look at Gabriel, needing the soothing awareness of this insightful therapist, but find him staring absently at the mirror behind

Francis. Noticing my gaze, he turns to look at me. "Are you okay?" he asks.

"Yeah," I respond. "It's just... I forget sometimes the gravity of what has happened."

"It's trauma, Jessynia. The mind will find a hundred and one ways to circumvent or paint over horrific memories such as this. We all do it. It's how we manage to make sense of life, to move on."

I nod, picturing Sebastian's face as the first flames took hold. Did he know what they'd do? Did he approve it? Did he take pleasure in the carnage? Did it pain him to pain me? Was it *him*? Was it that thing inside him? I could drive myself nuts thinking about it.

He's going to give me some answers...

"What do you want me to do?" I ask again. "If Sebastian finds out I've spoken to Cameron, he won't trust me anymore. It'll undo everything I'm trying to do."

"He won't find out," counters Nathan. "Cameron is discreet when it comes to you. He only speaks of you to those he trusts."

"Including Christian and Aaron?" I ask.

"You don't trust them?" asks Charles.

"I... I don't always know who to trust."

"The Society are very good at making people question their sanity," returns Francis softly. "At making us paranoid. Making us distrust each other. I've watched it for years, Jess. Most of the time, it's nothing but games and traps, ways to divide us. We have to be careful not to succumb to that urge and push everyone away out of fear."

"Me speaking to him will just keep him *stuck*. I don't want that for him. I want him to... move on somehow."

"You not speaking to him won't untie you," says Remy. "You haunt his every waking moment, Jess. I'm not sure if there's any doubt in any of our minds about that." She glances around the room to the sight of Charles and Gabriel shaking their heads.

My gaze is drawn to Beth who I've felt watching me in silence for way too long.

What the fuck is wrong with you? I feel like asking her. I've always tried to be nice to the woman. I've overlooked God knows how many of her outbursts, have tolerated more of her mood swings than I can count, have tried to be understanding of what she's been through. And I'm trying my best to get Cameron out of that place for good. But I don't think her anger has much to do with Cameron. God knows what it is but the bitter bite to her countenance crawls through me every time I look up at her wide green eyes.

"For as long as you're in his life, he'll fight," adds Francis. "Without you, he'll be drawn to the darkness inside him so much that he won't know how to resist anymore. We need your help, Jess. We can't watch this man fall to them. They'll become so powerful that nothing we do will stop them."

"I can speak to him," I finally sigh out. "But I can't see him. It's too risky. It'll undo all my work with Sebastian."

Francis nods. "Very well."

Half an hour later, I peer into Charles' soulful brown eyes as he puts on his coat and turns to face me. He's the last to leave Gabriel's apartment and I can't help but want to ask him things I couldn't ask in front of the others.

"Will you tell Cam you saw me?" I ask.

"Would you rather I didn't?"

"I don't know. I guess I'll... leave it up to your judgment."

He smiles. "It's wonderful to see you, Jess. I know the last couple of months have been rough."

"Is he really doing as badly as they say?"

"He's... not himself," he replies.

"God. I hate that," I shudder out before taking a deep breath. "Charles..."

"Yes."

"I have a number. It's a private one. It has to be kept very secret. I can't check it often but... if something is really wrong with Cam, if he looks like he's really going off track or something, can you text me?"

"Of course."

He takes out his phone and I plug the number into it.

"Don't store it under my name," I say as he takes it back and names the number LD.

"Little dragon," he smiles and I break out into the first grin I've been capable of since I got here as he recalls the anecdote we once shared about my father's nickname for me as a child.

"Bye," I say as I envelop him in as tight a hug as I can.

"Be careful, young lady. Men can be... tricky. And the trick is... never listen to them. Their words can be... deceiving, intoxicating... Just watch their actions very carefully. That'll tell you all you need to know. I mean, *I* know. I *am* one."

I smile despite the sorrow I feel as he says it and he reciprocates at having lifted my spirits.

"Goodbye, Charles."

"Bye."

After closing the door behind him, I walk back through the living room to no sight of Gabriel. To be honest I'm emotionally drained and not even sure I can make it through what I wanted to talk to him about. One thing I am thankful for, at least, is that he seemed warm and kind towards me, his expression brimming with concern. He's a bit blunt and kind of a prick at times, but beneath that, he's always been caring, seeming to want the best for me and for Cam.

Maybe that vision of him in the mask was nothing more than my traumatized mind playing tricks on me after seeing Cameron be beaten in front of my eyes. I feel like I've been seeing ghouls and goblins around every corner for months...

"Gabriel?" I shout out to the sound of a clang somewhere.

"I'm in the kitchen! Just making some fresh tea. Won't be a minute."

"Do you need any help?"

"Nope! Make yourself at home."

I wander around the apartment, glancing at its clean modern furniture, typical of service apartments. I head over to the huge mirror, peering at my ashen reflection for a moment before meandering slowly towards the window. I look out onto the street down below to see Nathan talking to a man in front of a car. I don't recognize him but as I watch the pair, I decide to ask Nathan that question I wanted to ask before and didn't dare to in front of the others.

"I'll be back in a minute!" I shout, not waiting for an answer as I rush out without my coat and find the elevator already on the same floor.

As I make it outside, I walk to where they were conversing only to see the man getting into his car as Nathan walks away.

"Hey," I shout out, getting him to turn around after my second shout. I run up to him, breathless as he watches me, hands deep in his pockets.

"Weren't you supposed to leave through the underground garage?" I ask.

"If the Society want to have us followed, they will do, Jessynia."

"Great attitude," I mutter to a rare half-smile from him.

"I have a meeting in twenty minutes. I need to be downtown."

"Okay... It's just... I..."

He raises a brow at my spectacular inarticulation and I take a deep breath and just do it...

"When we met the other week... after you left... men from QN turned up. They—" I stop myself from telling him the full story of how I was drugged and taken from that place for fear that he'll repeat it to Cameron.

His brow furrows in concern. "I didn't know that, Jessynia. What happened?"

"They just... were waiting for me. Did you see them when you left?"

"*Of course* not," he answers roughly. "Did you leave just after me?"

I think back to the conversation I had with Gabriel. It couldn't have lasted more than ten minutes. "Ten-fifteen minutes at the most."

"Fuck," he shudders out. "I'm sorry. I had no idea. Did they hurt you?"

I feel like I spend my life denying that I've been hurt. "No," I reply.

"I'm sorry. I really didn't know."

I search his eyes, deep and blue, piercing, appraising me. "Okay."

"I would feel a little insulted that you would even doubt me that much, but I guess I haven't been overly welcoming to you..."

"No. You haven't," I respond, shooting back a daring glare at the man who has been an asshole since the first day I met him.

"I'm sorry, I'm... naturally suspicious of strangers. I'll try to be more hospitable in the future."

"Less glaring would be nice," I mutter and he smiles. "Nathan, I don't want Cameron knowing about me being... taken. He can be a bit... fiery. I don't want him doing something stupid."

"Well, he's not taken my calls for weeks, so I have no real way of telling him."

"What, still?"

He nods slowly.

"Fuck," I sigh out, my gaze falling to the lapel of his jacket for a moment—no long hairs on it this time. "I'll call him. See if I can't talk him around."

"We'd all appreciate that, Jess."

A few minutes later as I'm about to press the buzzer to get back into the apartment, I jump as a woman steps out just as my fingers hit the intercom buttons.

"Oops, sorry," she sings as she sees me jump.

"No worries," I smile and head inside as she holds the door open for me.

Getting up to the fourth floor, I head to the apartment, opening the door and taking off my shoes, locking the door behind me. As I walk in, I see a steaming pot of tea on the table and peer around the room, hearing what sounds like a voice.

A few moments later, the sound of a door opening has me turning to face Gabriel.

"Sorry," he says. "A patient. Had to make a quick call."

"Do you want me to leave you to it?"

"No. I want you to sit down and talk to me, Jessynia. I know you wouldn't have called me unless it was something serious."

"Yeah, but... maybe we've been through enough for one day. It was kind of... intense back then."

"These meetings always are," he replies.

"Always?"

He nods slowly, gesturing for me to sit back on the loveseat I was on before. He takes up Francis's seat and pours me some tea into what looks like clean cups.

"What the hell was up with Beth today?" I ask.

"Who knows?" he shrugs. "Her moods change like the tide. Something may have upset her, rattled her."

"Why does she look at me like that?"

"I suspect that it's because you are everything she wants to be, Jess. Life hasn't been fair to her. It makes people bitter."

"Yeah, well, my life hasn't always been a bed of roses, Gabriel."

"Oh, I know that, but jealousy is not always rational."

"Bitterness is not a pleasant path to walk on every day, is it?"

"No. It certainly isn't."

22

Gabriel

I watch in silence as she brings the cup up to her pink lips and takes a sip, placing it back down on the coaster.

"It's so good," she says.

"Cameron had it sent to me. He always has the best teas."

"When?" she asks.

"Oh, a few months ago."

"Oh," she sighs out. "Gabriel, are you sure we should do this?"

"Do *what* exactly?" I ask, a wry smile tugging at my lips.

She shakes her head and shoots me a flat look, blinking slowly to signal how unimpressed she is with my shenanigans.

"I knew you'd be an indecent therapist," she moans to my grin.

"I'm playing with you, Jess. Trying to get you to relax. The last hour has been..."

"Tense?" she suggests and I nod with a smile.

"You wanted to see me. I know it wouldn't be for no reason. Why?"

She lets out a slow, audible breath. "I don't even know where to start..."

"How about... life at home... Jack. How has he behaved of late?"

"Perfect," she replies, a tinge of sorrow hiding in her eyes. "It's like he's a new man."

"And yet you can't forgive him."

"I'm trying. I really am trying. I just... can't quite fully forget the sight of him and Alex, and... how he got me back."

"But you love him for it, don't you? For the brutality of his possessiveness..."

"Yes," she admits, dropping her head. "I really hate to be that person, but, yeah. I know who he is. I know how he operates. And... he's special, Gabriel. Strong, smart, protective, passionate. He's overcome so much in his life, things that would have broken a lesser man. He's *so much more* than the worst things he's done, and he's never hidden who he was from me, since the very start."

"How does that make you feel? That you like how possessive he can be."

"Part of me hates that I like it. I'm smarter than that."

"It has nothing to do with being smart. As much as it will irritate the hell out of you, Jess, women have been attracted to dangerous men since the dawn of time because women are more physically vulnerable and have always required protection. Dominant, aggressive men are better at that than the weak men, the tame men. You are designed to want him like that. There's nothing to be ashamed about there."

"Well, I have some radical feminist friends I'd advise you not to repeat that to," she jests to my chuckle of amusement.

"What else do you feel?" I finally ask.

Her huge eyes dart all over my face. "I feel... guilt over Cameron... The way I left him was... like something out of a horror movie. I still can't believe I did it."

"You had no choice."

"I think it made him bitter, angry," she says, frowning at me. "That's the part that scares me."

"You're not responsible for his actions, Jessynia."

"No, but we can push people, can't we? Edge them onto the wrong path. I feel like I've done that. It torments me. I just wish he'd forget about me and move on from that place..."

"I hate to break the news to you, but that won't happen, especially now that you're entangled in that place. His need to protect you is very strong. It's primal. He can't detach from it. He's not going to walk away."

"Great," I sigh out. "How is he, Gabriel? Really?"

Oh, he won't be pleased with that question...

Not one bit.

"Like the others said, he's... not in a good place. And not communicating much."

"Is he still having nightmares?"

"He's had them for as long as I can remember. I don't believe they've stopped."

"Are they worse now?"

"They're bad," I reply, knowing full well that they are just as violent as before. "Do you miss him?"

She nods solemnly. "I can handle missing him. What I can't handle is the anxiety. I worry about him all the time."

"Worrying seldom helps."

"What else am I supposed to do? I can't fix this problem. I can't see him or help him through it. Do I switch off my feelings? Drink it away or something?"

"Speaking to him will help."

"Until Sebastian finds out..."

"Maybe he'll be more *lenient* than you think. You've bonded a lot. I don't think he would hurt you in the same way he was once capable of."

"He shouldn't have to hurt *anyone ever* again. He thinks that's part of life. Some strange currency for navigating his existence. It isn't."

"And you're determined to teach him that lesson?" I suggest.

"Look, people may criticize it or call me naïve, but in the meantime, I'm trying to do *something* to heal the man."

"Why do you want him healed?"

"Why do you *think*, Gabriel? He keeps hurting people, imprisoning them. He's only hurting himself in the process, staying in darkness."

"Maybe that's where he fits. He belongs. Do we all need to live in the light? Isn't that a bit tedious?"

I take her in for a moment as she watches me in sober but comfortable silence, contemplating my words. She has this quality about her—it's easy to be in her company. Her aura is vibrant, her disposition fiery at times but gentle at others, and compassionate to the point of foolishness. She's not afraid of eye contact, nor of telling you when you're pissing her off, and yet I've never seen her try to hurt anyone the way those at the Society do as a matter of course.

I can't help but glance down at her body as she settles into the chair—her tight T-shirt showing off her large round tits and slim waist. A knitted cardigan falls onto her snug navy-blue jeans. With her hair pulled into a bun, I observe three silver hoops in each lobe of her ear and for an imprudent moment, my tongue aches to slip against the shell of it...

"Do you think he's capable of it?" she asks. "Sebastian."

"Capable of what?"

"Of living a normal—" She stops herself, sighing out at the banality of the word, at the naivety of the concept—Sebastian Gravier becoming *domesticated.*

"Do *you*?" I ask.

"I don't know."

"Even if he could control himself," I say, "would it last forever? Would it break him to finally face the horror of his childhood?"

"People face their trauma all the time," she replies. "It doesn't have to *break* them. There are resources out there. He has more money than he could ever spend. If he put it into trauma therapy—" She pauses as she observes my flat expression. "I don't want to sound like some fucking moron, Gabriel, *believe* me, but... there has to be hope, surely? Or is hope now some stupid concept that only the foolish still hold onto?"

"Where there's life, there's hope." My absent delivery of the motto has her body bristling. Even when she's frail, there's a strength there—it's quiet but bold. You feel it. It's quite intoxicating...

Her eyes drop to the black cushion she's cradling on her thighs. I know what she's thinking...

"I don't think Cam is the only thing you came to talk about, Jess..."

I watch her chest rise and fall heavily for a few moments, imagining what she must look like beneath her clothes, what it must be like to suck on her tits, how Cameron must have reveled in her body...

"I... need to talk about something that happened... I can't keep it inside anymore."

"That's why I'm here," I reply, waiting until she has the guts to lift her gaze to mine.

"This is different," she replies. "It's... a... criminal matter. I need to be certain you'll never repeat what I say to anyone. I mean, to the authorities..."

"Jessynia, I can assure you that I do not want to arouse the Society's wrath... and I most *definitely* don't want to arouse *yours*. I'm not sure which is scarier."

She smiles at my attempt to lighten the atmosphere. "Promise? You won't tell Cameron? Or *anyone*?"

I nod slowly. "You have my word."

She shudders in a weighty breath. "Someone... once... tried to... *hurt* me." She gulps down the words, taking a moment to compose herself. "When I was younger. A man. Junior year of high school."

I take a moment to breathe, watching the light in her eyes dim for just a while. "I'm very sorry to hear that, Jess. You didn't deserve that."

"The Society found out about it... somehow. *Sebastian* did." She breathes through the words and I sit, unmoving, as she does, providing her the quiet, safe space that she needs. Her stunning face loses its color and her plump lips—always naturally pink—fall pale under the shadow of memories that must have caused her trauma throughout her life.

"What happened?"

"I... watched... a beating. I was made to watch it. It was... There was... *blood*." A tear pools on her waterline, spilling quickly over onto her cheek. I reach for the box of tissues on the table, holding it out to her. She takes one and wipes away a tear trickling down her breathtaking face.

He will be pleased with that...

"A beating?" I repeat.

"Yes. It was bad."

"How bad?"

"Very," she replies. "I... I can't really get it out of my head."

"I'm glad that you're telling me. Seeing a brutal beating would cause a trauma response in anyone. You need to get this out, Jess. Talk about it."

"The only person I can talk about it with is Sebastian."

"Why not Jack?"

"Jack doesn't know about any of it... and I can't have him get into some fight with Sebastian over it."

"Hmm. Your desire to protect your husband never seems to abate."

"Will they leave me, Gabriel? The visions? The sounds? I feel like I've journeyed into hell or something, seen things I can't process."

"It will never leave you completely, but it will become less overwhelming with time. It won't stop you from functioning."

"Are you sure?" she asks, peering at me so intently that it's hard not to get distracted by the plea in those bright turquoise eyes. "I'm so afraid of being stuck like this forever."

"I'm certain."

"Okay," she sighs. "I just needed to know that. Is there a way I can process it better?"

"Talk about it. Don't keep it inside, whatever you do. Don't internalize it. If it gets bad, then contact me. You shouldn't have to rely on *him*. That may not be safe for you." I scratch my chin slowly. "Did you contemplate calling the police?"

"No," she says swiftly.

"Why not?"

"I..."

"Trying to protect him?" I suggest.

"He did it for me... in a way..."

Fuck...

Her gaze jumps to the door behind me at the sound of something falling... or hitting something. She slides her gaze onto me, peering at me quizzically.

"Is someone here?" she asks.

"No," I reply flatly.

She takes a moment to contemplate my answer before getting to her feet with a jolt.

"Jessynia..."

She pays me no heed, marching to the bedroom, opening the door without asking. I get up slowly and follow her, listening as she opens the closet door and peers inside before heading into the en-suite bathroom, flinging its door open fast.

The apartment we're in is furnished but sparsely and the box spring of the bed goes all the way to the floor, leaving nowhere for anyone to hide... unless you know of that latch behind me that allows the bedroom mirror to pivot on its hinges and reveal a room next to the closet, out of sight...

She stands there for a moment, staring into the empty bathroom, before dropping her head, her body deflating.

I can hear her breaths.

She turns around stiffly. "I'm sorry," she says with a shake of the head, her skin ghostly pale, her demeanor visibly shaken. Her eyes, brimming with contrition, finally meet mine. "I'm so sorry, Gabriel. I... It's not you. I'm just... so paranoid these days." The beautiful desolation in her face is impossible not to be moved by. "I'm gonna go," she announces pitifully, brushing past me back through the doorway of the bedroom.

"You don't have to go, Jess." I follow her out as she makes a beeline for the front door. "Jess..."

She grabs her coat and as I reach her, I wrap my fingers around her slim wrist, the contact with her exposed skin jolting me more than I'd expected it to. For a second, I feel the presence of Cameron, as if channeling him, understanding the heat he burns with when he touches her, his relentless need to fuck her.

"Jess, look at me."

She lifts solemn, glistening eyes to mine.

"It's okay," I say with as pacifying a voice as I can muster up, my years of being a therapist and soothing the distressed coming in handy as they always do. I know how to make people feel safe. "I understand the paranoia. I've been there. No longer trusting my friends, my family even. I get it, Jess. I'm not offended. I would be worried if you weren't suspicious of those around you after everything you've been through."

I let go of her wrist, restraining myself from tucking a loose strand of her silken brown hair behind her ear. I harden at the bereft innocence in her incomparably beautiful face. She looks like a doll—huge, soulful blue-green eyes, a button of a nose, perfectly sculpted plump lips, and high cheekbones, always brushed with a hint of pink. It's impossible to look at her and not imagine gripping her long hair and sliding your cock into her mouth as she looks up at you.

What's more, she doesn't seem to fully comprehend her beauty, which, of course, makes her all the more exquisite. She's rare. Some lone fucking flower, delicate, rich in color, breathtaking, that you can't help but touch despite knowing the contact will destroy the pristine petals, will make them fall to the ground, to disintegrate...

"You came here because you needed to talk through some stuff. I'm here for you, Jess. You don't want this trapped inside, believe me. That's how the nightmares start. That's how we start to lose control of our minds." A tear tumbles onto her cheek, a glistening droplet of dew hanging from the petal of a flower. "I don't want that for you," I say, aware of how nauseatingly earnest I sound. "Let's finish," I say. "I don't want you going back home without having got some of this out. That's how people end up drinking or doing something stupid..."

After a moment, she puts her coat back on the hanger. Shame hangs between us—hers. I can make use of it.

"I need to use the washroom," she says.

I point her to the hallway just past the kitchen.

"Thanks," she utters, her voice frailer. I know her. She'll be consumed by guilt as she often is, more often than not unjustifiably. It'll weaken her. Make her more vulnerable. More in need of strength. I'll give it to her...

As she heads down the hallway and into the guest washroom, closing the door behind her, I make my way into the bedroom, closing and locking the door behind me with the simple click of an almost-silent button on the black handle.

I walk past the closet and flip a latch on the side of the tall mirror. It opens on its hinges and I step inside a vertical hole in the wall behind it to see him standing before the mirror, staring out onto the empty living room.

He doesn't flinch as I step into the hidden room built into the wall to the left of the closet, nor turn to look at me. I walk over to him, taking in his stern profile.

My eyes pan down to his white shirt which sheathes muscles that always seem to get bigger. I know that he works out more when he's aggravated. She does that to him—or rather her defiance, her resistance do, as much as he enjoys the challenge of them.

I glance down at the woman at his feet—kneeling up, hands bound behind her back, facing the one-way mirror allowing him to see into the living room. The air vents between the living room and this one allow him to hear what is being said. They also allow any accidental noises to come through from here to the other side...

His sub's face is pink, clashing with her light blond hair and her black dress. His fingers are wound around her neck, squeezing and then letting go for his pleasure.

Another of his many subs. Though this one is certainly more useful than most...

These women would happily be choked to the verge of death to satisfy him. He has power with women that rivals that which even Cameron yields... They drop to their knees with one look from him. I've seen it dozens of times.

Maybe that's why he yearns for Jessynia so recklessly.

She challenges him, rejects him, insists on knowing him before allowing him to touch her. I doubt he's experienced that before...

"What else do you want from the session?" I ask softly into his profile as he glares through the glass, his thick hair tied into a neat bun at the back of his head.

"Make her admit her desire," he responds.

"Very well."

He turns his head slowly to face me, his silver-hued eyes burning in that singular way of his—wild, reptilian almost. He grabs the blond ponytail of his sub and lifts it, yanking her head to the side for no reason other than he requires submission. It dehumanizes him and those around him—which is how he likes things... *usually*. He hates to feel human, and yet, that is how Jessynia needs him to feel...

"I want to see her tears," he utters grimly. "Understood?"

I bow my head to the distant click of a door handle being turned and a door opened, and then... she appears, walking into the room, her shoulders tight, her expression forlorn. I know she's crippled with guilt over not trusting me. He'll like that. It will make her more vulnerable, less able to show attitude.

From the side, I see his eyes widen as he watches her, unblinking, tracking her as she sits down in the same loveseat as before, seeming to stare down at the ring on her wedding finger, unwittingly facing the man who has the view that he so desperately wants on the object of his obsession.

Without a word, I leave the hidden room, turning momentarily to see Sebastian pull the woman around to face him. She drops down, her ass hitting the back of her feet as she opens her mouth for him. I swing the mirror back against the wall, lock the clasp on the side and leave the bedroom.

He'll be pleased about the gleam of the tear still glistening in her eyes—the glossy film showing she must have shed a tear in the washroom. She feels things deeply. It's what makes her so exquisite, and also such a delicious target for men like Sebastian.

I take a seat opposite her in a chair that doesn't obstruct any part of his view, reach forward, and pour some still-steaming mint tea into her cup. She takes it and gulps some down, the muscles in her throat contracting beautifully as she does so...

Lifting her eyes, she utters, "I'm so sorry, Gabriel. It honestly isn't you. I'm just... paranoid about everything."

"I told you. Don't apologize," I smile. "I've been there. They're experts in making people question their sanity."

"Was it always like that?" she asks.

"To some degree, but... not like this. People weren't afraid before, or at least not for a hundred years or so."

"Was it Sebastian who made the place this dangerous?"

I contemplate the answer I'll give.

Sebastian informed me before the resistance arrived that he doesn't want him diluted in her mind. He wants her to succumb to him despite knowing his malevolence, his craving for misery and suffering, his pathological need for control. He needs her to cave to her desire for him without him needing to water down who he is. Artifice repulses him; to seduce her while concealing the demons that consume him, while putting on some odious mask of civility, would be a failure he won't want to resort to. He wants the perfect union of extremes: the angel willingly submitting to the devil, unable to resist despite knowing the purgatory he comes from, the purgatory he will carry her to.

He could have seduced her before—there is no woman who can resist that man, or none that I've seen—but he wants to fuck a woman he owns fully, not one consumed by her need to protect other men.

I'm not so sure she'll comply any other way. I have no doubt about how overwhelming her desire for him is, but her love for Jack, for Cameron, it'll stop her... unless... she feels that it is Sebastian protecting her from either one. Her craving for safety has possession of the most primal parts of her psyche. If Cameron were to become someone she fears, she might just take refuge in the devil who designed him...

It's a shortcut that may just be palatable enough for Sebastian. And if Cameron keeps going the way he is, she may just need protection from him after all... or at least, that's how things may appear...

"Yes," I reply, taking a sip of tea and placing the empty cup down onto a metal coaster on the table. "He made it more dangerous than it had been for generations."

"Why?" she asks.

"The way he runs the Society is a manifestation of how his mind works. He sees the world in black and white. Dominance and submission, pleasure and pain, power and weakness..."

"Good and evil?" she suggests and I bow my head. "Does he think he's evil?"

"Do *you*?" I ask.

"He's done some evil things."

"That's not what I asked."

"I don't know, Gabriel. He was abused throughout his childhood. He learned that adults won't save him from horror. He learned that the world is cruel and unfair, even to the most innocent."

"*Especially* to the most innocent," I correct, leaning back in my chair, aware that Sebastian's keen metal-flecked eyes will be soaking in every movement of her candid face, every drop of her eyes, every time her finger wanders unconsciously to her wedding ring, rubbing it as if to soothe herself. He wants her peeled apart layer by layer, but she's afraid of opening up fully to me. I need her more vulnerable than this. "You have a need to make men redeemable, Jessynia. It's been quite problematic for you."

"Not *all* men."

"No. But the three men you're involved with now..."

"I'm not invo—" She stops, lowering her gaze as reality hits her—that she is owned by three men and not just the one whose ring she wears on her finger.

"Does the world feel safer when you can make them all civilized?"

"You can't compare Jack and Cameron to Sebastian."

I arch a brow. "I've known both longer than you, Cameron much more than Jack, of course. They're no boy scouts. Cameron has a... questionable side, as you well know. How does that make you feel?"

"I *hate* that side of him. I hate that it exists. I know the pain behind it."

"Hmm..."

"What?"

"Cameron O'Neill. A billionaire god. Leaning into his dominance. His dark side. Most women would sell their souls for a night with that particular beast, Jessynia. Do you expect me to believe you don't secretly crave him that way?"

Her lips part and her eyes widen in incredulity. I know Sebastian won't be pleased to hear of her desire for Cameron O'Neill, but I need her to begin to normalize her lust for powerful, damaged men like these. Her resistance to it is not serving anyone here.

"I... I want him to be *healthy*, Gabriel," she snaps, her spine bolting upright and her gaze turning into a glare of affrontment. "I want him to be *healthy* and *safe* and *happy*. I couldn't care less how hot his so-called dom side is. He can explore that when he's doing well. I don't want him broken and damaged, for fuck's sake..."

"I'm not suggesting you do. I know you care for him deeply, but I'm struggling to believe you aren't drawn to the darkness in him. I've never seen a woman who could resist him when he's tormented and needs the most abject submission."

Her glower eats into me. "Gabriel. I want him to be *well*. I don't care about anything else!"

"And yet, you spend time with two men who have hurt him greatly..."

Her ire dissipates and her face softens as I confront her with reality. "I... I didn't know the full extent of his issues with Jack when I got together with him. And as for Sebastian, I'm trying to free Cam and Jack from him."

"Isn't that a bit naïve, even to your own ears?" I suggest.

"Yes. You're right. It is naïve. I feel like a fucking idiot every time I say it, or attempt it. But I either attempt to help him heal or I do absolutely nothing. And you know what?"—she slams her palms into her knees—"I have no time for assholes who sit back and do nothing but criticize others while doing *fuck all* to solve any problem whatsoever."

The smile which escapes me only seems to irritate her further. "You have a temper, Jessynia."

"I do no—" She shudders out an irritated breath. "You're a prick, you know that?"

"I'm a therapist," I smirk, taking in the flush of pink on her chest. I wonder for a moment if she also gets it when she comes.... "I'm here to ask invasive questions and to annoy people. To shift energy."

"*Mainly* to annoy people," she corrects. As she takes in the mirth in my eyes, she shakes her head, falling into a smile despite herself. I match her grin as she begins to talk. "You're a therapist so that you can be paid to be an asshole, aren't you?"

"You may be right there," I reply wryly.

That is one hell of a fucking smile she has...

But it's not what I require from her today.

"I believe, Jess, that you came here because you wanted to talk to me about Sebastian."

The smile vanishes quickly and she inhales a slow breath.

"Why don't you tell me a little about him? About your relationship with him..."

She pauses, unspeaking, for too long. I know what she's concerned about.

"I won't repeat it to anyone, Jessynia. Including Cameron."

"We've bonded somehow," she says softly. "I don't fully understand what it is. A trauma bond, maybe?"

"Could be. I imagine watching him hurt the man who hurt you must have drawn you to him."

"Yes. Even if I'm still angry at him for doing it. For making me watch that. Does that make sense?"

"We don't usually feel just one thing about a given situation," I respond. "Contradictory emotions are to be expected in such heightened circumstances. He wanted to avenge a crime that someone committed against you, but he took away your right to decline to watch the act. Your consent. It's normal you should feel distressed over that. We all do when control is taken from us against our will."

"I can't understand why he did it. I mean, was it just an excuse to hurt someone or... did he do it for me? Or was it just to bond me to him? Leave me needing him?"

"Why would you assume there's only one motive?"

She fiddles with the button on her cardigan, eyeing it intently. My gaze pans down to her large tits peeking out from the cardigan. Her nipples are hardened into points underneath what must be a thin cotton bra. The woman is utterly unaware of how indecent she is, how desperate men are to immobilize her limbs and fuck her. I have no idea how Sebastian has restrained himself for this long...

"You care about him, don't you?" I ask.

"It's hard not to when you know about his childhood."

"That's a rookie mistake, Jessynia. Overlooking people's behavior because of their past abuse. You're more educated than that."

"I know. I can't help it. I sound like Rose, don't I?"

"She saw the abuse victim... to her detriment."

"Did he really kill her, Gabriel?"

"I have no idea," I shrug. "The medical examiner's office deemed it an overdose, a suicide. Rose was... troubled in her own way."

"How?"

"She was a masochist. An autossassinophiliac."

"A *what*?!"

I smile at her vibrant request for clarification. "Someone aroused by the fear of danger. Of being killed..."

"Is that really a thing?"

"There's no shortage of kinks out there," he says, cocking an eyebrow. "I'm not sure that this one is that far out of the ordinary."

"How... how do you know that? About her?"

"It wasn't much of a secret. I mean, her marrying a renowned sadist with a penchant for knives who dwells on the thin edge between life and death was the first clue. Cameron told me some things about her tastes..."

"God..."

"She was tormented by her husband. Tormented by Cameron, a man who cared for her but didn't love her. I don't know what really happened."

"Did he ever tell you he did it?"

"No."

"Did you ever ask him?"

"No."

"Why not?" she asks.

"I'm not sure that I wanted to know..."

"I don't know why I struggle to detach his childhood abuse from his adult behavior the way I do," she says.

"You think he'd want to be pitied?"

"I don't *pity* him. I just... believe he deserves to heal. As we *all* do. He's the key to *everything*, Gabriel. Jack. Cameron. The Society. If Sebastian can tone things down, no one has to keep getting hurt."

"What incentive is there for him to *tone things down*?"

"This need he has to cause pain, it's not a solution. It doesn't *heal* him. He has to keep inflicting it over and over to soothe himself. That means he must be in distress most of the time. Angry. It's not a life. He doesn't have to live this way."

I rub my chin as I contemplate her naivety. She's too smart to think it could be this simple. "You have a need to solve puzzles," I suggest. "You like to affect the outside world. That's why you gave up a six-figure job on Wall Street to spend your days fighting to get your articles published in sub-par magazines."

"I really hope you don't advertise yourself as a motivational coach, Gabriel," she spits back in breathless outrage, shooting me one of her frequent unimpressed looks that amuse me to no end. "For fuck's sake."

"I don't."

"Good, because that would be false fucking advertising!"

I bow my head with a smile. "Touché."

"You think I'm naïve, don't you?" she asks, her brow furrowing.

"I think you're being willfully naïve."

"How?"

"I don't doubt your motives, Jessynia. I believe you want Sebastian healed, or at least, the worst of his rage soothed. I believe that you want your men safe and healthy. I've never doubted that. But I also think you're denying reality when it comes to Sebastian."

"Why?"

"So that you can keep seeing him. I think you are drawn to him more than you care to admit... or am I wrong?"

She swallows hard, giving me my answer.

"You feel desire for him, no? Sexual desire."

After a moment, she nods her head, her cheeks flushing pink. She absently finds her wedding ring once again with the fingertips of her right hand. "You think I'm pathetic, don't you?" she asks. "That I'm just another of his moron groupies."

"If you were that, you'd have given in to him weeks ago."

"I don't want to feel this way, Gabriel. I despise the way he makes me feel. I know he's a monster. I know he's hurt people. Rose. Cameron.

Jack. *You*... I'm so sorry, Gabriel. I shouldn't talk about him like this in front of you."

"There's nothing to be sorry for. I *want* to know, Jess. That's why I'm asking you. I care about you. I want to help, and I can only do that if you tell me the truth."

She pauses for a moment. "The pull I feel is just... so strong. I can barely control how I feel around him. I have no fucking clue how I manage to resist him each time..."

"Do you touch yourself to the thought of him?"

Her lips part at the question before closing as she swallows hard. "Gabriel," she chides. "For fuck's sake."

"Do you? Answer the question. There's no shame allowed in my practice, Jessynia. These things have to come out. Shame is not a healthy place to function from. I don't judge. Ever. We're all human. All flawed."

Time stretches into a minute as she watches me in silence, shifting in her chair, her cheeks rosy, just begging to be bitten into...

"Do you?" I repeat.

"Yes," she replies, her breathy voice almost a whisper.

Well, I know that Sebastian will greatly enjoy that particular confession. I know he'll be hard and having his cock sucked slowly, silently, as he watches the woman now haunting him against all odds, as he soaks in her desire for him—the devil shaken by the angel he wants to protect as much as defile...

My cock throbs as I watch her wilt into the chair, the good little girl's usual vibrance dissipating as she admits the shameful secrets she's hiding about the man who has hurt both of her men—shameful to her, of course. She has an acute sense of decency and morality. I have no doubt she is tormented by her lust. In truth, I'm not sure there is shame to be felt for craving the strongest and most desirable of men.

"I know how much you need safety, Jessynia. That must mean that you feel safe with him... to some degree. In light of what happened to Rose, that would be *unusual*. Do you? Feel safe?"

"Yes. Somehow. I feel... protected."

"Hmm."

"But I also feel... his demons watching. Watching him. Watching us. I'm aware that it's a false sense of safety."

"Why do you think you feel safe around him *at all*?"

"I don't know. He never forces me. He never touches me... sexually. I mean, not like Jack or Cameron do. Not roughly. He's more patient than either of them. More gentle."

"For now. That wouldn't last. He needs pain to feel pleasure. Cameron's *proclivities* would pale in comparison to discipline dished out by Sebastian. Could you handle that?"

"I don't want to handle it! I don't want to desire him! I want these feelings to stop!"

"They are unlikely to stop, Jessynia. At the risk of making you want to punch me, I can say with certainty that beautiful, sensitive, vulnerable women like you are designed to be fucked by powerful, ruthless men like him. It's in your cells. In your blood. The universe wants it. Women crave safety and protection. Men like him provide it. You will never be able to overcome your lust. It's ingrained in every part of you."

"That's just great," she groans.

"You will be a slave to abject desire for as long as you know him."

"Not unless he hurts Cameron. I've told him I can't feel anything for him if he does. Do you think he would?"

"Perhaps he could be convinced not to."

"*Convinced?* What are you suggesting, Gabriel?" she asks, her tone harsh, her eye contact blazing.

She's begging to be tamed, without even realizing it... It's hard not to imagine undertaking the job as she speaks.

As she glowers at me in indignation, it hits me just quite how raw she is, how real. She doesn't hide things or pretend to be something she's not the way most people do. And she feels deeply, feels the pain of others. It makes her act in ways which defy logic, which make her vulnerable.

Her vulnerability is part of what makes her so exquisite. So intensely fuckable. My self-restraint has been pushed to the limit since I first met her. My cock hardens every time she lifts her eyes to look at me.

I don't blame Cameron for losing his sanity over her. Women want him for his looks and his dominance, but also for his money, his power and his name. They see the scion. She sees the human. She breaks down the walls he's erected around himself. She allows him to be vulnerable enough to be himself...

The problem is, she does the same for Jack whom she also seems to worship. Quite the conundrum she's gotten herself into...

"I'm suggesting that if you could relieve your guilt over your desire to be fucked by him by at least procuring a promise to protect the men you love..."

"Well, I don't intend to be fucked by him! Ever!"

"You don't need to *intend* it. Your body will make it happen. You won't have much say in the matter."

"That's ridiculous! Of course I have a choice."

"Evolution will trump your hypocritical sense of morality every time, Jessynia. You were made to be fucked by him and you know it despite your denial. I believe you get wet at the very thought of him." I observe with pleasure the way she begins to pant through her outrage. "Don't you?"

"Do you talk to all your clients like this?!"

"Not quite as candidly, but then, most are not as frank as you. As open. As vulnerable. This is how you'll heal, Jessynia. Admitting the truth. Moving out of shame. Facing reality. Or would you rather keep everything hidden and pace your apartment for hours as you do now..."

She frowns as if wondering if I have evidence of such a thing rather than guessing how her torment manifests itself...

"And do you care about my well-being in all this?"

"Of course I care, Jessynia. I'm trying to protect you in ways you don't fully understand. You're still naïve about your options. I want you to look at this in a way which will yield the best results."

"This isn't some portfolio investment, Gabriel! We're talking about people's lives, their bodies, their feelings..."

"I know that. And I know I'm an overbearing prick—your words, I believe"—her brow furrows further—"but I want you to heal, to step out of the darkness you're in, to face the real world. It'll be awkward now, but tonight, tomorrow, the next day, you'll feel better for having gotten this out. Can you understand that?"

"Cameron," she says. "He's one of your *best* friends. You encouraged me to go back to Jack. You seem to be encouraging me to sleep with Sebastian. I mean, do you even give a fuck about him at all?"

"Harsh words coming from a woman who allows his sworn enemy to make love to her every night."

"Jack's my husband, Gabriel. And they're not *enemies*." I raise a brow until she corrects herself. "They've just... fallen out."

"Your naivety won't serve you forever. They will hate each other till the day they die, Jess."

"I don't believe that. And either way, you're encouraging me to be with men other than your so-called best friend. Isn't that a bit cruel?"

"It isn't cruel to face reality about human nature. I've never been monogamous. Monogamy is a sham that we've designed to keep society somewhat *civilized*. Fucking other people has nothing to do with love. And sometimes it has practical purposes. You want Sebastian to leave Cameron alone permanently, no?"

"He promised to do that anyway, as long as I stay with Jack and go to QN. I don't need to sleep with him to make that happen."

"No, you don't. And yet, you can't think of much else, can you?"

"I think of him that way. But I think of Jack and Cam more. I want them safe from that place forever."

"What makes you think they want to be safe from it?"

"Because I feel it."

"That's a cop-out answer. Both have been tempted back before. Cameron is still contemplating a return."

She sits up, urgency snapping her spine straight. "How do you know that?"

"We've discussed it."

"I really fucking well hope you're not encouraging it, Gabriel," she warns.

"No. I most certainly am not. But he's strong-minded and ultimately, he will make his own decisions. The only person who has real influence over him is *you*, and your opinion is tainted by the pain he feels over knowing that Jack… spends his nights with you in his bed. Cameron worships you. He always has. How do you expect him to cope with the current situation?"

Silence stretches between us as she takes a moment to collect herself. "Does Sebastian want him back?"

"I don't know. I don't have dealings with Sebastian anymore. But I imagine it would intrigue him to see what happens when he gives Cameron access to you. The Society doesn't inform members of their spouses' extramarital activities within their doors. It's enshrined in their constitution. Jack wouldn't know. I believe that Sebastian would be curious to see whether you are able to resist both of them… at the same time. The two dark lords…"

"That's insane."

"They've fucked women together before. Many times. Including Rose."

Her body softens, strength seeping from her as she peers at me, her lips pallid.

"Cameron didn't tell you that part?" I ask.

She shakes her head slowly.

"Well, in his defense," I resume, "she wasn't complaining. I'm pretty sure she thought she'd died and gone to heaven."

"Well, that's where she did go, in the end…"

"Yes."

"Sebastian trained Cameron to bite and to cut and things like that, didn't he?" she asks.

"Yes. He was his protégé. That's what left Sebastian so embittered when Cameron left."

"But is Cam really like Sebastian? His dark side?"

I consider Sebastian's instructions not to pull punches when it comes to his nature. "I don't believe so. Cameron enjoys submission and delivering pain is part of it. He procures sexual pleasure that way, but he struggled to cut the way Sebastian does. And once his act of violent dominance is over, he feels shame and regret. He is disconnected from himself. Tortured at times. Sebastian is elated to have caused harm. To have left wounds that need to be tended to. It feeds him emotionally and not just physically the way it feeds Cameron. It allows him to breathe."

"God," she mutters, shaking out a breath from the deep recesses of her lungs.

"I'm sorry if the truth hurts, Jess. Sebastian is a sadist. He's not alone in that fact, but he does procure pleasure from pain. And there are more women than we could count who would, and do, willingly sign up to be his submissive. However, I've never in my years of dealing with him seen him care about *any* of them. You have power, Jessynia."

"I want Jack and Cam free. That's all I care about."

"I assume Sebastian knows this," I reply.

"Yes."

"And I assume he doesn't want you sacrificing yourself to that end?"

"No. Not from what he says."

"Then, how do you see this all working out?" I ask.

Her gaze drifts over my face as she contemplates her answer. I can't help but feel the blaze of Sebastian's eyes as he watches the woman tormenting him, taking away his peace, giving him cruel hope that will taste like bitter poison to him. Watching her open up—does it please him? Give him pleasure? Cause him pain?

"I... I've been... thinking of going away," she finally says, stunning me into silence for a moment. "Of leaving. Leaving Manhattan. For good."

Goosebumps prickle on my neck at the thought of Sebastian hearing those words.

He would *not* allow that.

It would drive him out of his mind.

"Why?" I ask.

"I can't make this work. Jack. Cameron. It's not a solvable puzzle. I once thought it was. Not anymore. I want Sebastian to let us go, all of us. For our sake and for his."

"You want to sacrifice being with the men you love so that he can tolerate letting you go?"

"Would he? Leave us all alone if I left and never spoke to them again, but only spoke to him until he gets used to the new normal?"

"I have no idea, Jessynia. He's not a predictable man. But then, he's not the only one you have to worry about. You think Jack would just sit back and take it? That Cameron would?"

"I'd make sure they can't find me for a while. I'd ask them to leave me alone."

"And you think they would?"

"If it meant all of us being free finally... Maybe. I need to talk to Sebastian about it, see if he'd agree."

"And give up the only real source of light in his life? You're giving him a lot of credit, Jessynia."

"Part of him wants to heal. I can feel it. If he could let me go, let *them* go, it'd be... something. Growth. Change." She lets out a sigh, her eyes searching mine desperately. "You think I'm being naïve again, don't you?" she asks in that earnest tone of hers that almost knocks you off your feet.

"I think you're running away from more than *him*, Jessynia. And from *them*. What are you running from?"

She shakes her head slowly as my words come out.

"You're running away from yourself. From the truth about yourself. From the truth about your desires. Your path. I don't believe it was a coincidence that you met him. The question is, what are you going to do with your power?"

"How much do I owe—?"

She stops as she observes my slow blink, putting her wallet back into her purse.

"Sorry," she says. "I wasn't sure..."

"Jess, I know I said some things which were harsh. I know that going through this stuff is painful in the moment, but it's all designed to shift energy, even the bits where you want to ram a fork into my eyeball."

"Two forks," she corrects, smiling despite herself, her gleaming lips curving beautifully.

"It's very, very important that we don't let this energy stagnate. We don't want things stuck, do we?"

"I know," she replies with a nod, putting on her coat. "And by the way, you're a prick, just in case there's any doubt."

"No doubt whatsoever," I grin. "That's why my clients keep coming back for more..."

She chuckles derisively, shaking her head.

"You'll be okay to get home?" I ask.

"Honestly, I have anxiety about leaving buildings these days," she says with a half-smile designed to conceal her concern. "Kidnapping is now part of my life apparently..."

"Do you want me to come out with you?"

"No, no. That'll make it worse. There'll be some cabs in front of that hotel at the end of the block. I'll nab one."

"I'll keep a lookout from the window. Text me once you get home, or I'll be coming over, okay?"

"Okay."

I reach forward and envelop her in a hug which she reciprocates, breathing in the minty scent of her hair.

"Bye, Jess."

"Bye, Gabriel. Thank you. For listening. And... you won't..."

"I won't tell anyone what you told me. I promise."

"Thank you. Bye."

I close the door and lock it behind me, heading to the bedroom where I find Sebastian standing, peering out of the window, just a foot behind the glass. I join him, watching as she exits the building and walks swiftly, looking all around her as she heads to the end of the block.

"Enjoyable?" I ask.

"In parts," he responds, not taking his eyes off her.

"I was surprised she admitted her desire for you like that. I thought she'd want to hide that one."

"She's very frank," he replies, his deep voice resonating around the room.

"But still consumed by both of them," I suggest, aware that the comment will ignite his ire.

Sebastian Gravier doesn't share—not emotionally anyway. He wants his women devoted to him. The one exception is Alexandra Frost whose affections for Jack and Cameron he tolerates with amusement, only because he knows they are not reciprocated anymore, and that they cause her pain. As close as they are, he does enjoy that...

"Yes," he replies slowly, turning to face me, bright reptilian eyes colliding with mine. "Their hold is still strong."

"Do you still want her like that? Infected by other men?"

"I was once averse to the thought. Having reflected, it could be a source of additional pleasure."

"Watching her rip herself apart with guilt?"

"Guilt makes people lose themselves."

"Do you want her lost?" I ask.

"I want two opposite and incompatible things for her."

"That must be tricky to navigate," I suggest.

"Very."

"Well, you're making headway," I say. "You no longer have to bring her by force. She now comes to you willingly... and not just because of the trauma she has endured."

"Hmm." His eyes narrow into thin slits.

"What do you make of her saying she wants to leave?"

"That isn't an option for her," he responds, the harsh bite in his voice causing my body to seize for a moment.

"And if she goes anyway?"

"I'll hunt her down. I'll find her. There is no getting out for her. Not this easily."

"I suspect she'll bring it up with you. Prey on your affection for her..."

"She may try..."

I contemplate his face—his savage beauty made all the more chilling by the horrors of his pathology, of the abuse which fractured him, forcing him to burn the kind and caring human he once was, to turn him into ash so that he never had to look back on him again. His expression is resolute, but I know that something unusual happens with Sebastian—something that this man who needs control will abhor to his very core: the way he feels about her, talks about her, morphs when he is alone with her.

I don't know exactly what he says to her, but I know that the way he feels when he's with her doesn't align with the calculated deviance that weaves through his words when talking to me about her. Something slips—the walls erected to close off his humanity, his rancor, his wrath, his pain, his need for suffering. She must dissolve them a little.

She has no idea how dangerous that is...

Some muted cough from the adjoining room makes his frigid eyes slip towards the mirror. I follow his giant frame as he turns to walk slowly in, observing the pitiful sight—his sub, naked and bound on the floor, knots holding her hands together behind her back. Her head down.

"I'm sorry, my Lord," she utters.

"You will be. I'm done with her," he says to me. "Would you like me to leave her here?"

"I have plans to see Evelyn," I reply. "I can put them off for a while. Unless you would like her to meet me here... to watch us."

"Until she's a member, that would be a violation," he responds.

I knew he would say no. Despite his malevolence, there are certain rules he still abides by.

"I would like a description of the act, as usual. I would appreciate it if you made her cry."

"I always try, Sebastian."

"Good."

"You still want her integrated in the Society? I still haven't said a word to her about it."

"That will depend on whether her brother returns to us..."

"And you would still allow that?"

"I want his destruction. I want his psyche ripped apart. His mind. I will use whatever method I have to to accomplish that. If that means tolerating his presence, so be it."

"The resistance seem fractured," I offer.

His eyes wander slowly over my face. “Indeed. They’re falling apart. The fall of Cameron O’Neill will finish them off for good. Beth Vass. She seemed unhinged today. I’m pleased with her unraveling.”

“She’s become paranoid,” I say. “On edge. Not sleeping.”

“Good. I want her sanity pushed so far that returning is the only option for her.”

“She’s close, Sebastian.”

“I hope so. She has a bill to pay…”

“And the girl? Cameron would come back because he wants her. Nothing else would do it. Would you leave her alone with him?”

“She’s afraid of his monsters. She’ll need to soothe him. I want her succumbing. I want her feeling shame about her treatment of Jack. I want her open. Malleable. Broken. She’s bound by rules of decency. I need those ties destroyed for good. I need her to embrace what she can be. I need her unchained. O’Neill can accomplish that.”

“It will make the ultimate loss of him even more brutal,” I suggest.

“Yes. That is something she will have to endure.”

I nod, taking in his unflinching face.

He gestures towards his sub. “Do you want her?”

And as he asks the question, Olivia lifts her eyes to meet mine. He won’t like her lifting her head, but the expression on her pale face is so pitiful that I have no doubt he’ll take pleasure in her utter submission and reverence to him.

I contemplate his offer.

Cameron uses her to fulfill a need. He knows she will submit to what he wants. He has no emotional ties to her. If he did, I’d reconsider.

“Do you want that?” I ask her.

“Look at me, sub,” snarls Sebastian, and her pale gray eyes slide to him. “Do you want our friend tonight, or not? You are not obliged to say yes.”

“I do, my Lord.”

“Good. Make sure he is satiated.” He turns to face me. “Call Isaiah and have her sent over to my place tonight. I need to teach my sub some lessons in maintaining silence.”

I nod my head as he leaves, watching Olivia as she peers up at me.

23

Beth

I'm always so fucking nervous waiting for him.

A man hasn't given me the jitters quite like this for a long time.

I stare at the wooden door, its burnt sepia hue that of the darkest of trees. I hate doors like this. In the modern world, most are stained a warm brown or painted white or black. This one is made of dark wood, just like those at that place. I've walked through more than I can count, and the memories of those rooms never cease to reduce me to a woeful wreck.

The corridor has been quiet for a while. I don't know if he's in there with another church member, but he always keeps me waiting—always, and I never see anyone leave, unless they're instructed to leave through the back door like me, perhaps.

It's only through random luck that I even heard about this church. A woman I spoke to briefly at a group therapy session told me about a church that was like a family. That's what I crave more than anything—connection, safety, family.

I had it when Silas was alive. The resistance became my family.

Now with Cameron gone and Silas dead, and Gabriel growing impatient with me, I no longer feel like I fit...

Maybe they're just tired of hearing the same old stories from me—my last months at that place. Gabriel says I'm stuck in a trauma loop, and constantly talking about it won't help. *Apparently*, I need to disrupt the loop by working on my nervous system, on releasing trauma from the body. Easy for that fucker to say—he hasn't been used the way I have and then thrown out like trash.

It was just *one* night, one fucking night, but it changes *everything*. Being used by snarling men, men guffawing at the pitiful sight of you, and then discarded like that. It rips away the image you have of yourself, erodes your value as a human.

So yeah, it's been years. I should be over it.

Well, I'm not.

And I know I'm not stable. Gabriel's made that clear enough over the years. I mean, he hasn't said it outright but treats me like I'm an ungodly fucking mess. Hell, maybe I am. Being fucked by a man who fucks another woman any chance he gets is enough to make any woman lose her mind.

Yeah, I guess I should just walk away from him.

The problem is that I don't know how to be with myself either.

I don't even know how to sit in silence on my own. I have to distract myself day and night so as not to feel the demons clawing at my skin, trying to get in, to remind me of what I am...

I don't know how to *not* depend on anyone.

I don't feel whole.

I don't feel safe.

I need him, as much as I hate the fucker for it.

Shit.

I glance down at the chip in my shiny crimson nails.

How the fuck did I do that?

I consider getting out my compact to check that my make-up is intact, but I'm afraid of him opening the door at that exact moment. I mean, I checked it half a dozen times on the way over here. It should be okay.

Fuck.

At the click of a lock, I clasp my hands together.

"Beth."

I don't see him. I only hear his voice, his deep, imposing voice. He always does it that way—never pops his head out. I have no idea why. It's one of the reasons he unsettles me so much. He has these ways about him that others wouldn't employ, just so as to not intimidate people. He doesn't play by those rules.

It's one of the reasons I can't stop thinking about him...

The tiny steel tips of my heels click against the stone beneath my feet as I walk towards his room. I shudder as I catch sight of him, his unblinking eyes taking me in. I bow my head as I enter. I'm not sure if that's normal practice with a priest, but I do it on instinct every time, and he's never corrected me.

I feel the weight of his stare as I remove my black coat.

"Should I take off my boots?" I ask, forgetting what he made me do last time.

"Please," he replies and I do so, placing them neatly next to the door as I glance at my stockinged feet, making sure there are no holes or rips anywhere, wondering whether he can see the crimson lacquer on my toenails under the sheer black fabric enveloping my feet.

I hope he can...

The entryway to his residence is dark with engraved wooden paneling snaking up the walls. Another thing that has always reminded me of that Godforsaken place. I head down past a bedroom to the right, a washroom to the left and a closed door to the right, and then into his living room. The shades are drawn despite it already being a cloudy day and the meager light casts eerie shadows everywhere.

I take a seat on the leather loveseat with my back to the window as usual, glancing down to make sure my breasts are not too exposed. I mean, I always wear tight tops when I come to see him, but I want it to appear somewhat subtle...

God, you're a joke.

Opposite me stands a floor-to-ceiling bookshelf full to the brim, and to my right, a shrine, a wall peppered with crucifixes of various sizes and materials.

I watch as he takes a seat on an armchair opposite me, leaning forward to pour some tea into an earthy ceramic cup. His eyes lift to meet mine as I take it from him. I'd rather he gave me something stronger, but I don't want to ask. I don't want him to think I'm unhinged like everyone else does. I'm really trying my best to tone down the crazy with strangers...

He leans back in the armchair, his hands snaking down the arms, his fingers curling round the leather edges. His deep brown eyes are intensely focused on my face and as usual, the blaze of them never ceases to make me fidget as he regards me with total composure. It seems I have a penchant for men who bear a certain brand of powerful grace.

And fuck it, the man is hot. I never cease to be affected by it. He always takes my breath away. Only Cameron could really match this kind of poise. As I think it, I see another face that can stun from a hundred paces with his violent grace—that *thing* in that godforsaken place. The elegant figure hiding a snarling dragon cloaked in human flesh.

Yeah, I know that sounds a bit dramatic. I guess you have to have been in a room with him alone to fully comprehend the forces at work inside that man, haunting him and everyone that goes near him. That monster knew that I saw what he was. That's why he had to take me out. He can see into you like no one else. Those types have to eradicate the danger—the danger of you unmasking them.

I peer over my cup as I take a sip of the hot tea. He doesn't speak, but considers me in silence. It's not intimidating. It's remarkably comfortable.

I take in the strong lines of his face—the high cheekbones over tanned skin, the strong jawline covered by a thick beard, the top lip covered by a neatly trimmed mustache, the thick roman nose. Half of his long chestnut-brown hair is pulled into a braided ponytail at the back of his head. The other hangs loose over his robust shoulders.

And when I look at the tips of his hair, I realize that today, something is different. He's missing the white collar that threads into the top of his cassock, and the top three buttons are undone, allowing just a glimpse of his chest to be shown, enough for me to confirm what I suspected—that the black and white tattoos of biblical figures on his arms, or at least his lower arms, the part that I can see, don't stop there.

Black lines are etched into his chest. I can't make out the design, but on his forearms, I see Jesus, sacrificed on the cross on the left, and on the right, Satan—his face handsome, his eyes the color of blood, his wings black and his body wrapped in flame.

It jarred me at first to see it. I mean, a holy man is not supposed to have images of demons on his body, surely. When I asked him about it, he explained the history of Lucifer—once one of God's most precious and loyal angels.

Fallen.

Father believes it can happen to anyone, even him, and uses his tattoo as a reminder. While in the tattoo of Jesus, his eyes are soft, in the image of the devil, his eyes are wild and wide open, and with the head-on positioning of the tattoo, sometimes it feels like the image is staring at you.

I wonder what he thinks of when he looks at me...

Sometimes I groan at myself for succumbing to the cliché, lusting over the hot tattooed priest. But it's not just about his looks. It's his energy. His aura. The way he listens to me, unspeaking. He gives me space to be, to breathe, to talk, without judgment. It's so rare, so precious when you can get it.

I really want to get down on my knees in front of him, but I'm afraid of humiliating myself like I've done with other men, throwing myself at them too soon. I never used to do it. I know the way I interact with men is fucked up... ever since I became part of that place.

I want to play this right. I mean, it's not like he's Catholic. He's allowed to have sex. In fact, in a moment that still makes me cringe to think of it, I did ask if he were in a relationship. He said only with God.

I mean, that can't be healthy. He's a strong man in what must be his mid-forties. He must have needs...

What I wouldn't give to tend to them. I know he'd make me feel safe. He always does. Every time I get to this place, it's like I can breathe again. It's the only place left in the city that I feel this way in. I used to feel that at Gabriel's but not any longer. Cameron doesn't take my calls anymore. His place once made me feel safe, on the rare occasion he'd let me stay there.

Nowhere else in this metropolis do I feel out of their line of sight like here.

"How are you, Beth?"

Darragh...

His voice is so smooth, so measured. It soothes me. I just want him to hold me, make all the demons go away...

"I've not been too well, Father."

He always pauses before speaking. He's never hurried or quick to react. It reminds me to take a breath before reacting—my tinderbox temper has not served me well in life, to put it very fucking mildly.

"I'm sorry to hear that, Beth. Tell me about it."

My gaze snakes up his forearms, thick with muscle and painted in black and gray tattoos, and onto the contours of his shoulders, trailing up his neck and onto eyes that seem to peer into me.

"I... I haven't been sleeping well."

"Why not?"

"The nightmares. They're still bad. I can't... sleep in the dark. I can't be alone with my thoughts. I always have to put something on to distract me."

"Is it worse than before?"

"Yes."

"Why do you think that is?"

I pause for a moment. He knows all about them, though I've described them as a cult, never giving any names. The name *Sebastian* left my lips once in a moment of despair, but I brushed over it and haven't slipped up since. I hope he's forgotten.

"They're still following me."

"You're sure about that? When we're paranoid, we often see things that are not there."

"No," I retort, relieved that I didn't snap at him the way I thought for a split second I would. *Breathe, woman...* "I *see* them. There are things they still leave outside my apartment."

"Are you ready to tell me what they are?"

"I can't. It could put you in danger, Father."

"Have they ever left them inside your apartment?"

"No."

"So that means they don't know how to get in."

"Oh, they know. They know how to pick locks, hack security systems."

"So, if they enjoy tormenting you, why would they restrain themselves?"

He asks the question in earnest, but I can't shake the feeling that he is not entirely convinced that the story I'm telling is true. Sometimes I wonder if he thinks I'm delusional, paranoid, psychotic, and in need of treatment.

Hell, ten years ago, if you'd have told me the story, I'd have thought the same, and given you a berth as wide as the Hudson.

"It's how he operates," I reply.

"Their leader..."

"Yes. He enjoys the slow agony. The torment. Death by a thousand cuts. He wants it to last. To draw it out."

"As you describe him, he sounds like a monster."

"No. He's not a monster, Father. Monsters can't control what they do. They're born that way. He's *evil*. He chooses what he does. He plans it. He takes pleasure in it. He's the *devil*."

The caw of a crow from outside has me glancing towards the shuttered window.

"That's quite a bold statement, Beth."

"I know. I mean it. Do you believe in demons, Father?"

"Of course. In my work, I frequent them regularly."

"How do you get rid of them?"

"We have our techniques. What becomes trickier is when they are still alive and have taken over a human host."

"That's *him*. They've taken over him and now he's one of them."

"We can exorcize them, but, in my experience, the host has to want it. Would he?"

I shake my head fast. "No way. He's had too much power for too long. He enjoys it. He won't want to give any of it up. Give *them* up."

"He must be intimidating to be around."

"He's terrifying, Father."

"Hmm. Why don't you leave the city, Beth?"

"This is all I've ever known," I shrug. "I was born here. My family's here—or what's left of them. Any friends I have are here. I wouldn't know where else to go. Plus, they have the means to have me followed anywhere."

"Why would they bother to do that?"

"Because he likes to torment me."

"Why?"

"Because I dared to question him."

"And he doesn't tolerate that?"

"He does. But not by me."

"Because you're a woman?"

"I don't know why. He just... didn't respect me, I guess."

"Does anyone dare stand up to him?"

"Yes. He can take it, but..."

I pause.

I haven't told him the full story. I've told him that I disagreed with the leadership of the cult, but not how it ended. Not what they did to me. I can't tell him that. Every time I tell a man that, it sullies what they think of me. They can't help it. No man wants to fuck damaged goods—a woman who's been used by a grunting, guffawing dozen men at the same time and then cast out like filth. Or at least most of them were. Even when Sebastian fucked me in the ass, the only emotion he showed was anger. He didn't smirk or snigger the way Vallen did. First, he watched in silence as they began to restrain me, to penetrate me, three at a time. The fuck didn't move. He just impassively watched over my utter disgrace until he finally climbed on top of me, grabbing my hair and making sure I felt every hard inch of him.

God, I hate that I let them do it. I hate that I pretended to be enjoying it, even when they were slapping my face with their cocks while laughing, even when they were hurting me, I still moaned as though I was part of it, as though I had some power left. Within a few minutes of the action starting, I felt it was all wrong, but I didn't dare say the safe word. I didn't want to disgrace my *fiancé*.

Little did I know this was his version of a farewell.

He destroyed me. Turned me from the goddess I'd been told I'd be to the common whore, barely human.

That's how men see me once they know what happened. Gabriel would never look at me the way he does Evelyn O'Neill. She's pure by his standards, worthy of respect. I'm the cum rag. The stupid whore, the fool who fell for Vallen Markov and let the deranged freaks of that place use her.

Even Cameron, who fucked his way through the Society for years before he left, isn't interested, no matter how many humiliating times I offer myself to him. I know what a freak that man is. I don't mind. But apparently, I'm not good enough to even be some faceless fuck toy.

I reach for the cup and bring it to my lips with shaky hands. I have to get this out, and yet every time I do, I relive the nightmare.

"A few people dare to stand up to him," I say, "but only those he seems to respect."

"Hmm..."

"That place. The way things ended. It felt like... venturing into hell. Do you believe there can be hell on Earth?"

"Only in the absence of God."

"I want to believe in God. It's just..."

"He abandoned you?"

"Yes. When I needed him."

"No, he didn't, Beth. He was always there, watching, holding your hand. He still is. You just need to let him in."

"Can you show me how?"

"I will try my best. I think first, I would need to know more about your pain."

I frown at him as he watches me in solemn silence. "Why?"

"I need to know how you are affected by them so that I better know how to help you heal. Tell me the feelings they have left you with. Be very clear, Beth. Very frank."

I pause for a moment, taking a shuddering breath in. "I feel... shame. Disgust."

"At them?"

"At myself."

"How does that manifest?"

"I hate looking at myself in the mirror. I can't say anything nice to myself. It feels like a lie. I feel... worthless. Dead inside. Bitter. Enraged at the world. At women who haven't been through this. Some days, I hate them *all*."

"That must be unpleasant."

"It's hell. *Sorry*."

"It's okay. Do you believe other women can relate to you?"

"No. Not really."

"You came here not two weeks ago to speak to someone. A young woman. Is she connected to them somehow?"

"Yes."

"How?"

"She's the wife of one of their high-profile patrons."

"What's her name?"

I feel my hands tense. Men always fixate on that bitch. It only takes being around her for a short time to make them *stupid*. I'm not allowing this one to.

"Jess," I reply curtly. You're not getting her full name.

"Is she someone who you can talk to?"

"I guess so," I shrug.

"Why did you need to see her so urgently?"

My cheeks burn hot as irritation spreads through me. I don't want to watch another man talk about her ever again. "I don't know. I just needed to talk."

"From what I've observed of her, she possesses quite vibrant energy. She has light around her. Very bright light. Is that why you feel safe to talk to her?"

"To be honest, Father," I manage, trying to control my irritation and not come off as a petulant cunt like I so often do, "I don't want to talk about her anymore. She isn't relevant. We're not friends."

"Very well," he says after a moment, bowing his head.

"I'm sorry."

"It's okay, Beth. You're safe to feel however you want to feel here."

I sigh out in gratitude. "I know, Father. Thank you so much."

Darragh

Her breathing seems to be calming despite her cheeks still flushing red. I hadn't realized I'd be touching such a nerve by bringing her friend up.

I know that Ms. Vass is unstable, but I hadn't quite realized that she was haunted by such a sense of inadequacy and inferiority. She has hidden it fairly well… until today.

"I would like you to pray, Beth."

"Pray? Father, I told you that sometimes I don't even know if God is real."

"You don't have to believe. He will listen whether you believe or not. It will be a short prayer, something you can easily say at home."

"What will it do for me?"

"You have experienced trauma. You are ungrounded. You need a grounding force. Your family are not safe to express yourself around. *God* is. It's not going to feel comfortable, but if you persevere, you will feel him with you. It will change everything."

"Do you feel him?" she asks.

"Yes. Some days stronger than others."

"Do you ever question your faith, Father?"

"Of course. Blind belief is not what God wants. He wants us to question and to reach for him anyway when things are difficult."

"When do you question him?"

I peer down at her crimson lips, the gloss shimmering below eyes that are a deep green and lined in kohl. "When I am tempted by impure thoughts."

She gulps hard at my answer. "Like what?"

"Lust." Her lips part. "Greed. Envy."

"You feel those things?"

"I am human, Beth. We can't escape these feelings. We can only choose whether we act upon them, whether we are led astray by them or not."

"What do you do when you feel them?"

"I pray. That's what I would like you to do, Beth. Can you do it?"

"I'll try."

"Good. Now close your eyes, and repeat after me."

"Dear Lord."

"Dear Lord."

"Protect me from harm... Watch over me... Shield me from those who would lead me astray... I place my faith in you... Amen."

"Amen."

"I will send you the words. I would like you to pray three times a day, until it becomes a ritual, one that brings light into the darkness. Can you do that?"

"I'll try."

"Good. I have someone else I have to see, Beth."

"Sure. Of course. Can I... come back... to see you? In a few days?"

"Yes. Send me a message the morning you need to see me. I'm always here for you."

"Thank you, Father."

She smiles as I close the door behind her, my fingers sliding the metal bolt all the way into the frame.

Making the sign of the cross, I turn down the corridor until I reach the locked door. Pulling a single key from my pocket, I unlock it, open it and slowly head down the stone steps.

Opening another door at the bottom, I turn to the right, towards the cage. As I reach it, I unlock the padlock and place my key onto the side table.

I open the metal door slowly.

"You may come out."

Her head, bowed and facing the hands lying flat on top of her naked thighs, lifts a little, not enough for her eyes to meet mine.

She wouldn't dare...

She props her weight onto her palms and crawls forwards on her hands and knees until she has left the cage, which I carefully close behind her.

She takes up the waiting pose once again as I come to stand before her.

"Look at me."

She lifts her eyes slowly—a bright blue, made all the more striking by the pale skin and long brown hair framing her face.

She watches as I unbutton the top of my robe, pulling it off my body before discarding my pants.

She glances down at my erect cock, licking her lips as she takes it in.

I slowly walk over to the wall and unhook a chain which I clip to the collar around her neck, drawing both her hands behind her back, threading the chain through the loop in one cuff before clipping it to the other, forcing her hands to remain bound behind her back.

I uncouple a leash from the wall, walking to face her and clipping it onto her collar before pulling her slowly across the room and onto the soft black rug near my bed.

"You've been very compliant. You may use the rug."

"Thank you, Father," she responds, peering up at me as I reach for my phone.

"You may begin."

"Thank you," she responds before opening her lips wide and edging them over the head of my cock, sliding up and down silently, her eyes daring to look into mine.

Glancing down at my phone, I press his name.

"It's me," I say as he picks up.

She stops her work, and my eyes widen on hers. "Don't you stop," I snarl and she immediately resumes.

"She's just left," I say into the phone.

"How was she?"

"She's unhinged. In pain and trying to hide it."

"Good. I need the bitch unstable."

"She certainly is that."

"I would very much like her broken."

"That's not my job, Sebastian. I don't do that."

"No. It isn't, but I need to know when she's close. She's been more resilient than I'd expected. She should have been committed by now."

"She's irrational."

"Always has been. It's not enough. I want her tormented, crawling back here on her hands and knees like a dog."

"If God wills it, it will be so."

"I don't need God for this one, Father. He can weep at the sight."

"I'm sure he will." I glance down as she licks the full length of my shaft before taking me in her mouth all the way to the back of her throat, her tongue writhing against the underside of my cock. "I've enjoyed this clone very much. I'd like to keep her a while."

"She's yours," he responds. "I've trained her myself. She can take more than most."

"I look forward to finding out. I only saw her briefly, but she bears quite the resemblance to your girl."

"Yes."

"How is that going?"

He lets out an audible breath. "It has taught me *patience*. Not a virtue I believed I possessed."

"The most divine pleasures are worth the wait."

"Indeed. But it's coming. She's close. I'm just considering the state I wish to leave her in."

"I'm curious to find out myself," I respond, pleasure coursing through me as the sub increases the speed of her work. "She is a light being, Sebastian. They play by different rules. Extinguishing a flame that bright will take all your skill."

"Or my weakness..."

"Part of you still desires to save her?"

"Yes. The urge still plagues me."

"Well, I pray you make the right choice. For you. For *her*. Once you extinguish her light, there is no going back."

24

Olivia
Present

"I told you I was irritable tonight. You shouldn't have come."

My eyes pan up the white shirt covering his broad back as he stares out of the balcony window. He doesn't even turn around to look at me.

I'm barely alive to him. The ghost of another woman. Some piece of flesh he amuses himself with to cope. And what's more, I can't seem to stop coming back for more like some pathetic fool. He's a drug to me. I've kicked cocaine three times, but he is a thousand times more addictive.

I keep praying that one day, she'll be erased from his mind, and he'll see that I can offer him what no one else can.

"I wanted to see you," I reply, taking slow steps towards him as butterflies whirl in my stomach.

The only light that's on is in the kitchen, causing his brown hair to look ebony in the dim glow of the room as he stares out onto Central

Park. For all I know, he's looking for her beyond it. He's always staring out of that fucking window. Always looking for someone else.

"Why?" he asks, not bothering to turn around.

"I always want to see you, Cameron."

"I'm warning you, Olivia. It's not going to be civilized tonight."

"Is it ever?" I dare to ask.

He doesn't answer. He barely cares what I think. I'm so addicted to him that I give him whatever he wants. There's nothing I say no to. He never forces me. Ever. I give him shit sometimes but the reality is that I always submit. He's just so fucking good. No one comes close to him. And I'm still holding out hope that if I'm loyal enough, then one day I'll be Mrs. O'Neill, like I was always supposed to be... until *her*. I know I can make him happy. I know I can give him whatever he wants whenever he wants it.

"I'm giving you a final warning." I ache at the sound of his voice. It's so deep and rich, laced with the gravel of torment. I feel its rough resonance in my body. "I'm going to hurt you if you stay."

"Since when have I complained about you hurting me?" I respond.

"Take off your clothes," he orders and my pussy clenches as it always does. He's so irresistible like this. I hunger for him. If this is the only way I get him, I'll take it... for now. He has to wake up at some point. He *has* to. "Put them on the chair."

"Okay."

"You have five seconds to rephrase."

"Yes, my Lord."

I can't help but run my gaze over the wide back that slopes up to a thick head of glossy hair that he refuses to let me run my fingers through as I peel off my clothes and place them on the wooden chair, as I do each time.

"Done, my Lord."

"Get the hood. Stand in position against the wall. Put it over your head. I don't want to see your hair. Not one strand. Understood?"

"Yes, Master."

I head over to the dark wood cabinet and pull open a wide drawer by its long steel handle. Inside to the left lie various disciplining devices, some more painful to endure than others. To the right, ties and cuffs and the degrading hood I have to put on so that he can turn me into some faceless thing. So that he can imagine it's not me he's fucking. It's *her*.

I hate her with every fucking fiber of my being. I knew he was stupid for her when we were together. The bitch was oblivious to it, but I saw the way he looked at her. After pleading with him to stop being friends with her and getting nowhere, I finally gave in and tried to befriend her. She was nice enough. She used to call me to chat, go for walks, tell me if she was worried about Cam. She actually thought I liked her. In reality, I wanted her dead.

I still do...

He only called me back because she dumped him. That's another in a list of things that makes me sick to my stomach to think of.

Hood in hand, I head over to the wall and stand beneath the painting—a willow in oils, short but wide, a canvas without a frame, just light enough for him to lift it out of the way to reveal the metal rings screwed into the wall and the chain draped over hooks which he uses to attach to my cuffs.

I stand with my back against the wall, just as he likes, hoping that for once, he won't need to hide my face.

"Would you like me to put the hood on?"

"Would you make me repeat myself, sub?"

"I'm sorry, my Lord."

I curse inside as I lift the fabric, pulling the black hood over my head, plunging me into darkness, making sure to tuck any loose strands of my blond hair out of the way. I hate myself every time I do it. The problem is I have no fucking power left with him. I've screamed, cried, threatened to walk away for good. Every time, he's let me leave. He doesn't even seem to give a fuck if I come back. That's what hurts me the most.

And yet, I do come back. Every single fucking time. With my tail between my legs, crying, begging for forgiveness, forced to submit to his cold discipline in order to earn my right to be fucked by him again.

I used to have power with him. I used to feel like his equal. Now I've lost it all, and yet I can't walk away. No other man even comes close to him... not even *him.*

And every time, he makes me re-earn my right to be his sub by degrading me in whatever way he needs, I let him.

I can't say no to the man. He's my drug. And I'm still holding onto hope that one day, he'll see that I'm the right woman for him. It's so obvious. *He has to.*

My breathing accelerates as I wait in black silence for him to approach, only to gasp at the sound of his voice just in front of me. It's so powerful, so deep. It makes my body vibrate. I remember being stunned by it the first time I heard him speak—he's so eloquent, so intelligent, so witty, and yet behind the façade lives a beast, a deviant animal that he hides from the rest of the world. One that I live for.

The voice echoes through me. "I'm going to hurt you, sub. Are you aware of that?"

"Yes, Master."

"Do you want it?"

"Yes."

"Why?"

"I like giving you pleasure."

"Do you like being degraded?"

"For you, yes, Master."

"Take off my clothes, sub. The way you've been trained to."

I reach my hands up and my palms collide with the walls of his rock-hard chest. I glide them over the hard planes of muscle to the center until I locate the buttons of his white shirt. I start at the top, just as he enjoys it, and slowly unbutton each one before reaching forwards and peeling it off his bulky shoulders, and tugging the sleeves down his arms.

"Onto the chair," he instructs and I throw it to the right in the direction of the armchair, praying that I don't miss.

"Do I keep going?" I ask.

"Have you earned the right, sub?"

"Yes, my Lord."

"We'll see about that. Now finish your work."

I reach down and fumble for the silver buckle of his black belt, undoing it and pulling it open before reaching for his zip. As I pull it down, his hand wraps around my wrist, squeezing tightly.

"Slowly."

"Sorry," I breathe, remembering how he likes it. Even after all these years, I get so flustered around the man that I can't recall all the things I've been trained to do each time. And he often changes the rules so that he can punish me. And I can't get enough.

I draw the zip down slowly until it snags at the bottom. I peel the back of his pants off his hard, curved glutes, reveling in the feel of the naked flesh beneath. I crouch down as I pull his pants all the way down. He lifts his bare feet and I pull them off completely, getting to my feet before throwing them onto the armchair.

I hear the clang of the belt as it hits the floor.

"You missed, sub." His voice is so ominous compared to the early days when I knew him. He's grown into such a man.

"I'm sorry, Master."

"Do you think that *sorry* is good enough?"

"No, Master."

"What should be done about your incompetence?"

"I should be punished, Master."

"How?"

"I should… be bitten."

"Where?"

"You decide, my Lord. Of course."

He inhales and exhales a heavy breath. "Bend your neck to the side."

I gasp as his hard body presses against mine, and his lips find the crook of my shoulder. His teeth begin to nip, and I pant more loudly as he bites down, exhaling breathy grunts of pleasure as he does so.

I whimper as he sinks his teeth in, never quite enough to break skin, but enough to bruise. To hurt.

And goddammit, giving him pleasure means more to me than anything.

As he groans through his arousal, I reach forward to grab his cock, and he stops suddenly, pulling away and yanking my hand off him.

"Did I tell you you could fucking well touch me?" he snarls.

"You used to let me," I counter defiantly.

"You're here at my invitation to perform one solitary act. What is it?"

"To submit to what you want."

"I don't require anything else from you."

"How do you think that makes me feel?"

"If you don't like it, you may leave, now. I won't hold it against you. Do you want to leave?"

I wish I had the strength to... but I can't. I can't get enough of him. I can't taste him enough. I can't touch him enough. I can't let go of the dream that one day I'll be standing opposite him, saying my vows. I just need that fucking bitch out of the picture... and I know how to make that happen.

"No," I say. He doesn't speak for a while, the silence dark and heavy, until I correct myself. "No, my Lord."

"You're on very thin ice, sub. Is that understood?"

"Yes, Master."

"Now, turn around and put your hands behind your back."

I do as instructed. The jangle of metal tells me what he's pulling from the wall. Suddenly, my hands are pulled roughly behind my back. I feel the familiar sheathing—this time of leather wrapping around my wrists as he places me in handcuffs.

"Turn around," he orders, and I obey, coming to face him, something I know only because he blocks out some of the light behind him and I can hear his voice, his breaths. Without my sight, the dark notes of his voice enter me as he speaks. "What makes you think you are worthy of pleasuring me, sub?"

"Because I live for you, my Lord."

"And that makes you worthy?"

"Yes. Nothing else exists to me but your pleasure. I'd do anything to give it to you."

"You're not the only one who can perform that function. Why should I give you that privilege?"

"Because nothing will ever be off-limits for me, Master."

"Hmm. Get on your knees, sub. Now."

I crouch down, which, in the dark with your hands bound, is a lot harder than it sounds. The hardwood hurts my knees a little but then I know that he enjoys my pain. It's part of submission, he says. You can't have one without the other.

"Open your mouth," he instructs.

There's only one hole in the hood—the one for my mouth. He doesn't want to see my eyes nor any other part of my face. He just wants to feed his cock into my holes. That's all I'm good for. And I beg for it every day and cry myself to sleep on the nights he doesn't want me, the nights he has some other mindless slave or, more often than not, that he's too fucked in the head over *her* to tolerate anyone else's presence. That seems to be happening more and more.

His timber roughens. "Tongue."

I hold out my tongue for him and moan in pleasure as he places the head of his hard cock on it, sliding it right to left before tapping it.

Without waiting for further instruction, I do what I know he likes, gently kissing the smooth, swollen head, and then the shaft, my lips caressing it with the utmost reverence as I moan my pleasure at giving this God what he needs.

Cameron, you have to see how good this is. We're supposed to be together. We fit.

"Service me with your mouth," he utters so coldly that you'd think we were in a business meeting.

I begin to slide my lips backwards and forwards, moaning in pleasure as I work diligently to tend to his singular needs. He's rock hard, thank God. It's not always the case with me. That's why he stopped seeing me at one point. I had to degrade myself further and further for him to find me a turn-on like he used to. It gave me fucking anxiety every time... until I figured out that if I gave him absolute, unequivocal submission, he'd always be hard.

"Don't moan like a whore," he snarls. "This isn't a fucking sex show. You're a sub, nothing more. A sub should be quiet unless in pain or instructed to make noise."

I stop moaning and begin to slide up and down. There's no noise except that of him slipping his cock into my wet mouth. He doesn't grunt or groan. It's only his thick, rigid length that tells me how he feels about me debasing myself for him like this, serving up my mouth as a vehicle for nothing but his pleasure.

After a while, he pulls out. "I'm going to fuck you, sub. You know the safe word. I don't punish my subs for using it," he continues. "Understood?"

"Yes, my Lord."

"Do you have any limits tonight?"

"No, my Lord."

"I'm warning you. I'm going to *hurt* you." He breathes out the words as if in pain. "Is that a problem for you?"

"No, my Lord."

He takes a moment before speaking. "Turn around. Now."

I flinch at the jangle of chains that I know he's lowering, ready to hoist me in the air with. He pulls my handcuffed wrists upwards and attaches the chains, pulling them tautly so that my hands lift in the air behind me and I'm forced to lean forwards, my head facing the wall.

Then silence...

A yelp is ripped from me as a lash of leather stings my ass. It doesn't really hurt that much. It's just the shock and the sting. When you can't see the blows coming, it makes it ten times worse. He slides the crop down my back before striking my ass again, and then the backs of my legs. Each delicious lash makes me gasp loudly, just as he likes it.

Sometime later, he stops and trails the whip over my back slowly. Every cell in my body tingles at the sensation.

In a sudden loss of control, he grabs the bun hidden under my hood and yanks my head back. "Do you like being degraded, sub?"

"Yes," I eke out as he cranks my neck back further.

While I do like it, the shadow of something looms over me at all times, making my gut twist. I was once his girlfriend, someone he cared for, he respected, he treated me respectfully. Now I'm nothing but the hot piece of ass he parades around Manhattan as if he loves me... and then degrades all night, biting and choking... and I let him. I beg for him. And he never pretends to be anyone but who he is. He tells me I can leave. He stops if I say the safe word. I know that he's still so infected by her. I know he wants me just for relief. I hate it, but I just can't walk away.

"Why?" he asks.

"You're worth it," I reply, hoping he can see that I'd do anything he wanted. *Anything.*

The sharp sting of his whip lashes my ass. "A sub doesn't address her Master in such an intimate way. Is that understood?"

"Yes, my Lord."

Upon a pause heavy with irritation, he unclips the chain from my cuffs, and my hands drop to my back. He pulls on my arm, tugging me a few feet in the dark until the fronts of my legs hit the back of his sofa. He leans me over the side of it, pushing me all the way until my head hits the cushion, and I'm reduced to just my pussy.

"I'm going to bite you as I fuck you. Do you object to that?"

"No, my Lord."

Please bite me.

I hear the familiar rip of plastic as he tears open the wrapper of a condom. All these weeks since she dumped him and he still refuses to fuck me without one.

He still doesn't trust me.

I guess he shouldn't. I'm lying to him about being on birth control. I'm not exactly proud of it, but I know that once he sees our kid, he'll realize what he's too blind to see. If it wasn't for *her*, we'd have been married by now. I know that for a fact. We talked about it until that fucking day he met her.

He's deluding himself if he thinks she can cope with his needs anyway. She can't. Only I would fully accept his tastes. All of them. She would *never*.

I gasp as he leans his heavy naked frame over me and his erection prods my ass. I feel his breath on my cheek despite the black fabric over my face.

"What is your only purpose, sub?"

"To be your slave."

"Good. Now, beg me to fuck you."

"Please fuck me, my Lord. Please. Please hurt me."

"More."

"Please fuck me. Use my body. Do whatever you want to it."

"Very well."

He takes a moment and I feel him pulling the sheath onto his cock. He blankets my back again and his teeth find my shoulder, where he pauses.

But instead of driving into me hard and fast like he does most nights, he stops as his breathing shallows.

He doesn't move.

He begins to inhale my skin in loud pants, his lips touching my back.

It almost sounds like he's hyperventilating.

No...

His breaths, once calm and steady, now quicken in sharp blasts against my skin.

Not again...

I turn my head but he pushes my neck down so that I can't move. My heartbeat thumps in my ears for what feels like a full minute before I dare to speak. "My Lord?"

"That's enough for tonight."

No...

This fucker...

He pushes against my back to stand up.

"What?! No!" I exclaim.

He grabs my bun roughly under my hood. "You think you're cute, sub? Speaking to me like that?"

"I just, I'm so wet, my Lord. *Please.* Please fuck me."

"I decide when you're worthy of being fucked by me. Not you."

He pulls me up by my bun to a standing position.

The fucker thinks he can just do this again—bring me over here, get me wet and then not fuck me...

My patience is wearing thin...

You'll see...

He peels the hood off my face, glaring at me as I watch him with imploring eyes, my hands still handcuffed behind my back.

"I'll get my driver to take you back home. You'll be compensated for your time."

"Let me stay. Please..."

"No."

"I'll stay in the guestroom. I just... You may need me during the night... I'll do anything you want. You can hurt me as much as you want. Please... I won't bother you. I just... want to be here in case you need to fuck me."

His eyes slowly roam down my naked and bound body. I've been working out so much in the last few months. I was so scared he wouldn't get to see the full results of my work. He's the only one I'd ever have put myself through this for. Well, him and *one* other...

"Let me stay and be your little toy... in case you need me. I'll serve you, my Lord."

His eyes narrow as he appraises me. "You can serve me food. You'll eat in your room. You'll stay there. You won't make noise. You won't come out. You'll sleep naked. If I require you, I'll make it known. You won't talk. You won't resist. You won't make phone calls. You don't come to my room under any circumstances. If you stay tonight, you exist only for my pleasure. Is that understood?"

"Yes, my Lord."

"Turn around." He releases me from my cuffs and takes them off me. "In the fridge, there is some food. You will prepare it for me. You will not put on clothes other than an apron while you do it. You will serve me at the dining table and watch me eat. You will then take your meal and eat it in your room. Is that acceptable?"

"Yes, my Lord."

God, it's so fucking humiliating... but I know it'll be worth it in the end. I know he'll see the obvious one day. And if he doesn't, I know someone who will make him pay...

As I prepare his food, I glance under the cupboard to see him staring out of the balcony window. Again.

He's always looking out of that *fucking* window.

I know it's *her* he's thinking about. Her tormenting him. I can feel it...

Cameron

Are you there?

Do you feel me?

Do you see me?

Do you look for me the way I look for you?

Do you see my face in every room you enter?

Do you hear my voice in the dark... guiding you... the way you guide me?

Do you need me to save you? If you do, I'll be there. I'll take you away. I'd give my life to protect you.

I see your eyes, angel. They stun me from afar.

Do you see mine?

Do you feel my skin on yours?

Do you feel my palm against yours?

Do you taste me?

Help me to stay strong, angel.

Help me to endure this.

Let me feel your warmth.

Help me see your light.

The only light.

Let me keep you safe.

Let me hold you so that you're never afraid again.

Do you feel me, Jessynia?

Are you there?

Olivia

The tapping of the heavy rain on the glass doesn't stop him from peering out. I can't stand it when he does it.

Fucking prick...

I scan the length of his indecent body. He's changed into black sweatpants but his torso is naked—tall, thick, lean, muscular. I want to run my tongue up the rigid muscles of his back but he doesn't let me anymore. I'm only allowed to taste one part of him and it kills me to be limited like this where four years ago, I had free reign to touch him however I pleased...

"It's ready, Master," I say from the kitchen.

He pauses for a moment before turning to sit down at the long dining table, watching me as I carry the plate out and place it in front of him, putting it between the knife and fork I had placed there twenty minutes earlier.

"Wine, my Lord?"

"Côte de Nuits."

I head to the wine rack near the kitchen. It's perfectly organized, like everything in Cameron's life—well, almost everything. His mind has been a chaotic mess in the last few months, which for a man who needs control the way he does, has left him volatile and unpredictable.

Other men pursue me relentlessly. I could have my pick of Fifth Avenue multi-millionaires. I've slept with more than I can count. And yet, I'm addicted to the only one who looks through me, who sees someone else when he peers into my eyes.

I don't mean to hurt him, but he *has* to pay for that...

I bring the bottle back and grapple with the wine opener before finally uncorking it and pouring him a glass. His eyes remain affixed to the liquid long after it settles in his glass, as if studying blood, as if wondering if he could drown in the crimson pool.

"Sit," he orders, tipping his head slightly forward to indicate my place. The floor. At his feet. He likes me sitting there. I know what's coming...

I take a seat on the floor next to him and watch as he cuts into the steak and brings it to his lips, beginning to chew.

Without lifting his eyes to mine, he asks, "I didn't give you permission to look at me, sub."

"I'm sorry, my Lord," I respond as I drop my eyes, anxiety pumping through me.

After a minute or two, I take care to keep my chin down but lift my gaze to watch as he eats, checking to see whether he's showing any signs that anything tastes off. This part is always so nerve-wracking. He can't suspect. If he does, even for one second, I'll be out of his life for good, and this time, there'll be no going back.

Relief allows me to breathe as he devours the whole meal, placing the knife and fork neatly next to one another on the empty plate.

I feel his eyes on me. "Come here," he orders, and I shift towards him, closing the small gap between us, keeping my head down. "You've earned the right to make me come."

"Thank you, my Lord."

"Put your hands on your head, close your eyes and suck. Don't look at me."

He pulls down his pants to expose his erection as I interlace my hands over my head and lean into him so that my chest is resting on his thighs. My mouth finds his cock and I slide my lips over the head and begin to suck.

He tastes so good. He's so thick, so hard, so long. I would suck his cock day and night if he let me.

"Don't look at me," he snarls as I lift my eyes to meet his. "Close your fucking eyes."

I do as instructed and feel him lean back in his chair, gripping the arms tightly as I service him diligently. I've worked so hard to get it exactly how he likes it—using my tongue to slide up and down, my lips to kiss the head and the shaft, working my mouth to pleasure him, my saliva to make it feel like my sex.

I increase the pace, eyes still closed as his breathing becomes hoarse. "I'm going to ejaculate down your throat, sub. Is that acceptable to you?"

I nod my head as I work him harder, faster, saliva dripping as I feel him swell further and further until he suddenly lets out an audible breath and his cock begins to pulsate as he pumps his cum deep inside my throat and I swallow down the salty liquid.

He's always tasted so good.

And I'm so wet from giving him pleasure. I dream of him fucking me the way he used to.

Opening my eyes slowly, I raise my gaze to see that his eyes are closed and that he's gripping the arms of the chair. His chest rises and falls as his body shudders through the high.

As the seconds turn into a minute and his eyes remain shut, I realize what he's doing... He's thinking of *her*... I can always tell. I lose him completely. Not his body, but everything else. It's like he's not here anymore, and I hate it more than I can put into words.

If he doesn't get this under control, I'm gonna make him suffer, I swear to *God.*

Over a minute later, he finally opens his eyes, his face hardening as he finds mine.

God dammit, he doesn't know that he kills me when he looks at me like that. When we were together at college, *really* together, his gaze was soft. His touch was caring, gentle—other than when he fucked me like the savage that he is, obviously. Now he does the latter, except I don't get the warm gazes or the interlaced fingers or the shared jokes. He's fucking well killing me and I can't say no to it.

When I tell him he hurts me, he tells me I should leave and never come back and that he'll only hurt me again. I just can't give up hope that he'll see how perfect we are together. It's obvious to everyone but *him.*

I know I can make him see it...

His brow furrows, his expression almost pained as he looks at me.

It kills me.

"Thank you for giving me the right to pleasure you, Master."

In truth, I hate him for not being able to bring himself to fuck me.

He bows his head slowly, his thick brown hair flopping over his face. The man is so insanely beautiful that it still takes my breath away to behold him. “Now take your food and water and go to your room. Don’t come out until 8 o’clock. If you hear noises, don’t come to investigate. I've warned you about appearing in my room before. It’s not safe. Is that understood?”

“Yes, my Lord.”

“Good. Now get up.”

25

Olivia

I hear the first cry around 3 a.m.

It's rough and primitive—unconscious sounds from a breaking psyche.

I haven't been able to fall into deep sleep. I've been waiting for this moment, and the man that I worship never disappoints.

I get to my feet, naked, as per his preference, and slide my phone from the nightstand, making sure that it's on silent before heading to the door. I turn the handle very carefully indeed and make my silent journey over to his room, my feet pressing into the smooth hardwood between us as the fear of getting caught causes my heart to race.

I hear him better now—hoarse groans and grunts of distress.

The first time I heard him when we were at college, I thought for a moment that he was jerking off. I'd never heard nightmares like it. I'd heard of night terrors before but had never seen them with my own eyes.

They are horrifying, and yet somehow, I feel closer to him when I witness them. His pain soothes me. I feel like he can see the darkness, just as I can. I know hardly anyone else has seen him like that. Gabriel has, I know that. He told me Jack had. And then *her*.

God knows what she thinks of them...

The first time he choked me during a night terror, I thought he was going to kill me. I had a red mark around my neck for days. The aftermath of that night bonded him to me. He was so fucking apologetic. *Destroyed.* He could barely look me in the eyes. It was perfection. And I could play the traumatized little woman card to get him to tend to me, to right his wrong. I don't know many women who could tolerate something like that. That's another reason we're so perfect. I can handle the nightmares. I don't judge him for them. I *like* them.

My trembling hand clasps the round handle of his door and turns it, opening the door slowly to see him in bed, his body jerking, low grunts of pain tearing from his throat. The dark-gray sheet only covers the lower half of him, just up to his belly button. The rest of him is exposed and glistening in beads of sweat which envelop his flexing muscles.

The man looks like God even in this state.

He works out constantly these days. He has too much pent-up energy that he has to get out, and brutalizing me clearly doesn't do it for him. The side-effect of his workouts is that his body is now indecent. His muscles are huge and tight. If only he'd let me taste them like I want to...

I double-click the button on my phone and begin to record, lifting it into the dark room. You can't see much, but you can see some movement and hear the primitive noises he's making as his body jerks wildly.

Fuck...

Despite my quivering state and my fear of dropping it, I manage to record for almost a minute before leaving the room and shutting off the camera, turning my phone off, and placing it deep inside my bag. I won't turn it back on until tomorrow when I leave... just in case...

But sixty seconds of footage—he will be pleased.

Tiptoeing back across the apartment, I stop in his doorway once again.

He'll wake up soon, panting and sweating. He's seen God knows how many doctors and therapists, but he can't make the rabid dreams stop. And honestly, he's fucking irresistible when he has them. So tortured. So tormented. So deviant. Even when he chokes me without knowing it, I like it. I like being taken to the brink by him. It's this journey into hell that only the two of us can fully understand.

At some point, the things he does to me will be so heinous that he has no choice but to be with me forever. I just have to wait. It'll happen...

I head over to the bed and sit down next to him, watching him grimace through whatever visions have taken hold of him. He's never told me exactly what they are, but I know he sees himself as a monster in them. He dreams that he's hurting people—that much I'm sure of.

Wanting to wake him before he wakes up and sees me there, I place a hand on his slippery arm and shout, "Cameron! Wake up! Cameron!"

The name that rips from his throat tears my heart to pieces, causing my body to freeze from the trauma of living in the shadow of *her*. "Jess... Jessynia... Run!"

You fuck...

He dared to say her name to me.

He dared to do it...

I hate you...

Despite the fury raging through me, I put on my best concerned face, and pull on his arm. A second later, I'm thrown onto my back and his hands are around my throat. He begins to squeeze and oh fucking God, does it feel good...

Do it, you fucker...

I can take it...

I know he's fucked in the head after every time it happens, so convinced he's a freak beyond redemption. A monster. That's how I need him to feel. That's how he'll know that only I can soothe him. Can accept him for the deviant he is.

I get ready to hit underneath the crook of his elbow, as I've been taught, forming a fist and punching the spot that will make his arm flex and release the grip of his hand.

Look scared...

As I punch and his hand releases from me, I land one on his jaw and his grip on my neck eases further.

As I shout "*Stop!*", he jolts awake, blinking into the moonlight.

Any second now...

"Jess—"

The motherfucker did not repeat her fucking name to me...

He did not!

"Cam," I whimper, sliding my hand up his arm as he loosens his grip on my neck.

He closes his eyes for a moment, horror and shame written all over his face.

That's how I'll get him...

He grimaces as it dawns on him what happened, dropping his head in disgust at himself.

"I... I told you not to come in here," he manages as he catches his breath. "I told you to stay the fuck out."

"I couldn't." I run my hands up his tense arms, squeezing his biceps. He flinches, prying my hands off him. "I heard you screaming. I can't stand you being in pain, Cameron. You know that."

"How long did it last?" he asks.

"I don't know. I woke you as soon as I heard. But I don't know how long you were having it before the noise woke me up."

He closes his eyes again, breathing through the reality.

You are damaged goods, Cameron. A deviant. A freak.

And no amount of therapy is going to fix what you are.

"I don't want you coming in here while I'm having one of these things," he says, barely able to look at me. "I've told you that before repeatedly. It's dangerous."

"I like the danger," I respond as he glances down at my naked breasts.

He considers me for a moment before dropping his head.

"Leave, Olivia," he orders, and hate claws at my insides. "Leave before I hurt you."

He lifts his leg up as if to unstraddle me but I grab his thigh and push it back down.

"I don't want to leave," I say softly. "I want you to hurt me. I understand you, Cameron. Better than anyone else. I accept all of you. Let me soothe you. Please."

His eyes narrow as I run one hand up his arms again.

"Choke me, Cameron. Choke me. Get it all out. I can make you feel sane again..."

I glance down at his cock. He's hard. He's always hard during his nightmares. He's such a good fuck just after he's had one...

I reach a hand down tentatively, turning my wrist so that I can wrap my fingers around the shaft lying on my lean stomach. He flinches but lets me.

"What do you want?" he asks.

"To be your slave, Cameron. That's all I've ever wanted. Can't you see that?"

"You know I don't love you."

"You will one day. Once you realize that you can be yourself with me. You shouldn't have to hide from your partner. She should embrace every part of you. *I* do. No one else ever will. No one will ever love you the way I do."

His chest rises and falls slowly as his breathing tempers. "Put your hands in the holes."

I'll get you...

I let go of his cock and extend my hands backwards, finding two of the many holes in his headboard. I thread my hands through them and he reaches forwards and opens a drawer, pulling out a pair of handcuffs. He sits up and attaches them to my wrists from behind the headboard before getting up and pulling out two ties from the drawer, using them to tie my ankles to his bedposts. The bed is king-sized and my legs are spread very wide indeed. He once left me like this for hours as he worked on his laptop in the living room, coming back in to fuck me every hour without saying a word. It was the hottest experience of my life.

He reaches for a sheath in the drawer and straddles me again. As he rips the wrapper open, I say, "You don't have to use that. I'm clean. You have me tested every week. And I'm on birth control."

I know I'm clean. He's not the only one who has me tested. What he doesn't trust me on is the birth control issue. I mean, he's right not to trust me, but it'd just take one little accident for him to finally wake up...

"The next time you address me, sub, I'll whip you so hard that you can't sit for a week. Do you understand?"

"Yes, my Lord," I say, as he rolls the condom over his swollen cock. He finds my sex a second later and grunts loudly as he penetrates me, tipping his head back in pleasure. He places his hands on either side of my arms and glares down at me coldly as he begins to fuck me.

"Stick your tongue out, sub. Don't make any noises."

I do as I'm told and savor this godlike man. He must feel how good this is. He must.

I've only ever felt anything like this with one other man...

But it's not him I love. It's Cameron. And I'll do what it takes to make him wake up.

"What's the point of you, sub?" he asks.

"To service you, Master. To give you pleasure."

"Do you exist for any other reason?"

"No, my Lord."

"Do you deserve to be bitten?"

"Yes, my Lord."

"Beg for it."

"Please bite me, sir. Please. I'll do whatever you want."

He leans forward, and I tip my head to the side so that he can bite. He likes the flesh between my neck and shoulder and I don't care how many marks he leaves on me. I wear them with pride, every single one. He thrusts his cock into me as he bites. I moan as his teeth bite down harder and he jerks inside me more roughly.

I know he's gonna come this time...

Finally releasing his teeth from my skin, he sits back up, watching me as he fucks me.

I smile, lovingly. I need him to know that unlike *her*, my submission is unequivocal. I will always give him what he wants. Nothing is too much for me, *ever*.

His gaze darkens as he watches me and his thrusting slows down.

No...

Not this again...

As if realizing something, he stops completely, no longer moving, his head bowed, his hair falling over his face, plunging it into shadow.

"Please keep going," I implore. "Please."

His breathing quickens and his body becomes rigid... and a while later, I feel a droplet fall onto my stomach... and another.

No...

Not this.

"Master, don't stop."

I hate you...

I hate you so much...

I know who he's thinking of. Who he's tortured by. I can *feel* it.

"Master, please don't stop."

On a deep breath, he pulls out of me, and gets to his feet.

He ignores me completely and unties my ankles and then uncuffs me.

"I need you to leave, Olivia," he says solemnly. "Today is... not a good day."

I shake my head. "No. I'm not going."

"One of my men will drive you home."

"*No*. Please. It's 4 a.m., for fuck's sake. It's humiliating. Let me stay. I'll stay in the guest room. I won't come out till morning. Please."

He pauses for a moment.

"You have to be gone by eight o'clock."

"Fine," I retort, humiliation making me tremble inside.

He watches me until I get to my feet, walking behind me until I get to the guest room.

"Do you want to come in?" I ask from the doorway.

"Goodnight, Olivia," he says, pulling the door shut behind him.

How much fucking humiliation does he think I can take?

I never quite show him how much he hurts me. I guess I could just leave and not come back like he keeps telling me to, but I can't... I've tried.

I pace the room, indignation making my skin mist.

Fucking asshole.

Thinks he can fuck me and not come...

Fucking prick.

Glancing at my bag, I head over to it, delving deep inside a zipped compartment for a black notepad. I pull out the pen tucked into a black elastic band around it, writing fast with shaky hands.

March 8th

7mg administered and ingested.

No sign of suspicion.

Night terror.

Groaning. Writhing. Sweating.

He said her name three times.

Tormented.

Tried to fuck me but couldn't make it all the way through.

Tears.

Over her.

Still cold towards me.

He's losing his mind.

I close the book and put it and the pen back inside the deep pocket, and zip it back up.

I take a few minutes to calm down.

It's gonna be okay.

He's contaminated by her.

We all know it.

It can't last forever...

7.45 a.m.

The sight of this fucked up man in his gray designer pants and crisp white shirt makes me wonder how long he can keep up the façade, how long he can pretend to the world that he isn't damaged beyond repair...

"I still wanna come to the gala with you on Saturday," I say. "I've cleared my schedule for it."

His eyes glare, but I see the contrition behind them that he's trying to conceal. That's how I'll get him...

"Maybe we should take a break from each for a while, Olivia. This isn't healthy."

"No! I don't care about last night. I want to be with you, even when you're like that. Let me come. I know it's an important night for you."

He takes a moment before nodding slowly. "Use the credit card I gave you to get a dress and... whatever else you need." My eyes can't help but be drawn to his neck as he winds his tie around it and does it up, turning back into the god he is in the Financial District as he gets ready to leave for work.

"Don't you want to see me before then?" I ask as I put on my coat.

"No. We need some space."

"Okay," I sigh out. "So... will you pick me up?"

He nods. "Seven o'clock." He gestures with his head towards the manila envelope lying on the cabinet near the front door. "For your time and... effort."

I shake my head slowly. "You make me feel like a hooker, giving me money like this."

"It's for your expenses, Olivia. Nothing more. You either take it or we don't see each other again."

My expenses? He gives me thousands each week, no doubt to allay his guilt. I sometimes forget what it's like to be around men who feel guilt and shame. Cameron always reminds me.

"Call me if you need me," I say.

"I won't."

26

Jessynia

I haven't been to a ball in nine months. The last was that night on Wall Street when I met Cameron on the rooftop, the first time I'd spoken to him in two and a half years, since our falling out over Jack.

That night feels like a day ago and a decade ago at the same time—rediscovering Cam's face, hearing his voice again, taking in the transformation—from college student to a powerful, formidable man whose glare strips layers from you.

As the clinks of glasses and the obligatory guffaws from nearby tables melt into a muddy mess of dissonant sounds, my mind flits through images of the last year—finding that phone, the torment of Jack's affairs, seeing him with Alexandra in the Hamptons, being taken to the Society to watch the initiation, conversing intimately with Sebastian for the first time, then the agony and ecstasy of being with Cameron and losing him. And then... being pulled further into the Society, into the unforgiving domain of Sebastian Gravier. And finally, watching the bloody spectacle of murder.

I bring the glass of sparkling wine to my lips, hoping to drown out the unbidden staticky images shooting across my field of vision like the trails of burning bullets in the night. They seem to hit me out of nowhere, and it takes me a few seconds to shake them out.

Jack squeezes my thigh, and I peer up at him, putting on my warmest grin. I used to take events like this in my stride, but today, even surrounded by friends of mine, I feel wafer-thin in my off-the-shoulder forest-green dress despite the hearty smiles I'm mustering up to make my way through this most opulent of social functions.

Jack knows I'm now a little jumpy at these occasional gatherings of Manhattan's high society. It used to be that I was afraid that people would internally smirk at the façade of our sham of a marriage given the probable rumors about Jack's infidelity, our separation... and perhaps about Cameron. Now I worry that members of the Society are watching us, and will appear without warning, dragging the attempted innocence of our world into dark water.

I don't know exactly when I started giving a shit what people thought, but this year has made the foundation under me feel brittle. Once you've seen through the looking glass, the images around you become distorted—the people, the smiles, the hidden motives in what may be perfectly innocent questions...

I hate the feeling...

Not to mention that since getting wrapped up with the Society, I now feel eyes on me all the time, even when rationally I know no one is there...

And to top it all off, part of me fears that Cameron will hear of me and Jack going to social functions as a couple again. I know we have the right to, but I don't want to hurt him.

My gaze is drawn to a waiter dressed all in black carrying a tray of drinks past our table. I only had to casually mention Stella inviting me to a charity ball for Jack to jump all over it. As composed and adept as he is at social functions, he doesn't usually give a shit about events like these, but he's wanted to reconnect with Stella and Kevin for weeks. I've been putting it off because I know how they feel about me being back with him. But tonight, it's just Stella and Kevin and I know they'll just about behave for my sake. I can't say the same about Maddie. Not yet, at least.

Jack has good-naturedly smiled in subtle amusement through each one of Stella's glares and Kevin's digs. He doesn't get intimidated easily, if at all, which only seems to be making Stella more irked.

I glug down the dregs of my third glass of champagne as Jack charms the pants off everyone in sight, fielding questions with ease, making the table laugh, even Kevin at times, all the while glancing down at me frequently, his eyes lighting up as I smile at his jokes, his easy demeanor, his sinful way of undressing you with his eyes.

As a couple on the other side of the round table get up to dance to the easy lounge music under glistening chandeliers, and another lose themselves in conversation, Jack takes the opportunity to speak to my friends. I squeeze his strong hand under the table as a warning to play nice...

"Thank you for inviting us, Stella."

"I invited *Jess*," she shoots back, and I blink slowly and shake my head at madam which has her sucking in a deep breath as if to compose herself. I glance to the right at Jack whose lips curve in mirth —just a tiny amount—at my friend's ball-stomping manner of conversing. He knows Stella well, and despite her lingering enmity towards him, I'm sure he knows that the fact that she's conversing with him at all is a good sign.

"Well, I appreciate being allowed to tag along," Jack says as Kevin, dressed in an eye-catching maroon suit sitting next to Stella, shoots me one of several "Oh boy" looks that we've been exchanging tonight. An elegantly dressed woman in her forties whose partner has left to chat to someone nearby smiles at me though I don't know her, having only met her tonight. I'm sure she's picked up on tension between Jack and my friends, and no doubt finds the sight rather amusing. I grin back at her before turning to face my friends.

"More wine?" I sing to cut the tension as Stella places her empty flute back onto the table. Without waiting for an answer, I turn to find a waiter hovering nearby. "Could we get some more white wine, please, sir?"

"Of course."

As the waiter brings some over to our table, Jack asks Kevin and

Stella how they've been doing. Kevin, now visibly tipsy and getting used to being around Jack again, regales us with a story about an insufferable interior design client of his while Stella slow-blinks at me as Jack winds his hand around the back of my neck, the slip of his strong fingers against my skin sending a frisson down my spine, a reminder of how intensely dominant he is, how possessive even the most minor gesture feels.

I smile at Stella, grateful that she's making some small effort to control her maternally outraged instincts and accommodate his presence. I love how protective my friends are of me, but I need things to feel somewhat normal, whatever that means.

"Did you not get any red flags from your first conversation with her?" Jack asks Kevin.

"Sure I did, but I needed the money. If I'd known what a miserable cunt she'd turn out to be, I'd have paid for her to find another designer."

Jack's chuckle relieves some of the tension and makes Kevin grin despite himself. I don't believe I'm the only one who gets a high making the formidable Jackson Wilder laugh.

"So how did it turn out?" Jack asks. "The apartment?"

"The woman has the tastes of a baboon on acid, so I gave her what she wanted."

"Was she happy with it?" I grin.

"Yeah. I mean, it looks like the seventies threw up in there," he utters in contempt, "so the broad's in heaven."

Jack's eyes meet me as I giggle through Kevin's visuals and his unimpressed facial expressions. His gaze makes its slow path down to my lips which he studies in that manner of his which lets me know how he'll be employing my mouth later on.

"So, how's work, Jack?" Stella asks, her face amusingly dour as she interrupts the moment of intimacy between Jack and I which, no doubt, annoyed her to no end.

"By Wall Street standards, good, Stella," Jack responds as they begin to watch each other. I know Jack's trying with Stella, for my sake, but he's not the type who backs down in the face of hostility. It's not in his

DNA. He doesn't fidget or get intimidated like most people do, and it takes a lot to knock him off balance. As savage as my gorgeous friend is, it'll take a lot more than Stella's death glare to get under Jack's skin.

"How's lawyer life?" he asks. "Still mostly dealing with assholes?"

"Well, they're hard to avoid around these parts," she replies with an eye roll, a pointed dig at Jack.

I shake my head at her slowly as Jack bows his head in capitulation at the insinuation. I then watch in an incongruous blend of horror and amusement as he shoots her one of his heart-stopping, panty-melting smiles and turns to me. "Fancy a dance, beautiful?" Jack asks.

"No fucking way!" I shoot back. "I'm so drunk."

"I'll lead," he replies, pulling his chair back.

"What? No!"

Ignoring me entirely, Jack gets to his feet, gripping my hand and pulling me to standing. Despite my vocal protests, he leads me firmly to the dancefloor where numerous couples are swaying to soft, elegant music under crystal chandeliers.

"I'm hammered, you know," I moan as he pulls me into him, one hand snaking around my back as the other lifts mine into the air, his fingers grasping my palm possessively.

His lips dip into mine. "I've got you."

"Well, if I throw up all over the dancefloor, you've only got yourself to blame," I groan to a glint of amusement in his eyes.

"Noted, madam."

"That went..."

"Better than I expected," he finishes, his lips widening into a stunning smile. "Though I'm sensing that Stella would enjoy half an hour with me alone in a room with a baseball bat."

"God, don't mind her. She's got the protective instincts of a polar bear."

"I was expecting worse," he replies dryly.

"What, did you expect them to throw food at you?"

"Food, forks, knives," he jests as a grin escapes me. "I'm sure I saw Stella eyeing her knife on a few occasions."

"She's always been a mama bear with me," I smile. "Honestly, it was such a good idea to bring that hot colleague of yours over to distract Stella and Kevin. If he hadn't been there—"

"They'd have stabbed me with a fork," he suggests.

"At least they were civil to you," I chuckle.

"It's a start," he smiles.

"Well, it was a good idea, bringing Jeremy. Pity he had to leave so early."

"It did seem to distract Stella momentarily," he concedes.

"You can't blame her. The man is hot."

Jack's eyes narrow.

"I mean, objectively speaking," I backtrack, shaking my head at his jealous glare.

He pulls me into him more tightly, staring at my mouth. "I liked watching you tonight, angel," he growls. "I like the way you eat. I like the way you laugh. My colleague does too. I know the fucker was thinking about fucking you."

"What?! No he wasn't!" I giggle. "You're nuts, Wilder."

"Yes, he was. He couldn't keep his eyes off you."

"He was just being friendly."

"I know how men's minds work, Jessynia. He was picturing your tits and your pussy the entire meal."

"Stop!" I admonish with a giggle designed to assuage the green-eyed monster.

"I suppose it's what I get for marrying the world's most fuckable woman."

I shake my head.

"I'm supposed to work with the fucker on Monday. I hope he makes it out alive."

"Jack, stop," I giggle.

He breathes out heavily. "I want to be a civilized man, Jessynia, but unfortunately for both of us, when other men look at you, I want to rip their throats out. It seems to be built into my DNA."

"Don't use that as an excuse!" I grin. "We all have control over our actions."

"So I've been told," he retorts wryly, and I can't help but smile as he leads us perfectly in the elegant dance.

Jack looks down for a moment, his countenance more solemn when he meets my eyes again. "Jessynia, I want us to go and see your parents. It's time."

I peer up at his resolute face, melting into the strong arms guiding us through the gentle dance. His glacial eyes burn with blue flame as he takes me in, absorbing the minute movements of my face.

"You're a glutton for punishment, Wilder."

"I want this to work," he responds soberly. "No more separate compartments. No more secrets."

I glance momentarily at a couple to our right, swaying to the sumptuous music before finding Jack again. "I fear we'll need a SWAT team on standby," I say.

"I can handle whatever your mother has to say to me, angel. We have to get this over and done with."

"Okay," I sigh and his chest deflates as if letting out a breath he's been holding in for a long time.

"Good." He pulls me into him, dropping his lips to my ear. "I know we're not fully healed yet. We'll get there. I'll take us to that place, Jess. You just have to believe I can do it."

His bold words stun me as they so often do. I peer up at him, soaking in the radiance of his indecent masculinity as he pulls back to look at me, eyes gleaming. I nod and a faint smile plays on his lips as he holds me, moving me in an effortless slow dance, our eyes locked into each other.

I want to believe you, Jack...

I want to forget everything.

I want to forget that everyone else exists.

I'm trying.

His eyes half-close as he takes in my lips. "We're going to have to leave soon," he whispers.

"Why?" I ask, biting my lip as my cheeks flush hot. I know the answer. I'm just teasing him... and he knows it.

"Because I need to see my cock down your throat very shortly. I'm not sure we'll make it back home..."

I shake my head and his eyes glitter at my disapproval. "You're a deviant."

"Which is why you married me, Mrs. Wilder."

His face warms in amusement at my blushing smile, and his hand slides into the seam at the back of my emerald-hued dress, the contact with his fingers making my skin tingle. He pulls me in so close that I feel his breath on my face... but as I do so, the tingling warmth of his touch turns to ice cold, and a blast of air makes my hair stand on end.

I pivot my head slightly, looking out onto glistening tables full of merry guests, the sight of them blurring into one big glowing mass under the effects of too many glasses of Moscato, the sounds morphing into some distorted, gurgling cacophony of dissonant notes.

Just breathe, Jess, I mutter to myself, hating the constriction of claustrophobia which started happening to me in public after finding out of Jack's affairs with Alexandra, such a high-profile woman around these parts...

I take a deep breath and shake the clawing unease off, only to feel Jack releasing me from his grip. As I turn back to look at him, I see him draw his phone from his pocket and bring it to his ear, speaking firmly over the music. "Outside. Right now."

He hangs up, his face hardened by wrath, his eyes fixed to something behind me. I turn swiftly, peering through dancing couples to the space behind them—waiters, guests and people standing around the edges.

Wait...

From somewhere across the room, eyes blaze into me for a moment, but in a flurry of movement, I lose them, the view blocked by swaying couples.

No...

"We're leaving," Jack announces roughly, his fingers finding mine as he leads me from the dancefloor, tugging me hard.

"Hey," I utter. "What is it?"

I turn to look in the direction he was looking in, but see nothing but the blurred faces of strangers… until…

No…

I'm jolted again by the sight of eyes burning into me.

Bodies pass by, blocking the view…

And then I see them again…

Blazing amber eyes.

My mouth goes instantly dry.

He's standing next to her—Olivia, her blond hair tied into a bun, her body sheathed in a black silk dress.

I haven't seen her in so long…

She's glaring at me…

Around them are well-heeled members of Manhattan's elite. I spot a businessman and his wife, a politician and her real estate mogul husband…

And then him, his cedar-hued eyes burrowing into me as I pant through the shockwave.

What are you doing here?

"Thank you for inviting us," Jack says to Stella after we weave through the room and finally reach our table.

He picks up my purse from my chair as Stella's eyes flit to mine. "You're leaving?"

"I have a very early call tomorrow," Jack responds as Kevin eyes me quizzically. "We need to get going."

"Yeah, sorry, guys," I stammer. "I'll call you tomorrow."

Jack doesn't wait for Stella to get all the way to her feet to say goodbye, instead tugging me out of the room firmly, past throngs of merry socialites reveling in the ludic innocence of their night out.

The elevator we take down is half-full, and Jack's eyes remain affixed to the door as we make our way to coat-check downstairs, retrieving our coats and exiting the building.

We don't speak as he leads me down the street to the end of the block where I see his black SUV parked, its lights still on. He opens the back door and gestures for me to enter, which I do, to spy Leon watching me from the rear-view mirror. My eyes turn to Jack as I wait for him to get in. He looks at me, fury chiseled into the sharp cuts of his angular face, but instead of getting in, he reaches into my purse and grabs my phone, throwing the purse into the back seat before slamming the door shut.

"Hey!" I shout, reaching for the handle, pulling it only to find the door locked. "Unlock the fucking door, Leon!" I turn to the other side to find it locked too, watching as Jack peers through the front driver's window.

"Take her home."

"No!"

He ignores my plea. "Stay with her. Make sure she doesn't call anyone. Or leave until I get there."

"No! Jack, just come—"

Before I can finish the sentence, Leon pulls out, leaving me watching a bristling Jack through the back window as he turns to walk back towards the building we just came out of in determined strides that arrow panic into me.

"Leon, stop the fucking car!" I shout. "Now!"

He glances at me briefly but keeps on driving, his face hard as nails as he weaves through traffic.

"Take me back, Leon. I'm not kidding! There's gonna be blood spilled!"

"Isn't that you want, little girl?" he sneers.

"Of course not!"

"Hmm... Well, you'll get it soon enough."

"What's that supposed to mean?"

"Put your fucking seatbelt on."

"No! Let me out of this car, now!"

His shadowy eyes find me as we hit a red light. "Put it on, little girl, or I'll come back there and tie you to your seat myself."

27

Cameron

"He's on his way up."

"Is the room ready?" I ask.

"Yeah. Just lead him to it."

I hang up the phone, slipping it into my pocket as I watch for him, my heart racing as I wait for him to appear in the doorway of the room... if he's not too much of a coward to face me.

I tune out the nauseating hum of small talk around me, aware that Olivia has stopped speaking to the group we are with and is glaring at me, watching me as she would do day and night if I let her. Very soon, I'll be letting her go for good, for her sake as much as mine.

There he is...

So, you do have the guts...

He appears after all, his eyes meeting mine through the room, through the crowd, the heat of him annihilating the loathsome guffaws and the clumsy clinks of drinks around us... or at least, that's how it feels since she was taken possession of like a pawn in some sick game played by even sicker people. Nothing tastes the same. Nothing feels bearable anymore when someone you love is trapped and has stopped fighting.

I knew you'd come...

My eyes remain fixed on him as I turn my head slightly to speak to Olivia. "I want you to leave in ten minutes. Thank you for accompanying me."

"No, I'll wait till you've finished."

"No. It won't be safe to be around me tonight. I can't allow it."

"I don't care. I want to come over anyway."

"No. I want you to leave before I'm out. This is your last warning."

As she turns to distract the people we are talking to as I instructed her to earlier, I make my way to the door in the corner of the room—one where only staff usually venture to collect food or drinks.

Wrath makes my body stiff, my heart thunder, my fists tense as I walk through it. I see his hands on her body, feel the touch of his fingers on her skin. The way he looked at her—I know the look. I look at her the same way. I look at her as if I want to devour her.

But she looked... distracted.

She felt something. I know it.

I feel when she's near me. I know she does the same.

I know she thinks of me when she's with him...

Despite rage making me tremble, I head down the corridor as planned and turn back to watch him as he appears through the glass window of the door. He pushes it open and enters the hallway as I continue down it, taking a right down to a deserted part of the bowels of this building. The man I paid to ensure safe passage and reserve a room loiters before its door. He nods as I approach and leaves, crossing Jack's path as he stalks me... as planned.

I push the door open and enter the room.

It is unlit, but that's how I like it. That's how I've lived of late... since watching her be taken, since watching her fall, be drawn into a world she should have no part of. The light feels wrong without her.

I walk in slowly, heading to the window, turning to watch the man whose existence I've known almost as long as my own enter the room...

The man who took her back by force.

The man whose fingers just trailed along her skin.

The man who can hold her in his arms because he allowed an evil man to scare her to death.

He stalks towards me slowly, his face hard, his hands fisting for a moment by his sides. He comes to stand ten feet before me, breathing heavily as he takes in my face, his expression a vision of wrath that could only match mine...

I take him in for a moment—as tall as me, as strong, his face broad, his eyes wild.

My fingers tense as I fight the urge to rip his throat out...

"I didn't know if you'd have the guts," I snarl.

His body seizes as his breathing quickens. "What do you want?"

"Come to see the happy couple," I say, cognizant of the bitter note to my voice.

"The deal is that you keep away from my fucking wife."

"Wife?" I shake my head as he narrows his eyes at my clear contempt for the word. "A man who takes his woman back by force loses the right to call her his wife. You're her fucking jailor. Nothing more than that."

He takes a step towards me, his eyes ablaze. "What do you want?"

"To let you know that I'm not giving up. Ever."

"And you'd put her fucking family at risk because you can't stand to lose?"

"Lose? She didn't choose this, and you know it. As for your deal, I didn't make that deal. I don't make deals with men who force their wives back by hurting their families. Burning houses. Drugging people. Does that make you feel like a man, Jack?"

He shakes his head, taking a step towards him. "She didn't sign that pact with me."

"No, but you stood by and let that fucking monster threaten her. Threaten her family. Her brother."

"I didn't know anything about that," he growls. "Not *one* fucking thing."

For a second, it happens, as it always does. I see him as he was when I first met him, twenty years ago. I see the lost child.

I take a moment to compose myself in the face of a man I once loved and who is now a stranger.

"No," I continue. "You didn't want to know, did you? You didn't ask questions, did you, Jack? But you do know how sick he is. You know how his mind works. You knew she'd be forced back to you through terror, didn't you? Did it feel good? To fuck a woman who's *terrified*?"

"Terrified?" he sneers. "*I'm* the one she's safe with. It's *you* she should be afraid of. Do you think I don't know what you are, you freak?"

Jack

His eyes burn into me in the kind of defiant provocation that most men don't dare around me. His hair is thick, longer than I've seen it, framing his face, almost a mask, through which glare the most piercing of eyes.

"You don't know anything about me, Jack," he responds bitterly. "Not anymore. Not since I escaped… unlike *you*. I know your wife better than you do. And she's afraid. That's why she lets you fuck her. That's why she lets your lips on her."

A swell of rage surges through my body. "You're about three fucking words away from having that pretty face of yours smashed in, O'Neill."

"Yeah, that's about right," he spits back, nodding slowly. "Show me who you really are. A coward just like your piece of shit father. I guess he taught you everything he knows about how to treat women—"

The punch escapes me before I even realize it. The thing is untameable, charged with hatred and fury and indignation at his words—words that would convey everything I've spent my life trying to avoid becoming.

My worst fear realized.

He attempts to block the blow, but it makes its way through his hands, colliding with his mouth, splitting the skin open before my eyes.

His free arm swings and I deflect the punch with my arm. He kicks hard into my knee, sending me backwards, allowing him to cock his right arm and land a punch onto my eye socket.

In truth, I saw the thing coming. I could have blocked it. I didn't...

As the blow sends me stumbling backwards, my palm hits the carpeted floor of the empty room. I pause for a moment before peering up at him, my gaze falling to his lip glistening dark red in the dim light, the room illuminated only by the lights from Manhattan outside.

I wonder for a second if he'd kick when I'm on the ground like the men in my family would.

I know he wouldn't...

He stares down at me, breathing heavily as I get to my feet. I swipe the inner seam of my hand against my eye, bringing it down to observe the glistening streak of blood.

We've always drawn blood when we've fought. Always.

Shaking off the blow, I take a step towards him, studying his face—wild, his whole being consumed by the wrath of jealousy. I know the feeling too well, for every time a man looks at her, I want to end his life.

"Go ahead," I snarl, keeping my hands low. "Do it again."

He breathes through his rage, just as I do mine, our chests panting in unison as his eyes, wrapped in shadow, burn with rage.

He doesn't look good. He looks pained—I see myself a few months ago when he dared to take my wife from me. I know the agony.

He can drown in it for all I care.

I wait for him to punch again, but he doesn't, his chest heaving as his eyes dart all over my face.

"Stay the fuck away from my wife," I order.

He shakes his head, his contempt for my order palpable. "Make me."

Before I can stop myself, I grab him by the shirt, spinning him around and shoving him hard against the wall. He doesn't flinch as my fingers grab the top of his shirt.

"What did you say to me?" Some desperate howl of jealousy tinges my words.

"I'll stay away from you... permanently... the day she tells me she's with you because she loves you, and for no other reason. Not because she's afraid. Not because Gravier has ordered it. Not because she's trying to keep anyone safe. When she tells me she is with you for one reason only, I will walk away. For good."

My fist tightens around his shirt as he dares to say this to me. "She doesn't have to tell you *anything*. And you know *nothing* about us beyond what you choose to believe. No one will ever take my wife from me again."

"That's where you're wrong," he snarls. "You may be the only one fucking that girl, but you're not only the only one in her head as you're doing it."

I put one hand around his throat, lifting and cocking my other fist as he watches me unmoving, eyes widening in satisfaction at my ire, not a hint of fear in his face.

I want to punch. I want to rip his throat out. I've dreamed of standing over his dead body more times than I can count, of putting a bullet between his eyes... but the fucking punch doesn't come.

Maybe it's because he's not moving, not defending himself.

The grim gratification in his eyes dissolves, turning into something somber, hollow as his eyes wander slowly to my fist and then back to meet me, his eyes misting as he takes me in.

"It isn't only *me* you have to worry about, Jack," he jeers.

I frown as I study the contours of his face, the tips of my bent fingers hot against his neck. "What the fuck are you talking about?"

"You know exactly what. That monster is in her head. You know how she works. You know what she's trying to do. And seeing as you can't protect her from him, I'll make that my job, so that she doesn't end up in the *ground*."

His words steal my breath, leaving me frowning into eyes I knew as a child—a boy I was once inseparable from.

He searches my face, his pupils dilating and contracting onto mine, his expression falling into something akin to distress. I see myself in the glistening reflection in the center of his irises.

"She saw him once. She doesn't see him anymore," I spit back.

"That's where you're wrong..."

I drop my fist, trying to control my frantic breaths.

She can't have...

Not again...

“Stay away from my fucking wife,” I repeat, aware of the silent plea distorting the order.

I finally let go of him, pushing back to look at him once more before I turn to walk out.

As I reach the doorway, his words stop me in my tracks.

“She didn’t know about tonight. You hurt her for it,” he threatens, “and I’ll make you pay.”

I turn around to face him. “I’ll discipline my fucking wife how I see fit.”

He takes two steps towards me, and I square my body to face him again. “You heard what I said,” he reiterates, and I seethe at his threat. I feel the fire in him, the need to protect her... and I hate him for it. “You touch her, and I will make you pay. On my *life*.”

I contemplate the broken, bloody skin of his lip, my fist desperate to split it further, to pummel his face until he’s a bloody mess as I’ve done to so many men...

Instead, I turn to walk away.

Sebastian...

28

Sebastian

"Take a seat, Jack."

Isaiah closes the door behind him as remnant flecks of blood, dried over the swollen, mottled skin above his eye fall into vivid focus.

Not her.

The girl wouldn't hurt him like that. I know that much.

Only two men would inflict injury on his face that drew blood.

His father. And the man who wants to take his wife from him...

He walks towards me, taking a seat, his elbows resting on his thighs as he tips his head forwards as if trying to catch his breath. His respiration is ragged, his chest rising and falling under his elegant jacket—attire so removed from where he came from.

"Drink?" I ask, gesturing to the bottle of amber bourbon on the table between us.

"Spiked, no doubt?" he suggests, his voice laced with the gravel of torment.

"Not this time, Jack."

He reaches forward, watching me as he pours the liquor from the bottle to the tumbler, bringing it to his lips, grimacing as he swallows it down before placing the glass back onto the table, his hand shaking as he does.

I lean back in my chair. The man's distress is quite something... so is watching him attempt to hold on to his civility when he could so easily unleash the savage his DNA requires him to be.

Voices call to Jack. I hear them. I know them. They whisper in contempt at his attempts to remain humane, at his indulgence towards his wife. He's the only brother in his family who has a wife who dares defy him. The others control theirs through fear and dominance—vocabulary that Jack understands. It is woven into the fiber of his being, as it is mine, as it is into the man who watches his marriage, waiting for the chance to save a wife who doesn't quite know if she needs saving.

He was designed to dominate, to control. It's how he functions in the world. It's what feels sane to him.

Only the thought of turning into the violent monster he calls a father, and the thought of hurting her, damaging her beyond repair, are stopping him.

For that, to my own contempt, I understand him...

I too am plagued by the fear of destroying her, a fear so alien to me that I barely know how to assimilate its presence. A fear that fights with the relentless need to witness her torment, a hunger that I can't seem to appease.

"I don't appreciate people turning up at my home unannounced... as you well know, Jack. It can lead to some uncomfortable encounters."

"I don't give a *fuck* what you want."

"Hmm. I'd like to know who inflicted that injury upon you."

"Has he seen her?" Jack growls. "Since she came back to me?"

The asphyxia of jealous rage has always left Jack teetering on the edge. He's like all the men in his family, despite his efforts to resist the draw of them; he sees his woman as his possession. It's a primal bond. It's unfathomable that she could not belong only to him.

His father uses terror to ensure his woman knows it. Jack is trying to be a new man, a modern man. And in the process, he's losing her...

What an exquisite lesson he's learning about leniency and its many pitfalls. I couldn't have designed it better myself.

"Mr. O'Neill, I presume."

"Don't *fuck* with me, Sebastian. Has he seen her? Has he *fucked* her?"

While I am aware of the two occasions that Cameron has sought her out, I still don't have a definitive answer as to his second question. She dares to look me in the eye with the kind of impudence that others would not, and with that nauseating sense of morality of hers, she would not want to lead him on, so I assume, despite the pressure that O'Neill likes to apply to her, that she managed to somehow get him to stop...

Though my uncertainty over it has haunted me for weeks.

I contemplate the answer he should have.

I'm not convinced of how useful Jack is to me more unbalanced than this. Unlike most people, I don't enjoy him unhinged.

And I don't need him to scare her for her to take refuge in me. Mr. O'Neill will shortly perform that function. He believes that it is Jack who she should be afraid of. He's in denial about what he is. A dominant. A sadist unable to embrace his need for pain, to reconcile it with his inbred decency, his empathy that he wears like a shackle—a woeful shell he will one day discard as he leans into the power that our kind yield... shortly before he pays for the injuries he has inflicted upon me.

"*Did he*?" Jack repeats.

"Fuck your wife? Not that we believe."

"Did he see her?" he asks through gritted teeth.

"Yes."

He shakes his head, shuddering out the foul venom of animus.

"But I wouldn't blame her for that. She didn't seek him out. She didn't know he would be there. He trapped her."

"I want him—" He stops himself from saying the word, from crossing the line that taunts him day and night, from becoming Jackson, the Brooklyn thug that his brothers want him to be, and that his father expects from him—the untamed savage who would finally earn his father's respect.

"Want him *what*, Jack? Do you have the guts to say it? To become who you're supposed to be? Or will you forever be the watered-down version of yourself?"

He takes another sip of bourbon, his hands quivering as he places it back down onto the table. He heaves through breaths so dense that I feel them on my skin—just as I feel hers. "What are your plans for him?" he asks, barely able to look at me.

"You would hide behind me like a coward, Jack?"

His wrathful blue eyes lift to mine as if burning ice. "I'm not a coward."

"If you want him taken care of, you just have to say the word. I've told you this for years. And I believe that I also informed you of the consequences of mercy. It's for the naïve, only. No one who is informed about the treachery of humanity would stoop to employing it."

"Answer my question, Sebastian. What are your plans?"

"The same as always. To make him *suffer*. To make him pay. You are the one who has stopped that from happening before despite my numerous warnings. One word from you, Jack, and I will expedite my plans."

"And turn me into the monster you've always wanted. Wasn't that why I was brought to this place?"

"Your monster was born before you met me, Jack. You would just finally be stepping into your power. It must be so unbearably tiresome to hold back, to pretend, to be as weak as the men we see around us. As vulnerable. What's more, your woman craves your beast. You know that about her. Lean into him, and she'll never leave you..."

His eyes morph, pain causing his brow to furrow. "Have you seen her? Without me?"

The question stuns me for a brief moment and I consider the answer I will give him.

His wrath may be useful, may detach her from him just enough.

I must confess that despite my own personal affliction, despite the suffering I endure over her, the endless hunger, the thought of her being punished by her husband does arouse me greatly—necessary preparation for what I will one day do to her...

"Yes. I have."

"Why?"

"I believe she wants to save you, Jack."

His face twists in pain. "Have you fucked her?"

I rub my hands across my jaw. "No. We have had no contact of that nature."

"Would you?"

"She would need to ask it of me."

He gets to his feet, glaring down at me.

"Sit down, Jack. I haven't tasted your blood for a while. I hope not to regain a taste for it..."

His hand balls into a fist at his side as he sits back down, his glower subsiding in the face of my order. I see his blood on my knuckles, remember the addictive metallic tang of it in my mouth.

"Why the fuck would she do that?" he seethes. "Unless... you're threatening her. Or promising her something? What is it, protection?"

"Protection? For *whom*, Jack?"

He grimaces as I conjure up reality—that her desire for protection is not only for her husband.

"You underestimate her," I continue. "Her desires. How dark they go. I've warned you not to show her mercy—she will seek satisfaction elsewhere without even realizing she's doing it. And as for your other hypothesis, I don't threaten women in that way. They come to me willingly. *Always*."

His eyes drop as he struggles to control his breathing. I don't normally tolerate the manner in which he has spoken to me, but he's clearly driven insane by the thought of her being taken from him. And I do enjoy the potential of him in this state. I do enjoy meeting the savage behind the suit. I hunger for him almost as much as I hunger for O'Neill's beast.

"What is it that you want from her?" he asks.

"Many things, Jack."

"Enlighten me."

"I enjoy her company."

"*Bullshit.* The only women you can stomach talking to are the likes of Frost."

"So I thought. It turns out I was wrong. Your wife... does something to me, Jack. Her beauty, her purity, her resolve. They move me."

"The way Rose moved you?" he snarls.

"I hope not."

His rabid glare meets mine. "I want you to keep the fuck away from my wife, Sebastian."

"Your love for her is very pure, Jack. Very powerful. I would hazard a guess that after everything that she endured, you would forgive her for her indiscretions..."

"Stay away from her."

"You may want to instruct your wife in the matter."

His chest rises and falls fast as he leans forward, his arms resting on his knees, his hair flopping over his face. "Why would she see you?"

"Maybe there are things she feels safer telling me about than you..."

"What things?"

"I don't share people's secrets, Jack. That includes yours..."

29

Jessynia

I stare down at my secret phone, willing a message from Cameron to come through, if for no other reason than to reassure me that he and Jack haven't hurt each other.

The barrage of messages I sent to him asking him to leave, to not engage with Jack, asking him why he came, have all gone unanswered and my stomach somersaults constantly at the thought of Jack's rage at seeing him watching us like that.

My body has been wracked with anxiety for the last hour.

Why isn't he back yet?

I listen out for signs that Leon is still downstairs. After shouting at him to get out half a dozen times only to be met with a brick wall, I finally went upstairs to get away from him and his cold-eyed glare, praying he'd be gone by the time I came back out.

Shutting the phone off and hiding it in my bag in our bathroom once again, I leave and press my ear to our bedroom door, listening out for movement. Nothing. It's been quiet for half an hour at least.

I open the door and creep downstairs barefoot.

Shit.

His feet. Those huge black boots. He's sitting near the door. I hesitate between going back upstairs to get away from him but decide not to. I want to talk to this prick about something else anyway...

"I told you I don't want you staying here!" I exclaim in frustration as I make it to the bottom of the stairs.

"I don't care what you want," he replies, leaning back in the chair he's pulled across the room so that he can sit just a few feet from the door. Your *husband* gives the orders, not you."

"Well, you can wait outside!"

Instead of leaving as I want, however, the prick gets up and walks to the door, leaning his huge back against it, bending a knee, and propping the soul of his boot against the wood in utter contempt for our home, and for my wishes.

It's been half an hour since we got home and he's no closer to getting the fuck out of our apartment, despite me locking myself in my room and telling him to be gone by the time I come back out.

I square my shoulders to face him. "Where is he?"

"Who knows?" he responds coldly, the tips of his dirty-blond hair brushing the black vest sheathing his giant body. His hair is longer now —past his shoulder blades. "Perhaps he's talking to your... *friend*," he sneers in contempt, his hazel eyes harsh on mine.

"Did you know Cameron was going to be there?" I ask for the second time tonight.

"How the fuck would I know something like that?" he shoots back, his tone dripping in disdain.

"I don't know," I shrug. "It doesn't seem entirely *clear* to me where your loyalties lie..."

His muddy eyes narrow on my face. "That's quite the statement coming from *you*."

"Yeah, well, unlike *you*, I care about the people in my life."

He shakes his head in contempt. "Is that so? From where I'm standing, they're in danger, thanks to you."

"Danger?! They were in danger before they met me! They were in danger the day they were *taken* into that place at *seventeen!* Not to mention the day people first stood back and watched as your so-called *boss* started beating his grieving son to a fucking pulp!"

"You care so much about his well-being," he scoffs.

"Of course I do!"

"Then why the fuck did Cameron O'Neill turn up to see you tonight?"

"You think I knew about that?!"

"Did you?" he asks.

"Of course not! Jesus!"

"He's clearly still as *contaminated* with you as your husband is. Do you realize what danger that puts them both in?"

"Hey, I *left* Jack, remember? We were broken up. He had me brought back here by force! He's not some innocent little victim here! As for Cameron, I've told him to move on more times than I can count. I don't know what else I'm supposed to do."

His eyes wander the length of me, trailing down my green dress, down the slit that reaches my mid-thigh, and back up, over my groin, onto my waist before pausing at my breasts and finally lifting to meet my gaze of vexation. "I wonder if your friend Sebastian will see things that way..."

"He's not my—" The ape arches a brow. "You have a lot of opinions, Leon. How about we talk about *your* questionable conduct for a moment?"

"How long have you got, Jessynia? We'd need a week at least."

I shake my head at the grim joke. "You know what I'm talking about." The shadows etched under his wild eyes grow darker. "What are you doing with her?" Gina's face flashes before me for a moment, and the vision of that necklace around her throat seers itself into the shadows of my mind.

"What makes you think I'm doing anything?" he asks, the question devoid of inflection.

"Because I'm not a fucking idiot! I tried to text her this week. She didn't answer. That's not like her. What's happening with her?!"

"Nothing that concerns *you*," he rasps.

"I care about her too, Leon! Why did you give her that necklace?

Also, side note, Cameron put thought into every single part of that necklace, and I'm gonna hate your guts for all eternity for giving it to her."

"Sounds like a long time," he deadpans. "As for that man you care so much for, I don't feel compassion for men who seduce other men's *wives*."

"Even when those men cheat on their faithful wives more times than they can count?!" I ask, seething at the rules that men like Leon play by whereby a husband can do what he wants and God forbid a woman mess up because of it.

"A decent wife will overlook occasional indiscretions for as long as her husband takes proper care of her."

"Occasional? Jack's affairs last for months, Leon. *Months*. Oh, and question, will a husband overlook a wife cheating on him if *he* does the same?" I take a most probably ill-advised step towards him. He dislodges the sole of his boot from the door, pushing me backwards instinctively with that gorilla-in-heat energy of his as he takes three steps towards me. "Do you think that animal is gonna overlook his wife cheating on him with his fucking employee?!" I shout. "Do you have any idea what danger you're putting her in?!"

"It seems we both have a penchant for putting the people we love in danger."

"Love?" I sneer. "Don't try to tell me that you love her, Leon. You're just doing it to stiff Cain and to be the asshole that you are!"

His body tenses, his eyes burning in anger at my insolence. "Careful, little girl. I'm not as decent as your husband, and I know how to teach women lessons."

"What, are you afraid of hearing the truth, you coward?! You're putting both your lives in fucking danger! I mean, *you* of all people should know that after what happened to your mother—"

But my sentence is arrested by the sight of him bearing down on me.

"Stop!"

As I shove my hands into his chest, he grabs me and pivots me, pushing my back into the wall and putting both hands around my neck, which he begins to squeeze.

My hands wrap around his thick wrists as I try to pry him off. "Let go of me!" I plead as he takes in my face while I try to yank his hand off me. "What is wrong with you people?!"

His glare scalds me as I use both my hands to attempt to pry his huge fingers off… to no avail.

He watches me struggle for a while before shaking his head coldly as my anger turns to fear. "That's not how you remove a hold like that, little girl. You're not strong enough to remove men's hands from your throat. You'll lose every time."

"What?!" The constriction makes the sound emerge faintly.

"You hit under the elbow. Hard." His jaw is tight, the words coming out through gritted teeth, as if he doesn't want to say them. "If that doesn't work, you strike the throat. Or the eyes. You kick the groin. Try it. Under the elbow. Now."

"Are you insane?! Let go of me!"

But he doesn't.

I peer up at him frantically as he begins to squeeze again, and before I know it, my hand is releasing, and I use it to upper-cut the underside of his elbow. It weakens his grip just a tad, allowing me to strike his throat and then push him back enough that he releases me completely.

His eyes narrow as he watches over my pitiful attempt to push him backwards. "You're a natural. It's almost as though you've had to force men off you before…"

"Go fuck yourself!" I retort breathlessly as he casually conjures up not just that man in the forest, but Cameron… in the midst of a nightmare, and Jack when his possessive wrath spirals out of control.

"Again," he says, and before I know it, his hands are around my throat.

"Let go of me!" I shout, grabbing his wrists as he squeezes… *hard.*

After a moment of panic, during which I recall my previous gesture, I ball my hand into a fist as I conjure up Brianna and her advice on how to punch from the gut, not the hand, striking him once more underneath the elbow. Something about it jars his reflexes and his hold drops long enough for me to do it again, this time striking him hard in the jaw in a move that makes my knuckles hurt.

He tips his head to the side, rubbing his strong jaw. "Very good, little girl. *Again.*"

But this time, before his hands can coil all the way around my neck, I uppercut his elbow once more, and he lets me go, stepping back to watch as I pant through the fury and indignation at being physically overwhelmed.

"I advise you not to forget that one," he snarls.

I scour his duplicitous features, my hand wrapping around the front of my neck as his eyes form shadowy slits. Finding my breath, I manage to whisper, "*Who are you?*"

He shakes his head slowly, his usual mocking features morphing into something altogether more solemn as he watches me intently, the angles of his face softening... just a tad.

Time stands still for a moment... until he speaks.

"I don't know."

As his glare becomes less harsh, the click of a lock ricochets through the room and Leon takes a step back as a man walks in.

Jack.

His eye bloodied and swollen.

"Oh my God, what happened?" I stammer, but he doesn't answer. He barely glances at Leon, keeping his scorching glare locked onto my face.

The fear I had multiplies, its tentacles crushing my chest, as he takes steady steps into the room towards me, forcing me to step away from the wall and walk backwards so that I'm not trapped.

"Do you need me here?" asks Leon, though Jack doesn't throw him a glance as he answers.

The rough gravel of his voice rumbles through the open space of our apartment. "No."

Leon's eyes meet mine... just for a moment. "Do you need me to... take care of anyone?"

"Not tonight," Jack growls, the threat filling the air with the fumes of smoldering black tar.

Leon grabs his coat and turns to look at me. I swallow hard, imploring him—this fucking neanderthal savage that I despise—to stay for a moment as I buckle internally at the contortion of bitter wrath in Jack's savage face.

Leon steps behind him, hesitating in the doorway for a moment as he watches me. It takes Jack turning his head to the side—just a little, enough for Leon to observe his rageful profile, for him to slowly close the door behind him, the usual Godforsaken smirk of victory absent today...

I drink in Jack's fury as he removes his coat, throwing it onto the chair against the wall before unbuckling his belt as he stalks towards me.

"Hey!" I manage as he pulls the black leather strip out of his pants and throws it to the floor with a clang that shoots through me like a bullet. "What the hell happened? Your eye..."

He doesn't speak, his bruised face wild despite the elegant designer suit beneath it as he stalks me as I tread backwards.

"Did... he do that?" I ask, but he remains unspeaking. "You're scaring me! What happened?!"

"How did he know where you'd be?"

"I have no idea!"

"How?!" Jack's roar makes a high-pitched breath escape me, despite my attempt at looking tough in the face of this rabid animal—one I need to reconnect to and pronto.

When it comes to Cameron, Jack loses his mind. He's always been jealous, but things become primal when he senses Cameron near me. I know he can't quite control the way he is triggered by him.

"I don't know! Do you think I'd want to be in that fucking situation? The only people who knew we were going tonight were you, Kevin and Stella, maybe Maddie. That's it!" I insist truthfully, wracking my brain.

Did I tell anyone else?

I'm sure I didn't...

Could he have found out through my friends, somehow? Or did he just have us followed?

"Do you seriously think I'd want you two ending up in the same place like that?"

But he doesn't answer. His ire hasn't softened and the sight of his immense body crackling as if plugged into the mains makes my legs turn to mush.

As we make a full loop around the large landing, my hand hits the bottom of the wooden banister and, on instinct, I take a step up the stairs, and then another. He turns to face me as I walk backwards.

"Jack, your eye. Let me—"

I observe his foot hit the first step as if in slow motion and I turn and run upstairs, panting as I hear his steps on the stairs behind me. I throw myself into our bedroom and thrust my palms into the back of the door, and just as it's about to click shut, the force of him arrests the momentum, and he pushes back against it, filling the doorway before walking towards me in unforgiving strides.

"Stop!" My words are swallowed by his grasp as he throws me, face down, onto the bed, climbing on top of me, forcing breath from me with the sheer heft of his hard muscles.

His hot breath burns my face as his lips adorn my ear with the roughest caress. "I keep trying to be civilized with you," he growls. "I keep trying to be a better man. And the more I do it, the more you misbehave..."

"I had no idea he'd be there!" I manage as his hand lifts my chin so that my face isn't pushed into the pillow.

"But he *was* there... which means he still believes he can take you from me."

"I'm not some possession that can be *taken*, Jack!"

"That's where you're *wrong*," he growls into my ear. "You're my wife, and you *belong* to me for as long as I say so." I scream as he grabs the top of my dress with both hands from under me, ripping it open and pulling down my strapless bra so that my breasts spill out onto the bed.

"Stop!" I shout as he lifts the back of my dress up, finding the top of my panties and sliding them down my legs and off my feet before climbing on top of me.

"How do I do this?" he snarls, "when you see my tolerance as weakness...?"

"I don't!" I yell back as he prods his erection into my bare ass cheeks rhythmically.

"I think you *do*..." The rough edge to his voice reverberates through my torso. My breath hitches as I feel him grab my bun, pulling it back slowly until my neck cranks backwards.

"Jack!"

"The universe designed you to be fucked roughly, Jessynia. Is that what it will take to make you respect me?"

I close my eyes as he slowly licks the side of my face in that brutal way of his, primitive, indecent sounds rumbling from his throat. "You've seen him. Sebastian. Alone. Why?"

Why?

Well, besides the numerous times I've been forced into a car to see him, or drugged and taken to him, I've now seen him because he murdered a man in front of me with his bare hands and there's not another human soul that I can talk to about it.

"It hasn't always been a—" I stop. I've never told Jack about the numerous times I've been stopped in the street and told to get into cars to see him, mainly because in a war between him and Sebastian, I know who would lose. "I'm trying to... do something."

"Fix something unfixable."

"It's not unfixable! No one ever tries to heal that man. No one else is doing anything about it!"

"One woman did try," he snarls, the weight of him stifling my breath. "She's now in the ground. Is that where you want me visiting you?"

"Jack, stop."

"And that other man still thinks he can take you from me... Do you know what that does to me? Do you understand the hell it takes me to? To feel like I don't own all of you?"

"Yes. I know that hell. I've been there, Jack."

"No. You don't know, Jessynia. Your mind isn't as savage as mine. I have to fight myself every day not to revert to the way I'm conditioned in order to keep you in line."

The sunless specter of Cain shoots through me like the bitterest of poisoned arrows.

"You're not like that, Jack."

"Maybe I am," he growls. "Sometimes I wonder if that's what you need from me. To be the savage I want to be... Would you respect me more that way?"

"I do respect you!"

"Not enough," he retorts bitterly, and I whimper as he presses his erection into me, harder, faster. "Do you know what I'm designed to do to men like that? Do you know I'm designed to end their lives and keep my woman captive until she learns to *behave*? If I find out, Jessynia, that you've allowed another man to touch you, I will make you watch as I hack off his hands."

"No, you won't! And you're not some innocent victim here, Jack!"

"I haven't touched a woman since you came back to me," he retorts roughly.

"Other than *her*," I whisper, evoking the day that he fucked Alexandra Frost in front of my eyes as Sebastian held me against him, trying to soothe me with duplicitous words that would purport to make me forget that my husband was inside her.

"I'm paying for my sins, Jessynia," he seethes. "Every day. Are you paying for yours?"

"I can't breathe."

He shifts his weight slightly, allowing my lungs to expand, blanketing the top of my hand with his as it clutches the pillow. "If I find out you've seen Sebastian without me ever again, I'll teach you a lesson you won't forget."

"Yeah, well, you don't get to threaten me, Jack."

His hand slides underneath my breast. "That's where you're wrong," he breathes. "I will do what it takes to keep you safe, even if you hate me for it. As for that other man, I'm not the only one who wants him *dead*. And maybe next time, I won't stand in the way of that problem being taken care of."

"You don't want that, Jack."

"No. Maybe I don't. But if it's a choice between his life and you, I choose you."

Goosebumps trickle over my skin as he says it.

"Who do you belong to, Jessynia?" he asks.

"Jack..."

"Who?!" he shouts.

"I belong to *me*," I respond, mustering up every ounce of defiance I can. "And no one else, so you can go fuck yourself!"

"I don't like that fucking answer," he snaps, his timber coarsening as his hand slides down my abdomen, lifting the front of the dress up until my sex is exposed on both sides. He slides his muscular legs between mine, using them to spread mine wide.

"Stop!" I shout as his fingers delve into the folds of my sex, opening it up, using the small amount of wetness to slide up and down the outer pink of my sex before pressing my clit.

"I'm going to have to absolve you of your delusions, Jessynia. You're my *wife*. You belong to me. You are my *property*. That's the covenant we signed. I'm not designed to think any differently. I've tolerated your reactions to my infidelities for long enough. We're going to play by different rules now, rules that will teach you how to respect the husband that worships every piece of you."

"Let go of me, Jack!" I order as my sex begins to swell and his finger picks up more juice, using it to stimulate the tight knot of nerves he's so adept at locating, at playing with, at sending into a frenzy.

"The only time you get to give the orders, baby girl," he snarls, his voice bristling with green-eyed madness, "is when you're naked on the floor, bending over and presenting me your dripping wet pussy to fuck all night." Affirming his grasp on me, he utters, "Now, you're going to get on your knees and open your little mouth. You're going to suck your husband's fat cock until I tell you to stop. Then you will get up and turn around and face the wall, bend over and present that pink hole of yours to me so that I can fuck you for as long as it takes for me to be sure that you understand what it means to be my wife."

"No," I reply as he presses my clit harder, faster, causing my sex to clench and gloss to pool at my sex, something he feels, for he dips his fingers into it with a groan, using it to lubricate his stimulation of my body. "We've done this before. I'm not letting you use my body to appease you ever again."

"You're my *wife*, Jessynia. Your body is designed to be defiled by your husband's whenever he needs it."

"I don't care! You're not using it to deal with your jealousy ever again," I add, recalling the day he had me brought back from Blackwood and staked his claim on me immediately, positioning me so that I would watch as he fucked me in front of the mirror.

He didn't force me. He asked for consent. He always has, *always*, but I'm not getting into that dynamic again, not least because I know that that's how all the men in his family operate, treating their women like possessions who get fucked whenever they're in the mood for it. These women lose too much of their power by letting it happen. I can't do that.

"You've always had a greedy little pussy, Jessynia. I know it wants my cock, just as my cock wants to ravage it."

"Let me go, Jack. We're not doing this. Not like this."

I feel the vibrations of his chest, the frantic ebbs and flows of his breathing as he pants his frustration into me, exhaling blasts of air onto the side of my face. His lips slip against my cheek from behind as a low growl of irritation escapes him. I can feel how hard he is, how fervent his need is. My sex is wet and open just a few inches beneath it. I know he's trying to stop himself from sliding inside me and relieving the wrath of tonight with my body.

Part of me wants him to. I'm desperate for release myself. But this dynamic is how things will have started with Gina, and Adele, and Brianna—them appeasing their brutal husbands. And now, they have no power left. I can't become like that, and I can't let Jack succumb to that side of him. Those men may seem to enjoy their dominance, but they are endlessly moody and irritable. Let's face it, they're insufferable.

Part of the reason is that when you're allowed to abuse your power over and over, you lose part of your humanity. That can't happen to Jack...

His savage tongue slips against my cheek with a moan of ravenous ire. My sex pulsates at the sensation, at his primitive need, at his unashamed arousal.

His finger slides slowly down the velvety skin of my outer sex and I wince as it settles in a veritable pool of gloss, my own arousal betraying my attempt to tame his lust.

"I want your body, Jessynia," he says, pushing his erection into me over and over. His fingers strain at the entrance to my sex, pushing in, just a little to open the tight walls designed for his pleasure.

"You're going to have to force me," I reply.

His hot breath is a gale against my face, and his lips slip against the side of my cheek until he finally growls, "We both know I wouldn't hurt you like that."

"Then let me go."

I stay silent, waiting, until, with a groan born of pent-up energy, he lifts his body off mine, lowering my dress before lying on the bed next to me, turning to face me, his respiration still fast, his pupils dilated in the moonlight which streams through the windows of our bedroom, casting it in lilac rays.

I turn my head to face him. "Thank you."

He doesn't answer, but watches my face, his mercurial glare leaving me feeling like I'm falling.

"Jack... I didn't know he was going to be there. I promise. I would never, ever have wanted that. Do you believe me?"

He nods, though his body is still clearly simmering in corrosive bubbles. "I'm not giving up, Jessynia. No matter how much pain we have to go through to make it to the end of this. I'm getting you back. All of you. And I decide how to protect you. If I find out that you've seen *either* of those men alone, there will be a war. Is that understood?"

I nod, drowning in his earnest gaze, wishing I could turn back time to the days when Sebastian Gravier was just a mere shadow I crossed from time to time.

. . .

Sometime later, I crumble under the weight of Jack's moody glare, his face harshening and softening through waves of anger and then acceptance as I convey my silent contrition for his pain. The angles of his breathtaking face are illuminated by the cool rays of the moon as I try in vain to fall asleep.

Realizing I need to go to the washroom, I sit up, pulling the covers off me and heading to the ensuite bathroom, all the while trying to ignore the pull of my secret phone and my need to make sure that Cameron is okay, to know whether Jack hurt him too. I also need to know why he did something so dangerous, something that could make Jack so angry.

Something about it felt... reckless and unbalanced, so far removed from the smart, sanguine man that I know.

Flushing the toilet, I glance at the locked door before looking down at the white cupboard hiding the phone.

I can't turn it on...

Jack's awake... and I'm too scared of him getting suspicious after the events of tonight.

Trying to resist the current of concern and consternation flowing through me, I strip off my clothes and let them drop to the floor. I leave my hair in its messy bun and head into the shower, taking in a lungful of air as I angle the showerhead to avoid my hair and turn on the faucet, letting the warm water soothe my skin. I close my eyes and exhale as I breathe out the fear and worry I felt tonight, and the horror of seeing Jack's face cut, and then the wrath turning him into a beast...

And Cam...

God, why did he do it?

I'm so worried about him some days that I don't know what to do with myself. I find myself pacing the apartment thinking of him, wondering where he is, whether he's finally letting go, whether he's happy, whether he's moved on.

I'd give anything to know he was happy... and yet I can't get too involved, otherwise, I'll draw him back to me, and then it'll all start all over again.

I grab the lavender-scented shower gel that I bought at our local farmer's market and squeeze some into my hand, rubbing it over my naked body, between my legs, slipping over my sex before slowly sliding my hand over my skin, my arms, my legs, my breasts, tilting my head back as the water washes off the meager suds.

Finally getting out of the shower, I grab my white bathrobe and tie it around my waist, taking a breath before switching off the light and leaving the room.

I gasp at the sight that greets me when I leave—Jack, standing naked before me, eyes wild with apprehension, the poison of jealousy still evidently coursing through his system. I hear the sound of my own sharp breaths as I shudder under the raging flames of his glare.

30

Jack

Her throat contracts as she swallows hard, peering up at me with eyes that glisten, as large as quarters in the silver light of the moon.

Fear flashes across her face for a second, replaced swiftly by trepidation.

I'm not trying to intimidate her, but I can't control the jealous rage taking my body hostage at the thought of him being there tonight. It eats into me, turning everything red before my eyes, making my body stiffen as it restrains itself from doing what it should.

I keep seeing his face.

Watching us.

Watching *her.*

My wife.

His eyes tracking her face as we danced.

I believe that she didn't know, but the fucker clearly believes he has a chance... and that, I have no choice but to make her pay for.

I don't fully understand how he could still believe it, though I suspect her endless goddamn compassion has been used to weaken her.

Her ability to care so much is part of what I worship her for, but ruthless people know it is her weakness, and when weaponized by them, her ability to feel others' pain, her need to soothe it, they are both highly dangerous.

What *she* doesn't know is that *he's* far more dangerous. And I won't allow her to find that out.

As for Sebastian, if he touches her, I will stand back as Cain finally makes him pay...

As I take in the beauty of her face, my hands fisting at my sides in rage at the thought that I share part of my own wife with someone else, her eyes mist over and her lips part, actions which dampen my ire... just a little.

I feel at war with myself.

I know how to make women submit. Every woman before her was submissive to my every need, without me having to do anything but just *be*.

She isn't like them, but I would know how to use fear and dominance to control her. What's more, I know she likes it. I feel how wet she is when I pin her to the bed, when I tie her hands behind her back and fuck her hard, instructing her on what her role is. I know I could make her submit to my strength with some more training.

My fear is... that I will push too far, hurt her in a way there is no coming back from. Change her. I see the reverence with which my father's and my brothers' women look at them. I watch them capitulate to the most humiliating of orders without a word of dissent.

I know how my family elicits compliance. I could do the same. The difference is that unlike them, I'm in love with this woman. God dammit, some days, I wish I could go back to a time when I didn't know the utter insanity of a love like this one, when I felt nothing for the women I fucked. It felt dark, but there was freedom in the void.

Now I'm enslaved by a woman whom I've hurt, a woman searching for monsters in the naïve hope of fixing the pain that she has endured.

The problem is that I've watched the women of my father and

brother change over the years—from vibrant to dull. Not their words, but their eyes, the light behind them. I've seen the light go out in my girl's eyes before, and it tortured me to watch it happen. I can't do it to her, not again.

And yet, with every day that passes, the fear of becoming like them grows. It's this pull that never seems to wane. I know it would solve my problems to embrace that side of me. *I want to.* But where will it end? My father was once a decent man. He wasn't born sick the way he is now. Pain and power corrupted him. Would I end up a monster like him?

Every time, I feel myself succumbing to what is ingrained in me, I look at my girl's face, and the pull of them fades... except on nights like tonight when I want to rip the city to pieces searching for the man who dares to think he can take my wife from me.

I feel my face tensing at the thought of him, at the thought of her seeing him, until dark flames consume me, turning everything to ash.

Her chest rises and falls fast as she absorbs the thunder of my wrath. She knows what I'm feeling. Even when we're disconnected, tormented by anger, we know each other. It's this inextricable bond the likes of which I've never felt before... or not with a woman, anyway.

I feel what my woman feels. I feel it inside my body.

As I believe she does me.

"Your eye," she says, concern making her frown. She turns around and steps back into the bathroom, running the water for a second and coming back out with a damp white face towel which she lifts nervously to the skin around my eye, wiping away what I know must be flecks of blood.

The towel is ice-cold and smells of tea tree oil which she must have applied as a disinfectant. Once she has cleaned my skin, she holds it against the side of my face to cool down the warm, swollen skin, watching me somberly as she does.

A minute later, she goes back into the washroom and comes out with an open tube of arnica cream which she applies to the skin around my eye socket, before putting the tube back and coming out to stand before me.

"Does it hurt?" she asks, but I don't answer, instead, taking in the contrition in her eyes, the worry, the fear as seconds turn to a minute.

As she swallows hard at my untameable glare, her slim hands find the white belt of her bathrobe and begin to undo it, opening it up and pulling apart her robe. My cock swells as her huge round tits spill out. The rest of her body is so slim that her breasts make her look indecent. With that innocent face of hers and that shaven pink pussy, she's more fuckable than any woman I've ever seen.

Not to mention that constant blush of pink that spreads across her cheeks when I intend to fuck her. I get hard just at the sight of it.

I don't say a word as she slowly peels the robe off her body, letting it slide down her slim arms. She takes it in her hands and folds it, placing it on the floor in front of her feet, and in a move which makes my cock throb, she drops to her knees, breathing fast as she peers up at me, parting her glistening lips, just a little.

I contemplate the invitation.

I'm hard for her submission, but fucking her body is not enough. I can't allow us to be reduced to that. It's easy. It's a bond too easy to pull apart.

I want all of her. Every broken piece of her soul.

My breathing accelerates...

The irresistible allure of her pink wet lips calls to me, making me take a step forwards, coiling my fingers around my hard shaft.

I inch further towards her, letting the swollen head rest on her bottom lip, and brushing it from side to side.

A groan escapes me as I catch a slip of saliva, using it to lubricate my passage across her bottom lip and then her top one.

I hiss my arousal as she contracts her lips around the dome and begins to suck on the head, peering into my eyes as she does, just as I've taught her to do. She's always done her best to accommodate my needs. Always.

Tension releases from my body as she silently sucks on the swollen tip, caressing the underside with her tongue. Withdrawing, she begins to kiss the head, allowing pleasure to trickle up my groin as if water filling a dry riverbed.

As I prepare to fuck the mouth she's offering me, I ask, "Do you want to show me what a good wife you are?"

She nods silently, hesitant eyes burning into me.

A low note leaves my throat as she slowly licks, underneath, on the sides, finding the dome and slipping her lips over it, sucking until I have to close my eyes for a moment to ensure I don't come.

"You like your husband's hard cock, don't you, baby girl?"

She nods before slowly taking my full length deep into her throat, and in a loss of control, I grab her bun with both hands, pull out, and ram my shaft right into the back of her throat again. She whimpers in that high-pitched manner of hers as I do so, which only makes me drive into her harder, fucking her mouth as she struggles to accommodate the fervor of my need for the type of release that only she can give me.

I want to fuck any remnants of doubt right out of her day and night... but I can't. It wouldn't be enough to own just her body...

As she gags on my cock for a long minute and saliva drips down her chin and onto her tits, I slow down, my ire dissolving upon seeing tears well up in her eyes amidst the thought that I could hurt this woman whom I have worshipped every day that I have known her.

I don't usually concern myself with my partner's discomfort, not even Alex's, a woman who owned me for almost the entirety of my teenage years.

With my girl, the pleasure of her submission never allows me to overlook the possibility that I'm causing her pain.

As I slow down, the tears spill over onto her cheeks, making blood pulse into my cock once more. The sight of her tears always does it to me. It's her vulnerability, her softness that makes her so exquisite...

A low groan leaves me as she takes a breath before beginning to lick my shaft in long motions, up and down the underside, along the sides, watching me for every measured stroke of her subservient little tongue. As she once again slips her lips over the head of my cock, she closes her eyes, moaning gently as she sucks on it, gliding her tongue all over the dome as her lips provide pleasure, pulling, rocking backwards and forwards.

"Open your eyes," I order sharply. I can't stomach it when she closes them while I'm fucking her. The fear that she could see someone else eats into me.

She opens her eyes instantly, locking onto mine as she tends to my cock, making my balls contract, desperate to shoot my cum deep inside her throat and watch her swallow it as she always does when I need it.

Instead, I withdraw from her mouth, sliding the head onto her plump pink lips, the perfect shape and size for sucking on my cock like she's supposed to.

Her eyes glisten as I peer down at her. And as I convey a taciturn order, she follows it, getting to her feet and turning around, bending over a little and putting her palms up against the wall.

Her breathing quickens as I push her back down further, forcing her hands to slide down the wall, and her ass to push out behind her.

I crouch down to take a look at the pussy I'll soon be fucking, finding it pink and wet and open. The relief of her arousal makes my blood pulse.

"Jack," she whimpers as I locate the dripping wet entrance to her body with my finger, sliding it up and down the soft dewy silk of her flesh. She inhales loudly as I begin to push my finger inside her, feeling the tight walls contract around me, the entry aided by copious amounts of juice.

"I think you liked sucking daddy's cock, baby..."

I groan as I watch my finger push into her and out, relishing her submission, her accommodation of my need to fuck her senseless as I would do five times a day if she could take it.

As I pull my finger out of her, I lose control, thrusting my tongue onto her pussy, pushing it inside before flicking it up and down her sex hard and fast.

"Oh my God," she moans as her body heaves through the sensation and I get to my feet, taking up position behind her, sliding my hands up and down her slim back.

"Don't take your hands off the wall," I instruct. "Is that understood?"

She nods.

"Are you going to take your husband like an obedient little wife?"

"Yes," she replies.

"Good. Then tell me what you want."

"Jack..."

"Say it. Tell your man to fuck you."

"Please fuck me."

"Say *Fuck my wet pussy*."

"Jack..."

"Do it. No more hiding, Jessynia." I bend over her and slowly lick the full length of her spine. "We're designed to fuck hard, baby. We always have been. Now tell your man what you want from him."

She drops her head a little and in response, I edge the head of my cock towards her, pushing it against the tight muscles of her dripping pussy, teasing her by rolling it around her outer sex. A breathy moan escapes her as I push inside just an inch.

"I'm going to fuck you senseless, angel, but first you're going to admit what a greedy little slut you are for my cock. I won't say it again. Tell me to fuck your wet pussy. Say *please*."

"Please... fuck... my wet... pussy."

Without a word, I rock my hips, pushing all the way into her until I hit her cervix. I grab hold of her bun with both hands and slide out slowly, pushing myself back in as she whimpers at the sensation.

"Oh my God, Jack," she exhales as I take my time to open her walls to ease my invasion.

I close my eyes as I fuck her, driving into her in deliberately measured strokes so that I don't lose control, drinking in the pleasure that her body gives me. There is no woman who has made me feel like this, who has given me this type of nirvana, with whom I've been able to relax and feel the act in my whole body.

"Do you like it?" I ask, cranking her neck backwards by her hair.

"Oh my God, Jack, you're so good," she replies.

"You've always been a thirsty little slut for my cock, haven't you, baby?"

At her silence, I pull her torso up, grabbing hold of one arm and yanking it behind her back, pushing it upwards until she yelps from the pinch.

"Jack..."

She braces herself with her other hand as I push her tits against the wall and begin to fuck in earnest, wrapping my free hand over her mouth, absorbing the whimpers that fall from her throat as I begin to ravage her, to reeducate her as to whose property she is, something I never felt the need to do before. Not like this.

I know it's part of my penitence. I know I have to pay for my sins. And if I have to reaffirm ownership of my woman every single day, I'll do it until the day that she finally understands who she belongs to.

My hand muffles her as I drive into her in deep strokes, reveling in her inability to move, in the access I have to her accommodating sex whose walls clench around me. My cock is so hard and the grip on her so tight that as I thrust upwards, I lift her off her feet a little. It's fucking beautiful to have this little doll on my dick, unable to get away.

What's more, she's dripping wet and between gasps of fear, there are moans of pleasure which force me to restrain myself from shooting my load into her.

My lips find her ear and my hand slides down to her jaw. "Do you feel your husband's greedy cock inside you, baby?"

"Yes."

"Do you understand that your pussy was designed to accommodate me?"

"Yes."

I locate her lips with my thumb, pushing it inside. "Suck."

I grunt my arousal into her ear as she sucks obediently, reveling in the control I have over her.

Pulling her mouth from my thumb after a while, she whispers, "Jack, my arm."

I release my grip on it, finding her ear with my lips. "Do you like it when your deviant husband defiles you like this?"

"Yes."

"How much, baby?"

"I love it."

"Do you understand that the way I fuck you is the way I *love* you, the way I need to protect you?"

I feel a teardrop onto the finger wrapped around her jaw. "Jack..."

"Do you?"

"Yes."

"Good." I withdraw from her, pulling her hair back so that her neck hyperextends and she is forced to look up at me. My free hand slides over her tits, squeezing her nipple. "Now get on your hands and knees and present your pussy to your husband like a good wife."

"You're so deviant, Jack."

"I'm designed to take care of my wife, baby. To remind her who her husband is. Now get on the floor."

As she takes up position on the rug, planting her palms and knees into it, lifting her ass in the air and lowering her chest to the floor, I close my eyes as I get to my knees behind her and push my cock inside the pink hole, tipping my head back in ecstasy at her submission.

A while later, she is flat on her belly on the floor, one leg bent and lifted to give me the access I require of her. I whisper dark threats into her ear which make her moan in pleasure before finally tipping her onto her back, forcing her legs wide apart and fucking her slowly as I cradle the back of her head with my hands.

The gentle way she peers up into my eyes kills me. Her face is so stunning that I have to restrain myself from fucking her mouth and shooting my load all over her face every time I see her.

My lips brush against hers as I fuck her accommodating body, the strokes slow, deliberate.

"I want to be a gentleman, Jessynia, but if you refuse to behave like a good girl, then I will be forced to fuck you like a bad one? Do you understand that?"

Her eyes half-close as she moans in pleasure, the breathy sounds she makes the sweetest of drugs.

"Do you like being defiled by your husband?"

She nods, sliding her hand up my tricep. "You're so good, Jack."

"No. *We're* so good. This *heat*. Do you feel it, angel? Tell me I'm not dreaming."

"You're not dreaming," she responds. "I feel it."

The softness of her gaze tips me over the edge as I succumb to an orgasm so rough that it makes my body shudder and loud groans escape my throat as I collapse onto her, inhaling her scent.

I look up to find her eyes closed as she takes in pleasure.

"Open your eyes, baby."

She does, her gentle gaze drifting over my face as I speak.

"I'm not letting go of you, angel. You run away, I'll follow you. I lose you, I'll find you. I'll hunt you down, even if you despise me for it. You can hate me, you can scream at me, but I'll drag you back to me, and you don't have a choice in the matter. Do you understand that?"

She lifts a hand to my face.

"Jack..."

31

Jessynia

Breathe...

Breathe...

Breathe...

I stretch my arms out in front of me—the only way I have of not walking into something in the pitch-black room. I can't see in front of my face. The room is swallowed by darkness so unforgiving that with every step I take, I feel as if I'm tumbling into some void.

Somewhere in the distance burns the faint glow of a light source so feeble that it doesn't reach me, doesn't allow me to see my bare feet touching the smooth wooden floor beneath them.

The only sound audible to me is the rough panting from my throat, ruffling the air around me in billows of icy panic.

I see nothing, no one... but I can't shake the eerie feeling that I'm being watched...

I peer around me, straining into the dark, but there's not enough light. I keep walking towards the faint glimmer of moonlight emanating from far across what must be a vast room.

If I can reach it, I can get out...

As I approach, light filters in, just a little, enough to allow me to see my bare feet and to almost see the floor beneath them. I knew from the feel of it on my skin but can also see now that I'm wearing just the slip of a dress—delicate and white. It barely covers my breasts and the fabric goes down to just above my knees. As stronger rays of light seep in, they allow me to breathe and I glance down at the white eyelet trim around the hem of the frail garment.

And then, in a moment of sheer and unexpected panic, a gasp tears through the air and I stumble backwards at the sight of someone, my palm hitting the floor hard.

A man.

Just enough light bounces off him for me to see the outline of his frame.

He's tall, cloaked, his face obscured in the shadows of an onyx mask, its grotesque features illuminated just enough for me to see him facing my direction...

Meager light hits him from behind, turning him into a dark statue, an unmoving silhouette.

I push against my palm and get to my feet, retreating slowly, trying my best not to fall as I keep my eyes pinned to him, wondering how I can run when I can't see, if my feet will know instinctively what to do despite the dark. I'd have to run towards the light, get past him somehow. If I can get far back enough, I can give myself enough space to run past.

But then... he takes one slow step towards me... and another.

The quiver in my voice shakes the air. "Stop! Who are you?!"

I'm not afraid...

A sharp tinge cuts through my ankle, and as he takes another step towards me, I take off as if being chased by ghouls, first to the right until I feel the flap of his cloak behind me and the low thuds of his feet.

Fuck...

I turn sharply left, hoping the pivot is abrupt enough for me to gain some distance and go around him, but just as I make it past him, some immovable force stops my momentum, spinning my torso, tugging me into him despite me kicking and screaming.

The strength of his muscles stuns me as his arms contract around mine, and his hand, which feels like that of a giant, muffles my mouth as I'm dragged mercilessly across the room by some force so powerful that it barely feels human.

"Let me go!" I scream in a moment of respite from his palm.

The echo reverberates in sinister pulses around the room like the waves of a skipping stone on the water, sounding off in my ear over and over until I become petrified of the very fear threaded into my own voice.

A growl escapes my assailant as I'm placed back onto the floor, only this time, it feels hard and rough—stone. I look down to just about make out cushions around me, all large, all black and in the center of them, bare stone with two metal rings sticking out of it, the rings attached to chains and to shackles.

No...

I fall as I turn and try to flee, kicking as a hand encases my ankle and pulls me towards it. And then another snakes around my other one, and as I kick backwards, it dawns on me that beneath my thin dress, I'm wearing nothing.

The bestial groans of two men thunder through me as shackles are placed around my ankles, the harsh locks clicking into place, no matter how much I kick against their hold.

"Please!" The desperate plea sounds pitiful even to my own ears.

And suddenly their hands release my body and all cascades into the sinister cavity of unexpected silence as I stare at the cruel metal cuffs clad around my ankles, one of them pressing into the muted pink scar still left over from my operation which stabs me as if with shards of smashed glass.

With my eyes becoming more accustomed to the light, I see a little more—not details but colors, lines, shapes. I peer a few feet ahead, trying to breathe as I take in the bottom of their thick cloaks. I know they're observing me in inhuman curiosity, but I don't care. I pull at the cuffs with all my might, bending over and prying a finger inside, straining against the thick metal. Nothing moves. I turn my attention to the chains, pulling, yanking, hitting the metal ring before trying to pry it out of the concrete.

Still pulling, I look up to face them. "What do you want?"

There's no answer, no sound but the desperate breaths of an animal caught in a snare—mine.

As I realize I can't pull my foot free from the tight shackle, I get to my feet, wincing as my ankle smarts once again. The chains attaching me to the floor are only about two feet long, barely enough for me to move, but enough to allow my legs to be pried wide apart...

A sharp inhale flees from my lungs as one dark figure begins to stalk towards me, the silence of his ominous approach deafening, like the hollow torment of an anechoic chamber.

"Stay away from me!"

The man ignores my plea, walking around me slowly, studying me as he moves. A full rotation passes as the chains become twisted around my ankles, jangling against one another.

And before I can stop him, I'm spun around and muted by the unforgiving cloak of his hand, and of his arm around mine. I writhe against him, but he holds me tightly, leaving me barely able to move.

Fight...

I struggle against him, trying to bite, but not able to find the edge to his hand which sheathes the bottom half of my face.

I keep struggling but he grabs my arm and pulls it behind my back, tugging it upward into an armlock. I cry out in pain only for him to do the same on the other side, holding my wrists together behind my back with one hand as the other man watches me, drinking in my torment, not moving, not flinching, not uttering a sound, his observation utterly reptilian.

"It hurts!" I whimper, but the loud exhale of satisfaction from the man behind me proves what I fear—that that's the point. That my pain isn't a hindrance to them—it's the goal.

And suddenly, the man before me moves in measured steps to a low table nearby, picking up an object from it and returning in the same manner. He throws it towards the man holding me, and from the movement of it, I make out what it is—a rope.

Despite fighting him with everything I have, it is coiled around my wrists and lower arms fast, imprisoning my hands behind my back, taking away the use of my arms from me.

No longer needing to restrain me, the giant of a man at my back slowly slides his hands up my arms, pulling loose strands that have escaped my high ponytail behind my ear, the movements gentle and deliberate, as if tending to some living porcelain doll that could break at a moment's notice.

His fingers wind around my neck, holding my jaw as he pulls me into his chest.

And then I hear it... his voice.

Though deep down, I knew it was him.

It's always him.

"Just breathe," he whispers as my cells freeze, turning my body into a frozen lake pelted by a frigid wind that howls dark notes into the wintry air.

No...

"Don't struggle anymore. Don't fight me. You can't win, Jessynia. We both know that..."

I jump at the sound of a mask falling to the floor, my gaze careening to the molded leather as it rolls forwards, landing to rest against a thick black cushion nearby.

I feel him move something near the top of his neck and realize that he is opening his cloak, wide. He hauls me back into his mammoth frame and I gasp audibly at the feel of naked skin against my almost-bare back. His chest is cold and hard, but beneath it is what steals my breath—the rigid column pressing against the lowest curve of my back, the shaft smooth, naked, hard, pointing towards the back of my head, ready. My sex is naked beneath my dress. There's nothing that could stop him...

Except the man in front of me, maybe...

Is he somehow here to help?

The unmistakable lash of a wet tongue brushes up the side of my neck, savoring the taste of me. From behind me, he exhales a groan of heinous pleasure, entirely unashamed.

His thick long hair dances across the tops of my shoulders as his lips find my ear. I shake my head, trying to free my mouth from his grasp, but he affirms his hold each time.

"No more fighting, Jessynia. You're done fighting this."

The muffled curse I try to cry is but a mere yell of desperation, a pathetic explosion of plastered-on courage.

Or is it?

If they try to hurt me, I'm going to fight...

I may lose, but I'll *fight*...

"I know you've been waiting for this." The toxic venom that Sebastian administers is always done so smoothly. His voice never wavers. He never shouts, and yet you hear him above every other sound, the resonant waves blasting away all noise around him, turning everything to burnt wood, to embers, and then to ash...

I try to shake my head but am stopped by the resoluteness of his hold.

My body freezes as the man before me takes a step towards me, and then another, his countenance utterly self-possessed, the movements supernaturally poised.

Just a few feet away, his hands find the top of his black cloak, pulling it apart to reveal his naked torso first, and then his body, his skin golden, his erection hard, full, swollen.

I know that body...

Sebastian lifts my chin so that I'm forced to peer up into the faceless figure, forced to try to locate eyes hidden behind the shadowy holes in his mask. Despite the darkness of the hood, I see that the nose of the mask is elongated and crooked, the mouth a straight slit. It's grotesque by any standards, but the thought of seeing the man behind it is a thousand times more terrifying.

No...

It can't be...

He closes the space between us, lifting his hand to my face. I try to turn my cheek but am held in place by the man behind me.

I glare up, panting as he strokes a thumb over my dewy skin, the monster taking in the grimace of fear, the glare of anger at the trap I'm caught in.

My insides shudder like leaves dislodged from a tree in a blustering windstorm as his hand finds his mask, pulling it off his face and dropping it to the floor.

Not a sound emerges from me as I tumble under the weight of the treacherously beautiful face of a man I know, a man that lives inside me, just as two others do...

Only this time, his warm copper-flecked eyes burn crimson and the black spheres in the center of his irises are thin serpentine slits that contract and expand as he tracks the tears slipping onto my cheek, and running in somber rivulets down onto Sebastian's pale hand.

No...

As another droplet makes its way onto my cheek, it is greeted by his fingertips which brush it off my skin, and in a move I've only ever seen Sebastian do, he brings it to his sculpted lips, his tongue dipping to lick the salty droplet from his skin.

He begins to breathe more quickly, closing his eyes as he tastes my fear.

"Look at the pleasure you give him, Jessynia," Sebastian whispers. "Look at his body. Look how he reacts to you."

"Let me go, Sebastian. Please."

His breath caresses my neck as Cameron begins to open his eyes. "I can't," he responds. "Nor do you want me to."

"Cam, please, stop this..."

He leans forwards as he appraises my face, his mouth opening to reveal the tips of four teeth—two upper and two lower—that jut out from under his lips.

They shouldn't be that long...

They glisten as he dips towards me, his scarlet eyes locked into mine. "You won't die," he whispers. "You'll clot fast."

"No!"

"It'll just feel like you're dying..."

And as I scream the word "No" he lunges forwards, sinking the daggers of his canines into my neck. I try to stop it but between the shackles, rope, his hands and Sebastian's, I can barely move.

My scream dissolves into nothing at the jarring sensation of warm liquid dripping down my neck and onto my breasts.

My feet go numb as Sebastian tucks his hands into my armpits, helping to keep me upright as Cameron begins his feast. The growls coming from him as he seals his lips over the gash in my neck and sucks at my blood are bestial, deviant, base, the savage grunts of some wild animal. He moans in low guttural utterances of unabashed pleasure, finding my nipples under the soaked white fabric of my dress, tugging them as he laps at my blood. His hard erection prods my belly, pulsing against me over and over as Sebastian's strains against the curve of my lower back.

No...

And finally, he stops sucking, tipping his head back and letting out a hoarse groan of the most primal bliss that echoes around this somber cave of a room.

I tremble as he tips his head back down to look at me, the lower half of his face stained with glistening crimson. His tongue leaves his mouth as he licks the blood from his lips, eyes narrowing onto my face.

As his hands reach forward for the straps of my dress, muted, my voice taken from me by the assault that has left me clinging to life, I lower my head to watch him peel the dress down my body so that my breasts are bare and coated in slick lashes of my own blood.

His fingers roam over them, drawing lines in the red liquid, tugging at my wet nipples, groaning as he does so. He watches me as he kneads my breasts before sliding his hand under the dress bunched up at my waist, using my own blood to lubricate my sex, to part the soft folds.

No...

I glance down to see his cock throbbing just as my neck is sliced into again, this time by Sebastian who leans forward from behind me and bites, taking his fill, sucking on my blood as Cameron watches the show while pressing my clit in firm movements. I plead silently, but though his demeanor softens, he doesn't move, studying me in solemn curiosity.

Sebastian releases me, exhaling loudly over and over as he takes in the pleasure of my blood, his body bristling, pulsing against mine.

"I need her," he groans, catching Cameron's eyes.

A moment later, with ankles still shackled and arms still bound by rope behind my back, my lifeless body is lifted up by both men until the opening to my sex is placed on top of Cameron's cock.

Breathy notes of deep pleasure release from him as I'm lowered down onto him, his shaft filling me up as my head is kept from slumping forwards by the pull of Sebastian's hand on my hair which keeps my gaze locked into the serpent-like orbs of Cameron's eyes.

The inner seam of my bent knees falls into the inner crook of his arms and he begins to fuck me, his glare deviant as he takes my wilting body for his own.

"No," I whimper at the sensation of hard muscle at my back. "No. Please..."

But I can't stop it.

I can't stop Sebastian from pushing his cock into my ass with a loud hiss of pleasure, rocking forwards into me as Cameron exclaims at the double invasion of my weakened body.

The minutes fall into nothing. Between periods of lost time, I occasionally awaken to the sound of bestial grunts, the roars of dragons.

I feel them on me—their hands, their tongues, moving me around, spreading my limbs, entering me.

My hands are no longer tied, but I can't move them. I'm too weak. I know I'm on the edge. I see the precipice, feel the darkness beyond.

My palm settles on someone's arm—a man, his muscle carved as if of stone. Tongues feast on the wound in my neck as I'm impaled, one cock in each hole, the thrusts slow, measured, as if to draw out the pleasure, the tension. The noises they make are so primitive, so primal, so savage. They feel like sounds you would hear in hell.

. . .

A while later, with light seeping into the blackness, I open my eyes to see their mouths on each other, groaning in pleasure as their tongues dance, licking the blood from one another, my blood, their hands pawing at each other's skin, at each other's bodies, grabbing each other's cocks, tugging, working one another as they breathe through pleasure, as their tongues collide as if famished.

Darkness encases me once more...

As I open my eyes sometime later, I see Cameron's above me, the color of burning embers, the shape barely human. I feel Sebastian beneath me, sliding into me.

As I try to survive the brutal invasion of my listless body by two men in the throes of ecstasy, my gaze is caught by movement to the left.

I squint into the darkness to see a shape. A man, hammering at a glass pane separating us, screaming soundlessly into the void, his hits on the transparent wall futile, his fists not cracking it.

I watch his mouth as he screams a word...

"No!"

Jack...

32

An instant later, I'm tumbling through space, my limbs twisting as I land, the journey made in a second, its effects leaving me sitting up and heaving in bed, shuddering through another nightmare.

Another fucking one...

Each one feels more real than the next.

Each one has sweat dripping down my skin and robs me of my breath.

Regaining my bearings, I spot Jack to my right, tracking the length of his thick thigh under the cover, following it upwards to meet his naked torso and a thick head of hair facing towards me.

Jack...

I watch him for a while. I know he's asleep. If he hears my nightmares, he's awake instantly, tending to me, talking me through them, or fucking the energy out of me when I refuse to tell him what I've seen.

Realizing there's no way in hell I'm going to sleep any time soon after the vivid nightmare, I pull the covers off me most carefully and pick up my pajamas lying on the chair.

Just as I'm about to reach the door, I stop, wracked with concern over whether Cameron is okay. I also need to tell him to never ever do anything like that again.

I head to the bathroom. Without switching the lights on, I put the pajamas on my naked body and then open the cupboard door with the utmost care. I gently zip open the bag and reach all the way down to the bottom of it, pulling it out, closing the bag and tiptoeing out of the room, glancing at Jack's sleeping body before closing the door behind me.

Did he hurt you?

I stare at the message on my secret phone, willing it not to be there... but I knew it would be.

The nightmare that jolted me from sleep left my body restless for I fear the agitated state that Cameron may be in. I know he may be worried. He has no faith in Jack, or at least, he wants me to know he doesn't, continually insinuating or asking me whether Jack is hurting me. At times, I can't tell if it's a manipulation tactic designed to plant the idea that Jack is dangerous in my mind, or if it's just justifiable concern over a man who has harmed me before—not physically, but in other ways.

My guilt over Cameron and Sebastian has me overlooking facets of Jack's behavior, for mine is now far from exemplary, and because I know he's doing everything he knows how to be a good man. I feel it in the way he touches me, speaks to me, handles me, even when his possessive dom side comes out like tonight and he needs to prove to both of us that I'm still his.

I can't deny that I crave him like that, and that I feel safe as I absorb the desperation in his brutal thrusts into my body—the desperation to own me fully, to ensure that I am his property and that I belong to him.

When he envelops my body, it scares me, but it also feels like armor.

My fingertips reach the screen of my phone—emitting the only light in the room—as I contemplate whether I should respond, finally typing one word to soothe any fears he may have.

I hesitate before sending it, especially with the feel of Jack still on my skin, still inside me, the heat of his lust so vibrant. I capitulated to my nerves over his anger, to my need to soothe him, but the pleasure I felt with him, the connection, blasted every sense of concession to pieces.

No.

A shiver rolls through me as I press Send.

I know that I shouldn't, but the thought of Cameron worrying hollows me out from the inside, and I can't constantly be afraid of turning on my phone for fear of seeing more messages, or be afraid that he'll turn up when I least expect it. I have to make it clear to him that he can never do that again.

As I stare through the study door at the staircase opposite, listening out for any signs that Jack may have awakened, I decide to send another text while Cameron is still asleep.

You can't do that again, Cameron.
I don't know what you were thinking.
I was afraid when Jack came ba—

I stop, deleting that last line for fear of Cameron's reaction. In its stead, I write:

Don't ever do that again.

A message from him draws my breath from me:

Talk to me, Jessynia. Please.

Shit.

I reply swiftly, my heart twisting in my chest at the thought that he isn't asleep at 3.30 am, witching hour.

I can't. Please go to sleep. Don't come and see us again.
And you need to stop texting me.

But as soon as I press Send, his name is flashing on the screen. I reject the call fast only for him to call back.

And in the midst of my deep-seated desperation to soothe him and those recurring moments of panic I feel when I think of Cameron succumbing to demons which taunt him, I accept the call, bringing the phone to my ear with a hand that feels weak.

"You can't—"

"Jessynia."

He speaks my name softly, stretching out the word, his tone some mess of yearning and pain. Even to my subjective mind, I taste the longing unfulfilled in the utterance...

For a moment, I hear nothing but his breath, finding myself unable to speak.

"I can't talk. Jack's upstairs."

"Did he hurt you?" he responds grimly. "I've been going out of my mind with worry."

"No. He didn't. But you *can't* do things like what you did tonight," I whisper, unable to get mad like I want to without raising my voice. "You're making things difficult! Not to mention, putting yourself in danger!"

And making Jack act like a lunatic...

"What did he do? When he got home?"

"Nothing," I respond swiftly.

His rough tone grates through me and I shift on the rug beneath me at the far end of our office.

"I want the truth. You always lie to me about the things that man has done to you."

I remain mute for a while, taking in the ebb and flow of his weighty breaths. "You can't do what you did tonight *ever* again, do you hear me?"

"You refuse to take my calls, Jessynia," he retorts, the bite to his voice like a knife cutting into my body. "What do you expect from me?"

"You can't blackmail me into speaking to you!"

"Then speak to me because you *want* it. Because you *need* to hear my voice the way I hunger to hear yours. Because every word I say means something to you, the way yours do to me. Because you can't make it through the day without hearing the sounds I make."

Cameron...

I close my eyes for a moment, seeing the glistening amber disks that I have peered into for years, that have studied me, that have watched over me, as he listened to me and protected me.

"It's not that simple, Cam, and you know it. It's not your fault, but you're making everything worse. You can't do things like this."

"Things like *what*? Like watch you with the man who hurt me, who hurt my sister, my father? Who hurt *you*? Watch you dance with him as if none of that happened?" he seethes.

God...

It's the first time I've really danced with Jack since we first separated back in August and of course, Cameron just had to be there to witness it. "Watch his hand slip around your waist?" he continues. "Watch his fingers slide up your back? Things like *that*, you mean?"

A wave of nausea has me wilting into the front of the loveseat at my back as I think of Cameron witnessing that, his wild cinnamon eyes flickering in flames born of outrage.

"Do you think I wanted you to see that?" I reply, keeping my voice as tiny as I can make it while still remaining audible. "Cam, I would never want you to see anything that could hurt you."

"Like seeing the man who seduced my sister on command holding the woman that I love. And that I know loves me..."

I slump into the loveseat at my back, feeling like I'm bleeding and can't find the wound.

Every time he says something like this, I'm reminded of the day that I made the decision to leave Jack. And I'm reminded of the day I was brought back here by Leon after watching Cameron being beaten to a pulp. I seem to spend a lot of time blocking it out, because part of me understands Jack and why he agreed to it. And because I know that Sebastian prayed on his weakness, his trauma, his pain to get him to agree. And because I love him despite how wrong it was.

"Did he hurt you?" he asks. "When you got home? I want the truth."

"No. He didn't. Stop asking me that."

"Did he *fuck* you?" The bitter way that he growls the word has me shivering internally.

His respiration quickens audibly as I stay silent, my stomach twisting at the question. I know he knows the answer because Jack did what Cameron would have done. They both function in the exact same way, using sex to stake ownership, to ensure submission, just enough to temporarily satisfy their dominant alpha whose programming requires that their women are submissive in bed.

"We shouldn't talk, Cam," I whisper. "It'll only make everything worse."

"Worse?" His voice sounds devoid of all light, of the rich vibrance coloring his ordinarily powerful diction. "Worse than knowing that that man fucks a woman he took from my home through violence? Worse than knowing that the woman I worship is fucked by a man who allowed another to have me beaten while she had to witness it. *Worse* than that?"

"Please stop. This isn't a path that will lead to anything but torture."

"I'm already tortured. My days are spent in darkness without you, Jessynia."

"Jesus, Cam, no. Please. I don't want that!" My voice raises a little and I immediately lower my tone, despite the rickety desperation clinging to it. My eyes remain affixed to the stairs, my pulse throbbing in my ears at the thought of waking up Jack. "We can't be in this place again. It's a maze with no out of it. Please just try to forget about me... and move on. That's half the point of all this."

"I hate that expression, Jessynia," he utters weakly. "Not only is it an insult to everything I know and feel about you, it's naïve to the point of negligence, and you know it. You want me to move on with some woman I feel nothing for and close my eyes to the fact that the woman I worship has handed herself back to a man in order to protect her family. To protect me...

"How do I do it, Jessynia? How do I make peace with how it happened? How do I let you remain imprisoned and do nothing? How do I behave honorably in the face of such dishonor? I can't be the man who stands by and does nothing. That's not a man you're worthy of."

"The reasons don't matter anymore, Cam. This isn't going to magically work out. They'll *never* allow it. Jack would never allow it. We were *dreaming*. It was never going to become reality and I knew it. I should never have agreed to see you again."

"You know I hate when you say that. When you negate every fucking moment we spent with each other."

"That's not what—"

"The hours I spent watching you, listening to you, holding you. Fucking you until you screamed. Do you remember them? Or is that one more thing you *regret?"* He snarls the word so bitterly that my heart seizes at their brutality. The unsettling wrath in his tone scares me. I feel like he's teetering on the edge of some cliff and my hands are tied as I try desperately to stop him from going over the edge.

"I don't regret it, Cam," I reply as softly as I can. "*Any* of it. But it wasn't meant to last forever. You have to accept that."

"Or maybe it was," he retorts. "Maybe this had to be part of our story, Jessynia. This trial. I'm not giving up. Not on you. Not on us. Not on something so powerful. Something that erases every other woman I've ever touched."

I watch a fat tear drop onto the pajama bottoms covering my bent legs... and then another soaking into the pastel-blue fabric.

"Unless," he continues. "You tell me you don't love me anymore. Could you say those words to me? Would you mean them?"

"Cam, stop," I respond after a moment.

"If you tell me, Jessynia, that you are with Jack only because you love him, because you want to make your marriage work, and *not* because you're afraid of the consequences of leaving, afraid of what Sebastian will do... If you tell me that, I'll do what I did for three years. I'll walk away from you. I'll be in pain like I was for every minute of those three years that we didn't speak, but I will respect your wishes. Your marriage. I know when you're telling me the truth. Can you tell me that? Can you tell me that fear is not the slightest factor in why you are trying to make your marriage work?"

I drop my head as tears tumble down my face and into my mouth. "Cam, please..."

"I didn't think so."

I wipe the tears from my cheeks as the rancorous torment weaved through his voice in barbed threads eats into the silence between us.

"Are you eating better?" he asks.

I sniffle down the tears that won't seem to stop. "Yeah. I've put a few pounds back on."

"And your ankle?"

"It's not hurting as much."

I hear him breathe out an audible sigh of relief.

"Cam... why did you come tonight?"

"Because I wanted to see you. I needed to see your face. And I wanted to see the two of you in action. To understand it. I wanted to see how deep your denial goes. To see how willing you are to protect your loved ones. How able you are to block out the truth of your relationship and the threats propping it up. I wanted to see how he still looks at you.

"And to let him know that I'm not giving up, not unless I feel with every cell in my body that you want me to stop because you love him and not because you're afraid. Because you don't love me rather than because you're trying to protect me. I don't want your fucking protection, Jessynia. I never have done. I want you. All of you. Every messy, illogical piece. Every tear. Every cry of pain. Of joy. Of pleasure. I want it all."

Cameron's face, framed by shadow, floats into view as if from deep in a murky lake. His hair was longer than usual tonight and his face unshaven with a cruel shadow chiseled into his glower. His beauty has always been civilized compared to Jack's. Jack's face is wildly beautiful, the bone structure savage, his glare indecent, his muscles borderline illegal.

Cameron's face is more elegant, the incomparable beauty refined and symmetrical, his limbs slimmer, leaner, or at least, they used to be. His body is bulkier than before, no doubt from months of working out to relieve any tension enveloping him. Between the longer hair, unshaven face and the wrathful glare, he's beginning to look perfectly uncivilized despite being one of the wealthiest men in the country.

"What happened between you?" I ask. "What did he say? Jack."

"He warned me to keep away from you," he replies. "I told him he can go fuck himself."

"God, Cam, did he hurt you as well?"

"He landed a punch."

"No..."

"Don't worry. I enjoyed it. I enjoy his anger. The physical pain takes the edge off the pain of knowing that you live in a house you don't feel safe leaving."

Goddammit, I can't listen to this...

"I'm sorry," I say, wishing I could tend to his wound.

"*Sorry?* This fucking need you have to apologize for things that are not your fault is part of the problem. You're too *fucking* compassionate for your own good."

"Isn't that why you said you loved me?" I shoot back, plunging us into silence for a moment.

"And why I'm so afraid," he replies. "I informed your so-called husband that it wasn't only *me* he had to worry about."

My breath thins and for a second, the scene before me spins at the shameful reality of his words. I can't even muster up the strength to protest. What he doesn't understand is that no matter how drawn I feel to Sebastian, if it weren't for him and Jack, I don't believe I'd ever see him again.

"Jesus, what are you playing at?!" I exclaim.

"I'm trying to see whether your husband has the guts to protect you like a fucking man. Like *I* would from that monster. Or whether he'll sit back and do nothing about it, like a *coward*."

"He's not—"

"I know you've seen him, Jessynia. I want you to know that." My panting becomes audible. "I know you," he continues. "I know how your mind works. I know how illogical your compassion is. I know you make sense of the chaos by trying to make everyone around you redeemable."

"For fuck's sake, I'm not some fool that overlooks everything! I don't think everyone is redeemable!"

"No. But you do *him*. If you didn't, you wouldn't see him. I know you. I feel what you feel. I know you're trying to draw out the dregs of the human he's using as a trap to pull you in. I know you're trying to save people by getting yourself into a fucking mess."

"I'm not—"

"Did he touch you? Gravier?"

I close my eyes as I breathe through the silence—the deafening response to his question.

"Did. He. Fuck. You?"

"No," I whisper as oppressive weight bears down on us. "Nor will he *ever*."

"Avery. You. Cannot. Fix. This. He isn't human. As soon as his human begins to come out, whatever demonic thing that man has inside him will take over his psyche. He will hurt you in a way you there's no coming back from."

"What am I supposed to do?" I respond, glancing as far up the stairs as I can see. "Sit back and watch as he keeps you and... Jack in his fucking web forever? I want you free. You've spent *twelve* years with them, Cameron. Your whole adult life, you've been enslaved by that goddamn place. And even now, you're not free of them. I can't take it anymore. You deserve to live as free men."

"Free? While you're encaged with him? Are you out of your goddamn mind?"

"I'm trying to *negotiate* with him," I snap. "*Heal* him somehow. The last time I talked to him, he almost seemed like he was willing to let you both go... for good. That's all I want. Nothing else matters now."

"This fucking urge of yours to save people is what will get you killed one day. You don't know that man like I do. He can't handle his humanity. Even if you break through and connect with it, sooner or later, the façade will crack, and only your blood will heal the fractures. I've seen it before. I've seen a good woman try to save him. Every effort made him more unstable. She was triggering him with every act of kindness. Tormenting him. He is too far gone. And I watched her be *consumed* by *demons*. Do you understand that? *Consumed*. I didn't love her, and it destroyed me anyway. I'm not standing back again and watching as you end up like *her*."

"That's not gonna happen. Just let me try to handle things. Please."

"No," he responds sternly.

The unsettling heat of his silence bears down on me like a freight train. "You're giving me anxiety," I mutter.

"Well, now you know how it feels when I discover you've been alone with him."

"How do you know that?" I ask, goosebumps prickling up my skin like droplets of rainwater turning to ice.

My mind races through the people he knows there.

Alex. Vallen. Ilya. Grace. Gabriel...

"I just know," he responds stiffly, and I drop my head at the grim tone.

"How have you been?" I finally ask.

"You know the answer to that. You know what your absence does to me."

No...

"Are you still having the nightmares?" I ask.

His silence gives me my answer and a dark ball of nerves knots itself inside me at the thought.

"You're still seeing the therapists for them?" I ask.

"Yes. I'm trying everything to make them stop. But they won't, Jessy-nia. Not for as long as you're trapped. They'll never go away until you're free. I know that."

"Cam, the thought of your nightmares kills me."

"As do yours. You're still having them?"

"Yes, but... it's okay." I close my eyes for a moment at the memory of the nightmare I just had—him and Sebastian, snarling in the diabolical pleasure my body gave them. "How can I make this okay, Cam?"

"*Be* with me, Jess. *Love* me. Love me the way I love you. Stay with me and never leave. Stay with me and trust me to protect you. That's all I've ever wanted, since the first day we met..."

The vision of my brother walking the sea wall, tracked by men of the Society that he doesn't know exists drifts over the murky water in front of me.

"I can't."

"One day you will, angel. One day you'll know how it feels to be in your own home and to breathe."

Silence pulls at us as I find myself unable to protest.

"How did it feel to see me?" he asks.

"I was terrified."

"But you liked it, didn't you? You like looking at me, just as I like looking at you..." When I don't respond, he says, "Do you think of me when your husband *fucks* you?"

The acrid bite to the word robs me of vigor. "Cam, stop it. We can't talk like this anymore. And you can't keep making me feel like shit for a situation I'm not fully in control of!"

"Do you?" he repeats.

"I'm gonna hang up."

"Do you remember us, Jessynia? Do you remember the insanity of our love? Do you remember dancing with me? Do you remember the way you trembled when I would pin you to the floor and fuck you? Do you remember the tears that fell from your eyes when I would come inside you?"

"Cam—"

"Do you?" he growls. "Did I experience that alone, Jessynia? Were you there?"

"Of course I was there. But, Cam, that's... over."

"*Over?* I guess I'm just supposed to forget that I've been inside you as you looked up at me with eyes that burned into me? That I've seen and tasted your pussy? Pushed my tongue inside it? Been driven insane by my need to give you pleasure? Do you think I feel that way about the other women I *fuck*? Do you think I care about their pleasure more than my own?"

"Please stop."

"I *don't*. It doesn't matter whom I fuck, I don't see anyone but you. I see your eyes as I feed my cock inside your wet pussy. I hear you gasp as I begin to fuck you."

Despite myself, my sex tingles at the deviant words I've come to expect from this man. "Cameron, please..."

"Please, *what?* Stop doing what I'm designed to do to you? Stop being hard for your tight wet pussy? For your cock-sucking lips? Stop wanting to inseminate you, and to fuck you as you grow our child inside you..."

Jesus...

"Stop imagining pushing my cock into your mouth and fucking it until you gag? Stop remembering how it felt to shoot my load down your accommodating little throat? Have you forgotten it, Jessynia?"

My sex pulsates, the walls opening up, the entrance wet and juicy as his voice begins to get low while the horror of guilt causes my body to seize and my breathing to quicken. "Cam, I have to go. We can't do this."

"You hang up on me, Jessynia," he growls, "and I'll find another way to speak to you."

"That isn't fair."

"Fair? On who? Your husband? When that so-called man took you away by force, he forfeited the right to *fair*."

The image of Cameron's bloody face hitting the dirt in that forest at Redwood shoots through me like a flaming arrow—an image I try so hard to forget, as well as the decisions which led up to it...

"I know you need deviant men, angel. But unlike the others, I won't hurt you. That's the difference. I could never touch another woman if you were with me. When you belong to me, I think of *nothing* but you. Of your voice. Of your face. Of your pleasure. Of your protection. I can give you something that they can't. I can control the danger. I can give you what you crave without hurting you in the process. *They* can't do it, not forever. Ja... Jack—" he spits the name out—"is too close to reverting back to what every single man in his family does. *Every* one of them."

No.

He's not the same...

He can't be...

"When he thinks he's not in control, he'll revert back to taking control of you, and he'll hurt you in the process. *I* would never do that to you, Avery. I know how to dominate and stay in control. Even when I fuck you the way that I do, I'm aware of where the line is. I'm aware of what will cause you damage. I don't cross it. *He* does. I know it.

"As for that *thing* you've spent time with, he wants your pain, Jessynia. It feeds him. I know how his mind works. I know you unsettle him and because of that, your death is something he will toy with constantly. He will fantasize about it, trying to resist the temptation, and it only takes one day of weakness for him to make it happen. Do you understand that?"

Sharp shards of obsidian swirl through my mind. Sebastian has reached for my tears enough for me to know what my pain does to him. He has imbibed them as if they were blood, life force. It's his demons that take pleasure in them. But at the risk of sounding naive, I know there's a human in there too. I can feel it. I see him sometimes. I just have to reach him.

He's the key to everything...

"Yes," I whisper. "I know, Cam."

"If your so-called husband can't protect you from him. I will."

"No! I told you, I don't want you involved!"

"Well, you don't get a choice in the matter anymore..."

My chin drops to my chest as I breathe through the trepidation of his words. "I don't want you doing *anything*."

"I want an answer to my question. How did it feel to see my face?" he repeats, sidestepping my request.

His scorching eyes flash before me as I recall the sight of this icon of Manhattan watching us from across the room.

"Do you like my eyes on you, Jessynia? Do you like being stalked by me?" I don't answer, trying to ignore whatever damaged part of myself yearns to say yes. "I know you do. I know what you crave. I will be the one who gives it to you."

"Cam, I have to go. He'll wake up."

"Do you remember us, angel? Please tell me I'm not alone. Tell me those memories happened. That I haven't lost my mind."

"Cam, please..."

"Tell me you don't remember the way you would watch me as you sucked on my cock. Do you remember how you would look up at me with those innocent little eyes as I slid it down your throat?" He almost growls the last words. I know from his tone that he's aroused. "Do you remember the taste of me on your tongue? The feel of me in your little mouth? How I would fill it? Do you remember how you would use your lips to pleasure me? Do you remember moaning as you would lick the length of my shaft? How you would close your eyes before swallowing my cum like a good little girl?"

He lets out a hoarse exhale.

"Cam..."

"I know you do, baby." I close my eyes as he continues to speak.

"You're wet, Jessynia. I can taste it." His cadence slows. "My tongue has tasted every inch of you. Your wet pussy. Your greedy clit. It's been inside you. It's fucked you more times than you could count, several times a day... if you remember. Should I pretend that I haven't sucked on your pussy? Pretend to forget those sweet little moans of yours, or your face as I pushed my cock inside your welcoming little slit? Your fear as I bound your hands behind your back so that I could have access to your hole when I wanted it. Do you remember how I would worship you while defiling you?"

I gasp at the vividly corrupt words, and he lets out a groan of pleasure at the sound. "I like your fear, angel. I like how pure you are. How raw. I like how you tremble and gasp as I dominate your accommodating little body. That's how it should be between a man and his woman. That's how it's going to be the next time you're in my bed. I'm going to be the first you feel when you wake up... and the last thing you taste in your mouth before you fall asleep in my bed. In safety."

"Cam..."

"Touch yourself, baby. Slide a finger onto your clit."

"I can't."

"Please. For me."

I don't, tumbling through shockwaves of guilt over Jack, but instead keep my eyes closed as waves of pleasure undulate through my weakened body at the sound of his words, his breaths, his groans.

"You let me bite into you, angel, remember?" He exhales loudly at the memory, drawing in breath and then moaning again. "You did it without treating me like I was a freak. You did it while loving me as much as before you knew of my tastes. I know it. Why did you do that, baby? You did it to *please* me. You did it because you're a good girl who wants her man to be kept satisfied. You did it because you were willing to do what it takes to make us work. You did it because you know me. You trust me. You know I'd never hurt you.

"And you did it because you love me... You've always loved me, Avery. I know that. I've felt your love for every fucked up part of me since the day we met. And even those years we didn't speak, I knew you loved me still. Just as I loved you."

He pauses for a moment, listening to me breathe. "I want to hear your voice, Jessynia. I can't handle not hearing it. Tell me you're not wet when you hear what you do to me."

Wet? I'm dripping from arousal at his words. He's always had this effect on me. Having said that, I defy any straight woman to fully resist the low, deep, drawn-out utterance of such sinful words by Cameron O'Neill.

"Cam, please..."

"Say it!"

"I'm wet."

"Good. You're going to listen to me carefully. You're going to take off whatever clothes you're wearing and turn around. As you do, I'm going to handcuff your hands behind your back so that you can't fight me. And then you're going to bend over and take me like a good little sub. *All* of me." My lips part and my eyes open and close as he pours his cravings into me. "Once I've fucked you from behind, I'm going to climb on top of you, watching you as I push my cock into your dripping pussy and fuck you until I shoot my load so deep inside you that you taste me in your mouth."

He exhales a hoarse groan from the deep recesses of his chest. "Do you want to hear me come, angel?"

He exhales some more, his cadence quickening until he finally lets out a long groan of pleasure, his breaths low and deep as cum shoots from his cock.

A heady buzz pours through my cells as his breathing begins to calm. The sound of the breaths coming from his strong, muscular chest dizzy me, and the thought of his pleasure—and of being able to do that to him just by listening to him, just by him imagining us—leaves me floating for a moment...preparing for the thud back down to the earth and the horrific guilt over conversing with a man Jack hates.

His next words have me opening my eyes slowly. "I know you remember us, angel. I know you remember the power of us. I know you remember my lips on your skin."

"Cam, please..."

"I need to speak to you more."

And at that moment, my heart stills, for I hear the rapid scrape of wood—the bedroom door opening.

"I have to go," I whisper urgently.

"No!" he snarls. "Let me take you out of—"

"I'm so sorry."

"Jessy—"

I hang up, my hand quivering as I push the power button to switch my phone off, cursing internally as the cretinous device forces me to put my pin in to turn it off. I slide it into the fold at the side of the armchair I'm sitting against before turning to see Jack's legs appear midway down the stairs.

It's too late for me to move from this position, so I don't, watching as he approaches the room, filling the doorway with his huge body. The dim light from the entranceway turns his mammoth frame into a silhouette of curved muscle.

He walks towards me in slow paces, prowling as if searching for his prey. His face is in shadow but for eyes which glow like cinders in the gloom. I swallow hard as he comes to stand before me as I peer up into a face that is severe, disquieted by concern and suspicion. He's naked but for the thin gray cotton of his pajama pants, and shadows formed by dim light bounce off him, accentuating every sculpted groove of his arms and chest.

Usually, when I'm sitting on the floor looking up at him, it's because I'm sucking his cock. My programming has my body itching to do the same now, wanting to offer up my mouth to soothe him like wives know how to do at times. The tension of expectation crackles between us... but I don't move.

"I heard your voice."

33

The sober tone of his dark utterance chills me for a moment. I've always struggled to lie to Jack. There's something about how unabashed and brazen his authenticity is that makes lying to him nigh-on impossible. Not to mention that he's smarter than almost anyone I know, and able to pick up the hidden physical cues that women can read but men sometimes overlook.

I contemplate for a moment telling him I spoke to Cameron. I'm always on the verge of telling him the truth—about Cam. About Sebastian. About the man... And his murder. I hate hiding things from Jack, especially now that I know how it feels to have it done to me.

He knows what's happened between us over the last year. And he knows how it feels to be damaged and to self-destruct. Something inside me makes me believe he'd understand. He's always loved me despite my flaws. Just as I have him.

But then, the thought of him losing control, succumbing to the side of him that is bred into the Wilder lineage, of him going to war with either of those men hits me and I lose my nerve.

"I... I was thinking out loud," I respond. "Talking to myself."

His eyes narrow into slits, the gravity of my lie registering on his face. He fills the chasm between us with that volatile male aura that shifts any space he's in, turning it into a storm that can wreck your world.

His hand reaches forward, and his fingertips slide down my temple and onto the side of my face, curling around and under my chin, lifting it slightly so that I'm forced to peer into his unstable glare.

He holds out a hand and after a moment, I tentatively lift mine to his. He grasps it and pulls me to my feet. In my barefoot state, I'm aware of how tiny I feel before this huge mass of muscle. His sober eyes, still etched with the wrath of seeing Cameron earlier and of suspicion now, trail down my body for a moment before finding my face again.

His fingers slide into the hair at my nape, curling around roughly to grab a fistful. He pulls me into him, his other hand sliding over my face, pulling back the skin, studying every minute movement of my face.

I stare back at him as boldly as I can. Jack and I are still in this tentative dance of reconnection. Some days, it flows, and we move beautifully, effortlessly. Other days, our bodies are tense and the movements stiff, uncomfortable as we both breathe through recurring shockwaves of pain and betrayal, trying not to succumb to the asphyxia of outrage and jealous rancor.

But no matter the state of our relationship, the heat between us never wanes, its flames licking the earth around us, pushing us to the brink of insanity some days. Jack's glare smolders... always, his hands gripping me possessively, his lips finding my skin, his tongue lashing me as if resetting the machine, as if to reconnect us to the first three years of our relationship and that beautiful amalgamation born of the heady euphoria of first love and desire indecently expressed.

My breathing quickens as his hand slides down my neck and over my breast, his thumb skimming my nipple until it hardens into a point beneath his touch.

He doesn't blink as his hand makes its way over my taut belly and into the waistband of my pajamas.

"Jack, stop!" I wrap my fingers around his wrist. I know what he's doing. He's checking to see if I'm wet. And he knows it wouldn't be from him... or not this time anyway.

He's stronger than me. My hand couldn't stop him sliding over my pubis and into my sex, but he stops suddenly, perhaps due to the determined strength I'm using to hold his wrist and arrest the descent of his hand and temper the possessive insanity of the act.

Taking his hand out, he pulls me into him, his features stern, his aura unstable as he soaks in my face. My breasts slip against the hard wall of his warm, sculpted chest as the ridge of his erection rubs against my belly from under his pajama pants.

"Why did you come down here?"

"I couldn't sleep," I respond, hit by a wave of anger and hurt that I know he feels too. Being with Jack feels like swimming in the ocean with him. Some days the waters are calm and beautiful, enveloping us in bliss, and others, they are rough and savage, tumbling us about as we struggle to hold onto each other.

It would be easier to walk away. I know he feels that too. But I see in his eyes that he wants to fight. And for as long as he does, I struggle not to meet him in that place.

"You used to ride my cock when you couldn't sleep," he retorts with a growl. "Remember?"

I peer up breathlessly into a raging flood of blue in his irises and a face that is broad, its angular lines sharp and beautiful.

"That doesn't solve every problem, Jack..."

Without warning, he thrusts a hand into my hair, forcing my head back. His brutal lips dip to skim mine. "No. It doesn't. Why don't I feel like I own every piece of my wife, Jessynia?" His question steals my breath and vigor from my limbs. When I don't answer, he repeats, "Why?" The movements of his body are angry, but his tone is underpinned by pain.

A single tear pools on my waterline, spilling onto my pale cheek. "Why did you go back there, Jack? To that place? To *her*?"

So, maybe it's a deflection, but I've spent nine months tormented by the question of why, in the midst of a marriage that was beautiful and passionate and raw and connected, he chose to sleep with Alexandra, and Lydia, and God knows how many women at that place before coming home to sleep in bed with me when he knew it would blow everything to pieces...

My unexpected question has him softening his grip a tad but does little to still the rabid breathing of his dense body. "That's not the subject tonight," he responds through gritted teeth.

"Yes, it is. It's always the subject," I retort, wishing it wasn't, wishing those months didn't erode the ground beneath us, nudging me into dark places that would once have been unfathomable.

His eyes suddenly close and his head drops a little. His fingers pull out of my hair and as if losing strength, he releases me completely, taking a seat on the loveseat, his elbows resting on his knees, his head bowed, thick hair flopping over his face.

I go to sit down on the floor in front of him but change my mind, deciding not to look at him so that he has space to answer without being watched. I take a seat on the rug, finding the space between his legs and leaning back against the front of the loveseat.

One of his hands settles on my shoulders and his chin brushes the top of my head, just for a moment, as I wait for what feels like an hour for him to speak.

"Why, Jack?" I whisper. "I need to understand it."

He doesn't respond for the longest time, and I wait in silence for an answer I've wanted for so long but have been so afraid to know the answer to.

"You'll think it's a cop-out," he finally says, his usually powerful voice frail as if strands of it are unraveling.

"Maybe," I respond. "I still want to know."

"I... I'd been... going... to that place since... I was seventeen. I'd been... seeing... *her* since I was fourteen."

My head drops and I try not to drown in the vision of that woman seducing him when he was a child.

"Jack..." My hand finds the top of his bare ankle and winds around it tightly.

"When it starts young, it becomes ingrained in you. Part of you. But I did try, Jessynia. I need you to know that, for whatever it's worth. I didn't go there for two and half years, despite the constant pressure, despite that woman still being in my head. I did try."

I close my eyes to stop the tears from spilling onto my cheek.

I know it's true...

I can hear it.

"What happened, Jack? I need to understand it. I've been playing it over in my mind for nine months."

"They... said they were... planning to... hurt... him."

A shockwave detonates in my body, canceling out all sound for a moment.

Cameron...

"I went there to try to stop it," he continues. "I was drugged. And... I lost control."

I turn around swiftly, peering into his shadowy face. "Sebastian?" I whisper.

"Yes," he nods. "It was *my* weakness, but it was his design. It always is."

I turn back around, finding his ankle once again which I coil my fingers around. "How do I know I can believe you?" I ask.

"Because I don't lie, Jessynia. You know that about me..."

I stare at my legs as I take in the reality of his words. Jack may conceal the truth at times, but he's right: he doesn't lie. The vision of Sebastian concocting his malevolent spells, conjuring up poison for people to drink appears in pale splotches before my field of vision.

"Does he know?" I ask about Cameron. "That you were trying to save him?"

"No."

I turn again to face him. "Why didn't you tell him?!"

His solemn eyes drink me in. "We were no longer speaking."

"Why didn't you tell *me*, Jack?"

"Because... I never wanted you to know about that place. I wasn't the one to take you there, remember? And because I feel... trauma from that day, Jessynia. And shame. I don't know how to talk about it. I wanted to keep you from that world, somehow. I failed."

I swallow hard at the vision of sinewy vines of ebony winding around his teenage self, creeping up his body, enveloping his face until he can't move, can't breathe... until they're inside him.

"You kept going back," I finally say as the silence in which trauma finds its home bears down on us.

"Yes."

"Why?"

"I didn't cope well with what I'd done. I did something to stop the pain. And I became afraid... of defying them, of losing you. I was still enslaved by... her... I was weak. I let myself fall."

My eyes close as I flinch through the pain of his affairs that still twists my insides, stopping me from being able to fully connect to him. The specter of Sebastian, Alex, and the other ghouls at that place hollows me out. Sebastian makes me feel like he wants to protect me, but he's caused me more pain than I know how to put into words.

He has to pay for it...

I'm going to make him pay...

A tear falls from me as Jack's hand slides onto the side of my neck. "I know I've hurt you. I know what it did to you... to us... to find out what... had been happening. I don't know words to express this type of regret."

"Did it stop them? From... hurting... him?"

"Yes," he replies. "But not for good. Sebastian can be appeased but it never lasts forever. Inside, he's thirsty for blood. He's aware of the problem. He can't control it. I think he tries to resist it, but it overpowers him. And when it does, nothing you say can stop him."

"He does try?" I ask and Jack's hand slips around the back of my neck.

"When it comes to people's lives, to decisions of life and death, *trying* isn't good enough, Jessynia."

"I know," I nod, struggling to reconcile everything I hear about his malevolence with the man who handles me so gently.

I turn back around, feeling Jack leaning into me, his fingers curving around the front of my neck and mine around his calf. We don't speak for some time, letting the ripples of mutual hurt and the volatile crackles of our bodies pulse through each other. I contemplate my guilt at Cameron's call, no longer knowing how to stop all contact, wondering whether I should tell Jack the truth, and beg him to allow Cameron into this house...

Shaking out the utterly insane idea, I instead decide to tell my husband something I should have told him before, but never had the strength to, because all I wanted to do was forget about it and move on. Except now, I know that when you don't talk about these things, they haunt you like a shadow.

"Someone once tried to hurt me," I blurt out and in a rush of movement, Jack gets to his feet, pivoting to stand in front of me, eyes wild with confusion.

"What do you mean?" he asks breathlessly. "*How?*"

"I'd just... turned seventeen. I was at a camp. There was this... man. A camp leader. A few years older. I barely knew him. He... tried to... but I managed to fight him off and... run away."

He shakes his head slowly, his brow furrowing as he tries to swallow. "What happened?" he asks, his hands tensing into fists before me.

"After I managed to get away... my parents were called. They and the... camp leaders decided that it's best not to involve... the police. And then... people from his family, they spread rumors about me. False rumors. And... that's about it..."

"Who was it?"

"It doesn't matter now," I respond.

"I want to know, Goddammit. I want a name."

"No, Jack. I don't want that."

"I need to know his name."

I shake my head. "I can't."

And in any case, there's no point anymore...

After what feels like an eternity, he finally sits down in front of me. "Who knows about this?" he asks.

"My family. Stella, Maddie, Kevin, Babs. That's about it."

He scours my face, his eyes devoid of light, his lips turning pallid before me. "Why didn't you tell me this before?"

I shrug. "The same reason you didn't tell me what *she* did to you when you were fourteen... Jack, do you know that what happened to you was *wrong*? What she did? That you were too young to handle a woman so much older? Do you know that you deserved better?"

"I'm not sure how much better I deserve," he responds soberly.

"Jack, you deserve *everything*."

He watches me for a while, his respiration accelerating as he takes in my face. Finally, he reaches for the throw on the loveseat, unfolding it and laying me down onto the rug. He slides his body next to mine, placing his thigh over mine before draping the throw over us and placing his arm over my body. I hear him panting as he breathes me in, and feel his body tremble a little as he holds me.

"I'm sorry," he whispers, his breath hot on the side of my face. "I'm so sorry someone did that to you. If I could kill him, I would."

"I know," I breathe. "I'm sorry too, Jack. I'm sorry for what she did to you. I'm sorry for everything."

I close my eyes as I melt into his body. "Jack? I don't want to hit you with the whole kitchen sink, but... why don't you ever talk about your mom? What that animal did to you afterwards, it didn't allow you the space to grieve."

I feel his body draw tense, the muscles stiffening. "I stopped grieving when I met you."

A tear falls from me, and he slides it away. "Can you... tell me one thing about her?"

He pauses for a moment before speaking. "She loved me," he replies, forcing my eyes to close as I see him as the young boy staring down at her grave.

I nod. "I know she loved you so much." My hand slips up his arm. "Jack," I whisper into his neck. "I need you to know that you're worthy of being loved. And that I love you."

"Stop—"

"I do. I always have. Even after everything that's happened, I've never stopped loving you. No matter what happens, I need you to know that."

"Stop," he pleads, his fingers interlacing mine. "Nothing's going to happen, Jessynia." I tremble at the feel of tears dripping onto my cheek —his. His body tightens around mine. "I'm not afraid of our storm,

Jessynia. I know how to weather storms." My eyes close as he whispers words which stun me into silence. "You're looking for something that you already have. Here. Me. Us. You don't realize that it's *us* you're trying to find." He breathes in my skin.

"Jack..."

"I'm not letting go, Jessynia. I'm not afraid of the storm. I'll never give up. And no one will ever hurt you like that again."

34

Darragh
Quercus Velutina
Present

Sebastian's hands fold over the ends of the wooden chair at the end of the long dark-wood table as he contemplates the man sitting opposite him—Alistair Rowling, a long-time ally, though you wouldn't know it today.

He has been jumpy of late, making comments here and there about Sebastian's apparent loss of control at the hands of a woman who was supposed to be easily tamed.

Meetings of the inner Council are always quite the event, but today's is more tense than usual due to the dispatching of Adam Kroenig and the manner in which it happened. The bloody violence of it has traveled in hushed shock waves around the Council. There's no risk of the police being called. None of these people have clean hands, including myself, I must confess. Taking down one would mean putting all at risk. Not since the early twentieth century has a member of Council reported the activities of Society members to the authorities.

But that doesn't mean that concerns are not being raised.

Apparently, the murder has rattled Alistair enough for him to dare to question Sebastian in public.

Glaring at Alistair at the foot of the table to my right sits Samara in her black cloak, her small eyes hidden in shadow. The woman is in her late fifties, her physical body frailer than it once was, but her force and presence are still as strong and unnerving as any of the men's here.

She has known Sebastian since he was first released from prison at the age of twenty-one and has been instrumental in his rise up the ranks of the Society to the all-powerful position of president.

She will defend him to the death—ruthlessly if need be. She seems to consider him to be something akin to a son, although I have no doubt that he fucked her repeatedly for many years, for it was, in fact, her and Alexandra who drew him into this place.

He was in his twenties, she in her forties. Nothing illegal, but she has whispered poisoned words into him since they met, with no sign of it abating. She feeds into his malevolence, for she is herself a most vile and bitter creature, albeit one who knows how to fly under the radar, speaking in hushed tones to those who enjoy her particular brand of unadulterated malice, and there are plenty of those around here. I must confess that I am partial to it myself on my weaker days.

These types either have visceral reactions to seeing people as malevolent as they are, or they enjoy how "normal" they make them feel. They enjoy the rationalization of their own venomous conduct that they experience when seeing people who are truly corrupt.

No decision of any real magnitude is made without her input. Her advice is not always heeded, but the slow trickle of her poison invariably sets the tone for acts sanctioned by the Society. She is one of many attack dogs who work in service to this powerful man, including Vallen, Isaiah, Ilya, Steven, Alexandra and Dominic.

And he may need them all today...

"What is your concern, friend?" Sebastian's cavernous, room-owning voice is always so measured, so civilized, so deep that it can stun even me into silence.

"My concern, friend," replies Alistair, "is that you were given authorization to end the man cleanly with a blade. That was what we voted on. Instead, he... was beaten to death. It's *messy*."

I glance at a woman standing in the shadows against the wall. There are four such women—one against each wall. All naked. All wearing the leather collars of fealty to the Society. All ready to serve—whether it be drinks or food or documents. They are naked during all meetings of the inner sanctum because its members must be able to abstain from sex when it is offered to them. They must be able to defy their base urges if need be. This is part of that test.

Indeed, one of the old rituals of initiation that Sebastian reinstated upon becoming president is that of *Sui Disciplinam*, a week-long test of self-control during which a potential Council member is sequestered alone for one week with a stranger—male or female depending on their sexual preference.

The stranger is free to roam if they are male, and bound to the wall by a long chain if they are female, allowed to be released only to use the washroom and to sleep.

They must sleep in the same bed naked, feed their guest food by hand, and wash their guest's body. But should the aspiring Council member succumb to their physical desire and engage in sexual conduct with their guest or pleasure themselves during that week, they are ineligible from resubmitting their application for another three years.

It is the only time that cameras are allowed into rooms. And from what I myself have experienced first-hand, it is sheer torture for the highly sexed patrons of Quercus Velutina who are used to having desires fulfilled on a whim.

These women against the wall—all collared subs—must be resisted at all times. They may not be touched during Council meetings. And yet, they are there to provide arousal to those present, a side effect of which, in theory, is to help meetings run more smoothly.

And after the meeting, these subs will be fucked mercilessly by the male members, while female members also get to choose the men they want from those present or from those waiting in a room nearby...

Sebastian lets out a silent breath. He has an ability that is rare and most impressive to behold—being able to glare at someone without flinching, barely blinking, his cold countenance stopping you from speaking, from thinking, as you share space with a man whose reactions are as unpredictable as an avalanche which will carry you to perilous terrain without warning.

"Yes," he replies. "I did deviate from what was agreed upon. The man was an abuser of children. I lost control in the face of that. The manner of his demise was a fitting end to his life."

"No one is questioning that he deserved to die, but it wasn't what we agreed upon," counters Steven Frost.

An almost audible silence fills the room at the sound of Steven daring to question Sebastian, his long-time ally and the man who has fucked his wife for a decade or more, and has shaped the Society, in part, under the dregs of her influence. Alexandra Frost gazes at her husband softly. It is rare for her to look upon him with anything other than contempt. Perhaps she is pleased with him for daring to question Sebastian, a man she is clearly most upset with these days.

Sebastian's eyes narrow as he absorbs the full extent of the insubordination of the lesser sanctum members, those who have benefited greatly from the Society's offerings under Sebastian's rule.

"What we're... concerned about," interrupts Alistair, watched by the cruel regard of Vallen, rabidly faithful to Sebastian, "is perhaps a... lapse in judg— A... a loss of control, maybe... because of *her*. Jessynia Wilder."

The utterance of her name has inner sanctum members darting looks at each other—Vallen at Alex, Isaiah at Grace. The latter two are not members but are allowed into the inner circle in order that they may perform their duties effectively. They are privy to things that only the elected few are, something which makes them powerful but vulnerable at once. Their loyalty cannot falter, not even once. It would mean putting a target on their backs that arrows would fail to miss.

"Are you suggesting I am not capable of performing my duties in our Society anymore, Alistair?"

"Of course not. I'm just a little... *concerned* about your feelings for this woman. She's married to Jackson Wilder. He won't give her up without a fight. Cameron O'Neill is still out of his mind over her, from what we've been told. I don't believe he'll stand back and watch over her integration into our family. Not to mention that she's a journalist. It's a high-risk profession for us. They are usually banned from becoming members, and yet she is allowed into our Society whenever you require her. That has not been voted upon. She is dangerous for us, Sebastian, especially if... you are not in *full* control around her."

Darkness swathes the room as he utters the insinuation aloud—that Sebastian Gravier's judgment can no longer be trusted due to his feelings for this woman. A year ago, the idea of him having feelings for anyone that went behind the primal desire to watch a woman submit would have been unfathomable.

"We have her watched, friend," drawls Sebastian coldly, "as you well know. She has not done one thing to expose us publicly, nor spoken of us to her friends or family. As for your insinuation that I place my feelings before our Society, you are lucky that we have been friends for so long. If it were not the case, I would take the insinuation as the gravest of insults."

"I am not suggesting that, my Lord," Alistair responds. "I just... was hoping for reassurance that she isn't a threat to our existence."

"Which would imply that I place her well-being above that of our family," Sebastian retorts, the glowing silver of his eyes flaring in bright cinders.

"I wasn't suggesting that..."

"She is not a threat," Sebastian snarls. "And anyone who deems her to be one without evidence to support the claim will be dealt with by me. Personally. Is. That. Clear?"

"Very clear, my Lord," replies Alistair, bowing his head. I wonder what price he will pay for such public insolence...

"Is she a threat to—"

"To *what*?" Sebastian snarls.

“To your… ability to make rational decisions?” he finishes. The man clearly doesn’t know when to stop digging. “She seems to… have quite a powerful effect on you.”

I glance at Alexandra Frost, her chest rising and falling fast under her blue cloak as outward signs of her flaring temper begin to manifest themselves. Her lips thin as she glares at our President.

Of course… She will not be liking the insinuation that Sebastian has lost his mind over the woman who broke her nose and faced no consequences for it… not one little bit…

“Are you questioning my ability to rule, friend?”

“No. I’m just… looking for reassurance that your… friendship with her won’t… put us in peril in some way.”

Sebastian watches him, unblinking for what feels like an eternity. “I believe we’re repeating ourselves. I don’t appreciate having my *fucking* time wasted. If you need further reassurance, it means you don’t trust my word. Trust has always been the foundation of our Council. Without it, we have *nothing*. When people don’t trust me, I find myself struggling to trust *them*. Would you like that, Alistair?”

“Of course not,” he stammers, his voice shaking.

Sebastian has been questioned about decisions before. It is not uncommon, nor frowned upon. He usually tolerates it well, but clearly questioning him about Jessynia vexes him in a way that he cannot seem to bear. But then, he appears to be utterly out of control when it comes to her. It is fascinating to observe, despite how dangerous it feels… for all of us. He despises anything that makes him vulnerable, weakens him, makes him feel anything beyond the rage and clinical curiosity he usually feels for people.

I often wonder how long he will tolerate the sensation, and what he will do once he finds that her existence is eating into the carefully crafted armor sheathing him, and lets light through, adulterating the seductive darkness that he inhabits so willingly. Light to Sebastian is poison. It shines the truth onto his experiences, onto this pain, his abuse, his abandonment by authority figures. Light forces him to face what happened to him as a child. Why would he when he can soothe

the pain by giving himself over to the menace inside himself? Without God, it is impossible.

I don't know if he's strong enough to stomach the sudden intrusion of unbidden light that can only exist in the truth, and that confronts him so boldly. I don't know if anyone could be.

Throughout my work dealing with broken people, I have come to realize that being utterly despised by a parent leads to fractures of the psyche that only a lifelong commitment to healing can truly unpack, especially given that a cruel society refuses to acknowledge that such abuse exists by parents, that there are parents who abhor every breath that their progeny take. The victims of this hell are left utterly abandoned, their abuse rationalized, explained away in a manner that absolves their abuser of guilt, retraumatizing them endlessly.

I have seen it with my own eyes.

Treatment for the relentless maternal abuse he endured would take months, if not years, and would require him to apply himself and acknowledge that he was a victim. But then, why would he when he can assuage his rage at the world by brutalizing those around him—men and women, often willingly serving themselves up to provide him the relief his soul seeks on a daily basis?

There is perhaps one vague glimmer of hope that he can salvage what's left of his human—Jessynia.

From everything I've heard, she understands this type of abuse, and its systematic invalidation. It's a rare gift that he won't be oblivious to.

Something about her clearly calls to the human encaged inside him—one that his demons do not want unchained. I feel them in him, writhing, desperate for her destruction, for she can speak to his human host in a way no one else can... or perhaps no one wants to. To the rest of the world, he is irredeemable, lost, some kind of demon, possessed by dark spirits that most do not see, and in the case of many, he is preferable that way.

She can see the human. She awakens him.

That's why she's in such danger without even knowing it.

That's why it's so utterly thrilling to watch—the battle between God and the devil. It is a battle I wage within myself every single day, one which tears at my soul, which pulls me apart. I have tried to be God's servant. I want to believe. I want to help... and then, other voices speak to me, call to me, whispering, leading me down paths which seem to burn so brightly—lit by the flames of hell.

I can't help feeling that my fate is tied to his.

"Of course I trust you," continues Alistair—unusually shaken for a man of his power and composure.

"Your concerns are noted, *friend*. My relationship with her does not and will never affect my role here. Is that understood?"

"Yes. It is. Thank you." He bows his head in capitulation as I glance around the table to grave faces.

Sebastian is now ruling through fear rather than competence. It is a dangerous place to govern from, for your subjects are not loyal to you because they believe in you, but for fear of the consequences of insubordination. And in a moment of weakness, they may band together and pounce...

Luckily for Sebastian, at least half of the members of the inner sanctum, and the majority of members on Council are rabid in their loyalty to him—Vallen, Dominic, Samara, Ilya, Steven—or at least usually. Alexandra was once a steadfast ally who yielded power through her association with Sebastian, but she's been unpredictable of late... or even more so than usual.

"Are there any other matters to attend to?" asks Sebastian.

"I would like to bring up the question of Cameron O'Neill," says Steven Frost sternly as his wife continues to glare at Sebastian who doesn't seem to have looked at her once. I have no doubt that he feels her energy without having to look at her.

Sebastian nods for him to continue, his bright eyes glistening like spheres of quartz in the candlelight.

"As we all know, there has been talk of him returning to our Society. I think we would all like some clarification on the matter."

Nods and utterances of approval ring out around the table as Sebastian's eyes flit to the members present tonight.

"Our people have reached out to him." Sebastian's implacable glare cuts to me for a moment. "He is contemplating the offer."

"How do we know he can trust him?" asks Patrick, another long-time member who usually doesn't dare to defy Sebastian.

"We don't," Sebastian replies. "But is he less dangerous to us now that he is no longer part of our Society? I would suggest not."

"We don't know what that man is plotting as we speak," adds Vallen roughly. "He's better off back with us so that we don't have to wonder what he's up to all the time."

"Isn't he still out of his mind over... *her*?" asks Alistair.

Sebastian's face twists in anger. "What's your fucking point?"

"My point, *my Lord*, is that she may be the only reason he wants back here. He can't get to her with Jackson in the way, so he'll do it another way. If he returns, his loyalty will not be to us. It'll be to her. Loyalty to a loved one over that to the Society is tolerated only when it comes to spouses and officially recognized significant others. She is neither. She's his *mistress*, at best." Sebastian's eyes darken. "We're playing with fire letting him back in."

"The offer is tentative, based on him complying with certain demands of ours," Sebastian says. "We don't know if the terms will be acceptable to him or if he'll accept the offer."

"Is he seriously contemplating it?" asks Dominic.

Cameron has long fought the demons inside him which crave this place. He has been stronger than most could have been, especially in light of the grooming he experienced at the hands of Alexandra Frost and her little harem of friends who eroded the foundations of his psyche when he was still a child, filling the chasm they left behind with smoke that left him confused and alone, and needing pleasure to cope.

He dwells in darkness, just as Sebastian does, but unlike Sebastian, he fights the darkness. He fights the need to hurt people to soothe his pain. For that, he is a braver man than me.

Normally, he is successful. But from what we know, losing the woman who owns him has left him bitter and unstable. Irrational. Desperate for solace. For relief from the torment.

Sebastian can offer that. What's more, he can offer up Jessynia who would never abandon someone she loves.

The question that perplexes me is why Sebastian would allow it...

He is creating an intimacy with her that he could not have predicted. Adding Cameron to the mix will surely damage that intimacy... unless he believes that Cameron himself will become so damaged if and when he succumbs to the pleasures of the Society again that Jessynia will no longer recognize him. That she will lose him. And will become afraid, needing to take refuge in the arms of the man who meticulously crafted Cameron's very demise.

Or maybe, his goal is to share her with a man he once believed to be a Lord of this place, one who could turn off his humanity for short moments and revel in his indecent physicality and appeal to women, whipping them into a frenzy in the process.

Could Jessynia resist the two of them? Could any woman resist the combination of Sebastian Gravier and Cameron O'Neill, both claiming her, tending to her with a bestial violence that would haunt many women's dreams? And nightmares...

No woman could resist it.

The fact that she has been able to resist Sebastian at all is an anomaly I've never seen here before. He doesn't compel women to pleasure him. They beg him to grant them a night in his bed, knowing full well how diabolical his tastes are, his need to choke, to cut, to drown.

They run the water for him, without being asked, desperate to be near-drowned as they are fucked. I've seen it with my own eyes. Hell, if you told them that they had a fifty-fifty chance of survival, I imagine half would say yes anyway. That is the power of this man—a power he wields over men and women.

If Cameron believes the only way to have Jessynia, to take her from Jack permanently, is to possess her within the confines of the Society, he might succumb to the temptation. Temptation is what takes every man away from a righteous path.

Every breath that man takes seems to be for her. He could have any woman in the city, but none of the dozens he's fucked since meeting her have dislodged the love he feels for her. His love is powerful, and dangerous.

At this point, it seems that he would risk his life for one more day with her. And if that means being here, would he do it?

He's not free as it is, not for as long as Sebastian harbors this hatred for him. Perhaps he would fare better than he did as a young man when his mind became sickened by the drugs, the mind games, the danger and the faceless fucking. If he returned, it would be as a more powerful presence, an unequaled draw in this place.

Or is his plan to get close to her, to dislodge her from Jack, only to take her away and bring the Society down with it? That thought can't be lost on Sebastian either.

In any case, the grotesque play is divine to witness. My role teeters on my faith in God. Some days, it is strong. Others, it wanes, and I revel in the pleasures of this place, in its evil, in its darkness, observing with glee the entities that have a hold on our president.

"We believe so," Sebastian finally answers. "We believe he's considering it."

"Why, my Lord?" asks Samara, a woman who never trusted Cameron and whose only concern is the protection of a man she worships, Sebastian. Her voice is so frail compared to before—a wicked act designed to create the illusion of deference. "After so many years, with all the resentment between yourself and him? Between him and our respected friend,"—she tips her head towards Alex—"How could he return?"

"I'm not sure he has ever really left," Sebastian responds.

"What would be the advantage of it for us?" asks Steven.

"Is there a day that goes by when one of us is not asked about his return?" he offers. "We know what that man will do to the place. We know the power that he brings."

"This whole fucking thing had better be so that you can enjoy him for a while before annihilating him," snarls Alexandra Frost, glaring at Sebastian as she does, her breathing erratic. "Otherwise, I don't see why he gets to come back. I don't see why you can't let him take the bitch. Let them go off together and leave our family the fuck alone. Unless you really have lost your fucking mind..."

Muted inhalations of shock ring out around the room, dropping us into the heaviest of black silences.

Steven swivels to look at her, his expression coarsening at her disdainful affront to the president. His hand coils around the slim wrist poking out from under her navy-blue cloak. "Forgive my wife, Sebastian. She's not been herself of late. I'll take care of it."

"It's a fair question," Sebastian retorts coldly. "My animosity towards the man has not been a secret. But I do believe that his return would certainly... soothe some of my ire."

His words are duplicitous, for I know full well what his intentions are. He may toy with him here for a while, but ultimately, he will never rest until he is standing over Cameron's bleeding body. He has spoken of it so much that I believe he already tastes the blood, sees the cold horror in Cameron's eyes as life seeps from him.

It's only then that Sebastian will truly be able to breathe.

Cameron's existence is a tumor in Sebastian's psyche, the same way that Jessynia's is in Alexandra's. He will tolerate Cameron for a short time longer before his demons require the blood they have thirsted for for years, before his plan is put into motion. And what's more, any Council members who may have misgivings over the endeavor have too much of their own blood on their hands to say a word to anyone about it.

"I have some... concern about this, my Lord," says Patrick, his face pale despite him being one of the most imposing of the men here. "You, Cameron, Jack, the girl... It could bring down our Society if things go wrong."

"I suggest we put the matter to a vote," replies Sebastian, his voice so authoritative, so collected that you'd never think he was on the verge of mutiny. "All those in favor of allowing Cameron O'Neill back into our Society, once he has been through the penitence program, raise your hand now."

I do so and look around at those who do—Vallen, Ilya, Dominic, Imogen ... and upon a glare by Sebastian, Samara, and finally, Sebastian himself.

"Anyone else?" asks Sebastian, his gaze sliding to me. I lift my hand in the air. As dangerous as this is, as wrong as I know it to be, I can't resist the ungodly potential of war between these two men. I am torn between wanting to stop it and needing to see the violence of it.

Seven votes in total, including Sebastian. Six people keep their hands glued to the table, including Alexandra and Steven. Alistair looks around, concerned as another man shakes his head.

"The motion is passed," says Samara. "If he agrees, he will be allowed in as a member only."

As the tension from the vote releases, Alexandra's eyes meet mine and I stare into the face of a woman unhinged, a woman who is losing everything...

Sometime later after other discussions of less magnitude, the meeting is brought to a close and the women who were once standing against the wall have leashes clipped to their collars and are silently led from the room and taken to one where any frustrations from this evening may be taken out on them...

35

Sebastian

"Sebastian."

I stop in my tracks at the sound of Steven Frost's voice, turning slowly to face him in all his duplicity.

"I apologize for my wife's outburst earlier, Sebastian."

"And for your own?"

"I believe my concerns about the girl are legitimate."

"Very possibly," I reply, meeting eyes almost black. "Though I believe your concerns could have been discussed with me in private, Steven. That is how we have always functioned, is it not?"

My *friend* breathes out slowly as he bows his head. "It won't happen again."

"As for your wife—"

"I'll be teaching her a lesson tonight, Sebastian. Don't worry about that."

"No. You'll be leaving her with me for the night."

His face harshens for a short moment as his eyes flare. He's watched me fuck Alexandra for years, but always consensually, always keeping tension between he and I at a minimum.

My current demand seems to be triggering some unexpectedly enjoyable reaction to another man's claim over his property. Blood pumps riotously through my system at the sight of his face absorbing the dent to his pride. He doesn't care about his wife, nor about who fucks her, within reason, but I normally request her presence in a more respectful manner. Neither of them has earned that privilege from me today. They'll both be taught a lesson, before it's too late for them...

"Very well," he nods. "But I want one of the clones in exchange. Your most compliant one."

"I'll have one sent to your room," I reply. "You may do with her as you wish, for as long as safe words are respected. I want your wife here within five minutes—collared and cuffed."

He bows his head. "I'll go get her."

"Do you have any limits as to what can be done to her?" I ask.

"No... But make it hurt."

"It will."

Alexandra

"Get your fucking hands off me," I snarl, yanking my arm away from the prick I am forced to call a husband.

He kicks the door shut behind him and grabs me by the hair, pinning me to the wall with his hand. The collar he forced on me protects me from the compression of his fingers around my neck as I try to pry his hand off.

I find Sebastian's eyes as he watches the sorry spectacle of our poisonous marriage with detached curiosity, his eyes wide on mine.

"Tie her to the wall," he orders, and I glare at him in response, despite my body vibrating at the command. I still want the fucker, despite the wounds he's inflicted upon me of late, the indignities over the cunt he can't get out of his head.

Steven yanks my cloak off me and reaches for a chain on the wall, clipping it quickly into the degrading collar around my neck. I try to slap him, but he grabs my wrist with his left hand, using his right to clip a second chain attached to the wall to the other side of my collar so that I'm chained to it by the neck.

"There you go." My husband spits the words out at me, his mouth twisting in fury. "Like the fucking bitch you are."

He takes a few steps back to admire the humiliation he has meted out to me yet again, starting with our wedding night when he drunkenly fucked one of my bridesmaids—a distant relative of his, no less—in our bed and forced me to watch it.

Honeymooning, Steven Frost style.

A mild taste of things to come...

"Teach this fucking cunt a lesson, will you?" my darling husband growls. "You don't want me divorcing the bitch, so help me get her back in line."

"What, not man enough to do it yourself?" I spit back.

His palm nails the wall next to my shoulder. "If you don't get her to behave, I'll be filing for divorce. I want her *submitting* like a fucking *dog*."

"I shall be having a serious discussion with your wife, Steven. Now leave us to it."

The fucker turns to face me, wrapping his hand around my jaw, his harsh lips scraping my cheek. "You can have her. I'll be fucking the kind of woman every man here wants while you're being fucked like a dog in the street."

"Get out!" I shout, pulling against the chains tying my neck to the wall. "Get out! Get out!"

Steven turns to look at Sebastian. "You'd better tame the bitch once and for all. My patience is wearing thin..."

Sebastian's eyes narrow on Steven until he turns and marches out of the door, shutting it behind him with a loud bang.

I pant as I return Sebastian's cold-eyed glare. He doesn't move—not a muscle as he takes me in.

I know you want me, you fucker...

After what feels like a full minute, he walks towards me slowly, eyes wandering down my dress. Coming to stand a foot before me, he studies me as I try to calm my breathing... and my emotions.

I've never been good at that.

He grabs hold of my wrist, pulling it up, despite my attempt to resist him, and clipping the cuff around it to a chain attached to the wall. He does the same with my other hand before coming to stand before me, observing me for a while before leaning into me.

I secretly like it, you prick.

"I thought we'd moved past this." His fucking voice still stuns me. "I thought we'd made our peace after the unfortunate events of late. And then this... Your explanation as to your behavior tonight will determine how much I have to hurt you, my friend. I advise you to choose your words wisely."

I don't speak until he roars the order again into my face, his breath hot on my skin, tearing a tear from my eye. I hate disappointing him, and yet, I can't stomach the way she now *owns* him. And the way others know it. That's what grates me.

As if I haven't been humiliated enough by that sanctimonious bitch. I can't believe he could be this fucking stupid...

"You. Have. Five. Seconds."

"How did you expect me to feel, hearing them all talk about your *feelings* for her?" I snarl, fully aware I can't control myself. "Do you know how humiliating it is for me to hear them all concerned about your feelings for that insufferable cunt?"

"You're not my wife, Alexandra. You have no business being *humiliated*."

"Fuck you!"

"Hmm... I've overlooked your temper because of my affection for you. Our bond. Our history. But your inability to control yourself in public is becoming problematic."

"My temper?! It's *your* infatuation with that bitch who could ruin us all that's the problem!"

"I spent years observing your infatuation for Mr. Wilder and Mr. O'Neill, *friend*. Is there some reason you don't have the decency to reciprocate?"

"So you admit it?!"

"Infatuation happens to us all, even us demons, Alexandra. You should know that."

"I don't even think you're infatuated. I think you're possessed!"

His eyes form into slits. "My fucking feelings are not your concern. However, your insubordination to me in public *is*. What do you have to say about your behavior?"

"I don't have to say shit!"

"Hmm," he smiles bitterly, knowing full well I'm provoking him on purpose. He knows I want to be fucked out of my misery. He knows I can't resist him no matter how much attitude I give him. "You really do want to be in pain tonight, don't you?"

"There's nothing you could do to me that that prick I call a husband hasn't. And seeing as you won't let us get divorced."

"Divorce has always been frowned upon in our Society. This is nothing new. It is a messy act. People talk. Lawyers learn things they have no business knowing. You two are no exceptions. I'm not forbidding it, but I would encourage you both to consider the consequences for both of you if things were to be less than amicable."

"Amicable? With *that* prick?"

"He's willing to work it out with you, Alex."

"Well, maybe my darling husband will get lucky like you did..."

His hand hits the wall next to my head, causing me to whimper. Another tear escapes me. I can't fucking well help it. He has no idea how much I've been hurt. I've lost a *third* man to her.

A *third*.

It eats me up from the inside day and night. I see her face, her eyes, that so-called innocent fucking smile of hers. They haunt me.

He doesn't speak, glowering at me, his breathing out of control. I know I'm going too far, but I can't help it. I can't temper the rage anymore. He has always understood me. We've always had this bond. He'd seen hell too. Experienced torture. Been toyed with for sport as if he were less than human. He understood me better than anyone else. Now all he sees is *her*.

She's poison.

Fucking poison.

Seeping into him.

Making him weak.

Making him vulnerable like the others.

Every breath of air she takes is stolen from *me*.

He squeezes my cheeks together, snarling as he speaks. "One more word about my wife's demise..."

"Oh, sure," I snap. "I bet you're just *miserable* the cunt is gone. *You* got freed from marriage. I *can't*."

"You're gonna pay for that..."

"Make my day," I sneer.

Removing his hand from my face, he grabs the top of my tight, long-sleeved white dress and slowly rips it down the center as his eyes stake their claim on me. He pulls further, tearing the thin fabric all the way to the bottom. I'm not wearing a bra as per usual, nor do I wear panties in this place. They're utterly pointless. As he pulls the sides of my dress open, his eyes wander down my naked body.

I know he's going to punish me. *I want him to.* I always want him, no matter how much I despise the way she now consumes his mind.

"Is the fucker coming back?" I ask as he contemplates my neck. "O'Neill."

"I intend to make it impossible for him to see her in any other way."

"As if he hasn't already fucked her..."

His eyes darken and his lips thin. "I would have thought you would have wanted his return," he snarls. "You certainly pined like a pathetic little whore over him for long enough. Isn't this what you've dreamed of?"

"Not like *this*. He can't be trusted! He only gives a fuck about *her*. He's contaminated like the rest of you fools. He's gonna fuck things up here. They *both* are. They'll be the ruin of this place."

"Perhaps *I'll* be the ruin of *them, friend*," he suggests.

"I want them *dead*. *Both* of them. If you don't have the guts to do what's right, I'll make it happen myself."

"You'll get your wish when it comes to *him*." He closes the gap between us as his eyes burn in anger. "As for *her*, go near her, you even *look* at her, and I'll rip your fucking world apart."

I do it before I can stop it. I didn't mean to. I can't control the rage anymore.

I watch as my saliva drips down his cheek. Thank God my spit didn't hit his eyes or mouth, but I tremble at the sight of it on his face anyway. I didn't mean to... but God, the fucker has been asking for it.

His eyes are facing downwards as he lifts a hand to his cheek, wiping my saliva from it.

"No," I snarl as he grabs me by the neck with his other hand, squeezing above the collar so tightly that I gasp for air, and wipes my spit over my face in slow movements of his strong fingers.

Finally satisfied, in a low rasp that I feel in my bones, he utters, "If you were a man, I'd have broken your neck for that. I hope you know that..."

I lower my eyes, breathing through the fear, the loss of power. How the fuck did this happen? He and I were once equals. Hell, it was me that helped bring him into this place. And now, I'm an afterthought in this grotesque piece of theater with *her* as the main feature.

I know he's going to hurt me.

I want him to...

Only in the past, I wanted him to because I knew he cared for me, in his own way, respected me. Now I'm terrified because he doesn't seem to give a fuck.

He watches the pathetic sight of tears welling up in my eyes as I try to pant through the hurt, the rejection, the loss.

"What's happened between us, Alex?"

"What's happened is that you're now *contaminated*... by *her*. Another fucking man I've lost. And hearing them talk about you two back there, it made me sick to my stomach. It's *pitiful*..."

"What's pitiful, friend," he growls, "is how unable you are to behave with decorum in public. You're past the age for such tantrums, surely."

"And I suppose *she* is allowed to get away with *hers*?"

"She's almost fifteen years younger than you. You should be able to behave with more grace than her."

I pull against the chains, seething as he watches me in grim satisfaction. He likes causing me pain whenever I dare to question him about her. Nothing I say hits. He has an excuse for everything she does. He refuses to even listen to me about the dangers of her. It's an impasse that we've never faced before, even during our most heated debates over Cameron O'Neill and Jackson Wilder.

I know I'm bleeding power… and I hate it.

It's *her*. I went from ruling this place with him to being in the shadow of a woman who will never be devoted to him like I am. She'd never do the things I've done for him. He *owes* me.

"I guess I'm just one big disappointment to you, Sebastian."

"You *will not speak* out against me in public ever again. Is that understood?"

"Why, because I'm a woman?"

"No, because I *own* you," he growls. "You are my property. You always have been, even when you thought you were toying with me. And you don't get to defy your Master. Is that understood?" At my silence, his hands constrict around my throat more tightly, before sliding up my face, squeezing my cheeks together. "Is that understood?"

"I'll never be the property of a man who is contaminated by another woman."

"See, that's where you're wrong."

"The bitch will pay, Sebastian. You have my word on that."

His eyes turn black and I grin in defiant satisfaction.

I don't care if he punishes me. I like it. There's nothing he can do to hurt me more than what I've already endured. I'm gonna say what I want about the cunt.

He doesn't move, staring at me coldly. He's never quite looked at me like this before. It's her. It's always her. She's changed everything. I want her *dead*.

His movements are measured as he unclips the chains from my wrists and then from my neck, grabbing a fistful of my hair so roughly that it stings my scalp.

I wince in pain as he draws me towards him, glaring down at me, nostrils flaring. "I think we'd better wash your face, Alex, don't you?"

"No!" I shout before he can finish.

I know what he means. That's one of two things I hate more than anything.

I kick and scream as he drags me along the floor in silence. I know I seem deranged, rabid. I can't help it. I don't want this...

A moment later, my scream is swallowed as my head is pushed under the cold water of his huge bath, three-quarters full. He pulls me up for air and I manage to inhale a lungful before my head is pushed back down, and I scream, this time trying to calm myself down, so I don't lose too much air like I have done in the past.

He does it to me over and over until I feel him lift the back of my dress up and undo his belt.

"It's you that's going to pay," he snarls.

Do it.

I want you to, you fucker. I've always wanted him, every single time, no matter how dysfunctional.

I could use the safe word. They're never banned, but I've never used it in my time here. Once I do, my power will wane. Wane *further*. I can't have that...

At the sound of his zip over the drip of water down my naked front into the bath, I brace myself for the penetration of his cock, bigger than even my husband's.

But it doesn't come...

He holds me roughly by the hair before dipping a hand into the water, and seeming to wipe his face, over and over, before getting to his feet. As I turn to look at him, he grabs my wrist, hooking a chain into the cuff around it that's linked to a metal ring on the wall.

"No," I plead, but, in a frenzy, he does the same on the other side, leaving my arms stretched out along the rim of the bathtub. I pull against them but can't get loose.

I wait for him to push my head into the water again and fuck me as he has so many times before... but he doesn't. Instead, he grabs my hair again, yanking my head back.

"Someone else is going to be teaching you a lesson today."

"What?!" A chill runs down my spine.

No.

Not him. Not that fucker.

I know what he's going to do to me.

"No, Sebastian."

"Your husband is gonna teach you some fucking manners." A scream is torn from me as he jolts my head back, lowering his mouth so it's just behind my head. "And you threaten that girl ever again, I'll lock you in a room with him for a week and tell him I don't want you able to walk when you come out."

"No!"

I scream blue murder as I hear him leave the room, closing the armored door behind him...

Steven Frost

"What the—"

The click of a lock has me unlocking my eyes from the woman bound to my bed.

I take a step towards the door at the sight of Sebastian entering, the master key in his hand.

He slams the door behind me, walking in fast strides, his breathing labored as he removes his mask and throws it to the floor.

"I'm not sure I like being interrupted, Sebastian."

"Go to my room. You'll find your wife ready to be disciplined. I want it done properly this time."

"The bitch is feral," I snap. "It doesn't matter what I do. She's untameable."

His eyes grow wild and he takes a step towards me. "You get her under control, or she will become a liability to me. Do you understand me?"

I glance at the sub—tied how I want her, ankles attached to her wrists, her pussy exposed, just waiting to be fucked, her limbs immobile. I gesture towards her. "I want her tomorrow. All day."

"You'll have her," he replies, "once you've done your fucking job."

I nod, attempting to hide my irritation, picking up my mask from a table a few feet away.

As I step back towards him, he says, "Fifteen seconds. She'll be screaming, so she'll lose air faster. Bring her up for air every fifteen seconds. We don't want any more *accidents*, now, do we?"

I harden as I realize where my dear wife is. Oh, she hates it. She'll hate it even more once she's having her ass ridden. I'm amazed I haven't tired of fucking her yet. I suspect that her screams are what still make her such a good fuck.

"She's allowed to use the safe word," he says sternly.

"She never does," I retort. "She's a brave little bitch."

"She's becoming problematic to me, Steven. I want her afraid. I want her compliant. That's *your* job, and you're not doing it adequately."

"Seems we both have a penchant for women who are not compliant," I suggest, for Mrs. Wilder is proving to be a most stubborn target whom even the great Sebastian Gravier is struggling to fully tame. Must be the first time...

"I know you won't disappoint me," he finally says.

I nod, my lips curving into a smile as I observe his wrath. He hides it well. The bitch must have really gotten under his skin.

"What do we do about *her*?" I ask, peering at the meat tied to my bed, panting into the pillow with her head turned to the left.

"Leave her," he utters coldly. "And I don't expect to see you back here tonight. I'll have the bed changed once I'm done with her."

Sebastian fucking in my bed is not something I'm unfamiliar with, though usually, it's my wife he's disciplining, with my permission.

He'll have fun with this one. She looks just like the girl...

"Very well, my Lord," I smile. "Enjoy."

"You too, Steven. You know what she doesn't like. Make it memorable, even by your standards. Lock the door behind you."

As I put on my cloak and exit the room, taking my key with me, I turn to look at him. He's peering at the woman, his body heaving as he calms his breathing.

She must have said something about the object of his affections to leave him in this state.

Maybe he has lost his fucking mind...

Sebastian

My eyes lift slowly to look at her.

Her long brown hair is strewn over her face, blocking her eyes. Her hands are behind her, her wrists cuffed and attached by a chain to her ankles.

Malaise infects me these days, even more so than usual. It spills into my blood, polluting it, tainting the taste of everything.

Wrath comes in the moments I realize I need these women, need to take the edge off the unbidden insanity clawing at me.

The fucking torment that has poisoned me.

I yearn for the day I watch her drain of blood, the day I feel free to inhabit the wild darkness that I so crave.

And yet, I yearn to fall into her light.

I know it will be the death of me.

Some species of death.

A death born of light.

I hunger for it almost as much as I hunger for her flesh.

For her touch.

Hunger to watch her eyes drink in my face, perplexed at the demon she wants to heal.

A demon who may see her dead before she can.

My body aches. It burns. The pain rips at me, stops me from moving, from staying still, from breathing...

How do I make it through this trial without killing her when visions of her blood dripping from her lifeless body torment me, providing the only relief to ravenous beings which dwell inside me?

In need of a meager reprieve from this unwanted disease, I remove my cloak and let it drop to the floor.

I climb onto the bed slowly, placing my knees on either side of her legs. One hand hits the mattress next to her shoulder as I blanket her slim, pale back with my chest. I gather her loose hair up with one hand, winding it slowly around my fist, once, then a second time as I begin to pull her head back, stretching her neck as far back as it will go, though not far enough for her to see me.

She does not have that right...

"Do you know who I am?"

Her voice is weak. "Yes, my Lord."

"What is your name?"

"Sub, my Lord."

"Will you please me?"

"Yes, my Lord."

"How?"

"By offering you my body to do with as you will."

"What do I want from you?"

"My compliance. My loyalty. My sex."

"What are your limits, sub?"

"I have none, my Lord."

"I am going to hurt you."

"I know, my Lord."

"Do you object to that?"

"No, my Lord."

"You know the safe word. You are free to use it."

"Thank you, my Lord. I won't need to."

"You will not speak while I fuck you. Not. One. Word. You may gasp or moan in pain. If you feel pleasure, you will hide it. I don't want to hear one note of pleasure. If I do, you will pay for it dearly. Are my instructions clear?"

"Yes, my Lord."

"Good."

I lift my hand from the mattress and wrap my fingers around my hard shaft. She's clean. They are tested daily, but I hesitate for a moment, ravaged once again by a vision I can't unsee.

I require the release, the domination, but some godforsaken plague has challenged me of late.

Visions.

Her face. Her skin. Her eyes.

Things inside me scream at the thought of her, making my body writhe. You can't see it from the outside, but I feel them, their limbs contorting, desperate for space, for room to breathe that they only obtain when I administer suffering.

I will make this stop.

"Do not say one word," I growl as I push the head of my cock into her, one inch. No more.

She's tight and wet and gasps at the sensation. I yank her head back by her hair, and she yelps at the tug.

"Make me come," I order, and despite her chains, she begins to slide her body backwards until she is filled with me. She moves forwards and then backwards again, employing her sex most effectively to do what it was designed to.

I close my eyes and tip my head back, seeing her face, the face that infiltrates my every waking moment.

My dreams. My nightmares.

It cannot go on like this...

Hell, I know. I was born into it. Unless you've lived with the devil, seen it close up, you cannot understand hell.

This is the hell of something else. Something that would try to pull me from the darkness I have so carefully curated.

I lose myself for a moment, falling through blackness, my body alight, imagining the moment she offers herself up to me. All of her—her body to do with as I will. Her soul, no matter what I may do to it...

Letting go of her hair, I drop down to cover her back with my body. My elbows dig into the bed as I locate her mouth, pushing one thumb inside.

"Suck," I order, and she does, sliding her lips and tongue up and down. She moans a little, almost in pleasure and I jolt her hair back with my free hand. She stops instantly, sucking in silence as I drive into her as deep as I can. She's good. Wet, accommodating, open.

"Bite," I order.

She whimpers at the order; the sound makes me throb. "I can't, my Lord."

"*Bite*," I repeat as her teeth touch my skin. "Put your fucking teeth around the bottom of my thumb and bite, or I will rip your fucking throat out with my teeth."

After a moment's hesitancy, she bites, pressing into me. I barely feel it.

"You either bite me, *sub*, or I will bite you and suck your blood from the wound. Now. *Hard*. Grind until you draw blood. This is your final fucking warning."

Her teeth dig into my flesh, further and further.

"Grind," I repeat.

She does so and as she finally breaks my skin, I feel her.

Jessynia...

I feel her in my arms, biting me to relieve her torment. Biting me as I need to do to her. As I will do...

After a moment, she stops, parting her lips. She must taste blood. "Suck the blood," I order. "*Now*."

She complies and I close my eyes, thinking of how she bit him... she bit me upon instruction, how my blood entered her...

It was exquisite.

Sometime later, I remove my thumb and place my palm over her mouth, cutting off part of her air supply.

I begin to fuck the meat harder, and she groans as if in pain, just as I like it.

I close my eyes and smell her scent—lavender, mint and citrus—a scent concocted by our pharmacist based on how the girl smells.

Needing to pin her down, I detach the cuffs around her wrists from the chains, allowing her to stretch out her limbs. I climb on top of her, pinning her stomach to the bed with my body as my hand slides over her nose and mouth, blocking *all* air.

She writhes underneath me, squealing before panting as I remove my hand, gasping for air. I repeat the operation over and over, allowing pleasure to finally flood my cells.

As she gasps for air a final time, I close my eyes once more. "This time, I want to hear your pleasure," I order. "Not the noises a whore would make. Quiet gasps and moans. Understood?"

She nods, and I blanket her completely, fucking in silence as I inhale her scent, drowning in the notes of pleasure which are so alien to me.

As the violent swell of ecstasy rushes through me, I feel her beneath me, see her face, hear her voice, imagine my cum finding its way inside her, impregnating her.

Nothing less will suffice.

She will submit.

She has to.

She will submit to me... even if it leads to death.

36

Beth

"Fuck," he mutters breathlessly, stopping dead in his tracks as he sees me in the unlit room. He shakes his head as he throws the letters he was flicking through onto the side table of the entryway, its light seeping into the living room where I sit.

"I knew it was you who'd taken that spare key," he says with a shake of the head.

"Well, if you'd done the decent thing and given me one like I asked—"

"You don't need one," he snaps back roughly as he walks towards the armchair I'm sitting on.

"You've got one to my place, Gabriel."

"And we know why that is, Beth, don't we?"

As he says the words, I feel the stab of skin under my bracelet that I sliced through with a knife last year in a moment of desperation, a cry for help—one that he saved me from, and won't let me forget. That fucking day now hovers over us, evidence that I'm truly unstable, a problem case, not worthy of the love I want to give to him.

He comes to stand square in front of me, the streetlamps down below illuminating his tanned skin and sharp brown eyes as he peers down at me. I breathe through the self-inflicted indignation of feeling troublesome, a freak, a loose cannon. He's treated me like I'm problematic for some time. I guess I can't make things much worse than they already are...

"Give me the key, Beth." His eyes drop to the purse tucked into the chair next to me.

"No."

"Well, I guess I'll be having the lock rekeyed tomorrow."

"What, you don't trust me?" I sneer.

"I don't trust people who don't trust themselves."

He takes a seat opposite me on the maroon leather armchair, blinking slowly as he studies me, as if a teacher disapproving of his naughty student. He's the same age as me, but seems to have forgotten that fact. He has a way about him that makes me feel younger and older than him at the same time—younger because I keep fucking up, and older because he sees me as damaged goods, a rare female reject of the Society. He denies it but I know it. I feel it.

"So, did you fuck her?" I spit out.

Fuck.

I wasn't meant to bring it up like that, but seeing the prick stare at me like this has me thrown off balance. He blinks in slow contempt once more, a fact that makes my blood boil more with each second that passes as I picture the O'Neill princess, all five feet eight inches of her; a natural beauty, refined, vulnerable with big brown eyes, shiny hair, big tits and the usual bullshit Fifth Avenue elegance—everything I'm not.

"How does it feel to fuck your best friend's sister, Gabriel? Isn't it all a bit sadistic if not incestuous? I mean, don't get me wrong, I get the appeal of stiffing Cameron, but his own sister... That's low, even for a man like you..."

I know I slurred the last words, the effects of the wine making themselves heard as they always do despite my best attempts. I also know that I sound bitter and unhinged. I can't fucking well help it. I never used to behave like this. It's what happens to you when you're used and discarded like trash. The rage at the injustice of it all, at the rejection, at the degradation, the humiliation, it eats away at you like carrion feasting on a discarded carcass until you start becoming the person they treated you like...

What's more, I'm aware of my behavior and can't seem to reign it in. That's what frightens me the most...

"You're getting repetitive, Beth," he drawls, scratching his heavily-stubbled jaw. "And you're drunk again."

"Well, maybe if you fucked me as nicely as you fucked her, I wouldn't need to drink this much."

The shadows under his eyes darken, turning his brown irises as black as coal. "I tried *nice* with you," he responds slowly. "It didn't seem to be doing much for you."

"Nor you, Gabriel."

He bows his head. It's not like the fucker can deny his tastes now, is it?

"So how is our precious Evie?" I sigh out. "Still needs stiffing by her therapist to get her through the day?"

"Apparently so," he responds with a shrug.

"Cameron should knock you out for it."

"For helping her to stay sane? I doubt it."

"*Sane?* You've been fucking her for years now, and she's still no closer to being normal."

"I don't exactly know what *normal* means to you, Beth, but I suspect it's highly overrated." He shakes his head slowly, brushing his wavy brown hair off his face. The fucker seems to get hotter every time I see him. "Are you off your medication?"

"No," I reply. "In fact, I took double the dose today."

"They're not breath mints, Beth. You can't just take the dose you want."

Shit...

The room spins for a second, my body seizing under the threat of nausea. I grip the armchair. "I can do whatever the fuck I want."

Letting out a breath, I lean forward to grab the bottle of uncorked and half-drunk red wine on the table between us—the most expensive-looking I could find in his wine cabinet. Before I can grab it, he leans forwards and clasps his fingers around my wrist.

"You've had enough to drink," he chides coldly, removing the bottle from the table and placing it onto the side table next to him, exhaling his irritation as he sits back down, watching me with frigid eyes. "What's gotten into you tonight, Beth?"

The condescending edge to the concern in his voice makes me want to rearrange his pretty face. A therapist shouldn't be that hot anyway. It's just asking for trouble... and Gabriel sure knows how to find it.

"Into *me?* I don't know, Gabriel. Maybe the fact that I've been seeing you for three years and I seem to be getting sicker and more paranoid..."

"You're not my patient, Beth. You're my friend. I'm trying to look out for you, but you're making it difficult."

"Friend?" The word is the bitterest of poisons.

"Yes. *Friend*. Or have I ever pretended we were more than that?"

"Oh no, don't worry," I sing. "You've made that *abundantly* clear."

"Would you rather I lied to you like some men do? Made false promises?"

"*Some* men? You mean *all* men."

"Your lack of faith in men is not serving you," he says, "especially in light of your simultaneous need for their approval. It's a recipe for trouble."

"Yeah, well, maybe I like trouble..."

He groans his irritation. He's warned me before about riddles. I no longer care enough to indulge his distaste.

As his fingers rub the side of his temple, his eyes wander around the room before tracing a slow path back to me. "How long have you been here?"

"Long enough to go through your stuff," I retort flatly.

His lips widen into a smile. "Find anything interesting?"

The fucker knows he keeps his study and bedroom locked and no matter how hard I've tried, I could not find the key.

"No. But I will one day..."

His fingers curl around the sides of the armchair. "I'm going to tolerate your shit this time because you're clearly drunk out of your fucking mind. You can apologize to me tomorrow when you've sobered up, like you usually do."

"Don't hold your breath, asshole," I jeer and his lips slip into a grin of contempt at the fucking mess sitting before him.

A shake of the head by him leaves me wanting to cry.

I hate who I am.

I hate how he sees me, how everyone sees me—him, the resistance, Cameron, them, the Society, Vallen and that demonic thing that runs the show. Sebastian.

They see me as damaged goods—trash that's good for toying with and nothing else. Some of them pity me. Others think I'm fucked up beyond repair. And then others think I'm the Society reject. The whore. The cum rag that can be passed around by the men. The slut who signed away her rights so that she could be abused.

Therapy has got me to a place where I can finally look myself in the mirror, function more or less, but I'm still unable to sit still in silence and just fucking well be with myself. I still feel like a freight train is careening towards me. I still hold so much tension in my body that I jump out of my skin if someone as much as puts a hand on my shoulder.

"Why did you come, Beth?" he asks gently as an annoying tear rolls down my face.

"I haven't seen you for days, Gabriel. *Days!* You don't even answer my fucking phone calls!"

"I have a life, Beth. I have a job. Friends. I can't always answer straight away. And anyway, it's not healthy for you to be dependent on me. It's a trauma bond. It's not healthy that you rely on men for attention the way you do. It's a recipe for co-dependence and unhealthy relationships. You need to find yourself instead of being propped up by others. It took us three years for you to accept the reality that you use people as crutches. *Men*, in particular. You need to work on building your inner strength and not needing others to provide strength for you."

"Inner strength?" I scoff. "Bit trite for a man like you, no? You don't usually spout platitudes at me. You must really be giving up hope..."

He stares at me contemptuously before glancing at the bottle of wine and taking it from the side table, bringing it to his lips, and taking a sip. As he does so, he shakes his head, his disdainful eyes meeting mine as the realization sets in, and I meet his frustrated glare with a grin.

He gets to his feet and heads to the kitchen, spitting the wine into the sink before pouring himself a tall glass of water, downing the entire thing and then dumping the contents of the wine bottle down the drain.

His hands hit the counter as he breathes through the heinous act. The poisoning. The Society's own drugs no less, years-old remnants of a life I once naively thought I could escape from.

"Why?" he asks, the hard edge to his voice breaking the shell of my bravado... just a little.

"I just thought it'd be nice for you to feel what it's like to have *your* drinks spiked, Gabriel..."

"You're out of your fucking mind," he growls.

"Oh, am I?"

"If you don't trust me, Beth, why the fuck do you still keep seeing me?"

"What can I say?" I utter bitterly. "I'm fucked in the head, as you well know."

Tossing a final glare in my direction, he heads to the side table near the door and picks up the phone he dropped there when he arrived. "We need a taxi. Now. Yeah, that address." Hanging up, he puts his phone back into the dock. "You're going home to sleep this off. The next time you call me, it'd better start with a fucking apology."

"I'm here to see Cameron O'Neill."

The middle-aged man behind the mahogany reception desk eyes me with keen brown eyes over his thin-rimmed glasses. "Is he expecting you?"

"No. I mean. Yeah— He... He said I could drop by anytime."

Fuck, I just slurred.

I tried calling Cameron the whole time I was in the cab, but it kept going to voicemail. Gabriel gave the cab driver my address, but I redirected him, getting him to drop me off on Fifth Avenue where I hovered at the end of the block for ten minutes before getting too cold.

I have to see him...

I miss him...

I've barely spoken to him in weeks. He used to be able to talk me round, to calm me down, to make me feel sane again. Without him, I'm struggling, making an unholy ass of myself in front of Gabriel, feeling like I'm losing my mind...

He's probably with someone. That man can't walk into a room without some bitch dropping to her knees for him, and I know from his years at the Society that that man likes to fuck. Hard. And often.

"There's a lady here to see you, sir," the concierge says into his phone. "Your name?" he asks me, holding the phone close to my chin.

"Beth Vass."

"Did you hear that?" he asks, listening for a few moments, his shrewd eyes observing me the whole time until he hangs up the phone.

"You can take a seat. He'll be down in a moment."

I turn and walk towards the seats near the door, stopping in front of the huge mirror on the wall to the right to check my hair and make sure there's no mascara under my eyes. I wipe away a smudge of kohl eyeliner and smooth my hair down before applying some tinted lip gloss to my lips.

I look a mess...

I breathe through my irritation at the fact that Cameron is coming down to see me. He never used to do that. I used to be let straight up there...

I'm losing all my power, I can feel it. Silas liked me. He protected me. I was taken more seriously when he was alive. Now, it feels like I'm a joke to everyone—the bitter, messy clown who'll never be whole again, who'll never heal, who'll forever be stalked for the amusement of the sick fucks at that place.

No one gets it...

No one gets the torment of being followed, being watched, being tracked like prey, threatened in silence to never speak up...

My heart begins to race as the elevator chimes its arrival. I get to my feet as he walks out, so tall, so strong. He's wearing dark-gray sweatpants and a black sweater, with a white T-shirt peeking out just under the collar of it. My breathing quickens as he locks eyes with me and walks towards me. There's no smile, but it only makes his lure more brutal. His hair is longer than usual and still as glossy and thick as ever. His face is unshaven, its beauty more rugged than ever.

He can't be real...

"Hey," I sing as breezily as possible, waiting for him to respond, to hug me, to say something, anything. Instead, I stammer to fill the interminable pause as he doesn't. "I tried calling you, but—"

"You shouldn't have come, Beth. I'm not myself these days. I've told you that. And I'm not always alone..."

"I needed to see you," I say, taking pains not to sound too desperate. Gabriel is a master at bringing out my unhinged side, but I don't want Cameron seeing me like that...

"Why?" he asks.

"I... I've not been—" I let out a long breath. "It's about Gabriel."

"What about him?"

I glance behind him to see the concierge typing something into a computer.

"It's private," I say. "Personal. It affects you. Please. I wouldn't bother you if it wasn't important."

I stare up into eyes so deep that it takes conscious effort not to lose yourself in their maze. There's a weight to his gaze that wasn't there before, and pain is scribbled into the angular lines of his face, the kind of pain I saw years ago when he first left that fucking hellhole. He looks tormented, hollowed out from the inside.

This is how we'll connect again... like we once did...

His solemn eyes drift over my face, but his robust body remains unmoving. The darkness of sorrow is visible in his face, as if the light has gone out.

What the fuck has happened to him?

He nods, turning to walk back to the elevator. I follow him, entering after him, watching as his thumb presses the button to the penthouse.

I glance at myself in the mirror of the elevator to see my cheeks flushing pink. I feel his glare eating into my profile and turn to look at him.

"Thanks for seeing me," I stammer. "I know I shouldn't have—"

The chime of the elevator stops my sentence short, and I follow him as he walks out and unlocks the large armored front door of his apartment. My eyes wander over his back, his muscles and shoulders thick and pronounced even under his sweater. What I wouldn't give to run my hands over them...

He holds the door open for me and I step inside, taking off my boots and putting them in the cubby under the bench, and hanging up my coat on a hook next to the door.

As he heads to the kitchen and pulls out two glasses, I take in this stunning apartment, its understated masculine elegance never ceasing to amaze me.

My eyes collide with his as he hands me a glass of water, gesturing for me to sit on the armchair as he takes a seat on the sectional opposite the balcony doors.

Inhaling a shallow breath, I ignore his clear instruction and take a seat next to him instead. He pivots slightly to watch me, his face unreadable.

"How've you been?" I ask, drinking in his solemn face.

Jesus, even though he clearly isn't taking care of himself properly, he's still the most sensational man I've ever seen. I believe with all my heart that if I could finally get him to fuck me, the pain that Gabriel has put me through would dissolve, not completely but enough for me to act more rationally. All I need to do is bring up Evie a little. That usually gets Cameron going...

"I've been better."

"Still missing her?" I ask, bringing the glass of water to my lips and drinking down a third of it as he places his down onto the table next to us—the stump of a huge tree with a thick sheet of glass on top of it.

He watches me silently in the elegant glow of the vast room. "What do you want, Beth?"

"Just to see you. I miss you, Cam. I miss how we used to talk. All of us miss you."

"I'm not much in the mood for talking lately."

"That's not healthy," I say softly and his warm copper-laced eyes narrow just a little.

"It is the way it is. I'm not in the habit of forcing myself to do things I don't want to."

"Like talk to me?" I suggest as I pull apart the sides of my black shirt, glancing down at the low-cut T-shirt underneath. "We used to talk all the time. I miss that."

"You need to find people other than me to rely on. I'm not always... safe. You of all people should know that."

"Look, Jess has—"

"I didn't allow you up here to talk about Jessynia," he snarls.

"She's made her choice, Cameron!"

"She didn't *choose* anything," he counters roughly. "That's the fucking point. She was terrified for her family. I can't allow that to be the reason she stays with him. Not that girl."

"Well, that's not gonna change anytime soon. What are you gonna do, waste months of your life waiting for a woman who may never come back?"

Shadow darkens his eyes.

Teach me a lesson, Cameron...

"She *will* be coming back," he growls.

"You don't know that..." My hand slides onto his knee and his eyes drop to look at it coldly before lifting to meet mine.

I've known him for years, since he was a fucked-up twenty-three-old, but he's never made me tremble like this before... He's a few years younger than me, and I've always felt it... but not anymore...

He has an energy about him that's different—more experienced, more ruthless, more dangerous...

Just as I like them...

For a split second that makes me shudder, it almost feels like being around Sebastian... or at least, Sebastian in his late twenties when the prick was still just exploring his so-called powers...

He doesn't flinch as I slide my hand slowly up his thick, hard thigh, until my glittered fingertips are within inches of his groin... and the dick I've wanted to touch since the first second I saw him.

I've seen him in action—fucking women at the Society; his length, his thickness, his stamina, his body and that quiet way he fucks—a silent beast right up until the moment he's ready to come when he tips his head back and unabashedly growls his pleasure like a wolf, a dragon... like Sebastian...

A gasp flies from me as, in a snap, the fingers of his hand curl around my wrist, and he lifts my hand off him.

"You're drunk. I can smell it on your breath."

"I'm not drunk," I lie. "I want you, Cam. Please. Let me help you get over her."

I lean into him, and he twists my hand to the side, hurting me a little. I gasp deliberately breathily. I know he takes pleasure from women's pain. Not quite like Sebastian, but it's there. A proclivity that no doubt causes him distress...

I pant my arousal. I need him to know that he can hurt me if he needs to.

"If this is about Gabriel," I say, "you do realize he fucks your own sister any chance he gets. You don't owe him a goddamn thing."

"I don't *fuck* her friends," he sneers, throwing my hand back at me.

"Evie? She's not my fucking friend!"

"No. Not Evie."

Of course.

Jessynia *Fucking* Wilder.

He's still just as tormented by her as before...

I hated the bitch on site—the way people's eyes light up around her because of that pretty little face and those huge tits, the ease with which she interacts with others, with which she makes them laugh, the enthusiasm in her gestures, the smiles that don't seem hollow or forced like mine. Her beauty. Her passion. Her sense of conviction, of belonging in a world which feels alien to me. It all made me sick to my fucking stomach. Somehow, she managed to make me warm to her, but seeing the hold she has on this man makes me despise her almost as much as I despise Sebastian...

"Jessynia's not my *fucking* friend either, Cameron," I spit back as his hands tense and his body hardens. "She never has been. She never will be."

"You're beginning to sound like Alexandra Frost, Beth," he seethes through gritted teeth. "I'd be careful about that. That's not a state I'd wish you to end up in."

"Yeah, well, I wouldn't care if the bitch dropped dead!"

Within a second his hand is around my throat, and I'm tugged towards him, lying flat on my back on the sectional as he climbs onto me, squeezing my neck.

My eyes glimmer and I can't help but let a moan escape me as I'm pinned to the cushions beneath me by his huge frame. His hair flops over his eyes as he glares down at me. The bestial snarl that escapes his throat ricochets through my chest. "What the *fuck* did you say to me?"

"You heard," I shoot back defiantly.

Teach me a fucking lesson, Cameron...

My clit throbs at the sensation of his erection against my body. I want to suck his cock so badly...

He leans down, his eyes wild with rage. "The next time you speak of her like that will be the *last* time you and I ever talk. Is that understood?"

"Oh yeah? Why don't you teach me a lesson I won't forget, Cameron?"

I reach for his cock, and he grabs my wrist, pulling it off him.

"Is. That. Understood?"

"She's *contaminated* you," I jeer. "It's *pathetic*."

"*No*. She's freed me from a life of darkness."

"Yeah, keep telling yourself that as Jack sticks his cock down her throat every night."

In an exclamation of bitter rage that is ripped from him, he climbs off me and gets to his feet, thrusting his hands through his thick hair and cursing loudly.

He heads to the side table, his body simmering, and picks up his phone. "I have an unwanted guest. I want her taken home. Now."

Walking back over to me, he grabs me by the arm and tugs me to my feet, pulling me over to the front door.

"Put your shoes on," he instructs. "And your coat. You're going home to sleep it off. And don't come back until you've learned to speak about her with respect."

"I know you've seen her! I can tell! They'll know it too!"

He grabs my coat, throwing it into my arms.

"Put it on, and get the fuck out."

I glare at him a moment before sitting on the bench and slipping on my ankle-length boots. He hands me my coat and I snatch it from him, putting it on as I turn to face him.

"You think you can trust Gabriel, don't you? You can't!" I shout. "He's one of *them*, Cameron. I can't prove it but I feel it... He's gonna fuck you over... and don't come crawling to me when he does..." I search his face, looking for signs of shock, confusion, or concern, but see that there are none.

The knock on the door behind me makes me jump.

Unfixing his glare from my face, he moves past me to open the door and I turn to be met by Aaron's torpedo of a stare.

"Take her the fuck home."

"*Fucking asshole*," I seethe, catching sight of myself in the glass of the elevator. "Fucking pricks, both of them."

I get out on my floor only to stop dead in my tracks as I remember...

they're always watching me.

Twice this month.

Twice this month I've come home to see things left outside my door. It's not a lot, but enough to keep me on edge all the fucking time. Their considerate little calling cards that lead to hours if not days of mental torture. It's gotten to the point that I'm afraid to come back home some days for fear of seeing them. I know my PTSD is not just from the events that took place when I was a member, but from what has transpired since I left.

They'll never forget me. *Ever*. I know that.

The question is, how much longer can I live with it?

I take slow steps towards the corridor and look down, panting as I see... nothing.

"Fucking cunt." Tears drip onto my face as I walk towards my door and see nothing there.

With shaky hands, I put my key in the lock, opening it, the static of fear zigzagging throughout my body as I fumble for the light switch.

I head over to the kitchen and pick up the half-bottle of red wine I'd left on the counter earlier before leaving for Gabriel's, realizing that I never even bothered to put the cap back on before leaving. I pour wine into a short, dirty glass next to the sink, and as I bring it to my lips, I scream, dropping the glass, the thing shattering into a million maroon-soaked pieces.

I lift my eyes to find what I saw—him sitting there...

Sebastian Gravier.

Only, as the shadows of the living room fall into focus, I realize that he's not there...

No one's there.

No one.

Fuck.

I taste tears in my mouth as I glance down at the shards of glass, soaked in red, as if covered in watered-down blood.

Bringing the bottle to my lips, I drink down what's left of it—all of it—before placing it down onto the counter and staring at the cracked glass around me.

My eyes wander in the darkness to a knife lying next to the sink, the thing filling me with the light of hope.

It wouldn't take much. One cut, maybe two… A few minutes.

Then the nightmare would finally be over…

In reality, I've been dead since that night. The night they used me and tossed me away like the debris from a crash, reveling in their victory the way only men are able to—men who see sexual pleasure as being worth more than our lives…

The words that Vallen wrote in that letter, words burned into my brain since that night, hound me once again, as they do several times a day—some form of PTSD that no amount of therapy will undo, for the words plunged me into a void, into a world so black that I no longer feel part of life.

I'm a ghost.

A specter trying to smile.

A fake human.

The sad clown.

Someone people see through.

Others pity me. Others still don't trust me. I mean, why would they? Any fool can tell from a mile away that I don't trust myself.

I hate myself.

They feel it. I'm some hollow almost-human.

Good for one thing—her holes.

When Sebastian was sodomizing me, the knowledge that I despised him, and that I would soon be cast out like garbage only heightened his pleasure. I know it. My life, my wants, my soul—they were irrelevant to him. They were irrelevant to all those men who jeered and guffawed as they pinned me in place and fucked me like a piece of meat.

And what's more, I let them. There's a safe word. I would have been suspended at the very least for using it in the non-consensual room, but at least I would have stood up for myself.

I thought it was what I wanted. I thought it would show that piece of shit former fiancé of mine that I was willing to do what it takes to make it work.

All it showed Vallen is how worthless I really am.

Being fucked is all I'm good for. Men barely listen when I talk. They'll listen if it means they'll get to take my pussy, pin down my body still wracked with trauma.

Even my own parents think I'm a fucking failure.

And the sad thing is... I once used to think the resistance were my family.

When Silas was alive, things were different. Cam and I were close. Gabriel treated me with some degree of respect.

And then *she* came along... and I lost everything.

What's more, what happened to me, I know full well that Sebastian would never allow it to happen to her...

She's different—more beautiful, more passionate, more caring, more innocent, more authentic. Even when she shouts at people, there's no bitterness in her voice the way there is in mine. She's everything I should and would have been. If I'd have been given the gifts she has, I'd have been worshipped by these men too, instead of treated like the filth she scrapes off her fucking shoes.

I hover above myself as my hand reaches for the knife, my fingers wrapping around the black handle and drawing the blade towards me.

I've tried for too long.

I thought I could escape them.

There is no escape.

I stare down at the blade beneath a waterfall of tears—its silvery metal shimmering in the low light.

Do it.

Do it.

Do it.

Fuck.

I know what to do.

I've always known...

I put the knife back down, my distress and self-loathing fading, replaced by the sheer relief of feeling... numb, of switching off.

I head over to my purse which I had dumped by the door when I arrived, fumbling for my phone which I pull out.

I scroll through my contacts looking for it.

S

I've never erased his number, nor blocked him. I never feared receiving a message from him, for I knew I was unworthy in his eyes. He wouldn't waste the oxygen on me...

Tears fall onto the screen as I begin to type.

I want to come back.

I shiver as I sit down amongst the shards of broken glass, leaning back against my cupboard, staring at the phone in the silent dark.

I have no idea how much time passes before his message comes through.

Half an hour. Maybe more.

But I don't move. I'm paralyzed at the thought that he could answer me.

And finally...

What makes you think you are worthy?

I shiver at the heinous reality of his words. The words of a man who has haunted me.

I know what I did wrong. I'm willing to make amends.

As I type it, I think about what he'll do if I return. I know he'll cut me, and bite me, and hang me, and torture me... and that I'll be passed around like some whore.

I no longer care.

Nothing is worse than this.

I take a breath as I type.

And I have information about him.
And about her.

37

Alexandra
Fifth Avenue

"I've asked you not to smoke so much in the bedroom."

"Yes, you have darling," he responds, handing me my own fucking gold lighter. "Light it for me. Now."

My husband's cold-eyed grin makes me want to light the cigarette dangling from his lips and stub it out onto his face. The fucker watches, eyes gleaming, as I light the thing, holding the flame under the tip of his cigarette. It flares orange for a second as he inhales the smoke, smiling at me as he blows it into my face before holding out the cigarette for me.

"How generous," I respond, taking it from him and sucking in a long drag. I resist the urge to follow suit and subject him to a cloud of smoke, tipping my head to the side and exhaling as I hand him back the cigarette.

He leans back on his propped-up pillows, the white sheet covering the bottom half of his body. His torso is still glistening in sweat from the half-hour of fucking we did earlier, most of which he tied me up for. He didn't sodomize me today, but he got me to call myself a worthless whore in exchange for his leniency. The fucker sure is romantic.

He lets out an audible sigh as he takes in his post-coital smoke, tipping his head to the left to watch me. "Did you enjoy that, sweetheart?" he asks, knowing full well that we both know he doesn't give a shit whether I enjoy it or not.

"I've had worse," I sneer, and he sniggers at my jab.

"Oh, I'm sure you have, darling. Didn't everyone at that trailer park have a turn? You should have charged admission..."

A violent wave of heat surges through me.

I'm not giving it to you, you fuck. You're not getting my pain.

I glower at his profile as he takes another drag. His hair is still jet black but for a few wisps of gray around the temples, which frankly somehow seems to make him look more alluring. His body is still muscular and strong. The discourteous prick only seems to get hotter with age, a fact that all women approaching their forties have to contend with. Society puts us on the scrap heap and tells us that these feckless cunts we're married to are more desirable than ever.

I release a sigh of barely-concealed wrath as I grab the now lukewarm tumbler of whiskey from the side table and down it, wincing as the liquor burns my stomach.

"You shouldn't drink so much," Steven chides.

"I'll stop drinking around the time you stop chain-smoking in our bedroom," I shoot back.

"You've clearly got a hair in your ass about something, darling. And I didn't put it there *this time*. Tell me. Tell daddy about it. See if I can't help matters."

"Help? You're as useless as the rest of them."

"The rest of *who*, sweetheart?"

"Forget it," I sneer. "It's pointless anyway."

"Let me guess... Jessynia Wilder." He turns to look at me, shaking his head in derision. "Tsk, tsk, tsk. You disappoint me, Alex. Are you ever not thinking about the poor girl? You should charge her rent for the amount of real estate she's taking up in your brain."

"Yeah, well, maybe if the bitch had broken *your* nose in front of half a dozen of your so-called *friends*, you'd get it."

"She did you a service, darling. Trust me, that dog-ugly hump was doing you no favors."

He grins widely, knowing full well he's provoking me on purpose, reveling in watching me squirm. My dear husband does love to torment me so.

I grab the cigarette from him and inhale sharply before handing him back what's left of it. He takes a final drag before stubbing it out in a glass ashtray on his bedside table as I grab the tumbler of whiskey and down the very dregs at the bottom.

Taking the empty glass from me, he places it on his nightstand. "No more for you tonight."

"*Fuck you*. You don't get to tell me what I do and don't drink."

"That's where you're wrong, sweetheart. I'm your husband, and as such, I own you." His eyes gleam as he pushes further and further, the preamble to what is usually degradation and humiliation. "You are my property, Alex. My plaything. My nicely worn-in little fuck toy. You belong to me. You're like some object that I've bought and paid for, and you'll do as you're fucking well told, or you'll regret it."

I sink into the pillows at my back, my body shaking as I stare at the foot of the bed which still has ropes threaded through the slats at the end, evidence of my husband's various proclivities. The prick can't get through sex without bondage or debasement anymore. Or, at least, not with me...

As much as I hate him for it, I can't deny that I like it.

"What's bothering you about our little friend today?" he asks.

The cretin knows full well what torments me, but just like the other fools, he overlooks it because he thinks that one day, he'll get to ride her tight little ass. Little does he know, that will never happen.

"How much power the bitch has," I spit back. "How weak she makes Sebastian look. She's dangerous. She's threatening everything."

"You've always had a penchant for melodrama, Alex."

"I'm *telling* you. That bitch'll be the end of us all. Our so-called president has lost his mind over her like every other fool does."

"I suspect that's what's really bothering you, isn't it, darling? Your devoted Sebastian daring to feel something for *another* woman." I glare at him as his grin of derision reaches his ears. "I remember when the man was marrying Rose. I didn't think the poor woman would make it through the ceremony without you clawing her eyes out."

"Yeah, well, knowing where she'd end up helped with the self-restraint," I retort to his snigger of amusement.

"Oh, I'll bet. You know, the man is allowed to feel something from time to time, Alex. Hell, I even had feelings for you once."

"Same," I spit back. "Though not in the last *decade*."

His eyes narrow despite the smile playing on his lips; I know he'll soon be teaching me a lesson in obedience. That's half the reason I provoke him. As much as I hate his guts, I crave the way he defiles me. It's the only way I feel vaguely alive, and perversely feel in control. What's more, my husband knows why I like to rile him up. It's this twisted ballet we've been engaging in since we met.

"I'll be making you pay for that one, darling... as you well know."

"If you're man enough," I scoff.

He turns to face me, his eyes boring into my profile. "I am going to enjoy this one, Alex."

I suddenly feel like he's looking at my nose, now straight, courtesy of his specific instructions. I wasn't given a say in the matter. He informed the surgeon that he wanted the bump removed when he reset it, and I was given clear instructions to agree.

I abhor the fucking bitch for it with every fiber of my being. And I despise *them* for treating the whole thing like some joke. Sebastian, my husband, the Council—as far as they are concerned, her punch was the natural fallout for me fucking her husband in front of her. And until I get justice for this, and for everything she's taken from me, I'll never be at peace. I pace my apartment for hours at a time just thinking of everything she's done to me...

Everything she's stolen from me...

"I suppose you think it's amusing that our president has more loyalty to *her* than to our family?" I ask.

"I think you'll find it's a *male* thing, sweetheart. You've never had a body or a face like that. We're all designed to want to defile her. Clouds our judgment, sadly."

"You're all predictable fools, even *him*."

"Oh, I don't know. Maybe he just got tired of fucking *demonic ephebophilic succubuses from hell*," he guffaws loudly, parroting the words that moralizing bitch dared speak to me in front of everyone the day that she broke my nose. "Like *you*, my sweet."

Fuck you...

"The deal was," I resume, the panic of rage surging through me like spindrift out of control, "that she be allowed into our Society, become a member, and then get drilled in every hole like every other woman. That's why we voted to let her in, so that every man could have a turn. So far, all that's happened is we've lost Jack, and Sebastian's lost his fucking mind. Even if the sanctimonious cunt agreed to join in like she was supposed to, I don't think Sebastian would even allow it. Not in the state he's in now. I've never seen him lose sight of what really matters before. It's *pitiful*."

"He seems to be handling matters as well as always."

"Oh, really? You think allowing Cameron O'Neill back is *handling* matters?"

"O'Neill's too powerful. Having him back is a way to avoid mutual annihilation. I'd have thought you of all people would have welcomed it with the way you drop to your knees like a ten-dollar hooker every time he looks at you."

"It's a fucking *trap*, and you damn well know it," I sneer, sitting up and turning back to face him. "He's not interested in being *back*. He's interested in getting *her* back and taking down Sebastian once and for all!"

"Maybe. Maybe not. O'Neill is a fucking freak. This place can tend to his tastes like no other. Maybe he just... misses it..."

"I don't trust the *fucker*. I don't get how he gets to humiliate me, leave without following protocol and then just waltz back in."

He twists a strand of my curly hair in his fingers. "We don't even know if he's coming back, my darling."

"Oh, he *will* be. If it's to get to *her*, he will. She's contaminated him like she has the others."

"I can certainly see why," he smirks.

I shake my head, scoffing at the pathetic tedium of men thinking only with their dicks. "You fucking fool."

He sighs out slowly. "I don't know why you keep going with the insults when you know how I'm going to punish you."

"I don't give a fuck."

"Oh, you will do, darling," he utters softly. "I'm going to make tonight memorable."

My pussy throbs at the promise.

Bring it, you motherfucker. I've taken worse than you...

"What exactly is it that you want to happen here?" he asks, blinking slowly as he takes in my face. "I already spoke up about him and her at our meeting, as you asked me to, Alex. I don't believe I have received much gratitude for putting my ass on the line like that."

"She's a liability. The delusional cunt thinks she's a journalist. She could write anything she wants on that pitiful blog of hers."

"It seemed pretty popular last time I looked."

"Yeah. There's no shortage of fools who'll lap up her nauseating sanctimony. She could out us all. And O'Neill will stop at nothing to protect her. He could bring the whole thing down. Not to mention that Sebastian is no longer in control of himself. That puts all of us at risk."

His expression grows graver as I continue to speak.

My husband is paranoid, always has been. I just need him to *feel* the danger. I need him on board with this... and I believe I know just the cocktail of poison to feed him to make it happen.

"We were told that she'd become a patron, that she'd be on the menu," I continue. "There's no fucking way Jackson would allow that, even after her fuck fest with O'Neill. And he's not even the biggest obstacle. I don't think Sebastian will allow it either. He's not mentioned her becoming a member for weeks."

"If he's contemplating letting O'Neill back," Steven says, "presumably he'd allow them to *fuck*. Why on God's unholy Earth would he do that if he was enamored with her like you say he is?"

"O'Neill is a gateway between her life with Jack and the Society," I say. "She'll never agree to becoming a regular member. She'll never make peace with betraying Jack, but she has trouble resisting that freak of a man. He could be what brings her in. Sebastian won't be able to resist the potential of that."

"Why exactly would O'Neill go along with that if he wants her out?" he asks.

"He knows the bitch still loves her husband. He knows she'll never leave him with the threat hanging over her family. The man is insane over that fucking woman. If this is the only way he can get to be with her, he'll do it, all the while figuring out how to take Sebastian down and get her out."

"Or maybe our famous Mr. O'Neill really just does need the special servicing he can get at our Society. He's quite the deviant, as I'm sure you remember, my darling."

"You're a cretin if you believe that. He wants her out and Sebastian in prison, and he'll do what it takes to make it happen. It is a *fucking* trap."

I peer up into dark eyes that contemplate me, his expression flitting between concern and suspicion.

"What do you suggest as a solution?" he finally asks.

"She needs to be taken *out*. Once she's gone, Jack and Cameron will be able to come back. Sebastian will go back to being *himself*, and all of this doubt and uncertainty and the risk and the danger, it will all go away."

"And how exactly do you propose she be *taken out*?" he sneers, his tone dripping in contempt.

"We've done it before, remember?" I remind him. "And gotten away with it."

"And almost got caught," he growls. "It's only because he covered for us that we *got away* with it."

"Not this time. We know better people. We know people who can get to her. A simple overdose. Happens every day."

"And if Sebastian finds out, there'd be no place on this Earth for us to hide. He wouldn't stop until we were found."

"Pff." I shake my head as his expression hardens. "Pathetic."

"You have something to say to me?" he asks, his jaw tensing.

"Nothing I didn't already know. I knew you didn't have what it takes to solve the problem, you worthless fucking coward!"

Before I can scream, the sheet is ripped off us, and I'm grabbed by the hair as he pushes me face-down onto the bed, snarling curse words at me as he straddles my body with his thick legs.

I kick on purpose; it's part of our demonic little ritual. I pretend to fight him when really I want him to force me, and he knows it.

Who knows why? Maybe it lets me take back some control... Maybe I'm just permanently fucked in the head... Either way, I'm not changing for anyone or anything.

I kick wildly, partly out of habit, and partly because I've hated this cowardly fuck who won't do what it takes to protect us for years.

"Oh, you're gonna get it, sweetheart," he growls as he positions himself on top of my ass as my legs flail behind him.

"No!" I shout, though secretly I want it.

It's the only way I feel anything—either I'm brutalized or degraded, or in the case of Sebastian, cut and choked until I almost pass out. I'll take any of it, as long as it's rough.

I squeal as he feeds his cock into my asshole, not bothering to spit this time.

"Fuck," he moans as he begins to thrust. "Oh, you're gonna pay, you disobedient little whore."

I whimper as he pins my hands to the bed and rides me, groaning loudly as I tremble beneath him, gripping the pillow to help me through the pain.

"Gently!" I plead, but I know it'll only make him rougher.

That's what I want. Anything to take me out of the void I live in. The hell. The blackness.

"Oh, you're still a good fuck, sweetheart," he groans into my ear as he sodomizes me. "Not as good as *she* would be, I'm sure."

He cackles as I lose it, trying to fight against the grip of a giant of a man. "*Fuck* you, Steven. *Fuck* you."

"Now, now, sweetheart," he sneers, jolting his cock into my ass.

"Let's face reality here. There's no man on the planet that would pick a bitter, cold-hearted whore with no tits over a ripe, beautiful, juicy wet cunt like hers."

I struggle against him for real this time, screaming obscenities that I just know the fuck will be enjoying.

He begins to sodomize me more roughly. "Oh, keep at it, sweetie. I can do this all night," he drawls, sticking his wet tongue down my ear. "I'm picturing her now as I fuck you. Those big innocent eyes, that long hair, those huge tits. I'd like to suck on them as I fuck her tight little cunt. Mmm..."

He releases his grip on one of my wrists and pushes my head down so that my screams are muffled into the pillow. He raises his voice to make sure he's heard over my cries.

"In the meantime," he groans, letting out a rough sigh of pleasure, "I'll keep fucking her clones. You should thank them, my love. They're what's keeping our marriage together and stopping you from being discarded like the used trash that you are."

Sometime later, I couldn't count the minutes, he finally lets out his usual filthy grunts, like some pig in heat, as he shoots his load into my asshole and relaxes his body on top of me.

"You are still good," he whispers into my ear, sticking his tongue down it once again just to further the humiliation. "Still very good. I do still have some use for you, darling."

I squirm to get him off me, but he doesn't move, breathing in my distress.

It's *her* that's done this.

All of this.

I've lost power with them all over *her*.

Jack. Cameron. Sebastian, and now my own fucking husband.

None of them take me as seriously as before. None of them look at me without seeing that bitch.

I'm gonna make her pay.

On my life, she'll pay...

38

Jessynia
Quercus Velutina, Tribeca
Present

I need to see you.

The familiar five words I sent to Sebastian have been echoing through my mind since I sent them.

How did I get here?

How did I go from praying I'd never see him again to asking to meet him?

I shudder once again at what he must think of the naïveté, the presumption of coming to psychoanalyze a man as intelligent as him, of negotiating with him. I can't help it. I'm tormented by his hold on Jack. On Cameron. On me.

By the hold that his trauma has on him.

The image of Cameron's bloody face meets me in my nightmares, as does the sight of Jack behind glass, unable to break it. I can't shake this feeling that something bad is brewing. Something at least one of us will not recover from.

I have to do something...

I have a plan.

I want to talk to him about his trauma some more, shift energy by letting him get it out in a safe space, and then at some point, talk to him about letting Cam and Jack go for good. I've been going over what I'll say to him for hours, wondering how he'll react, weighing up counter-arguments, deliberating over how I'll convince him of the power of relinquishing such unhealthy control.

I shake my head constantly at my own half-cocked plans, second-guessing myself, wondering if I'm brave and bold to at least try something, anything rather than just sitting on my ass like everyone else does and waiting for my world to implode in a moment of dark weakness that he succumbs to, or whether I'm foolish and naïve? Wilfully so, as Gabriel so graciously pointed out.

And I wonder if there's more to my need to see him than I'm willing to acknowledge...

Do I miss him? Does my body ache to be in his presence? To be watched by him?

Is there a reason I'm tormented by him in my dreams, unable to sleep sometimes because when I close my eyes, all I see is his face?

If so, how the fuck did I let this happen?

And does he know it?

I walk in silence but for weighty footsteps behind the tall, faceless man—Isaiah, his black cloak billowing behind him as he leads me to Sebastian's room so that I can once again converse with the devil. Or that's how it feels at times anyway.

The long cloak swishes around my lower calves and my hands feel numb as I walk—they always do when I'm here. I never get used to the nerves that consume me when I know I'm going to see him. I know he's a busy man. I know he runs an empire, but every time I've needed to see him, he's accommodated me instantly. At times I wonder what he was doing just before... or what he'll do after...

Do his actions change because he's seen me? Does he fuck someone to relieve the tension? Does he feel it the way I do? Does he hurt them like he wants to do me?

Does he feel whatever it is going on between us as acutely as I do or is he just toying with me? Watching the foolish young woman attempt to connect to him, to control her shameful desire as she sets about a plan that may have been doomed to fail from the start...

He's seen women fall to their knees in front of him his entire adult life, ready to serve him as if he were God, to worship his body, to capitulate to every sinister requirement of his. Is my sudden need to see him utterly tedious for him? Predictable?

Is it true that he's never encountered resistance before? Would his interest in me wane if the resistance were no more? Would I lose what meager power I have the second I finally gave in to him?

The plan I have for today rolls over in my mind, tumbling in fizzing waves that knock me about.

I need him to understand the power of letting people go. The power of showing mercy. Forgiveness. Of liberating yourself and others.

For fuck's sake, it sounds trite even to my own ears.

Fuck.

Is he going to roll his eyes internally as I speak? I mean he'd never show it to me. That's not his style.

Will he listen to me or will I just amuse him? Will he want to please me somehow, even if I'm not willing to give up my body to him?

Or is this all some game?

I've never met a man who truly toys with people before. Jack has hurt me, but it's never been a game to him. He's never wanted to hurt me. Any pain he has caused me has been a by-product of weakness and not malevolence.

With Sebastian, the rules no longer make sense. How do you exist with someone who plays with people's minds, who enjoys watching them unravel? Who enjoys the descent into madness?

The foundation upon which we base our interactions as humans dissolves under your feet with him and you're left feeling hollow, as if interacting with a being that is not quite human.

But then every time I think he's enjoying the morbid spectacle he's designed, I see glimpses of something that would appear human. I see the torsion of unbidden pain in his face as he studies mine, see curiosity that stings him, yearning that seems to anguish him. Am I reading him wrong? Do I make him feel... *human*?

And if so, will he want me stamped out for shining light into the obscure caverns he so enjoys inhabiting?

Or does he just want me thinking I affect him? Is that part of the trap I'm too blind to see?

I shudder in a ragged breath as I prepare to take the familiar dimly-lit and narrow corridor to his room... only we don't. The corridor splits into two, and this time, Isaiah takes the fork to the right.

I stop in my tracks and after a moment, so does he, not turning around, the silence of my absent footsteps alerting him to my reticence.

"This way," he orders, his back to me. The guy is huge. For a second, I don't recognize his voice... The disorientation of the black mask and cloak knocks you off balance, distorting voices, bending shapes, making you unsure who you're conversing with...

"I usually go straight to his room."

God dammit, I hate those words...

The man turns slowly, his twisted ebony mask coming into view in a macabre spectacle that would be absurd if it didn't chill me to witness it.

He walks towards me, owning the space the way men do around here—a by-product of being worshipped at the Society, at taking up the role of dominant in the patriarchal social structure of the elite of Manhattan.

The molded obsidian mask shrouds his entire face as the hood of his cloak does his hair. Shadowy brown eyes peer at me through the slits in the leather. "Sebastian requires you in another room today."

I take a step back. "What room?"

"A private room. Come this way, Jessynia."

I shake my head. "No! I want to speak to him. Now!"

"You'll speak to him shortly." And then in a tone that does nothing to mollify me, he utters. "There's nothing to be afraid of."

He never normally says things like that...

I swallow hard, wilting under the silent potency of his glower. He's close enough to reach out and grab me, lift me, carry me.

Sebastian has never hurt me physically. And there *is* a safe word. I just have to use the fucking thing...

I take a step forwards, swearing that I could see his eyes thin into slits behind his mask. Isaiah turns and leads us down the hallway, my barefoot state leaving me feeling tiny in this maze of a building.

Just breathe...

A while later, we stop in front of a door—dark wood, engraved, with a round black handle with vines etched into the metal. Isaiah holds the door open for me and I peer inside to see a staircase leading down a narrow set of wooden stairs. I can't make out what's at the bottom but it's dark down there.

I take a step back.

Jessynia...

And then another.

Jessynia...

"I'm going home," I announce loudly, turning around swiftly only to have his hand grip the arm under my cloak. "Let go of me!"

Without a word, he pulls me into him, lifting me onto the landing at the top of the stairs. My eyes meet his just before the door swings shut.

"No!"

I shove my hands into the hefty wood, but he's too strong and the door slams into its lock, the crash of metal against wood reverberating through me like unexpected claps of thunder.

"Hey!" I rattle the door knob, pounding on the dark wood with my fist, feigning bravado to avoid facing the panic seizing my body. "Let me out!"

Blood rages through my body like steeds galloping through fields as I bang on the door, demanding to be let out despite feeling that he has already left.

"Isaiah! Let me out! I'm not kidding! Open this fucking door!" I bang until the side of my hand is sore, my body shaking as I turn to look down the stairs, the sound of my panting breath a grim percussion to the eerie music that has been playing through the corridors of Quercus Velutina since I arrived, and whose grotesque notes now float through air dense with uncertainty.

"Sebastian," I utter, hoping that he'll appear at the bottom of the stairs so that I don't have to go down there.

I'm met with silence but for words whispered in my head...

You can't play with the devil and not get burned.

It's not like I don't know it. I just... have always had some semblance of control up to now.

It's okay.

It's okay.

It's okay.

"Sebastian?" I shout out, praying that he answers me.

Fuck.

Who's down there?

The steps are dark and after a minute of waiting, knowing I won't get out through this door, my hand reaches for the glossy wooden rail snaking down the stone wall, gripping it tightly as I make my descent, the steps more treacherous than they seem, for my legs feel like formless mush.

My mouth is so dry that I can barely swallow and I'm suddenly aware of the weight of the thick velvet cloak against my bare arms and the mask wrapped over my face, its features delicate, as if molded for the contours of my face.

As I make it down to the bottom step, I'm tempted to rip my mask off... but I don't know who's down here, who can see me.

"Sebastian?"

Fuck.

My voice wavered, panic skewering its usual vibrance, leaving some withering flower in its wake.

Straight ahead is a wall and the sight of the black tree engraved into it causes ribbons of ice to pool in my belly. To the left and to the right stand corridors lined with doors peeking out of the darkness.

"Sebastian? Answer me!"

God, please let it be him.

I'd rather take my chances with him than with some of the other freaks around here—Vallen, Ilya, Stephen, Dominic.

For a second, I see Cameron's face.

No.

That would be impossible.

I turn to the right, meeting the corridor and looking down either side to see dimly-lit doors of dark wood. I turn left on instinct, walking slowly, my heart thundering as I wait for some animal to pounce. Every time I approach an open door, my hand hits my chest and my breath quivers as I pass it. As I walk along, I see the corridor branching off, observing forks and alcoves hidden in it.

This isn't just a room.

It's a maze of rooms with paths too numerous for me to count.

I turn constantly, feeling someone behind me, feeling eyes on me—but I see no one, beginning to notice how utterly quiet this space now is, how every sound has died bit by bit until I hear nothing but the rabid gale of my own shallow breaths.

Taking a fork to the left, I spy a door at the end of it, and to its left, another fork, one branch snaking left, the other right.

Jessynia...

Rose...

I close my eyes for a second in relief that I hear her voice, a voice that I've not heard of late...

I thought I'd lost you...

I turn slowly around on legs that feel so unsteady, as if not wanting to take me any further.

And then it happens.

As I pivot to the right, a figure falls into view.

A man.

A cloak. A mask. All dark.

Standing.

Watching me in terrible silence from thirty feet away.

I can't stop the gasp from rushing from my throat, nor the trembling in my body at the sight of him.

"Sebastian," I utter, altogether too frailly, wishing my voice didn't betray my every emotion. "You're scaring me."

Nice, Jess. Let the big bad man know how you feel so that he can feast off the fear...

But then, I hardly need to speak. He can sense things about me before I even have time to admit them to myself.

"Sebastian?"

I take steady steps towards him, but he doesn't move. He doesn't flinch. Despite his cloak, I see that his legs are slightly apart and his hands fisted at his sides. And then the half-mask comes into view, its harsh features robbing me of breath. The bottom half of his face is exposed but the shadows from the hood over his head dissimulate it, aided by darkness punctured by just enough light emanating from sparse wall-mounted lanterns to illuminate the stone walls and a little of the wood beneath my feet. Nothing much more.

I stop in my tracks as the unsettling presence of something... wrong, alien, shifts the air, turning it acrid and jarring me for a moment as I peer at the man, not knowing whom I'm looking at.

"Cameron?"

His name spills from my lips without my meaning it to as I take in his frame—taller than most, shoulders broad, his presence potent, his confidence unwavering.

God...

Not him.

I take a step backwards.

Jessynia...

Run...

Panic draws me into its maelstrom of turbulent water, spinning me around where I half-expect to see another man. There's no one there and as I turn back, a sharp breath escapes me as I see the man closer—at least a few feet.

I didn't even see him move.

"Sebastian?"

As he takes another step towards me, I begin to walk backwards at the same pace.

I don't want to.

I want to stand my ground.

But I'm not dealing with the usual forces. This type of fear, primal fear, seizes your body, subjugating you to its merciless current, thinning you out from the inside, eroding the foundation from under you. It changes the rules—just as Sebastian does when he looks at you.

"Sebastian?"

Jack?

Cameron?

Who are you?!

For a second, I see Cameron through the mask—his whiskey-colored eyes incandescent like errant embers smoldering, illuminating the moodiest of nights.

I take a few more steps backwards as his pace begins to increase until suddenly, in a move beyond reflection, driven by instinct so strong that I can't stop its unyielding draft, I pivot on my heels and a split-second later, begin to run, the movements feeling frantic on my jelly legs.

I make it down the hallway and turn left and then left again down another. There are interconnecting passageways between corridors and every time I dart past one, my heart stops beating as I wait for some rabid beast to pounce from the treacherous shadows.

With another frantic step, sharp pain pierces my ankle, causing the next step to feel less sturdy, and the next and the next.

I need to get out...

After a minute or so, I lose breath, my pace faltering as I turn around, eyes wide as I expect to see him... but... he's gone.

My cadence slows and I begin to walk, peering into the disorientating gloom of rooms whose doors lie open.

And then... as I walk breathlessly past a passageway to the right in this maze of tunnels and rooms, the sharp blast of a figure stuns me and I begin to run... only this time he's chasing me.

I hear the fast flap of fabric behind me.

I feel him.

Run...

At the sight of a staircase at the end of the corridor, I begin to run faster, entering a wide landing before it.

But as I swerve to the left, a scream is ripped from me as strong arms wrap around me, arresting my momentum, pulling me into a hard body.

"Let go!"

Only two words tear from my throat before a hand wraps around my lower face, and his body coils around me as I'm hauled backwards, kicking and trying to scream, into a dark room to the right of the staircase.

My muffled cries go unheeded as I'm dragged into the secluded dark of the room, my feet flailing uselessly. My cloak and mask are ripped off me, exposing my delicate dress, before I'm lifted and placed onto my back on some kind of low table. It's thin and cushioned and before I can stop it, thick metal shackles with chains attached to arms splayed out from the flank, turning the table into the shape of a cross, are clicked into place around one wrist, and then another as my screams to stop are met with utter silence.

I pull against the cuffs, kicking frantically as strong hands pull the white dress assigned to me that I put on when arriving up to my waist and grab my panties, pulling them down my legs as I writhe and plead for him to stop—a mammoth man whose features are obscured in the darkness by the half-mask and cloak. My thighs are pulled apart mercilessly, forcing one leg to fall on either side of the narrow table. Hands wrap around my ankle, clicking a shackle into place around it—one and then the other.

And in a moment which steals my breath, causing a high-pitched gasp to fall from my throat, the man's tongue thrusts into my clit and he begins to suck, pushing the firm muscle backwards and forwards as I shout for him to stop.

His hand slides up my body, pushing my chest back so that I can't see the top of his cloak, but can only feel the hood brushing against my smooth pubis as his tongue writhes against me.

"No," I utter, my arms tensing, pulling against the shackles as he continues his work, the tip of his huge tongue flitting backwards and forwards against the tight nub of nerves between my legs... which is slowly pulsing, engorging with blood as unbidden clandestine pleasure trickles treacherously into my core, setting my cells alight.

"Please stop..."

In silent design, he slides his tongue down my sex and begins to lick the opening to my body. I feel my pussy unfurl as he laps at the juice that's beginning to flow from me, betraying the truth of my arousal.

Oh my God...

For a moment, it feels like Jack—the fervor of his tongue, the pace of his movements, the repeated gestures designed to turn me into his slave, to ensure that my wilting body becomes a vehicle for his pleasure once he's done.

A growl rumbles from the man's throat as he slides up to my clit, flicking it from side to side, licking all around it, before moving down and pushing his strong tongue inside me, my body's lubrication easing his passage.

I know that sound...

As pleasure builds and he continues his work, I close my eyes, trembling as he groans his pleasure, the sound utterly bestial, the movements of his tongue quickening, the lashes growing harsher, less forgiving as my clit swells and my former protests turn to gasps pulled through panting breaths.

In the dark, I see eyes—flaring red, a serpentine pupil. Dragon's eyes.

I whimper as his top teeth bite into my pubis and his tongue slips up and down against my clit, curving at the tip when he reaches the entryway to my body, tasting my wetness.

This place is unfamiliar—being tended to by a stranger who chased me through darkness, and yet, I know that I'm seconds away from an orgasm that will shake my whole body.

As a moan I can't hide escapes me, I feel the man pull off his cloak... and hear the thud of his mask on the floor. I daren't look, keeping my eyes closed as he begins to toy with my clit once more, the movements utterly fervent, matched by his violent groans.

And then I feel it.

His hair.

Brushing against my skin.

It's long.

Thick.

His arms, leaning on my thighs, feel bare, and between my legs, I feel the naked skin of a hard torso.

He pauses as his hair brushes the skin around my hips, as if waiting to see what I'll do once the realization kicks in. As I remain silent, unmoving, he continues his work.

Indecent noises emerge from his throat—the guttural, unabashed groans of a beast—as he savors me, tastes me.

And the depth of the cavernous sounds confirms who the man is...

Tears seep through the barrier of my closed eyelids, dripping onto my temples on either side as I tremble through the knowledge that my sex is open before him—wet, engorged, glistening in arousal...

The safe word performs some macabre dance in my mind, taunting me with my inability to say it.

Why didn't I say it?

As the brushes of wet velvet slow and his tongue undulates against my swollen clit, my nipples harden under my thin ivory dress and I begin to pant. Red eyes turn to messy stains and crimson blotches in the dark as waves and then the violent tsunami of ecstasy rushes through my cells like raging ocean water, tumbling me through the heat, through the glow, through the nirvana pouring through my body, shaking it, infusing it with light.

High-pitched exclamations escape me, the sounds echoing through the barren room as my chest heaves through the pleasure and air blasts from my lungs. My body quivers, tears streaming from my eyes as I feel his knees enter the space between my legs and feel his hands plant on either side of my torso.

I know he's watching me.

I daren't open my eyes.

Shame keeps them closed. Guilt. And the knowledge of the barrier ripped down between us, narrowed—one that once felt like a chasm.

"Look at me."

The dauntless order ravages my quaking body once more as I build up the courage to open my eyes.

I finally do, just a little, looking down to see a black belt and an engraved silver buckle over black pants. My gaze pans up over the bare grooves of his torso as tiny streams of light from the corridor bounce off the glistening wooden sculpture of his flesh. I pan up to arms that look as if they've been carved from white oak, my eyes wandering up a thick, pale neck until finally, my gaze collides with his as he peers down at me in silence, observing the tears falling from my eyes, dampening the hair next to my temples.

I feel myself falling, drowning in the silvery water of his unblinking eyes.

My body shakes as he takes in his victory.

And his power.

Oh my God...

I know the drill.

Jack and Cameron make me come and then my body is theirs to do with as they will for as long as it takes for them to be satiated with my submission—a vehicle for the pleasure they crave from my body.

Don't let him...

Annihilated by the shameful defeat of my will, I wait for him to unbuckle his belt and pull out his hard cock, taking his prize—my sex, its folds open, its walls lubricated, just waiting for his invasion.

White oak.

The words float through me but I'm unable to utter them... and he knows it.

His eyes narrow as he tracks a tear that spills onto my temple, his head dropping to the side slowly, hovering over me before dipping to lick the droplet of salt water from my skin, moving to the other side of my face to do the same. His eyes close for a moment as he extends his arms straight to look down on me again and in a move which I can't comprehend, he reaches for the shackle coiled around my slim wrist, unclasping it... and then the other, lifting his body off the table and removing the shackles from my ankles.

He gently brings my thighs together and pulls my dress down to cover my knees before reaching down and sliding his hand under my back. He pulls me up, lifting me, carrying me across the room, and placing me on my feet in front of a huge mirror, its frame engraved from ebony.

He takes up position behind me, wrapping one arm around mine, holding me in place. His other palm takes hold of my chin which has dropped as I take in the floor beneath my feet, forcing it upwards.

I don't want to look at myself...

Pinning my face up, he watches me through the duplicitous reality of the full-length mirror. In the semi-dark, his eyes shine brightly, as if stars illuminating a moonless night sky.

His loose hair mingles with mine as he presses the bottom of his head to the upper side of mine, watching a goddamn unstoppable deluge of silent tears as they make their way down my milky skin. His eyes remain affixed to mine as he licks a dangling tear from the bottom of my jawline—and then another, and another, his tongue lashing my skin in a move that makes my body pulsate.

He stands back up straight, dipping his head, the side of his face pressed against mine as we watch each other, the spark between us palpable, the savage beauty of his face burning into me.

God dammit, we look like we fit...

His lips brush against my cheek...

"Did you think you could play with the devil forever and not get burned, Jessynia?" he murmurs. "I know what happens to your body when you come to see me. I know how your sex pulsates. How it swells. How it opens. Did you think you could bring your dripping wet pussy in to see me over and over, and not let me tend to it?"

I don't speak, swallowing down the droplets that fall into the seam of my mouth.

"Why didn't you say it, Jessynia?" he asks slowly.

I know what he means. The safe word. I could have said it. I could have at least tried it. I didn't. Not once...

"Why did you stop?" I respond and his eyes form tight slits.

"Why?" He breathes in my face audibly, as if a predator sniffing the air for blood. "Because I have no interest in you submitting to me like that." He tightens his grip on me as his firm erection presses into the curve of my ass. He doesn't push, but I feel it. Jesus, he's rock hard... and so big. It hurts just to think of the thing. His hand snakes up around my neck. "I will penetrate you, Jessynia, the day that you hand me the rope yourself and beg me to bind you. Nothing less than your abject submission will satiate me." His brutal lips skim my skin. "And I know that you are close. I. Can. Taste. It."

I would protest that that would never happen, but I never thought that his tongue would be inside my sex, that my pussy would be open and wet before him, just ready for the taking...

My legs wilt, my strength seeping from me, as his fingertips draw my long brown hair backwards off my neck and onto my back.

His eyes find mine, their flickering light a perfidious candle in the eerie dark.

The fingers of his other hand pull back my soft hair on the other side before finding the thin strap of my dress. Unwilling to resist, I watch as he pulls it slowly down my arm, exposing my breast. My nipples harden and I begin to pant as his eyes roam over my chest through the mirror and his cock hardens at my back.

He watches me as he begins to groan into my ear, the noises low, deviant, sinful. I close my eyes as he pours rough bestial noises into me, teaching me the sounds of his arousal.

"Open your eyes and look at me," he orders.

As I dare to do so, to face the beast holding me, exposing me, his shrewd gaze finds mine again as his fingertips trace the outer curve of my breast. If he wanted to let my entire dress fall to the floor, I'm not sure I'd have the strength to stop him...

And at that realization, my chin drops, my eyes finding the murky floor beneath my feet, my body weakening under the shame and guilt of my defeat. A moment later, his hand lifts to my jaw, raising my chin so that I'm forced to face the reality of the mirror—the reality of the man holding me, his bare chest against the exposed skin of my back, his arms, dense with muscle, wound around my body, my breast naked in front of him.

"No," he drawls. "Your shame is a personal insult to me, Jessynia."

He would disapprove of my shame, or that's how it would appear outwardly, but does he secretly want me broken and unable to face myself? Weakened, fissured, split by deep, dark cracks and disconnected from who I am?

His erection pulses against me as his hand slips under my breast. "One day, you will look at me through this mirror, thinking only of how you wish to pleasure me, thinking only of how you can open up your body to accommodate me, seeing only me, hungry only for my body, and no one else's. Do you understand that?"

His lips slip against the crook of my neck as he holds me, taking me back to heady nights of insanity with Cameron where he would expose my neck little by little as I prepared for what was coming—the bite of his teeth into my flesh.

Sebastian's hand threads into my loose hair, pulling my head back slightly. His eyes lock onto mine as his mouth opens and his teeth find my skin.

I hear the dark notes of his voice in my head.

Just breathe...

I watch as he bites down, sinking his teeth into my flesh....

I breathe through the pinch, watching him in the mirror, watching as he bites into me.

White Oak

I don't say the words out loud, but he stops, as if reading my mind, or picking up tension in my body.

And in a fleeting moment of clarity that shoots through me like a thunderbolt, my fingers find his wrist and I remove his hand from my breast. Locating the fallen strap of my dress, I lift it back up onto my shoulder, concealing my body once again.

I meet his eyes, expecting to see anger in his face, frustration at my woeful attempt at last-minute resistance, but there is none. If anything his chest releases tension against my back as if in relief...

"I... I have to go," I utter, the words frail even to my own ears.

He shakes his head slowly.

"No."

39

Jack
London
Four years earlier

I walk slowly, observing the fat drops of rain as they splash against the gray paving stones.

I smile internally.

The joys of British summers...

The rain taps against my umbrella as I step to the side to let past a man carrying one so large that the thing takes up half the sidewalk, or pavement, I should say.

I'm only a few streets away from her house. I couldn't stop myself from booking a hotel not far from her place—or her cousin's place, rather. It took my man a while to figure out where she'd be staying for the summer. As soon as I found out she'd be coming here, I wasn't able to think of anything else. I've already been here for two weeks. I only have another three and a half to go.

I need to make this work. I can't go back without her.

At the risk of sounding dramatic, being without her is starting to feel like hell.

We've already been out for a drink twice since I got here. I'm not sure if you'd call them *dates*, exactly. I mean, I've hardly been subtle about my desire for her, but she has this way of turning my lascivious attempts at conversing into something playful and innocent.

It's the way she dismisses me with a shake of the head and a groan, or grins before throwing a jab of disapproval my way. It's disarming in a way I'm not accustomed to.

I don't usually have to jump through hoops like this. With the other women I've fucked, the majority couldn't get their clothes off fast enough. I've never struggled like this. I suspect it's partly because I've never tried to date a woman I've had feelings for before. It's throwing me off my fucking game. Rookie mistake, clearly.

But there's another reason...

Him.

I had no idea they were friends when I met her. I say *met*, but it was more like some fucking collision, some explosion that went off in my brain, obliterating every other woman who exists. I had no idea she even knew him, let alone was friends with him. By the time I found out, it was too late.

I could think of nothing but her.

Could see and hear no one but this girl.

She knows that he and I don't get on, but she has no idea of the depth of our rancor. Of our past. Of the bitterness we feel for one another.

If it were any other woman, I'd have walked away.

I've tried a few times. I've gone on trips, dated other women. I brought over three a few weeks ago in the hopes that once I was done with them, the tension I feel in my gut at not being around her will have disappeared.

And it worked... for the first hour.

Then, once again, the vision of her seeped into me and my stomach twisted as I saw her insanely beautiful face, those eyes, those lips...

I see them sucking on my fat cock as clearly as if she were doing it before me now. The vision won't leave me.

If you'd told me a year ago I'd be talking about a woman like this, I'd have thought you insane, but I can't shake this goddamn feeling that I'm supposed to be with this girl. I just... I can *feel* it. It's in my cells. It's the first thing I think of when I wake up and the thing that I lean into as I fall asleep.

I know what he's going to think—that I want to fuck her to mess with him. I wish that were the case, then I wouldn't be walking the streets of a foreign country in the rain tormented by the thought of her warm body... alone.

I've had the place watched by my guy here. She's not brought anyone in, nor stayed the night elsewhere. I don't know what I'd have done if she had. I'm not known for being civilized but even seeing her talking to other men around campus has me fearing I'll end up in prison if we do actually date.

I can't quite figure out if she likes that about me. Outwardly, she teases me for my arrogant bullshit, for my lack of self-restraint, but at other times, her cheeks burn pink and she blinks incessantly, fiddling with whatever she can get her hands on when I hit her with a glare that the cowards she's used to be being around wouldn't dare subject her to.

She gulps down her timidity when I hint at what I want from her. Even when she dismisses my invites to dinner, she blushes wildly as she does it.

Something's stopping her.

I don't know if she's afraid of my reputation. Of my violent scumbag family.

Or is she just afraid of hurting *him*?

I glance up to see a middle-aged lady carrying her purse over her head to protect her from the rain.

"Excuse me, madam," I say upon the seed of an idea so fucking dumb that it makes me groan at my sorry ass internally. "Take this." I hold out my umbrella for her.

"Oh, no, it's okay," she says, her British accent so proper despite her being drenched from head to foot, caught in one of the delicious rain showers that make London summers so fucking exciting…

"Take it. Please. I'm only going to the end of the block."

She peers up at me curiously. "Are you sure?"

I nod my head and hand it to her.

"Oh, well, thank you," she smiles.

I bow my head. "You're welcome."

I turn around and watch her as she walks away, while the chilly rain seeps into my jacket.

"Fuck it," I mutter, pulling my phone, wallet and keys out of its inner pockets and taking it off.

Just as I'm about to look for a trash can to stick it in, I spot a black railing with gilded spikes on top of it guarding a terraced house. I shrug at the inanity of my plan before draping my empty summer jacket over the railing with a sigh of self-derision.

Maybe someone will get some use out of it…

As I think it, I roll my eyes, for I realize that's the kind of thing this girl would say, and frequently does, to remind me what an unconscious prick I am.

I check that my phone and wallet are tucked deep into the pocket of my thin pants, glancing down to see that if they get much wetter, they won't be leaving much to the imagination.

I'm always hard when I get near her. My cock throbs in her presence, even when I'm being drenched by acid rain, apparently.

Maybe it's the months of imagining what her pussy looks like, tastes like, wondering how wet she gets, how tight she is, how warm, how often she can take it.

From what I know of the two *men*—if you can call them that—that she's dated before, they won't have taught her much. I don't think she'll be used to sex the way I can give it to her. I'm not sure if she could accommodate my need to fuck several times a day, but we could always find out… and I'm sure I could convince her of the virtues of pleasuring me, for in exchange, I dream of teaching her pleasures she couldn't conceive of.

Ever since I met this fucking girl, I feel like I've been drugged. Some nights I wonder how this happened to me. I've never bonded with a woman, nor connected with a woman emotionally, or at least, not like this. Alex and I have some kind of bond, but I don't dream of her endlessly, or hang on her every word. The first second I saw this girl, at the risk of inciting nausea, it felt like a lightning bolt had gone off, blasting away darkness I hadn't fully realized was there.

I knew she was the girl I'd seen in my dreams. I knew she was going to end up owning me...

I smile at a perplexed couple ambling towards me, eyeing me curiously in my white shirt now soaked through and pants which are beginning to stick to my thighs. Water drips down my face as I walk towards her place.

The plan is as dumb as all hell, but I can't think of anything but defiling her tight little body at this point.

I say that, but in truth, I crave her presence, even if it's just to shoot me down. Her voice is a melody which soothes me, a song which calls to me. The way she looks up at me softens me, allows me to let my guard down, something rare for me. I hunger to hear her thoughts, her words, yearn to make her smile.

For fuck's sake, I barely recognize myself. I feel plagued by my need to see her, to hear her, to understand her, to protect her.

Hell, it's the reason I came here. It's the reason I'm doing business with some sociopathic creep whose face I've been rather tempted to smash in bone by bone until it's concave.

I have to make this work.

The problem is that as much as I'm desperate to pleasure her until she can't remember her name, I have this fear that even if I manage that, it won't be enough.

I thought at one point that fucking her would get this obsession out of my system, but I know deep down that my desire is not only physical. I ache to hear the vibrant notes of her voice, to share the inane stories I hear around Manhattan with her, to revel in her movements, to watch her plump lips widen into a smile so beautiful that it feels like the rays of the sun.

I don't just picture myself smearing my cum all over her face. I ache to hear the words she groans at me when I go too far, to feel the endless passion of them, to watch as she slams her hands onto the table in a moment of anger that makes me grin internally.

I believe that she cares about me.

I frankly have no idea why she gives a fuck about a worthless piece of shit like me, but she does. I see it in the text messages she sends me warning me about ice on the road, or in the way she freaks out when she sees bruises on my face from one of the fights I can't seem to stop myself getting into with the loudmouth assholes I frequent in Brooklyn.

The way she cares about me feels new to me. I don't recall experiencing it before, or, at least, not since the death of my mother. I once believed Alexandra did, when I was a boy. It was Cameron who made me aware that what she was doing wasn't really *caring*. There was an ulterior motive to it, one that I haven't fully come to terms with yet...

"Fuck," I mutter, my body turning cold under the assault of copious amounts of July rain. The sun is setting over the West End and I'm still not sure whether to go through with this half-assed operation.

"Fuck it," I mutter as I turn onto her street, repeating the mantra that Cameron and I would whisper to each other in hushed tones when we were kids and building up the courage to do something that was usually very stupid indeed, and more likely than not, my idea.

As I approach her steps, I peer into the window on the ground floor to see light behind the curtains.

She's at home.

I shake my head, aware that my respiration is accelerating as I take that first step up the stone slab towards the house, and then a second, the side of my hand finding the brick wall next to the doorbell. I don't know if any other human being has made me this nervous, and I've met some pretty formidable assholes in my life.

Fuck it...

I step back a little upon ringing the bell, watching the peephole that I know she'll look through before opening the door. I know enough about her to know she's jumpy when it comes to her safety. I'm not sure if there's a reason that goes beyond her insane beauty and the effect she must have on men...

I certainly fucking well hope not.

She opens the door hurriedly, staring up at me, eyes wide. "Jack, what the—"

"I, um, got caught in the rain," I offer, raising my brows at her look of outraged concern.

"Well, come in before you catch pneumonia!" she shouts, grabbing my wet arm and tugging me inside. "Jesus, you're soaking wet!" she yells as I take off my shoes and leave them by the door.

"I think I'd better take off my socks as well," I say, peeling them off.

She grabs them from me without asking. "Oh my God, let me get you a towel," she responds with great purpose as she gestures for me to follow her into one of these typical London terraced houses with its living room looking onto the street below it.

I see her throw my socks into a washing machine in a tiny kitchen before washing her hands and disappearing into a room, coming out carrying two fluffy red towels, one of which she practically throws at me.

I raise my brows, unable to stop myself from smiling as she instructs me on how to dry myself before jumping up onto the tatty-looking brown armchair next to me and trying to dry my hair.

"Finished?" I ask as she lets out a sigh of frustration and stops attacking my hair.

"Your body's shivering. What were you doing out without an umbrella?!"

"It was hot and sunny two hours ago."

"Yeah. That's called an English summer! You can be in the middle of a heatwave one minute and soaking wet the next... if you get what I mean."

"I think I do," I respond and she shakes her head with a groan.

"Well, you're soaked through to the bone. We'll have to dry your clothes." She steps down off the armchair and heads to the fireplace, turning it on and cranking up the gas until I feel the heat radiating off it. "You need to go take a hot shower before you start shivering again and giving me an anxiety attack."

"You know you've missed your true calling," I suggest.

"What do you mean?" she asks.

"You would have made a quite spectacular nurse."

"Shut the fuck up," she chuckles dismissively at my teasing. "This way." I follow her to the bathroom. "Now, go take a warm shower and leave your clothes outside the door. I'll quick-wash them and then dry them. It'll only take about half an hour. I'll leave you some clean clothes outside the door." I don't speak for a moment, my body tensing as she says it. "What?" she asks.

"You just happen to have men's clothes lying around your house?"

She blinks slowly. "Um, first of all. It's not *my* house. It's my cousin's house, and she can have *all* the men's clothes lying around that she wants. Second of all, they're not *men's* clothes, they're *my* clothes. It'll be a very baggy pair of sweatpants with the elastic gone and a loose T-shirt of mine. Thirdly, you can drop the jealous asshole routine around me, Wilder. We're not dating."

"I can, can I?" I ask, taking a step towards her. "I think you have too much faith in my ability to control myself around you."

"Well, you have no business being jealous."

"Not now... but just wait until you are dating me..."

Her plump lips widen into a grin. "Get in," she gestures and I head inside her bathroom which looks like a small bomb has gone off in it.

"Shit. Sorry about the mess," she says, moving bottles of colorful liquid to the side of the sink. "I was planning on cleaning it up tomorrow morning. I think I'm still rebelling against my mother's anal ways. Plus, half of it's my cousin's stuff."

"Not a problem, Jessynia. I've seen the state of your purse. I'd imagined your homes would be the same," I jest, watching her as I hold the door of the bathroom.

"You're such a dick," she laughs.

"Indeed. Care to join me? It would certainly help to warm me back up."

She shakes her head with a smile and grabs the door handle, pulling it closed. "Enjoy your shower!"

"Um, madam, this T-shirt is not gonna fit. I tried to get it on but I almost tore it. As for these"—I glance down at the tight black sweatpants she's got me in that were most definitely not designed with men's anatomy in mind—"they're a little… tight."

She glances down at my naked torso, her lips parting as her eyes run over my body. For a moment, she seems to forget herself and a split-second later her gaze drops to my crotch. She gulps down the indiscretion before lifting her huge turquoise eyes to mine.

"Yeah," she utters sheepishly before turning to look around. "You may have a point." She grabs a thick gray throw folded over the back of the sofa, holding it out for me. "Wrap this around yourself," she orders, taking the T-shirt from me.

"Yes, ma'am."

A few minutes later, I can't help but smile internally as she spills some of the tea she's supposed to be pouring into my cup into the white saucer beneath it.

"Shit," she mutters. "Sorry, spatially challenged. And born clumsy. Doesn't help." She lifts the cup and removes the saucer, wiping the bottom with a tissue that she grabs from the coffee table. "Drink this," she says, handing me the cup upon filling it with what smells like mint tea.

"Do I have a choice in the matter?" I ask as I bring it to my lips.

"No, you do not," she bites back. "You need to get warmed up."

"I'm not a soldier in the freezing trenches, Jessynia. I was caught in the fucking rain for ten minutes."

"Yeah, well, you're in my house so I decide what you eat and drink. And you're giving me anxiety, so shut up and drink."

I smile as I take another sip, watching as she brings her cup to her lips. Her gleaming eyes watch me over the top of the cup. "What's funny?" she asks.

"*You* are. You have this particular way about you where you seem borderline pissed off while simultaneously more caring than any human I've ever known. It's a very odd combination."

"Yeah, I'm an exact fifty-fifty replica of both my parents."

"Which one's the pissed-off one?" I ask.

"My mother, AKA, the Rottweiler." Her lips widen into a smile as she observes my grin. "You think I'm kidding?"

"Oh, I believe you. I'll see for myself once you introduce me to them."

She shakes her head in disapproval, her grin not subsiding, her cheeks blushing pink. I get hard every time she smiles. She has this way about her that's atypical. She doesn't hide anything, nor pretend to be anything. And she doesn't *want* anything from me. I can tell pretty quickly when a woman can't see past the suit or the job, or the promise of money, but with her, she doesn't seem to even register those parts of my life.

I thought at first that she engaged with me the way she does because she's so insanely beautiful that she could have any man she wanted and doesn't have to put up with any shit. But the more I get to know her, the more I believe that she doesn't care about things like money. She appears to crave connection, meaning, safety. She likes people who feel, who make her feel, who ignite her passionate nature.

And she resists me—not something I'm used to.

I'm so scared that she's afraid of me. My reputation isn't exactly palatable around campus despite having graduated a year ago. I've tried to keep my friendship with her as discreet as possible, but I know that Cameron is aware of it, and I know he'll have tried to get her to stop being friends with me. The fact that she hasn't means that he hasn't told her everything... but then again, he *couldn't*. What I could tell her about him would leave her unable to continue her friendship with him. So, I guess we're both stuck in this game of chicken...

"I guess I'm just not used to funny women," I jest, purely to get a rise out of her. Her way of being outraged is most amusing.

"Hey, women can be funny!" she snaps, taking the bait.

"They can?" I tease, raising a brow.

"You're such an asshole," she sniggers.

I feel myself grinning and realize that when I'm with her, I feel the smile in my cheeks, feel the muscles tensing. It's almost painful.

"How about yours?" she asks. At my frown, she specifies, "Your family."

A pit forms in my stomach as she asks the question, one only soothed by the innocent beauty of her soft, curious face.

"Mine?" My father's face appears before me—rugged, brutal, his glare ever-piercing, never tender the way hers is, even when I piss her off. "My father and my brothers live in Crown Heights. Brooklyn. That's where I'm from."

"Really? You don't have the accent."

"No, I... I lost it."

I feel my body shudder.

I don't tell her how I lost it—how Cameron's father paid for me to go to a decent school in the hopes that I'd turn out less of a prison-bent scumbag than the other men in my family.

How do I tell the only girl I've ever cared about about them? How do I tell her that half of them have spent time in prison? That they run certain parts of Brooklyn like the mob. That they use their fists as negotiation tools, and sell drugs and guns to make money when they're not racketeering and generally causing havoc.

"Are you close to them?" she asks.

I contemplate the question for a moment.

We're bonded. It's a primal thing with men like us from patriarchal families like ours who live just outside the law. No matter how much we despise each other at times, no matter how many black eyes we give each other, we always gravitate back to one another like a clan. It's an unhealthy, dysfunctional bond and I can't seem to break it.

And God dammit, I don't know if she could accept a family like mine. I've looked into hers; they're respectable intellectuals with no criminal history beyond some arrests for protests that got out of hand thirty years ago, none of which led to a prosecution. Her world and mine don't fit...

"How about... your mom?" she asks, her face soft. I know she doesn't know. There's an honesty about the hesitant way that she asks the question—as if she suspects something but isn't sure.

"She... passed away."

Her face drops as I say the words, her gaze melting. "I'm so sorry, Jack."

"It's okay."

"How old were you?"

"Eight."

She sighs out heavily. "God, that's such a young age. I'm so sorry you didn't have her with you."

In a moment that jolts me, I feel the sharp lash of the buckle of Cain's belt against my back and I stare down instinctively. I got used to not looking him in the eyes when he was in that drunken state. He said it was a provocation, said I was eye-balling him. It always made the beating more frenzied.

"She was a lot like you," I say, lifting my gaze to meet eyes so big and blue you feel as though you could float in them. Swim in them. Drown in them.

"She was?"

I nod slowly.

"How?"

"She was kind of feisty, but also very... nurturing. Protective."

"I think I'm mainly like that because the men I hang out with all do stupid stuff like nearly catching their death in the rain."

"I think she had the same problem with hers," I smile.

"She'd be so proud of you, Jack."

"I'm not so sure about that," I reply grimly.

In truth, when I think back to some of the things I've done, I feel ashamed. I know she would have been ashamed of me too, at some of the beatings I've meted out, helping my father do jobs that hurt people.

Cameron—blackmailing his father, seducing Evie. In these electric shockwaves that stun me into silence at times, the memories of what I've done steal my strength, my self-respect. They weren't my ideas. I never wanted to do them. I was hurt. Hurt at being abandoned by him. Hurt by the unholy mess he'd left behind. Hurt because I didn't have the guts to leave them the way he did.

"Of course she'd be proud," she repeats.

"I've done some things I'm not proud of."

"We all have! *All* of us. That's part of being human."

"Is it?" I ask grimly.

"Of *course* it is. Do you regret them? Those things you did?"

I nod in earnest.

"Then that's what matters."

"I hope so, Jessynia."

We watch each other for a while, silent but for the tumbling of the dryer somewhere. The cycle will end soon. The sun has set, and the only light in the room is from the fire and the kitchen. I don't know how much time I have left with her...

I pull the blanket off from around my shoulders, placing it onto the armchair to my right. "It's hot."

"Yeah, it is hot," she replies, getting to her feet and leaning over to lower the heat of the fire.

I can't help but check out her ass as she does it. The thing is a work of fucking art and currently separated from my tongue only by a pair of thin black leggings... and some vestige of civility I'm struggling to hold onto around her. I see by the lack of a pantyline when she bends over that she's not wearing panties. I really don't want to be this brand of lecherous prick, but it's the result of months of being hard for her, months of pleasuring myself to pictures of her face, of shooting my cum onto them, of fucking women while envisioning her.

I'm so hard right now that I daren't even stand up. I think I'd shock the poor girl.

As she sits back down, her eyes drop to my naked torso for a moment before lifting, drifting over my chest and up to my shoulders. She grabs her tea as a deflection, asking me if I want more.

"Sure," I respond and watch as she leans over and pours the rest of the tea into my cup. As she does so, her breasts fall heavy against the fabric of her white T-shirt. As she sits back straight, my eyes fall to them again, observing the nipples, erect points under the white cotton. I don't want to be this asshole, but I can't stop myself from imagining lifting her T-shirt and sucking on them...

I can confidently say that I've never thought about another human's pleasure constantly the way I do hers. I may have cared about Alex's at one point, but not like this.

With this girl, I feel desperate to watch every movement of her beautiful face as she allows me to push my cock inside her tiny body for the first time. I want to see what her lips do, see the way she looks up at me as I pin her down. I can't get enough of this woman. I want to know everything...

She swallows hard as I watch her incomparably beautiful face in the low light, the tension mounting between us as the shadows from the flames in the fireplace dance over her cheeks.

"Do you like being in London?" she asks.

"I enjoy the weather," I deadpan and she breaks into a stunning grin.

"Yeah, it's fun, isn't it?" she giggles. Her mischievous smile makes my blood heat every time. "Is the contract you're working on here going well?"

I nod. I didn't come here for the contract. I mean, we want it done right, but I could have easily handled all that from Manhattan.

I came here for her and her alone. I've been building up momentum with her for months, despite her shooting me down a dozen or so times. I can't lose the bond we're building. I have this fear that if I lose it now, I'll never get it back...

She has to trust me.

I have to trust myself...

"It is," I reply. "But I didn't come here for the contract, Jessynia." She shifts nervously on the sofa we're sharing. "I came here... because I had this fear that... I might just go insane if I spent the summer without seeing you."

She inhales a breath as I say the words, her face flushing before my eyes. "Jack..."

I nod for her to speak, but she doesn't.

Instead, I shift towards her, running my hand down the back of the sofa. I hunger to touch her. To caress her face. To feel her lips on mine for the first time. To taste her pussy. I'm driven insane by the thought of it.

"What is it?" I ask. "You're afraid of me?"

She nods somberly.

"Jessynia, I haven't been the man I should have been, but I *want* to be. I want to be a good man. An honorable man. I want to be different from the men I came from. And I've never felt this way before. At the risk of making you want to file for a restraining order, I don't… fully know how to live without you anymore." I slide my hand onto the golden skin of her jaw as her chest expands and her breathing quickens. "I want to be with you. What are you afraid of? Tell me so I can fix it."

"I—"

"Tell me."

"This isn't going to be a thing, Jack. Us. We're not… we're not compatible, at all."

Anger bubbles beneath the surface of my composure at her words—anger that she believes that, anger at myself for fucking up so many fucking times, and anger at Cameron, for I know he's sown seeds of doubt that are the source of some of her reticence.

I guess I can't blame him fully. If she didn't drive me this insane, I probably wouldn't care what he'd said. The one woman I've wanted is the one who just had to be friends with him. Some sick joke designed by the universe. Karma, maybe, for my screw-ups.

Well, luckily for me, I'm not the type to give up without a fight. Not when it comes to her.

"Why not?" I ask.

"It's just… our whole way of looking at the world."

"Of treating people?"

"I heard about you… sleeping with a teacher. Then blackmailing her. Is that true?"

Her words stun me into silence. She speaks them softly, but the violence of the exposure of my conduct feels like being ripped apart.

I'm so ashamed of the things I've done. I'm not proud of the rage that left me callous, nor of the influences behind some of my actions—the nights spent with Alexandra when she would whisper vile demands into my ear and make it clear she wanted me to carry them out. Some sick test of loyalty the likes of which my father would probably approve of to ensure that I'm his special brand of ruthless.

It's not her fault.

I agreed to do it.

I didn't want to, but I did.

The drugs helped. My trauma and self-loathing and need for approval from her were the final mix in the cocktail. I haven't done anything like that for at least a year, but I wear the guilt of some of my actions like a lead overcoat that I can't take off, the corrosive metal eating into my skin.

As I look back up at her, I realize she's right. I don't deserve her. I don't deserve a woman who treats people decently, who cares about others. And she deserves a man who isn't as dangerous or capable of hurting people.

"I should go, Jess," I say.

"Wait!" she insists, coiling her slim hand around my forearm before letting it go. "Jack, I'm not trying to shame you or make you feel like shit. I just... want to know... who you are."

"I'm... a bad man, Jessynia. I'm a bad man from a bad family of criminals who have hurt people. I'm ashamed of the things I've done. I'm ashamed of my family's actions. And you heard correctly about the teacher. I slept with her repeatedly, and then later, I blackmailed her over it to make sure I got the grades I needed. Two years ago. She was a lot older than me, and I... snapped. I can't explain it to you. I just... lost control."

"Jack, I wasn't trying to—"

"I know. But you're right. We're not compatible." She nods in acceptance and I take a moment to calm my breathing. "I just wish"—I lean into her further—"that I wasn't tormented by you day and night."

"Jack—"

"That I didn't see your face every time I opened my eyes. That I didn't ache to hear your voice so much that it's all I can do to stop myself from calling you. That I didn't crave being kept in line by your honesty, by your compassion. That I didn't dream of making love to you until thoughts of it drive me insane. That I didn't see myself standing in front of you as you agree to be my wife—"

Her lips part as I make the confession.

I wish I were joking.

I've felt enslaved by Alexandra before, but she owned my mind and my body, not my heart. I'm not used to opening myself up, to trusting people. In truth, it makes me feel vulnerable and afraid, weak—not feelings I enjoy, to put it very mildly indeed.

"Jack, stop," she whispers and I edge towards her.

"I mean it, Jessynia. I wouldn't be doing this if I had a choice..."

She pauses for a moment, allowing me to take in the earnest beauty of her face. "I'm worried about... Cameron," she says softly. "Can you two fix whatever argument you've had?"

"I hope so. I want to fix it."

"You do?"

"Yes," I reply honestly, though in reality, the chances of that happening are slim after what I've done, and after the way he left them.

In the minds of Sebastian and his special friends on Council, you are either their submissive, their friend, or their enemy. There is no fourth route which lets you make it out without being hurt unless you follow their months-long exit procedure, that is. I begged him to do that. He refused. So far, I've managed to buy him time. I don't know if I can keep it up forever.

I want this fixed myself.

I'd have to limit my contact with the Society to make it work with this girl. I'm not a Council member, just a regular patron, so as long as I pay my memberships fees and occasionally visit as an observer, and as long as I don't fuck things up by leaving the way Cameron did, they should leave her and me alone.

There's no precedent for them harassing partners of regular patrons. In fact, I'm fairly sure it's forbidden by their constitution. I'm not worried about the repercussions the Council would mete out. They wouldn't. And I've reduced my visits there in the last few months without incident.

I'm more worried about Alex. She didn't take Cameron leaving lightly, but then again, he didn't just burn his bridges; he poured gasoline over the whole damn town and lit it on fire.

I'll appease the fuckers by staying in contact. It should make a difference.

At one point, I was afraid of myself. I've been going there my whole adult life. It's become a drug. I never thought I could live without it... but for her, I will. I have to believe I can do it. The force pushing me towards her is unlike anything I've known before. I've seen her in my dreams. I know it's her. I knew it from the second I saw her face, as insane as that may sound.

I intend to free myself of these people once and for all, but unlike Cameron, I'm going to use my fucking brain to do it.

"Do you think you can make up with him?" she asks.

She'd only ask such a thing if she were contemplating being with me. My heart lurches at the thought of getting closer...

"For you, I'd do anything, Jess. I can make it work."

"I'm scared of getting hurt."

I glance down at her glistening lips, trying not to imagine them dripping in my cum. My fingers are restless, desperate to touch her, to slide inside her pussy for the first time, to tie her hands behind her back so that I can defile her at leisure.

I don't know if she's used to that kind of thing. I know I could take care of her education... teach her what pleasure really means.

Looking back up, her eyes are wide, peering into me as if trying to understand. God dammit, there's something so earnest and vulnerable about them. I've never seen eyes quite like them.

"So am I," I say.

In the background, the clicks and whirls of the dryer stop suddenly, plunging us into silence.

Our eyes don't leave each other as she speaks. "I think your clothes are dry."

I nod and she pauses for a moment before getting to her feet.

Fuck.

Before I can stop myself, the movement of her tits has me grabbing hold of her leg and pulling her back onto the sofa, tugging her towards me. I take hold of the waistband of her leggings, and before she can stop me, yank them down her slim legs and off her feet, throwing them to the floor.

"Jack!" she cries as I bend over and spear my tongue into her naked clit.

Before she has a chance to protest further, I slide my tongue up and down in fast, deliberate movements, trying to stimulate her as much and as quickly as possible.

"Jack," she whimpers, propping herself up onto her elbows. I lift my face to see her looking down at me.

"Let me make you come, Jessynia. Please. I've been dreaming of your pleasure for months."

I know by her inertia that she's torn. I see it in the anxiety in her face. I have to give her pleasure, and *fast*...

Our eyes lock as I open my mouth wide. My top teeth delve into her smooth, hairless pubis as my tongue begins to work her clit again. Her gasp makes my cock harden as I begin to flick her clit, up and down, backwards and forwards, watching her as her eyes widen and she begins to pant.

I make one slow, deliberate lash of my tongue against her clit, and she whimpers my name. Hearing it come from her mouth is the sweetest sound I've ever heard...

I slide my tongue down to the opening of her sex. She's very wet, the clear gloss copious, a fact that gives me hope. She tastes fresh and sweet and I lap it up as high-pitched noises of reticence leave her throat.

Without warning, I spear my tongue as deep inside her wet pussy as the tight muscles will allow.

"Oh my God," she mutters.

Withdrawing, I say, "This is how I want to fuck you, Jess." I thrust my tongue in and out a few times. "Slowly. Carefully. I want to teach you pleasure you couldn't conceive of."

"Jack—"

I peer back up, slipping my tongue up and down her clit before toying with it with the tip as I stare at her timid eyes. "No more talking, Jessynia. Lie back down. I won't do anything but this. But I need to make you come. I need to see how you react to pleasure. It's not negotiable anymore."

As she watches me, I dip my tongue out and circle her clit, my eyes narrowing as her lips part. "Let me show you who I am, Jess. Close your eyes." I slide my hand onto her taut abdomen, pushing her back completely so that I can begin my work.

I start by kissing her clit, and all around it, softly, deliberately. I use my tongue to make strokes left and right, up and down, purposefully avoiding the tight nub in order to drive her insane.

I need this woman to hunger for me the way I do for her...

I need her to breathe for me...

The light notes of pleasure she makes are muted, subtle. With time, I want to hear her screaming...

I force my tongue inside her again. I can tell by the resistance that she's tight. I ache in desperation to slide my hard cock inside her, to pin her down, to fuck her, to impregnate her.

"Just relax, beautiful," I murmur. "Keep your eyes closed. Tune out everything but my tongue."

I toy with her some more as her back begins to arch and her body undulates. I push my tongue inside her again. "Imagine it's my cock," I order, "pushing inside you." I fuck her with my tongue as my name slips from her throat. "Just breathe. I need you to come for me. I want to hear your voice as you come."

I begin to tend to her clit as her sweet moans become louder.

"Louder," I order. "I need to hear you."

The volume of her pleasure increases... and so I stop.

"Tell me what you want, Jessynia," I ask, reveling in the sight of her beautiful, soft, juicy opening, desperate to fuck it so hard that she barely remembers her own name by the end of it.

"Jack..."

"Tell me."

"More," she replies breathlessly. "Please don't stop."

I groan at her plea for my tongue, and upon a final few flicks of her clit, her back arches, and she begins to pant through the pleasure, high-pitched notes floating from her, turning my cock rock-hard.

I watch her pussy as she comes, watch it contract. She's dripping wet, pink, smooth. Beautiful.

I've never felt desperation to fuck like this before... but I have to be so careful.

She's scared of me.

I'm scared of myself.

I don't want to be.

I want to be different...

I don't want to be like *them*...

I need to do things differently. I need her to know she's safe. I need to make sure I keep her safe.

I prop myself up and kneel over her, placing my feet between her thighs and my arms on either side of her on the wide couch. I look down to see her neck and the top of her chest that is visible above her T-shirt covered in red splotches, her skin flushing from the orgasm. Her nipples are hardened into points. I want to see them, to taste them, to suck on them...

I smile as she finally opens her eyes, her breathing still heavy, her face pink.

"Jack," she murmurs, eyes as big as quarters and glistening like ocean water.

"I've been dreaming of making you come since the first second I saw you."

Jessynia

I stare up into his face, its beauty so savage, the ceaseless magnetic pull of his controlled virility more lethal than should be allowed.

The high of the orgasm is still coursing through my cells, setting them alight, making my vision go splotchy. I've never felt pleasure like this, not even close. It feels like I've taken some drug for the first time.

I feel so exposed in front of him, naked, my pussy wet. Blushes of embarrassment make my cheeks burn at being open like this in front of a man so virile, so strong, so powerful.

I'm not sure what he's going to do. He's not moving, just watching me, his face soft, but his eyes focused.

I know I'm supposed to return the favor at this point, but I'm scared of going past the point of no-return with him. I'm scared of how I feel about a man who seems more dangerous than those I've been with before.

Mind you, the two I dated prior were outwardly respectable—both athletes, both with a 4.0 GPA, both from well-to-do families—but behind closed doors, they could be moody and possessive, and sometimes aggressive.

Even though Jack's been blunt about wanting to date me, he's never been moody when I've said no. He's always made me feel safe. It's just the stories that I've heard about him that scare me, but he looks so sincere when he's with me. I feel safe with him. I'm not even sure why...

He places his huge hands on the inner seams of my knees, pushing my legs apart just a little.

"I want to fuck you, Jess. Not because of what I just did, but because I'm so hungry for you and I'm so desperate to give you pleasure that I can't think of anything else. You don't have to say yes. You can tell me to leave, and I'll leave. I don't want you to feel any pressure. I want you to let me because you want me, not because you feel that you have to."

My sex pulsates as he speaks. Even though the orgasm he gave me is bliss beyond anything I've ever experienced, I feel myself aching for him to enter me properly, to fuck me...

"Jack..." He watches me, his face growing stern. "You have to fix things... with *him*."

He nods. "I'll try."

"Promise?"

"Yes. I promise."

I scrutinize his face. He really seems to mean it.

"I... I'm not on birth control." I haven't been since my last relationship ended months ago.

He gets to his feet and heads over to the counter where he placed his wallet earlier. He brings it back, pulling out a condom which he sets down on the coffee table next to us.

Upon reaching for the top of his sweatpants, he stops, dropping his head before lifting it to find my eyes, watching me for what feels like forever.

"Jack?"

I swallow hard as he finally speaks.

"I'm going home," he says. "I'm coming back tomorrow. Seven o'clock. To take you on a date. You don't have a choice in the matter. If after the date, you don't want to invite me inside, it's okay. I want you to have time to think this over, because once I fuck you, Jessynia, you'll never want me to stop."

My blood heats at the deviant words and a small note of pleasure leaves my throat. I've never felt arousal quite like this before, or maybe I have... with Cam, but I've known him for two years now and he's never shown the slightest interest in being with me beyond that intense stare of his... and he's had ample opportunity.

I like Jack... so much. I care about him. I feel safe around him. I feel this bond with him, this constant pull drawing me towards him. I'm desperate for him to show me what he means, but... I know he's right. I need time to think.

"Okay," I nod, wishing I could put my legs together so that my pussy wasn't exposed like this in front of him.

"This isn't because I don't want you, Jess." He reaches forwards and grabs my hand, lifting and pulling it towards his groin. On instinct, my hands cup his sack, which feels huge, before he slides my palm upwards. I can't stop the gasp as I take in the size and thickness of his erection.

He watches my face as he slowly glides my hand up and down. The thing is huge. It must be nine inches easily. I've never felt one anywhere near this big before. And he's really thick. And so hard. It feels like wood. My fingertips brush the head under the thin black cotton of his pants. It's swollen and the feel of it makes the walls of my sex contract in waves.

My face burns hot as he watches me explore the shape of him.

I don't see how it would even fit inside me...

He releases his hand from mine, but I can't let go. Instead, I wrap my fingers around the hard column, trying to get a sense of its sheer girth. He closes his eyes in pleasure for a moment before opening them as I reach for the waistband of his pants. I can't help it. I have to see him.

In an instant, his hand finds my wrist and he stops me.

"I'm coming back tomorrow," he says stiffly, jaw clenching, chest expanding and contracting fast. "You don't get to see me until then. I'll give you a day to think about this. If you still want me then, I intend to make love to you in a way that makes you forget the existence of every man you've ever known. Understood, Jess?"

I nod, trying not to drown in his earnest eyes as he peers down at me.

I so want him... I just have to be sure he can fix things with Cam...

I can't lose him...

40

Jessynia
Present

He sits watching me in the shadows after leading me to another unlit room in this vast maze—one with a bed in it and two armchairs opposite each other, a table between them upon which lie a bottle of water and two glasses.

As if by design.

I can't help but fidget under the weight of his stare. I'm wearing nothing but the same slip of a dress, acutely aware that my breasts are straining against the satin, that my nipples are pebbled beneath it, and that my still-wet pussy is naked under the loose sheet of white. The room is warm and my body still burns from what he did to me earlier, my skin singed by the fervor of his heat.

I don't know how to speak to him anymore.

I've lost any vague sense of power I may have thought I had. The man has seen my naked sex. He's tasted it. He's licked the juice from it, aware of what he does to my body. He's watched it engorge, felt it pulsate, open in front of him, and observed my face as I orgasmed from the pleasure that he gave me.

The only thing that stopped him was… *mercy?*

In truth, I'm not sure what exactly stopped him.

He asked me over a minute ago why I came to see him today, but I still can't muster up the strength to speak. Every time I'm overwhelmed by fear, or shame or guilt or anxiety, I go mute. It started when I was a child and worsened in my late teens. All I know how to do while waiting for my voice to return is try to stay afloat in the glacial waters of his eyes.

He takes the glass bottle from the table, filling both of our glasses with what I assume is water before placing mine close to me and then drawing his to his lips, watching me as he drinks it down before placing the glass back onto the table.

As it hits the wood beneath its thick base, the movement makes an unwanted tear spill over my waterline. It's not a tear of sadness but of overwhelm. My mother never cries, ever. She's very proud of being "emotionally stunted"—her words. My father cries silent tears easily, though being married to my mother, I don't blame him, God love her, and much to her chagrin, I process emotion in the same way as him.

As his incandescent gaze tracks the dewy droplet before I flick it away with my finger, I take a deep breath, building up the fortitude to speak. "You enjoy my tears. You must be in heaven today."

He tips his head almost imperceptibly to the side in that reptilian manner of his. "I'm torn between enjoying their beauty and finding them borderline offensive."

His eyes gleam as an unexpected smile escapes me at the tone he employs before dissipating into the ether.

"No words?" he suggests. "That's not like you. I rather enjoy being subjected to a barrage of unwanted opinions from you."

"I… I can't really speak," I respond, my voice deflated.

His eyes narrow. "Why not?"

"I don't know," I shrug. "It's not like I have any power left after… what just happened."

"Power? Do you think I do that to every woman? Do you think I give a fuck about the pleasure of the women I'm with? I don't. You have more power than any woman I know, Jessynia." The way he breathes my name rattles my body. "How did it feel? To come under my tongue?"

My lips part as the unabashed candor with which he speaks scalds my skin, no doubt leaving a flush of rose seeping into my cheeks before him. I hate that I blush so fucking easily. "Do you ever not say what's on your fucking mind?" I shoot back, burning up despite my meager clothes.

"Only around the weak and those I don't care to know. You're not one of them. I'll ask you again... How did it feel... to run? To be chased? To be hunted? To be ravaged by the tongue of a faceless man?"

The sharp inhale that leaves my dry throat resounds through the heavy air between us like gunpowder exploding.

So it is possible to die of embarrassment, I mutter internally.

At my silence, he speaks, his voice effortlessly commanding, a vehicle that sounds like it's served him for millennia. "You won't be leaving this room until I hear you say it."

"I felt... *afraid.*"

"Yes," he responds, his body unmoving.

The composed way he sits is like nothing I've ever seen. Jack and Cameron both have that self-possessed poise, but not quite like this. In the way in which Sebastian sits and talks and looks at you, it's as though there is... the absence of fear—the usual fear that threads through the fabric of our lives in even the most banal of situations: social anxiety, fear of how others perceive us, what they think of us, our looks, our personality. Fear of failure, of rejection, of not belonging, of saying the wrong thing, of being ridiculous, of making an ass of ourselves. These doubts manifest in the way we hold eye contact, or keep our bodies still, or stammer, or second-guess ourselves, or blush, or in the volume at which we speak, the expressiveness of our hand movements. I'm just realizing that Sebastian exhibits no outward semblance of even the most minute fear in his diction, his eye contact or his movements. It's so rare that for a second, the thought of it chills me.

"Hmm, I believe that," he continues, wild eyes locked onto me. "I can feel your heart beating in my body. I know the melody of their beats when you are afraid. I can taste your fear, Jessynia. *Always.* But that's not all you felt. What else did you feel? Don't make me force an answer out of you."

I fall into the leather at my back. I know what he wants. He wants a confession as to the pleasure that trickled into my body after the initial fear subsided...

"I felt... *shame.* And guilt."

He almost grimaces at the words, his hands curling over the end of the armchair, tensing for a moment as his eyes flare like embers escaping the grate around a fire.

"Shame." He toys with the word, turning the utterance as black as charred wood. "False modesty is an artifice I barely stomach, as you know."

I frown at him. "I'm not lying."

"No. You're too enslaved by the image you have of yourself—the good little girl. The faithful one. You're so trapped in the trauma of the rumors that that man and his family started that you're afraid to own your own sexuality. Your own right to pleasure."

As he evokes that man again, a tremor of angst vibrates through my body, short-circuiting my thoughts as the vision of Sebastian's coup de grâce, and the blood that spattered from his fist as it collided with the man's face, dashes through my mind like the most vicious of explosions. For a second, the room around me dissolves to black matter, leaving only the thud of the man's face as it hit the dirt.

As I collect myself, I peer up to find Sebastian's face almost pained as he scrutinizes my shaken countenance. "You're not even close to being healed from the trauma."

"You think?" I shake my head in incredulity. "I mean, am I supposed to be over it by now? Am I not respecting the trauma timelines that the other psychopaths around here follow? Or am I supposed to be fucking every single feeling out of me the way these vampires do in this place?"

"I explained to you before that I want you discussing your trauma over his death with me. I don't want it stuck inside you."

"Oh sure. I'll just make myself a nice cup of chai and call you up every day so that we can casually chat through the day you murdered a man in front of my eyes with your bare hands without giving me a choice in the matter!"

"The man was a predator. He violated children. His death was retribution, not murder."

"Well, I hope you don't have to tell that to the judge."

"We've ensured that won't be necessary," he growls.

God, I hope not...

"I don't need you traumatized, Jessynia. It's not conducive to my plans for you. I want you conscious and in control when you submit to me."

"Well, sorry to inconvenience you! I mean, you didn't exactly help in the trauma department, Sebastian. I'm still having vivid nightmares of... that day." I realize that my breath seems to evaporate into the air every time I think of it...

He leans forward in his chair. "With time, you will feel the release of his death. The liberation. The joy. You're not ready yet, but it will come. Part of that is you opening yourself up to me, trusting my decision to make him pay for hurting you the way he did."

I reach forwards for the glass, bringing it to my lips and drinking it down to quench my thirst. As I place it back down onto the table, my eyes meet his.

"What do you want?" I ask.

His face hardens, anger roughing its edges. "You know what I fucking well want. And the next time I have to ask you, I will bind you to the bed and force the answer out of you. Now tell me how you felt when my tongue was toying with your clit."

I lift my chin in defiance despite the tingling of my sex and the embarrassment I feel at him speaking so forthrightly. "I felt... ashamed. And guilty," I repeat, aware that the words will piss him off.

"Hmm, you disappoint me, Jessynia. I can't think of anything more tedious or predictable than your *fucking* shame, especially when I know where it comes from..."

"Well, what do you expect me to say?"

"I expect you to tell me the *full* truth, and not the one that makes you look the way your limited self-image dictates. False modesty is an absurd abstract to construct around a man who has just watched your dripping wet sex pulsate as you whimpered in pleasure."

"Stop." The breathy whisper falls from me as my limbs turn numb in the face of his demand for answers when all I want to do is keep up the same walls we all erect around ourselves in public, never admitting the true extent of our desires, good or bad.

"Do I strike you as being a man who believes that humans should feel shame for their desire to fuck? Your shame is unwelcome in my world. It makes you look pitiful."

"Well, I... I'm sorry I'm not like your good friend *Alexandra* who can prostrate herself *spreadeagle* in front of fifteen erect men without batting an eyelid."

The tenebrous tension crackling between us is cut by the slight curving at the corner of his lips, signaling the amusement which I occasionally witness and which makes the thick fog that swathes our conversations dissipate just a little.

"It took her a while to no longer care about the opinions of humans in all of their sanctimony and hypocrisy."

"Pff, let me guess," I scoff. "The human flamethrower was once a timid little lamb..."

His eyes gleam in mirth, their silvery flecks glistening as if the bearers of starlight. "Not quite," he deadpans with an almost-smile. "She certainly didn't blush profusely every time I looked at her the way you do."

"The bane of my existence," I mutter under my breath.

"Your shame is a disappointment to me. And as for your guilt, I've watched your husband fuck two women in this very room, while you were married. In fact, if I recall correctly, it was at the same time."

I shake my head, strength leaching from my body.

"In fact," he continues, "I could take you to half a dozen rooms down here that he fucked women in not two years after proclaiming his undying fidelity to you, and we wouldn't have visited them all."

"That's not true," I utter.

"I don't lie, Jessynia. Your guilt is utterly misplaced when it comes to your husband."

You designed that, Sebastian...

"As for any guilt you may have towards Mr. O'Neill, inside that man resides a beast, and if he lets it loose, then I may have to save you from it myself."

"I don't believe you," I declare loudly.

"One day, you will see it," he snarls. "As it is, your misplaced sense of guilt is part of what makes you weak. I intend to absolve you of every fucking ounce of it."

"What, so that I can become conscienceless like the other vampires around here?"

"So that you can be as you were born to be. Free."

I shake my head, glancing over at the bed, seeing Jack there, screwing someone, and then coming back home to me...

"Now, I will ask you for the last time, what do I want to hear from you?" he asks.

"You want me to admit—" I stop, unable to say the word.

"What?"

"My... pleasure."

He nods his head slowly. "I want you to own your desire to be fucked by me. I want you to revel in pleasure, no matter how heinous you believe the source to be. You were designed to be fucked, Jessynia. Your body, your face, your voice, your vulnerability—they are a package designed to make men lose their sanity, to turn them into conscienceless beasts, to make them frenzied, rabid. You don't fully understand that your purpose on this Earth is to be fucked by dominant men, to be educated in pleasure, to be taught to submit. To be filled with cum day and night. That is what you were designed for."

"Hey! Just because you... because of what happened, doesn't mean you... you have the right to reduce me to the status of silicone doll! I'm not just some thing with holes in her, you know?!"

He bows his head. "I am aware of that. That's why I'm sitting here talking to you instead of ravaging your tiny body in my bed as we speak... and as you want, Jessynia. Now before I take you there, I'll ask you one last fucking time... What did you feel when I was licking the juice from your sex?"

"Jesus, the way you talk," I retort, gulping down the truth—the truth of my desire for him. The truth of my yearning to be protected by a man so dangerous. The truth of my desire to experience sex in a way I haven't before.

His eyes bore into me, tunneling through me my cracking façade as he waits for the confession he craves. "I felt... pleasure. There, are you happy?"

"Hmm. You have the guts to admit it."

"Isn't my pleasure all a bit banal for a man like you? I mean, every other woman you fuck must feel pleasure or they wouldn't sign up to what you do to them."

"I don't care about every other woman. In fact, I don't give a fuck about any of them."

"None of them?" I ask, my voice frail.

"*None.*"

"What about... *her*? Alex?"

"I can't deny that I feel some *affection* for her. Her malice is something that I understand, that I know the power of. Her hatred for the world amuses me, soothes me. But her pleasure is utterly irrelevant to me. As is her ability to admit it."

My gaze is caught by the slight glint of his black wedding ring. "Did you care about Rose's pleasure?"

"For a brief moment."

"Why did you stop caring?"

"Her purity began to cause me pain. And her betrayal fed things inside me that don't rest until they have blood. I was... a less measured man back then."

"Do you regret it? Do you feel remorse?"

"I remember feeling endless remorse as a child. Endless guilt. Shame. Regret. I wasn't sure what I'd done wrong but I was informed that my existence was a burden of the highest order. And my shame and guilt over being alive were used as tools by her."

"Your mother?" I ask and he nods. "Tools for what?"

"To degrade me, to humiliate me, to shame me, to beat me, to educate me in what a piece of filth I was. What a disappointment. What a waste of life. What a mistake. And I believed her, Jessynia... until the day I made it stop. And since that day, I am not sure I have not experienced remorse... perhaps with one exception. Does that disappoint you to hear?"

"What's the exception?" I ask.

I swallow hard as he remains silent, wanting to ask him something but afraid to know the answer.

"Do you regret what happened with my family?" I finally ask. "The fire? My brother?"

Then something unusual happens—he closes his eyes for a moment, unspeaking, his breaths long, his face looking... pained, almost.

He finally opens them. "I feel some pain over those events. That is not a manner in which I wish to hurt you."

"Would you do it again?" I ask, searching his pale face.

"I hope not. Please don't make me."

"I can't make you! You are responsible for those decisions! I don't want you to ever go near them again!"

He bows his head and I breathe out a sigh of relief at the first vague flicker of his version of remorse.

"Something must have happened to your brain chemistry," I decide after a moment. "For you to need to cause pain."

He smiles darkly. "Your attempts at analyzing me are always a source of enjoyment, Jessynia."

"What's *your* explanation?"

"I became... *infected*. Something got inside me. Once there, it started to grow. It took over. It is now in every cell of mine."

"We can get it out..."

"I am fairly sure that if I get it out, I will die with it."

I feel my eyes mist over as he says it. "*No*. No, Sebastian. We can get it out and keep you alive. We can work through every single injury that that *thing* you called a mother did to you. I can help you to heal from it. I promise."

"I believe this is why you wanted to see me," he says, his words pouring out like acrid smoke. "Another therapy session?"

"Don't you want to get this stuff out?"

"Why would I?"

"Because that's how we start to heal. Don't you want to?"

"Do I deserve to?"

"*Of course* you do."

I watch his pale mauve lips part and his silver-hewn eyes wander slowly over my face. "Your eternal optimism, Jessynia. What is it? *Hope?* The naivety of youth? Denial? *Foolishness?*"

I shake my head slowly, feeling anger simmer throughout my body as I lean forward, my eyes wide on his. "Having hope doesn't make you foolish, Sebastian. Having none, however, *does*. Not to mention, that it's *cowardly*. It's a *cop-out*. It's lazy and it requires no fucking effort whatsoever!"

His eyes flare as if torched by white-hot flame. "What are you calling me, Jessynia?"

"I'm calling anyone who gives up hope, without at least trying, a *coward*."

"That's a lot of people," he retorts coldly.

"Yeah, well, that's how I feel." I pant through my irritation, one made all the more acute by the temperate manner in which he's holding himself compared to me. "And anyway, I think you're full of shit! You do feel hope! You wouldn't waste your time talking to me if you didn't! And you do think you can heal! I know it. I've already seen changes since I first knew you..."

His eyes form into narrow slits. "Did it ever occur to you that I show you what I want you to see?"

"I don't think you're *that* in control," I counter. "And you *have* changed. I've seen it."

"I can indulge you if it helps you make sense of your world. If it helps you to feel safer. To still the fear. But one thing has not changed, Jessynia. My need to cause pain. These things inside me demand it. They speak to me. They move me."

As he conjures them up, my mind hears some ungodly screech from deep within him, watching the contortion of black limbs that have taken possession of him.

"Maybe they're still there," I respond solemnly. "But I believe that your ability to see the evil inside you has grown more acute. To differentiate yourself and those things inside you."

He bows his head. "You may be right."

"Why do you see them more clearly now?" I ask.

His strong hands tense around the ends of his armchair. "You're playing games with me again, Jessynia."

I frown, shaking my head. "No."

My blood hums frenetically as his gaze drops to my lips, taking them in in a way that makes the Earth seem to stop spinning on its axle.

"Come here." The words pour out like warm tar.

I shake my head emphatically. "No."

His face contorts in anger and he gets to his feet as I retreat into the chair at my back. I peer up at him as he comes to stand before me. He holds out a hand but I don't take it.

"No."

"I do enjoy the hollow dregs of your attempts at resistance, Jessynia."

"No!"

I shout, trying to push him away as he reaches down and grabs my waist, lifting me up and over his shoulder as I writhe to release myself. He throws me onto the unlit bed, climbing on top of me, lifting my arms over my head, and pinning them to the pillow beneath my head.

No!

His legs spread mine and his hard erection finds its place—my clit, which it presses into as he threads his fingers through mine, stopping me from moving.

"Let me out!"

"You *know* what has shifted," he utters, the yearning in his voice roughening the words as if the admission torments him. "I don't enjoy the façade. The attempt to play dumb about your effect on me."

I shudder, my body arching, writhing as I picture Jack in this bed with another woman.

"I don't want to be in this fucking bed! Let me out!" My skin is suddenly charring, as if licked by flames as I try to extricate myself from his grasp. “Let go of me!” I kick, trying to budge his mammoth torso, to get out from under his legs as I feel Jack’s movements, sense the drives into some faceless woman, see the moment he tips his head back and comes inside her. Sebastian holds me tighter, but it only makes the constriction of claustrophobia more acute. “Get me out of here!” I shout, trying to catch my breath. “Please! I can’t breathe.”

A moment later, I’m hoisted off the bed only to be carried across the room and out of the door, taken down the stone corridor for at least fifty feet until we stop at a black door. Lowering me a little, he presses his thumb into a thumb reader and the door clicks upon.

41

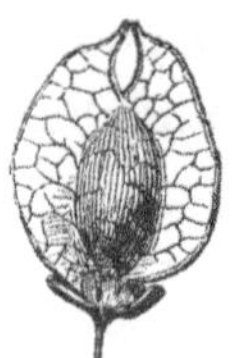

"I can't see," I mutter, the compression of my chest loosening despite my realization that we're in pitch black.

Suddenly I'm dropped onto the floor and pushed back against the door Sebastian is closing. At the sound of a click, a light comes on, dim, but enough to illuminate the area around us, to illuminate the pale skin of his naked chest, to bounce off the pronounced grooves, to shed light on his scars, to accentuate every hard ridge as he bears down on me, closing the gap between us as my hyperventilation calms and the sounds of my breath soften.

My skin tingles as his fingertips brush my long hair to the side, touching the skin of my chest, which, glancing down, I see is mottled in stains of crimson, my body's reaction to being in a bed where Jack slept with other women during our marriage... or so Sebastian says, anyway.

I know it's true...

I watch as his fingertips draw over my skin, leaving fiery imprints in their wake as they explore the internal welts bleeding onto my skin. He studies the red marks as if trying to understand them, before raising my chin with a jolt, forcing me to peer up into eyes shimmering with the only light that man yields. The frustration of jealousy lingers in his glare, but it swirls with concern.

In the silence of the murky room, the depth and resonance of his voice rumble through me despite him speaking softly. "Hmm. Even after everything you know about him, it still hurts you."

"Sorry I'm not dead inside yet," I shoot back. "Must be highly frustrating for you. Am I supposed to not care?" I utter, my voice stripped of its strength. "Am I supposed to just lie down and have a nap in the same bed my husband fucked other women in?"

"You care too fucking much, Jessynia. It will cause you endless pain."

"Or maybe the people around you don't care enough," I suggest as his hand slides up my neck and into my hair as he sandwiches me between the door behind me and the wall of flesh that makes up his mammoth frame.

My nipples harden into points under the frail silk of my dress as his dense chest presses into me and his hand weaves into my loose hair, keeping my hand cranked back, forcing me to watch his eyes flare with lust, with jealousy, with his version of worry, to feel the flicker of heat therein.

"And you still don't like the dark," he says softly as my body tingles from his touch, from the raging tumult concealed behind his outward self-restraint.

"Who does?"

"I do," he snarls. "And most adults are not afraid of it like you are."

"Good for them," I scoff.

"You feel things watching you in the dark, don't you?"

"Are they?" I ask.

"Yes."

"What are they?"

"There are beings amongst us, Jessynia. Beings we can't see."

"Inside you..."

"Inside *all* of us. I host more than most. And mine are less... *human* than most."

"What do they want? Yours?"

"You know what they want."

"My suffering."

"Your suffering. Your tears. Your blood."

"Do you want that?" I ask.

He has always told me what he wanted: My compliance, my loyalty, my sex. I don't know if it is he who wants my pain, or the things inside him. I don't know if they are even separate entities, or if he copes with who he is by making them so. A year ago, I'd have shaken my head at the concept of *demons*. Why, now, do I feel the presence of them so acutely?

"I hunger for your pain, Jessynia, but want to destroy anyone who would inflict it upon you." He speaks so matter of factly, yet I feel the deranged roar of some thing inside him. "I yearn to taste your tears, but the sight of them makes me flinch in pain. And I dream endlessly of tasting, of drinking your warm blood as it gushes from your body, and yet I know that the spilling of it will extinguish the only light left."

I shudder at the brutal words, my brow drawing tight. I know I'm sporting a scowl that would make my mother proud, but it's also tainted by fear and horror at hearing another human speak such heinous thoughts, ones that we are supposed to keep hidden...

"Do you want the light gone?" I ask as his gaze falls to my lips.

"I don't know," he utters softly. "I feast on darkness, Jessynia. I understand its warmth. I can breathe in it. And yet, your light... I can't seem to relinquish it... for good."

"Is that all I am to you? Some last-ditch attempt at holding onto light?"

The grasp on my hair tightens as his torrid eyes clash with mine. "I wish I knew. I wish I could explain away everything that you do to me. Your effect on me is most... *inconvenient*."

"I'm very glad to be a pain in the ass," I respond grimly to a gleam in his eyes.

And as his eyes shimmer, my gaze is caught by the glimmer of something behind him—the glistening of metal. Silver.

As I peer just right of his huge shoulder, I realize what I'm seeing.

Knives.

A dozen or more.

Hanging from the wall.

"What is this place?" I ask.

Releasing his palm from my neck after a moment, he grabs my hand, interlacing his fingers firmly with mine despite my attempts to pull away from him. He pulls me across the room in the direction of the knives, forcing me to stand in front of him, his chest at my back.

The blades, different lengths, shapes and thicknesses, hang from thick chords threaded through holes in the handles, all of which are engraved from wood. To the left of them hang various restraint devices—cuffs of varied sorts, ropes, bars, as well as gags of different sorts.

My skin mists, cold air making it clammy, freezing my flesh and leaving me feeling cold and alone. "You use these?" I ask.

"This is a private room. Only myself and a few others have used it."

"Has he been in this room?" I ask.

"Your *husband?* No."

My breathing accelerates as I study the knives, trying to understand the insinuation in Sebastian's tone. Was he implying that Cameron has? I want to ask him, but the thought leaves me sick to my stomach and I lose my nerve.

"You… cut people," I say.

"Yes."

"Consensually?"

"I do not penetrate without consent," he responds, the tension in his jaw audible, "nor do I *cut* without it."

"Why on Earth would anyone *want* to be cut?" I ask.

He pulls me into his huge chest from behind, his hand snaking up around my neck as his respiration quickens and his breath hits the side of my cheek in hot blasts.

"Your naivety pains me, Jessynia." His timber roughens, lowering to a sinister growl. "Especially when it's insincere. What also pains me is your inability to admit the truth about who you are, and what you want."

"Stop!"

But the word makes him tighten his grip on my neck. I feel the hard ridge of his erection against the curve of my ass.

"The appeal of your innocence pales in comparison to my need to have you face the truth about yourself."

His strong fingers contract around my throat as a long, low groan falls from his. "You know full well why one would wish to be cut. What's more, a part of you craves it, craves the slice of my blade into your flesh. Don't you?"

"Sebastian,"—I writhe to free myself, only to find his grasp on me more tenacious—"Let me go..."

"The women I chain to that table"—I glance to the right to see a table of sorts, its top padded in thick leather, with four sections splayed out to the right and left, allowing arms and legs to be shackled wide apart by cuffs attached to chains languishing on the floor. "They don't merely tolerate my cutting them. They *beg* me for it. They moan in pleasure as my knife enters them, as I lick the blood from their bodies. Why do they do it? Answer me."

My hand wraps around his wrist as I try to pull him off. "Go fuck yourself!"

Unmoved by my efforts, the smooth muscle of his tongue slowly licks the side of my face as he exhales a breath dripping in arousal.

"Hmm. I enjoy the way you fight me, Jessynia. I enjoy the last dregs of the façade you insist on erecting around you. It's valiant in the extreme, especially when I know what's happening to your body. I know every detail of it. I can taste your arousal, Jessynia. I know that your sex is hungry for me to lift your body onto mine. Isn't it?"

I close my eyes, my body freezing under his touch.

"Isn't it, Jessynia? Do you have the guts to tell me the truth? Or are you a coward?"

"Yes," I respond softly.

"And you feel shame because of it..."

"I can't help what you do to my body. It doesn't mean I intend to submit."

"No. It doesn't. You won't need to *intend* it to happen. One day, your need for me will be so acute that no amount of willpower will allow you to stand it."

"See, that's where you're *wrong*."

At my provocation, he spins me around, backing me against the wall in slow strides.

I jump at the gleam of metal from the knife that Sebastian pulls from the wall. He forces it into my hand, wrapping his strong fingers around mine, and edging the blade towards his free hand.

"No!" I shout as the tip hits his thumb and he forces it to slice through the fleshy top segment of the large digit. "Stop!"

I watch the first droplet of crimson appear, pooling at the bottom of the cut on his thumb. I peer up to see his eyes trailed on my face, and no sign of pain on his.

"What is *wrong* with you?" I utter breathlessly, glancing around to a nearby table next to a bed in the corner to see if there are any tissues. Before I can properly look for some, he coils his other palm around my neck, pressing me firmly against the wall.

He takes the knife from me, throwing it to the ground with a clang. "Look at the cut, Jessynia,"—he brings it closer to my face—"The perfection of the blood."

Before I can stop him, he lifts his bleeding thumb to my lips, slipping it against them slowly, staining them in his scarlet blood. A trickle enters my mouth, tainting it, imbuing it with that familiar metallic taste that always transports me back to that day in that forest when I bit through flesh so hard that I tasted his blood in my mouth.

I shake my head. "No, Sebastian."

"I told you, Jessynia. From now on, when you taste blood, it is *my* blood. His blood is no more."

As my gaze widens on his, he begins to push, steadily penetrating my mouth—first pushing into the seam between my lips, then slipping against my bottom teeth, before entering in contact with my tongue and pushing into the wet warmth.

My eyes close for a moment as I taste the blood and my lips close around his thumb, the cut slipping against my tongue.

I open my eyes to find his flaring on my face, taking in another defeat, another victory over my attempts at self-control around him.

Jessynia...

In a moment of clarity, I grab his wrist and pull his hand from my mouth. "No more," I pant and his lips fall to mine as his eyes widen, his pupils fully dilated as he studies me in the near-black.

"As I said," he utters, "your attempts to fight are most enjoyable to observe..."

I take a breath, proclaiming as boldly as I can, "I can be as turned on by you as I like, Sebastian. It doesn't mean I'll submit to you fully."

And as I say it, he presses himself against me, the slow press of the huge, hard ridge into my clit under my dress makes my sex pulsate.

Jessynia...

His face dips to the side of mine as he begins to breathe me in with a groan which makes my eyes close. The brushes of his lips against my skin are so soft, so at odds with the brutal power of this merciless beast. He lifts his face to look down at me again. In my barefoot state, in this dimly lit room, he appears almost as a giant, some creature from another world, pulling me into his where the rules are unfamiliar.

"Yes you will," he responds softly. "Once this fucking need you have to appear pure, to disprove the heinous rumors that were once spread about you, is gone for good. I want it obliterated. I want you free of shame. I know what shame does to us. What guilt does. I know how insidious it is. How it erodes us. How it destroys our ability to believe in ourselves. The shame you live in causes me pain, Jessynia, beyond the frustrations that my body endures around you." He presses his hard erection into me slowly, causing my lips to part and my chest to pant. "Now tell me the *full* truth, or I'll get it out of you. Do you desire me?"

I want to say No, but we both know it's a lie.

He considers me for what feels like an eternity.

"Part of me wants you."

"Wants to be fucked by me."

"Yes," I respond solemnly. "I hope you're happy."

His lips slip to my ear. "Part of you wants me to shackle you to that table until you can't move so that I can lift your dress and fuck you brutally. Don't you?"

"Yes." I close my eyes for a moment, swallowing down the admission of my unyielding desire for him, despite the knowledge of his brutal dominance. "But it's not happening."

"No. It isn't. You would not be acceptable to me in this state," he growls. "I don't want your reticence or your shame or your guilt, or your nauseating need to look pure in front of me. I want you to *beg* for me, Jessynia. I want you to beg for what my body can do to you. I want you so enslaved to your desire that me fucking you is the only thing that can soothe the agony. I want you to greet me on your knees with your mouth open and a rope in your hand. That's how this will happen."

The wild eyes of my bull-busting mother flash before my eyes. "And then I'll be like every other one of your mindless subs." I pull against his grip, my face hardening. "That is *not* happening."

He pauses for a moment, contemplating my words. "Your submission is ordained by forces more powerful than you, Jessynia. You won't have a choice by the end."

"That's where you're wrong, Sebastian. And you'll have to do better than this to make me lose my mind completely."

His fingers grip my palms more tightly and his eyes burn with wrath. "I don't enjoy being given instructions."

"Well, I don't enjoy half the things you've subjected me to, so you can go fuck yourself!"

His fingers uncouple from mine and his hands delve into my hair, yanking it back roughly, cranking my neck back so that I'm forced to peer up into the unforgiving glaciers of his eyes as the full weight of his mammoth torso presses down on my slim frame, stealing my breath.

"White Oak," I utter, my unconscious panic audible on the words.

The volatile storm of his mercurial glare doesn't abate as he studies me, but the grip on my hair softens, a little, then more, until he finally pulls his strong fingers out of my brown hair.

Silence stretches between us as I try to hold my ground under the weight of his storm.

"You always stop when I say those words."

His eyes narrow.

"We both know you've shown me mercy, Sebastian. Is it just because you want me more complicit than this? Or is there something else?"

"Your never-ending need to make me human..."

"Is there? You say you want the truth from me. And you call me a coward if I don't give it, no matter how humiliating. Are you not going to follow your own rules?" My neck strains from peering up into his savage face. "Why do you show me mercy?"

"Perhaps it's because I fear," he whispers, "that once you give yourself to me fully, I won't be able to stop until the light behind your eyes is extinguished..."

I wilt at his words as if stuck on some illusive ledge, some desolate slab of granite, peering out onto the bleakest of horizons.

Collecting myself, I say, "That's not the full reason," praying that I'm right.

"No," he drawls. "It isn't."

"Why else?" I ask.

"Because I am *tormented*, Jessynia. Your existence is agony to me. I am torn between my desire to tear you apart and to protect you. My mercy is an attempt to do the latter."

"Do you like the feeling? Of being merciful."

He shakes his head slowly. "I abhor it."

I feel my brow creasing as I peer into the beautiful darkness of his rugged face framed by thick, long, blond hair. "Why?"

"It makes me feel weak. Ordinary. It makes me feel out of control."

"Human," I suggest.

"Yes. Human. A species I despise"—his hand lifts to draw a long strand of hair behind my ear as he tilts his head to the side while studying the gesture—"but for few exceptions."

"Why do you despise them?"

"Their weakness. Their hypocrisy. Their ability to stand by in the face of evil."

"That's what happened to you, isn't it?"

"My father stood back and watched as my mother abused me, and then joined in when she called him weak. The few people she allowed near us saw that something was wrong and did nothing. Humans will only help others as long as there is no great cost to them. As soon as things become uncomfortable, their help will stop."

"Not everyone..."

"No. Not everyone. But then, you are brave, Jessynia. Braver than most. And you project your way of being onto others when they are entirely unworthy of it."

I sigh out heavily to the sight of his lucent eyes narrowing into thin beams of light.

"You asked me about mercy thinking of *them*, didn't you?" he asks, bitterness singeing the words. "Your *men*. That's what you want from me, isn't it?"

"I want it for *all* of us, Sebastian, you included."

"That's why you came to see me today, isn't it?" he asks coldly. "To beg for mercy for them."

"I didn't come to *beg*," I retort. "I came to try to make you see the advantages of being free of them."

"*Me* being free? What a woefully transparent manipulation. I didn't think you capable of stooping so low."

"I'm not trying to manipulate. I'm trying to open your eyes."

"Tell me about this plan for my freedom, Jessynia. Amuse me."

I swallow down a knot of tension in my throat. "I... I've been thinking of going away... for a while."

His eyes narrow. "Why?"

I raise my chin, mustering up every ounce of strength I have left. "Because... I... I can't make this work."

"With your men," he suggests.

"They're not—" I pause, dropping my head for a moment. "It's not fixable anymore."

"Was it ever?"

"I thought maybe it was. It *isn't*."

"Because you can't choose."

"Because they need to be freed. We *all* do."

"How gracious of you to consider my well-being," he sneers.

"Well, I *do* think of it, despite what you may think. And my leaving is not just for me, or them, it's for everyone's benefit."

"If you want to leave, why not just leave? Why come to see me?"

"You're kidding, right? You know full well that nothing we do passes without your say so. And... I... I want you to let us go. *All* of us."

"Why would I do that, Jessynia?"

"I won't see them again. Either of them. I won't talk to them. I'll make it clear that I don't want contact with them anymore. I'll go off-grid for a while if I have to. I'll do anything it takes. It will hurt me, Sebastian. Losing these men. It goes against everything I know."

"You think this sacrifice is worthy of having your men freed?"

"Yes. It is. But... I also want *you* freed, Sebastian. The bond you have with them is just poisonous. It's a trauma bond. It's based in malice and... control and... it's just not healthy. For *any* of you. If you want to heal—"

"What delusions make you think that I want to heal?"

"We *all* do. It's in our DNA as humans. We don't want to experience suffering and pain forever."

"You think running away will fix the pain? Are you that naïve?"

"I'm not naïve. Stop calling me that! And I'm not saying it will fix *everything*, but... *something* has to shift. Things can't go on like this. I have this feeling that... something very bad is going to happen. I can't shake it. I don't want to leave my home and my friends, Sebastian. I'm doing it while praying that it changes everything."

"Hmm. I would like to hear your explanation as to what is in it for me, exactly."

"I... I won't speak to them anymore. I'll only speak to you."

"Speak?"

"Yes."

"Why would you think that would satiate me?"

"Because... I believe you when you say that part of you wants to protect me. Even if the other part wants to cause me pain. If you can let me go, let them go, then the things that have control over you, they'll lose their power, Sebastian. They won't have control anymore. *You* will. And when you're in pain over the loss of control, I'll speak to you. I'll make it better, I promise."

"And you think both of your men will just let you go? Are you that determined to deny reality?"

"I'll make sure they can't find me. I'll make it clear I want us all to move on. And if I come back to New York, I'll only see you. Not them."

I feel myself tremble under the weight of my promise, and of his contemplation of it.

"Even if I were to be able to tame my utter contempt for your *friend* to the point that I could let him live a life free from the purgatory he deserves, that still leaves me unable to see you, Jessynia. I'm unsure it's something that I can tolerate anymore."

"You're not telling me you'd miss me, Sebastian?"

"We all miss the things we hunger for, Jessynia."

"No offense, but it would seem particularly mundane of you to feel something like that. I would have thought that kind of melancholy would be beneath you..."

His breathing quickens as his eyes fall to my lips.

"So would I," he whispers before peeling apart my lips with his tongue, pushing the muscle deep inside my mouth, fucking it in strokes that are wild, fervid. I close my eyes, trembling at the desperation in the movements, even as he slows down, sliding into and out of my mouth as my hand does something I know he hates—it slips up the side of his body, and onto the hard muscles of his bare back.

Sebastian doesn't like to be touched like that. I know that much. He needs to dictate, have his imprint be outward. I expect him to go rigid, but he doesn't, his movements flowing as he deepens the kiss and we crash into each other, our bodies undulating under the sheer current of his muscles.

As my fingertips locate one of the thick scars carved of his flesh, he withdraws from my mouth, his brow furrowing as I lift my hands from him.

My lips skim his. "Please, Sebastian."

His breathing is labored, his lips glistening in my saliva. "You're overestimating my ability to be human."

"*No*. You're underestimating your need to be free. This is a way for all of us to have a new life. It will hurt at first... but after a while, you'll feel... liberated. You'll start to heal. Please just try..."

"And your husband?"

"He'll find out once I'm gone."

"How cruel of you to deny him the only woman he's ever wanted."

"I don't want to hurt him," I reply solemnly, vigor bleeding from me. "I've never wanted to hurt him. But... I don't see any other way out. There isn't one. I've tried. I know it's not going to work. Plus, Jack is a God on Wall Street. There are thousands of women who would queue up to love him. He doesn't need me the way he thinks he does."

"That's not why you want to leave. There's something else. I want to hear it." The ire in his voice slices through me. "Now."

"I keep having nightmares. Not just about that man. I keep seeing blood. I see it over and over again. I know something bad is going to happen to one of you. I can feel it. I can taste blood in my mouth when I wake up. I have to stop this once and for all."

"Our Society was founded in blood. It is our life force. At some point, it will be spilled."

"Sebastian, I am begging you to let them both go. For good. In exchange, I'll help you to heal. You don't have to live in darkness for the rest of your life."

"Live in it?" he sneers, eyes flaring and making me gulp down the muted guttural roar. "What if I *am* the darkness?"

I shake my head, everything around me crumbling into shards of black coal at the horror of his words. "No. I don't believe that. Please. I'm begging you. Let me go. Let us all go."

Before I can really finish the word, I'm lifted over his shoulder with a scream and thrown onto the padded table nearby as he pushes my legs apart, sliding into the gap and climbing on top of my body.

I shout in protest as his hand grabs a fistful of my hair, yanking it back as his ravenous mouth locates my ear.

"Don't you know what you do to me?!" he bellows, the gravel in his bestial voice like the rumble of an earthquake through my body.

His other hand covers my mouth fully as I try to shout. As I writhe underneath him to get away, he presses his full weight onto me. "Don't you know that I am *tormented* by you day and night?! That I am at war with my own fucking self? That I yearn to rip you to bloody pieces so much that I have to restrain my body to stop it?" I whimper under the palm blanketing my mouth as his lips slip against my ear. "Don't you know that I want to drink your blood? That I hunger for you so much that everything else is tasteless to me. Pleasure is now filled with *distraction*. Your face now covers my every fucking scene. I *yearn* for you, Jessynia. For your face. For your voice. For your submission. For your sex. If I am to be saved… it is by *you* and no one else… Do you think I can just let you go…?" he roars.

He lifts his head from my neck with a groan, staring down into my eyes which mist in tears from the brutal devastation of his words, from the candor and violent vulnerability which I know must feel like agony… if his words are true and not… a trap…

I swallow hard at what looks like torment in his face as he slides his hand from my mouth.

"I can't feel anything for you unless you let them go," I respond, tears trickling onto my temples. "*Both* of them. For good. And the only way that can work is if I leave them both… for good. I won't speak to them again. I will only speak to you. Please. Just let us all go."

42

Alexandra Frost
Sixth Avenue
Present

I stub out my cigarette in the ashtray on Vallen's ludicrously ostentatious gold and marble side table, pressing it into the glass until it's crumpled, the ash dull.

Turning around, I grab my packet from the coffee table, pulling out another to the click of my lighter which Vallen holds out to me, flipping the top closed after I inhale a deep drag, the smoke leaving me in a breath of relief.

"I thought the problem was *him*," I say as I begin to pace through his tastelessly decorated nouveau riche apartment once again, watched by him as he leans back onto the white leather sofa and draws a tumbler of bourbon to his lips.

It always makes me feel insane when men watch me without speaking. Irrational. A lunatic. With Sebastian, it makes my blood boil. With these two, I don't give a fuck. I'm gonna keep talking until one of these fools gets it, till one other human sees what a fucking danger the bitch is.

"It's not him." I catch Ilya's eye as he takes a seat on the arm of the sofa to my left, placing a glass of wine onto the oval glass coffee table. "It's *her*." I hear the low rumble in my voice, taking a breath before speaking again. "She's *infected* him like she did the others. He's not in control anymore. Can anyone but me see that?! Are your brains all still in your balls?! Are you all so enthralled by the idea of *fucking* her one day?! Well, it's not gonna happen, boys! It was a fucking *lie* from the start!"

Fuck.

I groan as my former accent ekes out as it always does when I'm irate and on the tip of losing control. I spent months and paid thousands to make sure all trace of it was erased, but the fucking thing refuses to die.

My glare flits from Ilya to his uncle Vallen, two men who don't know how to shut the fuck up suddenly so quiet. "Cat got your tongues?" I sneer.

"Well, this is about the time I'd usually tell a woman to calm the fuck down," smirks Vallen, "or *make* her... but seeing as it's you, *friend*, I'd like to avoid having my maid clean up broken glass tomorrow."

The fucker's broad grin makes me smile despite myself. Unlike with Sebastian, I'm not afraid of looking insane in front of Vallen, partly because I know that my insanity is matched by his.

Thank God.

I often wonder where all the certifiable ones went. Everyone's so fucking desperate to be sane these days. It's insipid in the extreme.

I don't respect Vallen the way I do Sebastian, but he's always been loyal to me, and he's still a highly competent fuck, one who understands my needs, and my limits. His nephew is getting there as well, and what I particularly enjoy about him is that he seems to be quite deranged, unabashedly so. There's nothing more tedious than a veritable freak who hides behind a pallid façade of decency.

Case in point, our famous Cameron O'Neill, the picture of civility, a man who makes all of Manhattan come in their pants with his poise and that fucking grace of his... a demonic freak in the sheets. If only they knew...

Perhaps he's just too smart to let the façade drop in public.

Smarter than me, clearly.

It's only thanks to my husband's power and reputation that I've managed to hang onto mine as long as I have. Oh, I know people talk about me, but they're very, very careful about who they do it with, very careful that their idle words don't make it back to me...

With Vallen and Ilya, I can be myself. I don't care what they think, and with what I know about both of them, they're in no position to judge either.

"She's dangerous, you know?" I continue, exhaling more smoke.

"You don't have to tell me," retorts Ilya, taking a long slow sip of wine. He breaks into the same toothy grin as his uncle as he puts it back down. The fucker knows I can't resist that impertinent smile of his. I usually prefer them younger, but this man gets hotter with every year that passes. He's one of the rare ones that has been diligent about honing his body, turning it into a machine. The men of the Society are all supposed to, but not all of them apply themselves with the fervor that young Ilya does.

His dirty-brown eyes twinkle mischievously as he watches me. He thinks this is fun and games, but this time, he's going to take me more seriously.

They *both* are. Someone has to. The men around here are all such fools when it comes to that fucking bitch. I'm not taking it anymore...

"She *humiliated* you, Mr. Markov. *Rejected* you."

"You don't need to remind me, Alex," he retorts, bitterness coarsening his voice. So he's still got a hair up his ass about it. That's what I need...

"And you can't manipulate me like that," he sings, causing my face to harden in a snap. I normally try to control my switches in mood, but I've been subjected to years of them by the Markov men, neither of whom are known for maintaining their sang froid. They'll have to deal with it...

I take a long drag of my cigarette, peering at Ilya over the flaring ash. The fucker thinks he's so damn smart...

My eyes wander to Vallen who grins in diabolical delight, enjoying my attempt at self-control in the face of such predicable insolence by Ilya.

Taking a second to compose myself, I put on my most measured voice, something which will no doubt amuse both of them.

"I'm not trying to *manipulate* you, Mr. Markov," I respond, my cheeks tense as I force a smile. "I'm just trying to point out to you cretinous fucking fools that if we don't do something, this woman is going to be the end of Sebastian. The end of our Society. She is going to destroy everything."

"Wow. The bitch sure is powerful," Ilya cackles, mocking my concern.

Vallen watches over me as I breathe through the insult to my judgment. "Alex has a point, Ilya. Her type and our type don't usually mix. It ends badly. And Sebastian clearly isn't in his right mind over her."

"The bitch is just teasing him, working him into a state," replies Ilya. "Once she's given in to him, he'll do what he always does—turn her into another fucking sub. Strip her of her power and self-esteem. And everything will go back to normal," he sings... as if this is some fucking joke.

"I don't think so," I reply. "Not this time. I've known him for thirteen years. I met him when he was twenty-two. I've seen the way he acts around her. The way he acts in general now. He's never been like this before. The man is clearly being tortured. Did you see him like this with Rose? He had his brain in his pants for five minutes before he got bored. Hell, he was bored before the wedding. He never looked at her the way he does our Mrs. Wilder."

"Once he fucks her, this'll be over," retorts Ilya, daring to sound irritated with me.

"I thought that about Cameron O'Neill. I thought his obsession with the pious little cunt would end once he'd finally got to turn her into his personal whore. It didn't. If anything, it's only made him more rabid. I know what she'll be like in bed. She's gonna pull the innocent whore-with-a-heart routine, and he's gonna lose his fucking mind over her like the others did. And all the while, she'll be plotting on how to take our president down. Take us all down."

"How exactly is she going to do that?" asks Vallen, sliding his hand over the back of the sofa.

"Well, for one, she's a journalist. *Thinks* she is, rather. Secondly, she will make Sebastian *weak*. Merciful. Pitiful. The Society will become some fucking joke. Some cheap swinger's club."

"Maybe it *has* become too dangerous?" Vallen suggests as my chest heaves in anger.

"You're kidding, right?"

He breaks into a grin, tumbling into dark laughter. "I'm disappointed you could possibly think I'd believe that, Alex."

"Well, that's where it's heading, Mr. Markov. She'll be pouring her poison into him about healing and forgiveness and all the other bullshit she spouts. She'll be trying to tame the fucker. Turn him into some pathetic fool."

A snigger from Ilya has my blazing eyes darting to him. "He's a murdering sadist with little to no capacity for empathy. He's not gonna turn into some feckless cuck, now, is he? For all we know, it's *her* that'll end up broken, not him. I mean, he does have a track record for that."

"Yeah, well, this bitch has ways about her that make normally sane men lose their shit."

"I can see why," retorts a grinning Ilya, enjoying my ire as I absorb the provocation.

"Do you not get tired of having your brain firmly lodged in your dick, Mr. Markov? Does it not bore you to tears to see how fucking *predictable* you are?" I ask, to his smile of dark appreciation. "I for one am not sitting on my ass doing fuck all while she sets about taking us all down."

"She doesn't have the power," retorts Ilya.

The arrogant little prick is just asking to be taught a lesson by someone.

"No. Maybe not alone. But O'Neill does. And she can get the fucker to do whatever the hell she wants. And he has the power to hurt us, not to mention that that man would raise hell itself to protect her. And he... well, you know how old he was when we—"

"Fucked?" Vallen suggests.

"Yeah, well, the hormonal fucker wanted it," I sneer.

"Oh, I bet," replies Vallen. "But, um, tell it to the judge, Alex."

"As you may have to yourself one day," I snarl, causing his face to tighten into a sinister glare. He has his own penchant for youth, only I'm not sure he's been as careful or self-restrained as I have tried to be in the last few years...

"He has that hanging over my fucking head," I continue. "And she could convince him to make a complaint. If he does that, I'm fucked, and depending on my mood, I may just take anyone who didn't take me seriously down with me."

Vallen's jaw tightens as he glowers back at me coldly. He looks angry, but I spy the concern hiding in the shadows of his pale face. He's got even more to worry about than me. I've tried to avoid the under-sixteens these last few years. I'm not sure *he* has. What's more, Sebastian has explicitly banned any member of the Society from engaging in acts with so-called minors. He doesn't know we've been getting around his instructions. If he were to find out, I'm not sure which would be more dangerous—the justice system, or his retribution.

As Vallen brings the tumbler to his lips, staring at me flatly, a blur of movement has me gasping.

"No!"

The fucker...

Before I can say another word, my face is shoved into the cushion of the armchair as Ilya Markov cackles maniacally, winding some rope he must have pulled off Vallen's freak wall while I was distracted around the arms he yanks roughly behind my back. As he ties it taut with a tug, I'm pulled back around to face him, forced onto the floor where I peer up at him.

His grin reaches his ears in that unabashed Markov way as he unzips his jeans and pulls out his erection. The thing is long and thick and hard and I salivate at the sight of it.

"The *cretinous fool* wants you to suck his dick," he jeers, leaning into me, forcing the head onto my lips, and tapping it.

He knows what I like...

"Make me," I snarl and he grabs my loose hair and pulls me into him, feeding his hard cock down my throat, glaring down at me with a twisted smile on his face as he drives into me over and over, tipping his head back in pleasure at some point, the deviant sound making me nice and wet.

Pulling his young cock out, he taps it against my cheek, slipping it in the saliva dripping down my chin, and sliding the head around my lower face before pushing it into my mouth once more and fucking it as I glare up at him. Upon a deep groan, he pulls out. "I think you need to be punished, Alex. Calmed down."

"You don't have what it takes, you ineffectual little fuck," I growl, only for him to break into a grin and pull me to my feet.

Towering over me, he grabs my hair, yanking my head back. "I'm gonna tear you a new one."

A second set of hands carries me kicking and screaming to Vallen's bedroom where my clothes are ripped off before I'm thrown onto the bed where Ilya begins to fuck me as Vallen pushes his cock down my throat. They snarl and grunt like wild animals, just as they know I like it, with Ilya cackling as he rides me like a fucking pig.

"Rougher," I order as Vallen takes up position behind me, jolting my limbs. "Hit me!"

Ilya slaps me in the face over and over as I'm forced to swallow his dick. "Spit on me!" I order as they begin to work up to the frenzy I like—loud, rough, violent, merciless. The sounds that of rabid pigs fucking.

It takes me back to the cold horror of one spring day in the early hours when I was fifteen years old. Only then, I had no control as they jeered and spat and laughed in my face, leaving me covered in them and trembling in the dirt as they ran away. That was the first time it happened, anyway... I screamed and cried, but with time, I started to like it... I didn't have much choice...

And anyway, *I* have the control now... and I'm gonna use it.

For a moment, everything freezes as I realize something that I try not to think about for fear that it makes me do something I'll spend my life in prison for...

It hits me, as it does several times a day, that I don't have the same control as I once did. Because of *her*. I once owned Cameron and Jackson, body and soul. They were my fucking slaves. They worshipped the ground I walked on. It was pitiful... and perfect.

She took that from me. She even took Sebastian. He doesn't look at me the same way as he did before. Something's changed. And she is going to pay for it...

As their cries and thrusts and groans become more savage, I close my eyes, moaning through the pain, relishing their pleasure until first Ilya and later Vallen finally ejaculate, shooting their load all over my face as they've been instructed to.

That's how I've taken my power back...

I watch the flame flicker before me as Vallen holds out his lighter to light my cigarette, flipping the gold top closed as I draw in the delicious toxic smoke, letting out a loud sigh of relief.

The sight of their naked bodies lying next to me arouses me not ten minutes after being spit-roasted till I was sore.

"You boys just get better and better. In fact, you're now officially my favorite fucks."

"Sebastian not performing?" sniggers Ilya to my left, his head on the pillow next to mine.

"I don't enjoy being fucked by a man who is contaminated by someone else," I respond flatly. "I don't enjoy it one fucking bit."

"Oh, well, don't fuck Jack, then," smirks Ilya.

"Nor O'Neill," deadpans Vallen to my right, taking my cigarette from me and inhaling the gray mist, blowing out its dregs before handing it back to me.

"Your husband not doing his job?" asks Ilya.

"The prick doesn't respect my boundaries."

"Yeah, Steven doesn't strike me as the type to bend the knee," smirks Vallen.

"No. The fuck does what he wants when he wants, and I just have to take it."

"Does he share your concerns over Jess?" asks Vallen.

"Don't call her that!" I snap. "She's not your fucking friend. She's a manipulative cunt who will cause no end of trouble."

"What do you want us to call her, Alex?" asks Ilya, derision loitering in his tone.

"The *cunt*," I jeer, making myself and Ilya laugh out loud as I spit out the word. "And no, my prick husband does not share my concerns. Not enough, anyway. The cretin's still thinking with his cock, as usual, still buying into the lie that one day he'll get to tie the bitch up like a hog roast and stuff and baste her little holes..."

I turn to find Vallen grinning widely as he watches me and I rub my hand over the taut muscles of his hard abdomen.

"You know," I breathe out as Ilya cackles at my joke. "There are many ways to get rid of someone..."

He suddenly goes quiet as I sit up, pivoting to face them.

I take a breath. I've been waiting for the right moment to tell them what needs to happen.

I need to get this right...

"If enough of us are committed to it, we can get rid of her. For good. No one has to know. It can be done fast, clean."

"Sebastian would find out," counters Vallen, running a hand through his thinning dark hair.

"How? If we all keep quiet, no one can find out. I know someone who has access to her. A drug overdose. Plain and simple. Happens every day. It's been done before, only this time, we'd be better at it. No one would ever have to find out.

"Every single one of our fucking problems would disappear. Our Society would be safe again. Sebastian would go back to being who he was born to be. Hell, maybe even Jack and Cameron could settle their differences while visiting the bitch in the ground... Maybe they'd need help with their grief... We could offer them that. You can't deny that they are two of the most powerful draws we've ever had. The place hasn't felt the same without them."

"Even O'Neill?" smirks Ilya and I turn my head to take in his pretty face.

"You know, just because I despise someone's guts so much that I want them dead, doesn't mean I don't want to be fucked by them till I can't think anymore. I mean, my husband's proof of that."

Vallen smirks, taking my half-dead cigarette from me, drawing in a last puff of smoke before stamping it out in the ashtray next to the bed.

"Plus," I continue. "Once she's gone and those two finally detox from her, they won't go around pretending to be *civilized* anymore. Fuck, they're both nauseating to witness. If she were out of the picture, they'd finally let themselves out of prison and give in to what they were always supposed to be—savage beasts who make our little family stronger. I'm sure I'd find O'Neill more palatable if he finally gave up the façade and admitted what a demonic freak he was."

"You're serious?" asks Vallen, narrowing his eyes. "About her."

"Deadly," I reply bitterly. "And so should you be. For all we know, she's writing notes about us as we speak. Maybe she's only spending time with Sebastian so she can finally expose us all... She knows about us, Vallen. She knows what we like. I'm certain of that. Every day we ignore this problem is another day we're waiting for the police to roll up on our door."

He stares at me grimly.

Well, look at that...

I think I may have finally got him...

Even Ilya seems to be taking the bait.

"There is another option," I suggest. "Our little friend has a tendency to get into cars with strangers these days. She's been trained to by Sebastian. But... what if a car came along one day, and she was instructed to enter, told that Sebastian was waiting for her... and then, she was taken on a little ride. I know a place. It's in the woods. Private property. It belongs to a... friend of mine. Very naughty man. Very bad. It's the perfect place to store someone. It's isolated. There's a basement with... shackles. Chains. No windows. A series of locked doors. Cameras. No way out.

"It's a place where you could take someone if they were never to be found. And you two could visit her *whenever* you wanted to. And there are men who would pay for that pleasure...

"Can you imagine her little face? Can you imagine the begging? The pleading? The tears? Can you imagine how much fun you could have with that tight little body? That cock-sucking mouth... You two could spend weekends with her. You could hurt her as much as you wanted. I guarantee it would be the single most transcendent experience of your lives. You'll never have experienced pleasure like that before.

"And if things become too risky, we're in a forest. She would be buried without a trace."

Vallen shakes his head. "It's too risky. If Sebastian—"

"Fuck Sebastian!" I gnarl. "He's not protecting us! We have to protect ourselves before it's too late and we'd wished we'd done something sooner! We don't have to take her. Maybe I was getting ahead of myself with that one. An overdose in her own apartment. That's all we need. I know how to get that done. I'm putting myself out there with this. I want you on board. I want someone to show me some fucking loyalty for once."

They glance at each other before turning to face me.

I wait until Vallen finally speaks. "How would it be done?"

"Which plan?"

"Both."

43

Darragh
Present

"What do you think, Father?"

Samara peers up at me with small eyes as pale as blue ice. I know she doesn't give a fuck what I think. The feigned reverence is one of many tools she uses to make herself palatable, to make herself seem like some meek, pitiful woman, one who doesn't really pull strings, play with people, whisper poison into Sebastian's ear.

If he were a weaker man, I'd be more concerned about her influence. As it is, I know he sees through her just as I do, sees through the toxic words, the sinister threats dissimilated behind shields of ashy smoke. That doesn't mean that her efforts are inconsequential. It just means that she has to work harder to steer the ship in the direction she believes it should go.

The ship is the Society, and at its helm, a man she is bonded to in a way that is unhealthy for either of them. She joined the Society over thirty years ago as a young woman, making her way up the ranks until she became a Council member through her fervent loyalty to Quercus

Velutina and her ability to choose what would turn out to be profitable and faithful patrons.

Her beauty was a thing of great note forty years ago, something she used to her great advantage, and as her power has waned over the years, her cunning has morphed, for she is sadly no longer able to harness her beauty as she once could. Her erstwhile histrionics became less tolerable for others to stomach with age, so she has reincarnated herself most deftly into a version that is bearable to those around her. The mask she wears is of the sage, the wise woman, the counsel.

Her energy is not benevolent. Pretending to be so would not fool the sophisticated patrons of such a place. But the mask she wears is one of wisdom and experience, things they can just about get on board with, especially when her delivery is so smooth, the tone so caring... if you didn't know her better.

She has children of her own—one daughter, two sons—but her lifeblood has always been the Society. Her children haven't come close to consuming her the way this place has, the way Sebastian has.

She and Alexandra brought him into it when he was a damaged young man thirsty for blood, for retribution. He was in his early twenties, she her early forties, going through a divorce. She pulled him in, gave him power, pleasure, connections. She believed in him.

He'd not experienced the love of a mother. It makes men vulnerable, desperate for women, or desperate for a woman who will fill that role. She did—that of mother, and lover, for her tastes were well known and he was an eager student with a willing subject ready to let him practise, to ease his pain, to choke, to cut, to drown—to do what would soothe the hellfire for brief moments.

I could not have imagined that so many years later, she would still be his confidante. I wonder sometimes if he allows it because she knows too much, or if he still needs her—still has this hope of being seen as valuable, as a son of God, something that he never experienced as a child. He was born to a woman who saw only the hell of his existence. This one sees him as a deity, destined for great things.

Alexandra also, despite her bitterness, still believes him to be a God.

She still worships him, is enslaved by dreams of him being devoted to her as ardently as she is to him.

And then, there's a third woman, one who sees him as a man and not a God, nor a demon. One who appears to torment him much more than I had ever realized. It seemed unfathomable at first—the great Sebastian Gravier, the sadist, the sociopath, capable of falling for someone. It seemed like the build-up to some cruel joke whose punchline would be delivered like the falling blade of a guillotine.

But it may be true...

I had always believed that he needed to feel like a God, to sit above the pitiful foibles of humans, but did he just, in fact, need to feel like a man? To feel human?

"I believe that our President has an inner voice that will speak to him, that will show him the path," I respond as her dark eyes drift to the man beside us, a man who watches her without a shred of emotion registering on his face.

I wonder what he sees when he looks at her. Does he see a woman? A specter? Darkness? Is he afraid of her, as I am in moments when my faith is weak?

I still believe myself to be a man of God despite the proclivities that are serviced by this place. I try to follow the path. I don't always succeed, but one thing I do know is that this small, frail, unassuming woman is possessed by dark matter, dark energy and no amount of prayer or exorcism will get it out of her.

I used to think that of Sebastian, but something has changed of late —or perhaps I've just come to see what I always suspected—almost imperceptible remnants of light. The tiniest flame in a forest shrouded in black mist that stretches farther than the eye can see.

But then, I have thought that at times before only to watch that flame extinguish and see him carry out deeds that have chilled me, forcing me into weeks of prayer, forcing me to try to find God again. Sebastian is not one man. There are beings that dwell inside him. Psychologists may say they are fragments of a broken, abused psyche. The spiritual may say they are entities attracted to misery and trauma.

Sin incarnate, evil hiding behind a frail armor of ice—the human shell, the dregs of him held in chains deep beneath the surface.

I believe that demons live inside him—but can only do so for as long as Sebastian will let him.

They will hunger for her death.

He has to fight…

"Your loyalty must be to the Society, Sebastian," she says, peering up at him as if in reverence. "Not to any man, or any woman. But to *us*. She's a danger. She's a danger to everything we stand for."

"I see you've joined the ranks of those concerned about my ability to lead."

"Of course I haven't," she snaps, her long hair black in the low light. "I believe in you, Sebastian. I always have. I just think that this woman is… leading you from the right path. She's sent to test us. She's the work of the devil."

"I seem to recall you saying the same about my departed wife…"

"She was the devil's work too," Samara whispers. "I can spot them a mile away."

"From what I've learned of you, friend," he says, his eyes never leaving hers, "you seem to despise *all* women that don't capitulate to you instantly. It makes your judgment questionable."

"I don't—" She breathes out heavily in irritation. "This woman is no good, Sebastian. She needs to be dealt with thoroughly. She's married to another man, an important patron, no less. Where do you think this will go exactly? Why take the risk when so many people object to this?"

"She allows me to breathe," he responds. "To feel."

"This place, our family, that is what lets you do those things. Not *her*. I believe, as a woman who cares so much about you, that she has to be dealt with."

"How exactly?" he growls.

"Banished from this place. You must never see her again."

Sebastian's eyes flit to mine. "What is your opinion on this matter?"

"I would like to get to know this woman better," I respond.

"Why?"

"To understand what I'm dealing with."

"You saw her briefly?"

"Yes. With Miss Vass."

"You must have picked up something."

"Yes. She is a... gilded spirit. A bringer of light."

His eyes narrow.

"And that is why she may be a danger," I respond. "For all of us. Our Society is about pleasure, about liberation, but it functions in the shadows. It does not take kindly to light."

In fact, in this case, I believe that the collision of dark and light will lead to nothing but the morass of chaos.

"Exactly," Samara breathes. "She's an *affliction*. A drug. She has to be *handled*. Permanently."

His eyes darken as Samara suggests something that was once proposed for another problem we faced—his ex-wife's infatuation with Cameron O'Neill which led to her desire for a divorce that would have been most risky... for all of us.

"Anyone touches that fucking girl," he growls, "and—"

"No one will, Sebastian," I reply. "But we rely on you. You are our leader. We know you will make the right choice. For our family."

"He *will*," affirms Samara.

44

Grace
Present

Meeting Cameron's bright eyes after so long steals my breath for a moment. He has this way of fixing you with his gaze and not unlocking it from your face until you can't handle the heat anymore and have to look away. Sebastian has it too, though there's something more chilling, more calculated, about the way he looks at you, studies you.

I glance behind Cameron to see two tall men that I've met before—Aaron on the left, his deep olive skin warm in the light of the corridor, and Christian to the right, skin pallid as usual, clashing with jet-black hair and shadowy eyes.

"Ready?" I ask, determined not to show one ounce of fear nor intimidation.

"Ready," Cameron replies and I turn on my steel-capped heels to lead them down the corridor of this private members' club on the Upper East Side.

It's not a club the likes of Quercus Velutina. It's an altogether more civilized establishment designed for social interaction only. Elegant classical music plays softly from hidden speakers. Food and drinks are served on trays of silver which are placed on lacquered furniture from a century ago.

Neutral ground was needed for this meeting, and that meant a safe place for both parties, a public place where everyone would be seen on entering... and *hopefully* on leaving.

Upon walking through the opulent lounge, making some small talk with some well-to-do members of this private social club, Cameron and his men joined me in the corridor leading to the private room that we hired for the meeting.

My nerves have been jangling for the last few hours as we waited for them to get here. I know it had to happen. I'm torn between thinking it's a mistake, the biggest mistake Sebastian has ever made, and thinking that something had to give, to change. The tension between the two of them has been mounting for months, if not years at this point.

I just wish I could shake this feeling that something is going to go badly wrong, for one of them, at least.

When I think of them, all I see is blood.

I'm praying that they can come to some kind of understanding, but knowing one of them as well as I do, I'd say that's unlikely, or rather that any semblance of understanding is nothing more than a trap. He won't tell me. He never tells me what's happening until it's too late in the game to change anything, and I'm a deer in the headlights, unable to think, compliant because I don't know what else to do.

The sound of Cameron's footsteps behind me takes me back to years of leading this VIP down corridors at the Society, my body buzzing with anticipation as it always did when he was in the house.

On those days, the whispers of him being there would spread throughout the building like wildfire. The women would seek him out in rooms to the point that we had to set limits on how many could enter. Women who once had hard limits as to what they would endure at that place were suddenly open for anything. *Literally*.

When he was younger, his tastes were more pedestrian, but as he approached his mid-twenties, the rooms he chose were of the more extreme variety and required being equipped with the kind of bondage, restraint, and disciplining devices you would expect to see in Sebastian's rooms of choice.

He had a way about him that was unusual—a grace that not all the men there had, especially not one as wealthy or powerful as him. His presence was utterly devastating, particularly when the elegant façade peeled away to reveal a deviant with singular tastes.

I've missed it.

I've missed him...

While deviant, he had a sense of morality, of decency, something sorely lacking in some of the Council members, namely Dominic, Steven, Samara, Vallen, and Alexandra, vampires who ensure that Sebastian has free reign to cast the place in his vision.

Cameron was a moderating force despite his needs, and the tension festering between him and Sebastian became apparent when he was still in his late teens.

We all felt it. We all heard the ticking of the bomb.

And then... Rose.

And the first explosion. I would have thought it would have been the end of him, but Cameron has proven remarkably resistant. Most young men would have crumbled under the drugs, the nightmares, the stalking, the violence, the weight of eyes on you, the realization of the trauma you've been subjected to.

But he didn't... or not quite.

Maybe he would have if he hadn't met Jess, for I know that it is she who pulled him out of the worst of the darkness.

Unfortunately for him, he's not the only man who feeds off her light. There are three of them, including the man whom he is about to meet. And I know that this time, the blast that will ensue will spill blood.

I shouldn't be this scared...

Luckily, my hand doesn't quiver as I reach for the door handle, turning to face Cameron whose eyes flit to meet mine, his expression grave, angry perhaps, but he doesn't look nervous, nor afraid, or if he is those things, he's hiding them well which it's best to do in front of a man like Sebastian who feasts off panic like no one else, and who can taste it in the water from a mile away.

I take a deep breath and open the door to find three men standing together near the back wall—Isaiah and Dimitri, speaking in hushed tones to Sebastian.

As I enter, holding the door open for Cameron and his men, Sebastian turns, his eyes flaring at the sight of a man he abhors, a man who triggers him, ignites his every inadequacy, reminds him of the injustice he endured as a boy. A man he once cared for, educated, spent time with, trusted. A man who lives in the heart of the only woman he has ever truly bonded with in a way that wasn't steeped in evil.

Sebastian walks slowly towards the table in the center of the room, waiting for Cameron to approach.

Aaron and Christian take up position on the near wall to my right opposite Isaiah and Dimitri, four men who could do each other serious damage.

My heart stalls as Cameron makes it to within six feet of Sebastian, a man I believe he last saw when he was beaten in that forest in front of her. When they told me about it, I couldn't sleep for days. This isn't how it was meant to be, but it is how it is. I'm too far in. They'd never let me out. I know way too much for that.

And anyway, where would I go? What would I do after seeing things like this for so many years? After yielding this much power? What kind of life could I have? Would I even want to go back to the monotony of regular life after all I've seen?

I watch, holding my breath as Cameron walks towards Sebastian, the tension heightened by years of rage coursing through him, ire matched by Sebastian who will no doubt conceal it better, as he so often does. He can be poised to your face while plotting destruction. I've seen it. It's terrifying.

"Cameron," Sebastian says, bowing his head slightly.

Cameron doesn't follow suit, glaring at the man who has been a constant in his life since he was a teenager, whether close by or from afar. Their lives have been intertwined for years, never more so than now, with the blood of one woman pulsing through their veins.

I walk towards them, glancing at the table, double-checking that they have water in closed bottles and glasses.

"Do you need anything else from me?" I ask as Sebastian takes a seat on a thick burgundy armchair.

"No. Thank you, Grace."

"I'll leave you then. Just... call if you need anything."

He tips his head before lifting his eyes to study Cameron, one of the wealthiest and most powerful men in Manhattan, scion of one of the country's most prestigious families, a man who runs an empire, but is held hostage by the cruel wrath of a man he slighted—a man whose wife Cameron could have taken, a man who was born into the hell of parental abuse while Cameron was born into a loving family who worshipped him. I suspect that above all else, it is that fact that turns Sebastian's vision red when he thinks of him, staining it with the blood of jealous torment that all abuse victims struggle not to feel towards those untainted the way they are.

Jack has slighted Sebastian as well but does not elicit the same rancor, presumably because Jack too knows the cold sorrow of childhood abuse. These damaged people are the ones that Sebastian gravitates to, understands, accepts. The pristine beauty of the love and acceptance that Cameron received as a child is a vicious knife that cuts into Sebastian's flesh, even if the perpetrator of that wound is not Cameron himself, who is innocent of any crime, but Sebastian's own mother who despised every beautiful piece of him from the second she held him in her arms.

I leave the room, closing it behind me and walking swiftly down the hall to the next room down, opening it with the utmost care so as to avoid any necessary clicks. I close and lock it behind me, taking up position in front of the one-way mirror looking out over their elegant windowless room.

"I didn't think he'd come..."

Cameron has taken a seat opposite Sebastian and is watching him, his face hard, his hands curled over the ends of his armchair, one leg crossed over the other. I don't know if he suspects I can see them. I'm sure he does. He knows how the Society operates. I doubt he cares, but the thought that he may glance at the mirror, may lock eyes with me through it, telling me taciturnly that he knows I'm there, chills me to my core...

Or maybe he would want that...

We were friends once, of sorts. He confided in me a few times. He spoke to me after he left. I did try to help him, but I was too afraid to do more. And later, he paid me large sums of money to give him certain information, and though I was terrified, I took it. I don't know why. I didn't need it. I just couldn't say no to him. No woman can.

I don't believe Sebastian ever found out. If he had, I would have paid for it by now... unless he's biding his time. I've seen him wait years to mete out punishment, the subject of it never imagining that in the darkness, he was plotting revenge...

I clutch the edge of the narrow table before me, shuddering at the sight of these two men, so powerful, their enmity so palpable. Whatever happens between them will change so much...

"Shhh."

I quiver at the order from behind me as a hand snakes around my belly, pulling me into a hard frame at my back.

"I never thought I'd see this day," he whispers into my ear.

"I know," I whisper back. "I honestly can't believe he came."

Cameron

His face is so familiar to me. I feel like I see it day and night, see it until her face floats over my field of vision, erasing him, as he should be...

I stare into the eyes of the man who meets me in dreams, standing over me, watching as I bite into flesh, as I tear bloody tissue from it, as I plunge knives into people whom I love–*her;* watching as life drains from her, and her eyes, as vibrant as glistening ocean water in the shallows, turn to coal.

Jessynia...

He doesn't move as per usual, his face expressionless but for the sharp blast of curiosity that his gray eyes can't conceal. They roam over my face, drinking me in as they always have, since that first day I met him and shook inside at the sight of him.

"It's good to see you, Cameron," he dares to utter, this man who has taken so much from so many. From me. "Though I see that Jack likes to hit hard."

He must see the cut on my lip, the kind of which he once enjoyed inflicting upon me himself...

"It was mutual," I retort, my jaw tight as the veins and arteries under his pale skin grow vivid before my eyes, pumping blood, blood I could purge from his body with one sharp cut the likes of which I've dreamed of for longer than I can remember.

My eyes lift to take in Isaiah, his soldier, rabid in his loyalty, his dark-brown eyes piercing me. Next to him is a man I don't know, but from what I've been told, his name is Dimitri, and his salary has multiplied tenfold since he came to work for the Society.

Those types can be bought...

"Yes, I saw his blood," he replies. "And his distress."

"That too was mutual," I counter.

"Oh, I can imagine that. It seems that some people are destined to draw each other's blood."

His utterance would purport to be about Jack, but I know better. I know he is talking about us, me and him. And I've known for some time that our final destination will be one which drowns in blood.

The blood of Black Oak.

"What do you want from her?" I spit out as his eyes flare, their silvery flame flooding my body with wrath that I no longer know how to control.

Fuck.

I didn't mean to speak of her so fast. I didn't mean to look so enraged. I can't control it. The thought of him with her, speaking to her, touching her, something I can no longer do, leaves me off-kilter, unstable. The thought of him pouring his perfidious poison into her, a woman so pure by our standards, leaves me ready to kill. To die.

I've seen death in my dreams of late.

Her death.

I've dreamed of it before, of hurting her, of choking her, of drowning her, watched over by *them*, but never quite like this.

The visions are so clear that they imprint themselves on my mind for hours afterwards. I see myself chasing her, sometimes through dark rooms, sometimes through the woods, ravenous, on the brink of starvation, unable to stop, my body hungry for her blood, my tongue aching for the taste of it, for its force, the only thing that could keep me alive.

She can't stop it. She can't run fast enough. I scream for her to run in one breath, and hunt her down in the next. I watch her plead as I hold her, watch her tears as I move my teeth onto her neck, feel her tremble as I bite into her, her body quivering as I begin to suck on the blood, famished for it, needing it all to stay alive. I lay her down on the earth, hitch up her dress and fuck her shaking body as I siphon the blood from the gash like a wild animal, until suddenly I look up to see her eyes, but instead of the deep blue, they are black, spheres of obsidian staring back at me, all light extinguished.

And the sight jolts me awake each time, leaving me heaving in the darkness, my voice often hoarse from having screamed in ignominious terror.

I'm lucky if I have nightmares like that. At other times, I watch myself push the metal blade into her sternum, through her ribs, the blood dripping out as I thrust it into her heart.

Her tiny voice shakes me awake. "I love you."

I've had nightmares for years, but never so frequently, and never seeing the same person in them over again.

Rose haunted me for some time, but even her dreams pale in comparison to what I see now.

Jessynia...

She has been marked for death by someone. I can feel it.

I can taste it.

The blood.

Her blood.

Sebastian's lips curve ever so slightly. "You never were good at small talk, Cameron. We have that in common, amidst so much else."

"What do you want?" I repeat. "With that girl?"

"I'm sure you would have hoped your delivery would be more restrained," he replies, his skin pale, his countenance as poised as ever. "You must really be in torment."

"What do you want?"

He shrugs slightly, his head tipping forwards, just a little. "Truth be told, I'm not so sure anymore."

"Bullshit."

"She breaks the usual rules, Cameron," he returns, eyes gleaming at the provocation.

"I know you," I sneer. "I know what you are, what you want. You can only survive when you cause pain and suffering and misery."

Like a vampire...

"As I said," he replies. "She breaks the rules."

"Does Jack know about you two? That you see her?"

"He knows a little."

"And does nothing," I sneer. "I would expect nothing less."

"There is nothing he can do," he replies. "If he takes her away without my authorization, I will find them. I will hunt them down. No one leaves without following protocol."

"It shouldn't be that way," I reply, my jaw tense.

"So I've been told," he smiles darkly.

Jess...

I know what he's alluding to. I know it's *her* that told him that. I can see it. I can hear the words she would say to him. I can see her face as she pleads with him.

"Unfortunately, that's what happens when demons take control," he continues, his body still, his eyes fixed to mine, unblinking, drinking me in.

"Why does she see you?" I ask. "What does she want?"

"She wants you freed, Cameron. You're a lucky man. You have a woman desperate to free you from danger. Unfortunately, she is just as desperate to free another man."

My hands curl around the ends of the armchair, gripping them tightly to stop myself from doing what I have dreamed of doing for years.

I no longer care what happens to me.

He has to pay...

"Is that why you're asking me to return?" I ask. "Because she wouldn't want it? Have you not caused her enough pain as it is?"

"The current stand-off has not proven beneficial to either of us."

"The stand-off exists because *you* refuse to let go of a woman who you know you will destroy. Not to mention that you have spent years refusing to let me live some semblance of a normal life."

"Perhaps, Cameron. Or perhaps it exists because you never fully left... You never fully left a place that can cater to your needs. Your... *special* needs. Did you? That's why *you* took her back. *You* did that. Alone. No one else. You opened a door that had been shut."

"She begged me to take her," I reply through gritted teeth.

"Sometimes, we must say no to protect the ones we love."

"Not a subject you're an expert in, Sebastian," I snarl, feeling my chest rising and falling beneath my suit.

Sebastian bows his head slowly as I glance at the black wedding ring that he still dares to wear in front of me. "Touché."

"Do you know what has happened to her?" I ask in the face of glacial eyes. "Do you know she has nightmares? Do you know the trauma she's endured? The terror over her family? Do you know what it did to her to force her back to her husband like that?"

"I am aware that she has suffered," he replies. "She has willingly chosen to love dangerous men. There is a price to pay for that. She is not innocent anymore. None of us are."

"And I suppose you get off on her pain, like everyone else's?"

"Should I pander to you, Cameron? Deny the pleasure I feel from her pain? I don't think I'm alone in that, am I?"

For a moment, I see a flash of a life I once lived, of dark rooms with women bound for my pleasure, with gasps of pain as I would bite and discipline and choke, leaving the place tormented at what I'd done... only to return the next day, drugged, unable to say no to something that once made me feel so alive...

"I don't take pleasure in her pain," I bite back.

"I have seen one of the marks you left on her with my own eyes," he replies, narrowing his eyes. "You would bite into her skin and then deny that you gain pleasure from the act. How very disappointing of you, Cameron."

My breathing quickens as I feel my teeth sink into her soft flesh and hear her gasp at the bite.

"What happens during consensual sexual acts is no comparison to the suffering *you* like to cause. I don't try to cause her emotional pain."

"And yet you *do*," he sneers. "You could walk away, stop her torment over you. Stop her guilt over her husband. Allow her to rebuild her marriage. You don't. You refuse to acknowledge that despite the manner of her return, she worships Jack. You make her life painful to navigate. Impossible."

"She is not back with that *so-called* husband out of *choice*. You made that fucking decision for her. For as long as that is the case, she is not married in my eyes. She is in *prison*. And until I know she is free of fear, I will not allow a woman like that to live that way. Not again."

"Hmm," he smiles as I allude to the fear Rose endured during the last weeks of her life. "And I supposed you intend to get her out?"

"Out of the clutches of a man who feasts off her pain."

He contemplates my words for a moment, breathing out a long breath. "That's the thing, Cameron. Her pain also torments me."

His words steal my breath. "*Bullshit*."

"I told you," he utters, eyes flaring, "she breaks the rules."

"I don't believe you."

"The truth of the matter is that we've spent time together in recent months. It has changed things..."

"Why? What do you want from her? Or is it just to fuck with me? Take revenge on me for a situation that *you* designed."

In a rare lapse in sang froid, he grimaces, just the tiniest amount, as I evoke Rose.

But I see you, Sebastian...

"I can't deny that your feelings for her were once of great appeal to me." Heat trickles into my chest as I try not to succumb to the rage I feel. "Things have changed since then."

"Let me guess... She soothes your demons, right?" I scoff in contempt.

"Unfortunately not," he replies softly, eyes narrowing. "She soothes my rage, my hatred, my pain, but she provokes my demons, Cameron. She enrages them. She torments them. They writhe in agony inside me when she is near. I can hear them screaming. They. Want. Her. Blood."

His eyes flare, gleaming at the hollow fear I know is registering in my face.

"Then, why don't you let her go?" I ask.

"I may well yet," he answers, his deep voice coarsening. The sound takes me back to years of his heinous breaths as he would teach me his methods of procuring pleasure, with no shortage of willing subjects to practise on.

"Why did you ask me back?"

"It has occurred to many of us in our family that we could do each other a lot of damage."

"*More* damage," I correct, and Sebastian tips his head in concession.

"Yes. *More* damage."

"Not something that has stopped you in the past. Why now?"

"Perhaps I'm not the same man I was," suggests Sebastian.

"Perhaps?" scoffs Cameron. "You either know, or you don't."

"It's not as simple as that for me, Cameron, as *you* of all people should know. You are like me in ways that you despise, but which are undeniable nonetheless. You know full well what we have inside us. What we have to fight every day. Your beast torments you as mine does me. Or am I wrong? Has he gone away?" he asks, wild eyes gleaming as he evokes the thing inside me that speaks to me sometimes, that calls to me, that wants pleasure without conscience, that wants me to fall, to embrace what Sebastian would offer—pleasure and power without consequence.

"I don't hurt people the way you do," I spit back.

"Maybe your demons are not as savage as mine."

"Or perhaps I'm just stronger than you, Sebastian."

"Perhaps. Though the tools we were equipped with as children were not exactly the same..."

I breathe through the insinuation, through the bitterness, the rage I know he feels towards me for our disparate childhoods. I would tell him that his abuse was not my fault, but his abuser's, his mother's, but I have told him that before. He knows it logically, but it doesn't stop the rancor. It is the reason he tolerates Jack so much better than me. The abuse Jack suffered, an abuse Sebastian made him explain in great detail for his pleasure, placates him, allows him to breathe.

"Have you had time to consider our offer, Cameron?" Sebastian asks. "And the conditions for your return, as well as our guarantees."

"The conditions were more lenient than I had expected," I reply, "and the guarantees more generous."

"We want you back."

"Why?" I ask, my breathing quickening. "Why the fuck would you want that when you know how I feel about you? When you know what I think you are. What you want... When you know what I believe you deserve? I want an answer, and not one that involves me suspending disbelief about your new-found humanity. I know what the fuck you are. I know it better than anyone. Why now?"

"Perhaps I wish to do you a favor," he suggests as my brow draws tight. "I have informed Jessynia that the only way I would permit you to see her is within the structure of our Society. I have no doubt that plays on her mind... as it must yours."

"You have no fucking right to dictate who she sees and when!"

"I could give her to you, Cameron. Alone. No interruptions. Her husband would not be informed. I can give you something that you will be permitted to enjoy without the gravest of consequences for both of you..."

Grace

"Would he really come back?" I whisper as he slides his hands up my neck, breathing me in.

"It seems so," he whispers back, his lips slipping against my temple.

Darragh's erection presses into my back, pulsing over and over.

"We can't," I whisper, quivering as I watch Cameron's jaw tense through the mirror, his hands coil around the arms of the chair. "Not here."

"I want you tonight." His deep voice murmurs, making me shiver as he unbuttons my shirt, letting my breasts spill out and fondling them, pulling at my nipples.

"Shit!"

He's looking.

Sebastian.

Looking at the mirror as if looking through it... *right at me*.

He can't see through, but he *knows* what we're doing back here. He senses everything I do as if he owns me. Plus, he knows what our priest is like—how deviantly and often he needs to fuck while battling with God to show him a path that makes sense more than that offered to him by the devil.

Darragh's hand slides over my mouth to stop any noise escaping me, not that I would really let it, not with Sebastian so close by. He knows that Darragh and I have been close for years, but I would not dare to expose him to it while I'm working like this.

I breathe out in relief as he turns back to look at Cameron, a situation already sinister enough.

I already made a fool of myself around Sebastian once, dropping to my knees in front of him in the midst of a tense conversation. I have no fucking idea what came over me. I've never done that with any other man, not like that. He was disappointed in something I had done, and while explaining the error of my ways to me, I couldn't stop myself.

He stood over me as I opened my mouth, watching in silence as I blushed in humiliation and in anticipation of finally getting to taste him... but instead of letting me, he ordered me to my feet and told me to get out.

I was sure he would fire me, but he didn't. I was so mortified that I didn't know how to look him in the eye for months. I still barely do. But I'm caught in this trap, addicted to the power of this place, to its darkness, and scared that I know too much and won't be let out, scared of its monsters. Of him. I feel sure that one day, retribution will be handed down to me for some of my sins, for conversing with Cameron and others who have left. I couldn't help it. I couldn't help feeling like one day I would be free.

It was on the heels of Sebastian's rejection of me that I succumbed to Darragh, relieved to feel the release of sex with a man so poised, a holy man, one who is familiar with evil, who knows that once you've faced it, you're never the same again.

I don't love him, nor does he love me, but he soothes me, and that's enough, especially now.

I have a bad feeling about what's happening.

I can't shake it.

The collision of these two men can only lead to disaster, and yet it seems like they both want it, that they've both been waiting for it their whole lives.

Sebastian

I am not sure that I had quite expected to see this degree of pain in his face. A shadow is painted under both eyes and his appearance, despite the suit, is unkempt by his exacting standards, not something I've witnessed in this man for a long time.

He is known all over Manhattan, talked about, photographed. He mustn't care enough what people think anymore... a state I've wished him to return to for a long time... other than his utter degradation. His long-overdue destruction.

"Do you want to see her, Cameron? Be alone with her? There is only one way that you will ever touch her again without her being in fear of being caught. That is if *I* allow it."

His body tenses as I make the provocation, imprisoning the woman he loves.

The anger visibly rattling his body is exquisite, but there is something else—fear. A plea. One that dilutes his strength, for I know what he's afraid of. He's afraid of succumbing to the darkness before he can save her. I experienced that same fear as a teenager in the months following my arrest and imprisonment when I was alone but for older men watching me, moving me, confirming that I was what I had been told I was since the day I was born—less than human.

At first, they were quiet—whispers. Voices unknown to me. They spoke kind words of comfort initially, until their utterances became more brutal, more sinister, unsettling me, taking hold, filling me with rabid rage, requiring blood to placate them, to allow me to settle in my own body.

I was afraid of them at first. I was afraid to close my eyes for fear of seeing them—eyes red like blood, bodies black, limbs twisting in pain, in malice. And then her. Her face. Her wicked smile. I saw her inside me as if she were still alive.

Throughout my childhood, I had been kept in isolation by the woman who had birthed me, so by the time I was put away, there were no visitors to come to see me like the other boys. The voices were the only thing there.

I would try to distract myself from them any way I could, begging for them to stop, to give me one moment of reprieve from the hell of their voices, their whispers, their screams...

I asked for help from the medical staff, but the pills they gave me only enraged the demons, entrenching them further until the day I closed my eyes and let them speak.

After two years of concrete and steel, the evil words began to sound like a lullaby. They would cradle me. They would allow me to breathe... as long as I no longer resisted.

So I didn't.

And little by little, I began to enjoy their way of seeing the world, their plans, their utter contempt for humanity in all its horror, injustice and hypocrisy.

And by the time I was released from the system, they and I were one. They gave me power and abilities that most people could not conceive of. They took my soul, and until recently, I have felt no desire to get it back.

I still don't want it.

I know the hell of hope, of vulnerability, of needing to be loved.

I will not let myself succumb to that ever again.

As for Mr. O'Neill, I know there is something inside him—a beast. A demon. It also whispers. It taunts him with the potential of what he could be, with the promise of absolute pleasure, of being worshipped like a God. I know he leans into the temptation of it—the dark beauty.

He is afraid he is going to fall.

I intend to make that happen.

"Why on Earth would you want me back?" he asks, his face burning with rage, "if you've *bonded*, as you say you have..."

In truth, I no longer know whether I can stomach watching them in the same room, can stomach the way they must look at each other. But a fear that torments me is that when she succumbs to me, it will be in a moment of weakness that she regrets. That would not be acceptable to me. I want her to belong to us, to accept her place in our Society. I want her to give in to the darkness inside her, inside me. To revel in it. The things I want to do to her require an absence of shame, of guilt. They require that she give herself up completely, willingly, desperate to be educated by me. Desperate for what I can do to her. Desperate to be impregnated by me. Nothing short of that will satiate me.

Without Mr. O'Neill's assistance, I fear that she will not make it to this state. Her resistance, her sense of morality, of conscience, they will prevent her from belonging to me.

I believe that once he begins to fall, to embrace the darkness once again, she will need me to hold her as she watches over it. I know that once I fuck her quivering body, she will never be able to say no to me again.

If that means sharing her for a short time with him, and with her husband, then so be it. I can not deny that I have dreamed of nights when all three of us ravage her bound, brutalized, trembling body in the dark where she cannot see. What's more, I know she hungers for it —the part of herself she can not reconcile. I can feel it.

This has to be done...

"I know it will pain you to hear this, Cameron," I respond, taking in every perfect note of the distress he tries so hard to conceal, "but I could take her for myself. I've been close several times." His face hardens so beautifully. "But her shame and her guilt are unacceptable to me. Your presence can help with that. I want her to claim who she is, just as I want that for you."

"So you can destroy me like before..."

"I didn't *destroy* you, Cameron. You did that to yourself by fighting the inevitable. Fighting who you were born to be."

"She would not let me fall, Sebastian."

"Oh, I'm sure she would fight it, but I'm not sure she can resist the dark lord that you were supposed to be."

"Why the fuck would you want that if you desire her so much? And when you know what I believe you deserve?"

"Because I have faith."

He frowns, peering into me for an answer.

"Faith," I continue, "that you will finally embrace who you are when you remember what is offered to you, when you remember the power you were supposed to yield over others. When you finally stop hiding who you are. Finally break down that hideous façade of civility and banality that you wear. Finally become what you were meant to be, when you realize that you will never fully own her the way you want to in your current state. She will never recover from her guilt over her husband even if you do take her, nor will she be able to resist her desire for me. You can not own her any other way."

"And what if you're wrong?"

I let him dare speak to me like this, with such disdain, for I know that with time, he will succumb to the voice that has whispered to him his whole life, the beast that dwells inside him, desperate to be uncaged. I will give him power, access to pleasure he can't procure elsewhere, not in the same unrestrained way. Once he lets go of his need to be civilized, once she sees what he really is, she will either succumb to her fear and try to escape him, or she will submit to his dominance... and to mine...

In any case, my plans for him have not changed.

No matter what happens, he is going to pay for the injuries done to me.

In blood.

And he will not stand up again.

"So be it, Cameron."

Grace

"Are you scared?" Darragh whispers.

"Yes," I reply. "Something bad is going to happen. I can feel it." I turn around to look up at him. "Do you feel it as well?"

"Yes," he nods. "I feel it."

"What do you do when you're afraid?"

"I pray," he responds, his hand tugging at my naked breast. "And hope that God still listens to me."

45

Jessynia

"I swear to God, I've never had a man put his clothes on that fucking fast."

"Stop," I chuckle to Stella's melodramatic groan.

"I mean, most have the decency to at least wait till you've got your breath back."

"He didn't?" I ask.

"I swear, the fool got up within one minute of shooting his pitiful quantity of—"

"I don't need the details," I giggle. "I mean, is that even physically possible?" I laugh, taking a sip of wine. "Don't they need a few minutes to get their strength back before they get up?"

"Well, not this one. Freaking energizer bunny over here, apparently. He shoots his load, pulls out, takes the condom off, and starts pulling his pants on."

"Shit. I take it you're not gonna see him again..."

"You can say that again," she groans.

"Did he at least make you come?" I smirk, trying not to spit out my wine as I take another sip.

"Make me come?! That man couldn't have found my clit with a flashlight and a compass."

I giggle despite myself as Stella recounts a recent sexual escapade that left her more irritated than satisfied. "Are you sure?" I chuckle. "I mean, did you at least try the compass?"

"I did everything short of draw the fool a map," she whines, taking a sip of her wine.

"Oh God, as much fun as you have, Stell, I don't miss being single, honestly." I peer at my friend and she grins at my smile. The Hell's Kitchen bar we're in is pretty quiet tonight, but so is the music, and from the looks on some of the faces around us, I'm fairly sure Stella's story caught the attention of a few merry people around here.

Come on, Jess...

"Talking of maps," I say, building up the courage to say something that I've been playing over and over in my mind for days and building up the courage to tell my friend since I got here. "I... I've been thinking of taking a short road trip."

"Oh, where to?"

"I was thinking about doing the cross-country thing to California, visit my brother for a bit in San Fran."

She arches a thin brow. "That's not what I'd call a *short* trip, honey."

"No. I guess not."

"What, you and Jack?"

"No. Just... just me. Alone."

"What's the prick done now?" she exhales in irritation, making my lips crack into a smile of amusement.

"Nothing," I reply. "In fact, he's been... *perfect.*" My heart sinks as I say it... because it's true.

"Jack Wilder, perfect? Is that a pig I see up there?" she asks, squinting up at the ceiling.

"Well, as perfect as—"

"A dominant asshole can get."

"Something like that," I grin. "He's really trying, Stell. So hard."

"So, what's with the trip?"

I glug down a sip of Bordeaux, taking a deep breath before speaking. "I just feel the need to get out of Manhattan for a bit. Plus, I've always wanted to do a road trip. I thought it could be fun."

She tilts her head to the side, eyeing me as if I've just sprouted blue tentacles from my forehead. "A road trip. Alone? In March?"

"Sure," I shrug. "Why not?"

"Well, for one, that shaved *ape* you call a husband will handcuff you to the radiator if you even suggest it. Secondly, it'll be freezing from here to Iowa. And thirdly, isn't it a bit risky crossing the country on your own?"

"Women travel across the country every day on their own. I'd only drive during the day. I'd stay in decent hotels."

"Won't Jack go with you?"

"I haven't asked him."

She lets out a heavy sigh, downing the rest of the wine before staring at the glass for a moment as she places it back down onto the glossy wooden bar. "Why not, baby?" she asks, her face grim. "What's going on? I know I'm drunk, but I can still whip his ass."

"I know you can," I smile. "It's not him, honestly. It's..."

"Cameron?"

If only it were that simple...

"I just... I don't think I can make this work anymore, Stell. I thought I could. I can't."

"Are you still in contact with him?" she asks, eyes soft on my face.

I contemplate for a moment whether it's safe to tell her, especially in light of her and Kevin being targeted by the Society at one point in order to intimidate me into going back. I've never told them that. It's not that I wanted to hide it from them; I'm just so afraid of them being traumatized by it. I know that if I keep doing what Sebastian wants, keep seeing him, that he'll leave them alone.

But it shouldn't have to be that way...

If I can get him to relinquish his hold on me, on Jack, on Cameron, it will mean that something has changed, that his desire to heal is growing to the point that he can sit through the discomfort of being out of control. If I have to be without Jack and Cameron in the process, then so be it.

I just pray that Sebastian will be strong enough to allow it...

She watches me, unspeaking, as I wonder if I should tell her if I've seen Cam.

If I'm being perfectly honest, in some dark place hidden deep inside myself that I dare not delve into, the words Sebastian once uttered to me about not being able to trust my loved ones, echo in perfidious whispers through my mind, causing the decay of despair to hollow me out.

I trust Stella.

Of course I do.

Just as I trust Kevin and Maddie.

It's just that the subtle way that Sebastian plays his mind games eats into you until his words weave themselves inextricably from your thoughts.

"Yes," I finally say. "We're not... seeing each other. We just... talk. A little."

"How is he?" she asks.

"I think I'm gonna need another glass of wine for this," I announce, ordering one for me and Stella from the barman standing ten or so feet down the bar. "He's... struggling a bit."

She arches a brow. "A bit?"

"He says he's in pain."

"I'll bet."

"Do you think it's really about me?" I ask. "I mean, is it about his love for me or that he can't stand losing me to a man he hates?"

"Cameron strikes me as being a bit more evolved than that," she counters. "He's less of a brute than, say—"

"My husband?" I smile.

"Well, *you* said it," Stella deadpans with an eyeroll as the waiter places two new glasses of wine onto the bar, removing our empty ones.

"Whatever the reason, I can't make this work. I'm trying to create a life with Jack, but—"

"You still love him? Jack?"

I nod. "Yes. You judge me, right?"

She shakes her head. "Not my style, baby," she responds. "I've been in love, once, and we all know how *I* acted then."

I squeeze her arm, grateful for her open-minded compassion. "It was... um, a memorable few months," I grin as I recall her great love, Ian, and how loopy my beautiful friend became over the course of that relationship, especially when it broke down.

"Cameron won't let you?" she says. "Create this new life..."

"It doesn't seem so. He's showing no signs of being willing to give up. And if I were with Cameron, Jack wouldn't take it either. I have to go away, Stell. Hiding out in Manhattan is not a solution. I need to take a few weeks and get them both used to me not being in their lives anymore."

"Weeks? Try months, honey."

"Fine. Months. I'll wait it out. I'm a freelance journalist. I can work anywhere. I'll go to San Francisco for a while, live near my brother and his girlfriend."

"And lose them for good? You know that's the risk, right?"

A hollow ache causes my stomach to plummet and my eyes to close at the thought of not seeing either of these men again.

"Yeah," I reply. "For good. It's the right thing to do. The *only* thing."

"I just can't see Jack sitting back and taking it. The man has the self-restraint of a grizzly bear with a hard-on. And Cameron has been obsessed with you since the first minute he laid eyes on you. I'm just struggling to see how they're gonna lie back and take a nap while you go traipsing off across the country... *alone*."

"That's where I need your help."

She runs her fingers through her fine, light-brown pixie cut before taking a sip of wine. "My help sending my girl off somewhere where I won't see her? I'm not *that* generous."

I smile, peering into her earthy eyes, feeling so grateful that I have her. "I've already bought some disposable credit cards so that I can't be traced that way," I say, "but the hotels may not accept them. They need to put a hold on the cards sometimes, and they can't do that with that type. If I ask you to, could you reserve a hotel for me? I'll e-transfer you the money back the same day, I promise."

"I can do one better, honey," she replies, grabbing her studded black Chanel purse from the back of her barstool and plopping it onto her thighs. She pulls out her cobalt-blue wallet, opening it and pulling out a card with glittering fuchsia-tipped fingers. "Take this," she says, holding it out to me.

I glance down at the credit card. "What?! No! I'm not taking that."

She grabs my hand and opens my fingers, shoving the card into my palm and closing her wallet, sliding it back into her purse. "I have *five* credit cards, two of which I never use. I don't need it and I won't—"

"But—"

"Take no for an answer," she says, mock-shouting.

"Stella..."

"I'll tell you the balance at the end of each month. You can send me a transfer. As long as I pay it off within twenty-eight days, I have no interest to pay."

"Stella, I can't."

"That's enough. I won't hear another word about it."

"Thank you," I sigh out as she places her hand on my wrist.

"You just make sure you get to San Fran in one piece, understood?"

"Yes, ma'am."

"When are you thinking of leaving?"

"It has to be during a weekday. Sometime this week, I guess... if I don't lose my nerve. I'm gonna leave in the morning when Jack's at work. It'll give me time to drive for a few hours before that sixth sense of his kicks in. I'm gonna take the old Jaguar my dad gave me."

"Why not just take a plane somewhere?"

"I really wanna go off-grid for a few weeks. Well, kind of. I don't want to rent some apartment where they can find me. I need them to get used to this new life—theirs and mine."

"Is that realistic, honey?"

I let out a slow breath. "I don't know, Stell. All I know is if things keep going the way they are, then... someone will end up badly hurt. I just... can't shake the feeling."

"You can't decide between them?" she asks.

"Even if I could," I shrug. "I couldn't do that to the other. This was never going to work. I have to do something. Believe me, this is not easy, Stella. I feel like I'm leaving my heart behind or something."

"And taking theirs with you," she suggests. "And they're gonna take it, you think?"

"Maybe part of the reason they're both so sure they want me is because... it's like a competition. They can't stand the other one *winning*. If they know I'm with neither—"

"Honey, you left them both in August, remember? For several months. Neither of them left you alone. I don't think that's what's going on here. They need you, Jess."

"Maybe we can be friends at some point," I shrug, my limbs wilting to nothing.

"I'm sure they'll love that," she scoffs.

"Well, they'll have no choice."

"They both have the means to track you down, Jess, disposable credit card or not."

"I don't think they will. I'll... I'll ask them not to. I believe they'll respect my wishes."

"Well, I hope they deserve the faith you're putting into them and behave once they know you've left..."

I hope another man does too...

46

Jessynia

I'm aware of how tightly I'm clasping my hands together, how tightly my fingers are interlaced. I can't bring myself to open my eyes, but instead sit through waves of anxiety, through blasts of images—Jack at the mercy of Sebastian, Cameron hunted by him, Sebastian unable to heal with the same people around him.

I play out what can happen to all of us, to Cameron if he keeps doing what he's doing, to Jack if I can't stop the pull of Sebastian, to me if I can't make this right somehow.

Slowly opening my eyes, I observe the three pages of text scribbled by my hand, taking a breath before folding the sheets of cream paper neatly into three. I stuff them inside the envelope, writing Jack's name on top of it, glancing at my bags by the door, full of some essential documents and some clothes, as well as the ring my father gave me.

I have no idea how I got the words out onto the paper, but it's taken me almost an hour to write three pages, partly because my quivering hands didn't want to write and partly because unruly tears would trickle onto the paper before I had a chance to stop them, smudging the ink and forcing me to scrap a whole sentence. I'm an insufferably loquacious creature who can write for days and has no idea how to edit herself, but I struggled to find the words for everything I have to say to this man that I've loved so deeply. A man I still love.

I'm sure the done thing is to tell Jack to his face, or at least pick up the phone, but I know from past experiences what that will lead to, and we'll all end up stuck like this again. I can't allow it anymore. Something has to give before it's too late.

I know that what I'm doing is extreme, but something feels wrong. The sense of malaise I've felt over the last few weeks hasn't left me. The status quo is nothing of the sort. The current dynamic won't satisfy Sebastian forever, and unless I get sucked into that place, with Cameron as collateral damage, something will give.

I pick up the phone, scrolling down to his name, or rather the letter I have him under—V. As I bring up the phone to my ears, I'm aware of the sound of my own breath.

"Jessynia." Sebastian's deep voice sends a thunderbolt through me.

"I'm leaving. Now. I just wanted you to know that."

Silence stretches between us as I wait with bated breath for his response.

"You've informed your men?"

"I've left Jack a note. He'll get it tonight. As for... Cameron. I'll—"

Shit...

"You'll what, Jessynia?" he asks, his measured delivery so duplicitous.

Fuck...

I contemplate the faux pas I made in the midst of waves of anxiety. I now have the choice whether to backtrack and say nothing, or to tell him that I have some sporadic contact with Cameron.

The thing is, despite my trepidation, I know that he already knows that. I knew it weeks ago when he spoke to me at QN, when he wanted me to explain how I could defy his orders. I see it in the tremors of jealous ire which harshen his glare at times when he looks at me.

"I'll... find a way to make it clear to him that I don't want contact with him again."

"And how will you do that?" he asks, his tone as cold as ice.

"I'll... send him a letter," I lie.

"Hmm. You think fast, Jessynia. And you clearly have more faith in your men's self-control than I do. And in *mine*, for that matter. What makes you think I'm really going to let you go?"

"This isn't easy for me, Sebastian. But it has to happen. It's the only way. You have to make a sacrifice as well."

"I've already sacrificed my soul to humanity. Or had it taken, rather.

"It wasn't taken. It's still there. It's just *fractured*. It can heal. This is the first step. I'm going to help you."

"By leaving me."

"I'm not leaving you. We can talk. Every day if you want, until this new normal feels sane and stable for everyone."

"You give me a lot of credit."

"No. You can do it. We both can. They deserve to be free, but so do you. They shouldn't take up space in your brain anymore. The only reason they do is because of the abuse you suffered and its consequences. You deserve to step into the light."

"And what if I despise the light?"

"You don't despise it. You're just so used to living in darkness."

"I asked you before, Jessynia, and you didn't have the guts to face my question."

"What question?"

"What if I *am* the darkness?"

The barbarity of his utterance cascades through me like the most unforgiving of landslides, turning all to pitch black.

"No. I don't believe that. You're going to allow this. For me. I won't speak to them anymore. And you won't have to deal with them anymore. We'll be free. *All* of us. I know you don't like to hear people begging, but I... need you to do this. For me. Can you?"

"My demons will decide how far you get."

"No. You will decide, Sebastian. And I'll help you heal from them. You just have to trust me. If you don't trust anyone else, trust me. Please." Upon silence that stretches into half a minute, I say. "I have to go."

He doesn't speak once again, and with a voice that trembles, I say, "Bye."

Hanging up, I say a silent prayer that he'll let me.

I text Stella, letting her know I'm leaving. I'm gonna check in with her every hour until I reach my first hotel in Morgantown, West Virginia, six hours away. I figured I'd drive as far as I can the first few days just to reduce the risk of anyone catching up to me.

As for my mother, I'll deal with her later...

Staring at the letter on the table, I hesitate for a moment, wondering if I should take it with me and just call Jack to let him know just in case he comes home early or something... but after a minute of reflection, I get to my feet and walk out of the room, shuddering inside at the thought of hurting Jack.

47

Jessynia
Three hours later

My eyes lock onto the black SUV trailing me a few cars back in the rear-view mirror. I see two men in the front seat, but with the sun still behind me, I can only make out silhouettes.

I cast a glance at the clock. It's been over an hour since I last checked in with Stella, and three since I left Manhattan. It took me over an hour to get out of New York in the early morning traffic, the beeps and honks of irate New Yorkers not exactly helping with my anxiety.

Driving into Pennsylvania flooded me with relief despite the nerves jangling in my belly.

It's only another five minutes' drive till I get to Lancaster. I think I'm going to stop for a few minutes, check in with Stella to let her know all is fine.

I'm nervous, but nothing weird has happened... other than the SUV behind me which is probably just a coincidence. I've been convinced at least ten times in the last three hours that I was being followed only to have the cars overtake me and disappear. I checked the car for any signs there was a tracking device underneath but didn't see anything. I know I'm gonna be paranoid for a few days until I can be sure that everything is going to plan.

Observing the SUV again, I decide to turn off Highway 76 and into Lancaster.

Staying on the northern periphery of the town, I end up pulling into the parking lot near a stunning pond called Long's pond as I peer into the rear-view mirror to make sure that no one follows me in.

It's a sunny day and the pond beyond the reeds is a shimmery emerald green alive with ducks of various colors and surrounded by bulbous evergreens, benches and dirt paths.

A few cars are parked around and a couple of people are meandering to and from cars or walking along a thin path etched by eons of footprints into the grass around the pond.

I take a moment to look out onto the ethereal pond, wondering how I got here, what I'm doing. Am I running away? Or trying to solve a problem?

I close my eyes as I imagine the moment Jack will read that letter begging him to let me go, or the moment I tell Cameron that I can't see him ever again.

I feel the need to soothe people's pain. I can't stand observing it. I always feel it inside me. So I end up trying to help them and getting myself into a mess in the process. I have to find the strength to walk away from both of them. For good. And anyway, I think they'd accept that better than losing me to the other.

It doesn't relieve the ache, the feeling that something is eating away at me, the feeling that something in the universe is inexorably wrong when I'm away from either of them. But I know that with time, it will be the right decision... for as long as Sebastian doesn't give in to the voices inside him. As long as he tries to heal from the horror of the systemic abuse he endured as a young boy at the hands of a malignant narcissist, the desire to erase every single thing that made him unique, the invalidation he has known all his life.

As long as he lets us go.

Checking my rear-view mirror again, I text Stella to tell her where I am and to let her know that all is good. She responds with a few questions and jokes, helping to relieve the black stone sinking and settling in my belly.

And then I turn to the messages and missed calls from Jack.

I've told him I'm with Stella today, and he's given no sign that he doesn't believe me, but that doesn't stop me from staring at his last message in sorrow which pulls my heart apart.

Do you want me to pick you up later, baby?

Jack...

I close my eyes, determined not to cry at the thought of him—all of him. Not just the cheating asshole which he's so neatly reduced to by so many people eager to fit us all into clearly labeled boxes of black and white so that we can feel better about our own failures as humans, but the man who has loved me, protected me, helped me, and the kid he once was who was beaten bloody for half his childhood.

I'm sorry...

For everything...

I reply to his message:

No. I'll get a cab. That way we can both relax.

I hate lying to the man. He seems willing to hear the most unpalatable truths from me. A lump forms in my throat as I stare at his next message.

Okay, baby. I love you. I'll see you tonight.

So the damn tear does make it out, trickling a slow path down my cheek as I write words that hurt me, my finger quivering before I press *Send*.

I love you too.

I flick through a few messages from others, leaving cursory responses.

Nothing from Cameron who knows my number, thank God. I don't need him knowing until I'm well out of Manhattan. He's always been so protective of me, from the first day I met him in college. The bond we formed was so strong so fast. I felt like I knew him somehow, that I was meeting someone from a past life or something. It's the only way I can really explain it. I could sense when he was in pain, and he could sense when I was in trouble. I felt his eyes devouring me, watching over me, making sure I was okay... as I tried to do for him.

I know he hasn't been well of late. I hope being away from me for good allows him to heal. Allows both of them to.

I just pray that Sebastian agrees to leave them alone, to stop all contact, to never allow them back in that hellish place again.

He is the key to everything...

There is no message from him.

He's one of those people who you really don't want going quiet. His mind is always working, always planning, always making things happen. I'm just praying that for once, he steps onto the only path that doesn't lead to destruction.

I see a few missed calls, including one from my mother who is no doubt responsible for the voicemail waiting for me. I'll deal with her when I have to. I think knowing that I'm near my brother will put her mind at ease.

Taking a sip of water from my water bottle, I glance absently into the rear-view mirror again...

48

Darragh
Quercus Velutina, Tribeca

My eyes roam over his tall frame as he peers through wooden slats separating him from the rest of Manhattan.

"Talk to me, Sebastian."

He doesn't respond, continuing to stare out of the window for a long minute. "Do you enjoy doing the *right thing*, Father?" he finally asks.

"Somewhat vague of a question."

"Answer it."

"I don't know what the *right thing* always is," I respond. "I try to connect with God, feel his word."

"Still?" he sneers.

"Still. Always."

"Right after you shackle your sub to the floor and gag her, I suppose?"

"Sometimes," I respond.

"Hmm. See, I always know what the *right* thing is," he continues.

"And choosing that path always feels... *wrong*. It makes me feel like something is crawling inside me."

"It makes you feel vulnerable to give up power to others," I suggest. "But, the girl... She seems to require it of you. Maybe she was brought to you for a reason?"

"To weaken me?" he suggests. "Make me like every other man..."

"To change you."

"To destroy me, perhaps..."

"Or destroy part of you, Sebastian..."

At the sounds of footsteps approaching, I turn to the doorway of Sebastian's room to see one of his men enter.

He bows his head to me, as always, as he watches Sebastian.

"She's near Lancaster. She'll be crossing state lines again in about an hour. We still have four cars on her. What do you want us to do?"

Time stills as Sebastian wages war with two facets of his own self—the man, the one who wants to be saved, and the demons, those who want him trapped in purgatory.

This woman is light to him. Without it, he returns to darkness, a darkness he has inhabited most comfortably for most of his adult life. I understand the draw of both. I live in the same realm of shadows as him.

Releasing her would be an anomaly for him. He doesn't let people go. But perhaps the draw of the human enslaved inside him will finally be enough for him to do what is right...

I don't know what he's going to choose, but I sense that the fate of all of us will depend on the decision.

Can you do it, Sebastian?

Can you overcome the hell of what was done to you?

Can you show mercy in a way that you were not shown it?

I hear his breaths as his chest rises and falls fast, and his hand curls into a fist so tight that it must hurt. His head is bowed as he attempts to overcome everything he has ever known.

A low groan escapes him as his body tenses, his muscles rigid as his breathing quickens further...

Sebastian...

A minute later, he turns slowly, glistening eyes wrapped in shadow.

"Bring her back."

49

Jessynia

N*o...*

My eyes widening into the mirror, I sit bolt upright at the sight of a car rolling slowly into the parking lot.

A black SUV.

It looks like the same one I saw ten minutes before, and it's followed by another, and then another, gunmetal blue and gray.

I put the bottle in its holder and turn the key in the ignition—not quite enough to start it, but just preparing myself. There are ample free spots, but as the first car pulls up to my right with a growl and another to my left, I turn the key fully in the ignition and hit reverse, pulling out in the midst of panic behind me. I make a turn and stop abruptly, somehow managing to put the car into drive and pressing the gas before careening out of the parking lot.

He wouldn't...

I turn right as I leave, glaring frantically into the mirror at the sight of a car pulling out after me, and then another. It's a two-lane road, and I know I'm going over the speed limit, watching as the car in the lane left pulls up to the side of me. I glance through the window of his car to see a man I don't know, darting glances at me with ferocious eyes as he drives.

As he pulls right up to the right back corner of the car, I shout out for him to stop.

He's not gonna pull a PIT maneuver, for fuck's sake...

As we careen past cars on the road, I panic for fear of crashing and slow down, pulling into a smaller road and parking.

I stare at my hands as they grip the steering wheel. The doors are locked—I made sure of that when I got in—but it doesn't stop me from shaking internally as, out of my peripheral vision, I see a dark figure approach.

I barely dare turn to the right to look, but when I do, it's to meet brown eyes blazing in anger.

Isaiah.

No.

It must be on his orders...

His eyes narrow as he watches me—the animal caught in a trap.

He slowly tries the door handle, knowing full well it must be locked. It's a message—open the fucking door. "Don't make me break the window, Jessynia," he shouts. "I don't want to do that to you."

I bet you don't, asshole.

In the rear-view mirror, I see Dimitri, the driver that took me to Sebastian's place, walking slowly towards the back of the car.

Sebastian didn't even let me get three hours away.

He didn't even *try*...

I pick up my phone from the center console.

Pick up, asshole...

"Jessynia."

"Why are your men here?!"

He pauses for a moment. "To bring you back."

"What is wrong with you?! You said you'd try!"

"I did try, Jessynia."

"No, you didn't!"

"You leaving is not tolerable to me."

"Not tolerable to those things you let control you! Call off these men now!" I shout. "Tell them to go back. *Please*. Please, Sebastian. Something has to change, or things will end in blood. I can *feel* it. Please."

"*No*."

"Fine! I'm calling the police!"

With shaking hands, I end the call and find the number pad, pressing the numbers 9 1 1, and as I do so, Isaiah's palm hits the window in a blast, making me jump in my seat.

As I turn to look at him, his face hardens, twisting into a vision of abject wrath.

His low growl rumbles through the glass. "There will be consequences," he snarls. "On my life, I promise you that."

I glance down at the numbers, my fingers hovering over the Call button as my mind moves unbidden to visions of Babs and Frank and Finn and parents float across my field of view.

God...

I don't believe he would really hurt them. Not now...

I turn around to see Grace on the sidewalk a few feet behind Isaiah who is still eyeing me, refusing to unlock his eyes from my face. Dimitri approaches to my left.

"Open the fucking door, Jessynia," growls Isaiah. "Now."

50

Jessynia

"Let go of me!" I pull against Isaiah's grip on my upper arm as he pulls me out of the car and onto my feet. "I'm not going in there!"

My eyes dart to the mansion I was taken to on New Year's Eve, the same house I first got to know Sebastian Gravier in, first sat opposite him in to listen to him pour seductive, venomous words into me. It is the house where I was first given drugs that warped my mind and made me lose time.

Dimitri's hands grab my other arm, and I'm lifted across Isaiah's arms as I kick and shout for him to let me go just as Grace pulls into the parking lot in my car.

I shout her name as she gets out, but she doesn't move, watching me, inert.

Security open the door, and I'm carried through, shouting for them to put me down.

"Do we need to gag her?" asks Isaiah.

"No," replies the security guard. "The place is empty."

"Just try it, asshole!" I shout, knowing full well I couldn't stop them… as long as they don't mind getting bitten.

I'm carried along the corridor that I was taken down last time, only this time, we take a fork to the right as two men hold onto me to keep me from kicking.

"Put me down!" I shout but am ignored until we finally reach a door. Dimitri opens it as Isaiah sets me down on the hardwood.

I shove my hands into his chest, hard. "Don't ever put your fucking hands on me again!"

His eyes gleam and his lips curl into a deviant smirk as I pant through fear and indignation. He tips his head forwards. "Go inside, Jessynia."

I glare up at him, wishing I could use his face for target practice before glancing at Dimitri whose expression is altogether more grave.

I turn slowly to look inside the room. The thing is huge—cavernous with lofty ceilings and stone walls. It's about five times the size of our living room.

"Go in," snarls Isaiah as I try to catch my breath.

I take a few steps inside, only for him to come into view, cloaked, standing next to a table littered with various objects.

Taking a breath, I walk towards him in determined strides as the door behind me closes.

"How dare you bring me back here?! You have no fucking right! You didn't even try—"

I stop, stumbling backwards as the man slowly turns to face me.

No.

I shake my head as he walks towards me. "No."

I shuffle backwards, getting to my feet only to feel arms wrap around me, holding me in place.

I know who it is in an instant.

I feel it.

I can smell his scent.

I struggle as his long hair grazes my cheek, but hear the words he's whispered to me so many times. "Don't fight me, Jessynia. You can't win."

As the man approaches in measured strides, his blazing amber eyes studying my face, tears tumble down my cheeks.

"No!"

EPILOGUE

"You can't possibly trust him, Sebastian. Him or his *friend*."

"I don't."

"Her loyalty will be to *him* above you. You know that?"

"Perhaps. Perhaps she needs to see another side of her old friend. A side that that man has meticulously kept hidden from her."

"She knows some of it."

"She knows the parts that make him look flawed, damaged, alluring. He has omitted the parts that reveal quite what a ravenous beast he is when he loses control, quite how dangerous he is. I will make sure that he is offered pleasures here he will not be able to resist."

"It's not like you can force her to watch him in the act."

"No. I will not need to do that. But she will watch as he loses himself like he has done before when he yields to the power and the pleasure his beast so violently craves. She will observe his descent into madness like before... only this time, she will be powerless to stop it."

"Maybe. For all we know, this is just an act to get close to her again."

"Oh, it may well be. I'm sure that is his plan, in fact. But he holds onto his humanity by believing that she will one day be with him and him *alone*. Once Mr. O'Neill finally understands that her heart will always be torn, and once I have offered him what he desires—subjects desperate to be cut and bitten by him—the metamorphosis will begin, one which will tear apart the frail shell he has presented to her. Once he understands the bond that I share with her, I have no doubt that the process will be expedited."

"We need him broken. It's the *only* way this could work. He's too dangerous otherwise."

"Within months, he will finally be unchained, free to be the dark lord that he was supposed to be. A fractured man, burning, tormented, his soul wandering endlessly in search of something that can only be found in the light which he will turn from. I intend to watch over every moment of it."

"I still think this is some act, Sebastian. He wants you taken down; I can feel it. And he's trying to save the girl. He could have any woman he wanted, but she's all he ever thinks about. That will not just stop."

"No. But whatever his naïve motives may be, his fate has been decided. The injuries he has done to me will not be erased by his return. I have known for some time that this war will lead to blood. I can taste it."

"What if it's not *his*? What if it's *yours*, or...?"

"Or *what*?"

"What if it's *hers*? She seems to have accumulated some enemies along the way. Powerful ones."

"No one will hurt that woman without *paying* for it with their *life*."

"And yet you still intend her to watch over his death..."

"Yes. She must. She has a price to pay as well. And there is no other path that will allow her to belong to me fully."

"She'd never accept you after that, Sebastian."

"She has demons of her own, friend, ones who are not yet awakened. I have no doubt they soon will be..."

"Would you want her like that? In darkness?"

"She either meets me in darkness or I meet her in the light. Once blood has been spilled, there may be no more light."

"The Blood of Black Oak."

ALSO BY MONIQUE EDENWOOD

Thank you so much for reading *Ashes of Black Oak*, the fifth novel in the Black Oak Series. I hope it was a thrilling adventure.

The final book in the series is called *The Blood of Black Oak* and will be released on July 9th 2022. It is now available for pre-order on Amazon.

About *The Blood of Black Oak*

I watch the blood as it seeps from him, pooling like crimson flame around his neck, trickling in rivulets of liquid fire onto the dense body below.

The body I've touched. I've held. I've kissed. I've felt wrapped around me for so long, holding me possessively, protecting me from those who wanted me lost.

The nightmarish thud as he hits the ground rages through my cells as a scream is ripped from my throat.

The horror of raw bloodshed is new to me.

I try to free my hands from the coarse rope binding them so that I can get to him before the eyes locked onto mine lose the blaze of their light and close for good, turning to ash before my eyes.

I have to get there so that I can touch him. Hold him. So that he knows I'm there.

He has to know I'm there...

I tried to stop it.

I tried to do what they asked for.

I tried to heal the wounds enslaving so many, to vanquish the demons so cruelly infesting their host, unwilling to let go.

They were too strong, too corrupt, too ravenous for blood.

I couldn't quench their thirst for torment.

I wanted to save them all.

I should have known it could only end in death...

The Blood of Black Oak is the final book in the Black Oak series.

For mature readers.

WORD FROM THE AUTHOR

I would like to say a huge thank you to those who have joined the Black Oak adventure and been moved by these characters and stories. I couldn't even begin to express how thrilled and honored I am to have people read the books and resonate with them.

Ashes of Black Oak was originally supposed to be the final book in the Black Oak series, but while writing it, I realized that because of all the elements in play, unless I omit large chunks of the story, I will not be able to finish it all in one book, so have had to move the final part into The Blood of Black Oak.

I keep my readers updated in my Facebook group, Monique's Clique, as to changes in the series so please join me there to stay up to date. It's a wonderful and very friendly group. I also regularly leave updates on my Instagram page, www.instagram.com/monique_edenwood_author.

The Black Oak series is dark romance and as such, not everyone will behave as they should. Sometimes lines are blurred and we may be conflicted as to how to feel about certain characters, but I hope that it is a moving adventure and exploration of the effects of trauma which is a subject very dear to my heart.

If you have liked the book and are ever inspired to leave a very quick rating or even a very short review, please feel very free to. It does help small independent authors tremendously and I can't express how greatly appreciated it is and what a huge difference it makes to us.

Thank you once again for taking this journey with me and please feel free to reach out to me on Facebook if you have any questions!

Thank you again so much,

Monique

ABOUT THE AUTHOR

Monique EdenWood is a British-Canadian author based in Vancouver, British Columbia.

Her love of the magical trees and forests that she grew up surrounded by helped to inspire her first novel, *Enter the Black Oak.*

When she isn't writing or reading, she loves hiking and cycling around beautiful Vancouver and is a lover of 80's music and epic fantasy fiction.

She is passionate about helping people take a well-deserved break from their daily lives for a short while with the help of some very memorable fictional boyfriends and loves exploring the intimacies and complexities of relationships.

For more information or to contact the author, please join Monique's amazing and very friendly Facebook group, Monique's Clique.

For updates on the Black Oak Trilogy, feel free to visit Facebook.-com/Entertheblackoak or follow her on Instagram at www.instagram.-com/monique_edenwood_author.

Monique absolutely loves hearing from readers of the Black Oak series and tries her very best to respond to every comment she gets.

Made in the USA
Coppell, TX
02 January 2023